The Good Guy List

Russ Vanderboom

Pepper Seed Publishing
2445 First Street NW
Rochester, MN 55901

For information about special discounts for bulk purchases, please contact
Pepper Seed Publishing at russvanderboom@rvanonline.com.

Edited by Annie Vanderboom
annie.vanderboom@gmail.com

Twins art by Chuck Weber
http://weberportraits.com/

Cover design by Gustavo Estrada
animaturas@gmail.com

Printed by Worzalla, Stevens Point, Wisconsin

Library of Congress Control Number: 2014904705

Vanderboom, Russell
The Good Guy List/Russell Vanderboom
Pepper Seed Publishing
Pages cm
1. Families farm – Fiction. 2. 1960s – Fiction. 3. Dairy farming – Fiction. 4. Families and war.-5. Vietnam 1967-68 – Fiction.

ISBN 978-0-9916421-1-3 (pbk)
ISBN 978-0-9916421-2-0 (hard cover)
ISBN 978-0-9916421-1-3 (ebook)

10 9 8 7 6 5 4 3 2 1

For the guys at Bethesda,
and to those left behind

And to Janny, Rita, Anita and all who lived
so that others who followed
could have better opportunities in life

The Good Guy List
Book One
Twin Brothers

Oh very young
What will you leave us this time
You're only dancing on this earth
For a short while
Oh very young
What will you leave us this time

— Cat Stevens

If people bring so much courage to this world
the world has to kill them to break them,
so of course it kills them.
The world breaks everyone and afterward many are strong at the broken places.

— Ernest Hemingway, A Farewell to Arms

Chapter One
American Lady

A FLUTTER OF COLOR caught her eye, and Elle Joyce traced the flight of a butterfly lifting from the cosmos in the garden along the porch. The satyr dipped and dallied, touching down ever so lightly on Michael's will, the decree that confined Elle to North Freedom.

"Fly away, little lady," she whispered to the butterfly as she fanned her hands in wide sweeping arcs to send it along its way. Her eyes scanned the farmyard for swallows and jays as it flew its bouncing course along the garden, north toward the orchard. "Be gone."

Elle glared at the will sitting atop her thick, leather-bound journal on the porch railing. *The power in those pages,* she thought, absently asking, *Why?*

She slipped her journal from under the document in which Michael had defined the limits of her life. She perched the book atop her belly and opened to where the pen marked her last entry. Elle shook her head as she read. *Three days,* she thought. *So much to absorb from these three long days past.*

Elle's focus melted into the blank space below the words she had written. With her thumb and fingers, she massaged her eyelids gently, squeezing each side of the bridge of her nose and pressing softly on her eyes. Then, deliberately, she took up her pen and set it on the paper. As a blot of ink spread slowly from the stylus, she wrote:

June 18, 1946

He gave me so much. And he took it all away. He's gone. How can that be? Is he really gone? Will he not somehow return?

For so long, I feared as much. That he would not come home. That he'd be lost to the War. It was reasonable to believe, to worry, to fear… that he would never return. But he did. Only to be swept away now, so suddenly. Lost not to a war, but to the river. Gone. Not a trace to be found. He is gone. He slipped away. Am I to accept what I saw? Unbelievable! How can it be? How can it be!

He gave me so much. He left me nothing.

Elle glanced again at the papers on the railing beside her rocker. She felt a sudden tumbling motion from deep within, and watched as the nascent life inside her jostled the journal that rested upon her belly.

Almost nothing, she added, closing the book.

Chapter Two
Twin Brothers

ELLE'S TWINS WERE BORN early in the morning on Friday, June 21, the first day of summer, the longest day of the year. The next day, Michael's body was found mired in reeds along a sandbar on the Wisconsin River, miles downstream from where the Joyces had held their picnic. The twins' father had been adrift for six days.

∞

Elliot Pritchard sat with his elbows propped on his rosewood desk, his forehead resting heavily in his hands. The patriarch of the little country hospital, Dr. Pritchard had seen many Joyces into the world—at least those who had been born in Baraboo. He reflected on the long night he had spent with Elle as she gave birth to her two sons. The first of the boys was born at 3:05 a.m., after a full twelve hours of labor. The birth of her eight pound, nine ounce boy left Elle spent. And yet, after just a few minutes, her contractions resumed. Her second son birthed easily; the boy was tiny next to his brother.

Dr. Pritchard consulted with Kate Joyce, Elle's sister-in-law, in his office after the twins' birth. "I've never seen anything near to this," he confided. "She was so silent. It was like she had nothing left. I knew it would be tough after losing Michael, with her grieving and being in mourning during the week. But I just don't know. It was like she wasn't even there."

He rubbed his chin, frowning, and then he sighed. "And now, with twins. The challenge lies yet before her, especially for the smaller one." He leveled an eye of caution at Kate. "She will need to be more than stoic, either way. If the little one dies, or if he survives."

∞

Before she caved to exhaustion, Elle shared her despair with Kate, her closest friend, the woman responsible for drawing her into the Joyce family.

"So, there are two. And boys," Elle said softly. Kate took her hand. "Well, that big old house won't be nearly so empty after all. It would be so much easier if there were only one. How unfair it will be for the firstborn. Or if one had been a girl," Elle whispered. She looked out the window at the rooftops of the houses below. Along the horizon, darkness faded to a luminescent blue as the sun stalked the night from the east. "Why does it have to be so unfair?" she asked, as her eyes fell closed.

"Oh, Elle," Kate whispered to her sleeping friend, touching her cheek and taking her hands. She felt a senseless blame for Elle's predicament. She had introduced her college roommate to Michael, her younger brother, who swept the innocent co-ed off her feet with his charm and magnetism. Kate had been thrilled when her best friend became her sister, but now she bore the pain of Elle's isolation on the farm during the war, her early widowhood, and now this, the foolishness of the Joyces' inheritance tradition.

Kate grit her teeth in anger at the injustice her younger brother had put upon his wife and sons. She had talked at length with her older brother about the pain that he, too, had known, and had buried, and which was now renewed. Paddy had been a victim of the same travesty—the family legacy that Michael had honored.

Elle's husband had left all that he owned to his second son, just as his father had passed over his eldest, Paddy, and willed the farm to Michael. The tradition had been honored for five generations, ever since Sean Patrick Joyce was cast off the family farm in County Clare because it was willed solely to the oldest son, his only brother. Sean Patrick had rectified that injustice by inverting the same provision, once he settled his land in Sauk County and started a family of his own.

Elle, now, was the most recent victim of the Joyce tradition. Elle, and her oldest son.

∞

When Elle awoke, Dr. Pritchard was waiting by her bedside.

"Can I see them?" she asked, timidly.

"Of course. The nurses will be bringing them in just a few moments. I wanted to check on you first." He glanced at his wristwatch. "You must have been exhausted. But the babies were just as tired as you. They woke up only a short time ago." He chuckled. "It was as if they were scheduled to wake up together. Mrs. Daly said that they awakened within a few seconds of one another.

"They are quite a bit different from each other, Elle," he said, his tone wary. "Fraternal, not identical. One is much bigger. And the smaller one has a crop of long dark hair that he must have gotten from you. The big fellow is light featured, like the Joyces. The twins don't look much alike, but they seem to be synchronized in their sleep cycle. Twins can be that way, you know."

Elle didn't know. She knew nothing of babies.

∞

When she first saw her sons, Elle was startled by the mix of fear and tenderness that stirred in her heart.

The big, rosy-colored fellow with the plump little fingers and full cheeks yawned sleepily as the nurse handed him to his mother. She took the boy in her arms and held him, but he quickly settled back into sleep.

She asked for her younger son. The lightness of the swaddling sent a wave of shock through her. The bundle was less than half the weight of the firstborn. When she peeled back the nursery blankets, she saw a tiny body not much bigger than her cupped hands. The boy's head was larger in size than his torso and limbs combined. He lacked his older brother's healthy pinkish coloring; his skin seemed thinner, darker, varying from a deep red to blue. Elle quickly reswaddled him. But the baby jerked his tiny arms in spasms of excitement. He opened his deep blue-black eyes and tried to focus on her. His mouth opened, his head craning on his tiny neck toward his mother's breast. When he couldn't reach her, he wailed in a mouse-like squeal.

"Your little boy is hungry," Dr. Pritchard said gently. "Would you like to try nursing him? I think he is ready. He certainly doesn't have the reserves that his sleepy brother has." The old doctor's manner was gentle and reassuring.

Mrs. Daly helped Elle unsnap her hospital gown and lowered the shapeless garment to expose her breast. Dr. Pritchard carefully returned the boy to her. Elle followed the twin with her eyes, missing Dr. Prichard's slight wince as he visually examined her breasts, neither of which were swollen as he would expect a new mother's to be. He knew that some women, for reasons he could not explain, could yield little or no milk. So it seemed with Elle. She would not be able to meet the needs of both her sons.

"The worst is over, Elle," he assured her. "But we have quite a challenge before us, if we are to keep both boys alive. You need to see if you will be able to nurture both of them with your milk."

The doctor was encouraged to see that Elle's youngest knew his business. The babe latched onto her nipple and suckled with gusto. The little fellow had the gumption to try, and trying, Dr. Pritchard knew, was more than half the battle for tiny newborns. While Elle's younger son had nearly completed a full term of gestation, he was no larger than babies born six weeks or more early. He knew the challenge, and the dismal odds, of keeping a stunted baby from succumbing to one of a variety of illnesses if the youngster had no desire to thrive. This boy had the will to live, the doctor thought. He wondered if Elle was as determined.

"How big is he?"

Elle's hushed question jolted her doctor from his thoughts.

"He's a little fellow, Elle. Four pounds, maybe a pinch more," he exaggerated. The boy was two ounces lighter than the four pounds the doctor claimed. "But he's a scrappy young fighter, don't you think? Do you know what you are going to call him?"

She nodded, her eyes fixed to the babe at her breast. "David. I was just thinking he is a good David."

As his mother said his name, David left her breast, arched back his neck and again squawked with his tiny voice.

"Well, David, you are quite a feisty one," Dr. Pritchard said. "You probably want more foremilk, little one."

He helped Elle remove her arm from the other sleeve and bared her unsuckled breast. He compared her two breasts; they were sadly small. Neither was at all well-developed—not like he would expect of a woman prepared for the postnatal nurturing of babes. He leaned in to help her bring the fussing infant to her other breast.

She balked, blushing, feeling insecure and ignorant.

"Shouldn't I let Patrick nurse?" she asked, looking to the older twin, deep in sleep.

Dr. Pritchard shook his head.

"No. David needs everything you can give him." Settling himself into the chair by her bed, the old doctor carefully explained the challenges her younger son would face. "The average weight of twins is about five pounds five ounces for each baby," he told her. "Your boys together average closer to six pounds. That's because young Patrick there got more than his share of the nutrients these past few months."

Elle held her little one close, but looked curiously at her firstborn sleeping comfortably alongside her. A double-banded crease formed between her eyebrows, and she tipped her head as though she couldn't quite comprehend all this new information.

As Dr. Pritchard watched her with concern, a thought occurred to him. After Michael's death, Elle's sister Mary had traveled to the farm with her own infant, a six-month old son. In his consolatory visits to the family, he'd seen Mary nursing Jack easily and often. She could be a lifesaver, he reflected.

"David has an uphill battle," the old doctor continued, choosing his words carefully. "Chances are perhaps fifty-fifty, gauging from his zeal to feed," He stroked the boy's head tenderly. "We will know that soon enough. He has good suckling instinct, and the suckling muscles seem well enough developed.

"As for young Patrick, he will do quite well for the time being with your sister as his wet nurse." He watched her reaction closely. Elle seemed comfortable with the suggestion.

"Assuming Mary agrees, of course. Kate mentioned this morning that your sister will be staying with you for at least a couple of weeks. I suggest you concentrate primarily on David. And you do live on a dairy. There will be no shortage of milk for Patrick in any event.

"You can rest easy, Elle. The Lord has blessed you with two baby boys. I will do everything I can to help you raise them in good health. The rest is up to Providence."

∞

Dr. Pritchard kept Elle in the hospital for a week. He told Paddy and Kate that he wanted to give her a chance to rest, to strengthen both her body and spirit while he observed her youngest son for a few days. He did not add that he wanted to watch over her just as closely, to evaluate her. And to keep her away from Michael's funeral.

Mary had readily assented to nurse Patrick, so Dr. Pritchard suggested the boy go home where she could conveniently care for him. He thought the arrangement would be easiest on Elle as well; she could concentrate her strength and determination on the little fellow, the second born. When she arrived home at week's end, Elle gasped to see again the disparity in the twins' size. Patrick slept dreamily with a look of peace and satisfaction and a belly full of Mary's milk. The boy had gained twenty percent of his birth weight. Although she knew she shouldn't, Elle initially felt slighted by her son's attachment to her sister. He did not respond to her like David did. Instead, Mary and Patrick had bonded as if he were her natural son. Yet with the family gathered at the farmstead, Elle savored the healing days of summer. Mary was close by, and Kate frequently commuted up from her home in Madison, often staying for days, preparing her classes and working on her writing at the big kitchen table.

But summer was fleet. Mary's husband Paul arrived on the train from Indiana, and Elle understood that his visit would end with the Howard family's departure for their home on the shores of Lake Michigan. Then, a brisk Canadian cold front pushed across the state, and Elle realized it was already late August. A chill of anxiety slipped into her heart as she remembered the long, empty hours during the war when people everywhere went on with their lives while she hung suspended, alone on the farm, waiting.

As summer gave way to autumn's long afternoon shadows, Elle let the suffocating grip of lonesomeness creep back into her life. Day after day, she swaddled her sons, put them in their basket, and set them on the floor of the porch alongside the hanging swing. She rocked forward and back, hour after hour, waiting for them to cry so she could answer their needs.

Chapter Three

Raising Twin Boys

December 25, 1953

ELLE LAY SLEEPLESS in the dark on yet another Christmas morning. The house was still but for the murmurings of one of the twins tossing restlessly. Radiators clanked intermittently, cooling as the fire fell to embers. Elle listened mostly to the whir of worries spinning in her mind.

She had so much to make ready. Why did the whole family insist upon another Christmas gathering at the farm? Perhaps it was Paddy's doing. *Overwhelming*, she thought. She first needed to prepare the pies from the cherries she had put up last summer and the apples still crisp in cold storage. Then, she would dress the turkey. The fowl and a roast rib of beef must be in the ovens by mid-morning.

Elle rose when she heard Paddy in the cellar stoking the furnace on the way to milk his Jerseys. In his quiet way, Paddy did much to maintain the big old farmhouse, and he kept a gentle eye on the growing young boys as well. Elle should help more, she knew. But she did what she was able.

∞

April, 1954

From the time he was a toddler, Patrick was plagued with allergies to the animals, manure, and feed dust in the barn. His role on the farm fell short of his twin's, who loved the day-to-day chores of farming.

His brother didn't understand allergies. "It's our duty, too, you know," David often chided him. "Uncle Paddy is working our part of the farm for us. We ought to be helping out."

Patrick's typical response was to shrug, sniffle, and look for entertainment that didn't aggravate his hay fever. He didn't miss the barn work. He didn't like it. The exceptions were the jobs that promised adventure and challenged his strength, especially if the work didn't trigger a sneezing fit. By the time he turned seven, Patrick was bigger than the twelve-year-olds at school, and strong enough that he could handle the bales of alfalfa that his uncle tossed up into the hay wagons. He liked toting and stacking bales on wagons in the field, regardless of the heat, for as long as his hypersensitive nose allowed him to grapple with the fifty-pound blocks. In the hay mow, however, the dust was too fierce. But he enjoyed building fences and hauling and stacking firewood. Some rarer tasks were even more inviting. He especially looked forward to waging war against the beavers every spring.

In recent springs, a family of beavers had constructed dams across the creek along the back of the west pasture. Under Paddy's watchful eyes, the twins had helped break down the beavers' work when the creek backed up into the pasture. Patrick loved wrenching apart the piles of branches cemented together with mud and cheering with his brother and uncle when a critical mass tore loose and the stream gushed free.

The April before the twins turned eight, David spotted freshly scarred willow and poplar, hewn by the beavers' sharp teeth. Throughout Easter week, with the weather warming, the snow rapidly melting, and runoff flowing freely into the creek, David watched as a new dam took shape.

"We have to tear down their dam," David told his brother. "If we get it now, they won't flood the whole pasture again."

Patrick shrugged. "You know they'll just build it up again." He didn't care, though. Tearing the dam apart was a hoot.

On Saturday, after breakfast, Paddy asked the boys whether they would like to go with him to town to get soybeans ground for feed. Patrick locked his eyes on his oatmeal, avoiding David's glance. Paddy noticed, but said nothing.

"Think not, Paddy," David said, offering no explanation.

His uncle fixed his gaze on the bigger twin. "Don't you want to try to find a ball game in town? I can give you a lift."

Patrick shrugged, his eyes still down. "Naw. Thanks."

His uncle knew they were up to something. But then, they were always up to something. "Well, you boys be sure to be helpful here for your mom. You want to be pitching in, not just giving her more work to do. Understand?"

"Definitely," David agreed. "We'll take care of things."

Paddy grunted a general purpose warning before leaving the farmhouse and hopping into his pickup. The twins waited until the truck was well on its way toward town before heading to the tool shed.

As David and Patrick armed themselves with picks and pry bars, the Klemm boys coasted into the farmyard on their bikes, baseball mitts dangling from their handlebars. Chris and his little brother Lenny had hoped to fetch Patrick along for a ball game, but David had other ideas.

"Baseball can wait," he called. "Come on! It's war on the beavers!" Without waiting for an answer, he began passing out tools from the shed: a long-handled iron rake to Lenny, a short-handled pitchfork to Chris. Patrick took the long steel crowbar, while David grabbed a pickax. "We gotta bust up their dam before it gets too big," he declared.

"Too late for that," Lenny said. "The water's backed up halfway to the road. I could see it from my bike."

"Let's go," David said. "They're making better time than I'd thought."

The dam was a formidable structure. "How many beavers *are* there?" David wondered as the boys approached it. The newly formed pond behind the dam submerged several acres at the bottom of the pasture that had been dry just weeks before.

"Man," Patrick muttered. "It's as big as ever." He stuck his bar under a willow limb and pried. The branch bent and swayed, but remained firmly embedded in the matrix of the dam, which was mounded nearly six feet above the surface of the pasture. The beavers had packed the bramble tightly with mud, but the sticks in the center of the dam had been washed clean by the water escaping over them. There, Patrick saw, they could tear apart the tangle. They set to it, climbing up on the dam and picking, prying, hacking and breaking the supple wood that held the pond in check.

"Here, Patty. Work on this big piece," David directed his twin. "It's holding this whole layer in."

Patrick stuck his crowbar behind the three-inch branch. He wrenched the bar back and forth while David used his pickax to break away the smaller pieces that worked loose under his brother's efforts.

"Wow," Patrick gasped after a few minutes. "That's deep in there."

"Yeah," David pried against the woven branches. "They really know how to make a dam. But keep at it. Look at how loose this front part is getting," he said.

Patrick sucked in the clean, fresh spring air, his skin flush and his eyes aglow. Returning his brother's grin, he turned to see the Klemm brothers' efforts. Chris had stuck the pitchfork straight down into the bramble. He stood with both feet on the beam of the fork, holding tight onto the handle, rocking to and fro. It looked like fun. Patrick jammed his heavy crowbar deep alongside the branch at his feet. He shoved the bar forward and pulled back with all his strength. The bar held, but so did the dam. He jumped up onto the shaft of the bar, wrapping his arms and legs around the steel, using his whole weight to swing against the springing force of the willow branch.

"Hey, this is working." He gripped tighter and pulled harder as the bar began to arc more widely. "It's coming apart!"

David turned just as the dam shifted and a key section between Patrick and Chris tipped away. David, standing directly on top of the compromised structure, swung his arms above his head as he lost his balance. Patrick swayed again toward the pond, wrenching out the chunk of dam upon which David stood. Suddenly freed, the creek poured across the breach. Patrick watched and laughed as his twin tumbled into the runoff water. David's eyes flew open wide and he let out a high yelp as he plunged into the icy waters.

Patrick felt a sudden surge of alarm as the dam shifted beneath him. He lost his grip on the bar and fell backward, sticks and branches poking him on his butt. He crawled like a crab onto more solid ground as the center of the dam dissolved under a torrent of pond water. The water roared through the rift in the beavers' wall.

Chris and Lenny stood on the other side of the flowage, looking dumbfounded at the water pouring into the creek. Chris caught Patrick's eye. He pointed downstream and called out to Pat, but his voice was drowned out by the deluge pouring from the pond. *He looks scared,* Patrick thought. His eyes followed his friend's hand downstream.

David was gone.

Patrick leapt from the remains of the dam. The water in the pasture was over his shoes, but he ignored its iciness. He walked as close to the creek's edge as he could, searching for his brother. Nothing. He ran, covering fifty yards along the creek. There was no sign of his twin. He glanced back toward the dam. Chris was searching his side of the creek.

"Anything?" Patrick yelled. Chris shrugged.

Lenny remained atop the crumbling dam. He held his head at an odd cant, looking directly down into the tumbling spillage. The dam continued to unravel and the flow of water pouring down into the stream doubled in volume. Patrick worked his way back upstream, the water up to his shins along the creek's banks.

"Where'd he go?" Chris called across the flooded creek.

"I dunno," Patrick said, shaking his head. Branches and debris littered the water, but the spill-off remained clear. Where was David? Why couldn't he see him in this shallow flowage? A horrid sinking sensation filled his heart, and a fog settled behind his eyes, dimming his vision. He felt fear hurl itself into a panic within his chest, and his heart beat with pounding force; he could not bring himself to inhale. Standing immobile, he looked again toward the dam.

Lenny stood frozen, disfigured by his ungainly posture, looking down into the dam as if he were a robin eyeing a worm hidden in deep grass. He held his arm straight down, his finger pointing into the branches tangled below the tumbling water. He stood stock still, marking a single spot.

Patrick suddenly understood.

He gasped, sucking in the cool spring air, and the fog behind his eyes cleared. He found himself running, splashing, hurdling the surface of the current as he sprinted back to the dam.

He climbed onto the dam and looked down. "Where, Lenny?" he screamed above the water's roar. "Do you see him?"

Patrick followed the line from Lenny's eyes down his arm, his index finger pointing toward the edge of the spillway. He focused his gaze under the swirling surface of the water. Nothing. He looked again. And again. Lenny continued to point, a ghastly, ghostly pallor shading his face. Patrick dove into the tumbling water. It was stunningly cold, and the current swept him quickly away. He swam and fought against the water to get closer to the dam.

By the time he'd reached the dam's base and worked his way across its face, Chris had returned to his brother. Chris shook Lenny, talking into his ear. Patrick couldn't hear, but he saw Lenny answer, never taking his eyes from that spot below.

Chris peered down over his brother's shoulder. His eyes widened, and he yelled, "Below! His shoe! Davey's shoe!" Chris shimmied around his brother to the very edge of the spillway and plunged his arm into the water. It was too deep, and the water ran too fast. He groped behind him, yanking a long branch from the debris. He stuck it deep into the water, probing toward the base of the dam.

Patrick squinted into the chute flowing from the broken dam. Beneath the foam, in the swirl of bark, leaves and matter, he saw the bottom of his brother's sneaker. He hurled himself into the water, grabbing at the rubber sole of the Ked. The water swept him away like a flower petal in a gale. He gathered his feet beneath him and plunged again, challenging the rapids, diving and pushing himself into the flowage. He felt the shoe. It slipped from his fingers.

He splashed out of the water and crawled up on the dam, turning to approach the shoe from above. When he was as close as possible, he sucked a deep breath into his lungs. *Now,* he thought. And he dove once more.

He caught the heel of the shoe and he pulled. He felt the Ked slipping off David's foot, so he grabbed higher, wrapping his fingers around David's ankle and gripping like a vise. He tugged, and felt his brother move in the mire beneath the cascading water. Patrick planted his feet in the logjam that locked his brother beneath the spillway. He pushed and pulled, again, and again. He felt David's body shift under the current, and he pulled again with all his might. His brother popped from the tangle like a cork, and the rushing water swept the twins downstream into the creek.

Patrick clung to his brother's leg as he scrambled to gain his footing in the slippery mud of the creek bed. He staggered as he broke the surface and gasped for air, then fell beneath the surface, chugging water into his lungs. He fought on with all the strength in his legs and found the bank where the coarse grass offered traction. He crawled, tugging his brother's body, which drifted downstream like a log.

Chris and Lenny ran through the flooded pasture to help pull David from the creek. They hauled his limp body onto the grass, setting him face up. Patrick staggered behind, throwing up water and gasping for air.

His brother was pale and lifeless.

"Davey," Patrick called once, then again, and again, each time louder as if his volume alone would waken his brother.

The Klemms stood above them, looking hopeless. Patrick barked at Chris, "Run. Get Paddy." Chris sprinted toward the farmstead.

Paddy had gone to town, Patrick remembered. He looked at the frightened younger Klemm. "Grab his legs." Patrick reached for a grip under his twin's armpits. Together they lifted David, but he was wet and slippery and they couldn't hold him. His limp body slid onto the grass of the pasture with a thump.

Patrick stood at his brother's feet and pulled him by his hands, jack-knifing David's little body in half. He stooped down, scooping his twin up over his shoulder in a fireman's carry. His brother was light. *He's such a tiny guy,* Patrick thought, and he began sprinting across the uneven lumps of grass in the pasture. As he ran, he heard water spewing from his brother's lungs and stomach, and felt its warmth run down his back. He quickened his stride, running with the load on his shoulder like a sack of feed. He covered the quarter mile to the farmyard without breaking stride. As he carried his brother between the barn and the corn crib, he saw his uncle driving the pickup into the yard. He felt, for the first time, that his prayers had been heard. He felt hope.

Reaching the yard, he flopped his brother down on the lawn as he caved to his knees in exhaustion. David lay still, his eyes rolled back under his forehead, his color as bland as milk, unconscious. But he was gasping, coughing, his breath caught in the spasms of his diaphragm. Jostled by his brother's sprint from the creek, and his lungs emptied along the way, David was breathing, and his heartbeat was strong and even.

∞

Elle fretted and fumed over her sons' mishap in the creek. She was one minute irate at them, the next, stricken with overwhelming fright. Her mind spun as if she were being drawn into a whirlpool of panic and fear. She sat in helpless vigil with David during the two days he remained in the hospital under Dr. Pritchard's care. And returned, frantic, when he spiked a fever and coughed up blood shortly after coming home. Again she felt the grip of despair as she sat with him in the hospital, his limbs packed in ice, his eyes distant, his breathing shallow and uneven.

His words frightened her as much anything, when he was able to speak again. "It's okay, Mom," he'd said weakly in the hospital bed. "It's so peaceful. You don't need to be afraid, Mom. Just let go. Pure joy! It's neat. It's here..."

Elle wished she could relax enough to let go. To cry. To feel, if not joy, calm.

∞

December 25, 1954

The door on the wood burner clanked shut, and Elle crawled out from the warmth of the blankets to the chill of the predawn darkness. She could wait a few moments until the heat built up and the fans blew the warm air up into the house. But why? She may as well just get up. There was so much to do today. Another Christmas. Another gathering of her in-laws at the Joyce farm. In their home, in which she lived. She had so much to do.

∞

The children ripped the wrapping from their presents within moments, and then, as the men lounged in the living room after Christmas dinner, the cousins savored the novelty of their gifts. All but one of the children's presents had been opened. A single, large box, almost a cube, sat below the tree marked: "For the Kids." It was signed, "From Uncle Roger."

"Let's have one of the twins open it," Roger said, lifting the box and setting it on Patrick's lap. "Go ahead, Patty. It's for all of you."

Patrick's eyes widened as he surveyed his eager cousins and brother. He tore at the paper and slid off the top of the box to find four heavily padded brown mitts with thick, clumsy thumbs hooking over their palms. He held one up.

"Boxing gloves?" Kate asked incredulously as Patrick tried to jam his hand into a mitt. She heard a gasp from behind her, where Elle sat on the sofa.

"Well, if that don't beat all. What do you want these kids to do? Beat each other up?" Gabriel snapped.

"No, no," Roger retorted. "This is just for sport. It's good for them. They aren't big enough to hurt each other, and it'll teach them how to take care of themselves." He took the gloves from Patrick and untied the laces.

"Here. Hold up your hand with your fingers out," he instructed. He shoved the glove over Patrick's fingers, held his wrist firmly, and gave the mitt a couple of extra tugs. He squeezed the thumb and asked, "Your thumb in there? Wiggle it."

Patrick nodded. The thick stub didn't move. Roger grunted, then tied the strap around the boy's wrist. He repeated the process with the other glove. "Who's going to challenge?" Roger asked, looking over the bewildered cousins. "How about the twins, one against the other?"

Elle gasped again and murmured weakly, "No."

Paddy leaned forward in the great rocker by the windows, skeptical. He had stopped rocking, and pinched his chin between his thumb and fingers.

David watched his twin inspecting the gloves on his hands, like great balloons over the end of his arms. Patrick tapped the mitts together, first tentatively, then more boldly, making a dull thud. David got up, stood in front of his uncle, and held up his hands for the other pair.

"The ring will be the oval rug," Roger said as he cleared away chairs and littered wrappings. "Each round will be thirty seconds. If that's too long, we'll try fifteen. Let's see how it goes."

"What's a round?" David asked.

Roger cast him a dubious glance. "A round is the time when you can legally box. You can't punch your opponent before the round starts, and you have to stop hitting him when the round is over. No punching below the belt or behind the back. Try to keep your guard up," Roger said, placing David's oversized left mitt in front of his face. The stuffed pad bobbed when Roger let go.

"Any questions?"

"How do you tell who wins?" David asked.

"The boxer who lands the most punches, wins. Jerry, you keep count, okay? I'll ref the bouts. Paddy, you want to keep time?"

"Don't have a watch," the farmer grunted through the hand over his mouth.

"I've got mine," Cousin Dean piped in.

The women held their breath, apprehensive. Elle looked wan. Kate, outraged, got up and left the room. But as soon as the twins were squared off and the round began, she stepped back into the doorway, leaning against the oak frame.

The first round ended in a stalemate. After half a minute, neither boy had landed a punch, or even truly attempted one. They merely tapped at one another's gloves, unaccustomed to the heavy clumsiness, feeling their way.

After a brief rest, Roger called the boys to the center of the ring. "The idea of boxing is to take a few good swipes at your opponent," he told the twins. "Hit him. You're not going to hurt one another. These gloves have a lot of padding." He knocked the boys' hands together. "Come out swinging!" he cried, signaling to Dean to start a second round.

Patrick took his uncle's advice to heart, swinging his right arm back along a pendulous arc. David saw the punch coming and took it squarely on the cheek and nose. His eyes watered and his nose burned. He could see through his tears that Patrick was winding up for another volley. David staggered a step back and warded off the punch by pushing at his brother's arm with the clumsy mitts.

"Good punch. Good block," Roger encouraged.

The cousins cheered, though they picked no favorite. "Come on, Davey! Come on, Pat. Hit 'im."

David heard the cheers over the sound of air rushing though his nose to his lungs. He blinked away his tears, regained his equilibrium, squared himself before his twin, and started a flurry of punches. He launched the first punch high, toward Patrick's forehead, following with a rapid succession of jabs, each slightly lower as the gloves weighed down his hands. Three jabs and he needed to lift the trajectory of his punches again.

Patrick froze, befuddled. His guard slowly lowered, following David's descending punches. By the time David raised his second series of jabs toward his brother's head, Patrick stood defenseless, waving his padded hands in front of his belly. After David landed a third volley of punches, Dean called time on the round. Roger grabbed David's wrist and held it aloft, proclaiming him the winner of the bout.

Gabriel cackled at the outcome. "I'd have never thought!" he chuckled.

With good reason. Patrick stood more than a full head taller than his brother, and his heavy-boned frame supported much more flesh than his diminutive twin. At seven and a half years old, Patrick was off the growth charts. He stood well over five feet tall and weighed one hundred twenty-nine pounds, and the fair-haired twin carried his weight well. David, on the other hand, weighed a scant fifty-two pounds and was less than four feet tall. He looked like a sparrow on stilts. His barrage of punches did little more than draw tears to Patrick's eyes from a tap on the nose.

Much greater pain was dealt to Patrick's young ego. His face reddened and his eyes welled as Roger tugged off the gloves to prepare the next challenger. He wanted to go to his mother, but resisted. It was bad enough that he had lost; he couldn't act like a sissy. Instead, he sat cross-legged next to the ring and watched as his brother levied the same flurry of jabs against his seven-year-old cousin Daniel. When a flushed-faced David was again pronounced the winner, Patrick bound up, desperate for a rematch. "Let me have another try," he pleaded.

"You'll have another turn," Roger snapped, "but you'll have to wait for it. First let the others go a round."

David's spunk sparked the adults' enthusiasm. Gabriel softly urged on his young friend as though he was settling a young colt. Paddy laughed good-heartedly at the frenzy of punches that were as defensive as offensive. Kate even caught herself yelling support for the reigning champ as he defeated a third and then a fourth challenger. She noticed, however, that Elle sat frozen, apprehension frosting her pale face.

David embraced the fight. He sensed that his only hope resided in keeping his cousins so busy defending his jabs that they couldn't punch back. His arms grew heavy, as if he'd lifted a couple dozen bales of hay. Gabriel tended him, rubbing his shoulders and encouraging him with quiet praise. Hot sweat stood in beads on his forehead and nose. He inhaled deeply, gloved hands dangling heavily at his sides, staring across the ring at yet another opponent. Uncle Roger slipped one glove on the left hand of his son, Roger Junior, who was fifteen years old.

Uncle Roger stepped to the middle of the ring to announce special provisions for the bout. Young Roger would kneel during the round, keeping his right hand behind his back. Uncle Roger lowered a warning eye at his son, silently demanding discretion in fighting the little twin.

"Circle to Roger's right, away from his gloved hand," Gabriel murmured as he rubbed David's shoulders.

"Are you ready?" Uncle Roger asked the defender.

David nodded. He braced himself, considering Gabriel's hushed advice.

Roger brought the fighters to center ring, where they touched mitts. He signaled the start of the round, and David lunged sharply to his left, attacking Young Roger's face on the right with a frantic, desperate flurry of punches. He connected immediately with a left and again with a right, but Young Roger fended off the blows with his left hand and forearm. David launched another barrage, but the older boy, who even on his knees was as tall as the twin, extended his arm and pushed the tired punches back into David's face, making him hit himself with his own deflected punches. As fatigue gripped David's thin arms, panic set in. His muscles burned, and without the motion of the jabs, he could not keep the heavy gloves up in defense.

"Twenty seconds," Dean called.

David's supporters, who moments before had been exhilarated at his dominant outbursts, sat mute, sensing his doom.

"Stop it!" David heard distantly. "Stop." It was his mother. But Young Roger tasted victory. He threw a test jab at David's cheek, stinging his skin and bringing water to his eyes. Then, certain of the range, he smacked David smartly in the face. David saw the punch coming and braced, taking the full impact on his nose. Roger's next punch landed solidly on David's rib cage.

Patrick watched in disbelief as his brother took the beating. At first, he was disappointed that he wouldn't get another chance at David. Then, when he saw David take the blow to the face, Patrick's anger flared. The fight was over. His cousin had hurt his twin. He would not let this happen again.

Uncle Roger stepped in to stop the round before the final seconds expired. "Enough," he called, but his son's final blow was on its way, landing directly on David's sternum. David felt his diaphragm heave and invert, his breath forced from his lungs. He fell to the carpet on his back, his eyes rolling up in his head. He could hear the clamor about him, but it was muffled and distant. His lungs burned for air, yet he couldn't draw a breath. He caught glimpses of his relatives standing over him as his eyes rolled in their sockets.

"Give him room."

"He'll be okay. Just got the breath knocked out of him."

"Help him!"

"He's all right."

Slowly, David felt his breath returning. He looked up to see Uncle Paddy lifting him by his belt as he tried to inhale, then lowering him as he exhaled. A sense of calm came over him as he regained control of his diaphragm. By the time he could breathe normally, he felt relaxed but spent. His arms ached and burned and the skin on his face stung. He sat up, ready to have the gloves removed from his thin arms.

∞

Elle stayed seated as her boy responded to Paddy's care. Fear had hollowed out her belly as she watched David fight, and when he fell, despair swept in to fill her soul. She watched, ashen-faced, as her son gamely stood up, fighting tears. He walked directly to her, hunching stiffly as lingering spasms caught his breath. He took her hand, and led her out of the room. Elle held him close to her side.

"Who's next?" Elle heard her brother-in-law call as she followed her son to her bedroom. "We got a new champion, so who will be the first challenger?"

"Let me! Let me!" demanded the older twin.

David led his mother away from the action behind them, and they entered her bedroom without turning on the light. She sat in the big stuffed chair at the foot of her bed, and he climbed into her lap, his face resting limply above her breast. She felt him slowly break into sobs.

"You didn't have to fight," she whispered. She stroked his fine black hair against the grain, letting it fall forward randomly.

He sniffed, tears and sweat dripping from his cheeks.

They were still for a long time. More cheers filtered into the darkness of her bedroom.

"A new champion!" Roger proclaimed above the hubbub from the living room.

Then, as quiet settled into the outer rooms, the sounds of Gabriel's fiddle filled the silence.

"I have to, Mom," David said quietly. "I have to try. I couldn't not."

She thought about his words as she held him close. "No, you don't have to fight, you know," she whispered.

He tensed, then relaxed in the warmth of her embrace. After a moment, he shook his head.

"I do, though, Mom," he said, looking deep into her eyes. "If that is what is put to me. If that is what they expect of me. Then I have to fight. How else can it be? Aren't those the rules? Isn't that the game?"

Elle searched her son's dark eyes. She shivered, and he responded by collapsing into her embrace. She felt his breath in rhythm with her own, and wondered if even the heartbeat that she felt through the thin walls of his chest pulsed in time with hers.

After a while, he slipped off her lap and walked slowly toward the living room. At the door, David stopped and turned back to his mother. From across the room, he again held her gaze.

"It's not like I look to fight, Mom," he said softly. "It's just that sometimes, that's what they expect. I don't know why. But that's what it is, isn't it?"

She had no answer for him.

He stepped out through the door and looked toward the gathering of family in the front of the house. His eyes narrowed, and he turned toward his own bedroom.

Elle sat, oblivious of time or the sounds of family in the living room. After a spell, she opened the journal on the table alongside her bed. Entering *Christmas, 1954* the top of the next blank page, she started another entry, her script unusually shaky and uneven from the rage flowing through her:

It is as if they are bent on forcing the boys to become angry and aggressive. Certainly, if Michael was here, he would not support this type of activity, would he? He would not allow our sons to be molded into feisty, angry little Irishmen. The war changed Michael, and the scars that gnawed at him inside kept him from me. But that which remained, the part of him that could still reach out, was kinder and more honest and gentle than the arrogantly bravado boy who brought me here and left me all alone to go to war. And then, he took even that from me, too. I have nothing but the memory of him with which to raise his sons. His brothers and their families seem determined on shaping my sons to be just as their father was... before he was purified by war. How can I be both mother and father to these boys? Why did Michael leave me with this responsibility? Why did he leave me at all? Why did he even bring me here?

It seems that he married me simply to leave me waiting and worrying and raising a family that he will never know. Did he ever even know me? I wonder. I don't think so. How could he possibly think I could handle all this by myself? And yet, he left me with these boys to raise. The audacity…

Chapter Four
The Whitmans

June, 1955

EVERY COUPLE WEEKS, David accompanied Paddy on one of his trips into Baraboo. While his uncle ran errands, David roamed the stacks of the Carnegie Free Library. The volunteer librarian, Mrs. Whitman, often helped David locate books, and she was both amused and amazed at the subjects about which he inquired. No other nine-year-old asked for titles such as *Organizing and Planting Your Garden, Beef Cattle Farming,* and Owen Gromme's *Birds of Wisconsin.*

"Not the routine Hardy Boys reader, are you?" Mrs. Whitman quipped once.

"Read 'em already," David replied as he plopped *David Copperfield* and *Huckleberry Finn* on the librarian's desk.

"David, do you truly expect to finish both of these books in fourteen days?" she asked him.

"If it rains, I do," he smiled. "If it doesn't, I make hay."

During the following two weeks, Mrs. Whitman wondered often how he was faring with more than a thousand pages of literature. The summer skies had brought a lot of rain.

When David next peered at her from under the broad visor of his baseball cap, his nose just clearing the top of the tall check-out desk, Mrs. Whitman greeted him with a smile. "How did you like those books, David?"

"Gotta renew one, I'm afraid," he said. "I finished *Copperfield*. It was great! But I didn't get done with *Huck Finn.*"

Impressed as she was, Mrs. Whitman couldn't resist teasing him as she handed back his renewed copy. "We had a lot of rain, David. I'm surprised you didn't finish *Huckleberry Finn* as well."

"I would've, but I got to playing too much fiddle with Old Camp. We spent the better part of three days doing nothing but fiddling out in the hay mow during downpours. Thanks, ma'am." He stuffed the book into his pack and turned to leave.

"David!" She called him back, surprised. "Did you say you play the fiddle?"

"Yes, Ma'am. Old Camp's been teaching me since I was four. You know Old Camp, Mrs. Whitman? Gabriel?"

She shook her head.

"He's kin. He made my fiddle for me. Gave it to me for Christmas. He's kinda old, but he can still play a wicked fiddle. And he knows a million songs." David paused. Mrs. Whitman was staring at him. He frowned a bit, then turned to leave again.

"David," she called him back once more.

"Yes, Mrs. Whitman?"

"David, I'd like to hear you play. Would you, for me?"

He grinned. "Yes, Ma'am, sure will. Like Old Camp says, fiddlers usually go beggin' for an audience. I'd be delighted to play for you."

"What songs do you know?"

"Oh, I'm working on 'Lonesome Fiddler's Blues' right now. I can already play 'Orange Blossom Special' and 'Cripple Creek.' Then there are some tunes I don't know the names for. Things Old Camp kind of made up. And I really like 'Will the Circle be Unbroken.'" A sudden wave of self-consciousness crept up into his chest, and he broke off. Except for his family, he had never played for anyone before, and here he was boasting about his repertoire.

"If you really want to hear a fiddler, maybe I can get Old Camp to play for you. He's a lot better than I am."

"That might be nice, David. But I'd like to hear you," Mrs. Whitman said. She glanced down almost shyly, then met his eyes again.

"I play the violin, too. And I teach music. I'd be glad to play for you, too."

Well, that's fine with me, David thought.

"How about if I call your folks? Maybe they can bring you to our house. Or I'd be glad to come out to your house, if you'd prefer," she blurted. She cringed as she realized that she'd impulsively invited herself to his home.

But the youngster dispelled any discomfort.

"I'd like that. Then I could play along with Gabriel, too." He beamed another smile. "And I'd like to hear you play, too. Whatcha know?"

"Mozart, Bach, Vivaldi…"

"Never heard of it, 'less that's one of Old Camp's unnamed tunes," he teased. "I still want to hear you, though."

∞

A balmy June breeze rippled across the strawberry leaves. Elle had made shortcake, and David helped her gather the first ripe berries until he heard the crunch of the Whitmans' car on the gravel driveway.

As Mrs. Whitman parked the car, Paddy and Patrick joined Elle and David in the yard. The families exchanged introductions and Mrs. Whitman apologized that her husband had been called in to the hospital.

Her reaction to the boys was typical.

"My, I would never have guessed you to be twins," she said. "Why, Patrick, you stand a full head taller than David."

Patrick shrugged.

David looked at his feet.

"How old are you?" the librarian asked.

"Gonna be nine this week," Patrick boasted.

"Well, happy birthday! To you both," Mrs. Whitman smiled. Turning to her girls, she indicated her fairer daughter. "Wendy will be eight next January." The younger Whitman looked demurely at the twins, flashing lightning blue eyes below loops of creamy blonde bangs and braided pigtails above each ear.

"Jannie is ten," Mrs. Whitman continued. "She's a March baby." Jannie winced at the "baby" reference. She was no taller than her sister, and noticeably thinner. She, too, wore her dark hair braided, but in a pair of fine plaits that ran along the crown of her head and gathered in a single woven cord that reached well down her back. She pivoted her body to and fro on her heels as she stood in the yard.

David felt numb. He had seen Jannie dozens of times at the library, but never realized that she was Mrs. Whitman's daughter. While the two children sometimes nodded greetings, they always went their ways without as much as a word. Now, in his farmyard, she looked vibrant. The light on her face shone differently than in the library, almost as if she glowed. He nodded timidly, and she returned the nod, bowing slightly, meeting his eyes evenly.

"Didn't know you live on a farm," she said shyly. "I mean a real farm. Not like our farm. We have four animals. That's all."

David gazed at the radiant girl in her crisp white blouse under a pressed lime green jumper. He compared her clothes to his faded old t-shirt and bleached-out jeans, which he suddenly noticed were splotched just below his shin with a swatch of soupy green manure.

He crossed his ankles, attempting to hide the ruminated alfalfa, and answered, almost swallowing his words. "Thought you might'a been able to tell."

"Yeah," Patrick interjected. "Especially when you smell like a barn."

David shot his brother a blistering glance.

"I live on a farm, too," Jannie repeated, her voice as soft as a rose petal.

"We have horses now," Wendy added. "April, Joker, Dancer, and Cherub."

"Cherub is mine," Jannie said. "He's an Arabian. So is Joker. Dancer is April's foal. They're Morgans."

"Wow, neat!" David exclaimed. "Do you want to see my calves? I have two new ones, born this week."

Elle squeezed David's shoulder. "There will be plenty of time to take a look at your calves after you play your violin, David. And after we serve our guests some shortcake."

David's face fell. The cattle were his pride. And what was more, the Whitmans were ready to hear him perform, but Gabriel had not arrived. A strange hollowness spread in his stomach.

"Aren't we going to wait for Gabriel?" he asked his mother.

Elle hesitated. She knew that the old man's sense of time was uncanny, unconventional, and uncontrolled. Ask him at any moment what the time was and he could tell you within seconds. But ask him to be at the house at eight fifteen, and he might arrive at ten o'clock. Or noon. He could be anywhere right now, watching the flight patterns of feeding birds, the cattle munching their way across the pasture, or any of the intricacies of nature that unfolded before his eyes.

Paddy spoke up. "Well, unless you're in a hurry to get back to town, Mrs. Whitman, maybe the kids can go look at Davey's calves for a few minutes," he suggested. "That will give Gabriel a little while to show."

Before Helen Whitman had a chance to consent, the children burst into chatter and headed for the barn. David led his new friends and brother, laughing and running toward the barn.

"I think I'll go and keep an eye on them," Paddy said. "Coming along?"

Elle stood mute, her eyes fixed on the large bowl of strawberries cradled in her arms.

Against her inclination, Mrs. Whitman declined.

"I'd be glad to stay and help with these berries," she said. "When the children have had a chance to get to know each other a bit, perhaps David will be more relaxed about playing. If I'm not mistaken, he looked somewhat apprehensive."

"Could well be," Paddy agreed. "Although I've never known Davey to be one for getting butterflies over any sort of challenge, the least of which would be playing his fiddle." Paddy chuckled as he turned to follow the youngsters.

∞

Helen Whitman studied Elle as she followed her into the kitchen. After several clumsy attempts at initiating conversation, she began to regret not having tagged along with the children.

"Have you and Paddy lived here long?" she asked, immediately regretting her question as she saw Elle's entire body quiver and her face convulse in a what looked like physical pain.

"Paddy lives… there," David's mother said, pointing her eyes through the kitchen window toward the farmhouse across the road. "He's not… he's my brother-in-law. My husband died. Drowned. Before the twins were born."

Helen watched Elle's fingers work nervously, pulling the green stems and white cores from the strawberries. Helen reached into the large pottery bowl. She, too, needed something to do with her hands as she tried to talk with this timid, anxious woman.

"Oh, I'm sorry," she offered. "David never told me anything about his family, really. I assumed…" She paused. The conversation swerved into a cul-de-sac of silence.

"David is quite a reader," Helen started again. "I see him often at the library. I'm very impressed with his interests."

Elle visibly relaxed, and Helen probed for firmer footing. "I'm really quite amazed to see the selection of books he checks out. Dickens. London. Thoreau…"

"Thoreau? David is reading Thoreau?" Elle perked up, her gaze boring into Helen's eyes.

"Yes, he reads Thoreau. And Twain. James Fennimore Cooper…" She continued, slowly, listing the authors that the boy had explored over the last year or two. She expounded more on David's reading habits, how regularly he visited the library, and how he came in to study reference handbooks on livestock and agriculture.

Helen kept her eyes on the strawberries, stealing glimpses at David's mother only when she felt the woman relaxing. Then, as she sensed that she'd breached the barriers of Elle's unease, she continued.

"To be honest, Elle, David is an unusual young—," Helen hesitated. She was inclined to say "man," but that did not seem to fit her little friend. Although David was just turning nine, he was not a little boy, especially mentally. In ways, he was ageless. She selected her word, and modified it with tone, "—person."

Elle focused on the strawberries.

Helen considered the other twin, Patrick. "It's difficult to believe that David's brother is his twin," she mused aloud. "They don't resemble one another much at all."

"Patrick is bright, too," Elle defended her older son. "He is just interested in different things than David. He almost died, you know."

"Patrick?" Helen gasped.

"No, David. When he was seven. Almost eight. Pneumonia. The boys were doing some fool thing on a beaver dam. In April. It was cold. He caught pneumonia. And, of course, when he was born. I thought we had lost him. But he just fought his way back. He's a fighter."

As Helen processed Elle's words, the door burst open and the children returned with their raucous report.

"David has *six* calves, Mother! " Jannie said in awe. "He has a whole herd of cattle!"

"You should see the cute little ones," her sister chimed in.

"He's got three Angus calves, two Jerseys and a Holstein," Jannie continued.

"Oh, Mom, can we get a calf, too? Please, mother? They are so-o cute!"

Helen marveled. "How did you come to have so many cattle, David?" she asked the boy, who was glowing with pride.

"Earned them," David replied. "Got the Angus heifers for doing chores for the Mays, making sure the cows have feed and water when Mr. Mays goes to cattle shows and the State Fair. And he just up and gave me one of the calves 'cause she had the scours and he thought she'd die. So he said I could have her if I could bring her around. Which I did. And then both the heifers freshened a month ago, so that brought me up to three Angus calves.

"And the dairy animals?"

"Bought the Jerseys from Paddy in exchange for milking and chores," David replied. "They're the ones that just freshened with my two newest calves, the really little ones. The Holstein, I won. Got my name drawn in the raffle at the twilight meeting at Heatherstone Farms last spring. That's why I call her Twilight. She's a yearling, now, and not a little one. She's almost ready to breed. She's as tame as a puppy."

Helen was impressed by the clear, succinct background the boy had provided. David, however, felt as if he had boasted too much. With his report concluded, he stood silent, gauging the librarian's reaction.

Patrick, on the other hand, had his fill of cow talk, and he looked toward tastier subject.

"Is the shortcake ready, Mom? We gonna have it now?"

"Well, we could, if we're still waiting for Gabriel to show up," Elle said. "Where is your Uncle Paddy? He said he'd whip the cream for us."

"Paddy's tending things in the barn," David said.

Patrick shouted for his uncle from the door of the farmhouse. His bullhorn voice traversed the farmyard, calling his uncle to whip the thick, yellow cream skimmed from yesterday's milkings.

∞

Even after the kids had cleaned the last of the shortcake from their dishes and the adults had emptied their coffee cups, Old Camp had still not arrived. David realized it was time to perform for the Whitmans—and that he had to play alone. The shortcake suddenly felt like a lump of dry biscuit caught in his throat. In the lull after the snack, David left the porch to fetch his fiddle.

Without a word, David stood before Mrs. Whitman. He tucked his fiddle under his chin and looked directly at her. With a dip of the scroll and a flash of his bow, he danced his fingers along the neck of the homemade instrument. To start, he riffed through "Cripple Creek." Foregoing the customary ending tag, he skipped a beat, then picked right back up with "Turkey in the Straw." He kept his bow zinging through "Lonesome Fiddler's Blues." After a second hesitation, he then plucked his E-string: PING, pause; PING, pause; PING; PING; PING; PING. With two long strokes of his bow, David blended an E and an A to create the whistle of a train. He repeated the plucking, gaining momentum.

Paddy picked up the beat with his hand clapping against his thigh. Mrs. Whitman clapped, too; David's fiddling set her toes tapping. Puffs of rosin plumed from his bow as he blazed through "Orange Blossom Special," and wrapped up his debut with the classic bluegrass tag, "Shave and a haircut, two-bits."

Silence followed his last notes. David slowly lowered his fiddle, looking bashfully at Mrs. Whitman. She sat spellbound. He glanced at her daughter and asked, "Okay?"

Jannie beamed, her hands clasped together beneath her chin. But before she could say a word, a commotion like a squirrel in a paper sack broke the stillness of the moment. In a flurry, Gabriel scurried up the walk, admonishing himself to "Hurry, hurry, hurry, Old Gabe."

"Well, here he is. None too late to join the party," Paddy laughed. He introduced Gabriel to the Whitmans.

Nodding and bowing, Gabriel launched into an apologetic explanation for his delay. "First I forgot my bow, but I didn't realize it until I was halfway across the hollow," he said. "And then, I found this." He removed his battered felt fedora to reveal a scrawny, pin-feathered baby dove with big, innocent eyes, perched comfortably in the old man's fluffy white hair.

Elle jumped.

The girls cooed with delight at the little bird, begging to handle it.

"If you are gentle," Gabriel said. "And we all know how gentle little girls can be."

Patrick glanced briefly at the bird, looking bored. David, too, wished to be excused. He was peeved at Gabriel. Not only had the old man reneged on his word to accompany him, but when he did arrive, he acted like a buffoon. *No wonder townsfolk mocked the old man,* he thought. David concealed his chagrin, but his feelings were hurt.

Gabriel placed the tiny gray dove in Jannie's soft hands, and with a glance that seemed to see right through his young protégé, shouldered his fiddle and bowed a low, crooning note, simulating a dove's cry. The young bird sat still in Jannie's hands, curiously eyeing the old man.

David's misgivings melted in the hum of his mentor's music. How could he stay vexed? He shouldered his fiddle, and with long, even strokes, he played a background to Gabriel's avian imitations. David's fiddle whispered, like wind filtering through pine needles.

Gabriel screeched the scolding squawk of a Jay. Then, with the flick of his wrist, he tipped the bow to the A-string and carved out the long clear call of a cardinal: CHEEW-CHEEW-CHEEW-CHEEW. After several minutes of bird song, Gabriel blended his notes with David's, capturing the sound of the wind, soft and low, dancing through the leaves and needles of the forest. When they finished, there was, again, silence.

"I've never heard the violin sing like that," Helen Whitman said.

"I can't rightly say I have either, Ma'am," Gabriel laughed.

"Gabriel said the wind taught him, and the birds," David piped up.

"Squirrels, too. And flowers," Gabriel agreed. "I guess when you choose to spend a lot of time with certain friends, they teach you what they can. And when you hang around as long as I have, well, you can't help listening to the wind and birds and animals."

Helen asked to see David's instrument. Gabriel watched her closely as she studied his craftsmanship. She plucked the strings, listening to the fine resonance welling from the maple and spruce box.

"Would you like to do an encore" she asked David as she returned his fiddle, "now that Gabriel is here to accompany you?"

"An encore, is it?" Gabriel jumped in. "Then it seems I missed our gig. Ah, so it is." He set his instrument down resolutely on the floor of the porch next to a wicker lawn chair, in which he promptly sat.

"Will you play for us?" David asked with an impish grin. "It's your turn!"

Helen smiled and agreed. She unpacked her instrument and tuned the strings. Then, shouldering her violin, she brought the bow to rest on the E string, and with the lightness of a dandelion seed in a summer breeze, played the first measure of Bach's Concerto for Violin and Oboe; Gabriel's wind-music had brought it to mind. The playful violin part called for the complementary hum of the oboe, and Helen planned to play the simple melody for several measures, then improvise into another selection, much like David had done.

Gabriel, however, changed her intentions. He subtly shouldered his fiddle and began to fill in for the absent oboe. As Helen carried the melody toward a finalé of triads, he provided the lilting harmony in smooth, sweeping tones.

As when David finished, silence was the finest applause.

Paddy finally broke the stillness. "Gabriel, I've never heard you play like that."

"I suppose you're too young to have," Gabriel agreed matter-of-factly. Facing Mrs. Whitman, he turned the praise to her. "Nor have I heard anyone play like you for quite a spell. You have great command over Bach's finest music."

"As do you, Gabriel. I certainly didn't expect to hear what I did today from both you and David."

David winced. He realized that his skills were not in the same league as what he had just heard. "I sure can't play like you can," he said sincerely. "That was beautiful."

"Thank you, David. As was your playing. I am most impressed," she said. "I can see you have a good teacher in Gabriel. Which, I admit, disappoints me, because you see, I was hoping perhaps I could give you lessons."

David was lost for a reply. He looked to his mother, who was equally taken aback. She had not considered lessons for her son. Gabriel satisfied his needs, and besides, lessons would be expensive.

Gabriel, however, intervened. "Just what our boy needs," he nearly shouted. "I've taught him about everything I ever knew. Now he needs someone who really knows what violinin' is all about. And I just heard one. Not just a fiddler, like me."

Helen smiled, acknowledging the flattery, but knowing that they both understood his skill as well.

"I really don't know if we can afford..." Elle mumbled.

Paddy read her thoughts and jumped in.

"We can afford it. I'll pay for it. No questions asked. I agree with Gabriel, Elle. David can use lessons, if Mrs. Whitman is willing to teach him."

"Please, please," Helen protested. "I didn't mean to say I was going to charge him for lessons. I said I'd like very much to *give* him lessons. I play and practice myself, and I teach Jannie as well. If David is interested, if he would work and practice, I'd love to help him learn."

David approached his new teacher and extended his right hand.

"Thank you. When do we start?"

Chapter Five
School

PATRICK LOOKED through the motes of dust floating in the light filtering through the schoolroom's hazy windows. Beyond the glass panes, the air outside was clean, the sky an unspoiled blue. Patrick's thoughts traced the arc of a baseball up into the sky. The dream ball followed the same path as those he'd hit during morning recess on the field behind the single room schoolhouse.

Patrick had been at bat when the schoolhouse doors burst open and the little white building belched out a half-dozen youngsters and two eighth-graders, laughing and squawking, released at last from the tedium of lessons. Their appearance meant that recess was over for the middle grades. Patrick trudged to the schoolroom, touched by a case of fresh-air poisoning and dreading the teacher's demands.

"Get your readers out," Mrs. Hatcher ordered.

The children quickly heeded her instructions. They knew what the old disciplinarian expected. Patrick, however, followed along only briefly before his daydreams drew him back outside.

∞

David noticed his brother drifting off while Mrs. Hatcher helped Katie Blyth work through a difficult passage in her reader.

He quietly tore a thin strip from a homework assignment, slipped it into his mouth, and worked it like cud. When the spitball was soggy, he propped it on the edge of his reader. To his left, Petey Harnsdorf saw David's mischief and leaned out of the projectile's flyway. David aimed, cocked his index finger on his thumb, and launched the wad with speed and accuracy. The ball slapped messily into his brother's ear.

Patrick jerked, torn from his dreams, knowing exactly what had hit him and who had launched it. He spun to see both David and Petey intent on their reading. He reached to peel the spitball from his ear, but diverted his hand to his reader when he spotted Mrs. Hatcher's hawk-like stare beamed directly at him. He glued his eyes to his book.

The portly, gray-haired woman stalked down the row and planted her bulk between him and Petey. She reached down to Patrick's book, turned two pages, then jabbed her plump, wrinkled finger to the line where Katie had been reading.

Patrick felt her pudgy finger peel the soggy projectile from his ear.

"Ear wax, would you say, Patrick?" she asked dryly, the ball lodged conspicuously on her fingertip.

"No, Ma'am. Uh, yes, Ma'am," Patrick murmured. His ear burned where she had scraped it. "Must be ear wax."

"Patrick, I have been teaching in this school for forty-one years. I taught your father, all of your uncles, and your aunt. Every one of them. Never have I seen a Joyce appear in class with ear wax that so closely resembled a spitball." She turned away.

Patrick slumped, relieved that she trained her anger elsewhere.

Mrs. Hatcher walked to the head of the row, then strode down the next aisle until she stood between Petey and David.

"Well?" she demanded.

The boys exchanged wide-eyed glances. David broke the silence.

"'T'was my spitball, Mrs. Hatcher."

"See me at noon hour, David."

She returned to the front of the classroom.

"You may resume where Katie left off, Patrick," she commanded.

∞

The teacher could not recall another youngster who had ever galled her so. She wondered whether teaching was becoming too great a task for her. As a younger teacher, when she faced wave after wave of Joyces, she'd never lost her humor at a child's antics so frequently or sharply as she did with David.

He was too much, simply too much. And she was too close to retirement.

David had emerged as an exceptionally bright student during his first two years. By the third grade, he already had command of the material she presented to the fourth, fifth, and sixth grades—and he even grasped the early challenges of algebra, square roots, and other math that eluded the eighth-graders. When she asked for answers to new problems posed to the upper grades, only one student consistently responded: David Joyce.

Rather than nurture the youngster's gifts with academic challenge, as she once might have, she found herself attempting to harness his zeal with punitive discipline. His precocious skills, coupled with relentless enthusiasm and energy, disturbed the tempo of her teaching, and she urged the boy to conform to the norm of his peer group.

But regardless of her tack, David readily mastered concepts that tested and often tripped up the older students. Like his twin, they recognized him as the one certain to know the solutions to difficult problems, and often used him as a crutch when they were stumped.

This, too, annoyed her.

∞

Mrs. Hatcher interrupted the children's work by briskly ringing the shiny bell that stood on the corner of her desk—the same bell that David had once rendered mute by wadding with putty. As the students scurried outdoors with their lunches, Mrs. Hatcher eyed the tiny twin. She waited for the room to clear. Patrick was among the last to leave, glancing tremulously at his brother. He closed the door almost on his own nose, the heavy slam resounding through the room. Mrs. Hatcher watched him go, arms folded stiffly, eyes narrowed, a deep furrow upon her brow.

∞

David watched his teacher curiously. Would she be as angry as when he'd let the corn snake he'd found on the playground slip out of his shirt-sleeve to slither up the aisle toward her desk? Or when he'd sealed the seats in the outhouse? He'd given her plenty of reason to resent him with some of his more mischievous pranks, those motivated simply by the urge to amuse himself.

He had been in third grade when he first saw through the old school teacher's façade.

She had set the classes to work during a study period. When all were busy, she retreated to her desk, shuffled papers, and absently graded assignments, glancing up from time to time to lord discipline over any student impudent enough to dawdle.

When David had scripted the last sentence of the assignment on the coarse, green-lined paper, he looked up to see Mrs. Hatcher reaching for a handkerchief from her handbag on the floor. Her dumpling-shaped body balanced precariously on her sturdy wooden chair, one leg nearly parallel to the desktop, her arm extended.

With a loud *ka-LUMP*, the teacher disappeared, crashing onto the hardwood floor behind her desk. The startled students jumped, looked up from their work, and discovered her gone. Suddenly, like a cat peering through tall grass, her stern, piercing eyes popped up over the desk. As one, the students trained their eyes on their work, coughing back a few muffled snickers. Her thick forearm gained hold on the desktop, but her eyes never left the students. As she pulled herself to her chair, Mrs. Hatcher's glare zeroed in on David Joyce.

The youngster remained spellbound, amused at the spectacle.

Mrs. Hatcher demanded, "David, have you no work to do?"

"I'm done with the assignment," he responded, his eyes still wide. He couldn't wait for recess to detail the entire scene to his friends.

∞

Standing over him as she prepared to address disruption caused by his spitball, Mrs. Hatcher relived the scrutiny of his look as he'd watched her climb painfully off the hardwood floor. Oh, how she had longed for privacy, for the few sacred minutes of freedom that recess would allow. After excusing the students, she had allowed herself to relax for just a moment, free from the piercing gaze of the little boy who noticed everything.

Out on the playground, she saw him. David teetered on an imaginary chair, surrounded by his fellow students. Then suddenly, the tiny youngster crashed to the ground, convincingly miming the collapse of her massive bulk.

The students burst into an uproar, imploring David for an encore. He gladly obliged, spicing the performance with a dash of flagrant disrespect. As he imitated her expression as she peered out from above her desk, she'd seen her own emotions reflected back at her: He caught first her fear, and then the anger she wielded to reign in her class. Recalling the incident, her embarrassment burned anew. How could this mere child look through her, judge her? How had she lost the upper hand?

Glaring at him now, after the spitball, she broke the silence.

"Explain."

"I was just trying to get my brother's attention, is all, ma'am."

"And what business do you have disturbing your brother during study time, David?"

"He was dreaming again, ma'am." David avoided using his teacher's name when speaking directly to her. "If I'm going to spend so much time after school helping him do his homework, I hate to see him dreaming away the time he's supposed to be doing his work in class."

He had her.

Again.

She knew he was right, in principle. She could only attack his means.

"Under no circumstances is there justification for anyone to throw spitballs in my classroom," Mrs. Hatcher retorted. "That is dishonorable. You show no respect. Tonight, David, after class hours, you will remain behind. You will write a five-hundred-word paper on 'Honor.' You will not leave until you are finished. Do you understand?"

"Yes, ma'am."

"Go to lunch," she snapped. *Go to hell,* she thought.

She longed, momentarily, to be at home, relaxing, sipping the amber nectar that eased the burden of teaching.

∞

David reported the extent of the punishment to his fellow students waiting on the grassy playground.

"Five hundred words!" Petey Harnsdorf whistled. "Wow, I didn't think a little old spitball was worth that much."

"Bet you don't even know five hundred words," a younger student teased. "Leastwise not to write. You'll never get home tonight."

No problem, David thought.

∞

After dismissing her students, Mrs. Hatcher called David up to the front of the room. Handing him a thin blue notebook, she said curtly, "Begin."

David took his seat, looked briefly out the window, and put his pen to the paper.

HONOR
AND THE ACT OF BEING HONORABLE
By David Joyce

People act with honor when they are true to what they believe in. If people have no faith, if they have nothing in which they can put their trust, it is difficult to act with honor...

The words came easily. He focused on his resentment of his teacher, a fatuous, shallow educator. With a good start rolling, David paused and counted his words: one hundred sixty-six. He had been working for less than ten minutes.

Mrs. Hatcher sat idly shuffling papers at her desk, but when a woman drove into the school's parking lot, she went out. David heard the sing-song tones of their voices drifting in through the open windows. He recognized the intonations and hushed, rapid, Tommy-gun inflections of gossip. He curled his lip and returned to his work.

...There are many things that keep people from acting honorably. Lying, cheating, and stealing are actions that destroy people's honor. Getting drunk destroys honor. Killing destroys people's honor. So does gossip...

Three hundred twenty-four words. He was cranking it out. No need to pad much further. He wondered if he could contain it to five hundred words. He'd hate to give her more than she demanded. It was not yet four o'clock, he reckoned. Mrs. Hatcher and her friend were immersed in their conversation.

...I believe I acted honorably today when I tried to get my brother's attention back to his work. My brother is a dreamer. All he thinks about is playing baseball. My mother worries about him, because it is so hard to get him to do his schoolwork, unless I help him— or she does.

And he never likes to do any other kind of work, either.

Just play.

And daydream.

So when I do something to help my brother pay attention to his work, I do it honorably. That way, maybe he won't grow up to be a dumb cluck.

I know I don't always act honorably. I realize that the time I tacked cellophane over the hole in the teacher's privy, I was acting with less than honor. But it was a good laugh. And I paid for it with another detention. I can't figure out why a teacher who gets so mad at a student would want to spend so much time with him after school. Five hundred words. The end.

David closed the booklet and put it on his desk. It had taken him twenty-four minutes. He went over to the window to watch the two women chatting on the bench in front of the schoolhouse.

He went back to his desk. He knew that Mrs. Hatcher would expect his punishment to keep him a couple of hours. He sat idle for a minute. Then, like a magnet, his eyes were drawn to the sturdy metal bases on which the students' desks were mounted.

He had examined the steel frames before. The previous summer, he'd helped Paddy and the other students' fathers when they took the desks apart, stacked them in the vestibule, and stripped and varnished the floor. He remembered how the desks were assembled. A set of four screws held each writing surface to its frame. The seats were each fastened on the frame with a collar tightened by a single screw. The screw on Petey's seat was loose, with half of its threads showing. David turned the screw counterclockwise. With the collar loose, he easily lifted the seat off its frame, then replaced it.

Barely pausing, he walked to the coatroom behind the drapery at the rear of the room. The spacious vestibule held a large rubber kickball, several baseball bats, and a box of unclaimed caps, mitts, and singleton galoshes left during the previous winter. Pegs stuck like stubble from the wall; a single scarf hung, forgotten. A metal box with a heavy coat of dust sat on the sill of the coatroom's only window. He opened the box, examined the tools and selected a large screwdriver.

David returned to the window to check on his teacher. She remained in deep conversation. He went back to Petey's desk. The screws holding the desk to the frame turned easily. He took off the desktop and set it in the coatroom. He returned to the classroom, disassembled the desk closest to the rear, and stacked it on top of Petey's. Then he took the seat to the coatroom and leaned it against the wall. Moving faster, he returned to the classroom and worked on the next desk. And then the next.

After he had stacked the last desk and chair in the coatroom, David started on the frames. The cast mountings weighed at least as much as the book-filled desktops. David estimated that each one weighed as much as a bale of hay, but he wrestled them all into the coatroom in near silence. Only his desk and Mrs. Hatcher's desk remained. He stood, satisfied, inspecting the classroom, perspiration beaded on his forehead.

He snuck back to the window. The women, still chatting, were now leaning against the car. David went back to his seat. His stomach clenched with nervous excitement as he anticipated the look on Mrs. Hatcher's face when she entered the classroom. He opened the booklet, preparing to look as if he were still composing when she returned.

In just a few minutes, he grew restless. Peeking out the window again, he saw that the women had returned to the bench. He went to his desk, took out his blue cap with the long visor, picked up the booklet, and walked out to where the women sat talking.

"I'm done." He looked at her with interest. The conversation had softened Mrs. Hatcher's steely expression. Her eyes looked lighthearted, and her face was relaxed. She looked gentle and grandmotherly.

For an instant, David regretted the scene awaiting his teacher in the schoolhouse.

"That didn't take long. Are you certain that there are at least five hundred words?" she snapped, her eyes narrowing hawkishly. "You'll have to start all over tomorrow if you don't have enough words here."

"It's long enough. I counted."

Both women looked at the youngster peering out from under the oversized visor. The boy's little round face, with big brown eyes framed by dark brows, resembled a cherub more than a delinquent.

"All right, you're dismissed," Mrs. Hatcher said, accepting the book.

"David," she called as the boy turned away. Her face was hard. "I'll have no more distractions in my classroom."

David turned away from her glare and ran across the playground, taking the shortcut across the field toward home. Once into the pines, however, he took cover, quickly working his way back to watch her reaction when she returned to the schoolhouse.

The women remained on the bench. Mrs. Hatcher was reading his essay to her friend. Several times, she stopped, looked at her friend, and the two of them shook their heads in wonder. At times, they chuckled. At others, they frowned pensively. The friend made several comments. Mrs. Hatcher nodded in return, then continued reading.

David guessed that Mrs. Hatcher had neared the end when she suddenly appeared flustered and dropped the paper to her lap. Her friend's face lit up, and she grabbed for the paper. Mrs. Hatcher clutched her face in her hands.

David could see her flush all the way from his lookout in the pines. He knew they were reading about the cellophane in the outhouse. Mrs. Hatcher's friend fell back against the bench, her laugh ringing across the schoolyard. David watched a minute longer, then made his way through the pines and fields. He wondered how much more intense the storm caused by the emptied classroom would be after also leaking the story of the outhouse incident, which Mrs. Hatcher had been careful not to spread. He'd barely been punished that time, even though he'd freely owned up to the prank—one detention spent scraping gum off the underbellies of the desks, during which time his teacher had barely been able to look at him. He guessed that her fear of her friends hearing about the booby trap that had left her sitting in her own movement had been great enough to make her stifle her anger at him.

∞

At home that night, he waited for Mrs. Hatcher to race her car angrily down the drive, demanding to speak with David's mother.

But nothing happened. The evening passed peacefully, although David harbored a sense of foreboding. He watched his mother go about routine chores: folding wash from the line, washing up dinner dishes while the boys worked on their school assignments. Apparently Patrick had downplayed the spitball incident. When Elle asked casually why he had been so late coming from school, David explained his detention assignment, and she accepted his account with little concern.

Long after bedtime, David lay awake listening to tunes playing softly on the radio.

Before retiring, Elle entered the boys' room to turn off the music. When she found her younger son wide-eyed, she sat on the edge of his bed.

"Something bothering you, David?" she asked. "Something from school today?"

"Yep."

"You want to talk about it?"

"Kinda," David sat up slowly, his mouth twisted.

"I did wrong at school today," he began.

Elle waited patiently.

"I crossed Mrs. Hatcher. I don't know why, but I just went ahead and did something mean 'cause I knew it would irk her."

"You mean the spitball?"

"Naw. That was nothing. Though she made like it was something real big. It seems a lot of times I do things that one of the other kids might do, but she really gets mad if I do it." David shook his head. "Most of the time I don't think what I do is bad enough to get her that angry with me."

"What did you do this time?" Elle asked.

David peered into his mother's eyes. In the dim light from the hallway, they seemed bottomless. He searched her face for the resemblance he so often heard was mirrored in his own eyes. Instead he saw worry and burden, and most of all, loneliness.

"I took the desks apart. At school. The only desk left in the classroom is mine." He allowed a sheepish grin to sprout across his face.

Elle was puzzled. She tried to imagine the deed.

"That doesn't seem so bad," she said. "It's not like you destroyed the desks, is it?"

"It's not so much the desks, Mom, as what I meant by doing it," David said. "I just feel like doing mean things to old Mrs. Hatcher. She makes me feel that somehow she deserves it. Like she's getting by, without doing anything exceptional as a teacher. Nothing extraordinary. Just coming to school and doing the same stuff as she did back when my father was her student. But all worn out, with no enthusiasm at all. It doesn't seem fair. It's like she's not trying."

"Oh, David." Elle looked away, summoning up her words. She brought her gaze back to his. "That might just be the way it seems. You know, every person has his or her own gifts. And it's not really your place to judge her, you know. She has been teaching children in this town for many years. If she wasn't a good teacher, do you think people would let her continue?"

"Maybe that's just North Freedom," he said. "Everybody is happy with the same old thing."

Elle thought a minute, then replied gently, "That is not true, David. Just think of your Aunt Kate. She went through grade school under Mrs. Hatcher, and look at all she has achieved. Why, she's a professor at the University!"

David looked down at his hands. "Yeah. I guess that's just what I mean. I wasn't thinking. I just do things to her that are kind of mean." He leaned his head on his mother's shoulder.

"You are not a mean young man, David. I'll go talk to Mrs. Hatcher. Maybe she will have some suggestions. Now get some sleep, or you'll fall asleep during class tomorrow," she said, tucking her son under the sheet. "And then you would be in real trouble."

∞

To David's surprise, there was no trouble at school the next morning. There was no school at all. As David and Patrick drove the pony-cart into the fenced lot next to the schoolyard, they noticed several older students clustered on the steps of the schoolhouse. A sheet of paper was tacked to the door. While David unhitched old Fred from the cart and led him to the paddock beyond the pines, Patrick joined his friends.

"What's going on, Bobby?" Patrick called to a tall, lanky boy at the top of the stairs.

"No classes today!" Bobby Bluhm said, peering at the note. "Mrs. Hatcher left a message saying she isn't going to be here today."

David cringed as the students' chatter carried across the school yard. He ran to join the group inspecting Mrs. Hatcher's looping script. The note said simply:

School is closed. I will not be here to teach the classes. The children should return home.

Mrs. Elva Hatcher

David read and reread the notice, seeking subtle nuances in the words. A sinking feeling welled in his chest, and he sensed that this was much more than a day off from school. Around him, the other students wondered aloud about Mrs. Hatcher's motives for canceling class. As quickly as one boy or girl could suggest a reason for the teacher's action, the next student voiced a different thought. But they quickly lost interest, focusing instead on their newfound freedom.

"Hey, I know what I'm gonna do," Petey Harsdorf blurted. "I'm going fishing. I bet the smallmouth are biting on Seeley Creek today. Anybody want to come along?"

"Hold on," one of the Faivre boys called to Petey as he left to trade in his school books for his fishing pole. "I'm coming."

"Don't you want to get a ball game going?" Patrick called. "We'd have enough for two full teams, if we let the girls play."

The fishermen hesitated.

"Let us play? Baloney!" Annie Belter snapped at Patrick. The eighth-grader wielded a bat better than most of the boys. "Ask us first. Then see if we even *want* to play."

"The note says we should return home," Katie Blyth said meekly.

"Doesn't say we have to."

"Says we should."

"I say we play ball."

"Naw. I can feel them biting," Petey said. "I'm going fishing." He turned and marched out of the schoolyard, a half-dozen of the boys following along. The rest of the students headed home, alone or in pairs.

As the other students left, Patrick shrugged. "Guess we coulda just kept old Fred hooked up."

The younger twin scrunched up his face, squinting his eyes and puckering his lips. "I dunno. Maybe we ought to check things out." He sauntered casually around the school house. Then, raising an eyebrow, he said, "Wanna see why there's no school?"

Patrick looked both curious and confused. He shrugged. "Sure."

David tugged at the door, but it was tightly locked.

"Let's try the back." He took off around the side of the school.

Patrick followed in stride, but the rear door was locked as well.

"How about down through the bell steeple?" David suggested.

Patrick looked at him quizzically.

"If you give me a boost from the bench, maybe I can reach the roof. If I can get to the roof, I bet I can shimmy down through the bell tower," David said.

The twins grabbed each end of the bench on which Mrs. Hatcher had gossiped with her friend the previous evening. They carried it across the schoolyard and set it alongside the wall of the school.

Patrick hopped up on the bench, and David climbed his brother like a squirrel up a tree. The older twin lifted David's feet off his shoulders and easily hoisted him within reach of the rain trough.

"Hope it holds," David said as he grasped the gutter. He lifted his wiry body onto the roof and scrambled on all fours up the steep incline to the bell tower. The opening was little more than a foot square, but David slipped through, feet first.

Inside the steeple, David found a ladder fastened to the wall to service the bell from below. He climbed down to a trapdoor held closed by a small wooden turn-peg underneath. He tried it, but it held tight. Clinging to the ladder, David first jumped lightly, then more forcefully on the trapdoor. He felt the latch giving. Once, twice more he jumped, and the latch popped and the door swung open.

David grabbed tight to the rung of the ladder, breaking his fall, then lowered himself until his feet touched the top of one of the cabinets against the wall.

He climbed down the desks that he had piled up along the wall and headed for the front door, but without the key, he couldn't unlock it, even from the inside. He went back into the schoolroom and opened a window. Then he jumped down onto the soft grass of the schoolyard.

Patrick was waiting for him in the front by the door.

"Couldn't unlock it," David said. "Come on. Let's put this bench back."

After setting the bench by the parking area, they returned to the opened window, looking around one last time to see if they were being observed.

David considered the plan forming in his mind.

"Wanna give me a hand?" he asked, hitching his head toward the schoolhouse.

Patrick wrinkled his nose. "Whatcha gonna do?" he asked. "Can't image why we're going into school when we get a free day."

A grin spread across David's face.

"Oh, it'll be a bit different today, that's for sure."

David climbed back through the open window and inspected the empty classroom. The air felt stuffy and hot. He paused to admire the specks of dust floating in the sun-lit air. The blue composition booklet in which he had written his punishment lay open on the big oak desk at the front of the room. He perched on the corner of the teacher's desk, looking at his own desk alone in the classroom.

"Whoa!" Patrick cried as he hefted himself through the window. "What happened here? Where are all the desks?"

David smirked.

It took but a few seconds for Patrick to make the connection. A big grin spread across his face. "So this is why we have no school. Golly darn, Davey. Did you do this?"

David nodded.

"She made you take detention, and like magic, you made all the desks disappear," Patrick laughed. "You're going to kill that old woman!"

David winced at the thought, but turned to lead the way back to the coatroom.

"Holy mackerel," Patrick gasped when he saw the stacked desks. "How'd you do this all yourself?"

"Wasn't hard," David said, explaining how he'd helped prepare the floor for varnishing.

"You wanna just leave them like this?" Pat asked. "Maybe we won't have school all week then."

David mulled over that prospect for a moment, but his imagination was busy conjuring another idea.

"Nope. Come on, Twinnie. We gotta put these desks together before Mrs. Hatcher comes back. My guess is, she will be back." He set to work.

Patrick laughed, shaking his head at his brother's mischief. He could see how it was unfolding, and he wanted in. Old Mrs. Hatcher was going to do a somersault through reality, and she'd really be doubting her sanity by the time David finished with her.

Reassembling the desks proved more difficult than breaking them down. The screw holes seldom aligned. David positioned the pieces and carefully threaded the screws as Patrick held the parts in place. He replaced each desk on its frame, checked the contents to see whose possessions were within, and then placed the desk in its proper position in the rows. With Patrick lugging the heavy frames, they made fairly good time.

By noon, the brothers had restored the classroom to order. Perspiration dripped down their faces. They sat, a bit fatigued, on the last desk, joking and chuckling about the transformation, when tires crunched faintly on the gravel outside.

The twins moved quickly to the window.

Superintendent Gantner was pulling up to the building, Mrs. Hatcher beside him. She was talking earnestly, gesturing wildly as he parked near the front doors. Dr. Gantner nodded with understanding.

David glanced back to Patrick. He stood wide-eyed, his thoughts showing clearly on his face.

"Uh oh! We've been caught!" he muttered.

"Not yet!" David responded, shifting into action. "Come on."

He closed and locked the window. Exhilaration edging on panic churned his gut. He ran to the coatroom, turning to survey the classroom one last time. The screwdriver lay atop a desk near the front of the room. David sprinted to retrieve the tool. He danced back to the coatroom on tiptoes, fearing his footsteps would be heard. Replacing the toolbox, he jumped for the trapdoor. It was too high. He jumped again, but fell short.

"Come on," Pat urged, grabbing his brother and slinging him up to the top of the cabinet, where David caught his footing and stepped up through the ceiling.

With a surging leap, Patrick caught the bottom rung of the bell tower ladder. He hung briefly to stop himself swinging back and forth, then pulled himself up into the tower like a monkey. Propping himself in the chute with toe holds on the ladder, Patrick reached down for the cord that dangled from the top of the trap-door. As a key rattled in the front lock, he pulled the trapdoor shut.

The twins stood motionless, listening to Dr. Gantner's voice outside the schoolhouse door as he tried to calm the agitated teacher. The lock turned, the door creaked open, and the educators entered the schoolhouse. Mrs. Hatcher ranted on as they strode through the entryway, and then… silence.

David could hear only the buzz of wasps nesting near the bell, and his brother's deep breathing. Across from him in the narrow tower, Patrick grinned like a goon. He strained to keep the door closed. David couldn't allow himself to make eye contact with his brother; he knew they would both break out laughing. Sweat dripped from his nose, plopping in the dust on the floor of the bell tower.

David heard the muffled sounds of a calming voice as Dr. Gantner resumed the conversation with Mrs. Hatcher. Desks slammed closed with sharp reports, one after the other in succession, as she checked to ensure that they were in order.

As abruptly as they had come, David heard a set of footsteps hurry from the school. A second, heavier set of steps followed slowly, leaving the classroom, pausing in the vestibule.

He glanced at his brother. Patrick held fast on the rope to the door. His face, however, was scrunched up and red, his eyes watering and his nose twitching as he held back a sneeze. In the hot, stuffy tower, his allergies were raging.

David cupped his hand over his brother's nose, pressing evenly, hoping to thwart the sneeze. It came anyway, but his hand muffled the sound. Patrick's eyes opened wide; clear, watery snot coated the palm of David's hand. David grimaced, disgusted. Patrick squeezed his eyes shut and turned his head away to assure he couldn't see his twin. He shook, trying to control his laughter.

David grabbed the point of Patrick's nose with his index finger and thumb, pinching and twisting. He tipped his head in caution and mouthed, "Quiet."

The footfalls moved across the floor beneath them, hesitated almost half a minute, and then turned and left the school. They heard the door lock. Distant, surreal murmurs now drifted down through the top of the bell tower as the adults walked to the car.

"If you think I will step foot back in this schoolhouse, you are wrong. Wrong. *Absolutely wrong!*"

David listened to Mrs. Hatcher's shouts. Though her voice was faint, the intonations of her rage carried clearly. Dr. Gantner's voice, on the other hand, sounded calm and subdued, too low to carry clearly into the tower. The car doors slammed, the engine started, and the car pulled away.

Patrick let the trapdoor fall open and jumped to the floor. David dropped down behind him. He jimmied himself up on the file cabinet and reached over to pivot the peg that held the trapdoor shut, only to discover that the latch, loosened from its mount when they entered, had been forced off completely. Only empty screw holes remained where it had been fastened. He looked to his brother, who stood wide eyed, staring at the displaced latch. It had been set in full view on top of one of the cabinets.

"Wow," he gasped.

From the coatroom window, David checked to be sure that they were indeed alone. He turned and wiped his slimed fingers on his brother's shirt. "So gross!"

Patrick beamed, then rubbed his puffy nose on his shirtsleeve.

David fetched the screwdriver from the tool kit and returned the latch to its original position, relieved it still seemed strong enough to keep the tower door closed.

They returned to the classroom and slipped easily out the window, pulling it shut behind them. Peeking around the corner of the schoolhouse, David checked one last time for Dr. Gantner's car. Patrick chortled and snorted behind him. Seeing nothing, David cut across the playground to the shade of the pines, where old Fred waited, lazily chewing a wad of greens. The boys hastily hitched up the pony, hoping that neither their teacher nor the superintendent had noticed the animal grazing beyond the thick cover of the pines. They drove the pony on the shortcut back to the farm, laughing and recounting their adventure.

There were no classes on Thursday, nor on Friday. On Monday, they learned that school had let out for the year, and they would be sixth graders in the fall.

July, 1959

JANNIE WHITMAN LOOKED up from her reading and greeted David with a smile. Inspecting the books he set across from her on the wooden library table, she faked a yawn. He muffled his chuckle, then, raising his eyebrows, he eyed her book. She tilted the hardback up from the table to reveal its cover: *The Black Stallion.*

"Again?" David teased, widening his eyes in feigned disbelief. Jannie glanced again at David's titles. She smirked, then returned to her chapter.

David opened the first of his three books, *How to Feed Your Dairy Cattle.* He read a section on hay quality and evaluation, then scanned the chapter on "Feeding Grain for Increased Milk Yields."

He set the book aside and turned to a larger volume with smaller print and many charts and graphs. The print on the spine of the heavy book read, *Ruminant Nutrition.* David struggled through a section on forage, jotting unfamiliar words on paper he had snatched from atop the card catalogue. Later, he would copy them into his notebook at home, along with the definition from his mother's *Webster's.*

Finally, David turned to a short book, little more than a bulletin, *Buying Holstein Cattle.* He perused the introduction and the first chapter, "Genetics: Understanding Pedigrees."

Jannie interrupted. "We better go. My mom's going to be waiting."

Book bags over their shoulders, they skipped down the front stairs of the library, hustling to their violin lesson at the Whitmans'. Jannie was a nod taller than David, but was slighter in build. With similar dark features, the two could pass as brother and sister. Jannie's dark brown hair, long and shiny, dangled in a ponytail to her waist. Her eyes were larger than David's, and wider. Both had brown eyes so rich in pigment that the irises appeared indistinguishable from the pupils, except in the light of the sun.

David's sharp features mirrored his mother's. His lean, tight jawline broadcast his earnest determination, while Jannie's face was softened by her high, wide cheek, accenting her kind smile. In the mid-June heat, David noticed the fine hairs above her brow, highlighted by the bright sunlight. Tiny beads of perspiration glistened on the down across her forehead and under her eyes. Although she was a year older, she looked as young as David—who was a runt compared to his brother and his pals at school.

David relished the music classes he and Jannie had shared for the past four years. Mrs. Whitman was an upbeat yet demanding teacher, and she prodded her students to strive for the full satisfaction of their efforts. She was also patient, doling out gentle criticism when she knew how to build upon their errors. David reveled in the moments when Mrs. Whitman would hum a pure, precise tone, calibrating her students' ears before gliding the bow across the strings of her violin, teaching him to repeat an exact note, or melody of notes, on his instrument.

Music filled the Whitmans' home. David grew to appreciate the beauty of symphonic music performed by some of the world's greatest artists: Stern, Heifetz, Menuhin, and, of course, Fritz Kreisler. He always noticed the recordings playing in the background as he and Jannie busied themselves in their other interests.

David compared the music of the Whitmans' home to the silence of his own, occasionally broken by sparse conversation or the tinny tones of the bedside radio, which Patrick often listened to as he fell asleep. Sometimes after his twin started snoring, David rolled the dial to locate the public radio station from Madison, which he recognized by the sober-voiced announcers and the strains of classical music.

At other times, he tuned into the Reedsburg country music station, hoping to hear his favorites, like Patsy Cline's full, rich voice singing "I Fall to Pieces." Usually, David left the radio tuned to Patrick's favored rock-and-roll station, or the Milwaukee station that broadcast the Braves games. Occasionally they dialed in WLS from Chicago. He listened, intrigued, as the disc jockey issued warnings about overcrowded traffic conditions on the city's expressways, or, on hot summer days, reminded sunbathers on Chicago's beaches that it was time to turn over to tan evenly on their backs as well as their fronts.

The sounds from the shoe-box-sized radio were not as uplifting, David thought, as the stereophonic recordings that filled Jannie's house, but the rhythm still set his toes to tapping. Nothing touched his soul, however, like the music he and Jannie made.

∞

While David spent the summer of the twins' thirteenth year focused on lofty goals with his 4-H livestock projects, Patrick chased his dream of winning every Little League game he pitched. His team, the Baraboo Blues, was unbeaten after eleven starts. With one game left before the regional tournament, Patrick looked forward to pitching against new and tougher teams on the way to the state championship. Coach Bill Blackmon fed Patrick's ambitions and built up the confidence of his team.

"This is quite a group of ballplayers," Blackmon said to the parents watching their boys from the bleachers, well within earshot of his team. "If they keep their heads on the ballgame and continue to make the plays they've been making, we'll be right in the thick of things at the state tourney down in Madison. What we have here is real championship material."

Paddy would have considered Blackmon's praise merely morale-boosting lip service, had he not run into the coach at the co-op while he was having a load of corn ground. Blackmon was purchasing lime for the baselines.

"Paddy, this is probably the best team I will ever coach," Blackmon said quietly, "especially from as small a community as Baraboo. Every coach looks for a special team, one loaded with talent. This team has more than just ability, though. They have that spirit, that drive, you know, and the imagination that enables them to just keep on winning." He leveled an eye at Patrick's uncle. "And your nephew is the best of the bunch. He'll take us there. I fully expect we'll be playing in Madison next month."

∞

Patrick trembled. One fist clenched tightly at his side, the other thrusting a soiled t-shirt before her impassive face, he impatiently waited for his mother to answer. As he watched her slip deeper into the semi-catatonic fog he readily recognized, his frustration mounted. He wanted to shake her, to bring her to her senses. Couldn't she even keep his clothing clean? Couldn't she do something more than just be there?

He turned and left, pulling the grass-stained t-shirt over his head as he stomped to his three-speed propped against the porch. He pumped the pedals fiercely, gritting his teeth, his anger welling.

Why can't she be like some of the other guys' mothers? He didn't see Mrs. Graber or Mrs. Terry moping around like they were half alive. They were always at the games. They even had fun watching their kids! Mrs. Blackmon was neat, too, always real friendly to all the players. A lot of times, after away games, she'd ask her husband to pull the station wagon into an A&W and she'd treat everyone to a root beer. *Why couldn't I have been her son? Kind of sad,* he thought. *The Blackmons with no kids of their own, and Mrs. Blackmon being so nice to all the guys, and my own mother won't even look me in the face.* He couldn't figure it out. There seemed to be no justice in it. Nothing fair about it at all.

∞

Elle churned deep inside as her son pedaled angrily from the farmhouse. From her wicker chair on the porch, she watched him dissolve into the waves of mid-morning heat wafting off the road.

He is just a boy, she reminded herself. *He needs to express himself, to identify himself.* Only a slight frown hinted at the rage and guilt that battled within her. She felt like a caged bird, frantic and trapped. She was trying, so desperately trying, to control her emotions.

Almost daily, when faced with what she knew should be simple challenges, she experienced the sensation of bursting into billions of sparkling particles, spinning and spiraling at tremendous speed away from her center. She was so alone, left behind, trapped in dark, open space, seeing the lingering sparks of her emotional explosions fading, fading, fading… until she fell, abandoned, into the dark, empty shell of her lonely soul. Outwardly still, she spun in a vortex that swallowed the light, trying to stabilize herself, to stay above the darkness, trying, trying, trying…

She didn't know what to try for.

"You have to try," Kate had pleaded as she took Elle to the appointments with the specialists in Madison. "Please, Ellie, you must try."

Try. Elle had tried. She had tried and tried and tried and tried, groping recklessly at the shadows in her soul for hints of joy, happiness, peace, God grant it possible….

Her memories of joy and peace were waning and distant, echoes of echoes fading in a fog. Elle remembered joy as she remembered pain; she knew it well, but she couldn't recall the intensity of pain's color, nor the flavor of joy. She tried to recall happiness, to savor a taste of peace. What she inevitably conjured instead were leaden ingots of emotion, those that settled nearest and soonest: remorse, fear, dread. And they were gray and tasted of ash.

At her best, she dreamt of stars in the darkness. She had heard once that stars die, but that their light travels on continuously in long, shimmering, undulating waves that reached to and defined the ends of the universe. Abstractly, she pondered what it might be like at the source of that light, before it unspooled and trailed away. Was it possible to catch on to the tail of a beam of starlight and wrestle it into control—or at least cling to it for the ride? Could she gather fragmented waves, she wondered, first one beam, then another… Could she retrieve the strands of light that once lit her soul? *I would have to be everywhere, always,* she thought, *to be able to restore order to my being. Everywhere. Only God is everywhere.* That is what they taught, anyway. That is what she had learned as a child. Before she had witnessed her world blow up on her time and again.

If God is everywhere, she wondered, *why isn't He here, within me, where I am so alone? Dare He not venture here? Does He bother not with me? If He were here, would He bring back the light? Maybe that is where He has gone, to fetch the tails of all those light beams streaming across space. How long does it take God to be everywhere? What is keeping Him?*

Try, she remembered. *Just, try.*

Try prayer, a voice within her repeated.

How? she answered. She'd tried the worn shining beads that Michael's mother had given her as a baptismal gift, on the evening when the priest dripped water on her forehead. *Funny,* she thought. *The Catholics don't even embrace their sacrament of baptism as fully as my mother's church did.* Her husband had taught her to say the prayers: the Lord's Prayer, the Glory Be, and the Hail Mary, each on its appointed bead or gap on the fine wire chain. *Why does she get ten prayers for every one that I say to Him?* Elle had wondered when she first learned the ritual. *How come I'm praying to her? What can she do that the Lord can't? Does it take ten of her prayers to do what one of His does? Does she deserve more than He?*

Elle didn't know. All she really wanted to do was talk with Him. Or her.

And listen to what they said.

∞

Her prayers, she thought, were no more effective than her pills.

She did feel better, possibly. Sometimes. More in control, now and again, since she had started the medication the doctors in Madison prescribed. Apathetically in control. The ingots still weighed her psyche, but she just didn't care. She'd seen two psychiatrists: a Dr. Vincenti, who David's friend Dr. Whitman had recommended, as well as Kate's acquaintance, Dr. Goldman. Both men prescribed the same drug, Thorazine. She had taken the pills for two weeks, and while nothing seemed to be resolved in the whirlpool of worry spinning in her mind, she'd notice a decrease in her emotional explosions—until the argument with Patrick.

He criticized her so unfairly. He had stood before her on the porch, soiled shirt in hand, bare chested, lips pursed and eyes livid.

"Aren't there any clean shirts?" he demanded. "I've got nothing to wear."

"I'm sorry, Patrick, the machine is broken," she explained.

"Well, aren't you gonna get somebody to fix it?" he screamed, incredulous.

She sat mute in her wicker rocker. She didn't know who she could get to fix the machine that was older than her sons. It had been one of Michael's improvements the year he returned from the War. He would not go without clean clothes, he made clear, ever again. But he had not put the burden of the laundry on his wife. He enjoyed doing it himself, comparing the clean clothing to what he had put in the machine. David was like his father in that respect. He took joy into the little things, such as clean wash, and was willing to help get it done. Patrick expected it to be done for him.

She was afraid that she had worn out the machine, keeping the twins' clothes laundered their entire lives. If it was gone, how would she replace it? Even if it was reparable, who could she get to do the work? Maybe Paddy would take a look at it later. She just didn't know...

∞

When David returned from the barn after chores, he found his mother, her normally pallid face flushed and tearstained, wringing out a shirt amidst a sudsy mess in the kitchen sink. A mound of laundry was heaped on the counter next to the water basins, yet to be washed. A smaller mound of tightly wadded, wet clothes was bunched on the counter opposite the soiled heap. Elle scrubbed relentlessly.

David watched her rhythmic pushing and pulling on the garments, the splashing of the water, undulating in eerie accord with the bobbing and bowing of Elle's head and shoulders as she washed the clothes, oblivious of her son's presence in the kitchen. He stepped over to the sink and looked closely at the process, still unnoticed by his mother. There was a strange muttering and humming coming from deep within her throat.

"What are you doing?"

No reply.

"Mom, how come you're doing this?"

Nothing.

David reached up and dabbed at a tear running down his mother's face. Suddenly, she turned and focused on him. David saw an unfamiliar gleam in her eyes. Hope fluttered, momentarily, as he returned her look. He searched her eyes, wondering if what he saw was an inkling of passion, if not peace. He smiled, then laughed, a little warbling laugh.

"I'm doing the wash," his mother said, her voice pert and filled with pride. The lilting flow of her words startled David; he'd grown quite accustomed to her soft, monotonic murmuring.

"Why are you doing it in the sink?"

"The machine's broken. It won't work. I'm going to do it myself."

David stepped away as she returned to pumping and thrashing the sopping clothing. He walked into the laundry room where the wash machine stood idle against the wall next to the window. David turned the knob, but nothing happened. Not even the light on the control panel was on. He checked the plug; it was firmly in place. He pulled it from the outlet. The iron sat cool on the ironing board, its cord dangling. David plugged the iron into the outlet and turned it up to high. He waited a moment, then, wetting his index finger on his tongue, he lightly tapped the bottom of the iron. He frowned and touched the iron again, not quite so fleetingly. He placed his open hand on the heating plate. The metal was cool.

From the other room, he could hear sounds of fresh water pouring into the sink, and then a heavy, repetitive thud. He went to the kitchen doorway. His mother was pounding a bundle of wash the size and shape of a large batch of bread dough on the edge of the wash bin.

David returned to the washing machine and climbed onto it to reach the fuse box. He swung the door of the box open to reveal two fuses, both badly scorched. He reached for the dust-coated cardboard box sitting on top of the breaker. Inside were four fresh fuses, identical to the ones in the fuse box, but without charred tops. Seeing the threading on their narrow bases, David turned the spent fuses in the box. They stuck at first, but once he broke the caught threading, they screwed out easily. David inserted the new fuses, closed the fuse box, and hopped off the machine. He replaced the plug and he pulled the control knob again. Water sloshed into the basin as the control panel light flashed on.

His mother glided into the washroom. Her face was ashen.

"How did you do that?" The monotone had returned.

David held up a spent fuse. "I put some new fuses in."

Elle nodded and returned to the kitchen. David followed.

She gathered the wash, but the zest was gone. As David helped her move the mounds of laundry into the washroom, he regretted replacing the fuses. Elle remained in the washroom with the machine, feeding it items of laundry, dropping one piece at a time into the churning water.

Ravenous after his morning chores, David wandered back into the kitchen. He planned to meet the Whitmans for a picnic at the lake, but couldn't wait that long to have at least a snack. And he knew his mother would forget to eat if he didn't make her a sandwich.

Just a swallow of milk sloshed in the bottom of the stainless steel pitcher. David knew that it had held a quart or more, fresh from last night's milking, when he'd left for the barn at dawn. He could see the lip smudges on the rim where Patrick had chugged it. David set the container aside and inspected the contents of the refrigerator.

The choices were few. A bag with five slices of bread, including the crusts; a sticky, quarter-full jam jar; a covered pan; some old ketchup, caked with dark, condensed drippings on the neck of the bottle; a saucer with butter, half the stick melted evenly across the surface of the china, the other half gouged and chiseled, floating like a barge atop the lake of clear yellow fat. Three eggs, two beige and one brown, the remains of the dozen David had nabbed from Paddy's hens two days before.

David grabbed the bread and jam and closed the door. He opened an upper cabinet and found the peanut butter. Brown, sticky globs smeared the top third of the jar. The lid was missing, and a gooey knife was stuck against the inside of the rim. Only the dregs along the insides of the jar remained. David took a rubber spatula from a drawer under the counter and scraped the last of the peanut butter onto two pieces of bread and topped each with a smear of jam. He took the open-faced sandwiches into the laundry room.

"Here." He handed a piece to his mother.

"Thank you."

They ate their lunch as they watched the agitator pounding the sudsy water.

"I'll pick up bread and some peanut butter on the way home," David said. "Do you want anything else?"

"Bananas." Elle craved bananas. "Just bananas."

∞

Helen and Wendy Whitman were waiting at the beach when David and Jannie returned from their hike along the rocks on the east shore of Devil's Lake. Jannie launched into a detailed description of their adventure, but abruptly stopped short.

"I've got to go to the bathroom. Want to come along?" Jannie asked her mother. Her sister joined them as they walked along the beach toward the bath house, chatting happily.

David went to the wooden picnic table where they had parked their bikes. He rode Jannie's cycle over to the sand where her mother had laid out the beach towels, then walked back for his own. He'd almost reached the fat-tired bike when he heard the clatter of baseball cards slapping the spokes of a speeding bicycle, a racket that usually heralded his brother's arrival. David spotted Patrick and his buddies bearing down on him along the path from the parking area.

"Hey, Little Man," Patrick called.

David cringed. It irked him that Patrick used that demeaning nick-name, especially when they were away from home and in the presence of his friends. Billy Graber, Bobby Johnson, Bobby Schellinger, and Ricky Terry all followed close behind his brother, and they rode like a posse of vigilantes.

"Did you bring anything along to eat?" Patrick demanded.

"I didn't. Jannie's mom fixed us a picnic, but we ate already," David said, pushing the Baby Ruth that he and Jannie had saved for later deeper into his hip pocket..

His brother caught David's motion and peered over his twin's shoulder. "Whatcha got in your pocket, Little Man? Lemme see!"

Patrick cruised around his brother, turning his front wheel up against the heavy black tire of David's bike, trapping him. With his free hand, he grabbed David's shorts, pulling on the belt loop and reaching for the candy bar.

David hated being picked on because he was so much smaller. His brother wasn't like that at home, but around his friends he often acted like a bully. David backed away into his bicycle, keeping as far as possible from his brother's greedy reach.

"That's not yours. I'm saving it—" David protested, trying at the last minute to catch himself, "—for Jannie."

"Ooohhh," Patrick sang. "For Jannie. He's saving it for Jannie."

"Davey sure likes to play with girls," Ricky joined in.

"Rather be with the girls than play with the boys," Billy added. "Put your fingers in her pants, eh, Davey?"

David felt like a squirrel cornered by a pack of hounds, and his face reddened with anger, fueled by fear. He gripped the handlebars of his bike and forced it past his brother, but Patrick reached neatly into David's pocket and snatched the candy. David lunged for the candy as Patrick tore open the wrapper and stuffed an end into his mouth. As his bicycle crashed into Patrick's, his handlebars tangled in the spokes of his brother's front wheel.

Straddling his larger bike, Patrick lost his balance, staggering forward awkwardly. His pedal spun around, pinning his foot to the ground, and the big twin flipped hard onto the grass. His left shoulder popped like a cork as it took the brunt of his fall. Patrick's cry of pain was muffled by the candy bar sticking from his mouth.

"Arrgh… my shoulder!"

David darted around the pile of tangled cycles to where his brother lay helpless, crying, unable to sit up. Patrick's shoulder seemed caved in, and his arm lay limp at his side. A lump, perhaps an inch across, protruded up beneath his skin like a tentpole. It stuck a good two inches above the plane of his chest.

"Oh, boy," David murmured.

"Now you did it," one of the guys accused. David barely heard him. His brother lay hurt, and his mind raced as he tried to figure out what to do.

∞

Helen Whitman had spotted the boys' scuffle as she and her daughters walked back from the bath house. She saw David's brother bully him, and David's fear, then anger. Helen was annoyed when the bigger boy stole the candy, and then speechless when David reacted violently. When she saw Patrick trip and fall and heard the boy's ligaments pop from across the picnic area, she broke into a run.

As she rushed to the boys, Patrick rolled to his side, trying to prop himself up with his good arm. David had stepped behind his twin and supported his back as Patrick rolled onto his hips and sat up. Together, they got

Patrick onto his feet. Aside from his awkwardly placed shoulder, he could walk with David and Helen at his sides. They loaded him into her car. She wished she could phone her husband to tell him they were on the way to St. Claire's.

∞

David sat glumly at the kitchen table, listening as the adults discussed the extent of Patrick's injury.

His brother had broken no bones, but had torn ligaments and tendons. His clavicle had ripped from its joints at both ends and the ball atop his humorous had popped from the shoulder joint. A doctor at St. Claire's in Baraboo, one of Dr. Whitman's colleagues, had returned the dislodged bones to their proper conformation, taping the boy's shoulder and chest tightly. Helen Whitman had tried to reach the Joyce farm, but with Paddy in the barn and Elle not answering, she had urged the attending physician to tend the injury well enough that she could take the twins home, Patrick sedated and with his left arm in a sling.

When she had exhausted her explanation, and feeling as if she could do no more for the family, Helen got up to leave.

"If we can do anything, please let us know," she said.

Elle didn't respond.

Paddy frowned intently at his hands folded in his lap, then rose to his feet to see Helen out.

"David?" Helen said, stopping behind the chair where David sat, slumped. She laid her hands on his shoulders, and he tipped his head against her. He nodded several times, indicating he would be all right, and held back his tears. She put her hand on his head and brushed back his fine black hair, nestling him to her.

Paddy escorted her out to her car. David could hear their hushed voices as they crossed the yard.

He sat in silence, hoping his mother would say something. She remained quiet, rocking slightly, her eyes on the table between them.

"I didn't mean it," he said softly. "I didn't mean to hurt him."

Elle said, "It was not your fault alone." She got up and went into her room.

David heard her move about, then shuffle into the living room. He heard the scratch of pen upon paper. He listened as the engine started outside, Mrs. Whitman's car pulled away, and Paddy's steps approached the house. The screen door opened and his uncle walked into the kitchen, squinting in the light. He sat at the table next to his nephew, but remained quiet.

David quietly confessed his version of the incident. He accepted the blame, but again denied having meant his brother harm.

Paddy listened, but did not seem overly concerned with David's confession. When the boy had finished, he merely waved the boy's guilt away with a gesture of his hand.

"Things happen, David," he said softly. "Patrick got what he deserved, in a way. You hate to see it happen, especially when it's someone close to you, but sometimes people just bring things down on themselves. Patrick got his comeuppance. I'm just sorry that this happened between you two. It's not a good thing when brothers get bad blood between 'em."

"He told me I ruined his shoulder, that now he can't play in the tournament," David said, his voice breaking. He fought to hold himself back from sobbing.

"His shoulder will heal, David. He'll have many more baseball games, many more tournaments. I hope his spirit heals as well as his shoulder."

Again they sat in silence until David bowed his head and wept. "He called me a fucker. A goddamn fucker," David sobbed. "Right in front of Jannie. And Mrs. Whitman. A goddamn fucker."

Paddy got up and went to his nephew. He picked up the sobbing boy, cradling him in his arms as he would a calf. He carried him out of the house into the darkness, across the road to his own house. Sitting in his porch swing, he held his nephew in his arms until the last of his little-boy tears were spent. Then, as he heard the deep, relaxed breaths of sleep issue from David's rag-doll body, he took the boy into his home and set him to sleep on the sofa.

∞

In the morning, David woke to find Paddy already gone to the barn. He slipped on his sneakers and went out to join him.

"Hi," he said meekly.

"G'morning," his uncle chirped. "What a lazybones you are! Here I'm almost done with the milking, and you're just wiping the sleep from your eyes."

David smiled.

"You been to the house yet?" Paddy asked.

"Nope."

"Well, you'd better go see how your mother is doing. And your brother. To be honest, I'm more worried about her than him. I thought I saw her in the sitting room window, still sitting up where she was last night after Mrs. Whitman left. I went over to have a chat after you fell asleep. Let her know I had you, and all. Your mom's shook over this one."

Paddy left off to finish up the cow he'd been milking. He pulled off the suction cups and lifted the stainless steel milk bucket from under the cow's udder with one hand. With his free hand, he disconnected the hose from the Step Saver vacuum pipe. He poured the milk from the can into the rolling transfer tank. He set the can down and put his arm around David's shoulder, leading him to the half door looking out over the pasture between the barn and the river.

"David, your mother is ill. You know that, don't you?"

David nodded his head. He swallowed hard, his vision blurring with warm tears.

"I want you to call your Aunt Kate when you get into the house. I tried to reach her last night, but couldn't. Tell her what happened to Patrick and see if she can come up today, as soon as she can. Tell her we're going to need her, and that I'm more worried about your mother than your brother. She'll understand. If she can't come up, or wants to talk to me first, I'll be in as soon as I finish up. But she could just about be here by the time I'm done with chores, if she sets her mind to it."

Paddy took the boy by the shoulders, facing him. Looking deep into his eyes, he said, "David, what people lead themselves into is their own doing. Even if they are as close to you as, well, your mother. Or your brother. You can't take the blame for what is hurting them. You can't make it right for them. You can only do what you gotta do, what is right for you. Forgiveness included. Do what is good for you. And you pray you make choices that will benefit others by strengthening yourself. Understand?"

David nodded. "I think so."

"Okay. Go on now. Do as I said and let me know if there are any problems." He sent the boy running with a pat on his backside.

David hustled off, but stopped in the brilliant light seeping through the opened barn doors.

"Paddy?"

His uncle looked up as he stooped, reaching for the milking device.

"Is she going to have to go away?"

Paddy looked keenly into David's eyes. He nodded, almost imperceptibly.

David turned and ran from the barn, and, through the blur from his tears, saw the golden rays of the morning sun shining into the sitting room window where his mother was still rocking slowly.

∞

Over the dinner table, Kate, Paddy, and David discussed the family's options. Patrick remained uncomfortably bedridden, dozing under the influence of the painkiller the doctor had prescribed. Elle sat with the trio in the kitchen, but neither contributed to nor appeared concerned with the conversation concerning the breakup of her family.

"I want to stay here," David said firmly. "My animals are here. I can help you, Paddy. I can get myself to school. I always have. This is where I belong. This *is* my home."

Kate met Paddy's glance. He nodded. They recognized David's determination, and they did not for a minute doubt that he could actually remain there, with Paddy close by. They also understood David's emphatic remark about his home; he was heir to the farmstead. But were they being unrealistic about him living in the big old house alone?

"I could take boarders, like you do," David contended.

"David, I take boarders because there are many people in need of good housing while they attend the University," Kate replied. "Who do you think you could get to board way out here? And what about safety? You must believe that I'm very careful about whom I allow to share my home."

David turned to his uncle. "Well, why don't you live here with me?" he demanded.

Paddy leaned heavily on his forearm draped along the edge of the table. He rubbed his hand across his stubbled beard, three days long on his cheeks. He looked at his hands, turning his palms down, then up, then down again, aware of his little nephew's growing impatience for an answer, a solution to the problem that threatened his home.

"David, you must understand," Paddy started, his voice soft and kind. "I was born in this house. I grew up in this house. I was fourteen years old when your father was born. And do you know, when I learned that I, like your brother, could never plan to live in my home for the rest of my life, I made a pact with myself. I vowed that as soon as I could, I would leave and never sleep another night in this house. And I left when I was sixteen. I used to cry, David, thinking how this home would never be mine."

Paddy sat up, squaring his shoulders, inhaling fully. He took on a stronger demeanor. He spoke louder, and his voice deepened. "But I refused to be bitter. I wanted to be near my home and family, so when old Fred Bender died, I bought his land. I built my barn with my own hands, and I lived in it a whole year until I could cut the timber and earn enough to build the house I have now. I suppose I was selfish, making it so small. I didn't think I had need for bigger. There isn't enough room for anyone more than me—you know that. That is my home, now, David. I do not wish to live here anymore."

Paddy paused. "But, I do not want to see you leave, either. I cannot fathom how you could live in this big house all by yourself. I can be close by. But I cannot join you."

David bit his lip and nodded several times. He felt the strength of his argument slipping away. He fought back his tears, and with them the fear that his uncle would abandon him. Paddy was the only father he had ever known. Panic gripped him, and he could think of no way out.

Kate could see that the boy was about to cry. "Did you hear what your uncle said, David?"

David looked up, face flushed, a tear beginning to run down his cheek. He shook his head.

"I believe he said he is willing to try to help you stay here, if you can bring yourself to live alone."

Paddy nodded. "You mostly take care of yourself anyway. Not that we don't work, eat, and just plain be with each other a good bit of each day. But I don't believe I could handle you and your brother both. We don't know how long your mother will need... care."

"Katie and I have talked this over already," Paddy continued, turning toward his sister-in-law. "Patrick needs a lot of looking after. He needs to have a lot of things done for him. You do many of those things for him already, which is why I know you can handle yourself. But can you even think about living without your brother?"

"What would happen to Patrick?"

"Well, I think the first order of business is to let him heal. Doc Whitman said he'd be real sore for a few days, but that he'd probably feel like getting back into action by the end of the week, maybe early next week. We'll see how he does, and how it works with him here. Then, if we need to, and after we decide what you can handle, we will try to place your brother when he's healed. We can ask Jerry if he could take him in. Or Dean and Marley."

Elle stirred. In a hoarse whisper, she said, "My sister."

Kate's eyes widened. *It's a valid suggestion,* she thought, but then remembered that Mary Howard was in Oslo where her husband was on sabbatical studying Scandinavian literature. They weren't due home for a couple more weeks. Nonetheless, she thought, it may be best, and it seemed comforting to Elle.

"Yes. Certainly. That is a good option, for Patrick, and for you as well, David, if you discover it is just impossible to live here. Or that you want to be with your brother. You just have to remember, you have to hope and pray, David, that this will be for just a short time. We don't know how long your mother will be hospitalized."

Elle shook her head slowly, her eyes closed.

"If it doesn't work out at all, I promise you, you can stay with me in Madison," Kate reassured him. "I'll be up here on weekends at least. As often as I can. We'll try to make this work. Okay, David?"

The boy nodded, hugging his aunt and uncle. Then he hugged his mother tightly and kissed her cheek. She looked beyond him.

"David, David," she murmured.

And with his arms snug around her, she resumed her rocking, back and forth, again and again.

Chapter Seven
Separation

DAVID WATCHED from the hay mow as Kate loaded the car to take his mother away. Elle was in the house, packing the few things she valued. She'd surprised them all with the ease—almost relief—with which she'd agreed to commit herself into an institution near Madison.

As Kate slammed the trunk, the measure of the moment pierced through David: *Nothing will be the same after this.* He jumped down onto the hay bales in the cow yard and ran to the house. As he reached the porch, his mother appeared, carrying a knit satchel. Several of her journals jutted from the open flap. She had perched an old Easter hat atop her head and draped her mother-in-law's crocheted shawl across her shoulders.

David stopped short, straining to recognize the woman he knew was his mother. She looked lost in time, like the sketches of the women in *Huckleberry Finn.* Tiny, frail, more ancient than her thirty-six years. She took Paddy's arm and let him guide her toward the car where Dr. Whitman waited, holding open the passenger door. As she passed by David, she stopped. She looked around as if she were missing something. *She's looking for a parasol,* he thought. She pulled herself up and met David's eyes.

"Be careful to keep up with your readings."

David stood frozen. His mother glided to the car. A tremendous tension bunched like a knotted leather cord around his heart. His eyes filled, and he gasped a single, burning sob. He tried to cry out "Mother," but his voice withered before it reached his lips. Elle looked at him again, putting a single finger to her lips. *Keep the secret.*

Kate was suddenly, softly at his side, her arm around his shoulder. He watched Dr. Whitman's Oldsmobile lift a plume of dust from the drive as they sped from the farm.

∞

Kate and David swung with the breeze on the porch swing, watching Patrick pump his bicycle up the road toward the farm. They held their shared silence sacred for a moment longer. David sighed, and the spell lifted.

Patrick guided his bike one handed, his right arm resting in the sling. He rode to a stop, swinging his leg over the saddle as the bicycle came to a halt against the house.

"She's gone, then." His voice was flat.

David nodded. He sucked his lips between his teeth, tasting bitterness, and felt the lump swell again in his throat.

"Your mother seemed at peace with going," Kate said.

Patrick stomped across the wooden planks of the porch. "Yeah," he said as he yanked on the screen door to the kitchen. "Anything to eat?"

Kate exchanged a bemused glance with David.

"Denial," David whispered in a hoarse, throaty voice.

Kate couldn't keep a smile from her face as she got up to help Patrick in the kitchen.

"Does he understand?" David asked.

Kate stopped, holding the screen door open.

"I don't know. Seems unlikely," she acknowledged. "Can you do without him?"

"Sure. I got Paddy nearby. I mean, there'll be a whole lot less to do if Pat's not here, I guess."

Kate saw reality weigh down upon her nephew. His wounded, strong eyes broke away from her, and he looked out across the pasture beyond the barn. A calf, bleating for its mother, called from the meadow. Kate felt her heart breaking for him. But she knew—she believed—he would emerge from this stronger. Her concern was for his brother, who at the moment was crashing through the kitchen drawers and cabinets. How would he weather this transition? She turned and went in to help him make a lunch.

∞

In the days after Elle's departure and the weeks before Mary Howard's family returned from Oslo, two facts became evident. David would thrive on the farm under Paddy's guidance. Patrick could not.

When Kate arrived to stay with them each weekend, she could clearly see how the boys fared for themselves in her absence—or didn't. David took on Elle's daily tasks while continuing with his own chores and responsibilities, but he couldn't keep up with Patrick. A stack of dirty dishes built up in the kitchen from Patrick's meals and snacks. Bread, milk, lunchmeats, cereal boxes cluttered the kitchen. Apple cores littered the counter alongside unrinsed tuna cans. His soiled clothes lay strewn from the porch to the bedroom. Patrick had no concept of the wake he cast.

Returning early one Friday evening from the University, Kate stood awestruck at the disarray. David was still milking, but clearly, Patrick had eaten. Peanut butter-coated knives and plates covered the kitchen table. Kate reckoned that Patrick had eaten four sandwiches; four butter knives lay sticking to the counter. Brown, sticky smudges coated the rims of two glasses. The cap for the peanut butter jar left a trail where it had rolled off the table and across the kitchen floor. It had settled face down on the floor, with dust bunnies and grit clinging to the peanut butter smeared around the outside of the lid. Milk pooled on the counter where Patrick had overfilled his glass. It dripped slowly onto the floor near the peanut butter cap. Kate called out for Patrick. No response. She called again from the base of the stairs. Nothing. She shrugged, shook her head, and resigned herself to cleanup duty.

∞

David stepped in from the mudroom as Kate finished tidying the kitchen. She hadn't heard him come up from the barn. With an armload of grimy dishtowels, t-shirts, and jeans, she greeted David with a heated glance.

"Did you just come from the barn with those hands?"

"Yeah, but I washed up in the milk house, too," David said meekly. "I just always wash 'em again here, though, after I change out of my barn clothes." He turned on the water in the kitchen sink and began rewashing his hands.

Kate conceded a flicker of a smile and a nod as she reined in her temper. It was not this twin with whom she was angry; she needn't vent on him. "David, you're in no trouble here at all," she started. "You need not hang your head. I can see this is not your doing. But it is your problem, as it is everybody's problem around here. Where is he?"

"I think he biked over to the Klemms'. He shouted something into the barn as he rode off."

"He doesn't have any problems riding with that arm of his in a sling?"

David tipped his head to the side and scrunched his face.

"Kinda. He swerves all over the road," he said, gripping an imaginary handlebar and swaying widely to convey his brother's one-armed steering skills. "Klemms' isn't far. He'll be okay. He's done it a bunch of times."

Kate set the load on the washer and joined David as he began preparing supper.

"Paddy said he'd join us when he finished up."

She pulled a loaf of fresh bread from a sack she'd brought from Madison and set it on the counter. "Here. Cut some slices. I'll warm up the soup."

"It's gone."

"Gone?" Kate asked, incredulous. "Gone? All the soup? I made gallons of it!" She looked into the refrigerator, awestruck.

"Pat's a hungry boy, Auntie Kate." David started laughing. "And you made it too good. He ate it up. What he didn't eat last night for dinner, he ate for breakfast this morning. Or lunch."

Kate looked into her nephew's face. His beaming expression told everything about his good little heart. She couldn't suppress a giggle.

Laughter burbled up in Kate's belly as David mimed his brother shoveling huge mouthfuls of imaginary food into his mouth with his bare hands. David picked up the uncut bread and shoved it toward his gaping mouth, his eyes popping from their sockets like a trophy bass lunging for a fly. Kate doubled over, laughing until her stomach muscles began to cramp. David set the bread on the counter, took the empty milk pitcher and poured its emptiness down his throat.

"Stop!" Kate snorted. "Don't! No more!"

David swung the fridge door open, stuck his head in, snarled like a dog, and came out with the bone from the leftover lamb roast she'd made on Sunday. It already was gnawed on; Patrick had left his mark. David faced Kate, the bone jutting from each side of his mouth, his eyes wide and wild. He growled. Kate buckled at the knees, collapsing onto a kitchen chair and clasping her belly with both arms.

"Please! David!" she gasped. Tears streamed down her face. David viciously shook the bone in his mouth, a final growl dissolving into a giggle. His shenanigans overcame him, and setting the lamb by the sink, he, too, doubled over.

When Paddy came in from the barn a moment later, his kin were holding themselves up, gasping, laughing, teary-eyed.

"'Ungry," David muttered through his laughter, grabbing the lamb bone and pointing it at his uncle.

"Stop! Please! David," Kate gasped. Her belly burned, and she felt as though she'd melt. She rolled her eyes toward Paddy. Thank God he'd arrived. "Too much." she said, catching her breath. She struggled to her feet and stumbled over to Paddy, hooking her arm into his and leaning comfortably on his shoulder.

"This one's yours," she gasped, getting control of her laughter. David picked up the toaster and tried to devour it. "All yours. You up to it?" she asked, looking brightly into the dumbfounded face of her eldest brother.

∞

It took only four days to make arrangements once the Howards returned to the United States. It was time, the adult Joyces agreed, that the other twin become Mary Howard's ward in her home in the dunes of Indiana.

Patrick did not want to go. He complained bitterly to his brother. "I don't see why I can't just stay here. All my friends are here. And what about baseball? Who am I gonna play with in Indiana? They probably don't even have a team there. Leastways not that I can get on. I mean, why can't we both just stay here 'til Mom comes home? You know, this is just going to spoil the whole rest of my life."

David had no answers. He heard him out, shrugged, and moved on with the never-ending list of chores necessary to keep the farm running. He was relieved, however, when Kate relayed Aunt Mary's promise of a grand Fourth of July celebration upon the older twin's arrival in Dune Acres. While Patrick still viewed his move to Indiana as banishment, his complaining waned.

∞

"You all set to take off?" Paddy asked his nephew, who had made an uncharacteristic appearance in Paddy's barn as his uncle tended to his morning chores. Kate had already strapped his red three-speed to the roof of her shiny new Bel Air and helped him tuck his bat, ball, and glove securely into the luggage wedged into the trunk and backseat. The older twin appeared uncharacteristically cheerful, for once resembling his smaller, darker brother.

"I am, but Auntie Kate's still doing things in the house. She was calling the school office about my records, something about being able to take a copy of them down with us. Seems like they start school earlier in Indiana." Patrick talked easily about the imminent changes in his life. He glanced about, though, curiously, looking for his twin. "Davey around?"

"Think he's with his dairy heifers."

"Oh." He shuffled his feet in the fresh straw lining the floor.

"You know, Uncle Paddy, I'm gonna miss you." His features reddened.

Paddy draped his arm across his young nephew's sturdy shoulders and walked with him into the barnyard. "Things will look up for you, Patrick. And we'll make sure your mom is getting what she needs to get better. You'll be home in no time. Don't worry."

Paddy caught a shadow darkening his nephew's expression. The boy looked doubtful and pensive. But just as quickly, Patrick brightened. "Cousin Jack says they have flag football teams in middle school down there. When the season starts, I can try out for the team."

A lull settled between them, leaving each to his thoughts.

Patrick twitched anxiously, fidgeting as if he had something important to do. "Think I'll go find Davey," he said.

∞

Patrick found David in the heifer barn.

"You all set to go?" the smaller twin asked.

"Just about."

David continued spreading straw in the pens. He noticed that the bigger twin's eyes and nose started to drip almost immediately. "Let's get out of here, before your face blows up," he offered.

But Patrick preferred to remain in the barn. He wanted to share his brother's domain alone with David before he and his aunt drove away.

"How come you don't teach 'em to shit out there?" he chided as he leaned on the Dutch door leading from the barn to the yard where David's cattle huddled around their water tank.

"I did. That was easy," David laughed. He took a spot leaning on the door frame next to his brother. A fresh breeze wafted past them into the barn. "Just can't get 'em to not shit in here."

Neither knew exactly how to say what weighed upon their minds. The boys had never been apart before. They couldn't fathom what life away from one another would be like.

"It's kind of creepy thinking 'bout being away," Patrick admitted.

"Don't you want to go?" David asked.

"Oh, yeah. Going's okay. I'm all right with going, I guess," Patrick said. "It's not leaving here that's gonna be creepy. I suppose it's the being away. Missing…all this. Mom. An' you." He fell silent.

David mashed a lump of green manure with the toe of his barn boot, stirring and kneading as though it were a ball of bread dough.

"Yeah. It's going to be different, all right," Patrick added.

David wondered. "I s'pose Jack and Aunt Mary and Uncle Paul will keep you from missing home. Keep you busy and all. Don't you think?"

"Yeah. I s'pose."

While Patrick knew his kin would welcome him, he had no idea what his new home would be like. Where did they live? What would it be like living away from the country? On a lake—a big lake? How would it be living with the Howards? What would it be like having an Uncle Paul instead of an Uncle Paddy? Jack rather than Davey? He shook his head, staring vaguely at the glob of manure that his brother toed.

David couldn't imagine the old Joyce farmhouse without his brother and mother. Everything would be in its familiar setting, but it would be strange, eerily vacant, hollowed by the absence of his family. He had begun to feel the change already, with his mother at the institution in Madison, and with Patrick getting ready to leave. His brother, however, seemed strangely optimistic and light-hearted about changing his life so radically.

David couldn't grasp how Patrick could so easily accept a new life. Patrick said he thought it would be "creepy" being away from home, yet he did not envision staying on. David, too, thought it was going to be drastically different, but he could not bear the thought of ever having to leave the farm. He wondered how Patrick could do it.

"You know, this is more your home than it is mine," Patrick broke into David's thoughts.

"How can you say that? This has been your home all your life."

"Yes and no. I mean, I've always thought of going someplace else. Doing something different. I mean, sure, you love it here because you have all your animals and all the things that interest you, like the woods and Old Camp and Jannie and your fiddles and all that. Me, what I like to do, I can do anywhere. Maybe better somewhere else. If there are more kids around to play baseball, then maybe I won't have to ride all over just to get a game going. And, you know, there are other things. They got the lake there, so I can go swimming anytime I want. Jack says he'll even teach me how to play tennis."

Tennis, David wondered. *How does he even know he would like tennis?* The only time the twins had tried, it was a bust. A wild extravagance of expense for tennis balls. David had justified the purchase by finding alternative applications for the cylindrical cans. He modified them into tennis-ball launching mortar tubes that he used to torment his twin. But, he reckoned, his brother was such a natural athlete, he'd be good at tennis, or any sport, if he played it regularly.

Again, his brother broke his train of thought.

"I guess I just know that everything is always gonna be the same around here. I'm just ready to get on with some of the things I'm gonna have to do sooner or later."

But everything is changing around here all the time, David thought. *Nothing is ever the same. Look away from things for a minute and they'll never be the same again.*

"Everything *is* changing, Pat," he argued. "If things didn't change, then you wouldn't be going away. And Mom wouldn't be where she is. If we could keep things the same, then we wouldn't be going through what we are now. We'd be keeping it all the way it used to be. You just can't do that. Things are made to change. We have to be able to change with them. We have to grab on to what we have now, cause now is always changing."

Patrick fidgeted impatiently. "You know what I mean," he said shortly. "It's just that I think I have a better chance of doing things if I'm someplace else. Someplace where I don't have to throw a ball against the side of a barn just to have some fun."

He cut off his explanation, frustrated that his words did not deliver his sense of smothered confinement on the farm. He had come to the barn to apologize for the bitter invectives he had heaped upon David after his shoulder had been injured. His words had been weighing heavily on his heart. He had intended to ask forgiveness for bullying his twin and stealing the candy that led to the mishap. But now he felt that his brother was being condescending.

Lecturing him. David's know-it-all attitude irked him, and he felt his temper rise.

"Aw, never mind. You just don't understand. Things just come so easy for you. You make it seem so easy to get whatever you want."

David challenged that thought in his mind. But he didn't want to argue. Not at this point, so close to him leaving.

"*This* isn't what I want," he said. "What we have ahead of us isn't going to be easy. It isn't going to be fair." He turned the lump of manure at the toe of his boot, then smashed it flat. He looked directly into his twin's gaze. "Patty, I've been thinking. I've been wondering why it is that we—you, Mom and me—why it's been so hard for us here at home."

At the mention of his mother, Patrick narrowed his eyes, furrows wrinkling the skin between his eyebrows.

"I mean, what's been normal for us has been anything but normal. It's like normal is unreal. Right?" David asked. Patrick listened. "So now what we have, well, it's kinda our new chance. It's not fair and it's not easy. But it's what we have." His gaze riveted his brawny brother. "It's what we've been given. Now, we just gotta ask, what are we going to do with this chance? How are we going to make our new normal work for us? What good can we make of it? Where can we make this chance take us?"

Patrick studied his twin.

David shrugged. "I guess you're right, Pat. I do get what I want pretty easy," he conceded. "Sometimes it seems like all I have to do is dream about what I want, and it happens. Like with my cattle, and showing at the fair. I just kind of see myself doing it, and I keep dreaming of getting there, and sooner or later, there I am and my dreams are coming true. I mean, if things are going to change, I want to make sure my dreams help shape that change."

He paused, shaking his head. "I guess the hardest part is to keep on dreaming the same dream, and building on it. Building normal out of it. You know what I mean? Making dreams real?"

Patrick suppressed a surge of rage that raced through his body. His dream of leading his ball team to a Little League championship had crashed into pieces.

"The trouble with dreams is that they hang around when they're no good any more. They become 'if only I coulda done this instead' dreams. You end up following them around aimlessly, rather than using them to direct you on." He couldn't keep the cynicism from his voice.

You gotta let the old dreams go, David thought, seeing the pain in his brother's eyes. *You have to grab on to what you have now to let your dreams take you where you want to go.* "I'm sorry about your shoulder, Pat," he said aloud. "I know what the tournament meant to you. I didn't mean to push you off your bike."

Patrick was tongue-tied. He had meant to admit his guilt and apologize, and now his brother was making amends instead. He sucked his lips toward his gritted teeth, failing to offer the apology he intended.

The horn on Aunt Kate's car honked twice.

David glanced at his brother, worried that his words had only nurtured his brother's resentment. He was shocked, then, when Patrick grabbed him and hugged him, pulling him right off the floor. Crimson-faced, he set him down and backed away, looking at David as if he were searing his image into his memory. He said nothing, and the seconds passed timelessly. Then, abruptly, Patrick turn and ran from the barn. David walked out after him to send him off, his gait reflecting the lightness of his heart.

∞

Kate stayed the night at the Howards' home in the Dunes before saying good-bye to her nephew. "You take care of yourself here," Kate encouraged the strapping young man who so much resembled his father, her younger brother.

Patrick was tall enough now that he looked down into her eyes. He'd grown at least another inch over the summer. For a boy just starting his teens, he was alarmingly mature, she thought. Physically, at least. Kate noticed the down turning heavy and thick above the boy's lip. She hoped he could successfully grapple with the stress of adolescence, as well as with the break-up of his home and the illness that afflicted his mother.

At the very least, she reassured herself as she backed her Chevy down the Howards' driveway, he would be comforted and nurtured by his mother's sister and her family. Mary had been such a help after the twins' birth and had kept close ties with her sister's family throughout the years. She had held the boy to her breast and nursed him. Kate pulled onto the road feeling confident about her nephew's unfolding future.

Chapter Eight

Thriving, or Trying To

PATRICK THRIVED with the Howards. He found comfort in the regimentation of his aunt's discipline and complied with her house rules, even though she sometimes administered them unevenly between him and her son. He bonded quickly with his uncle, a warm man who was genuinely interested in Patrick's thoughts and feelings. And, after meeting some of his cousin's pals on the beach, he looked forward to making more friends at his new school.

Patrick was awed by the size of the school. Each grade was split into five or six separate classes, each in its own room. There were seven more students in his clean, bright new classroom than there had been in all the grades combined in the old one-room schoolhouse in North Freedom. His sole disappointment was that he hadn't performed well in the proficiency tests he took during the summer, and had been held back to do sixth grade again. He was particularly weak in science and math, and he admitted to himself that perhaps he'd depended too much on his brother back in North Freedom.

He'd already realized that he could not depend on his cousin as he had on David, at least for his studies. Jack's interests were much more social than academic, and although he was usually sullen and moody at home, his friends knew him for the cutting wit he unleashed when out of the house. Away from his family's strict regime, he was reckless and rebellious.

Patrick felt more comfortable with his aunt and uncle in their warm, welcoming home than he did with Jack and his wisecracking friends. Still, he entered the family circle much like he waded into the cool waters of the lake; slowly, deliberately, an inch at a time.

∞

Patrick ran down the steps from the house to the mailbox every day, hoping to find letters from his brother. After several months, though, he had sent off only two of his own. The first was brief:

August 15, 1959

Dear Davey,

Everything here is real neat. Lake Michigan is so big you can't see across it, and the sand is piled in big hills that people build their houses on. School starts next week. You should come here some time. Jack is crazy, but he's a blast.

Your Brother, Pat

His second and final note that year reflected how well he had settled:

November 20, 1959

Dear Davey,

I made the basketball team last week! We practice every night after school. It's a lot of fun. Everybody here is real big on basketball, a lot more than at home. Some guys are real good. You can tell they have played a long time.

Jack doesn't go out for any sports. He says he'd rather hang out with his friends. He would probably be pretty good at sports. He is a real good swimmer. You should see him water ski. Zowie!

School is ok. I have a real nice teacher, Miss Gerard. She isn't mean at all. I'm doing good. I can't believe they bumped you up a year. An eighth-grader already—man! All of a sudden, my twin is two grades ahead of me. Weird. I'm not surprised, though. You were doing all the work for the eighth-graders two years ago, already. Do you still have to do the same lessons over again?

Have a nice Thanksgiving.

Pat

In contrast, Patrick knew that on every Tuesday, he'd more than likely receive a thick envelope that his brother had mailed the previous Saturday. David's letters were usually several-page chronicles of the previous week. He wrote of the fall harvest, and of the production of his herd. He'd explained all about the new boarder, Miss Rose, who was also his teacher. She'd just moved to North Freedom to take Mrs. Hatcher's old teaching job, and she was doing a bang-up job of challenging David, he wrote. By Thanksgiving, Patrick had received seventeen postings detailing the progress of David's cattle, Paddy's well-being, the state of their harvest, all that David learned about his mother including his recent visit to her, and sundry news from the schoolhouse and community. There was always a note about Jannie.

When David's Thanksgiving letter arrived, Patrick retreated to his bedroom and read and reread his brother's words, hearing David's voice in his mind as his stories unfolded.

Saturday, November 24, 1959

Dear Pat,

I was real glad to get your letter telling me how nice things are at the Howards'.

The biggest thing going on around here is the deer season. Today was Opening Day. It was a cold opener. We got snow last Tuesday, more than three inches. It rained a little on Thursday, so the snow was crusted on the leaves. It was real hard to move quietly in the woods. That was good for the deer, if the hunters couldn't hold still. I sat out with Gabriel again. Sure enough, he got his buck, a nice six pointer. I'm glad he likes it when I go out with him. He is like a rock in the woods. He doesn't move a bit, until he sees or hears a deer. Or smells it.

Today, we heard them before we saw them, crunching through the leaves and snow, browsing on the tips of the maple seedlings. There were two does and three fawns that came walking on through right in front of us before we saw the buck. Gabriel told me later that he knew a buck was coming along behind them by the way the two does kept looking back the way they had come. I don't think they ever saw us. We were on a stand at the base of the bluff looking out over the river west of the house. We sat on a windfall stump that was leaning about four feet off the ground on its big hunk of roots. The tree had fallen through a lot of prickly ash, so we were real well concealed. I think that buck would have gone right into the prickly ash to bed down, if Gabriel hadn't shot him first. The buck wasn't more than ten yards away when Gabe let him have it. He just leaned that old 30-30 of his right over the top of a big root and waited for the buck to get closer. We watched him come for about twenty minutes, picking his way through the brush, real tense and alert all the time. I think he knew that people were in the woods. He just didn't know where.

I like being able to help Gabriel get his deer out of the woods. I don't know how he would do it, if I didn't drag it for him. But he pulls for all he is worth anyway. We got the deer as far as the fencerow along Paddy's cornfield, then I ran in to get the tractor. Paddy saw me coming, so he came out to help. We laughed when we saw Gabriel just sitting pretty right on top of that old buck's chest when we got out to him. He said it was the warmest place he could find. Then he told us about having to crawl inside the chest cavity of an elk he killed once, just to get out of the cold. He said that was when he was out in the Rocky Mountains in Colorado when he was young. He is quite a guy, old Gabriel.

We hung the buck on Paddy's grain scale. It weighed 152 pounds! It was a big one. Miss Rose cooked the venison tenderloins for lunch. Since she started living with us, she's pretty much taken over the cooking, and she's real good at it. Especially with game. Venison, it's the best. What a feast! Paddy laughed that we were already in from hunting long before noon again. He kids Gabriel about taming the deer all summer long, and training them to eat peanuts right out of his hand, and then shooting them when they least expect it. Gabriel swears he never feeds peanuts to the deer. He says they're "too expensive to give to the varmints." And I never have seen him feed the deer anything, other than maybe a nibble of grass or alfalfa. I have seen him get pretty friendly with some fawns at times. He says they have no sense about people when they are real young, until the does and bucks teach them to fear us. Still, I have seen bucks in full velvet show no surprise or fear when they come across Gabriel in the woods. I've even seen them sniff at him from about a foot away. He does have a way with deer. He probably would have them all tame, if he didn't shoot them to eat them. I wonder why deer aren't any tamer than cattle or sheep? They know we kill them, too, I think. They even seem to know when the renderer comes to take a dead one away. Paddy says they can smell death. I don't know. They sure can sense something.

Sunday, November 25

It is bitter cold out today, windy and gray. I'm glad I didn't have to go out in the woods this morning. We stoked up the wood burner in the basement last night when the temperature started going down. We had been getting by with the woodstove in the kitchen. It was 4 degrees when I did chores this morning. Cold!

Paddy drove me down to see Mom this afternoon. She looked okay. Kind of frazzled, maybe. She asked about you. Have you written her yet? She would really like to hear from you. I know I like it when I get a letter from you.

Anyway, she is still pretty quiet when we see her. Last time I saw her was toward the end of September, when I wrote you about it. She is a lot better than that time. Then, she had been having a lot of that shock therapy that I was telling you about. Man, I think that must have been hard on her. She'd be, like, gone. But even now, she still doesn't talk much, unless you ask her questions. Or make comments about something. I was sorry I told her about Gabriel's deer. I don't think she liked that too much. It's funny, after all these years of shooting deer and eating venison, to find out Mom doesn't like to see the deer get shot. She started crying when I told her about it. I felt real bad. Paddy said afterward not to be concerned. But it was hard not feeling bad.

She didn't know anything about when she could come home. It won't be for Thanksgiving, Paddy said. Probably not even Christmas. He said it is hard for her to get better, 'cause she doesn't know what better is. He says her doctor said that she has to want to try to get better, but that is hard until she understands what to try for. I asked her before I left to try hard to get better. I think it just made her feel uneasy.

Wednesday, November 28

Well, we got out of school early today because of a snowstorm. I was home by noon, but that didn't make a lot of difference because Miss Rose was all geared up to teach for the whole day and when we got home she had to let it all out on somebody, and that somebody was inevitably me. You asked if we were doing the same old lessons that the eighth graders did every year when Mrs. Hatcher was teacher. Heck, no! Miss Rose has her own idea of how to teach us, and she moves a whole lot faster, too. And we're always learning about different things, not just our lessons. With the extra time off today, we have been learning about how cows make hay into milk. Did you ever hear of butyric acid? I'm pretty sure that's not what we were going to study in school, but sometimes Miss Rose and I get off on "tangents," as she calls them.

It's fun having Miss Rose living here. Aunt Kate was really surprised when I called her and told her we actually did have a boarder. Gabriel really likes it, too. I thought he would miss living out in his cabin at Old Camp, but he seems to be real happy here. He insists it was his idea to be here in the first place, that it was no good for a "youngin" to be living all alone. I wondered if he would return to his cabin after Father Hanley arranged for Miss Rose to stay here last August. He didn't though. It is really funny to watch them, too. Gabriel is always teasing Miss Rose, making jokes and such. And I think she really enjoys having us fiddle after supper is done. She said she'd make us a deal. She'll do all the clean-up if we play our fiddles. Well, that just let us get more time to play, so you can imagine how fast we agreed to that!

Tomorrow is Thanksgiving, and we were going to have a turkey here, just the four of us. Uncle Jerry invited us to join them, and so did Uncle Roger. But none of the invitations included Miss Rose, or Gabriel, for that matter, and Paddy told them that we already bought a turkey and they were welcome to join us if they wanted. Nobody did. Except, you're not going to believe it, Jannie and her family are going to join us for Thanksgiving dinner! They called Monday evening to ask whether I could join them. Well, I hated leaving everybody behind, so I said no. But after hearing Paddy return the invitation to everyone, I thought it would be courteous to do the same. Was I surprised when Mrs. Whitman called back and asked for Paddy! He wasn't in the house, of course, so I let her talk with Miss Rose. Well, those two got to talking and after about ten minutes, Miss Rose gets off the phone and says that the Whitmans will be coming to join us. They'll be bringing some pies and ice cream and a bunch of vegetable dishes. Can you imagine? Miss Rose has had me and Gabriel scrubbing this place all week. I can't wait.

Thursday, November 29

I ate so much.

We had a great time with Jannie and her family. For eight people, we sure made a whole lot of noise with all the talking we did during dinner. I'm surprised we got much eaten, but we did a pretty good job there too. After dinner, I could hardly move, but Miss Rose said if I expected any pie and ice cream, I had to play some fiddle. So we got out our fiddles and dusted our bows and with the four of us, we had a real good time playing. It is amazing to hear Gabriel play along to songs Mrs. Whitman and Jannie and I have been practicing. Some of those songs he has heard me practice around here. Others, he has never heard, at least as far as I know. He says it doesn't matter how often you hear a tune, it is how well you listen that matters. Well, long after Jannie and I ran out of things we knew how to play, Mrs. Whitman and Gabriel played and played. She would start a piece by Mozart or Bach, and old Gabriel would listen a measure or two and then just improvise right along. Sometimes it would make for some pretty strange sounds, but mostly it was heavenly. You wouldn't believe it. We were going to go down to Madison to see Moby Dick *but we got carried away with playing music, and then after that we played charades. It was a lot of fun, and we played it until it was too late to drive to town. I don't think anyone wanted to go anyway.*

Friday, November 30

Jannie called to say her folks would take us down to the movie tonight instead. Wow, it was great. Have you seen it? Moby Dick *is this huge white whale. During the whole movie, Captain Ahab, this crazy sea captain, chases all over the ocean after the white whale. After searching and searching, they finally find it, but it attacks and sinks his ship. The way it ends, you don't know if the whale is killed, but it is stuck awful bad. But you do see that he takes the old captain down with him into the ocean. The captain was lashed to the whale with the ropes from the harpoon. There was a young guy from the boat that kind of told the story, Ishmael. You don't know if he made it or not, either, cause at the end he was the only one left, hanging onto a floating coffin. But in the end of the movie, the last thing to show was the coffin, floating all alone. Eerie! I have to get the book. Miss Rose said it is by a guy named Melville. I can get it in the library. I'm going there in the morning. I'll mail this then.*

Gabe moved back on out to his cabin. Said he was getting too civilized, and that Miss Rose was spoiling him. Said his cabin was lonely and calling for him. But he'd be back for dinner often, he added. And for fiddlin'.

I wish you could be with us for all these things we are doing that are so much fun. I hope you are having as much fun in Indiana.

Until next time,

Love,

David

Damn, Patrick muttered. David had told him the whole movie again. He always did. It was a good thing Patrick frequented the movie theatre more often than David and Jannie did. He'd usually already seen the movies that David would have spoiled after seeing them back home in Baraboo. But if David saw one first, like *Moby Dick,* and was that psyched up telling about it, well, it was probably worth seeing anyway. Patrick folded the seven pages of his brother's letter, inserted it back into the envelope and placed it in a box with all the others. He'd have to return a letter to David—an intention he often planned when he finished reading and rereading the lengthy writings, but seldom followed up on.

Chapter Nine

Rose Truewater

August, 1959

WITHIN A WEEK of starting her new teaching job, Rose Truewater recognized that David Joyce was more than precocious. The administration had bumped David up to the eighth grade, but he easily handled the material that challenged his fellow students. At the first opportunity, she expressed her concerns to the school superintendent.

"What do you suggest we do for the boy?" Dr. Gantner asked. "He's only got a year left at the schoolhouse in North Freedom. It wouldn't benefit him any, from my perspective, to bring him into town to compete in the larger classes. Do you disagree?"

He glanced curiously at his newest teacher. "You have a unique situation before you, Rose. A special challenge. David Joyce is more than a handful, but he's also a student who offers as much satisfaction as any you may ever encounter. He stands to make an impact on you. I hope you have the gumption to make as big an impact on him."

He shifted in his seat, leaning forward with both elbows on his desk. Rose thought he looked whimsically conspiratorial.

"You may recall that when I hired you, I suggested you would find opportunities to take on exceptional students in the classroom. I'd be less than truthful if I said I was not aware of David when I told you that." He paused.

Rose took in her boss's kind tone and noticed a hint of humor twinkling in his eye.

"Perhaps the Joyce boy is a product of the system," he continued. "Too soon, we will see the end of the small country schoolhouse and the wonderful opportunity for early exposure to and repetition of the basics that our children receive in the multi-grade classroom. You have a chance to enjoy the best of the past before it becomes nostalgia."

He left his desk to search through the volumes of texts stacked on the shelves lining his office. Finding his copy of *Ramifications of Centralized Elementary and High School Education in Rural Wisconsin School Districts,* he handed it to Rose.

"Ever come across this?" he asked.

Rose read the title and noticed the author's name. Mary Katherine Joyce. *Coincidence?* she wondered.

"Not unrelated," Dr. Gantner informed her. "This is the work of a local girl. One who graduated from the schoolhouse where you now teach. Though she is not by any means a girl anymore. You know her. David's aunt.

This is Katie's dissertation. She's a professor now in the department of education down at the University. Mary Joyce—we've always called her Katie."

Rose paged through the thesis, glancing up at her mentor, inviting more of his wisdom and advice.

"Take it. Read it. I think you will find it interesting, if not a bit frightening, as it focuses not just on what we gain, but what we leave behind when we consolidate. Perhaps you will see your responsibilities at the Freedom School, and with David, in a new light. For you see, I don't believe that education will ever again offer the freedom and flexibility that we have now in little schoolhouses scattered across the countryside," he said.

Rose found her situation inviting. She nodded, encouraging him.

"Not once we close them down and shuffle all the youngsters across miles and miles of country roads to run them through the chutes of centralized primary education. Oh, there will be advantages and efficiencies to the new way, once it is firmly established and all the pieces are in place. I wonder, then, if they'll prove to be merely economic advantages, rather than intellectual. Pity the students who are in the transition group!"

He mused silently for a moment.

"You see, Miss Rose, you are very young. And capable. I believe you would have made an excellent instructor in the old system. And you have the opportunity, for another year or two, to take advantage of that system, before Freedom School and others like it are closed for good.

"I believe in that system. I am a product of that system," he admitted. "I suppose I'd have been farming all these years, had it not been for a dedicated school teacher who spotted in me an ability to learn. Had she not cracked the whip over my head throughout the eight years I was under her tutelage, I may never have left the farm.

"Consider this Joyce boy your special assignment. He will break up the routine for you, I can guarantee that! See what you can do with him. And I hope someday, thirty or forty years from now, you will remember him among probably just a handful of students who excelled to levels others will never reach. He will be special, for he will be the only one you will be able to tutor the old way."

∞

Rose Truewater heeded her superior's words. She challenged David Joyce relentlessly. During school hours, she demanded that he persevere and focus more diligently than other children. She enabled David's fellow students to cope with the academic discipline at their own rate. At first, the students thought their new teacher was confused as to which grade David was in. Then, as the practice continued and they found that she had taken residence at the

Joyce farm, they resented her attention to him, thinking she favored David. However, when it became obvious that she singled out David because she expected a higher level of performance from him, their resentment faded. They thought that perhaps the peculiar little woman with the dark skin and straight black hair pulled back neatly into a bun or, sometimes, in a long, graceful ponytail, might be tasking their friend to do more than others to show that she didn't grant him favor because he boarded at his house.

David, too, noted the standard by which his teacher judged his performance. The semester started innocuously enough. On the morning of the first day of classes, their new teacher stood up front of the class, a strange, tiny-framed woman with deep, dark eyes. She moved nervously, like a junco foraging for seeds, alert for predators. But the students soon held no doubt about her authority. Her glance commanded respect.

When she spoke, he noticed her accent, as did every child in the classroom. They discussed the tang in her enunciation repeatedly during those first days of school, often mimicking her heavy *r*'s and long, loping vowels.

"She said she's from Canada. Maybe that's why she talks so funny," Danny Belter wondered.

"I don't think so," Anny Steive said. "My dad and brothers go fishing in Canada, and they say everybody there talks normal, kinda."

"Maybe she talks that way on purpose, just to be different," one of the younger students suggested.

"Naw. She's from Montreal," David said. "They don't speak English in Montreal."

"You're kidding! No? What do they speak then?" Tommy Graber asked.

"French."

David had guessed correctly. What brought her to North Freedom was happenstance, mere quirks of coincidence that brings souls together.

What kept her there ran deeper.

∞

June, 1960

After the end of her first year teaching at North Freedom, Miss Rose stayed on as a boarder at the Joyces' farm. But she asked David and Paddy whether she might pay a reduced rent in the months that school was out and she received no salary. David looked quizzically at his uncle. He spoke first.

"You know, for all you do around here, you probably shouldn't be paying rent at all. As far as I'm concerned, you can stay here for nothing."

Paddy added, "David's right. We should be paying you. I'm sorry we hadn't thought about it sooner."

Rose Truewater was an asset to the farm. She pitched in with haying, and she enjoyed working with the cattle, particularly with the calves. But her greatest contributions were in running the household. She quietly assumed tasks that the woman of a household typically handled—tasks that David and Gabriel neglected. Rose Truewater put a halt to the budding bachelor's quarter mess that spread throughout the house like moss on damp surfaces of rock. She did not allow clothing thrown randomly over the backs of chairs. She took over the laundry detail. Before arriving in North Freedom, Rose had always depended on either a laundromat or a washbasin and was now happy to have a washer in the house. She gladly included Gabriel's and David's clothing in the loads she ran. She was less receptive to Paddy's soiled farming clothes, until she realized his role in the Joyce farmstead. Then, she gratefully kept Paddy in clean work attire.

"I'm not sure the cows recognize me, so clean every morning," Paddy quipped to David as they started chores early one Saturday.

"I don't," laughed his nephew.

Paddy did not take the service for granted. He delivered his soiled clothing to the house in a five-gallon bucket, the bulk of manure, grease or heavy soil already soaked or scrubbed from the overalls and trousers. He would not abuse the generosity of this dark-featured young woman. But he had never before in all his years of dairying worn freshly ironed shirts and creased khaki trousers to the milk line. Even his jeans and overalls were pressed. He took, on occasion, to wearing a tie with his pressed shirts. He never felt so spiffy on the farm.

"'You going to church?" David joked as they met in the milk house early in the morning.

David noticed how effortlessly Miss Rose dealt with the laundry and other tasks of keeping the household on track. While David continued to do shopping at the grocery store, he did so now with a complete list prepared for him by the caretaker of his house. His bicycle was no longer sufficient for routine trips to the store; there were too many bags to put in his baskets. Instead, Paddy drove him into town, and David filled the shopping basket with canned fruit and vegetables, flour, beans of many varieties (kidney, black, and pinto were Miss Rose's favored requests), boxes and bottles of detergent and bleach, household cleanser, light bulbs, and so on. While David shopped, Paddy tended to business at the co-op or purchased parts for his tractors. David noted that his trips to the market were fewer, but that he purchased much more per visit. Miss Rose encouraged him to minimize the complexity of his housekeeping tasks and focus instead on his studies, his farming, and his weekly social time and music at the Whitmans'.

Once, Rose dropped him at the doors of the grocery, his list in hand.

"I will be at the library for one-half hour, David," she said. "That is plenty of time for you to finish the shopping. You do not want to spend any more time than necessary with this chore. There are other opportunities more suited for a boy your age. Now go."

She was waiting for him precisely a half-hour later.

"Good," she said flatly. She held aloft a thin book for David to inspect. The title read, *French for Beginners.* "Now we can accomplish something."

Chapter Ten
David and Jannie

December, 1961

OVER CHRISTMAS BREAK, Jannie and her family traveled to her grandparents' house. Each day while they were gone, Paddy or Miss Rose drove David to the Whitmans' to tend the horses and Jannie's 4-H steer. David didn't expect to see Jannie until the Saturday before New Year's, so when he saw the Whitmans' car parked in the drive on Thursday, his heart soared. Ignoring the hungry horses, he went straight to the house. His hopes were dashed, however, when Mrs. Whitman greeted him with an apology.

"I'm sorry, David," she said wearily. "Jannie isn't feeling well. She's had a bit of a fever since Christmas Eve. A virus, I suppose. That's why we're home so soon, because she was feeling so poorly. Perhaps we can get together for New Year's."

The Whitmans did invite David and his family to an afternoon dinner on New Year's Day. Reveling in the bustle of their warm kitchen, David thought of his mother. During the holidays, Elle often noted aloud that no matter how beautifully the dining room might be set or how comfortably the living room was arranged, people inevitably clustered in the kitchen, the focal point of family activity. David wished his mother was with him to savor the rich fragrances of cooked ham, spicy mustard sauces, pies, and breads, and to appreciate how everyone moved about as if choreographed, weaving and dancing with one another in the golden hue of the Whitmans' kitchen.

He fretted to see how pale and thin Jannie looked. But her eyes twinkled and her smile melted him. She demanded that he give an account of exactly how much her fine Arabian, Cherub, had missed her while she was gone. Had he exercised the horses?

David assured her that he'd treated Cherub with favor, handling and grooming the chestnut gelding daily, but that he had ridden him only twice, and then just bareback. He'd been busy making sure each of the horses had time in the paddock, and keeping their stalls spotlessly clean. He added an update on the progress of Dante, the steer that he had selected especially for her to show the next summer in the Sauk County Fair. The young beast was gaining rapidly, more than a pound and a half a day. David had kept both gelding and steer healthy and happy during her short trip away.

Jannie rewarded him with a grateful smile.

"How about you?" Jannie asked.

"Been good. Heard from Patrick Christmas Day. He called."

"And?"

"Sounds great. He sent me another ream of stationary, and told me to keep on writing. Ha! He should talk. And he got a boatload of gifts from Aunt Mary and Uncle Paul again. Sounds like they spoil him about as much as your folks do you!"

"I'm not spoiled," Jannie clarified. "I'm loved."

David nodded. "I think so."

"Davey, feel this," she said, taking his hand and moving it to up her neck, behind her ears.

Her hands were soft and dry, but warm to his touch. He let his fingers skim over the smoothness of her fine, creamy skin to a tight, pronounced lump behind her ear.

"Wow!" he said, softly palpating the swollen mass. "What's that?"

"Daddy said it's a lymph gland. I have one behind my other ear, too," she said, turning her head and pulling her hair back for David to inspect. "I've had them all week. Along with a fever. It's been nasty."

"Daddy says she's got mono," Wendy chimed in. "Kissing disease!"

David blushed. Wendy grinned wickedly.

After dinner, Paddy and David helped Dr. Whitman zip through the chores in the barn. When they returned from the horse barn, Mrs. Whitman firmly told Jannie to say goodnight, that she'd had enough for the day and would have plenty of time to see David the following day or any of the other days remaining in the break. Although he'd hoped to stay longer, David couldn't protest, seeing how pale and tired Jannie looked. He was mollified— but shocked—when Jannie hugged him, then kissed him gently on his lips as the families bid each other happy new year. He stood speechless. Paddy took him by the shoulders and pushed him toward the door, chuckling as they left. David ambled out the door and to the car as in a trance. The last thing David heard before the door closed behind him was Wendy's teasing peal, "Ew! Kissing disease. I told you so!"

∞

On the last weekend of the break, the Whitmans invited David to join them at a movie. Paddy assured his nephew that he could handle the barn duty. David stayed in town all afternoon, sharing dinner with the Whitmans and seeing Gregory Peck in *To Kill a Mockingbird*. Afterwards, they returned to the Whitmans' for pie and ice cream, and he and Jannie were allowed to watch part of a late movie without Wendy tagging along. Mrs. Whitman escorted her protesting younger daughter upstairs while Dr. Whitman left to make quick rounds at the hospital before taking David home.

Snuggling happily on the couch, Jannie and David didn't even notice the title of the late movie. Their emotions whirled. Breathless, David heard nothing when Jannie suddenly sat up, straightening her disheveled blouse and smoothing her hair. Dr.Whitman had entered the kitchen from the garage.

"You kids alright in there?" Dr. Whitman's voice sounded awkward. "You ready to head home, David?"

David was suddenly flustered. Taking his hand, Jannie led him to the kitchen, where Dr. Whitman was snacking on a chicken leg. Mrs. Whitman came downstairs and bid him goodnight. David reeled again when Jannie sent him off with a warm hug and kiss goodnight.

∞

School started on Monday. Two days later, any hint of a January thaw was a frozen hope. A cold snap set in deep and hard. For a stretch of twelve days, the thermometer remained at or below zero. Night temperatures dipped well beyond twenty below.

Many students returned to Baraboo High with a variety of viruses and colds, and sniffles raced through the school. By the time the cold snap eased in late January, close to 15 percent of the students were absent from classes.

David, however, was impervious to prevailing viruses. He routinely awakened before the alarm and was in the barn no later than Paddy. He milked the cows and wrapped up the chores before returning to the house to wolf down the hearty breakfasts Miss Rose had waiting, and then drive to school in Baraboo with her. While she was no longer his teacher, Rose continued to mentor him. His home life had become a blend of farm work and intellectual challenges, with Rose always in the lead. On Tuesdays and Thursdays, the daily routine was conducted in French.

He missed Jannie on Tuesday. He called after school and her mother assured him that she'd simply come down with the cold that ran through the student body. But after four days, she remained at home, and David worried. On Saturday, he called Whitmans' and asked if he could come visit Jannie.

"David, I don't think that would be a good idea. Jannie's got a fever again, and she's been sleeping most of the time," Mrs. Whitman explained. David heard concern in her voice.

"Well, ok. Let me know when she's feeling better," David requested. "Okay?"

"You know I will. Or as soon as she is feeling better, I'm quite certain Jannie will be on the phone to you herself."

When she did call on Monday evening, Jannie said she didn't feel very good at all.

"I just got too bored being sick," she complained. "I wanted to talk with you."

"I wish I could come over."

"So do I. But I guess I don't feel too pretty right now."

"I don't care."

"You're too sweet."

"Get better."

"Yeah."

∞

David lugged a hay bale from the wagon in the frozen pasture. *Paddy was right,* he thought. Dairy animals were a lot easier than beef to care for during the depth of winter. They pretty much were fed and handled exclusively in the barn. Yes, there was plenty of manure to move each day. But the barn was generally warm, not exposed to the bitterest of winter as the beef lot was. David rolled the bale near the herd and turned for another. Some of the cattle slowly ambled to their feed. Others reclined on the crisp crust of snow. *Twenty-eight degrees below,* David marveled. As cold as he had ever seen it. But the cattle didn't seem to mind at all. They preferred to bed down out in the open, especially when it was still, as it had been all that night. Still, except for the munching of hay, the crunching of hooves on the snow, and an owl hooting in the woods beyond the pasture. When the wind did kick up, the cattle often took shelter in the lean-to at the end of the paddock. Sometimes, they huddled in the shed or clustered in a tight circle for no apparent reason. But mostly, they lounged out back, ruminating lazily, each choosing a direction in which to view the open land around them.

David's beef herd had grown to nine cows, three heifers and two steers, not including the show steers that he kept confined in a pen in the dairy barn. He'd brought Jannie's Angus, Dante, back to the farm when she got sick so that he could manage the steer's growth. He wanted the show steers, both Dante and Bruno, to use all their energy growing, not fighting the extreme cold of Wisconsin's winter. He knew that each animal needed at least a half-pound of extra grain just to maintain his body mass. Without the extra grain, the steers burned energy from body tissue to keep warm when the temperature fell below zero.

With the hay dumped from the wagon, David threw the old Ford 9N tractor into gear and headed for the machine shed. It was colder driving the tractor than tossing the hay. He stood rather than sit his butt on the frigid tractor seat, and turned the steering wheel with one hooked gloved finger, except when the tires gripped the frozen ground and ripped it from his grasp.

After parking the tractor, David draped a heavy canvas over its front end and hung a drop light to burn next to the engine block. He stepped out under the late January sky. It was almost silent with the tractor's engine off. David heard only the soft whisper of the cattle tearing at the bales, and their hooves crunching in the snow as they jockeyed for position to feed. Above him was quiet and endless. Crystal clear, the sky seemed bottomless, deep into the darkest blues, littered with twinkling galaxies. He looked at a star, then took a long stride to the south. He wondered about the ray of light from the star as it followed him in his tracks. He pondered that for a moment. He took another step, and the ray followed him continuously toward the farmyard. He took a step to the left, and the ray was there as well. It was everywhere. He smiled, and wondered.

David stood in the still cold. It didn't bother him. There was no wind. He was bundled in layers, and the new boots he'd bought at the co-op were the warmest he'd ever had. Peace buffered his mood. The kitchen lights cast amber rays through the windows onto the glistening white snow. Miss Rose passed back and forth behind the glass, preparing hot breakfast for him and Paddy. David looked east. If dawn was prying its fingers into the seamless winter's night, it was only just beginning. The sky remained dark. The moon had long since set; it was the last thing David had seen from his window as he struggled to sleep the night before, wondering, worrying about Jannie. He remembered now. Would she be back in school today? He doubted it. It sounded like her folks were going to keep her at home regardless of how she felt, until after they took her down to Madison to see the specialists at University Hospital. David didn't count on seeing her again until the weekend, three more days. The Whitmans were going to Madison tomorrow.

∞

Sunday, February 11, 1962

Dear Patrick,

I guess I haven't written much since Christmas. This is only the second time I've used the stationary you sent me, and the first time was to thank you. Things are kind of slow, pretty much.

Jannie is sick. I guess real sick, Miss Rose tells me. She's got too many white blood cells. It's called leukemia. I guess it is real serious. The docs in Madison diagnosed it. Acute lymphocytic leukemia. I'm kind of scared for her.

She spent a good part of last week in Madison. Her mom went down every day. I haven't seen her for almost two weeks now. We talk on the phone. She called me from the hospital in Madison, twice! She actually sounded pretty good. She was on a floor with a whole lot of kids. Some were pretty sick, she said, but many were like her, where they just didn't feel quite right but felt good enough to fool around and have fun. She said the nurses were hollering at them for doing wheel chair races in the halls. Mostly, though, she says it was kind of boring.

She spent a lot of time reading. I just talked to her again a little while ago. She got home this afternoon. I wanted to go see her, but Miss Rose and Paddy decided I'd better wait until the Whitmans ask me. Jannie said that her folks are thinking of taking her to Maryland to a place where they specialize in treating kids with her kind of disease. That's what her Dad wants. They are going to see what the doctors down at Madison suggest, she said, before they know what to do next.

I saw Mom yesterday. Miss Rose took me down to Madison. Mom seemed alright. She even seemed kind of funny—I mean, she made a joke or two. She was telling me my pants were high water pants. I guess that means they were too short. Maybe you've heard that before. Seems like your pants were always too short. That hasn't been too big a problem for me, you know. I have grown a little, though, which is another thing that Mom was finding funny. I am 5'2" now. Miss Rose measured me the other day. She noticed I'd grown. She and I are eye to eye now. One morning, I came in from the barn for breakfast, and she said, "You grew last night." We got out the yardstick and sure enough. I was almost half an inch taller than I had been. I'd been stuck just over five feet forever, it seemed. How tall are you, now? Seems like you were five feet in about fourth grade!

Well, I guess I don't have much more news. Jannie's and my 4-H calves are doing incredible. Dante, the one we picked for Jannie, is huge. He is three inches taller than Bruno—my calf—and at least 100 pounds heavier. He is the one from that Argentinean bull that Mr. Spencer inseminated Bunny with. Dante is Bunny's first calf. She is out of Daisy, remember. Daisy is Marigold's daughter. I know you remember Marigold. She was my second heifer, remember? She's the one that chased you and Bobby Bluhm out of the pasture that day you guys were going to go fishing down by the creek and you didn't know she'd just dropped her first calf. That calf was Midnight, Bruno's mom. So I guess Bruno and Dante are cousins, kind of. But we bred Midnight with semen from an American stud. Bruno is a lot lower slung, real typical. I bet he shows better than Jannie's steer—but don't ever tell her I said so.

Let me know what is going on with you. How's Jack? Still crazy? Say hi to Aunt Mary and Uncle Paul.

Your Brother,

David

∞

Winter hung on through March and lingered into April. On Good Friday, the morning finally hinted of spring. The temperature breached sixty degrees, and the last of the hard, dirty crusts of snow melted into pools and puddles that stood on saturated fields and ran in torrents along flooded ditches. By mid-afternoon, however, David sensed a difference in the air. Leaving St. Mary's after the Passion reading, he could see a disturbance in the sky that cast an unusual pall over the land. The sky seemed potent and dangerous, eerily still, yet laden with suspended energy. The sky amplified the mood from the gospel reading. Paddy and Miss Rose hesitated before getting into the Packard, looking to the sky above Reedsburg.

"A storm," Rose said.

Paddy nodded, glancing southwest, then north again. Muttering to himself, he climbed in behind the wheel.

By the evening milking, the temperature had dropped to the low thirties. A sly wind kicked up, sending drafts through the barn. Even the cows anticipated something brewing in the weather, David noted. Several danced nervously, and others didn't let down much milk at all. Paddy noticed it as well, reminding David that it was better to let the cows hold back than to work their teats too much.

"It may take a couple milkings to get them back to normal, but we don't want to bring on any mastitis," he warned. A few precocious snowflakes swept past David's face as he walked back to the farmhouse after chores. *Scouts,* he thought, whimsically. *There'll be more to follow.* After supper, the mood was mellow. Miss Rose read quietly in the warm kitchen. Paddy hung around longer than usual, played a couple games of chess with David, and stoked the wood burner downstairs one last time before heading to his cottage. David noticed the barn light go on a few minutes after Paddy left: a last check on the girls. Still, no snow collected on the ground. Just a few flakes darted through the light coming from the barn. Perhaps, David thought, it would blow over.

He read late in bed. Just as he started nodding, an abrupt stillness snapped him back to wakefulness. He peered out the window. It was utterly dark. Tiny flakes of snow fell listlessly on the sill outside his window. Something Gabriel once said took on new meaning: "When starting out on a long journey, take small steps." He picked up the book he'd started, *Doctor Zhivago,* and read deep into the night.

The snow fell all the next day and well into Saturday night. David finished *Zhivago* and took up *War and Peace*. He'd been blazing through Russian authors lately. He was completely drawn into the complicated story lines and tangled interactions of intricate characters.

Late in the day, he wrote Patrick.

Saturday, April 21, 1962

Dear Patrick,

You would not believe the snow storm we are getting. So far, it's almost thirty inches, but shows no sign of letting up. The TV says it won't quit until late tonight. Seems like this storm front just got stuck here above Baraboo. Madison has only had several inches. Milwaukee got just rain. Chicago is still in the 50's, so you are probably having spring. I think the groundhog must have gone extinct in these parts this year. Looks like winter forever.

I talked to Jannie today. She's leaving for Bethesda, Maryland, on Monday, if they can get out on the roads. In some ways, I wouldn't mind if the snow kept her here forever. But only if she was okay. She says she's feeling pretty good. I'm hoping to see her tomorrow, if we can dig our way out of here.

Mr. Gooding called me into the guidance offices on Thursday. Seems he wanted to know what I was doing to choose a college. I said that was easy, I'm going to Wisconsin. He laughed, and said that yeah, that made it easy. Wisconsin is a great school. He just wanted to know if I had considered any of the other top tier schools. Stanford, in California (that doesn't sound half bad today, when I see winter still ruling in April!), or some of the schools out east. He says he has friends at Yale that are interested in me. I asked how they even knew about me, and he said two ways. The entrance exams—I got my SATs back and scored real high—and he had told them about me. It looks like I'll be Valedictorian. He said I could pretty much choose where I want to go to school, and probably get a full scholarship as well. I told him I want to go to Wisconsin because I want to study animal genetics and also 'cause I could get home a lot and take care of my animals.

I feel kind of guilty leaving Paddy with all the Holsteins. I have 19 cows milking now, and a dozen yearling heifers that will freshen this summer. Paddy has culled down to just fifteen Jerseys. We have been working on remodeling our barn, since it can only hold up to fifty cows in stanchions. We'll be putting a milk line in this spring, and probably convert the herd over to this barn sometime in the summer. I wonder if he'll fill his barn back up with Jerseys after we move the Holsteins over here, or if we'll keep the herd all together. He claims that his Jerseys have to struggle to get their fair share of silage when we dump it in the manger out in the cow yard. He thinks the Holsteins are too aggressive for the Jerseys to compete with. They sure milk more. We're putting a new cooler in this barn that is four times as big as the old milk tank in Paddy's barn. It'll hold close to two thousand pounds of milk! That's almost 300 gallons! The dairy pressured us to do that cause they said Jim Thompson wouldn't have to stop by every day to pick up the milk, but Paddy wonders if even that size tank will be big enough for every-other-day pick up. Mr. Thompson said not to worry. He'll pick us up as often as we need it. I sure hope he's right about that, cause by the time we milk tomorrow, the tank will be pretty full. I sure don't want to dump milk out in the snow.

Well, anyway, you can see I like my animals more than ever. So I guess I'm not too concerned with looking at schools other than Wisconsin. And besides, I can live with Aunt Kate. What could be better?

Well, let me know how things are going with you. I haven't heard much from you since you called in February. What's going on in the Dunes?

Your Brother,

David

By the time David finished his letter to his brother, the snow had stopped. The wind, however, picked up, clearing the skies and whipping the snow into mounds that buried the Packard in the driveway, reached high up along the side of the house, and covered the road to the farm with twelve-foot drifts that were impossible for the county plows to clear. David and Paddy dumped milk on Sunday morning, and again that evening and Monday morning.

After milking and a hearty breakfast on Sunday, David had the urge to explore. He waxed up and strapped on Gabriel's old cross-country skis. The wind had sculpted drifts and packed the snow so that David, with his weight distributed on the long, broad skis, skimmed across the glittering crust like a sand flea over little dunes of snow.

He headed west into North Freedom, gliding across the snow to the railroad trestle. He stopped, mesmerized by the flow of the river under the tracks. The Baraboo River cut a dark swath between snow-blanketed banks. The buildup of spring runoff from before the storm flowed hastily south, headed for the Wisconsin on the way to the Gulf of Mexico via the mighty Mississippi. David kicked snow from the ties on the bridge, wondering how long before the molecules from the flakes would mix with the warm waters of the Gulf.

In the village, no one had emerged from the snow-covered homes. The only signs of life were at St. Mary's, where Father Hanley shoveled snow from the steps of the small church. David watched the snow fly in great plumes above Father Hanley's head as he vigorously tossed the fine white powder off the walk. He skied swiftly across the blanket of whiteness into the churchyard.

"Morning, Father," he called.

"Good morning, David," Father Hanley said. "Happy Easter."

"Happy Easter," David replied, unstrapping a ski. "Got another shovel?"

"Inside the vestibule." Father Hanley set his shovel next to the door and turned toward the church. "I'll be glad to get it for you, if you're willing to help."

Working together, the priest and the young man had the walk to the parking lot cleared within minutes.

"A path to nowhere," Father Hanley said, his arms folded atop the handle of his shovel. He looked out across the undisturbed whiteness. The silence filled the air with sacred freshness.

"I don't think we're going to have many takers for Mass this Easter morning," the priest commented. David listened for judgment in Father Hanley's tone, but there was none. The priest sounded relieved. He looked at David, shrugged, and added, "Must be the way the Lord wants it. Well, let's go in. If you'll do the honors of serving, we can celebrate Mass on behalf of all those who chose to remain snug and safe in their homes."

David followed the priest into the church. With a flip of his hand, Father Hanley indicated not to bother with the alter boy's tunic and cassock. "That's just for showtime," he laughed. "Not necessary." Donning his mantle, the priest led David to the altar.

David could not recall so quick a Mass. One *Kyrie eleison* was sufficient for Father Hanley that morning, and forget the *Gloria*, even if it was Easter. Father Hanley did linger over the reading a bit, adding a few of his own thoughts—mostly in the form of questions.

"How do you suppose he rose right up through all those funeral wrappings?" he asked, waving his hands upward from the altar as he reflected on John's version of the Resurrection. "Did you notice, he appeared first to his women friends? Hmmm."

Then, solemnly, at the end of the gospel, he asked a final question. His voice was soft and inviting.

"Why do you suppose that the Son of God had to go through all the trouble of dying—especially in the way he died—just to rise from the dead again?

David met the priest's glance. It was difficult not to laugh at the burly Father Hanley scrunching his eyes and lips into grotesque convolutions, his mane radiating from his head like a shaggy halo. David wondered if he was hamming it up; would the priest be so irreverent?

"Well?" Father Hanley demanded. "Aren't you going to even make a guess at it? You can't just go through the motions if you're going to serve Mass. It's your role to respond."

David's mind raced for an answer, but he was distracted by the priest's comical expression. He blurted, "Et cum spiri, tu tuo!"

And you, too, go with the Spirit!

Father Hanley's eyes widened as if he were thunderstruck, his gaze searching the distance. He thought silently for a moment, then said absently, "Brilliant." He turned to the altar, muttering in a pleasant, surprised tone, and resumed the Mass.

But David's mind whirred like a roulette wheel, landing finally on an unresolved question of his own. He again blurted his words, but this time heartfelt, the pain stabbing deep within.

"But why did he have to die unjustly? And why does he make people die unjustly? Why is he letting Jannie die?"

Father Hanley stood still as a stone. David saw the priest shift his eyes, looking at him in his periphery. Again, David was caught off guard by the shaggy one's response.

"Now that is a worthy offertory, if I've ever heard one. You make this humble Jesuit ponder his radical faith. I thank you."

Slowly, the priest walked over to the chairs along the wall of the sacristy. David followed and took the seat beside him. David saw his eyes close, and wondered, after several moments, whether he'd gone to sleep. Suddenly, his eyes popped wide open, and he spoke with confidence.

"I think it doesn't matter to Him how we die. Just that we die," the priest said.

"What do you mean?" David croaked.

"Well," the lionish man continued, "the good Lord gives us time. And free will. And He lets us weave our own little acts of will into the grand mural of creation. I think He does particularly care how we live. I'd like to think he'd rather look at beauty in creation, of course, than evil and war and all the downsides of life. But in the end, He expects everybody's part in creation to be unique. And while He gives time, he doesn't guarantee how much. It's what you do with the time you have that He enjoys. Or values." He paused to reflect, sifting his beard through his fingers. "That's my guess."

"It sure hurts, sometimes," David said.

"Life?" the priest asked. "Yes. Probably much more so than death. And the dying itself, well, it's a killer," he added earnestly.

They sat, caught in contemplation. Then, Father Hanley rose and walked slowly toward the altar. He stopped, turned toward David, and said, "Let's finish it."

Together, they broke and shared the bread of Communion. The priest shared the wine with David as well.

Suddenly, the Mass was over.

"You have shared your blessings with me this morning, and I with you. Go, now, David. Seek peace along the way, and always spread the grace."

The curious fellow shepherded David to the door and watched him prepare to ski away.

"You've given me plenty to think about today, and it looks like the Lord intends that I won't have my thoughts interrupted," he said, gesturing across the white landscape. "Don't be a stranger, especially if you have some more testing questions."

David set back out across the snow, returning in the tracks he'd cut on the way into town. The ruts held their form, and the skiing was much faster. He was home again in less than an hour.

∞

That evening, during milking, David recounted the priest's unorthodox celebration of Mass that morning to his uncle.

"Ha!" Paddy laughed. "You witnessed Jack Hanley in his finest form. Unfettered from the burdens of pastoral politics. He's been called a heretic, you know. Preaching his Jebbie heresy on Easter morning, of all things. That's probably the Good Lord's reason for keeping everyone snowbound. He didn't want just anyone to have to listen to Jack's outlandish theology! No wonder the man's got himself in a stew of trouble."

David was amused by Paddy's reaction. He knew that Paddy was well acquainted with the shaggy cleric. His uncle had confided that the wayward Jesuit had been assigned the role of visiting priest at St. Mary's Chapel as much for his own mental health as to provide pastoral care in the little community. Before arriving in North Freedom, Father Hanley had been in Asia for several years. He'd walked the mountains of Iran and Afghanistan, preaching, sharing philosophies with Sufi monks, and contemplating the life of the young man Jesus in his years prior to entering public life. On his assignment in North Freedom, he continued his treks, covering miles every day, often ending up near Plain, Reedsburg, or Lake Delton. He particularly liked hiking to Sauk City or Spring Green along the Wisconsin River, where he'd set up on the banks, hypnotizing himself with the flow of the water, slipping deep into a contemplative state for a day or two before returning to St. Mary's. Sometimes, he would miss the entire set of weekend services; weekends were not a convenient chronological landmark for him.

Paddy had immediately bonded with the wild-looking priest. He often veered the several miles west into North Freedom to gather up the cleric and take him along on his errands. He'd treat Father Jack, as he called him, to a sandwich, and often a beer or two, while they were in town. Baraboo was the winter home of the Barnum and Bailey Circus, and Paddy loved to watch the priest interact with the circus animals on their daily exercise parade around the square. The rough-looking man with the blazing blue eyes and long, unshorn hair would quiet the camels, elephants, zebras, and other great beasts merely by his presence on the sidewalk along the parade route. Father Jack particularly liked the giraffes, and they clearly returned the feeling. Invariably, the father and mother giraffe, along with their yearling calf, would stop, spread their forelegs wide, and dip their heavy, bony-skulled heads low on their long necks, attempting to nuzzle the priest. He savored every moment, as did the trainers and townsfolk who came to appreciate Jack's peculiar but gentle eccentricity.

"Well then, why do you suppose the Good Lord chose to expose me to Father Hanley's scandalous theology?" David shot back to his uncle.

Paddy reflected for a moment, his eyes flashing. "David, the Good Lord's got something special in mind for you, I reckon." He nodded once, then again, confirming his own speculation. Then, laughing, he added, "Father Jack'll tell you exactly what he thinks the Lord has in mind for you, whatever that means."

David thought about what Father Hanley had said. He wondered what his part in weaving the creation mural would be. He knew that if it were up to him, he'd create a world in which Jannie wouldn't be sick. And his mother wouldn't be crazy. He leaned his forehead into the flank of one of his promising first-calf heifers. She was coming along, producing more than many in his herd. She'd be even better next year. David had faith in that. He reflected on how certain he could be about things like his cows, yet how weak he felt about the people he knew and loved the most. Maybe it was a matter of faith. Maybe it was more than merely existing; it was truly believing that one could really impact creation. He'd read about faith healers. Jesus certainly was one. How come he couldn't be one? He wanted to be a healer. *Where is a healer when you need one?* Paddy's words spun in his mind: *the Lord's got something special in mind for you.* They whirled and blended with Father Hanley's comments, confusing him further. If the Lord had something special in mind for David, and he was empowered by the Lord to add to the great woven tapestry of all creation, how was he supposed to know what was consistent with the Lord's will, when all he wanted to do was make Jannie and his mother better, and he couldn't? David shook his head in frustration, dried off his heifer's udder, and turned to prep the cow next in the milk line.

∞

May 21, 1962

Dear Davey,

Well, it's official. I'm as hairless as a worm. I can't find a single hair on my body. Not even you-know-where! (Don't tell anyone I told you!!!) Thanks for the Braves cap. I really love it. There are all too many Yankees caps around here. And worst yet, Judy Cheveck wears a Cubs cap. She's not even from Chicago! She says her uncle works for the Cubs. I hate the Cubs. But I hate the Yankees even worse. All the damn Yankees fans here think they are going to win the World Series again. That's sick. I'm not the only one with a Braves cap here, but I'm definitely the only one with a cap autographed by Henry Aaron. How'd you ever get that done? INCREDIBLE!

I can't say I've been feeling a whole lot better. But that's 'cause of what they are doing to me here. The medication is the pukes. And the shits. I don't know how something that wrings me out so much is supposed to help me. It's the bone marrow tests that are the worst, though.

But overall, it is pretty much the same. I have a really cool new friend, Mary Catherine. She's from Georgia. She's a scream. You should hear the way she talks! We hit it off from the moment we laid eyes on one another. Why is that? Sometimes it is so easy to get to know and like someone without even trying. You are that way. Getting to know you was as easy as getting to know myself. Seems like we've always known each other. Same way with M.C. She likes all the things I like. She's real artsy. And she can play beautiful music. She plays several instruments. She brought her guitar with her, and she's real good. And she can sing beautifully. She says her best is the cello, but she didn't bring it here with her. She says she is going to ask her mom to bring it. The Sergeant Major Head Nurse, in one of her benevolent moments, told M.C. that she would see about trying to get a cello in from somebody in Bethesda. I guess people are always doing nice things for us in here, or trying to. M.C. thinks that would be alright, but she'd kind of like to have her own cello. She says if she gets it, she'll help me finish learning the Air on the G String, then we could play it together when I come home. M.C. says it really needs a cello to be right. I don't know where she'd keep it. They have these big auditoriums and meeting rooms downstairs where we go to hang out so we don't disturb the kids who aren't feeling too good. God, there is nothing worse than when everybody starts acting up and making noise when you feel like shit. And that's just about how you feel sometimes. Then, the kids who are finally feeling good get yelled at and chased by the Sergeant Major, which is a lot of times half the fun of having fun. Finding new ways of bugging the Sergeant Major. I don't know how anyone could want to have a job around kids if she gets so annoyed by us. But she is here ALL the time. It's like she never goes home. Maybe she doesn't have a home. I don't know. But we are always trying to figure out how to make her go ballistic again. We do things like hide the chart she's been carrying around, or pick-pocket the scissors she's always carrying in her uniform. She's got these real loose pockets, and her scissors and pens are always just about to fall out when she's doing things on you, so if you're good, and it doesn't take a lot to be too good, you can just slide the scissors right out of her pocket and hide it under the blankets. Then when she's gone, you get somebody to take it back out to the desk and sneak it onto the counter, or put it someplace real obvious. Sooner or later, the Sarge comes snooping around, looking everywhere for her stuff. God, it's funny. We all about burst! Darcy Lemmons was the one who named Miss Crenshaw "the Sergeant Major." I guess Darcy's folks were both in the Army. Her mom was a Sergeant, and she always said Miss Crenshaw was more regimented than either of her folks put together. I really liked Darcy. She came here right after Thanksgiving, and she never went home again. Some of the kids go home. Some of them. I want to go home, and I told one of my doctors so. I want to go home and see you, and ride Cherub, and see Wendy. My doctor didn't really say yes, and he didn't really say no. But he kind of indicated that there was hope. He said if I kept working at it, and my blood counts kept getting lower, that maybe… Cracks me up. If I keep working at it! What is there to work at? The biggest thing to keep working at here is overcoming boredom. Man, either there is nothing to do, or you don't feel worth doing it. They have all these craftsy things to do, like drawing classes and art classes. It's like today's mantra shall be, "Basket weaving beats boredom!" Give me a break! Maybe the art will be more fun now with M.C. Tuesday, she did this thing where she drew what looked like a dozen eggs in a carton. But then she put these faces on all the eggs, and I realized they were us! I mean, I could even tell which one was me! I laughed so hard my sides were hurting. I thought I was going to burst! And she just kept on painting, a little smile on her face the whole time. The Sarge took a look at it and said it was mean to make fun of the patients. Hell, if we don't make fun of the patients, who are us, what fun is there?

Well, I gotta go. I gotta have a treatment this afternoon. Pukes!

Thanks for telling me about Zhivago. It was a great read. So sad! I felt bad for Tasha. She so loved Zhivago, and he really loved her, too, it seemed. But the passion he felt for Laura! Whew! Had me reeling at times. I don't quite understand it sometimes. I mean,

Laura had kind of a hard life, and was always on the brink of being a loser, kind of. But she was a strong woman, to get through so much, I guess. I don't know. Why was Zhivago attracted to Laura so passionately, but not to Tasha? I suppose it's kind of that kindred spirit type thing, like Anne of Green Gables always talked about. Or like I was saying about M.C. And you. Most of all, you. I miss you most.

Now I HAVE to go. They're coming to take me away, ha ha. Damn.

I love you, David.

Jannie

∞

David read Jannie's letter again for the third time. He laughed at the thought of her playing tricks on the nurse. *That woman made a big impression on Jannie,* David thought. He skimmed over parts, and reread others. She sounded so like herself, so spunky. That was good. Her letters weren't always that way.

He folded the pages of her letter, lifted them to his nose to catch her scent, kissed it lightly, and put it with the bundle of her other letters stored in the drawer of his bedside table. He turned off the light. Quietly, he cried himself to sleep, praying that Jannie would be among those who made it home.

∞

David flung the last of the spent bedding into the wagon he had backed down the barn alley. He'd been working all morning, and still needed to lime down the barn and freshen it with clean bedding. The cows would be spending most of their time in pasture now, so he was able to give the empty barn a thorough cleansing.

Outside, Paddy drove his old International pickup to a hard stop, kicking up dust that billowed into the alley. David heard the truck door slam, but at first he couldn't see his uncle in the thick dust cloud. As Paddy emerged, he strode with an upbeat pace. David studied his uncle, decoding his expression. Obvious joy. Almost glee. It was contagious. David felt a smile spread across his face. His uncle looked nothing less than jolly.

"What's up, Pad?" David asked as Paddy marched to a halt next to the tractor. He was positively beaming, David thought. His uncle's eyes sparkled, almost teary, with joy.

"Jannie—she's coming home, David."

David froze. The barn around him faded away. Paddy's joyous face floated before him, like a balloon on a string, smiling happily. Yes, David saw, a tear did stream unfettered down his uncle's face. The reality of the news hit him like a bolt. Suddenly, the world crystallized before him with alarming, beautiful clarity.

He leaped at Paddy, hugging him dearly.

"Yippee!" he screamed at the top of his lungs, dancing in bounds around the barn. "Yippee! Yippee!"

He stopped suddenly, grasping Paddy by the shoulders.

"When? How'd you know?"

Paddy wiped the tear track with his bare forearm. He could hardly talk through so broad a smile.

"Thursday. I ran into Doc Whitman in town. They found out this morning. Mrs. Whitman was trying to call the house all morning, but with you out here and Rose and I in town, nobody answered," Paddy beamed. "She's coming home, David."

The two men, face to face, disarmed by joy, hugged and cried, dancing in circles in the freshly limed alley of their barn.

∞

Late that afternoon, David called Jannie at Bethesda. The nurse who took the call had to search among the marauding teens cooped up in the ward to find the fortunate one. David waited eagerly to hear her voice.

"Hello?"

"Jannie, it's me. David."

"David! Oh, David, did you hear?"

"Yep. You bet. I can't wait to see you."

Jannie paused before responding cautiously. Her voice seemed halting, almost shy.

"Davey, I don't know…"

"What?" he demanded, his voice filling with surprise. "I'm dying to see you." He was immediately sorry for his choice of words.

Jannie noticed as well, and laughed, breaking the tension. "Oh, you don't have to do that just to see me. There's enough of that going on around here."

"What do you mean, though?" David asked. "Don't you want to see me?"

"Oh, yes! More than anything," her voice shimmering with hope. "It's just that, well, I don't know if you'd even recognize me, Davey. This hasn't been easy, being here. I don't look like me. I look… horrible!" she said softly.

David listened as she described her fears. He wouldn't like what he saw. She was thin—skinny. Sallow. And she was totally bald. She looked worse than she felt, she said. She was really feeling pretty well.

David waited for a pause, listened to her catch her breath, and said, "Jannie, how are your eyes?"

The question caught her off guard.

"My eyes? I dunno. Fine, I guess. Why?"

David took a deep breath. He felt himself on the brink of tears, and he didn't want Jannie to have to deal with that. Nonetheless, his voice rasped as he said in nearly a whisper, "Jannie, I just want to look into your eyes. I want to see you. I want to look in your eyes and I want to kiss you. I can't wait for you to come home."

Jannie was silent a moment on her phone in Bethesda. When she spoke, it was she who first spilled tears.

"Oh, Davey. I've waited so long. I'm coming home."

June, 1962

BY THE SUMMER he turned sixteen, Patrick had found a comfortable niche of existence in the Dunes. He was at home at the Howards'. While his aunt tended to be sensitive and high-strung, his uncle was a mellow, stabilizing factor in his life. He hung out with a few friends from the Dunes community, and with Jack and his circle of friends who drifted along on the hot, white beach.

Patrick had learned to be discreet about the time he spent with Jack, as his cousin so often provoked his parents with his erratic behavior and his inclination for mean-spirited mischief. While Jack could be fun and entertaining, his mood swings often left Patrick feeling uneasy and embarrassed. Patrick preferred to cast his own lot, focusing first and foremost on his sports and conditioning.

Patrick ignored the prescribed, regimented weight training that was the crux of his football coach's recommended preseason conditioning routine. He chose instead the aerobic exercises he could do outside. He loved to run. And he seldom tired of calisthenics, especially pull-ups or push-ups. He did endless push-ups. Jack watched in awe, or sometimes with mock amazement, as his cousin pumped out pushes without a break.

"What's your most ever?" Jack asked.

"I don't know," Patrick lied. He once topped two hundred before losing count, his mind wandering freely. He'd counted to 150 on several occasions.

Jack started challenging him to bear weight during his push-up sets. He placed a large potted geranium squarely on Pat's shoulder blades. Patrick pumped a steady hundred. Jack tried a bag of salt for the water softener. No problem; Patrick pushed another hundred. Another day, on the beach, Jack coaxed Alexander, Jim Manding's golden retriever, into sitting atop his cousin. The seventy-pound dog sat proudly and calmly through Pat's first dozen reps before spotting a gull swoop down at the shoreline. Alex suddenly bolted for the bird, raking raw claw-marks across Patrick's tanned skin. Patrick writhed and moaned on his belly as his cousin doubled over, howling with laughter.

On a lazy afternoon under the hot June sun, Jack boasted to the gang that his cousin could do a hundred push-ups with one of the O'Connor sisters sitting on his back. Eddie and Brad Sanderson jumped all over Jack's claim. Patrick sat back on his elbows in the sand, listening to Jack's blather. His cousin was digging him a deep hole again.

"I bet you your Cat for a day that he can," Jack wagered. He'd love to command the Sandersons' seventeen-foot catamaran out on the lake. He knew they would never let him have it, even for an afternoon, unless they took and lost his bet. And he knew the Sandersons loved to gamble.

"What's in it for us?" Brad, the older Sanderson, demanded.

Jack held up his surfboard. "Possession, all summer. It's yours, if Pat can't deliver," he smirked, egging Brad on. Jack's surfboard was his icon that summer. When the waves were up on Lake Michigan, Jack rode the crests of the breakers better than anyone. He'd paid a good price for the board, ordering it by mail from California. Nobody else in the Dunes had one nearly as nice. If he lost it this early in the summer, Jack would certainly forfeit heady bragging rights. But he knew he wouldn't lose it.

Patrick slowly lowered his head between his arms, lacing his fingers behind his neck. He closed his eyes. Why did Jack do this? He often roped Patrick into schemes, cons, and outlandish bets without even checking with him. Patrick shook his head. Just because. For no other reason. Just because. Jack pushed everyone to the edge.

But Patrick knew he could meet this challenge. He felt it. He'd just finished a run. He was warm. He was ready. He could probably rack up a hundred push-ups with both the O'Conner twins on his back, they were so tiny. He looked up, catching Jack's eye. He nodded, ever so slightly.

Jack was on the attack.

"In or out? Yes or no?" he demanded.

"In!" Brad burst out.

"You bet," Eddie chimed in. "There's no way he can do that. Not a hundred. No. You're on. Come here, sweet thing," Eddie latched on to the board.

"Hold it while you can, Eddie," Jack said. "It won't be for long."

Ginny O'Connor volunteered to be the sitter. Patrick smiled. While both Ginny and Molly, her twin, were small girls, Ginny was the larger of the two. And she was the cuter. Patrick had watched her often among the gang on the beach. *Well,* he thought, *if Jack's got me into this, least ways it's Ginny.*

"Come on," Jack urged. "Show these guys."

Patrick found a level spot on the beach, next to the calm lake where the sand was wet and firm.

"This'll do." Towering over Ginny, he coached her on how to sit: cross-legged, facing his feet, directly above his shoulder blades.

"Feel the flow of the push-ups," he instructed. "Ever ride a horse? Try not to rock or tip back and forth, just go with the flow."

Ginny's eyes danced as she nodded. "I'll hold real still," she promised.

Patrick got down on his belly and let Ginny get settled on his back.

"Try not to sit right on your heels, Gin. They dig in a bit."

He felt her adjust. Her bare legs were warm and soft on his back.

The challengers jeered, doubting that Patrick would do anywhere near the hundred push-ups that Jack guaranteed.

Patrick slowly pushed off the sand, feeling Ginny steady. She tipped a bit, then settled, and he lowered himself slowly. Each subsequent push-up was a tad quicker, until he reached nine or ten.

"Like riding a horse, Gin," he reminded her. He hit stride then, and smoothly, evenly lifted and lowered the young girl on his back, his triceps pumped into powerful bundles. He kept his neck straight, in the same plane as his back and legs. Ginny perched pertly on his shoulder blades like a tiny Buddha. Patrick hit twenty, thirty, forty....

In his periphery, Patrick sensed the others on the beach gathering and observing. The incredulous gang of doubters silenced as he reached fifty. He moved powerfully, oblivious of Gin's extra weight. She was gone to him. Muffled mutterings filtered into his ears.

"Incredible..."

"No way. No way!" It was Eddie. His voice was fraught with despair. He hated losing.

Patrick kept pumping.

At eighty-three, he felt the burn in his arms, and slowed his pace. The cynics noticed the change, and looked for him to falter.

"He's done. He's slowing," Brad cried, hope finding its way back into his tone. "He can't make it!"

Patrick persisted. He reached eighty-five, each push labored, slower than the last. At eighty-eight, he braced up, Ginny suspended high upon his shoulders, his arms extended, resting briefly. She was still as a sphinx on his shoulder blades, and he felt as if she were willing herself lighter.

He lowered himself slowly. Eighty-nine. Again. Again. He worked up to ninety-one and once again held himself up. He let his arms lock, extended, while he arched his head back. Sweat dripped from his forehead, down his face, falling freely from his nose.

The gang was wild.

"He's done. We got 'im now!"

Jack sat confidently, a few strides away, a knowing smile on his lips. He'd watched his cousin do too many of these stupid push-ups. Patrick's arms bulged, his shoulder muscles swelled. But he wasn't even shaking yet. He could do another fifty. Maybe more. He was giving Jack leverage. But Jack didn't need it, or want it, just now. Saturday on the Cat would be enough.

"Finish it. Do it," he urged quietly.

Patrick heard him, and smoothly, evenly finished the last nine push-ups. On the one-hundredth, he lowered his belly and laid his arms on the cool sand. He felt Ginny lift off his back. The cool air touched lightly on his skin where she'd been. He rolled over and sat up, facing the lake. He smiled to himself, feeling as smug as Jack. *I hadn't even started shaking.*

"Damn," Brad muttered.

"Saturday," Jack reminded them. The Sandersons understood. They would be good to their word. It was their boat, and their parents didn't care whether they let any of their friends use it. Even Jack. The brothers were confident he could handle it. It was more the loss of pride that smarted.

"It's yours. Saturday morning. Come and get it," Brad conceded, handing back the surfboard as the gang moved back up the sand.

Patrick scanned the beach. Some of the girls sat in the sand, clustered around Ginny, giggling and asking what the "ride" felt like. Several of the adults mingled a dozen yards away. Mrs. Simpson. Avery and Georgia Draper. A couple he didn't know. One of them was a woman, young. Very beautiful. Patrick could see that they were discussing his feat. Avery lifted his eyebrows toward him in acknowledgment, and he nodded back. The unfamiliar lady watched him closely. Patrick rolled to his knees and crawled on all fours like a turtle into the cool water. When the water hit his chin, he rose to his feet, his arms, shoulders, and chest still pumped, and waded deeper into the lake. At waist deep, he kicked his legs out and floated on his back, dangling his burning arms at his sides. He paddled slowly, watching the group still chatting at water's edge. There was something about the lady talking with Avery that fascinated him. He wondered who she was. He wondered when he would meet her. He knew that in the Dunes, it was only a matter of time.

June 21, 1962

DAVID STOOD on the steps of the county courthouse, examining his brand new temporary driver's license. He'd been driving tractors and the pickup around the farm for years, and he thought it was silly that he had to wait even longer to get his permanent license. He snapped back to earth as he heard Paddy's International rumbling down the block.

He hopped into the pickup and waved the document toward his uncle.

"Got it."

Paddy put the pickup in park, opened his door, and stepped out. He tossed the keys across the bench seat to his nephew.

"You drive."

David was all smiles as he circled three times around the square before heading for the co-op, where they loaded bags of cracked corn and some fencing supplies. With a full load in the truck and David proudly at the wheel, they headed out of town.

"What about all the alfalfa we just cut?" David asked guiltily as they turned into the Whitmans' drive.

"There's no rain in the forecast for several days," Paddy assured him. "I may just run the rake through the hay to turn it and let it dry more. There's no need to worry about hay, or milking for that matter, David. You just go have a good time with Jannie and her folks. That's my birthday present to you."

Paddy couldn't have given me a better present, David thought as he busied himself around the Whitmans' house on his brilliantly sunny birthday. He and Jannie played chess and cribbage. Then, she watched as he worked Cherub, who was a bit unruly for lack of exercise. Jannie laughed as her gelding sidestepped and shimmied under David's rein.

"You're egging him on," David protested. "You know he's just acting like this 'cause he's showing off for you." As if on cue, Cherub halted abruptly, launching a quick double-rear-leg kick.

Jannie laughed. "Get a lesson," she razzed back at him.

Later in the afternoon, David helped Mrs. Whitman prepare his birthday barbeque while Jannie napped. He chopped a head of cabbage for slaw while she worked on his cake. They chatted idly, but then, after a moment's lull, Mrs. Whitman braved more serious matters.

"You know she may need to go back to Bethesda, David," Mrs. Whitman said. "Most likely, they've warned us."

David studied the fine, undulating layers of leaf that he sliced from the cabbage. He hadn't considered that possibility.

"When?"

"We don't know. We really can't tell. I keep praying she won't ever need to. But...." She left the rest unsaid.

David moved the stack of shredded cabbage into a large pottery bowl.

"I kind of worry that I'm going to tire her out and make her sick again," David confessed. "I sometimes think I shouldn't be over here so much."

Mrs. Whitman looked up from her cake.

"Don't ever think that, David." Her eyes probed right through him. "You are extremely important to Jannie. She needs you as much as she needs me and her father."

Mrs. Whitman's expression softened. "In some ways, more. Sometimes I feel so selfish, knowing how much work you have to do at home, farming and all. And school. And how young you are. But I also know how good you are for Jannie. She lives to the fullest—as full a life as she can—when you are with her, David. She always has. I wouldn't take that from her for anything."

Tears filled her eyes, one dripping from her long lashes. She dabbed at it, sniffling.

"I'm sorry, David. I don't mean to break down on you. But I just think so much about Jannie, and what a vibrant life she's had until... this. And I think of how much life she might miss...."

Again, she dabbed at her eyes.

"David, I see how close you and Jannie are," she said, her voice strong. "When she is away, at Bethesda, I think that is the greatest threat to her, being apart from you. This may not be fair to you. It is definitely not fair to Jannie. You are both so young."

She moved away from the counter, approaching David. He'd grown enough that they were now almost eye-to-eye. With tears streaming freely down her face, she wrapped her arms around him, hugging him as she would her own son.

"I want Jannie to live more than anything in the world," she said. "But I can do nothing. Jannie may live, she may not. But as long as she can, I want her to live completely, joyfully. And you are a big part of her joy, David. I'm sorry. I hope we're not asking too much of you."

"Is Jannie going to die?" David asked outright.

Mrs. Whitman half shrugged her shoulders. Her bottom lip pouted out, and she shrugged again. "I don't know. Maybe." She fought back, refusing to say, *probably.*

David met her eyes. He understood. He shook his head, almost imperceptibly.

"I'm here because I want to be," he said softly. "I need to be. As much for me as for Jannie. I'd be crushed if you made me stay away, even if it was for Jannie's sake."

Mrs. Whitman wiped her eyes with her apron. She nodded knowingly and let out a little laugh. "I'm ruining your cake."

David smiled, charming her. "If you don't get it today, I'll be back tomorrow."

∞

Jannie slept late, and Mrs. Whitman put off starting the barbeque until she awoke.

But when Dr. Whitman and Wendy returned from the club, they brought along keen appetites whetted by two hotly contested sets on the tennis courts. They were hungry, and Wendy was more than a little dismayed that the barbeque wasn't waiting for them.

"I'm famished," she complained, her voice raised and her temper simmering. Mrs. Whitman cast a warning glance toward her husband.

"Well, the horses are as hungry as we are," Dr. Whitman said as he moved toward the door. "Come on, Wendy. Dinner will be all the more tasty by the time we get chores done. Want to help, David?" he asked.

David kept in step with Wendy as they followed her father to the barn. Chores didn't amount to much. David broke off a flake of hay for each horse as Dr. Whitman scooped out their grain. Wendy opened the door to the corral, then stepped onto the bottom board of the gate of Cherub's stall, her arms folded on the top rail. Her tennis outfit glowed impeccably white against the barn's dusty hues.

"Cherub was rather fractious this afternoon when we rode him," David told Dr. Whitman.

"Fractious, was he?" Dr. Whitman chuckled. "Well, we don't want a fractious horse, do we?" Suddenly, his head snapped in a double take. He glared across the barn at David, his brow furrowed. "What do you mean, 'when we rode him?"

David laughed. Jannie's father's concern was plastered all across his face.

"Well, I rode Cherub. Or tried to. Jannie just laughed at me," David said. "But I pretty much imagine that if she felt like it, she'd hop right on."

Dr. Whitman grunted, acknowledging the truth in David's opinion.

David stepped outside to herd the horses into their stalls. Joker strolled in leisurely, but Cherub resisted, cantering around the corral.

"Holy Minnie, Cherub!" David protested. "Horses always run to the barn, not away. Don't you know that?" He shook his head and walked out along the fence, circling behind the frisky gelding. He heard Dr. Whitman joke from inside the barn, "What are you doing out there, David, making him fractious?"

"He's fractious enough on his own, Dr. Whitman," David called back. Cherub danced and pranced, his neck arched and his mane flowing with every move. David held his arms out, moving slowly, herding Cherub toward the barn. "Any other time, I'd be working to keep you out of there," he complained.

Cherub spun, flicked his tail, and trotted into the barn. David followed. As he swung the doors closed, he saw the gelding stutter-step before entering his stall. In a flash, Cherub kicked back, catching Wendy on the chin below her cheek. David watched her head whip to the side. She crumpled against the wall of the saddle room.

David sprinted the few steps into the barn. Dr. Whitman was still tending Joker, his back to his daughter. The incident had been almost silent, except for the clapping of Cherub's hooves on the barn floor.

"Dr. Whitman," David cried as he slammed the stall door shut behind Cherub. "Wendy!"

A stream of blood flowed from Wendy's face, the flow of crimson spreading across her white tennis dress. Her eyes were rolled back in her head. David put his hand to Wendy's chin to stanch the flow of blood and felt her jaw bone give way under the slight pressure.

Dr. Whitman was at her side in a flash. "Oh, God," he muttered. He felt the same spot that David had touched, detecting the broken bone. He gently hooked his finger into her mouth and peered in, checking to see that her broken jaw and teeth weren't stuck in her airway.

David ran into the tack room. He grabbed the first aid kit and returned to Dr. Whitman. Ripping open the box, he found squares of wrapped gauze. He tore open the paper envelopes and handed Dr. Whitman the gauze.

"David, I'm going to lift her. Carefully, gently, keep these bandages on her cut."

David helped Dr. Whitman get his daughter in arm. She stirred, coming to, moaning. Her head rolled back against his chest. Dr. Whitman carefully started toward the house.

"David, quick. Run and tell Helen. Open the back door of the car on your way to the house. I'll be waiting for Helen in the car."

David raced for the car, opening the door with such force that it slammed on the rebound, pulling him along with it. He yanked it open again, then sped toward the house, ripping open the kitchen door. Mrs. Whitman and Jannie stood together, smiling, admiring David's birthday cake.

"Mrs. Whitman," David commanded. "Come quick. Get your car keys. Dr. Whitman needs you. Wendy's hurt. Hurry."

Mrs. Whitman hesitated for only the briefest instant. The urgency in David's voice and the wide-eyed seriousness of his expression set her heart pounding.

"What is it?" she asked as she snatched her purse from the chest inside the pantry.

"Cherub kicked her. She's unconscious. She's bleeding a lot. Take a towel. He got her on her jaw."

Mrs. Whitman moved quickly around the kitchen, grabbing a handful of clean towels from a drawer. Pulling her keys from her purse, she looked at Jannie, then at David.

"Everything will be alright. If you get hungry, go ahead and eat. When I know how things are, I'll call." She met each of their eyes. "It is alright. You two...will take care of each other."

Jannie reassured her. "Go, Mother. We'll be okay. Go."

Helen Whitman turned and hurried to her daughter.

∞

Just after seven o'clock, Mrs. Whitman called to report that Wendy had indeed broken her jaw and required fifty-eight stitches to close the horseshoe-shaped gap running from under her chin up along her cheek. She had regained consciousness on the way to the hospital, but was sedated now, waiting to go into surgery to have her jaw set and wired.

"Is everything okay there?" Jannie's mother inquired. "Have you eaten?"

"We're fine, Mom," Jannie said. "Davey barbequed the chicken. We didn't know how long you'd be gone, but we figured it would be a while. We kind of burned it a bit. But we ate. We thought you'd either eat, or would be hungry when you got home. His slaw was great. You'll like it."

Mrs. Whitman smiled on her end of the line. The kids seemed to be in good hands. Each other's.

"How long 'til you get home?" Jannie asked.

"I don't know. It will be late, though. Don't wait up. Tell Davey we're sorry about his birthday dinner. We'll have to do it again later. If he needs to get home, please ask him to call his uncle," she said. "But otherwise, I'm okay with him being there with you. I feel better knowing you're not alone."

"I'm okay, Mom. Davey and I were just getting out our violins to work on the Air," Jannie said. "Call me later and tell me how Wendy's doing."

"I will. Jannie…," she paused.

"Yes, Mom?"

Jannie listened to the silence on the phone.

"It's okay," she said, finally. "It's okay. Alright?"

"I'm okay, Mom," Jannie repeated. "Everything will be alright. I love you."

"I love you, Jannie."

∞

Jannie had made considerable progress on Bach's Air on the G String while she was at Bethesda. David was swept up in the intensity that Jannie evoked with each crystal note. His fingers moved independently of his thoughts, anticipating her every note, meeting and complementing the passion of her music.

"Wow," he said, searching for words as they finished. "You're amazing." His whisper was filled with awe.

Jannie smiled, visibly drifting down from a lofty place.

"M.C. knew the Air," she said. "She really helped me learn it. More than learn it—really *feel* it. Oh, David, you should hear it with M.C.'s cello. It is gorgeous!"

"You really found a friend in M.C., didn't you?"

"She was more than a friend. She was like a sister, but better," Jannie said. "Wendy is my little sister. M.C. was like having an older sister. Knowing M.C., I learned how to be a better older sister to Wendy. Least ways, I'm trying." She giggled.

Jannie turned her eyes to David's. He sensed she was measuring him. She put aside her bow, and set her hands over his. She spoke slowly.

"You know, what M.C. is all about is that everything is right now, this very instant, totally. When we played together, she played with everything she had. Ten minutes after we finished, we'd be eating a sundae and you would have thought it was the first time she had ever tasted ice cream. She'd be completely wrapped up in it. If she watched a movie, you couldn't even talk to her, she'd be so involved with the story. She just about never watched a movie twice, though.

Not enough time, she'd say. About the only thing she'd want to go over and over was our music.

"One time, when she was working with me on the Air, I was sounding just awful. I wasn't into it. I was playing like a spoiled, moody child. She tried harder and harder to lift me up, to inspire me. Her playing was just beautiful. I felt real bad, and I asked her how she could always keep her playing at such a high level. She just smiled, and looked right into my heart and said that she just wanted to play every note like she was playing it for the very last time. She said, you know, that might just be the last time she'd play that note, and she didn't want to leave anything from it. She wanted to use every bit of feeling and power she had to make it perfect.

"And that is just how M.C. is. She told me once, 'Jannie, we only have each moment once. And we may not have too many of those moments. Let's make them worthy.'"

She paused, looking at David.

"Yep, M.C. is pretty special. Even for a Yankee fan." She laughed.

David wrapped her in his arms and she melted into his hug. David kissed her gently. He felt her respond, pulling him closer. She felt thin in his arms. A wisp, like a feather. Her warmth felt good against his chest. He reveled in her fragrance. He broke the kiss, looking at her. She remained spellbound, eyes closed, his kiss emblazoned on her lips.

David led her to the couch. She lay upon the cushions. With open arms, she invited him to her.

David lay beside her on the overstuffed sofa. He slid his hand under her blouse, feeling the smooth skin across her belly. He reached behind her, and she arched, letting his fingers access the clasp of her bra. He fumbled. She started to smile, saying just as he popped the clips apart, "Out of practice?"

He shrugged, smiling into her eyes, a bit sheepish. He brought his hand around to cup her soft breast. She slowly closed her eyes, inhaling, the smile lingering on her lips.

Slowly, warmly, he caressed her, kissing her eyes, her ears, down her neck. She sat up and took off her shirt, dropping it and her bra onto the floor.

He slid his lips down from her neck onto the fine, smooth skin high on her breast. She moved, not suddenly, but sat up, breaking the moment. Her eyes remained inviting, but took on a determined, decisive edge. She looked down at her pants button, gripping carefully, opening the waistband. She lifted her hips from the couch and slid the pants down her legs, removing one foot, then the other. She sat a moment, naked but for her underpants, examining his expression.

David looked at her in wonder. They had played before. They had kissed and necked. They had caressed and probed, laughing, loving, breathing heavily in passion. But overall, they had always been chaste. Until now.

David allowed his eyes to move across her young body. She was thin, thinner than last year. But she was beautiful. He watched as she reached up and kissed him softly, then leaned back and removed her last piece of clothing.

As David kissed her, Jannie opened the buttons on his shirt. He drew his fingers lightly over her shoulders, gliding across her back and shoulder blades, then back up her neck and across her scalp. She slid her hands under his shirt and pushed it back over his shoulders. He kissed her again, holding her bare skin close to his. He moved his hands down her back and along the sides of her hips. He touched her thigh, first on the outside, then slowly, gently, tenderly up into the warmth between her legs. He felt her smooth, hairless skin and the soft plumpness of her mound. She arched slightly, pushing gently against his hand. He cupped his fingers and palm firmly across the front of her, pressing, rubbing, moving ever so carefully.

She lay back and enjoyed the pleasure of his touch for a few moments, then reached to unfasten his belt and trousers. David stood, peeled off his shirt, and drew down his pants and underwear in one motion. His erection sprung eagerly from his pants, bobbed up and down, then stood high and firm.

Jannie's eyes widened. She had felt him many times, but only through his clothes. She suppressed a gasp, then a giggle, but could nonetheless not help but look at him, seeing him for the first time. She touched him gently with her hand, wrapping her fingers gingerly around him. She pumped slowly, recalling M.C.'s words of experience and advice. She tried to not bring him to orgasm, although she didn't know when exactly that might be.

David was as enthralled with the sight of her as with her gentle strokes. He moved closer to her, clear that she wanted him, knowing that he would take her. He wondered how that would be. He wondered if he should just put himself in her. The sensation in his loins was mounting. He shifted, lifting himself to move above her.

Jannie took her hand from him and put it to his lips. She shook her head slightly, apprehension flickering in her eyes.

"M.C. said…" she whispered. "Davey, slowly. Please." She shifted slightly, and took his hand from where he softly caressed her nipple. She led his fingers back down her body, to her softness special to his touch. She held his fingers still and close, then moved them slowly in a tiny circle between the fold.

Again, he felt her arch and sigh. He watched her face, eyes almost completely closed, her head tipped back slightly, her lips parted. She moved slowly to the rhythmic motion of his hand. After a moment, she again gripped his penis, squeezing slightly with long, even strokes.

The sensation was overwhelming. David felt the first shutters of orgasm begin to well deep within him. Suddenly, Jannie tugged at him, pulling him above her, toward her.

She slipped her body under him, spreading her legs, opening herself to him. She reached down, leading him with her hand firmly around him.

David brushed against her warmth as her hand released him. She moved her hands gently to his hips, holding him back, then slowly, carefully bringing him to her.

David felt her brace as she drew him still closer. There was a tightness against his penis, her hot skin pressing against him. He let the pressure of her hand guide his hips as she pushed him slightly back and away, then in again. He felt her warmth become moist and slippery. His urge was to enter her, to bury himself in her. But he let her hands direct his movements.

He felt the release, heard her gasp, looked suddenly into her face, saw a startled, hurt expression, and then she pulled him further into her. She saw his concern, and smiled at him through eyes brimming with tears. Bringing her palms up behind his shoulders, she drew him to her, kissing him. She moved her hips up against him, pushing firmly, taking him completely. Her tongue lashed gently at his lips, and he surrendered to the pleasure of being one with her.

∞

They held each other, oblivious of the time, safe and happy.

At ten thirty, the phone rang, breaking the spell they savored.

"Jannie, is everything alright?"

"Yes, Mom. We're fine. Davey is still here. How's Wendy?"

"Well, she's medicated heavily enough to keep her comfortable. Dr. Morgan looked at her and said he thought we'd do best bringing her down to Madison, which is where we are now. We tried calling before we left, but the line was busy."

"Oh, Davey must have been talking to Miss Rose. Sorry."

"That's okay. I'm just glad everything is alright with you."

"We're fine," Jannie said, smiling at David, whose head rested in her lap. She stroked his hair with her free hand.

"Your father is heading back now. He left a few moments ago. I'm staying here with Wendy. They'll be operating on her in the morning."

"How are you, Mom? You sound so tired."

"Exhausted, dear. This has been quite a day."

"Well, don't let yourself get run down," Jannie quipped, imbuing the words with the exact same inflection she'd heard from her mother so many times over the past months. They shared a tired giggle.

"I'll be home tomorrow, Jannie."

"Good night, Mom."

∞

Jannie looked deep into David's dreamy eyes. A little smile curled her lips slightly.

"So why?" David asked.

"Why what?"

"Why did you...." He searched for the words. She knew his meaning.

"Well," she said playfully, "if I live to be a hundred, I'll still be loving you. So it doesn't make much sense to wait forever to show you that." Her eyes danced, and then she shrugged.

"And if I don't live to be a hundred, I couldn't see wasting one more day of my life not sharing all of my love with you."

They sat in stillness, pondering her words.

"Do you think you'll live to be a hundred?" David asked.

They gazed into each other's eyes. They were dancing around the fire, and they knew it.

"Davey, I don't know whether I'll live to be a hundred. I don't even know if I'll live to be eighteen."

He poked a finger into her ribs, careful just to tickle and not to gouge.

"You'd better live to eighteen. And nineteen, and forever," he countered.

Slowly, she shook her head.

"I dunno, Davey. Sometimes I don't think it's going to happen," Jannie said gently. "Sometimes it scares me. Sometimes I get real angry. It seems so... unfair."

David watched her face as her emotions blazed across it. Her eyes widened, and then narrowed to angry slits. But just as quickly, her face softened, going almost candescent, and she appeared filled with peace.

"You know, Davey, when I was at Bethesda, a lot of the kids didn't make it. Sometimes, they'd go home, and occasionally we'd hear later. One of the kids who might have been good friends with another would get a letter. Or a lot of times, the Sarge would come in. That was when she was at her best. She could soften the blow somehow. She made it seem so natural, like it was just another part of the day. Somebody was going to die. A lot of times, we never heard. Kids just left."

Jannie took a long, deep breath. She smiled gently at David. *She is so incredibly brave*, he thought.

"Some died right there. They never even came close to going home. One little girl—I don't even know her name, it seems like she had just arrived—she died after just a couple days. She'd just gotten her first treatment." Jannie's eyes widened again. "You know, Davey, sometimes I think the treatment was killing us as much as the cancer. Honestly."

David wrapped his arm around her waist, kissing her temple. She backed away, just enough to look into his eyes.

"When Darcy died, though, that really hit me," Jannie said. Her eyes were so earnest, David was compelled to hold on to her ever more tenderly.

"Darcy was my first friend there," she told him. "She was in the bed next to me. She was so kind and quiet. She never complained, even when she'd had her treatments, or… at the end."

David watched Jannie closely. Sometimes, it seemed like she was miles away. Then, with the blink of an eye, she'd be looking deep into his heart.

"You know, that's one thing you notice when you're around people who are dying," Jannie said. Again, her eyes focused far away, and she sat pondering her thought.

David gave her the moment. Then, gently, he leaned and kissed her cheek, just next to her lips. She smiled.

"What is it that you notice?" he asked.

She looked at him with unfathomable kindness.

"That when you die, it kind of doesn't matter. Like, sure, your mom and your dad, and your friends and everybody, everybody notices. And they cry and miss you and grieve. It's all a process, kind of. But you know, the clock doesn't miss a tick. Everybody else doesn't miss a heartbeat. The whole rest of the universe just keeps right on going. You're just a drop in the bucket, and the bucket is the ocean of all oceans, of all space."

They held each other, quietly absorbed in their thoughts.

David asked, "Are you scared that when you die, it means so little?"

Jannie thought a moment.

"No, not really. When I die, it won't make any difference to me at all, I suppose," she said with certainty. "I don't think that's what's important, really. After I die, there's nothing at all I can do about it, is there?"

She shifted her position, looking again into David's eyes.

"That's why it is so important to choose what I do while I am living. I'm sure of it, Davey. I don't know how much time I'll have. I just know it is important to choose carefully what I do with my time. It is how I choose to help weave this tapestry of creation that counts. It is what we do in life that is meaningful. That is why I wanted you—yes, I wanted you, I wanted all of you. I wanted to experience all of this love I have for you, and I feel so strongly from you. I didn't want to let another moment go by without you being... part of... me."

Tears welled up in Jannie's eyes, and he hugged her closely.

∞

When Dr. Whitman arrived home, his daughter was sound asleep in the arms of her young friend. David peered up over Jannie's slumbering head, wide-eyed. Dr. Whitman looked stressed and exhausted. The shock of finding Jannie so snugly wrapped up with David registered on his face. David's eyebrows lifted cautiously as he waited for Jannie's father to react.

Dr. Whitman's expression softened. He greeted David with a nod.

"Has she been asleep long?" he whispered.

"No, not really," David said. "Just a few minutes. But she's really out now."

Again, Dr. Whitman nodded. He reached around and under his daughter, gently lifting her from David's arms.

"Come on, Sweetie. Let's get you to bed," he softly murmured. With exaggerated facial expressions, he mouthed "I'll be right back." Within a few minutes, he returned.

"Let's get you home, buddy," Dr. Whitman said to David.

In the car, Dr. Whitman talked a mile a minute. He recounted the entire evening with Wendy, explaining all the medical aspects of her broken jaw and sutured laceration. After rehashing that, he asked a series of questions about David's perspective of the incident with Cherub. By the time they turned on to Joyce Road, he'd pretty much covered all the missing information he'd wondered about all evening. Then, he turned his questions toward Jannie's well-being.

David reassured him that Jannie didn't seem like she was overtiring herself. He related how they had worked on their music for a good long while after having made and eaten dinner. David made it sound like they virtually wore through the strings on their instruments, they'd played so long. He didn't know where else to go with his report, so he finished by saying they'd just watched TV for much of the evening.

Dr. Whitman listened silently, mulling over what David told him.

David thought about Jannie's talk with him as they quietly rode the last mile to the farm. Dr. Whitman turned into the driveway and pulled into the circle leading to the front porch. David hesitated before opening the door.

"Dr. Whitman," David started to ask, "do you think Jannie…"

He left the question open.

Dr. Whitman considered the variables. As he thought, a weary expression masked his emotions.

"David, Jannie is, well, was real sick. You know that. But I think we have done everything we could to beat this cancer." He faced David. "I'm optimistic. Guardedly optimistic."

David wondered. Was it the physician in Dr. Whitman that was optimistic? Or was it his hope as Jannie's father? Or both?

Chapter Thirteen
Dunes Solstice

June 21, 1962

PATRICK WOKE EARLY on Thursday, his birthday, feeling every bit a sixteen-year-old. After coffee with his uncle, he did his chores and then changed into running shorts and shoes. He loosened the muscles in his calves and thighs, and by eight-thirty, before the heat of midday waffled the air above the white sand of the dunes, Patrick was jogging down East Road, past the tennis courts, and out beyond the guardhouse to the highway. At the railroad tracks, he doubled back. When he got back to the guardhouse, he turned off the road and headed up the path through the woods toward the old golf course.

He picked up his pace. He planned his route to follow the outer loop of the course, through the woods and meadows that had reclaimed the abandoned seventh and eighth fairways. Then he'd climb the big blowout at the west end by the old Parmley place and cut down to the beach, where he'd kick it out and high-step it the last mile to home. He looked forward to the waves. When he left the house, he'd seen that the surf was decent this morning. He loved dodging breakers, racing to stay ahead of the water rushing in on the sand. The beach was always firmest along the edge of the water, and he'd dart in as each wave receded into the lake, then dash away from the ensuing froth as the next one rumbled onto shore. Sprinting along the shore, hurdling the whitecaps as they rolled across the sand, was among the most exhilarating runs that Patrick knew.

The humid stillness in the woods was a pressure cooker. Patrick sucked in the hot, moist air and headed up the hills below the line of houses perched on top of the dunes. He cut west, skirting the edge of the Parmleys' land. He'd heard it had finally been bought by a doctor from Chicago. Most Dunes people said it had been overpriced. Word was that the doc had paid the asking price—way more than most locals thought the place was worth. But Herb Parmley had really made it nice, and Patrick had helped him. Patrick had met Mr. Parmley two summers past, before the architect had taken the job in England and chosen to sell. He'd hired Pat to help remodel the den and living room and spruce up the yard before he'd put it on the market.

Patrick climbed the ravine leading up to the west edge of Parmley's land. Dune grass was waist high along the old path up the hill, and the coarse blades ripped at his legs and arms. He could see the first rows of raspberries less than a hundred yards up the draw. Patrick knew those barbed plants well. It was one of the tasks he'd performed last fall, cleaning out the old, mature stalks, trimming the plants back, and putting in new trainer posts. It was a job he'd seen David and his mother do many times on the farm, but not to the scale of Mr. Parmley's raspberry patch. Patrick had pocketed a hundred bucks for that particular chore. The vines had filled out nicely. They were lush and green. *The new owners must be watering them,* he thought.

Patrick reached the raspberries at the crest of the dune in full stride. The breeze off the lake greeted him with a gentle kiss of cool air. He stopped, taking in the view, lifting his arms to catch the full gust of breeze. He doubled over, hands on his knees, his chest heaving as he gasped the clean, lake-cooled air.

Patrick's eye caught movement. At the near end of the house, by the pool, a woman was painting a canvas perched on an easel. She dabbed from small jars of watercolors arranged on a stand next to the easel. As he watched, she stepped aside from the easel, looked out over the dunes toward the beach, then returned to the painting.

Dripping with sweat and panting, Patrick froze. The woman was bare, but for a scant bikini bottom. He glanced down at his running shorts and shoes. He had on more than she did. She was tanned evenly across her back, breasts, and legs. Her hair was pinned up in a flip. She moved lightly, like a shadow of a leaf in a gentle breeze. He recognized her from the beach. She had been with Avery that day he'd won the Sandersons' Cat for Jack.

Patrick slowly dropped to his knees, then to all fours. He moved up the rows of berries until he was no more than twenty-five yards from where the lady worked. He was flustered. He couldn't just get back up and resume his run, although he knew the path skirting the perimeter of the property was considered public passage for Dunes residents. But no one ever used it. Patrick was probably one of the few, if not the only, who ran hard enough and far enough to circle the entire old golf course to the beach. He studied the path and looked back to where the woman was painting. He'd be exposed for at least fifty yards before the path dropped down into the big blowout leading to the beach, which beckoned from another three hundred yards downhill. He could double back to the guardhouse, or circle out through the brush and dune grass to the vacant dunes beyond the west end of Dune Acres. He looked back toward the pool and assessed his situation.

The lady was lovely. Intent on her work, she moved with grace. When she stepped to look at the view down to the lake, she pivoted lightly, leaving a foot behind, on toe, like she was dancing. She shielded her eyes from the bright sky and examined the contours of the sand as it mounded and rolled into dunes. Along with her bikini bottom, she wore a plain white visor. Her shoulders and arms were fine, and her legs were long. Her calves were high and tight, and her waist was thin. *She could be a runner,* Patrick thought. Like the rest of her body, her breasts were tan and firm. The sunlight softened on her skin, accenting the smoothness from her shoulders to the curve of her breasts. The skin at her nipples shone, stretched thin over her full and supple areolae. Her belly was taut and smooth. A few tiny beads of moisture glistened on the skin around her navel and between her breasts. The blade of her hip caught the sunlight above the edge of her bikini.

Patrick had caught his breath, but he felt the dry dune air race through his nostrils anyway. He peered over the tops of the raspberry plants, entranced by the image before his eyes. A wave of guilt swept over him. His heart pounded. *What if I'm caught here?* He looked back down the path, then into the wilds to the west. There was no one.

His eyes were drawn back to her. She was like an elfin goddess. His eyes absorbed every movement, every aspect of her body. Patrick was overwhelmed by her beauty.

As he watched, she set aside her brush, took off her visor, and stepped to the edge of the pool. Facing him, not more than twenty yards away through the thick rows of raspberries, she sat down on the lip of the pool, dangling her feet. She scooped handfuls of water and splashed her face, her neck, her shoulders, the water flowing between and across her breasts. She planted her hands on the deck, lifted herself, and slid into the pool. She submerged for a long moment, then surfaced, face first. He could hear her expel the air in her lungs, and breathe in deeply. She floated easily onto her back, paddling smoothly across the surface. She swam the length of the pool, then back, several times. After her swim, she stepped from the pool. She wiped down her body with a towel from a table alongside the pool. She took a bottle of lotion from the table and spread it across first one leg, then the other, and over the rest of her body.

In the cool breeze from the lake and the shade of the raspberries, Patrick was no longer sweating. His muscles had stiffened up, having stayed low for however long he had been watching the lady. Twenty minutes? More? He didn't know. He wondered, again, how he could leave undetected. Then the lady put on a white pool robe, letting it hang loose. She brushed her hair back and stepped into the house.

Patrick was up and running. He cleared the raspberry patch and dipped down into the dune north of the pool. His timing was uneven, and his breathing out of sync. But he ran hard, stretching his legs as he sprinted down the trail. It took but a minute to reach the front dunes, where the dune grass and cacti could not hold out against the ravages of waves and wind off the lake. Patrick raced toward water's edge, where the sand tightened and the waves licked playfully along the smoothened beach. Shoes and all, he hurdled first one, then another of the knee-high waves. When the water reached his thighs, he plunged in. He felt the flow of cool water as he swam underwater toward the edge of the sandbar. He felt it first with his hands, then his knees. He crawled up onto the bar, ribs heaving, lungs pulling and purging air. He pivoted, sitting back on the sand. He wiped the water from his face and eyes. The waves broke rhythmically against his back, jostling him toward the beach.

He traced his path across the beach and up into the dune. He could see his steps dotting the sand in long strides down the slope from the house. At the top, movement once again caught his eye. The lady stood looking, her robe caught by the gentle breeze. She watched as Patrick cooled his body in Michigan's waters. Patrick slid off the sandbar and swam, underwater, as far down the beach as his lungs would let him before he surfaced again.

Chapter Fourteen
Mentor Jack

July 1, 1962

SLIPPING AWAY before starting evening chores, David drove the Packard into North Freedom, secretly hoping that Father Jack would be away on one of his rambling treks. But as he pulled into St. Mary's parking lot, he could see the door to the chapel propped open. Father Jack, uncharacteristically, was on time for Confession.

David parked the car and climbed the stairs of the country church. With each step, he felt his burdens weigh more heavily upon him. His anxiety festered over this encounter with his confessor. It was not that he feared the retribution Father Jack would demand. On the contrary, one of the appealing characteristics of Father Jack was that the penance he doled out often was spiced with the priest's unusual humor.

∞

When David had confessed, earlier that spring, to having taken the Lord's name in vain, Father Jack had demanded an exact recounting of the incident that provoked his ire.

"Well," David explained, "one of the fresh heifers is a dancer. I mean, she kicks, and she does it maliciously. She waits until you're convinced that she's really not going to kick you, and she winds up and just about takes your face off."

"And?" Father Jack led him.

"And what?" David asked. It was pretty obvious. He'd lost his temper and sworn at the dumb beast. And he could feel his anger welling again as he recounted the incident. "She knocked my cap all the way around so that the visor was over my ear."

"And?" Father Jack asked, demanding more.

"And I cussed her out."

"What did you say?"

David squirmed uncomfortably. He had felt miserable after the original incident, humbled and embarrassed, shrinkingly small in the eyes of his uncle, who had witnessed his outbreak from his place between the pair of cows across the barn alley, but said nothing at all. Paddy had simply nodded, put his head back down and focused on the cow before him as she finished her let down.

"I said, 'You goddamn whorebitch.' And I slapped her hard. On the belly."

Father Jack had sat in silence, pondering the situation. David groveled in shame, awaiting Father Jack's verdict on the severity of his sin. After a moment, he heard the priest whistle low and long.

"Whew," he said. "You were really pissed, weren't you?"

"She about took off my head, damn it!" David was pissed again.

"Yes, I see," Father Jack said.

David strained to see through the screen closure between his chamber and the priest's. He was certain that the priest was lurching in stifled laughter. It made him all the more furious.

"Well, it hurt!" David asserted.

That broke the priest's last line of resistance. He broke out laughing, low and muffled, but hard and gut-wrenching. David heard the priest stand up and open the door to his confessional box. He closed it again, and sat back down, his chuckling ebbing. "Oh, that's too much. I was worried somebody in line might hear me. Oh, forgive me. You say she had your hat turned all the way around over your ear?" The priest started snickering again. David, too, couldn't help a little laughter himself.

"Yeah, and worse, she snapped her tail in my face. And it was all wet with manure."

Father Jack lost all control. He howled with laughter.

"Assaulting the Dear Lord's beasts," Father Jack accused between gasps and laughter. "This is new ground for you, David."

"Hey, how come you know it's me? Aren't these confessionals supposed to keep you from knowing my identity?"

"Oh, David, the Lord sees all, knows all," Father Jack said as he regained control. "And He wouldn't really want His priests to be totally out of the loop with His sheep, now, would he? Besides, I don't have any other parishioners who confess to being animal-beaters."

"I wasn't confessing that I beat my cow," David protested. "I was confessing that I took the Lord's name in vain."

"Oh, yes. You did, didn't you? Well, I think the Lord is willing to forgive you that indiscretion. Probably more quickly than taking out your anger on his poor, dumb beasts. That may well be your more grievous error."

"But she kicked me," David reminded the priest through gritted teeth.

"Turn the other cheek, David," Father Jack retorted. David heard him snickering in his darkened cabin. "And I'm sure she'll straighten your hat out for you!" Father Jack lost it again over his own joke.

"Why do I confess to you?" David asked, shaking his head in the dark.

After a moment spent regaining his composure, Father Jack said kindly, "For perspective. Now, I'd say your animal inflicted penance enough upon you. Nonetheless, I encourage you to speak daily with St. Francis of Assisi. He has much to offer you. And if she kicks you again, ship her. You need to learn to avoid the near occasion of sin. How's that?"

David had left the confessional that afternoon after Father Jack's absolution shaking his head in wonder.

∞

On this occasion, David anticipated Father Jack's response to be more serious. He wondered whether the priest would condemn him. He was guilty of fornication, after all. And lust.

As he expected, there was no line for the confessional. David entered the dark closet and knelt on the worn, leather-lined kneeler.

"You awake?"

"In a fashion."

"You ready for this?"

"As ever."

David sighed.

"Bless me, Father, for I have sinned. I... have had sexual relations with a... woman... outside of marriage."

David stopped. He had wondered whether to say "with a girl," but there was little that was girlish about Jannie anymore. He waited silently for Father Jack to respond. He sensed an enormous energy of concentration flowing through the covered window from Father Jack's side of the booth.

After several minutes, David shifted his weight on his knees. He was just about to inquire if Father Jack was still there when the priest spoke.

"Well, that's not such a bad thing, is it?" Father Jack's tone was entirely sincere.

"Is too, in the Church I was taught in," David said.

"What do you mean?"

"Well, it's against the Commandments. It's immoral to have sex outside of wedlock. It's wrong," David said, getting a bit agitated.

It was Father Jack's turn to sigh.

"You are so hard on yourself." After a moment, he continued. "Let's consider this for a moment. Okay, so you're not supposed to have sex unless you're married. That's the rule. You broke the rule. But, you know, I hear this one all the time. And worse, it's usually married people who are having relations with someone beside their own spouse. And you know what the first thing I want to know from them is? I want to know if they love their spouse, and are they making love with their spouse as well?"

David sensed that Father Jack was getting excited. He could really work up a lather if you gave him the right load to draw.

"Now, some of them say, no. They don't love their spouse at all. They still might have sex with them, but they don't love them. Well, what in God's name is so decent about having a wife or husband, not loving them, and screwing them anyway?

"So if they don't love their spouse, and they go out and have sex with someone, is it 'cause they love that person? Well, a lot of times they say it is. But sometimes not. Now, those are the people who are just fucking for the pleasure of it. They probably screwed around indiscriminately before they got married, too. What can you say about them? They're dogs. But I guess I've known a few good dogs in my time.

"Then, there are others, those who are married but in love with someone else. Those are the ones living in hell. They can't find joy in the love they know, and they have no joy in the marriage they're in. Those are some sorry suckers."

Father Jack's in full stride now, David reflected. He could see him working his way toward David's case. He hoped he'd let the bit out of his teeth by the time he got there.

"And then, you have those who truly love their spouses, and they truly love their lovers, too. And they are caught. They don't want to hurt anyone, but they just have this enormous ability to love."

David could see Father Jack rubbing his beard, contemplating, behind the veiled opening between them.

"Those are the people I pray for the most. I pray that their propensity for love isn't smashed by the hard hammer of moral judgment. Sometimes, I hope and pray that they just don't get caught, and they don't hurt the ones they love. But those are usually vain prayers. I should use those prayers for the conversion of Russia, I suppose."

He fell silent again, contemplating. David listened to the silence. A minute rolled into two. Then three. Then five. David wondered if Father Jack had transcended.

"Hey, Father."

"Yes, David." The response came softly.

"Let's take this out onto the steps, okay?"

"Good idea."

David went to the front steps of the church. Father Jack stepped toward the sanctuary, motioning with an upraised index finger that he'd rejoin David in a moment. When he returned, he handed David one of the two cold root beers he was carrying.

The summer sun hung high in the northwest, shedding a brilliant light upon the lush green hillsides in the Baraboo River Valley. David heard the drumming of a grouse hiding in the trees on the hill to the north of the church. The air smelled of hay cut and laying in the fields.

The two friends sat sipping their sodas. Neither seemed in a hurry to speak. David knew that Father Jack would continue when he was ready. He sat patiently, content to watch the swallows swoop down after flying insects in the sky above the churchyard.

Finally, after a long draw on his nearly finished root beer, Father Jack asked in a soft tone, "Have you no more intentions to have relations with Jannie?"

David rocked his head back and looked deep into the blue summer sky.

"No. I cannot imagine holding back from her." He looked over at his confessor. "I suppose if I were sure she was going to grow old with me, and we had all the time we ever needed, well, I might not feel this way. But I'm not sure at all that she's going to grow old. She isn't either. I've thought about it, though, and I have to think, even if I knew she'd live to be a hundred, I would still feel the way I do about her. And now that we've... done it... I guess I can't see any way but to keep on loving her."

Father Jack took it in.

"So, if you think it is a sin, but you have no intention of repenting and changing your ways, why the heck are you here confessing?"

David thought a moment.

"Isn't that what we're supposed to do? Confess our sins?"

"Well, of course. But then you're supposed to 'go, and sin no more.' Remember, that's the prayer that ends a Confession?

"You love this girl, don't you?" Father Jack changed the tack of their conversation.

"Well, yeah," David answered, incredulous that Father Jack would ask.

"So, why don't you marry her?"

David scrunched his face in surprise.

"How can I do that? I'm only sixteen, and Jannie's just seventeen. And she's got cancer, after all! Can you imagine her parents even letting us get married?"

"Have you considered marriage?"

David set his empty bottle between his feet, then looked down into the neck of the brown glass.

"No." David fidgeted. "I haven't. I didn't think it was, well, something we needed."

David shook his head, holding his temples in his hands.

"I mean, I thought we'd marry someday, when we were old enough. When it was the right time. But I never doubted that we would. I can hardly remember what life was like before Jannie. It is like she has always been there with me. Like she is part of me, and I am part of her." He sat, then, in stillness, thinking.

Father Jack ruminated. "So what you're telling me then is that you and Jannie are like kindred spirits."

David took in the words. "Yeah. Exactly. More, even. When she looks at me, it's as if she sees right into me. Right into my heart. Right into my soul. It's like she lives right in my soul. She keeps part of herself right in my soul."

Father Jack rubbed his beard, his eyes focused on the distant bluffs west of Devil's Lake.

"David, what we have, I think, is one of God's little conundrums. It seems to me that sometimes people, like you and Jannie, were created just for one another. God made you for each other. So why, then, do these rules—these conventions—we have about marriage apply to you?" He chewed on the thought a few moments and continued.

"I mean, it gets right down to the issue of whether acting on your love for Jannie is honoring that love, or sinning." He swatted at a gnat buzzing around his eyes. "All things considered, David, I wonder if you wouldn't be dishonoring this love you share with Jannie by not acting on it. So how can it be a sin?"

David looked over at Father Jack, a quizzical frown furrowing his brow.

"What?" Father Jack asked.

"It's just so confusing," David admitted. "That's not what I expected to hear."

Father Jack laughed.

"Oh, come on! Give me a break. If you wanted to hear just what you expected, you'd go confess to old Father Hendricks at Saint Joe's," he chuckled. "You come here to me because you trust me to tell you what I think is the Truth. But you know, I all too often get in a lot of hot water for telling people what I think is the Truth. You go around telling people what I think the Truth is for you, and I'll be in hot water with the Bishop again before you can blink your eyes.

"But honestly, David, if God really wanted each and every one of us to obey one law meant for all, then why would he have made us individuals? Why would he have created us with free will? I give God a lot more credit for his Creation than to think it should all fall nicely under a single set of narrow-minded rules, conjured by old men who think they know everything God has in mind for each and every being He's made. Nope. I think God is a bigger thinker than that."

Father Jack sat, illuminated by his own good will. In a moment, the spell dissipated.

"Just don't go repeating these damn fool ideas around," Father Jack cautioned abruptly, raising his eyebrows. "I mean it. This is a matter of the confessional, you know."

David chuckled. "You afraid the Bishop will send you back to Iran or something?"

Father Jack rolled his eyes in exasperation. "Oh my God, no! I'd be afraid they wouldn't let me go back to Asia, David."

"You want to go back?"

"More than anything."

David raised his eyebrows. "How come? Don't you like it here?"

Father Jack hung his head a moment, reflecting. "Well, of course I like it here. But it is not enough that I like it. I mean, I like how beautiful it is, and how peaceful," he said, pointing at the countryside with a sweeping motion of his hand. "But I kind of fit in better there. I have a role there. I mean, everyone there kind of expects me to be different, so they accept me that way. So I fit."

"Don't you think you fit in here?" David asked, recognizing instantly how most local folk snickered and talked about the eccentric, exotic priest with the wild mane of hair who was in residence—probably in reprimand for some zany deed he'd perpetrated overseas—at the chapel in North Freedom.

Father Jack's expression indicated he was on the same wavelength as David. He didn't bother to answer.

"David, I think if I were in your shoes, I'd do exactly what you are doing with Jannie. I'd love her with my whole self. My whole heart. My whole mind. My whole soul. My whole body. Anything less would be holding back from the honor she deserves.

"But I'm concerned," he admitted. "Have you thought about the possibility of her getting pregnant?"

David shrugged.

"Well, yeah. Of course. Worried, more than anything, I suppose, especially with her having been sick and all. We talked about it."

Father Jack nodded. "Maybe you'd better do something about it."

Chapter Fifteen
Dunes July Fourth

July 4, 1962

A HOT BREEZE coming off the beach crackled with anticipation and excitement. Towels and blankets were laid out in a bright mosaic over the choice sand between water's edge and low slopes of the dunes bracketing the beach. Parents lounged on folding recliners under umbrellas, keeping watchful eyes on their youngsters playing in the shallow surf. The sun danced with all, further browning those lucky enough to already sport deep tans, and singeing the pale, unweathered noses and shoulders of holiday revelers freed from the drudgery of homes and offices. Throughout the day, parties and gatherings sparked like grassfires, spreading as if carried on the wind. Everyone looked forward to nightfall and the annual Dunes fireworks display over the water.

The Howards hosted their neighbors for sunset cocktails. Patrick and Jack were to make an appearance before they left for the beach and the company of their own peers. As usual, Jack disregarded his obligation, leaving Patrick solo to pay his respects to the adults.

From the upstairs window, Patrick watched the townsfolk bustle in preparation for the fireworks. Several men were toting cans and ice from the back of a pickup. Already, people were gathering along the lake front—he could see his cousin milling with the Sandersons, Robbie, and the O'Connor girls in a hollow where two dunes intersected and leveled out onto the beach. Another, much larger group had congregated to watch the official town fireworks committee check the launching tubes and ground displays dug into the sand. A small fleet of cabin cruisers and sailboats anchored offshore, with others still sailing in to join them.

On the porch deck below, the party hummed with chatter and laughter punctuated by the clinking of ice in glass. Patrick took a deep breath and braced himself to meet the adults, then galloped down the steps.

He recognized several of the Howards' friends. The Edmonds, the Whitakers, the Drapers, the Markmans. Others were unfamiliar. Patrick greeted the Drapers first; of his aunt and uncle's guests, he felt most comfortable with Avery and his wife Georgia. He lingered a moment, and then turned to make his rounds. His vision tunneled as he maneuvered between strangers. He spotted his uncle chatting near the steps down to the beach—his escape. Patrick worked his way toward Uncle Paul, intent on making a final show of politeness before exiting. Aunt Mary gestured for him to join the group.

"Patrick, I'd like you to meet some of Paul's friends from the University, and some of our newest neighbors in the Dunes," she began. "This is Professor and Mrs. Maher, from Paul's department."

Patrick exchanged handshakes. "Pleased to meet you." He still felt like a bumbling farm boy at the Howards' soirees, but he'd been through the routine often enough to know his lines.

"And this is Doctor and Mrs. North," Aunt Mary continued, turning her nephew toward the couple on the far side of his uncle. "The Norths bought Arthur Parmley's place on the west end."

Patrick froze while extending his hand to Dr. North, suddenly blinded by an intense, glowing presence in the periphery of his vision. Mrs. North. *The lady. From the beach. From the pool. Parmley's pool. And the raspberries.*

Dr. North was startled by Patrick's visible hesitation. He stepped closer to the boy, who towered over him, and took his hand. Dr. North was a small man, thin, and no taller than Aunt Mary. Patrick's hand engulfed the surgeon's delicate fingers and palm. Patrick forced his eyes onto the doctor's face, staring blankly at the bridge of his nose. He locked his hand around the doctor's, pumping up and down as if drawing water from a well. He avoided turning to the doctor's wife. But it was inevitable. Mrs. North stepped in front of him, offering her own hand to shake.

"Spare the good surgeon's hand," she smiled, brushing her fingertips briefly on her husband's wrist as he wrenched it from Patrick's grasp. "He may need to operate." She took Patrick's hand, meeting his glance evenly. She let her hand linger in his fingers.

"And you are Patrick? I'm so pleased to meet you," Mrs. North said with disarming charm. Patrick began to relax a bit, until she said, "I believe we may already have crossed paths."

His breath left him in a puff, as though he'd been hit in his solar plexus, and he blanched. As robustly as he'd greeted her husband, Patrick shook Mrs. North's hand timidly, as if he were clinging to the wings of a butterfly. Her grip was gentle, warm, and steady—and unrelenting. She held on to his hand firmly, pressuring ever so slightly when he moved to retract his hand from her grip.

"You'll recall," she said, turning to her husband. "Kelly and I were discussing Patrick last week."

She looked back into Patrick's eyes, his hand still in her keeping. "Didn't I see you…" She paused just a second.

Patrick writhed. He felt displaced from his body.

"…Didn't I see you down on the beach, doing some push-ups with a girl sitting on your back?"

Patrick gasped air, not realizing he'd stopped breathing. He snapped back into himself. Mrs. North peered deep into Patrick's eyes, and he was forced to focus on her. Her face was lit with amusement, warmth, and kind humor. She was enjoying herself.

"Oh, yes." Dr. North remembered. "Kelly couldn't quite get over it. What did she say, a thousand push-ups?"

"No, just a hundred," Patrick blurted. "That was enough. It was a bet, for Jack. Kinda burned my arms up a bit," he added, flexing his biceps and triceps reflexively.

The adults shouted with laughter.

"Only a hundred!" Paul exclaimed. "Must have been a big girl."

"It was Ginny," Patrick said.

"Ginny!! She's but a handful!"

"Ha! Let's see you do three push-ups, Howard," Jerry Edmonds joined in. "I was on the beach that day and saw Patrick doing Jack's dirty work. And making it look easy. A wager, you say?"

"Yeah," Patrick acknowledged. "The Sandersons' Cat for a day." To his dismay, Patrick had become the center of conversation. But he was trapped. Mrs. North stood her ground before him, gazing piercingly into his eyes. She still possessed his hand.

"Quite a feat," she confirmed. She examined the boy's features. He had the face of a boy on the head, shoulders, and body of a man. "Exactly how old are you, Patrick?" She released his hand so gently that he left it extended, suspended in the space between them.

"Just turned sixteen, ma'am. June twenty-first."

"Sixteen! Remarkable. I don't recall too many of my friends attempting a hundred pushups when I was sixteen—and that wasn't all that long ago," Mrs. North said. Indeed, she looked much younger than her husband. But for her strappy, summery party dress and casually sophisticated up-do, she would have blended more easily with Pat's peers on the beach than with her adult companions on the sun porch. She glanced at her husband, who'd turned to converse with several other guests as they looked out over the lake. Seeing that the surgeon was distracted, she returned to Patrick, squinting a bit, studying him.

"The twenty-first of June, was it? Longest day of the year. The summer solstice. A Thursday, if I recall."

Patrick squirmed. He didn't like where this line of questioning was going.

"Yes, ma'am." He forced himself to break his eyes away. "Thursday, two weeks ago now."

"Such a nice day it was. Warmer than usual for June, don't you think? A great day for swimming, or gardening. Or maybe going for a run. You're a runner, aren't you?" She didn't pause to let him respond. "I think I was painting that day. How was your birthday?" She changed course. "Did you do anything special?"

"No, ma'am. Not really." He tried to dodge. "Called my twin, though."

"Twin? Gracious, there are two of you?" She smiled, cutting him a little slack. Patrick's anxiety level was sky-high.

"David. He's my brother. He lives back in Wisconsin."

"So you have a twin brother. Are you identical twins? Is he as big as you?"

Patrick chortled. "Hardly."

"Patrick's brother David is about half the size of this giant," Mary said, handing Mrs. North a fresh drink. "You almost wouldn't believe the two are brothers, much less twins. David has hair that is almost jet black. He wasn't five feet tall the last time I heard."

"He's more than that now, Aunt Mary. He told me he'd reached five feet two. He was pretty happy about that. He's almost as tall as Jannie now," Patrick said. He felt a bit more relaxed with Aunt Mary by his side, and the topic changing to David.

"Five two! You must be a good foot taller," Mrs. North said.

"About. I hit six one just before our birthday." He grinned. "Davey grew four inches last year. I grew three. I guess he's catching up."

Just as Patrick sensed an opportunity to ask to be excused, Dr. North returned to the conversation.

"So you helped Art Parmley with the yard work last year?" the doctor asked. "You know, by the time I get home from the hospital, I don't have much opportunity for that sort of thing. Would you be interested in taking on the job again this year? We've got plenty to do, from watering and trimming to picking all the raspberries that are coming in. What do you think? I'll pay well for good work."

Patrick was dumfounded. His faced turned a deep red, as if he were choking.

Aunt Mary spoke for him. "Certainly, Patrick would like to help out. Wouldn't you?" she asked her nephew.

"Uh, sure," he murmured. He realized he wasn't breathing again, and inhaled fully.

"That's wonderful!" Mrs. North exclaimed. She looked impish. Patrick tried to look away, but she captivated him with the laughter in her eyes. "There really is a lot to do out in the raspberry patch," she added.

Patrick coughed. He had to find a way to leave.

"That would be great, working for you, Dr. North. Be glad to." He turned to his aunt. "Can I go down to the beach now? I'd like to find Jack and the guys."

"Sure, Patrick," she replied. "When would you like Pat to work?" she asked the Norths.

Patrick couldn't believe this was happening.

"How about Saturday morning, nine or so? I'll have a list," Barry North said.

"Great. I'll be there. Thanks. Bye, now," Patrick stammered. "Pleasure meeting you. Gotta go. Thanks again."

"Oh, the pleasure is ours," Lynn North said in her melodious, playful tone.

He ran down the stairs to the beach, aghast at what he'd gotten into. "Oh my God," he muttered, wondering, *what did she mean about the raspberry patch?* Did she know he'd been there? That he'd seen her? He was so embarrassed! How could she have known he was there? She couldn't have known. She wouldn't have acted so… unabashed. Oh God, he thought. She must have known. She looked like she knew. She teased him! She looked like she was having fun, and she looked so… young compared to the group of adults she was with. She looked so young for an adult, but she treated him so… equally. She teased him, but she didn't put him down. She let him grovel, but she didn't belittle him. She had not shamed, blamed, or ridiculed Patrick. He didn't know women could be that way. It had set alarms off in his head, one right after the other, until he escaped his aunt and uncle's cocktail party.

On the beach, Patrick settled down near Jack and the gang as he watched the fireworks flash. His anxiety dissipated as the explosions filled the sky with streaming colors. A thin blue cloud of smoke drifted from shore out across the lake. The people gathered on the beach applauded loudly, and those on the flotilla sounded their harbor horns. Then, when the last blast of the finale rolled like thunder out across the lake, the crowd slowly drifted away. Patrick wound his way through the dune grass to the steps to his aunt's house at the top of the dunes. He ran the steps by twos until he'd reached the sixty-fourth and final step. He knew his aunt and uncle were awake upstairs, but he quietly slipped in through the porch. He aimed to ease into his bedroom, read a bit, and fall asleep before Jack came home.

Lingering thoughts of Mrs. North distracted him, however, and he made no progress with his reading.

Chapter Sixteen
Making Hay

BY THE FOURTH OF JULY, Jannie was more like herself. She had regained both strength and energy. Her white blood cell counts were stable, and she had added a few pounds as well as a healthy tan. When her mother dropped her at the Joyces' to help put up hay, David saw that her old glow had returned. She'd taken to sporting colorful bandanas, folded in triangular halves, with the pointed corners tucked down into the knot tied behind her head. For the Fourth, she'd chosen one adorned with bright stars and stripes.

"It's a good thing the ladies are down in the creek pasture," Paddy said. "They'd likely get a mite excited to see so fancy a hand making hay, with all that red, white, and blue!"

"Truth be told, Paddy, if those cows of yours have a speck of patriotism in them, they'll double their production when you start feeding them the hay we put up today," she said. "Least ways, if you brought them up right."

Paddy rebuffed her sass with a hearty guffaw, but glanced anxiously toward his fields. He had twenty-one hundred bales of top-quality, high-protein, second-cut alfalfa drying in the forty acres along the road, and the sun was getting high. It didn't look like rain, but Wisconsin skies could change in the time it took to sigh.

Paddy laced his boots, the signal that mobilized everybody.

By noon, they had the first wagon loaded.

"One down," Paddy said, wiping his brow. His faded cotton shirt was drenched with sweat. He pulled back his cap, revealing the pale top of his forehead and balding scalp. Flecks of dried alfalfa speckled his deeply tanned, wrinkle-creased forehead. Paddy had the hardest task, walking beside the wagons, lifting each fifty-pound bale up onto the chest-high wagon bed. But, sweaty and dusty as he was, he was undaunted. He winked up at Jannie perched upon the Farmall seat. Some folk didn't like haying. Paddy did. These were some of his favorite days of farming.

"Four fifty?" Paddy ventured.

"Four hundred eighty-four," Miss Rose confirmed.

"Wow," David said. "A lot of bales on this load."

"I packed them a little smaller this year," Paddy explained.

Jannie drove the tractor right up to the barn and came to a smooth stop.

"We going to stack this load in the mow?" she asked before shutting off the engine.

"Not yet," Paddy replied. "Let's get a drink, and we'll load up another wagon—if you're feeling up to it."

"No problem with me," she beamed. "You're the one that has to step it up."

Paddy raised an eyebrow, unable to stifle a grin.

The day grew hotter and stiller.

By mid-afternoon, they had all taken on a deep bronze tone. Jannie was pink across the bridge of her nose as she parked the fourth wagon in line with the others outside the barn. They still had a short load, maybe two or three hundred bales lying in a strip bordering the woods along the bottoms, but all the wagons were full. They would have to unload one before bringing in any more bales from the field.

"Rose, I'd be obliged if you'd take this young'n on up to the house with you and make her get her rest," Paddy said as he went to take the wheel of the tractor from Jannie.

Jannie started to protest, but her words were met by the palm of Paddy's upraised hand and the most stubborn expression in Sauk County.

"Young lady, I know exactly what you're thinking, and I don't care one hoot. Your mother would scalp what little hair I have left on my head if I worked you one more minute," Paddy said, drawing a firm and uncompromising line. "Go." His lips curled ever so slightly. Just looking at Jannie Whitman brought a smile to Paddy's face.

"Come on, Jannie," Rose agreed. "We have cooler work to do in the house."

Jannie climbed off the tractor, grinning up at David still perched on top of the bales. He loved watching the interaction between Paddy and Jannie. His uncle could honestly have been her father, he mused. His own as well, he reflected. May as well be. "Well, I'm not even tired," Jannie called back to Paddy, looking over her shoulder. She turned and walked backward toward the house so she could pepper him with more comments. "I mean, how hard is it to sit on a tractor all day?"

"Don't start," Paddy called back. He cut off any rebuttal by firing up the Farmall and throttling the engine to a mighty roar. David tipped backward as the wagon lurched forward into the barn.

Unloading the hay was quicker than picking it up off the field, but it was physically tougher. Within three-quarters of an hour, David had all the bales off the first load, and they headed back out to the field with the empty wagon to load the last of the bales on the ground. Still hustling, they stowed those bales in the mow, and unloaded another of the wagons still waiting in the lot.

"We got 'em," Paddy said. He pulled out his pocket watch on its chain, wiping his brow with the back of his forearm. Dust and bits of leaf on his forehead smeared in a dark wet strip above his eyes. He glanced up at David, his eyebrows raised.

"Milking time."

David pushed the last few bales tight against the barn wall and climbed down off the stack.

"Let's do it," he said, nodding to his uncle.

The girls cooperated, and the Joyces were done with milking in near-record time. Stepping out of the new milkhouse, Paddy looked up at the July sun, still intense even at eight in the evening. An hour and a half until sunset, two until twilight. Plenty of time before heading to town for the fireworks.

"Tell Rose I'll be right up," Paddy said, heading for his small home across the road. "And tell her I'm hungry as a lion."

David trotted up to the house. He was pleased but not surprised to see Father Jack sitting peacefully in the rocker on the porch. The priest would be joining them for the fireworks. David sat on the porch swing, peeling off his boots and letting them plop heavily on the wooden deck. Miss Rose stepped out with a tall glass of ice and a pitcher of lemonade. David downed a glassful in one long series of gulps.

Rose smiled at the young man.

"Thirsty?" she teased. "Another?"

"Merci, oh wonderful redemptress," David pleaded in French, winning points from his teacher. "And where is my sweet one?"

Rose chuckled at David's buffoonery, happy that he chose to speak in her first tongue. He seldom limited his use of French to Thursdays anymore. It had become his language of choice when conversing with her.

"She sleeps like a princess." Rose replied. "Perhaps driving a tractor is harder than our fair one admits." David smiled, only a little wistfully. Jannie had a lot more energy than she did after returning from Bethesda, but she was still recovering.

"Would have enjoyed seeing you alongside my uncle Paddy, strolling around that hay field this afternoon," he said to Father Jack, returning to English. His eyes twinkled. "Maybe even hoisting a bale or two. You think?"

Father Jack met his glance with raised eyebrows, then turned and examined the long shadows creeping across the newly gleaned hayfield beyond the barn.

"Paddy ever explain to you his one-day theory?" he asked the boy.

"Yeah. He got it from Gabe. The bird over the North Pole thing? The eagle? Sure. Just one big day?"

"Right. 'Cept it's a dove. Regardless. I consider my one and only day to be Sunday. No servile activity on Sunday, in my Book. Nada. That's why I don't golf, either."

Rose snuffed.

David nodded, grinning.

"Yeah. Uh-ha. Exactly." His head bobbed, indicating his appreciation of Father Jack's logic. "Paddy deserved to hear that for himself. Direct. First hand."

Father Jack nodded once in return, and the friends fell silent, watching the shadows creep across the fields. "What do you know about remission?" David asked as the swallows swooped above the farmyard for evening insects.

Rose refilled his glass, set the pitcher on the porch deck, and joined him on the swing.

"Life is such a robust, fragile phenomenon," she mused.

David laughed. "You've been listening to Father Jack too much."

Rose allowed a wide, gentle smile to brighten her face. "Perhaps the good Father is the listener."

Father Jack stirred from his reverie. He let his thoughts bob on the surface of the moment for an instant or two, then returned to his distant contemplations. He did not feel compelled to intrude on David's conversation with Rose, although the sound of French was kind on his ear. As he mused, he heard them speak.

"Could well be," David agreed. He'd shared plenty with Rose in this porch swing, rain or shine, even during snowfalls. Or over coffee at the kitchen table. They'd covered wonders from the birthing of calves to the mystery of being a twin. They'd argued about God's role in people's lives, and in death and evil. David cherished Miss Rose's concepts of the integrated role of man in nature, tested and fortified by her life on the farm She often challenged him on the ethics of his "mischievous manipulations" of his herds' genetics, but she was insatiably drawn to his breeding charts and herd objectives. Miss Rose loved to ponder life and its many facets, and David was grateful that she was his teacher.

"So, what's your thought about this remission, and... Jannie?" he asked.

Rose looked to the horizon under the sun. David studied her face, her eyes, dark and complex. He listened carefully as she spoke.

"I do agree with Father Jack," Miss Rose said, switching to English, facing David and looking deep into his eyes.

"Death belongs to us all. We each have our own unique lives to give one another, to contribute to the Oneness that is us. We have choice. And we have death. It is the equalizer. More so than life. There is sanctity in death. We must honor that."

She paused.

"There is no remission from life," she continued, searching his eyes. "Life has its own turns. Talents and gifts are not distributed equally. Time differs for each of us. It is what we do with our time that matters. Jannie lives in the moment. Even as she naps, she slumbers under grace as powerful as the wind that sweeps across the face of our fields. She is whole. She is holy."

Rose gazed into David's eyes, and he felt as though she looked deep into his heart.

"You are blessed to be One with her."

Rose's eyes flashed, startling David.

Father Jack responded vaguely. Softly, absently, he muttered his agreement. "Amen."

"David, does it matter if Jannie is in remission, or not? Can we hold our breaths, waiting, always wondering, and fearing? I think it best to cherish her now, as she is, for as long as she will be."

She nodded.

"I don't think remission matters at all."

Rose returned her eyes to the distance, sitting peacefully, quietly. Then, with a start, she looked around, and returned to David. Smiling, she asked, "Aren't you hungry yet?"

"Oh, I'm alright," David said, still mesmerized by her words. Then he, too, looked up abruptly. "But I know Uncle Paddy is coming over as hungry as a bull, and I don't think a few berries will satisfy him." David arched his back, and sighed.

"Well, come, then," Miss Rose encouraged him. "You'll want to clean up, and you may find your appetite when you see the shortcake Jannie and I whipped up while you finished the hay."

She stood up from the swing, reached down and helped him to his feet. Slipping her arm gently around his shoulder, she added in French, "You need not fear. You will never be alone. One cannot be alone. One is all."

And she led him into the house.

∞

Later, as he lay in bed after the fireworks, David pondered the day.

Jannie had looked good, driving the tractor across the fields. He'd chuckled when she'd wiped off her scalp with her bandana drenched in cool water. Her hair had started growing back, and a soft, downy layer of fuzz grew in swatches across her skull.

"It'll be as long as yours in three weeks," she'd promised.

She'd worked like a trooper out there all day, running the tractor, never losing her concentration, always helping. But when he'd come in for supper, she was deep in sleep, her tiny frame curled upon itself, her arms hugging her body, her knees tucked up to her elbows. A soft glow of afternoon sun seeped in through the cracks in the window shade, illuminating her face with a honey-cast light. She looked angelic. And fragile. David felt his heart lurch. Sometimes, just looking at her, he felt fear reach up into his belly, into his chest, squeezing, twisting, tearing.

And in a breath, the fear would be gone. Jannie lay there so peacefully. When her eyes opened, she'd smiled just for him. And again, he'd known joy and peace.

He thought of what Miss Rose had said, pondering her words, and of what Jannie had told him on several occasions. How at Bethesda, people died, and nothing else missed a beat.

He thought of the hay they had put up, and the life it would sustain in the herd, the milk it would help produce, and how it would feed so many people, keep them living.

He thought of his brother, and felt a great loss. It left an empty spot in the peace in which he dwelt.

He grinned, recalling Father Jack's surreptitious motions as they drove into town for the fireworks, when the priest had carefully handed him a small cardboard carton with a dozen condoms. The priest said nothing to him, keeping his gaze trained ahead so as not to attract Rose's or Paddy's attention from where they rode in the front seat. After a few moments, Father Jack had looked over, nodded almost imperceptibly, then resumed his distant, distracted demeanor.

He thought of Paddy, and wondered once again how he could miss a father he had never known when his father's brother was so close to him. He wondered how his father and Paddy had been to one another.

He thought of his mother.

He fell asleep, praying gratefully for all those he loved so much.

Chapter Seventeen
Summer Work

SPRINTING BAREFOOT down the beach toward the Norths', Patrick pumped his arms and knees like pistons, his running shoes in his hands. He challenged himself on the climb up the last big blowout, where northerly wind gushing off the lake piled sand to shape the long steep slopes of the dunes. Patrick gulped in the dry, searing air shimmering above the white sands of the dune. At the top, he dropped the shoes and doubled over, hands grasping the legs of his gym shorts. A dark ring of sweat leached down around the collar of his gray t-shirt. Another larger band ran down the center of his back. He'd aimed to arrive at the Norths' at nine o'clock, and had made it by five to the hour. The sun already hinted at its blistering power; the day had the makings of a July steamer.

From the shade of the umbrella over the table on the pool deck, Bartholomew North looked up from an intense conversation with his wife. Lynn's back was to Patrick, and when Barry waved to his young helper, she looked over her shoulder.

"Well, here's our help now," Barry said. He eyed the boy curiously. "Don't tell me you ran here. Will you have the energy left for quality work?"

Patrick straightened up, savoring the cool breeze that followed him up the blowout from the lake.

"G'morning, Dr. North." A grin slowly spread across Patrick's face. "Oh, I still have plenty of energy. It was just sprinting the uphill that winded me, that's all." He looked back toward the path up the blowout.

"You sprinted all the way up from the beach?" Dr. North asked, incredulous.

"Oh, yeah. That's the best part of the run. Maybe not the fastest, but definitely the toughest," Patrick replied. "The beach is good for speed 'cause the sand is hard. But the dunes are something else. Good for power. The sand is soft and each step is a killer. I run the blowout by Aunt Mary's at least once a day."

Dr. North eyed the rippling muscles in Patrick's calves and thighs. The boy had already regained his wind.

"Well, as long as you still have an honest day's work in you, I guess it's alright." A note of skepticism lingered in his tone.

"As if he'll be too tired to pick raspberries and mow a swatch of lawn," Lynn chided her husband. "Good morning, Patrick. I think my husband underestimates the strength and endurance of a teenager, much less a teen who trains as an athlete."

Patrick blushed, but he felt pride that she viewed him an athlete.

"I'll do a good job for you, sir," Patrick assured the doctor.

"We've just been discussing what I'd like done, Patrick. My wife seems to think we can depend on you for far more than I'm inclined to ask," Dr. North admitted.

Patrick looked him squarely in the eye, then glanced at her.

"Well, let's see," he replied, rising to the challenge.

They put him to task, starting with the bounty of the raspberry patch. Lynn busied herself in the house, while Dr. North remained at the deck table reading a medical journal. Within minutes, Patrick approached with the colander they'd given him, now full of plump red berries.

"Where would you like me to put these?" Patrick interrupted.

"Oh, you're done already?" Dr. North seemed startled. "Well, take them into Mrs. North. She'll handle them. My, there are a good bunch, aren't there?"

"Well, this is only a part of them," Patrick replied. "I only did the outside half of the first row." From the deck, he could still see many perfectly ripe berries, ready to be plucked, and even more that remained green.

Patrick took the colander into the house, knocking first on the kitchen door and calling to Mrs. North. He put the berries on the counter next to the sink and looked around for another container. Lynn North was stacking clean, inverted mason jars on towels lining the kitchen counter.

"You're going to have a lot of berries," Patrick advised her.

"I would imagine so," she sighed. "Do you have many more to pick?"

"About ten times as much," Patrick guessed. "I just did the outside of the first row, and I could see where you'd already been picking. The other rows are untouched, except for the birds. What do you want me to put them in?"

Lynn fetched a couple more large bowls from a cabinet. "Let's fill these next."

She surprised Patrick by joining him in the berry patch.

By half past one, the first harvest was complete. Between them, Patrick and Lynn had amassed a huge haul. Scratched and pricked from the thorny canes, Patrick was relieved to be done with the task.

"Let's have some lunch," Dr. North suggested, joining his wife and hired hand in the kitchen as they brought in the last bowls of berries.

"Here," she handed him the bowl full of raspberries. "Add cream."

"Sounds good to me," the doctor said.

"God bless Abraham Levenson," he muttered as he poured on cream from the refrigerator and headed toward his study.

Patrick wondered who Abraham Levenson was, and what he had to do with berries.

"Dr. Levenson is a heart surgeon at Northwestern, where Barry works," Lynn explained, shrugging. "Barry can't simply enjoy cream on his berries. He has to consider the risk to his heart." She wagged her head sarcastically. "How about you? Are you hungry?" she asked.

"Well, kinda. But I've pretty much had my fill of raspberries."

Lynn laughed. "So have I. I'll fix lunch in a moment."

She leveled an appraising gaze upon him.

"Although hiring you was Dr. North's idea, I'm pretty certain that he'll lose interest in your work," she said. "He probably has already. That makes me your supervisor. So while I get us something other than raspberries for lunch, you get the lawn mower from the garage and mow the grass along the drive and up next to the deck. And I'd like you to weed and clean along the drive and the steps to the beach. Come on. I'll show you, then I'll get lunch on." She led him on a quick tour of the yard, pointing out his objectives, and left him to do the work.

While Patrick tackled the chores, Lynn fired up the charcoal grill by the pool. As Patrick's nose caught the first wafts of searing meat, his stomach rumbled, reminding him that he could not live on raspberries alone. By the time he'd trimmed the lawn behind the house, the aroma of the sizzling beef had him salivating. He pushed the lawn mower back into the garage and followed his nose toward the pool.

Patrick stopped in his tracks at the edge of the pool deck. Lynn North had changed to a bikini top. Her hair was wet, and her shorts were spotted with the dampened shape of her bikini bottom. She tended several massive steaks, a set of pincers in hand.

"Almost ready," she announced. "All finished?"

He shook his head. "Close. Gotta clean up the clippings."

"Later," she shrugged. Indicating a tall glass on a table in the shade, she invited Patrick to take a break. A bowl of potato chips and a smaller bowl with dip sat on the table next to his drink.

Pat took a long pull from the cold lemonade. She had squeezed it fresh, and a slice of lemon floated among the ice cubes in his glass. He took a handful of chips and excavated the dip. Creamy and rich, it was tangy, sweet, and chunky.

"Clam dip," Lynn said, watching his expression. "My mother's recipe. Like it?"

Patrick gulped a second mouthful.

"It's great." He shoveled another dip-laden chip into his mouth. "It's wonderful."

"Another boon to Dr. Levenson's practice. Keeps his patient load steady for years," Lynn quipped, flipping the slabs of beef on the grill. "You like it rare?" She didn't wait for his answer. She put the steaks on a platter, using the tongs to pick up a bundle wrapped in aluminum.

"I took a dip after I put the steaks on," she said. "Perhaps you'd like to cool off a minute before you eat. These need to rest a moment," she said, and set the food on the table by Patrick.

Patrick considered the option. He was hot, and dried sweat had caked on his skin and in white lines on his tee shirt. His legs were dirty, his arms scratched, his hands red from the berries, and he didn't smell altogether sweet. He looked at the pool, but as inviting as it was, he felt like he would pollute the water by jumping in. And he felt the hunger in his belly.

"I think I'll just eat," he told her. "I wouldn't want to mess up your pool." He laughed nervously.

"I'm treating it tomorrow anyway," she said. "Or maybe I'll wait 'til next week and teach you how, since you're the labor around here now. It's up to you. You can wash up your hands in there, if you'd prefer." She indicated the sliding door into the house. "On the right."

Patrick would have ignored his dirt, but felt obliged to clean up. He found the bathroom inside and rinsed his face, hands, and arms. All of the washcloths and towels hanging next to the sink were fresh and as pure white as Mrs. North's bikini. He wiped his face and dried his hands, leaving dark smudges on the towels. *Darn,* he thought. He washed again, lathering the fragrant soap on his face and hands. Using a different part of the towel, he dried again, satisfied that he left no further stains. He headed back to the pool. A soft snore caught his attention in the hallway. He stopped and listened, but heard nothing more. Patrick returned to the deck.

"Well, you *were* there under all that grime," Lynn North teased. Patrick grinned, blushing again as he watched her inspect his face, neck, and arms. "At least your face was under there," she kidded, running a finger along his neck, then turning it up into the light to examine it.

"My mother would say, 'You missed a spot.'"

Patrick laughed. He was feeling more at ease around Lynn North. Witty and humorous, her comfortable manner charmed him.

"Let's eat," she said, tearing open the aluminum wrap from a loaf of warmed, garlic-buttered French bread.

Patrick took the plate that she heaped with a huge slab of rib eye and a couple of slices of bread. He waited until she served herself, and hesitated further.

"Is Dr. North going to eat with us?" He looked across the deck toward the house.

"Dr. North is napping." Her tone was sharp. "He's going back into the hospital later."

Patrick let it alone. He concentrated on his steak. It was delicious, and he told her so.

"Thanks," she said, the humor returning to her voice. "It's pretty easy to grill a fine piece of meat and come across as a good cook."

"Everything's good, though," Patrick countered. "The lemonade, the dip. The bread is tremendous."

Patrick devoured the steak, and she served him more. He was stuffed, but the steak was too good to resist. And he didn't feel as though he could turn her down. He grabbed a last slice of the garlic bread, too.

"You eat like my brothers," she said.

He hadn't thought of her in terms of brothers. He asked about her family.

She had two brothers and a sister. The brothers were both older by nearly ten years. Her sister was younger.

"My parents thought I was a surprise, and then Ingrid came along," she said. "My dad said we kept him young, but I think it might have been quite the opposite."

She grew up in Minnesota, near the Twin Cities. Her father worked with computers. Her mother raised the kids and taught at Macalester. One of her brothers was in residency in Denver, the other a captain in the Air Force. Her sister, she said, was "wild and spoiled," but extremely close to her. Ingie was still at the University of Wisconsin, studying God knows what now, but having a wonderful time, Lynn was certain.

When Patrick had finished his second slab of rib eye, Lynn offered him yet another serving. He protested that he could eat no more. She laughed softly and settled back into her deck lounge.

"How about you?" she asked. "What is it like to be a twin?"

"Well, I guess it's kinda like anything else. I mean, I've always been one, so it's pretty normal for me," he explained. "Davey's real neat. He is really, really smart. And he's so much fun to be around because he's so...," Patrick searched for the word, "…into everything. He's a fanatic. Sometimes it drives you nuts, but most of the time it's just fun because you know that if something is going to get done, Davey is going to do it all the way and the right way."

"If you're gonna be a bear," she replied, her eyes twinkling, "be a grizzly!"

Patrick laughed. "Yeah. That's David. 'Cept Davey's about as big as a teddy bear."

He told her about David's animals and his music. And his best friend, Jannie. He found it easy to talk about Davey—easier than about himself.

"How do you feel about being away from your twin?" she asked.

"At times, I miss him a lot," Patrick admitted. He looked away, avoiding the feeling of loss that hounded him; there were plenty of times he'd been so lonesome for his twin and his mother that all he wanted to do was return to Wisconsin. He faced Lynn North with a stiff smile and narrowed eyes.

"Overall, I really like it down here better. I mean, Wisconsin is cool and all, and I had a lot of good friends, but it's super here in the Dunes. And I've got some pretty good friends down here, too, I guess."

He paused, caught in his thoughts. She watched a shadow pass over his face.

"Uncle Paul says that once you leave a place, it's never the same, and to just remember to enjoy where you are while you're there, rather than wishing for something that's no longer the way you remember it anyway. That kind of makes sense to me, really."

Lynn studied her new young friend. He was a paradox. Broad-shouldered and brawny, he looked very much a man. He moved and walked and worked like a young man. He ate like a man. She remembered her brothers, both strapping young men, devouring everything in sight at the family meals. But as she remembered them just before they left home, they were really closer to twenty, truly teens on the brink of manhood. Patrick was still very young, almost a boy. His expressions revealed his youth as he talked. His body concealed his immaturity. But his mind churned, working, probing, evaluating the world about him.

Their conversation faded when Dr. North joined them. He'd put on slacks and a dress shirt, and was looping a tie into a Windsor.

"So, you've completed the chores at hand, I take it?" he asked Patrick. "And you still have energy for more?"

"Yes, sir. Not a problem. Picking berries is nothing. I could probably even go for another run, if it wasn't for all the steak sitting in my belly."

"Yes, I could smell the barbeque, even as I slept. It made for some interesting dreams, I must say," he smiled, lighthearted and more relaxed than he had been earlier. "Very well," he concluded. He turned to his wife, and summoned her aside. "We need to talk more about this wall idea."

∞

Finished with the chores, Patrick stored the lawn tools and sauntered around the yard, avoiding the pool deck, where the Norths carried on an animated conversation. Finally, after glancing his way several times, they walked to the crumbling tie wall that ran the length of the driveway.

"Patrick," Dr. North called, his tone curiously apologetic and, at the same time, condescending. His light-hearted post-nap mood appeared to have dissipated.

"We need to replace this wall; as you can see, the dune's ready to collapse on our driveway. Mrs. North thinks you can do it, but I'm of the opinion that it's a job for a professional contractor. Perhaps you should give us your opinion before we get you in over your head."

Lynn surveyed the remains of the failing tie wall along the drive, her tanned arms folded resolutely. She said nothing while her husband droned on, pessimistic about the project, but she met Patrick's glance with determination.

Patrick examined the aged structure. The original railroad ties that made up its mass were visibly rotted. The lower tiers were crushed, sand spilling from the wood's eroded cores. He pulled at a scaling fragment of wood and it peeled off in a long, light shard that crumbled in his hand. He counted the ties. Ten tiers high, arcing at least fifty yards along the driveway. The old ties were the only barrier preventing the dune from sweeping in across the asphalt, and in places, sand already poured through.

With a confident eye, Patrick met the doctor's pessimistic glower. "I've built a lot of fences and corrals. Back home, I helped my Uncle Paddy build forms to pour concrete all the time," he exaggerated. He kicked at the wall like he was judging a used car. "I can swing a sledge. And set pins."

"See, there!" Mrs. North chimed in, victoriously. "I say that this is a job we do ourselves."

"I do not see why in God's name you think it is so important for you to build a damn wall," Dr. North complained.

"Because it's there to do."

Exasperated, he capitulated. "But if it gets out of hand, we call in Ed Clark or the Dorner Crew. Promise me," he demanded.

"Fair enough," Lynn granted, grinning.

Barry North stalked away. "I'll be on call through Tuesday," he tossed over his shoulder. "I'll be back out on Wednesday night, unless something comes up with my patients. But I'll be going back in Thursday evening." He walked briskly into the garage, started his Cadillac, backed out until his bumper tagged a broken-down tie, and drove away without a backwards glance. A stream of sand cascaded down where the Cadillac had bumped.

"Wow," Patrick said. "Dr. North sure seems ticked off."

"Oh, he'll be alright," Lynn assured him. "He's a surgeon. He doesn't like when stubborn meets stubborn and he doesn't get to decide everything. And if he doesn't understand how to get something done, he just figures you should hire someone who can do it for you. I think that takes all the fun out of things."

"So you think this is going to be fun?" he asked.

She looked at him in amazement.

"Of course. I wouldn't want to do it, otherwise. It will be a showcase of art."

He looked at the wall again.

"Do you know how to do it?"

"Well, if you're asking me if I've ever built a tie wall, I have to say no," Lynn admitted, smiling broadly. "But I watched my brothers and father build one at our cabin on the lake in Hackensack. They encouraged me to help, as much as I could. I watched them plan it out and lay every tie." She nodded. "If my brothers could do it, so can we. Whaddya think?"

Patrick couldn't keep a smile from slowly crossing his face. "Looks like fun to me," he agreed. "When do we start?"

"Monday we start ripping out the old wall," she said decisively. "Tomorrow, I'll go into the library at Valpo and see what I can find about building tie walls."

She looked at her young charge.

"Nothing better to do in the summer, eh?"

Patrick grinned.

"No. I suppose not."

"You want to come to Valpo with me to see what we can find out about building this thing?"

Patrick grimaced. In a way, he wanted to. But then, he was hoping to go sailing with Jack and Ginny and the other kids. He told Lynn so.

"That's fine then. I'll get things figured out, and we can get a good start on Monday morning. Early. Okay?"

"You bet. We'll build a wall Dr. North will be proud of."

She smirked.

"This wall isn't for Barry. It's for me," she said distantly. Then, flashing a beaming smile, she headed for the house.

"Well, come on then," she said. "You've got more to do before I let you go today. Have you ever made jam? I'd be glad for the help. It'll take a couple hours. Then I'll drop you off at home."

Why not? Patrick thought.

Chapter Eighteen
Cons and Conventions

PATRICK HITCHED A RIDE to the Norths' with his uncle, who dropped him off on his way to the South Shore train. The aroma of rich coffee met him as he knocked on the screen door and inquired, "Hello, anybody home?"

"Come on in," Lynn North's voice carried from within the house.

He heard a commotion from the back of the house as he entered the kitchen. Her arms filled with a stack of books and magazines, and a rolled tube of paper and her sketching pad tucked under her elbow, Lynn bustled into the kitchen.

"Morning, Patrick." She set her load on the kitchen table. "Coffee?" She nodded toward a carafe on the counter. Two cups stood beside it, along with a small crystal pitcher filled with thick cream. Beads of condensation swelled on the pitcher in the dense summer air.

Patrick poured the coffee. "Want a cup?" he asked, doling a large portion of cream into the strong, dark brew.

"Please," Lynn chirped, arranging her sketchpad and the books on the table. "I hit the jackpot in Valpo yesterday. There were several good books on constructing tie walls. These have a lot of information about footings and anchoring." She indicated the stack of library books.

"But best of all, I met a retired construction worker. He was volunteering at the library," she said, amused. "Orin Hoovel was his name. He said he had done his share of hard labor, so he was spending his retirement amongst books!"

Patrick served Lynn a mug of coffee and joined her at the table.

"I told him what we are doing, and he was very encouraging," she said. "He had no doubt that we could build this wall."

"Did you tell him how big it's gonna be?"

"I did. He didn't think that size would be the problem. In fact, he said we'd be pretty good at constructing walls by the time we finish," she laughed.

"The main thing he warned me about was having the right tools. He made me a list, and we'll go in to town later to get what we need. He told me where he'd order the ties, and helped me figure out how many it will take. Look," she said, spreading out her sketching pad.

"Wow," Pat gazed in awe at a drawing of Lynn's plans. Her charcoal sketch detailed a wall extending from the far end of the paved parking area along the driveway, curving gracefully along the low side of the dune below the scrub oaks, the raspberries, and the small swatch of lawn at the south end of the pool. The structure wrapped around the blacktop turnaround at the base of the stairs. Where the wall intersected the stairs to the house, Lynn had designed a three-tiered terrace of garden boxes. Her drawing was complete with plantings and light fixtures mounted on the ties.

She showed Patrick several diagrams she had made with Mr. Hoovel that illustrated how to link the ends of the ties together and how to anchor the wall deep into the dune to keep it from spreading and buckling.

"Looks like I'll be shoveling a bit of sand this summer," Patrick grinned.

"I'm afraid so," Lynn smiled. She squeezed his bicep lightly, forming a caliper with her thumb and fingers. "Won't hurt you, though. Get you in shape for football."

Patrick snorted, embarrassed, and looked away from Lynn's beaming smile.

By the time they had finished the coffee, Lynn had infused him with her enthusiasm, and he was eager to get started.

"I'll get Mr. Hoovel's list. We need to go to town," she told Patrick. "You come, too. You'll need to choose tools that feel right for you."

Lynn North turned on the air and left the top up on her shiny new Thunderbird convertible as they drove into Michigan City, ramping up the volume on the Beach Boys.

Stopping first at the building supply and hardware, Mrs. North ordered two hundred and fifty-four ten-foot ties with set pins and ten bags of Redi-Mix concrete for footings.

At the hardware store, she ordered a wheelbarrow, a couple of wrecking bars, a long crowbar, both a square-faced and a spade shovel, and another, smaller spade. She encouraged Patrick to choose his own hammers, several pairs of cloth and leather gloves, and some safety glasses.

"You'll need a maul, and probably a two-pounder as well, Mr. Hoovel told me," she said. "You choose the ones you like."

Lynn paid for the goods and asked that the wrecking bars, gloves, and safety glasses be bagged to go. Then she offered Mr. Seibert a twenty-dollar tip to take the heavier equipment to the lumberyard so that it could be included with the delivery, but Mr. Seibert declined.

"I tell you what, Mrs. North," the old merchant advised. "You keep your twenty, and I'll just get Fred to swing by on his way to deliver your lumber. He'll be glad to do it," he assured her.

Lynn charmed the old fellow with a smile as genuine as the gratitude she expressed. Patrick stifled a smile of his own to see the old gent's wizened features melt under Lynn's thanks.

"One more stop," she said as they got back into the Thunderbird.

"Oh, yeah?" Patrick asked, his stomach beginning to howl. "Where's that? The A&W?"

Lynn chuckled. "Oh, you must be hungry! I never thought—I'm so sorry," she apologized. "Well, then, maybe we'll need to make two more stops. But the next stop is at Ollie Rossom's. He's the Stihl dealer in Michigan City. "

"Stihl?" Pat questioned. "You gonna use a chainsaw?"

"I can if I need to." She took a stand, but then demurred. "I was hoping that you would handle the saw."

Patrick pondered the opportunity. Uncle Paddy had never allowed him to run the old chainsaw he used to remove downed branches from the fence line, clear fields, and put up firewood.

"Yeah, I could do that," he said confidently. "But I never have before."

"We'll fix that," Lynn said. "I'm not all that qualified to show you much about it, but I'm pretty confident that if Mr. Rossum wants to make a sale, he'll be more than willing to give us all the lessons we need."

Lynn was right.

At the Stihl store, Mr. Rossum eyed his customers, settling first on the strapping young fellow, then on the pretty little woman with the golden ponytail. As he assessed his customers, the lady flipped her sunglasses up above her visor. Mr. Rossum thought she was looking right through him with her amber eyes. He stepped out of the shop door, lobbed a wad of well-chewed tobacco onto the gravel, and wiped the juice from his chin with his thick, suntanned forearm. Most of his customers were farmers, construction workers, or landscapers. He didn't see very many buyers who were quite as fancy as this young woman, in her crisp white shorts and low-heeled sandals. He wondered for a moment about the young man she had with her. He eyed him once again.

"You'll be running the saw?" Rossum's question to Patrick was more of a statement. "Ever run one before?"

"We both will," Lynn responded with certainty. "I can run a saw."

"I've never handled one," Patrick added. "And I may never, unless you show me how." In the periphery of his vision, he could see Lynn smile ever so slightly, glancing at him briefly, then returning her demanding gaze upon the crusty salesman.

Returning Mr. Rossum's assessing gaze, Patrick noticed that the man favored his left knee; it was probably what kept him from working construction.

He wondered how he'd hurt it. Had Rossum taken a saw to his leg? Maybe that was why he was leery of selling the tool to a pair of novices. He knew it was no use to bullshit the fellow. Patrick figured the only way to earn his confidence was to stand right up to him and prove he could handle the machine. He wondered, just briefly, what Lynn was doing, demanding instructions for herself as well.

"You're not all that sure about selling us a saw, are you?" Patrick asked Rossum directly.

"Well, son, I've done crazier things in my life. But you're right. I damn well could use a sale, but I have to wonder about sending one of these machines down the road in the back seat of a goddamned Ford Thunderbird. This ain't no toy, you know. I wouldn't want to see anyone hurt—or killed—on a machine I sold them."

Patrick laid it out to Rossum. He explained how he'd been brought up on a farm, and helped with the heavy work. Yes, he had been too young to run the saw before he left the farm, but he'd seen how careful his uncle had been when he used the old Homelight. And that every time Uncle Paddy worked the saw, Patrick had heard every lecture on safety his uncle could think of. It was like Paddy was telling it all over again, as much to remind himself as to teach the boys.

"And I brought a lot of firewood in with my uncle." That was one thing he could do on the farm without sneezing, Patrick realized. "Me, my brother, and my uncle. We'd put up seven full cords every summer and fall. I've been around saws."

Rossum listened, fishing a crumpled pack of Camels from his shirt pocket. He lit the cigarette, looked through the door for a moment, then agreed to give them a try.

"If I don't like what I see about you handling this machine, I'm just not going to sell it to you. Understand?"

"If you don't like what you see, I'll pay you for your time and we'll get out of your way," Lynn countered.

Rossum nodded sharply and turned to his inventory.

After a half hour, Patrick and Lynn had heard about everything from kickback to blade sharpening. Mr. Rossum appraised Patrick's skills and strength, and figured the boy was good to go. He watched Patrick run the blade through thick rounds of oak, then knotty pine, feeling the difference in how they cut. He pointed out how to look at the wood and see how each piece would cut. And to keep an eye out for metal, like barbed wire embedded in the wood, or nails. Patrick had pretty much cut a short cord of wood when he got

Rossum's nod of approval. He took off the safety glasses and wiped sweat and chips of wood from his face.

"You'll do alright," the grizzly fellow allowed. "You just better pay attention every second you're running this saw. And don't run it when you're tired, or it's dull. Keep the blade up out of the sand and it won't dull as fast. You got it?" He picked up the equipment, ready to take it back into the shop and clean it up before the sale.

"My turn," Lynn demanded.

"What?" Rossum was taken aback.

"My turn. I want to run the saw. I'm buying it."

Rossum grunted in exasperation. He thought the young man's ability to run the saw was obvious, and he saw no need for this tiny young woman—girl, really— to work the dangerous piece of equipment. But he could see she was determined. Damn, if she hurt herself, he'd never forgive himself. Damn fool. She wasn't even dressed for it. Serve her right. She'd have wood chips from her toes to the top of that sassy ponytail.

Lynn didn't give Rossum the chance to say no. She took the saw and set it down to get a grip on the starter cord. Pausing, she slipped a pair of safety glasses from her shorts pocket, placing them deliberately on her face. She made a swipe at the side of her head as if pulling loose strands of hair out of her face, although none were displaced.

Patrick thought she gave him the slightest hint of a wink, and she said, "How do I look?"

Rossum's lower jaw fell open. It was difficult to tell since his skin was so deeply tanned, but Patrick noticed red flushing up Rossum's neck from his collar.

Lynn clipped the throttle into starting position. She didn't bother choking the machine. It was still hot from Patrick's use. She braced the saw with a stiff left forearm, steadied the handle with her right toe, and gave the pull cord a swift, tough tug. The saw buzzed loudly, and she leaned down, released the starter clip on the throttle trigger, and lifted the saw into position. The engine hummed as she revved the throttle. She ran up the RPMs and set the blade gently onto the oak log. Lynn guided the blade carefully, cutting a nicely squared disc. She eased the throttle, then tilted the saw ninety degrees and made a five-inch cut horizontally into the edge of the log, a third of the way down from the top. Then she made a second cut, parallel to the first but three inches from the bottom of the log. Putting the blade back on top of the log, she made a neat cut straight down, stopping at the higher of her horizontal scores. A semi-circular wedge fell from the top third of the log, its edges neatly squared. Finally, with the chain spinning on the oiled bar, she set the topside of the saw underneath the log, ramming the teeth into the oak's bark. She revved the engine once more and cut upwards from the bottom, again stopping cleanly at her lower horizontal cut. Another neatly trimmed half-circle fell harmlessly out of the way, leaving a flat, level tab protruding from the edge of the log. Lynn triggered the throttle twice, then idled the engine briefly before shutting it off and setting it on the ground.

Rossum examined the cut, his relief clear on his face. "That's a nice cut, Miss," he acknowledged.

Leaving her glasses on, Lynn looked through the sweat and chips caught on the lenses, gracing Rossum with her smile. "Thanks," she accepted cheerfully. "You were right the first time, though. It's 'Ma'am'. I'm a missus. And that is a nice saw."

Rossum laughed outright. "Well, I'll be damned! You said you could run a saw. I just didn't want to believe it."

"Well, don't you wonder why I chose your shop, and a Stihl?" Lynn's tone was almost flirtatious. "I mean, I could have gone to Sears and got a Homelight right off the shelf, no questions asked."

"You know, I wondered why you hadn't," Rossum admitted. "I even kind of wished you had, when you first came in." He laughed. "Why did you come to my shop?"

Lynn removed the ungainly glasses and wiped her face. She pulled back her visor and brushed the chips from her hair.

"Well, first off, I wanted a Stihl saw," she said. "My uncle has a saw and snowmobile shop up home in Minnesota, and that's the only saw my family ever uses. My daddy taught me to use a Stihl when I was in high school. They're the best.

"So, when I asked Orin Hoovel about where I could get a good buy on a Stihl, he told me that you ran the most honest business in Northern Indiana," she continued, again flashing her most gracious smile at the ruddy businessman. "Even if you are, in Mr. Hoovel's words, a 'stubborn, foul mouthed, red-necked son-of-a-bitch.'"

Rossum barked with laughter, bending over and slapping his leg.

"Orin Hoovel, that old bastard," Rossum chortled. "So you know that piss-ant?"

"I met Mr. Hoovel in the library at Valpo, and I found him to be enlightened and a gentleman."

"A gentleman! The library! I will be damned!" Rossum exclaimed, picking up the saw and heading for his shop, muttering and chuckling the entire way. "Son-of-a-bitch. 'Enlightened!' I'll be damned. Makes my day."

Lynn glanced over at Patrick. He was watching her quizzically.

"What?" she asked.

He grinned. "I think I've just witnessed a con job."

"Now, what do you mean by that?" she argued, trying very little to hold back her smile.

"You caught Mr. Rossum pretty much by surprise."

"Mr. Rossum set himself up for any surprise he got."

"Yeah. Sure."

"If you want to see a con job, let's go see what Mr. Rossum is going to sock us for this saw."

There were no more cons perpetrated that day.

Mr. Rossum sent the unlikely pair away with a good saw and a very reasonable sales contract. He loaded the gear in the trunk of the Thunderbird and offered a last couple bits of advice.

"Remember about that sand," he admonished Patrick.

"And always, always know where your partner is standing when you have that saw in your hand. I hear you touch up your pretty little partner here by not paying attention to that blade, and I'll personally come trim your horn with this goddamn chain saw."

With that, Rossum tipped his forehead with a grimy finger, nodded to Lynn, and said, "Pleasure doing business with you, Mrs. North." He turned and stalked off into his workshop.

∞

Patrick wolfed down his third hamburger, chasing it with cold, sweet root beer. By the time they had finished at Rossum's, even Lynn admitted to being ravenous. She had finished her burger and was enjoying a hot fudge sundae, watching with amusement as Patrick ravaged his lunch.

"So you really don't think you conned Mr. Rossum?" Patrick paused between bites.

"Of course not," Lynn said, eyeing her ratio of fudge to remaining ice cream. She plucked the cherry from the top of the scoop by the stem, and waved it toward Patrick. "Do you like the cherry?"

Pat popped the pulpy red fruit into his mouth, then bit off another mouthful of hamburger to cover the cherry's sweetness and semi-crunchy texture.

"Then why not just come out and tell him?" he asked. "I mean, about your uncle and everything. I still think you were trying to pull one over on him."

Lynn stirred the fudge into the soft white ice cream, looking into the distance through the windshield of the Thunderbird.

"It was a convention," she replied. Looking over at him, she asked, "Do you play bridge?"

"Nope," he shook his head. "Euchre. And Sheepshead. And I've played a bit of chess with David and with Uncle Paul."

"Chess, then," she said. "Do you know the defenses and offenses?" Patrick again shook his head, and she continued.

"Well, there are some tried and proven strategies that are part of the history of the game. The Latvian Gambit. The Sicilian Defense, or the Nimzo-Indian Defense. In bridge, there are conventions. You can play a Texas Convention, or the Manhattan Convention. People devise their own conventions, if they play together long enough. They're just ways of playing your cards so that your partner understands your strengths and weaknesses and knows how you'll play your hand."

She scooped a small bite of her sundae, drawing the spoon slowly from between her lips. Then she continued.

"I could have come right out and told Mr. Rossum all about how I would only buy his type of saw, and that I could handle it and all that." She waved the spoon dismissively, glancing over at Patrick. "It wouldn't have mattered to him, though. He had to find reason to respect me first. So, I was breasting my cards until it was time to play them. And when I played them, I came out strong in my trump suit. Sometimes actions are indeed louder than words, especially if you're short of trump. Now, I think, Mr. Rossum has some respect for me. He certainly gave us a reasonable deal on the sale."

She paused, thoughtfully.

"You don't always want others to know all that you know, or what you think. You want to wield your power in subtle ways."

Lynn studied her sundae again, dipping the tip of the spoon into the fudge and licking it deliberately.

Patrick watched her a moment, wondering if she would continue.

"So why exactly do you want to build this wall?"

She looked at him with confidence.

"Because I can. We can, anyway," she smiled. "I couldn't do it without your help. But I think we can together. And I can see exactly how it will be. It will echo the lines of the dune as it flows along the drive, with ivy and wildflowers dangling down from above." She pointed with her fudge-covered spoon at imaginary points in the space between them. "I'll put in soft lighting for at night, and slots and bunkers for planters. I'll fill it with native plants, dune grass, prickly pear, wildflowers. It will be art. It's as simple as that. Our wall will take nothing from the beauty of the dune—it will add to it. It will be part of that moving, lovely, living dune. It will be there for years. And, with your help, I will have built it."

She looked at him now from under her eyebrows. Her expression reminded him of a puppy. He stifled a laugh.

"What?" she demanded.

He dodged the question. He didn't want to confess his thought.

"So where'd you learn all that about chess? And bridge."

"Chess, from my father and brothers. We played endlessly," she said. "I learned bridge in college. And I played some with Barry and his doctor friends the first year we were married. Now, I play with the widows. Do you want this?" she asked, offering Patrick her half-eaten sundae.

"Thanks," he said, taking the ice cream. He hadn't ordered a dessert for himself, and the amount left in Lynn's dish was perfect. He spooned it slowly, dipping the tip of the spoon as he had seen her do. It was indeed a joy.

Chapter Nineteen
Foundations

THE EIGHTH OF JULY was long and bright. Back at the Norths', Patrick unloaded the gear from the trunk. He took the saw and gas can into the garage, put on a pair of gloves and, with wrecking bar in hand, headed for the wall.

"You're pretty eager," Lynn kidded. "It's nearly five o'clock!"

"You bet," Patrick said. "I was thinking on the way back. We have a whole lot of ties to pull out of the side of this dune, and a load of new ones coming on Wednesday. I think we have our work cut out for us if we're going to get these out by the time your new wall gets here." She nodded in agreement, and he continued.

"We ought to have the old ties out of the way for the delivery truck. Let's see how easy they come down off the dune, and where we can stack them down by the road."

Patrick went to work on the ties furthest from the house. As he got started, Lynn brought out a tripod-mounted camera and snapped pictures of the worksite. "We'll document our project," she told him.

They worked without much chatter, wiping sweat from their brows as they rolled heavy ties off the wall. By nine, when twilight had a toehold on the night, they had stripped a third of the wall along the driveway. Patrick sauntered back up to the house after depositing the last of the day's work in the scrap pile along the road. He turned on the garden hose, bent over, and sprayed down his neck and over the back of his head. He rinsed his arms and face, then held the stream gingerly on the palm of his left hand. He'd blistered the pads of his index finger and thumb. He flinched as he cleared the dirt and sweat from the raw skin. His right hand was better.

"Do you think we'll be ready for the ties on Wednesday?" Lynn wondered aloud.

"If we get an early enough start tomorrow, we ought to."

"Well, let me just clean up a bit and I'll give you a ride home. Or are you hungry? You want a bite before you go?"

Patrick declined both offers.

"I haven't run yet today. We did kind of take it easy this morning. I'd like to run the beach."

Lynn smiled, amazed. Her look said she thought he was off his rocker.

"Really," Patrick protested. "I'm not real tired out. Just warmed up. Honest."

Lynn laughed, taking the hose. She dipped her face into the spray, running the water down her arms and neck like she had seen Patrick do.

"Oh, my, that's heavenly," Patrick heard her say as he kicked off his sneakers and work pants. He hung the sandy jeans in the garage. He would run the beach barefoot. He stepped out of the garage as Lynn finished spraying the grime off her legs. Her skin glistened with water, and her hair was disheveled, dripping in wet strands that had loosened from her ponytail. Her face and neck were deep brown, as were her arms and legs. Her short-sleeved denim blouse clung to her body. She looked at the skin on her arms and complained, "Oh dear. I suppose I'm going to exchange my total tan for a farmer's tan with this project." She smiled and raised an eyebrow at Patrick. A burning blush raced up his neck and face. "Well, bright and early then," she said, bidding him goodnight.

"Uh, yes, ma'am," Patrick blurted, heading up the stairs and toward the path to the beach.

His last glimpse of Mrs. Lynn North before he ran to the beach was of her unbuttoning her denim blouse as she pulled it out of her shorts on her way to the pool.

∞

With a fresh start on Tuesday, Patrick and Lynn had the wall down by mid-afternoon. As she had the day before, Lynn snapped pictures now and again as they worked their way up the driveway. They didn't bother to move the ties to the scrap pile until they had torn them all down. By evening, they still had about a third left to move.

The lumberyard called early Wednesday morning to say that the deliveries—it would take two truckloads—wouldn't arrive until later that afternoon.

When he saw the first truck back up the drive, Patrick sucked in a deep breath. *This,* he recognized, *was going to be a big job.*

∞

On Thursday morning, with the cicadas chirping ceaseless crescendos as the day's heat built up, construction started slowly as Patrick and Lynn loosened sore muscles. Patrick dug deep holes for footings. Then, they mixed concrete in the wheelbarrow, filling each hole.

It was half past two before they finished the last footing. Lynn smoothed the surface of the concrete as Patrick washed the tools.

"Hungry?" Lynn called over her shoulder.

Patrick shot her a look of disbelief. How could she wonder? They had worked right through without a lunch.

"And thirsty!" he exclaimed.

"Well, we've earned a break," she said. "I want to take a few pictures of the footings, and then I'll go make some sandwiches. Do you want to sign the concrete?"

Patrick examined Lynn's surfacing. She had smoothed all the concrete, but on the footing at the head of the driveway he found an inscription: *Lynn N. July 11, 1962.* Lynn's lettering was clear and tidy.

Lynn offered a small, pointed trowel to Pat. She smiled, satisfied, before turning to hose the concrete from her hands. Patrick took the trowel and knelt by the footing. He used the point to scrape first a *P* and then a *J* in block caps.

"PJ, eh?" Lynn asked, peeking over his shoulder. "Well, PJ, let's grab something to eat."

As they sat on the bank overlooking the drive, eating sandwiches and drowning their thirst with fresh lemonade, Lynn explained how she thought the project should develop. Her face glowed with excitement and her slender hands danced first this way, then that, as she created her wall in words. She finished, looking first at the wall she saw in her mind, then to her helper, inviting his reaction.

Patrick considered Lynn's wall as he finished the last of the lemonade. Lynn studied him as he ruminated on her plans. After a moment, she prodded him.

"What?" she asked anxiously.

"I'm with you," Patrick nodded. "Let's do it."

EACH DAY, the wall's shape became clearer. Since he felt he was wasting time waiting for a ride from his uncle, Patrick started jogging the beach to get to the Norths' at first light. When he arrived, Lynn would already be on the job site, coffee in hand, examining and evaluating, planning and figuring, recording their progress with her camera. Each day she knew exactly what they had to get done. They worked until dusk, and sometimes longer. They didn't waste a minute.

Counting down the days until two-a-day football practices started, Patrick didn't think that they had time to spare. Four weeks remained until he reported for team training.

Their biggest delays were caused by the routine visits from Harriet Hamilton, the senior member of the Dunes widows' group, a potter and artisan who lived two houses down on West Drive. Harriet was Lynn's bridge partner and self-proclaimed guardian. Almost every day, Harriet tottered up the drive, lugging a basket of cookies or brownies, sometimes sandwiches, and a thermos of sun-brewed iced tea. She always arrived in a flurry of excitement, commenting each day on the beauty and progress of the construction. Sometimes, Patrick would hear Lynn mutter a word or two as Harriet arrived, but she invariably greeted her neighbor graciously and thanked her profusely for the snacks.

Patrick was particularly grateful for Harriet's snacks. At first, Lynn's zeal for their work precluded her intention to break for lunch. The second time Patrick saw Harriet approach with her basket full of goodies, he exclaimed, "Thank God for Harriet!" Lynn laughed and apologized, embarrassed at her oversight. Each day thereafter, she made certain that the refrigerator was stocked with sandwiches, pasta or fruit salads, and plenty of drinks. Pat wondered when she found the time and energy to make up the salads, and figured it had to be in the evenings after he ran home. He reckoned that if he still had the energy to jog the mile and three-quarters home, she probably cleaned up, made dinner, and still had reserves to plan for the next day. He noticed that she, like he, was getting a lean, sinewy physique from the hard manual labor. And she never complained.

Each day, they pressed on.

∞

On the last Sunday of July, a cold front swept in from the northern plains, chilling the sultry weather system that had held the Dunes hostage to oppressive heat for two weeks. The collision of the two fronts created a tremendous display of thunder and lightning crashing over seven-foot waves on the lake. Several funnel clouds were reported, none of which touched down. The Canadian air wrung four inches of rain from the humid summer skies in less than an hour and a half, washing several tons of sand down the embankment over Lynn's partially-constructed wall. Patrick's first chore on Monday was to shovel the sand back up onto the dune behind the wall. The task took him the entire morning. While he cleaned up the sand, Lynn strung the electrical wiring behind the fourth tier, splicing in connections for each of the light boxes that would illuminate the driveway.

Just before noon, Harriet arrived with her basket.

"Oh, dear, that dune *did* wash down over your wall. I wondered if it hadn't." Talking with Harriet was like resuming a conversation somewhere in the middle; she picked up where she'd left off on her previous visit. Patrick found her amusing.

"Morning, Mrs. Hamilton," he called, leaning on his shovel.

"That was a real gully-washer last night," Mrs. Hamilton said. "I meant to come over earlier and see just how much damage the rain did. You already have it pretty well cleaned up, though. Isn't it awfully heavy, shoveling all that wet sand?"

Patrick chuckled. "It's not too bad. When it's dry, it just kind of runs off the side of the shovel, so I feel like I'm shoveling it two or three times just to get it back up on the dune."

"I don't think Pat minds the extra weight," Lynn added. "I was thinking as I watched him that when we first had to move the dune back from the wall, it would have been a lot easier to spray it down with the hose. He's moved a lot of sand this morning."

"I thought he might have," Mrs. Hamilton said. "So I brought sandwiches and some extra brownies today, figuring you'd be quite hungry."

Patrick rifled through Mrs. Hamilton's picnic while she examined Lynn's wiring job. The brownies looked as good as usual, but Patrick was wary of her sandwiches. He enjoyed the plain baloney; it was pretty hard to do harm to a baloney sandwich. Same with the peanut butter and jelly, even if Mrs. Hamilton made all her sandwiches on a heavy-grained whole wheat bread, not the soft white slices that he preferred. Patrick hoped she hadn't made tuna again. She always mixed in as much celery as tuna, and she used Miracle Whip instead of mayonnaise. He didn't care for the crunchy, sweet tuna.

The worst, however, was the egg salad. Not only was there the Miracle Whip, but Mrs. Hamilton was atrocious about peeling eggs. He didn't know how she could miss the big hunks of shell, especially since she used brown-shelled eggs, which should have been fairly easy to spot against the bright cooked whites. They almost always got by her, though. Patrick cringed when he saw yellow filling in that day's sandwiches. He'd wait until later, after Mrs. Hamilton had left, to try one. Then, maybe, if he and Lynn were hungry enough, they would dare each other to take a bite of their sandwiches and carefully, gingerly chew, feeling the gag reflexes welling at the top of their throats.

Mrs. Hamilton scurried off, thoughtful about delaying their work. After chatting with Harriet as she walked her to the end of the drive, Lynn returned to join Patrick for lunch. She read the look of apprehension on his face.

"Oh, no. Egg?"

He nodded. He offered her the basket. "You first?"

She hesitated.

"Not today. I found shells first last time. Still not over that," Lynn wrinkled her nose as she recalled Harriet's last batch of egg salad. "I've got pasta in the fridge. Want some? I'll go get it. Lemonade?"

"You bet."

Patrick wanted to move the last of the sand before lunch. He plunged his shovel into the pile and quickened his pace. It was a good-sized drift, and Patrick put his back into it. Dune sand didn't take long to lose water, and the top layer had already dried in the sun. White sand poured freely from his shovel as he scooped it up onto the embankment.

A bright sparkle in the falling sand caught his eye as he lifted the shovel up over the wall. He stopped and looked for the glittering object that had fallen into Lynn's planter. A ring, encrusted in sand and minerals, lay almost hidden behind the ties. Patrick picked it up and examined it, rubbing off some of the deposit. The thin gold band held a setting of three gems, each shaped in a long oval with pointed ends. Patrick chiseled the crusty sand with his thumbnail. The center stone was clearly a diamond. He wondered about the deep green stones that flanked it, picking at them to get a better look. Were they emeralds?

Lynn returned, carrying a tray with the drinks and bowls of pasta salad.

"God bless Harriet," she was saying. "And bless her egg salad, too."

Patrick's focus on the ring caught her attention.

"Whatcha got there?"

He offered her the ring.

"It was in the sand."

Lynn examined it, pulling her shirttail from her jean shorts to rub on the stones. "Wow. Whopper rocks! This is beautiful. Somebody must have lost it. I wonder who? I wonder how long it has been here?" she asked.

She slipped it on her right ring finger. It was several sizes too large, and badly needed cleaning, but looked sleek and timelessly fashionable on Lynn's long thin hand.

"A lucky find," she said, taking it off and handing it back to Patrick. "Finders keepers."

Patrick was dumbfounded. "It's not mine," he stammered. "It was on your property. I just found it."

"Well, it's not mine," Lynn said playfully. "I already have one." She held out her other hand to display her thin wedding band and the diamond engagement ring her husband had given her.

Patrick felt funny about the ring. It belonged to someone, but not him. He suggested that they try to find its rightful owner. Lynn agreed that they could write Mr. Parmley and see what he knew about it.

"But you know, he had been divorced for more than fifteen years, long before he moved here. So it's probably not his. We can check, though," she said. "Here. I'll put it in the house so it doesn't get lost again. And I'll get it cleaned up and polished. We can ask around to see if any of the older neighbors know of someone who lost a ring here. Maybe Harriet knows. But otherwise, I think you found a real treasure, Patrick. You can give it to someone you love."

Patrick handed the ring back to Lynn. It was a lucky find, but he still didn't think he should keep it.

"Why don't you have it?" he asked her.

Lynn smiled, looking first at the ring and then at her helper.

"Finding someone to give it to may not be quite that easy," she advised him. He felt a blush run heatedly up his face. He really hadn't meant it that way, but she didn't let him explain.

"I know," she said gently. "I'll keep it for safekeeping now, and we'll take it into town and have it cleaned and polished. But you deserve it. You found it." The playfulness returned to her voice as she turned to take the ring into the house.

"Besides, you'll never know when you'll need it."

Chapter Twenty-One

Lynn's Wall

LATE AFTERNOON SUNLIGHT filtered through the canopy. They had two more ties in place and were ready to set in a third. They were at the top of the drive, the most curved part of the wall. Patrick cut a tie at precisely the angle Lynn had marked, and he began heaving it into place while Lynn guided the front end. The sharp corner of the milled log bit into his flesh as he balanced it on his shoulder. He leaned into the wall, bracing his knee against the lower tiers while he strained to position the load across his shoulder. Lynn tugged at the front end of the log, guiding it to fit square and tight. The tie bumped the dune, knocking sand and debris onto the flat surface of the lower tier, just where they were working.

Following the momentum of the massive wooden beam, Patrick was sliding the tie into place when, at the last second, he saw Lynn reach out to sweep away the fallen debris. The heavy tie was unstoppable. He felt the impact of the ties butting ends, buffered only by the small, gloved fingers caught between them.

"Awwgh!" Lynn cried. Her crushed fingers were trapped. "Pat!"

He'd lost his grip on the beam when he'd placed it, but yanked at it nonetheless, the leather fingers of his gloves slipping over the coarse grain. It was enough to widen the gap between the tie-ends. Lynn pulled again, freeing her hand. She spun away, clutching her gloved hand to her belly.

"Oh, oh, oh," she whimpered softly, pacing in circles around the drive.

"Are you all right?" Patrick asked, sprinting to her side. "Is it okay?"

Lynn stifled her cries. "Oh, Patrick, it hurts. It really hurts," she whispered.

"Let's see it."

She stopped pacing. Slowly, she lifted her left hand, still held gingerly in her right. She eased the glove off her wounded fingers.

Her middle, ring, and pinky fingers were swollen and purple. The nails were a deep, violent shade of maroon. There was no bleeding, but her fingers seemed to be growing as they watched.

Patrick looked at her blanched face before gently taking her by her shoulders and guiding her toward the house.

"Come on. Let's get ice on those fingers." He knew from the many smashed fingers and joints that he'd had from playing sports that ice might not make it feel any better, especially at first, but it would help with the swelling.

In the house, Patrick helped her to an armchair in the study before hustling into the kitchen. He grabbed a towel, dampening it and filling it with ice from the freezer. His vision seemed to narrow as everything rushed and closed in on him. He grabbed another dry towel and hurried back to Lynn.

She sat clutching her hand, rocking slowly back and forth against the pain.

Patrick laid the dry towel across her leg. He gently took her wrist, looking first into her eyes to gain her confidence. He slowly lowered the damaged hand toward the ice.

"Let me," Lynn said softly. She carefully set her fingers on top of the ice, palm side up. She closed her eyes, inhaled, and held her breath for what seemed a very long moment.

Patrick visually examined her hand. The little finger was blue, but not as extensively bruised as the next two. Her middle finger was bright purple, and so plump with blood that the ripples of her fingerprints were smooth and shiny. But her ring finger was the worst. Her wedding and engagement rings severely constricted the blood flow out from her finger. Her usually dainty finger was bigger around than her thumb knuckle, and the tight, swollen skin had darkened to an ominous shade of violet.

Patrick looked into Lynn's face.

She was watching him. Her eyes were puffy and tears wet her face. Her lips remained tight against the pain. But she was almost smiling at him. Her eyes were kind, grateful.

She wiggled each finger slightly.

"I don't think I broke anything," she whispered, her voice cracking. "Could be worse."

Patrick looked down at her fingers again.

"It will be worse, if you don't get your rings off, and soon," he said. He stood up, walked to the phone mounted on the kitchen wall, and dialed the number to his house. No answer. He'd hoped Aunt Mary, or Jack for that matter, could come quickly with the car and take Lynn to the hospital to have the fingers cared for. He tried Harriet, then Adam Smith and several others, but no one picked up.

"Should I call an ambulance, or the police?" Pat asked Lynn. "How about Gus the guard?"

Lynn studied her fingers.

"I don't think we need to," she said. "You're right, though. We have to get these rings off."

She thought a moment.

"Pat, bring me the wooden case from under Barry's desk," she said, tilting her head toward the large oak desk in the study.

Patrick found the case tucked in the chair well beneath the desk. He took it to Lynn, popping it open on the end table next to her chair. Inside was a collection of sleek electrical instruments. One resembled a dentist's drill. Another looked like a fine, miniature saber saw. A third looked like a rotor grinder, with a tiny, inch-wide grinding wheel.

"That one," Lynn said. "Plug in that grinder."

Lynn watched him inspect the exquisitely engineered instrument, testing its speed and heft. He switched it off and held it out to her.

"No. You do it."

Lynn held an ice cube directly on the bands strangling her ring finger. She cooled them until she couldn't feel the ice. Then she took a long metal probe from the case, inserted it under the band of her engagement ring, and gingerly pried it away from her swollen finger.

Patrick carefully placed the wheel near her ring, revving the tool only slightly.

"Run it on high speed. It will cut faster, I think," she offered.

Again, Lynn iced the ring and finger. When he was ready, she pried the ring away from her flesh and Patrick worked the grinder into the gold band.

He stopped twice to let her cool the metal. She cried when she let pressure off the prying tool under her ring, but urged him to continue. On the third attempt, he cut completely through the band. Using a needle-nosed pliers and forceps, he bent it back and peeled it from Lynn's ballooning finger. The wedding band was thinner. He made one cut and pulled back the loose ends from the finger as quickly and evenly as he could. He watched her wince each time he bumped her hand.

"Oh, God," she said when he'd freed her finger. She immediately plunged the hand back into the towel filled with ice. She looked up at him gratefully.

"Thanks. Nicely done."

He drew in a deep breath.

"There is one more thing," he said evenly.

"What?"

"We have to drill your nails." He removed another tool from the case of surgical instruments and plugged it in. The drill bit rotated amazingly fast.

"You must be kidding," Lynn said, her face paling again. Her fingers were swollen and numb, but her fingernails pounded intensely with her pulse. "The nails are the worst!"

"You've got to drill them to let the pressure out. Otherwise, they'll hurt more for a long time. I know. Uncle Paddy showed me how to do this a bunch of times when I smashed fingers. It's not bad. And this'll be easier. On the farm we had to do it with a hot sewing needle."

She looked warily at him, but consented.

She silently watched his every move as he carefully lowered the spinning drill onto the surface of her nail. He touched her middle fingernail just slightly, revving the drill. A spurt of blood gushed from under the nail, then flowed evenly. Lynn felt the pressure subside immediately.

Patrick gently pressed the pad at the tip of her finger until the blood slowed.

"Let's do the next one," he said.

She nodded. He drilled the ring finger, the one that hurt the most. Lynn felt the pressure release. The pain lessened immediately. Eagerly, she said, "Do the last one."

Patrick quickly vented the nail on Lynn's little finger, then watched carefully to be sure that the fingers continued to ooze and the holes didn't plug up, allowing the pressure to rebuild.

The color returned to Lynn's face as she sat quietly, icing her injured hand. After a few minutes, she started to pull herself up out of the chair, wanting to walk off the throbbing pain.

Patrick helped her, holding the ice-packed towel around her gruesomely crunched fingers. The sight of her, so small and uncharacteristically fragile, was a sudden, powerful emotional trigger. His adrenalin had surged from the moment he saw her gloved hand slip between the ties. Now, suddenly, after the worst had passed, his eyes filled with hot, stinging tears.

Lynn looked up at the young man, handsome, tanned, strong. She was startled to see his eyes flooded. She felt her own emotions unwind. Her eyes watered again as she watched his tears take shape.

"You," she said softly. She leaned into him, carefully keeping her wounded hand upright between her shoulder and his chest. She rested her cheek against him, took a deep breath, and sobbed quietly.

He felt her body shudder with a staccato of sobs, and he was awash in emotion. He wrapped his arms slowly around her shoulders and hugged gently, careful of her injury. He had hurt her once already. He never wanted to do it again.

She felt him lean his cheek down on her hair. He shook a moment, crying. She watched a tear drip down onto his shirt. Another splashed off her hair. She let him hold her, let him release himself from the emotion of the accident.

They stood for moments, quiet. They listened to each other's breathing, finally inhaling, then relaxing.

Lynn looked up at the boy. He started to speak, but could only produce a muffled croak.

"I...I'm..."

She stopped him, putting a finger from her good hand to his lips.

"It's okay, PJ. It's okay."

He breathed in deeply, and exhaled, forcing himself to relax enough to speak.

"It's that...," he made himself continue, "it's that, well, I'm so sorry."

He pulled her closer, gently.

"I'm just so sorry." His voice trailed off in almost a whimper.

She melted into his arms. She slipped her right hand further around behind him, pulling him close, careful of her fingers.

When she looked up at him again, he looked afraid. She let her eyes smile at him, and said, "Look at you. Crying for me. You are such a man."

His face showed his surprise so clearly that she laughed gently.

He couldn't believe she could laugh with her hand hurting so. Her pain had to be terrible. He'd smashed fingernails and fingers before. It hurt incredibly. And she'd crushed three!

"Tears on your face. Such a sweetheart," she continued. "Here I'm the one hurt, and you're sharing your tears with me."

She tilted up on tiptoe and kissed him softly on his lips. Then, gracefully pulling away, she led him to the kitchen. She got more ice for her pack, and handed him two bottles of soda.

"Open them, please?" she asked. "I'm dying of thirst."

Pat cracked open the Cokes and followed her out to the terrace. She sat in a lounge chair, elevating her hand, sipping from the soda he gave her.

He spoke. "I mean, I'm sorry I hurt you."

She was silent for a moment, weighing his words and looking into the distance. The sun was beginning its descent behind the Chicago skyline. She thought for a moment of her husband, working in the city. What would he say about this mishap? She dismissed the worry and looked at the anguished young man sitting before her.

"I know you're sorry. I know you didn't mean to hurt me," she said. "I didn't mean to stick my hand in the way, either. I just saw some sand and stuff and wanted to clean it off before we set in the tie." She sighed.

"It wasn't your fault, Patrick. Not as much as it was mine, really. I lost focus for a minute. That's when accidents happen, when you stop paying attention.

"It's okay, though. You really don't have to blame yourself. You don't have to be forgiven. You are, if you think it necessary. I forgive you for hurting me, even if you didn't mean to," she said. Her usual playfulness sparkled from her eyes, and her voice bounced with kindness.

"You don't have to worry. I still love you."

∞

They lingered by the pool until dusk, chatting, resting, and listening to the sounds carried up from the beach on the breeze. Lynn wrapped up in a couple of thick pool towels to keep warm as the day chilled.

Patrick went inside and made grilled cheese sandwiches, which they both gobbled down. Later, as it got dark, she asked him to pour her some whiskey. She directed him to a special bottle in Dr. North's liquor cabinet. An Irish whiskey from 1951, Knappogue. He brought her a half-full tumbler with no ice, as she had requested.

Lynn eyed the measure of whiskey and quipped, "Are you trying to get me drunk?"

Patrick shrugged. He didn't know how much she wanted. He knew his Aunt Mary could put away the amount of whiskey he'd offered Lynn in a reasonably short period.

She sipped the amber drink, and sighed. She closed her eyes, feeling the liquor warm her belly. She held the glass up to Patrick. "Want to try some?"

He took the drink to his lips, sniffing its fragrance. He touched the liquid to his lips and felt it warm his tongue and throat. It was potent, but very smooth and mellow. He handed it back to Lynn.

"Whew," he said. "That's strong."

"It is the only whiskey I've ever liked. Tonight, I think it will be perfect."

"You'll be all right?" he asked.

"Yes. You go now."

He checked her ice pack one last time, lingering a moment longer.

"Go," she repeated, laughing. "I'll be just fine."

Patrick went down to the garage, hung up his jeans, and pulled on his running shorts. He grabbed a shawl from the den before closing up the garage. Turning back toward the pool, he took the stairs up to the terrace by threes.

Lynn sat peacefully in the blue hues of twilight. He spread the wrap across her legs and lap. She peered at him gratefully.

"Goodnight, Patrick," she said.

"Goodnight," he paused, then added, "Lynn."

"See you in the morning."

He nodded, and took off across the dune, down the trail to the beach.

Chapter Twenty-Two
Patrick's Wall

ALL WAS STILL when Patrick arrived at the Norths'. He quietly peeked into the kitchen. No coffee had been made. There was no sign of Lynn. In the garage, her car remained parked as usual. Patrick slipped into his work clothes.

Everything was where they had left it the night before. The injurious tie was just inches out of place; Patrick easily pushed it into position. The next tie would need to be measured, but Patrick didn't want to start up the chain saw if Lynn was still sleeping. He busied himself by topping off the fuel in the saw, tidying up the work site, and moving some of the ties further up the wall to where they would be measured and set.

Within the hour, Patrick heard stirring in the house. When Lynn stepped out from the kitchen door, she looked haggard and pained. She cradled her swollen, sore hand upon her chest. Patrick could see the purple and blue of her fingers from across the driveway.

"Morning," he said.

"Hmmmph," she mumbled. She came over and sat on the ties he had just stacked.

"Still hurting bad?" he asked.

She nodded.

"I didn't get much sleep, I'm afraid." She looked dolefully at her fingers.

"I tried not to make much noise. I thought you might still be sleeping."

"I was. I woke up all night, every time I bumped my hand," she said, holding her fingers up in the sunlight for his inspection. "Not pretty."

"No. Not very," Patrick sympathized. He moved to the wall, fumbling with the tape measure. "I don't imagine you feel much like working today?"

Lynn looked down at the ties. There was no way she would be able to work on the wall that day, or probably any day soon.

"I've been thinking about the work we have left on the wall," she began. "I had a lot of time to think about it during the night."

She looked up at Patrick, pausing, not wanting to say what she knew she must.

"Patrick, I can't do anything with these fingers, and I don't know how long it will be before I can. I don't think we will be able to get done before you start football." She looked back down at the ties. After a moment, she added, "I think I'll have to hire out the rest of the work."

Her words surprised and stung him. He had worried about her hand, and had wondered when she would be able to resume work. But he had planned on keeping the project going by himself; she would be there to direct him. He could pick up the slack while she healed.

He sat next to her on the tie. He said nothing. He could see disappointment in her eyes. As he watched her, her eyes teared up.

"Lynn," Patrick said softly, in almost a whisper. "I can do it. If you can just tell me how you want it done, I'll do it. I'll finish your wall. But you can't just give it up. Not after we've done this much. Please, Lynn...."

She sat, shaking her head slowly, a tear dripping off her chin. She smiled, still shaking her head.

"How can we keep going?" she said. "I just don't feel like it's possible. Not this morning, anyway."

"Don't decide this morning," Patrick implored. "If you're going to need to hire this out anyway, you can do it later. Next week. Or after I go to football. Just let's see what we can do in the meantime."

Her voice was as soft as his.

"I was hoping you'd want to talk me into it," she said, almost to herself.

"You feeling good enough to supervise today?" Patrick asked.

"Well, let's just say that I feel too bad to do anything but supervise." She gave him a crooked smile. "I'm more tired than anything. My hand throbs if I move it much. But if I just hold it up like this, it'll be okay."

"Well, how about this next tie?" Patrick said, standing up and starting to muster the momentum to get the project back on track. "How do you want me to measure it?"

∞

Patrick persevered on the wall, with Lynn offering guidance from her new station in the lounge chair under the shaded umbrella. He regretted that he hadn't thought to bring it down from the pool deck until late in the afternoon on the day after her accident, when the discomfort of her perch on the ties became obvious. Since then, though, she'd been comfortable and relaxed, especially as she saw that he was perfectly capable of measuring, cutting, hefting, and placing the heavy ties on his own. As the wall grew, she continued to observe and direct but served more as company and entertainment than co-worker or boss.

Patrick enjoyed her new role. Complaining that her tan would fade if she spent too long in the shade of the umbrella, she often moved up onto the dune above the wall, legs crossed, reading. Sometimes, engrossed in politics or philosophy, she'd read aloud to Patrick, her voice filled with excitement at an author's argument. Other times, she shared her interests in fiction, especially the humorous passages. She read aloud an entire book about an immigrant, Hyman Kaplan, and his adventures in his new home in America. She followed that with another selection about a little Italian priest, Don Camillo, his spiritual conflicts with the Devil, and his worldly competition with the Communist mayor in their small Italian village. She would read until she couldn't, consumed with belly-gripping peals of laughter. The humor often interfered with Patrick's progress, but she didn't seem to care. Patrick found himself wiping his eyes, bent over in breath-heaving guffaws, as much at Lynn's contagious giggles as at the actual story. When Mrs. Hamilton made her daily visits, Lynn would flip back to dog-eared pages and re-read her favorite passages, subjecting her friend to the same gripping bouts of laughter.

At least once every day, Lynn would suddenly get up, without a word, floating like dandelion bonnets in the breeze, moving across the crest of the dune to her house. She'd come back with her big, clumsy camera and snap some photos. But often, she simply sat placidly, her knees tucked up under her arms with her chin resting on her crossed wrists, lost in thought, or merely watching him. They passed long stretches of companionable silence, broken only by an occasional suggestion about the length or angle of the next section of wall. When these passed, they began to chat about themselves. Lynn asked Patrick many questions about his family, his twin, his mother, his life in Wisconsin. Her questions often came in series, examining every angle of the topic she was consuming at the moment. She asked a lot about Patrick's mother. Did it seem to Patrick like she was mentally ill? How did she act? Was she close to Patrick? To his twin? What was it like having a twin? Did he miss being close to David? Did they think alike and act alike, as so many twins are known to do? Did Patrick want to return to Wisconsin? For every answer Patrick gave, Lynn seemed to have another question waiting.

When he needed his breath to heave the ties into place, Patrick diverted her with questions of his own. He learned that she, too, had some farm background, albeit more in the line of a hobby farm like Jannie's. Her father still lived on the acreage in a lake community west of Minneapolis. Lynn and her younger sister Ingie had been active in 4-H, showing rabbits and sheep and competing in the horseback riding events at county fairs. She admitted preferring the crafts projects in 4-H, and had earned more esteemed awards in art and photography than in animal husbandry. Her mother was an avid amateur photographer, and she'd mentored Lynn in the finer aspects of through-the-lens composition and the value of the full spectrum of light.

As teenagers, she and Ingie had shifted their interests toward social activities. Sailing, tennis, and golf became far more attractive pastimes than grooming animals and cleaning stalls. When Lynn was seventeen, however, her mother had developed ovarian cancer; the diagnosis had come on her forty-ninth birthday. She died within months, a week before Lynn's high school graduation. She promised her mother that she would get a good education and have a career. She enrolled at Marquette and committed herself to a nursing major, although art was her first love. Art and photography.

Lynn spent four years at Marquette, loving Milwaukee and its proximity to Chicago. She'd quickly learned how to commute to the Windy City. Weekend trips on the Hiawatha into Union Station and a short ride on the L put her in the heart of Chicago's art community. She loved frequenting the galleries and studios, and of course, the Art Institute. After graduation, she had focused intensely on finding a job in Chicago. That was how she'd come to meet her husband, just a week after starting her short-lived nursing career at Northwestern University Hospital. She had turned twenty-one just three weeks before graduation.

Patrick listened raptly to the events that shaped Lynn's life. She was twenty-three years old, just seven years his elder. Yet it seemed she had done so much.

Chapter Twenty-Three
Photo Finish

BY THE END OF THE WEEK, their routine was well established. The days remained sunny, climbing back up into the nineties, but a high-pressure system that had pushed down from Canada had dried the air. Patrick worked shirtless, his torso glistening with sweat as he lifted the heavy ties up onto the shoulder-level tiers. Lynn read, sketched, fetched lemonade and snacks, and snapped photos.

Patrick particularly appreciated one aspect of Lynn's adjusted participation in the project. While she was still around as much, her attire reflected the change. Instead of denim blouses, work gloves, jeans or khaki pants, and solid leather shoes, she often started the day in a light sleeveless blouse, shorts, and sandals, if she wore any shoes at all. As the sun rose and the heat began shimmering off the dunes, Lynn often changed to a bikini top. When she read or worked on her art, she inevitably wore a visor, or sometimes a white cap with an oversized bill. Patrick had thoroughly enjoyed working side by side with Lynn North, both of them sweating and grimy with sand and stain from the ties. But there was nothing lost in the trade for Lynn North in her present role, always prim and neat, and, when she passed close by, leaving a clean and fresh fragrance.

Her arms, neck and face were deep brown, while her shoulders, back and stomach were much lighter, a shade of tan faded from its deepest hue. The past few weeks of labor had left its mark on her even glow.

"You're going to lose your farmer's tan," Patrick teased her one morning as she sat on the dune, spreading coconut oil across her skin.

Lynn inspected the contrast between her bronzed forearm and pale stomach. She shifted her gaze to Patrick, arching one eyebrow.

"A lady should have no tan lines," she replied. "Not such as these, anyway." She smiled mischievously, then added, "You should know that." She resumed spreading the sweet-smelling coconut oil down her leg.

Patrick stood paralyzed. Clearly, he realized, she was referring back to that morning of his run, on his birthday. He tucked his head and began working industriously. He peeked up the embankment. She had pulled her visor down over her eyes and turned to her reading. A hint of a smile remained on her face.

"You know," he said.

She lifted her eyes to meet his, looking out from under her visor. The smile remained.

"You know, don't you?" Patrick demanded. "You know I was up by the raspberries that day. I was running…." His complete confession tailed off.

Lynn's smile spread modestly. She nodded once, briefly but firmly. Her gaze riveted through to his soul.

Patrick could not control the sheepish grin that claimed his face. He looked down, abashed.

"I'm sorry," he said, kicking sand up against the blade of the shovel.

Lynn was quiet for so long that Patrick was about to repeat his apology. Just as he looked up to say the words again, she spoke. Her voice was soft and gentle, but firm in its kindness.

"Once again, you're sorry for something about which you have absolutely no need to be," she said. "You meant me no harm. You did me no harm. You probably suffered much more than I did, with this self-imposed guilt and embarrassment that you wrestle with."

She laughed lightly.

"Then how come you keep teasing me about it?" Patrick asked. "How come you keep bringing it up?"

"Keep bringing it up?" Lynn's voice danced. "I recall only twice bringing it up to you. I couldn't help but see how you responded when I first met you at your aunt's. I had to see whether you were malicious in your heart. Did you mean to hurt me, even if it was unintentional? I could see you didn't, though. I bet you haven't even told anyone about it, have you? Not even your cousin."

Patrick met her look. He shook his head. "Of course not!"

She studied him a moment. "Your brother?"

He shook his head, slowly.

"Nope. Not even David."

She nodded, then shrugged. "So. There it is. You meant no harm. Why should I hold it against you if you happened to see me being me the way I am, and the way I enjoy being? I don't need to forgive you anything. Perhaps it is I who should be forgiven, posing such a shock to your fragile little adolescent ego." Again, she laughed.

Patrick shook his head. "No. You don't need forgiveness from me," he assured her, grinning. "I'm much obliged," he added, laughing.

Lynn stood up, wiping the sand from her legs. "Well, then, now it's in the open. We have nothing secret between us. You don't have to carry your baseless guilt around any longer," she said, "and I won't get to tease you about it anymore." She laughed again.

"It was just an accident," Patrick added.

Lynn reflected a second, and commented nonchalantly, "Harriet always says that the only true accident is a miracle. Do you believe her?"

Patrick's grin again conquered his expression. He laughed. "Well, I admit, seeing you that morning, it kind of felt like that!"

Lynn raised her eyebrows. "Makes you wonder." She walked to the house, asking over her shoulder, "How about some lemonade?"

∞

On Monday, Lynn greeted him with a cup of coffee. "You know, PJ, it looks as though you'll finish up this week."

He nodded. "Yep. We'll be done with half a week to spare before football."

"Ah, yes, football. Are you looking forward to the start of your season?"

He found himself grinning uncontrollably. "Oh, yeah. Definitely," he said. Then, after a moment's consideration, he added, "It's kind of funny. Last year at this time I couldn't wait for football to start. And you know, earlier this summer, I was already thinking nothing but football. But since we started this job, the summer has really flown by. I haven't thought about the season nearly as much as I usually would."

"Do you regret that? Has this project been too much of a distraction?"

"Oh, no," he countered. "Not at all. I guess it's been a great distraction! And it's gotten me in good shape for football, too. I really like working on your wall. It's a lot better than hanging out with Jack, believe me!

"Plus," he hesitated, meeting her eyes, "I've really enjoyed doing this with you."

Lynn appeared pleased. He thought he detected the slightest blush coloring her face.

"At least, until we nailed your hand with that tie last week. That was a bit too much," he laughed. He nodded towards her shorts and sandals. "Looks like you're not ready to get back in it. How come?"

"Well, a couple of reasons, I suppose," she said, topping their mugs with warmer coffee. "Of course, Barry went wild when he looked at my fingers. He went on and on about why I shouldn't have been doing that work in the first place."

"He should have seen you out here!" Patrick set his coffee aside. "He could have seen how this wall wouldn't be like it is, except for what you did."

She acknowledged his compliment with a smile. "Well, to be honest, I don't give a damn what Barry says. I'm here to help, if you need it. And supervise. But you're doing fine, and we're really close to finishing." She looked at her hand, flexing and bending her fingers. "I really don't hurt much at all anymore, so I know I could be helping you."

"So, why?" Patrick pushed her. "Aren't we going to finish this? Together? This is your wall."

She studied him a moment. "Yes. It is my wall. My project. My piece of art," she said softly. She looked at him steadily. "You are going to complete it for me.

"When I couldn't work on it last week, I watched you carrying the load. I saw the whole project from a different perspective. I very much enjoyed that perspective. If you are willing to finish…," she hesitated. "Well, I would be grateful."

What is there to argue? Patrick thought. He shrugged. "Sure," he said, a look of puzzlement on his face. "If that's what you want."

It was, and he was anxious to get back to work. While the end of the project was in sight, he could see that he had almost as much work as the week before. There really wasn't time to dally.

Lynn resumed her post on the dune above the wall. She read to him first from an article in the *The New Yorker*, and then from Steinbeck's *East of Eden*. Lynn loved Steinbeck. The reading she selected focused on Lee, the Trask family's Chinese friend. In his pursuit of understanding, Lee had taken a problem to the elders of his Chinese community. To resolve Lee's question, the elders undertook the study of Hebrew in order to comprehend the semantics of scriptural text. Finally, by learning the language, they were able to satisfy their curiosity and gain understanding.

"Remarkable, isn't it?" Lynn commented. "The extent to which Lee and his friends went to gain insight and wisdom! The passionate quest for knowledge! It is so… enthralling."

Patrick stretched the tape measure across a tie, and looked up at Lynn. "Seems like a lot of trouble to go to just to find out the meaning of a line of scripture."

"What a great thing Lee did!" She flung her arms about as if to take flight. "With this incredible humility, he sought out his mentors. He motivated them all to reach for something more. He aspired for something greater, some higher meaning. He gained something that he would never have had, had he not been curious and interested in the importance of life."

She was moved.

Patrick shrugged.

"The rewards were so satisfying, PJ." Lynn cast a kind eye upon him. "That knowledge enhanced Lee's entire perspective on life. It enriched everything he already had. And he was willing to spend the time and do what it took to reach that higher goal, that greater understanding and awareness."

Patrick took the measurement on the tie. Lynn's enthusiasm was captivating. She positively shimmered with excitement as she spoke. He shook his head, wondering, trying to grasp her excitement.

She spotted his doubt, and knew she had planted a seed. She hoped it would germinate and grow. "Oh, you'll have to read *East of Eden*," she said. "You'll love it."

She hopped up and headed for the house. "You want a brownie? I made some this morning."

When she returned, Patrick helped himself to a brownie. He grabbed another, and eyed it with appreciation.

"Now, this," he waved the treat at her, "is satisfying reward!"

∞

The wall was complete by mid-afternoon on Friday. The day was glorious, with crystal blue skies and fairly low humidity, a slight breeze buffering the intensity of the early August sun. Patrick tended the last details of work. By quarter to two, he'd pinned in the last of the ties. By four o'clock, he'd completely cleaned up the work area. Lynn had finished the wiring and was washing down the driveway with a tight, hard spray from the nozzle on the hose. She pretended to lose control of the hose, threatening him with a drenching. He warned her with a wary eye, knowing all along that she would spray him if she wanted to. She didn't, though her face beamed as though she actually had. He kind of wished she would've. Play after work appealed.

He gave the wall a final inspection as she finished rinsing the drive. It was a fine job.

She rolled the hose in a coil under the faucet. "You were looking kind of hot there for a second," she teased. "I thought I could help cool you off with a little shower."

Patrick laughed. "You'd have paid, though."

"I'm sure I would have." She laughed in return. "But that doesn't solve the heat. Let's go for a swim. I'll meet you up at the pool."

Perfect, Patrick reflected. He peeled off his jeans and shoes. He still wore his running shorts from the morning. He cleaned up his face, neck, and arms with hot, soapy water in the garage sink, and went up to the pool. He didn't wait for Lynn, but jumped right in.

She'd put on her white bikini. The last ten days had helped even out her tan, but she still had some pretty severe tan lines from the blouses she'd worn while helping Patrick with the labor. The skin along the edges of her top was pale; she'd clearly lost the even tan she'd sported earlier in the summer. He tried not to notice, or at least not let her detect him noticing. He looked away, around the pool, but finally always back into her face. She riveted him with the kindness of her eyes.

"I thought about what I might do with the money I've earned," Patrick said. It seemed like a comfortable subject for discussion.

Lynn bobbed lightly in the water, floating on her back, not a care or burden imposing upon her mood. She righted herself, sweeping the water back off her hair.

"What's that?" she asked.

"A boat, maybe," he said. "Maybe a Sailfish or a Sunfish."

Her expression lit up. "Why don't you build one?" She leaned back into a full backstroke.

The thought hit Patrick like a bolt. *Build one.* He had never considered it. It was an intriguing idea, though. "My brothers built boats," she said. "Canoes. They used them every summer up in the Ely flowage. They were beautiful boats." Her expression reflected the distance her thoughts had taken her. "I'll write Kenny and see if he still has the directions to make the boats. I'm sure he does. He learned from a pro—a guy my dad knew from Brainerd. I remember Kenny having to document every step of the process in a logbook. He really enjoyed it. He showed Ted how to build his canoe a couple years later." Again, she followed her thoughts into a peaceful reminiscence.

Patrick pulled an inflated float into the pool, bunched it against his chest, and drifted placidly. The sun was still high in the afternoon sky. He felt a sudden loss of direction. He wasn't used to having absolutely nothing to do at this time of day. His work was done. He watched the ripples on the surface of the pool. The quiet was lovely, but unusual.

Lynn suddenly burst into motion. Like a seal popping onto an ice flow, she slid onto the deck. She hurried toward the house, leaving a glistening trail of pool water behind her.

"What's up?" Patrick inquired. "You okay?"

"We have to photograph the wall, PJ! The light is great. We have to take photos on the day we finished it," she called as she disappeared into the house.

Patrick followed her into the house. He found her in the study, attaching her large, boxy camera to her tripod. With her light meter in one hand, she picked up the camera and tripod and headed toward the wall.

"Here." She chose a spot near the center of the wall's long, graceful curve.

Patrick stepped in front of the wall he'd built. He spotted the little flaws and flairs that only the artist sees in his own work. He watched her as she adjusted her camera.

"More to your left." She waved him into position. Looking up from the viewfinder on top of the Hasselblad, Lynn gauged the light.

"You know, when I started this whole project, I didn't know you were gonna be such a photo nut," he teased.

Her attention was fixated on the viewfinder. After a moment, she looked up at him, her expression a mix of intensity and humor. "There is a lot about me that you don't know, PJ." She smiled gently. "Except maybe that I can get a wall built. And that I take pictures."

Patrick flushed. A tease for a tease. He felt a wave of anxiety surge through him. Her eyes stayed steady on his. A flicker of a grin sprouted on his face, and he felt his shoulders shrug reflexively. He crossed his arms at his wrists, in front of his navel.

She snapped the aperture and quickly wound the film crank.

"Hey! Wait!" he protested, throwing his shoulders and head back with laughter.

She snapped another image.

Patrick left his assigned spot by the wall, approaching the camera.

"No fair!" he cried. "You should be in them. Show me how to work this."

Lynn explained how to work the aperture, the focus, and the shutter trigger. She focused the lens on a specific spot where the ties met the dune.

"I'm going to sit right up there," she explained. "When I tell you, click the shutter. Okay?"

Patrick nodded. He looked down into the viewfinder. He watched Lynn move into the field of vision in front of the vibrant wall, dune grass, and sky. Her hair and skin glowed in the filtered light of late afternoon. He looked up. Lynn had climbed up onto the fifth tier of ties. She sat gracefully, her legs at an angle to the camera. She leaned slightly back, an elbow draped casually on a tie. She was smiling brightly. Instinctively, he snapped the shutter.

"Are you sure the camera was in focus?" she enquired.

Patrick looked closely at the image in the viewfinder after cranking the film winder. He adjusted the focus ever so slightly. Lynn leaned back on the heel of her other hand, brushing her damp hair back from her face. For an instant, her expression was bland, removed. Patrick snapped another exposure and quickly wound the film. Lynn laughed at Patrick catching her at her own game. He snapped several more shots. Lynn moved the camera to different locations along the wall, where they took turns taking each other's portraits. Finally, she found a setting on the stairs that satisfied her sense of composition. The sun had moved beneath the low-hanging branches of the trees along the top of the dune, illuminating the parking area with an indirect candescence. Lynn liked the lines of the wall from this point. While the planter remained barren, it presented an ideal setting for posing.

She positioned Patrick on top of the planter, his legs dangling easily along the ties. He propped himself up against the back of the planter with his forearm stretched along a tie. She studied the setting carefully, wound a small lever around the perimeter of the lens, and pressed a button on the face of the camera. The camera hummed and buzzed, the lever moving clockwise around the lens. Lynn hustled into position alongside Patrick. Her back was to him as she sat with her arms around her knees on the sand in the planter. She leaned forward, just touching the side of his body with her back. The shutter blinked.

"Stay right there." She jumped off the planter to reset the camera.

Again, the Hasselblad hummed and Lynn scurried into position. "Look nice, now," she said brightly. Patrick tried to be in his best pose. The shutter again opened for the exposure.

"Again," she said, bounding off the planter. Patrick noticed some dark markings from the ties on her white bikini. She flicked sand from her bottom and quickly reset the camera. Before activating the timer, she studied her setting again. She hit the button. She took her time getting into position. Patrick felt her brush up against his chest. Then, she turned, looking up into his face, deep into his eyes. She paused a second, then said, "Thanks, PJ. I couldn't have done this without you."

Patrick was taken aback, moved by her words, and more so by her tone. He looked into her eyes. Once again, she had caught him off guard. The shutter clicked.

A jay in a sand oak at the top of the dune cackled, laughing.

Patrick remained frozen in place. Lynn's eyes were deep and liquid. She held his gaze for a moment, then said, "We have two more frames."

For the next image, Lynn sat squarely against him, her legs folded with her knees together, down and away, her heels tucked underneath her. She leaned snugly into Patrick's rippled abdomen and chest, facing the camera directly when the shutter snapped.

In the final image, she quickly assumed the same position, but reached up with her right hand and drew Patrick's hand off the tie. She brought it down across her, holding his fingers lightly between hers. Patrick drew her close with his forearm. Again, the shutter snapped.

They paused a moment after the last photo, neither wanting to move. Slowly, Lynn turned her face toward Patrick. She kept his fingers interlaced with her own. She gazed into his eyes. She let her look linger, saying nothing, saying everything.

Patrick whirled. He sighed lightly, leaning to her, kissing her gently.

She took his kiss, and returned it. He felt her lips meet his, then close slightly, clinching his kiss. Her lips moved gently apart, and he felt the slight flicker of her tongue just touching his lips, then again she brought her lips closed, snug with his.

He felt the surge in his loin. His penis protruded in a huge lump beneath his running shorts. He was disconcerted, almost afraid. Afraid of his response, his reaction, of what he would do next, of what he should do next.

Lynn backed away, still looking deep into his eyes. "I'm so grateful," she whispered. Her eyes welled with tears.

Patrick smiled sheepishly. "I am too."

She untangled her fingers from his, and unfolded her legs from beneath her. Kneeling, she faced him. A thought struck him, and she couldn't refrain from chuckling at his puzzled expression.

"What is it?" she asked.

He gave her a curious look. "What is it you're grateful for? The wall?"

She looked down the length of their completed project.

"Yes," she sighed. "The wall. Your help. Your confidence. Taking over when I pinched my fingers." She shrugged, and added, "Your company. This whole summer. I'll never forget it."

He bobbed his head in agreement. "Yeah. It was the best." He watched as her eyes teared up again.

"I don't know what I'll do, now that it's over."

Again, he nodded. "We'll make canoes," he grinned.

She laughed, wiping her eyes with the back of her hand. "Let's!" she said. "I'll write my brother."

Chapter Twenty-Four

The Fair

September, 1962

JANNIE'S HAIR HAD GROWN as long as her pinky finger by Labor Day, but it was uneven and thin. She wore her favorite bandana, a brilliant blue kerchief, as she helped David groom Dante for the open class beef show at the Sauk County Fair.

Jannie's illness had left David not only raising both of their steers, but showing them as well. He had entered Bruno in the Angus show, where he figured the heavy, low-slung animal would compete better for the style that was fashionable in the breed. He'd been right. Bruno won his class on the first day of the fair, and was barely edged out for the Angus Grand Champion ribbon. Runner-up was pretty good for Bruno, David reflected. He anticipated a good price for the steer at the auction.

Dante, he figured, would compete better in the open show.

They bathed the bovine with the hoses outside the cattle barn, and Dante looked sleek and shiny, jet black, nicely muscled. David fussed with the clippers, going over every square inch of the steer's body, looking for any hair just a fraction longer than it should be. He'd polished each of Dante's hooves and had groomed the tip of his tail into a bulbous black pomp.

As David tended to the last details with her steer, Jannie leaned back on several stacked hay bales, reading a new letter from M.C. "M.C.'s been playing in a youth symphony in Atlanta," she informed him happily.

David was keyed up. The open competition was the third event the next morning, but he already had Dante in top shape. He'd need to bathe and groom the steer again in the morning, but he felt good having him ready to show. More often than not, judges would wander through the barns to see how the animals were put together, and how they looked without the stress of the show ring. Dante looked good, and David was confident that he was ready for the judge's eye.

In spite of his excitement and his focus on his animals, David heard every word Jannie said.

"What do they have her playing?" he asked.

"Her cello, I think," Jannie baited him.

He looked up sharply to see if she was spoofing him. Her grin confirmed his suspicion. "Of course she's playing her cello. I mean, what music do they play?"

Jannie laughed lightly. She'd got him. "She didn't say. She had to try out for the position, though," she added. "Cool, eh?"

"You could play with the Baraboo youth orchestra, you know."

"Yeah, sure. It's more like a marching band, and you know it," she scoffed. "All they play is circus music and Souza."

David checked again to see if she was leading him on, but she wasn't. She had her nose back in the letter.

"Nothing wrong with Souza," David tossed her way, watching over Dante's neatly groomed backline for her reaction. She was far away, lost in thought; he wondered if she'd even heard him. She set the letter down on her lap and turned her head away. She sat motionless a moment, hovering, he thought. She looked up suddenly, snapping back into real time, her indignant expression indicating that she had heard his nonsense after all.

"Right. Souza," Jannie grumbled. "We used to swear that the Sarge marched around to Souza playing someplace in her weird little mind." She folded the letter and tucked it deep within her satchel.

"Wanna walk the arcade?" she asked. They had almost an hour before the grandstand show started.

"Let's go," he replied, grabbing a sweatshirt, more for Jannie than for himself, and taking her hand as they left the barn.

They strolled between the barns toward the bright lights and merry sounds of the midway. Jannie loved the arcade, David knew, and he paced their walk accordingly, in spite of the hunger rumbling in his belly. They bought hot dogs and icy sodas, sipping the sweetness and bubbling carbonation as they strolled. They visited with friends they met along the midway. Occasionally, David noticed a finger pointed their way. He knew people talked about Jannie's illness. She looked good, though, to him. She glowed golden brown from the summer's sun. Her eyes danced. He saw beyond her illness, and was aghast when a youngster, no more than four or five years old, passed by them gawking, his head turned completely around, his eyes bugged out. "Hey, mister," the kid said rudely, "You sure have a goofy looking wife."

David was crushed, and his anger surged. "I ought to whip that little shit," he muttered between clenched teeth.

Jannie looked at him and shrugged. She had become accustomed to odd looks. Young women don't show well with nearly bald heads and eyebrows so faint as not to be there at all, she knew. "It's nothing," she said. "I hope he never knows why. Plus," she giggled, elbowing him gently, "He thinks I'm yours!"

They walked the arcade, riding a few of the amusements. Jannie would not go on the Octopus at all, but she did enjoy the Ferris wheel. They both thought the attendant gave them an exceptionally long ride on the wheel, stopping it right when they were at the very top. It seemed that they had forever to look out over the fairgrounds, with Baraboo lit up to the west. The evening sky was crystalline, steeping in the intense indigo twilight. Noise from the midway filled the atmosphere above the Sauk County Fair.

"It's so beautiful," Jannie cried, the sparkling lights shimmering off her eyes. "Just so much… energy. I love it!" She snuggled close to David and gave him a kiss, but the wheel suddenly swooped into motion, their hanging seat rocking freely on its axle. Jannie whooped and screamed, and David burst into laughter. After many more revolutions around the wheel, the attendant stopped the ride with their cart at the bottom. He opened their safety gate and let them step free.

"Best ride at the fair," he said softly as they stepped by him.

David looked at the man. He was weathered, in need of a shave and haircut, but his eyes were clear and gentle. "You bet," David said. "Best ride we've had all night."

"That's the way it should be," the carny smiled. He offered Jannie a hand in getting off the Ferris car.

Jannie grinned. "Yep. It all evens out, doesn't it?"

David looked at her quizzically. "What do you mean?"

"Well, some things aren't so kind. Some things are even kind of mean. Or real mean. Cruel," she explained. "But then other things, little things, little acts of kindness that really don't matter, well, they make up for it. Don't you think?"

He stopped walking, tugging her to a halt. Sometimes she moved him so deeply, he just wanted to take her in, to say something to her from his heart. She stood, grinning at him like a fool. Her bandana had unfolded in the back from the breeze on the Ferris wheel. The pointed corner stood straight up, a swatch of fuzzy hair poking through. David reached up and tucked it back. "Feel a draft?" he asked.

"Thought I'd be an exhibitionist," she retorted.

Hand in hand, they made their way down the midway toward the grandstand. They were plenty early for the main show, although the first singer had already started performing. They heard the twang of his guitar and his gentle, warbling voice carrying from the stage on the infield across the racetrack to the ticket gate. Inside, they spotted Wendy, Mrs. Whitman, and a few of their friends. Sitting a row in front of them, Miss Rose and Father Jack waved with wide, arching motions to get their attention. David chuckled. "Pretend we don't see them," he teased.

Jannie ignored him and headed straight towards her family. David veered off to chat with Miss Rose and Jack. He greeted Father Jack as he climbed the bleachers.

"Howdy," Father Jack replied. "Haven't seen you for a couple weeks. Been busy?"

"Getting ready for the fair. Farming. The usual. How about you?"

"Covering ground, mostly. Been to Reedsburg, LaValle, and Loganville last week. Nice country."

"Meet anybody interesting?"

"A few. Mostly just walking, though. Thinking."

David glanced at the priest. He seemed a bit removed.

Father Jack caught his glance. "I'm feeling a 'calling,'" the priest said with a wily smile.

"I thought you already had a calling," David shrugged. "That's what got you into the priest business in the first place, eh?"

"Well, yes," Father Jack agreed. "I heard a calling, and I responded. That's different. That's my vocation. This is something else," he said, a pensive frown above his deep brown eyes. "I get these. Maybe you know what I mean. Sometimes, I just feel that life is, well, more intense, more real than usual. Something special is happening. Or is going to happen. It's like life is crystallizing right before my eyes. Or soul. It's like, creation happening." He looked at David, searching for comprehension in his young friend's eyes. "You know what I mean?"

David considered it. "I don't know. Maybe," he shook his head.

Miss Rose leaned around Father Jack. "He means that he's being a warrior," she said.

Both David and Father Jack shot her expressions of bewilderment.

"What on earth could you mean?" Father Jack asked respectfully, the slightest hint of satisfaction ringing in his voice.

"When you are a warrior, you become totally focused, vigilant. You are right here, right now, aware, ready, living for the moment in the moment. Then can you hear the calling. Then and only then, can you act. The rest of the time, you can only react to the echoes of now." She turned to face the lone singer strumming his guitar on the stage.

"She must be a real humdinger to live with," Father Jack said under his breath. "Good morning, David. Zen down your pancakes and karma your way into fruition," the priest laughed.

David chuckled.

"It's dharma," Rose interjected, grinning slyly as she kept her eye on the musician.

"Huh?" Father Jack asked.

"Dharma," Rose repeated. "One dharmas their way into fruition, if you must. Or, really, one dharmas their way into one's karma. You're missing a really good show here," she said, pointing her nose toward the stage.

Father Jack rolled his eyes back toward David. "She's using my own theology against me," he murmured.

David sighed. "You guys are a tag team. You know that, don't you?"

Jannie slid down the bleachers next to David, Wendy at her side. "Hey, are you listening to this guy?" Jannie asked, nodding down towards the lone singer perched on a stool with an acoustic guitar. "He's great."

The minstrel's heartfelt melody carried across the grandstands.

You might have heard my footsteps
Echo softly in the distance through the canyons of your mind
I might have even called your name
As I ran searching after something to believe in…

David straightened up, tuning into the lyrics. Jannie leaned against him, her head tipping onto his shoulder.

You might have seen me runnin'
Through the long-abandoned ruins of the dreams you left behind
If you remember something there
That glided past you followed close by heavy breathin'

Don't be concerned, it will not harm you
It's only me pursuing somethin' I'm not sure of
Across my dreams with nets of wonder
I chase the bright elusive butterfly of love…

"S'pose he writes his own stuff?" Father Jack asked.

"Haven't heard a note of it elsewhere," Miss Rose said. "'Cept for a little Dylan in his earlier songs."

David glanced her way. "All you ever hear is me and Old Camp fiddlin', or Jannie if she's playing with us."

"No wonder I've never heard anything like this before," Miss Rose replied, leaving David wondering if she had slammed him. Jannie's elbow in his ribs confirmed his suspicion.

The troubadour's song lingered in the group's thoughts after his last notes had faded, and they sat spellbound. "He must have really loved someone," Jannie whispered into David's ear. As the musician strummed the opening bars of another ballad, Paddy climbed up the grandstand with Old Camp a step behind.

"Been by the beef barn," Paddy said to David. "Your big steer is looking real fine."

David smiled. He had great hopes for Dante. "We'll see how he does in the morning."

∞

After he'd finished with the morning's milking, David left Paddy with the bulk of the barn work. Gulping down a few bites of breakfast, he bid Miss Rose a hasty goodbye, grabbed the keys to the Packard, and headed into town.

Jannie was waiting for him at the Whitmans'. She met him as he pulled to a stop, waved back to her mom at the porch door, hopped in the front seat, and slid over next to him. He turned out of her driveway and sped on down to the fair.

At the fairgrounds, he parked the Packard and they hurried past the midway to the livestock, hand in hand, laughing and chatting about their hopes for the day. In the barn, David went directly to unlock his tack box. Jannie opened the stall, stepped inside with Dante, and stood frozen, perplexed, her mind struggling to register what she saw. Sensing her apprehension, David glanced back to see her standing stock still, her hands suspended halfway to her face. She turned her eyes from Dante to David, puzzled and frightened. She pointed toward Dante's massive hindquarters.

An arc of dried blood matted the sleek black hair of the animal's belly and rump. David moved slowly to the steer's side, gently setting his hand on Dante's flank. The three-quarter ton beast lowed dolefully. David brushed at some of the dried blood. He moved quietly toward his animal's rear.

"It's okay," he whispered. "It's okay. You'll be alright, Dante. Whoa, buddy. Gentle. Whoa." The Angus turned its head back, eyeing his master, shuffling his hindquarters. David gently ran his palms over the steer's rear legs and hocks, finally working his fingers down the long, bony tail.

The cut had been clean, neatly severing a joint. Blood-smeared white bone now formed an abrupt and ugly end to Dante's tail.

"Oh my God," David muttered, stepping back from his steer. Jannie approached him, putting a hand on his forearm. He glanced at her, shrugging his shoulders in bewilderment. "Why?" he asked, simply.

Jannie shook her head. "What are we going to do?"

"I dunno," David said. He was near tears, and his voice cracked in anger and disbelief.

"Let's bandage up Dante's tail," Jannie suggested. "Then we can clean him up. Do you think Dr. Lander will be around this early?"

David rummaged through his tack locker looking for first aid supplies. "I doubt it. I'll go ask in a bit. You're right. Let's get Dante patched up first," he said.

He handed her a wad of gauze and a spool of white tape. Fishing clean towels from the box, he grabbed for a bucket to haul fresh water from the faucets outside the barn. Looking into the bucket, he froze. Glancing up at Jannie, he picked a teased mass of black hair from the bucket. Whoever had docked Dante's tail had thrown the bony tip into the bucket.

Anger welled in David's chest. His face flushed and his eyes closed to narrow slits. "Rotten rat," he snapped, removing the tail from the bucket and setting it carefully, as though it still had feeling, on a shelf above the supply box.

"Davey, I'm going to call home. Maybe Daddy's still there. He can help," Jannie offered.

David looked back at the steer. He couldn't see how much of anything could help at this point, but he nodded. Jannie ran from the barn toward the phones at the 4-H office.

David crooned softly to Dante, wrapping his arm gently over the docile beast's neck, comforting him. He drew peace from the big animal's warmth. Dante seemed unfazed by the injury. He bobbed his head up and down, demanding that David scratch the thick black hair on his forehead and neck. David rubbed the beast vigorously, chuckling.

"Well, if you don't care, then I guess I don't care. We can't afford to bitch about it now," David confided to his steer. "Let's get you ready."

David took the bucket out to the wash faucets. The initial stream of water into the pail brought out a big clot of congealed blood, which slid away over the bleached concrete slab. Adding a stream of liquid soap to the bucket, David filled it until thick white foam bubbled over the rim.

David left the bucket by the wash area and returned to Dante's stall. By then, a number of other exhibitors were up and about, preparing their animals for the day's shows. As David led Dante from the barn to the wash stands, several of his friends noticed the bloodied steer's newly bobbed tail and came over to examine the damage.

"Whoa," Rodney Kohlmeyer gasped. "What the hell happened, Davey?"

"I dunno," David said. "Sure wish I did. But I can't worry about that now if I'm gonna get Dante ready for showing."

"Man, you think you can still show him? He looks terrible with that tail," Rodney said.

David simply shook his head. "I guess I can only go with what I have," he replied. Fastening the lead to a rail by the water faucets, David grabbed Dante's halter, lifted the beast's head up and spoke right into his face. "Right, Dante? We'll go with what we have. If you can't show with a pound less tail, well, I guess you weren't going to show at all." Dante pulled hard on the lead, bobbing vigorously as if affirming David's words.

David was scrubbing blood from Dante's left flank when Jannie returned.

"Daddy'll be here in a few minutes," she said. "What can I do?"

"Well, let's get him cleaned up, first off," David answered, gesturing to a sponge and a stack of towels he'd brought from the tack box. "I'm trying to be careful not to get any soap or anything into that cut. It doesn't seem to bother him, but, man, you'd think it would sting."

Jannie swabbed the opposite side of Dante's huge body, scrubbing hard to dislodge the clots caked into his deep black hide. She worked quickly and thoroughly. After several minutes, David broke the quiet.

"Jannie, I really wanted Dante to show good today," he said, standing on the very tips of his toes to see Jannie over the steer's spine. "I mean, Dante would have been yours to show, if you wouldn't have been gone all spring. He was your project."

Jannie nodded as she continued to scrub at the blood. She looked up at David peeking over the top of his massive beast and couldn't help but smile. "I know, David," she grinned. "I know you wanted to give me the better of your two steers. But things are the way they are, and now you have him to show in the Open anyway. That must be the way it's supposed to be. He's yours, Davey. All yours. You bred Bunny just to get a calf like Dante. And you raised him and groomed him and halter broke him."

She paused. David dipped down off his toes behind Dante's tall backline. Jannie stepped around Dante's hindquarters to face him. "You were meant to show him. Dante is yours. He's like a pet to you, honestly," she said, lifting Dante's wounded tail to examine it. "You know, whoever did this, did it because they were scared you were going to win today. Well, Davey, you have to show like you are going to win. That's all there is to it."

David smiled. "I was just telling Dante something to that effect a little while ago."

Jannie dabbed gently at the blood-crusted tail. "It's kind of funny," she said, a twinkle sparkling her eyes. "Seems like all the critters you love go around losing their beautiful hair."

David laughed, then reached up and lifted the edge of Jannie's bandana. He peeked underneath. "Yeah, but looks like you're doing pretty well growing yours back," he nodded. "I don't think Dante's going to be that lucky." He gave her a quick kiss, thanking her for her encouragement.

"Let's get the big guy ready for the ring."

∞

David eased Dante back in line after drawing him out and walking him in a tight circle for the judge to assess the Angus's movement and frame. He set the beast in place, lightly touching the point of his stick at the split in each of the big steer's polished hooves to spread his mass wide upon its frame. Dante gently lifted each hoof, placing one after the other on the points that satisfied David's sense of showmanship. When David had the steer posed, he drew the stick's barb across the bottom of Dante's massive belly. The beast responded to the tickle, sucking up his gut and straightening his spine to a neat line. David mewed like a kitten and the steer's ears snapped forward.

"Atta boy," David purred, keeping his animal's attention. "You did your best, Dante." His voice was almost a whisper. Certain that the steer had shown well, David shifted his attention to the judge in the ring.

He'd seen this particular judge, Franklin Green from down near Lancaster in Grant County, work the Sauk County Fair before, as well as several neighboring county fairs. Once, when he and Paddy made the trip to West Allis, he had watched Mr. Green slap the rump of a fine, heavily muscled Limousine as he named it champion of the Wisconsin State Fair. Now, the tall, thin man wore a grim expression on his face, watching Elmer Nelson lead his short-legged steer in a circle in front of the line of exhibitors. He knew the judge was influential in the Angus Association. David wondered how he'd take to Dante's long, tall conformation.

David caught a glimpse of Jannie and her father sitting with Paddy and Miss Rose in the bleachers just beyond the judge. They watched as Elmer adeptly led his steer. As if drawn by David's glance, Jannie's gaze drifted slowly away from the action in the ring to where David waited, his steer standing proud, two in from the end of the show line. She smiled warmly at him and nodded.

David thought she looked absolutely beautiful. He loved it when she wore baseball caps, as she did now. Just before he'd led Dante into the ring, Jannie had called them to a halt.

"Wait!" she'd exclaimed. "We can't let him go in looking like that." She slid the bandana off her head, revealing her short, fine crop of downy hair. Folding the bandana, she wrapped it around the white bandages that her father had taped snugly on the stub of Dante's amputated tail. Tucking in the corners, the kerchief added pizzazz to the steer's burnished black finish.

David grinned. The white bandage was a distraction, but Dante wore the azure bandana like a stylish accessory—not as conventional as the classic tail puff, but a pleasing eye-catcher nonetheless. Taking off his Braves cap, David placed it jauntily upon Jannie's head, brim perched high and angled upward. She immediately adjusted it to her liking, her eyes smiling. David led the big bovine into the show barn, its blue-clad tail swinging gaily behind.

"Good luck," he had heard her call.

Seeing her across the arena, David realized how much she meant to him. Everything he did revolved around Jannie. From his music to his animals, he shared all the excitement of his dreams with her. As he showed the steer he had hoped would be hers, David realized how dearly he wanted Dante to take top honors in the open class. He wanted this championship for all it symbolized.

He snapped back into focus as Elmer guided his steer into line with the rest of the class. David looked at Dante, made some fine adjustments, drew the steer's belly up tight with the claw hook, and watched the judge.

Mr. Green paced the length of the class of steers, studying them first from the front, comparing both brisket and depth of chest. He noted the width of the animals between the knees of their front legs, as well as the girths of their bodies. Circling around behind, he paced up and down the class, again assessing the steers' differences. He stepped up to several animals, probing above and below their hip joints, eyeing the width at their pins. He examined the shape of their hooves and the set of their legs. He asked Robby Pollard to lead his Hereford steer out in a circle and set it again in line with the class. He asked the same of Elmer Nelson.

David watched the judge working, his worry increasing as Mr. Green paid ever more attention to Elmer's steer. Finally, the judge pulled up behind Dante. He stepped back, looking straight up the Angus's spine. David watched as the judge moved his eyes discriminately across Dante's physique. David drew the scratch claw sharply across Dante's belly and the big beast hunkered up, looking taller than ever. Mr. Green moved to the animal's flank. He dipped down slightly, bending at his knees, eyeing Dante's backline, which stood a full six inches taller than most of the animals in the class. The judge moved close to the animal, set his hand gently on its flank, and said something softly to the steer, so softly that David could not hear. The judge ran his hand down Dante's backline, pinching with his thumb and forefingers like calipers at the tenderloin above Dante's kidneys. He moved back further, lifting the tail gently, examining the bandana adorning Dante's stub. He looked up at the young man working the steer, keeping the Angus drawn and standing firm. Mr. Green set the tail gently back down and walked up to where David held the halter lead with one hand and his show stick with the other. "Pretty fancy tail job there, son," Mr. Green addressed him quietly. "Not the most conventional, I'd say."

David sensed every aspect of Dante's posture, keeping the steer in fine display as he riveted his eyes on the judge.

"Sometimes you have to make the most of the unexpected," he replied, pulling his shoulders back and holding himself as high as his steer did. "Things happen. You just have to move ahead."

The tall man nodded. "I see," he said simply. He turned on his heel and moved one last time along the line of exhibitors. The spectators crowding the bleachers watched in silent suspense. He took a few pensive steps toward the bleachers. Then, instead of indicating the champion of the class with his characteristic slap on the rump, Mr. Green addressed the crowd.

"What we have here today has made me look very closely at this class of steers," he began. Mr. Green spoke softly, in deep tones. His pronunciation rumbled across the sawdust bedding of the ring to the crowd raptly listening in the bleachers. David strained to hear his every word.

"I've been partial, in the past, to the more conventional conformations that are typical of the British-born breeds. The lower, compact animal with great girth but little waste. Perhaps we've bred these animals to carry much more muscle than they did some years ago. Nonetheless, they've been the staple of the beef industry in this state and throughout the Midwest. And we have some fine examples of that type of steer here today," he said, half-turning toward Elmer and Robbie at the far end of the class.

"Today," Mr. Green continued, picking up the volume and pitch of his voice, "I had to take a closer look at those animals, because we have a fine example of the newer conformation that has been gaining popularity among breeders and packers both. We have an animal here that definitely carries the influence of the South American breeders. It is taller at the shoulder and the pins. It carries an exceptional mass of flesh, promising the packer a fine carcass for cutting. This animal finishes well, clearly maintaining a tremendous rate of gain in the year since its birth."

The judge fumbled for a moment, looking for his words. He shifted on his boots, kicking at the sawdust in the ring.

"On another day, it may have been easier to overlook this tall animal on my left. I even admit, in the past, when I've attempted to judge a steer such as this in comparison to the more conventional types, it's been difficult. It's like looking at apples and oranges.

"But we had events here during the night that the Fair Master has called to my attention. For whatever reason, someone thought it best that this Angus lose the last foot of its tail."

Darkness filled Mr. Green's expression. When he resumed, he ramped up the volume of his voice, his words rolling like distant thunder.

"For the life of me, I don't know why a soul would take it upon himself to bob the tail of a fellow exhibitor's steer the night before the show. But I can say with all certainty, never once in my career as a judge have I seen an animal called to the front for the way its tail was puffed into the most outrageous ball of hair—or bobbed like a cat. I call this class solely on the merits of superior beef animals. And we have a champion."

With that, Mr. Green whirled about, heading to the far end of the line from where David stood with Dante. He rounded the end of the line and headed back up along the other side. As he came up behind Elmer Nelson, he held up his hand, three fingers showing.

"Congratulations, son, you have a fine third-place steer here," he said to Elmer. "Take him on forward and present him to the crowd." Elmer led his black steer to a spot in front of the class.

Mr. Green waited for Elmer to set up, then moved to the Hereford behind Robby Pollard. He held up two fingers. "Present your runner-up," he told Robbie. "You've done a nice job with him, son."

After Robbie had set his steer up next to Elmer's, Mr. Green continued his trek down the class. Stopping behind Dante, he looked quickly into David's eyes.

"Son, tail or none, this steer is a walk-away champion, today or any day. Fine job." Holding up one finger, Mr. Green slapped an open hand on Dante's hindquarters.

"You have a champion," he told the crowd.

"Thank you," David blurted as he pulled on Dante to take his position next to Elmer and Robbie.

The crowd went wild. Leaping to their feet, the spectators in the bleachers cheered the judge's call. By show time, everyone at the fair had heard about the tail-bobbing and the attendance was beyond capacity. Dante and the other steers danced and fidgeted at the commotion of the crowd as Miss Sauk County presented the championship ribbons to David and his runners-up.

David beamed as he held his ribbon for Jannie to see. The only spectator not on her feet, Jannie sat sobbing, her face buried for one moment in her hands, the next looking tear-stained and grinning at her best friend, who led the Grand Champion.

DAVID GROSSED more than eleven thousand dollars for the sale of his two steers at the fair auction. The manager of Eisenberg's Supermarket got into a bidding war with Mark Miller from Miller's Meat Market over who would buy Dante. What at first appeared to be a good-natured duel turned into a stubborn stare down between the two butchers. Mark Miller won out, setting a huge new auction record of four dollars and fifty-two cents per pound for the fifteen hundred and twenty-two-pound championship steer. After being forced to pay more than he'd reckoned for Dante, Miller drove up the bidding on the second-most-desirable steer in the sale, Bruno, who weighed in at fourteen hundred and seventy-six pounds. Miller teased and taunted Frank Knoble as the supermarket manager squirmed to maintain top bid on David's Angus class winner. When Mark was satisfied that the bid would top three fifty a pound, he sat back, grinning across the aisle at a red-faced Frank, who knew he'd been forced to pay more than three-quarters of a dollar extra due to the bluff of his poker playing buddy and fellow usher at St. Joe's.

The payday set David's resolve. He mulled over his herd records, critically examining the production and the genetics of each of his dairy cows and heifers. From there, he made two lists: the culled, nineteen cows and heifers; and the kept, twelve select milking head, and another eight fancy, genetically superior heifers, most of which would be bred to Orbit, his best proven bull. His herd currently averaged near fourteen thousand pounds of milk during their three-hundred-day lactation, about six gallons per cow per day. His girls filled the bulk tank every other day. If he reduced the herd, keeping only the highest-producing females, the herd would initially fill the bulk tank only once every four days. But if he sold off the bottom producers in his herd and replaced them with six to eight genetically superior pregnant heifers purchased from outstanding herds from Wisconsin, Minnesota, Vermont, and Ohio, David felt confident that his herd would be milking enough to fill the bulk tank every other day within a year. With the top producers he already owned and the young stock coming in with the bred cows he'd purchase, he calculated that within two years, between his and Paddy's cows, they'd be filling the new cooling tank every day,

He decided to do it.

∞

"You certain you want to go ahead with this?" Paddy asked, looking at the list of animals David had decided to cull. "You'll be cutting back on your milk check substantially this year."

"Yeah," David agreed. "But, look, within a year the new cows will just about make up for the loss in milk we'll see now. And besides, then you won't be stuck with so many animals to handle when I'm down in Madison next year."

Paddy looked up over his black-rimmed reading glasses. He'd considered herd size carefully, anticipating David's departure for college.

"David, we have forty-six head in the barn now, and I think we could pretty much handle a dozen more with you here on the farm," Paddy said. "Or with a hired man." He rubbed the stubble on his chin, looking over David's list, comparing it to the records on each animal. He nodded his gratitude to Rose as she topped off his coffee with steaming fresh brew. Aunt Kate slid a pan of frosted cake, already half eaten, across the table toward David, who sliced a sliver and stuffed it into his mouth. The cake caught Paddy's attention, and he followed David's lead.

"I dunno," Paddy mulled over the list. "What about the beef cows?"

"Sell them, too. Use the money to buy top Holsteins. Concentrate on the dairy herd. Look, Paddy," David said. "I think that if we cull the herd drastically now, and keep strict, high production standards for the next few years while I'm at school, and we do some real smart breedings, well, I think we can make this herd into something special."

Paddy once again looked over the rim of his glasses at his nephew. "Just what do you consider special?" Paddy asked, almost rhetorically. He thought he knew where David was going with his plans.

"Eighteen thousand pounds, Paddy," David shivered slightly at the thought. "I think we can reach eighteen thousand by the time I graduate. Four years. Whaddya think?"

Paddy studied the list, looking as if he were trying to find a missing element. "That's quite a goal," he said slowly. "I don't think we have a herd in the state averaging eighteen thousand pounds per cow. Do you think we can really get there?"

David nodded decisively. He had no doubts.

"Well," Paddy said finally, pausing to take a sip of coffee, "I think this. We keep the eight best from your cull list, milk them one more lactation, then cull them. That will give us twenty cows from the Holstein milk line, plus however many of these fancy genetics cows you buy with your earnings from the fair and the proceeds from the ones we sell. And," he said, taking a long deep breath, "we ship my Jerseys."

David's eyebrows arched high onto his forehead. "You want to get rid of the Jerseys?" he asked, incredulous.

"Why not?" Paddy shot back.

"I don't know," David said, puzzled. "I just have always thought that you and Jerseys, well… you know. You've always had your Jerseys."

Paddy sipped more coffee and kept his eyes trained on David's cull list. David, Kate, and Rose waited to hear Paddy's response. Finally, he looked up, shifting his glance from David to Rose.

"Well, it's not like quitting the Church, or anything," he said defensively.

David laughed. "Almost, you'd think. Maybe you'd better check this out with Father Jack before you make up your mind," he teased.

"That crazy rebel shaman! He'd probably tell me to take up sheep, for God's sake," Paddy burst out.

"Goats. Jack would suggest goats," Rose interjected, drawing looks of utmost disbelief from both uncle and nephew. They examined Rose's wonderfully neutral expression once, then again in a double-take. Only the twinkle in her eye gave her away. Finally, all four around the table erupted in laughter.

"Goats!" David gasped between waves of rib-cracking laughter. "I wanna milk goats!"

"Here we go," Paddy laughed, leaning back and stretching his legs out full length, preparing for David to go off on one of his routines. Sure enough, he squinted through tear-filled eyes to see his nephew slide off his chair and crouch down low, reaching between the chair's spindly wooden legs, pretending to milk the teats of a goat with the very tips of his fingers.

"There we are," he said, holding up an imaginary mug. "She gave me near a whole cup today," he said, his face wrinkled and red, his eyes bulging with intensity.

Kate rocked in her chair, pleading with him to stop. She was always particularly vulnerable to David's zany humor. "Oh, enough, David," she gasped between peals of laughter.

Rose laughed quietly, shaking her head slowly back and forth as she witnessed David's antics. She looked at Paddy, wondering if he'd keel over with mirth, or simply forget to breathe. The laughter ringing in the Joyce kitchen slowly quelled, until Kate sighed audibly, followed a moment later by Paddy. They all sat quietly for a moment, sipping their coffees, savoring the warm afterglow of a good laugh.

Rose spoke when the spell had all but dissipated. "There are things to tend," she said, looking directly into David's eyes. She turned to Kate, and then Paddy. "David's mother needs to come home." Rose sat quietly, letting each of the Joyces ponder her words a moment before adding, "Soon. It is time."

David softly said, "Wow." He shook his head.

Kate agreed. "I've been thinking the same, lately, Rose."

Paddy and David were caught off guard. Paddy asked Rose, "What made you think of that?"

She thought a moment. "Think what David's mother was missing last week at the fair, when we all were singing and celebrating. She is missing her son growing up. I prayed about it. And I realized, she should be home. We are better medicine for her than anything they can give her in... that place. She looked down at her coffee, and then back to her friends. "You are making plans for when David goes away next year. You are figuring out the details of taking care of his animals. You have never... asked of me," she paused, "...or demanded of me as part of my living here, to be responsible for anything with the herd. But I help anyway, because I enjoy it. I love the animals."

She turned her gaze to Paddy, and held his eyes with hers for the briefest moment. Then, she continued. "Next year, David will be gone. There will be no reason for me to stay here any longer. Unless it is to help David's mother. Will she need help staying here? I don't know. But if she does, I would be glad to be the person to make it possible for her to be here, and not be all alone. If she is to come home, she should be here at least for a while when her son is still at home, before he goes away to college. And if I can be of help with her, I can also be a help to you with the herd, Patrick." Rose folded her hands and placed them on the table before her. Her face once again smoothed into implacability as she let the others consider her thoughts.

David stirred. "How do we know she even wants to come home? Or can come home, for that matter? Will they even let her?"

Kate looked down into her lap, watching her fingers play aimlessly with the ring she wore. "David, Elle can come home any time she wants to. Well, any time she isn't too... apprehensive about it. Too afraid to come home."

"Too afraid?" David asked, bewildered. "What is she afraid of coming home to?"

Kate shook her head. "Maybe she's afraid of all she's lost. Maybe she's afraid of us, of what she thinks we think of her. I don't know. I guess I don't think she'll come home until she's ready. Until she feels it is time. Until she thinks she is needed here."

"How can we make her feel needed here?" Paddy thought out loud. "Especially if she is afraid of us?"

"She is afraid?" Rose asked. "Fear can be a wildfire. But fear can be controlled—by love. Fear is the opposite of love. Love can conquer fear, if it is nurtured. That is all we can do for Mrs. Joyce. Show her love, the love of this family. Every day. Right now. If she can live in our love, she will know no fear." Again, Rose sat erect and calm, her hands gracefully overlapping on the table.

Paddy smiled at the little dark-eyed woman. He nodded at his sister. "Rose's right. It is time," he said. "Before it's too late, before David goes away to school, we should bring Elle back home."

∞

September 12, 1962

Dear Patrick,

How's school? Man, isn't it amazing how school can make it seem like summer was months ago, even after just a week. I can't believe the fair was last weekend. School can do that, can't it?

Paddy and I are going to sell off about two-thirds of my Holstein herd and all of his Jerseys. We're going to use the money we get from the sale along with the money I got for Bruno and Dante to buy ten or twelve really fine Holsteins. We're selling thirty-nine animals, and replacing them with a dozen. Man, the barn will seem empty this winter! We probably won't even have to make hay next summer, with all the feed we'll have left over!

We were going to sell the beef herd, too, but Miss Rose suggested we keep them. We're kind of looking toward next year and after, when I'm at Madison. I thought we'd get rid of the beef 'cause I didn't want to leave all that extra work for Paddy. But Miss Rose said that she'd be glad to take on the beef herd. She's willing to help with Mom, too, if Mom comes home. I don't know if that will be happening, though. Aunt Kate and I went and visited Mom and talked to her about coming home. We told her how much we wanted her home, and how much she was needed here. She got kind of anxious about it. You could just see her expression getting kind of down and worried, just mentioning it to her. I don't know if she is ready yet, but Aunt Kate seemed optimistic about it. I don't know.

Anyway, that is what looks like will happen. Miss Rose will stay here and help with the beef herd and even with milking. She's going to be teaching still, but says that after I'm gone, she'll have a lot of time that she's been spending working with me on French and stuff. I have to admit, she really does spend a lot of time with me, always hanging in there with me as I do my homework, checking it, or even just observing while I do it. She was saying the other night as I worked at a calculus assignment that she never had to take calc, so she wants me to teach her what I'm learning. It takes a lot more time, obviously, but she is really interested, and I get a kick out of doing it. It really seems to help me understand what I'm learning if I have to teach her once I get the idea of the lesson.

I'm kind of looking forward to having more time this fall with the herd numbers way down. We'll have less than twenty cows in the milk line, so milking and chores will be nothing. We'll be out of there in less than an hour. I wouldn't mind spending a bit more time in the woods this fall, hunting. And spending more time with Jannie, too.

Jannie's been pretty good. She loves being back in school. They let her stay with the senior class, so she'll be graduating with me in the spring. We were kind of worried about that last spring when she was in Bethesda. But they figure she's as smart as anyone else in the class. She took a bunch of tests over the summer to show she kept up with the work. She probably would have been salutatorian if she hadn't have missed the whole last half of junior year. Wouldn't that have been something, if she and I had been salutatorian and valedictorian?

I wish I could get to one of your ball games. It sounds like you are tearing them up. Thanks for calling last week. It was good to hear you.

David

∞

The cattle sale went well for the Joyces. David's cows and heifers averaged four hundred and eighty dollars apiece, giving him another nine thousand dollars to invest in the type of Holstein genetics that he had in mind.

Paddy silently watched the last of his gentle brown Jerseys climb into the stock trailer. His entire herd had gone to one bidder from near Eau Claire. He remained quiet all that afternoon. As they worked together to complete the milking that evening in less than a half hour, David wondered whether they had made a mistake in getting rid of Paddy's portion of the herd.

"You alright?" he inquired.

Paddy fussed with the stainless piping in the milkhouse. He kept on working, looking briefly toward his nephew. "Yeah," he said with little conviction. He halted his work, still for a moment. "It's just that I am going to miss the girls. Old friends, you know. But I'm alright." He looked into his nephew's eyes. "Sometimes you just have to let go. And move on."

Fall, 1962

A WEEK AFTER setting the final tie in the wall, Patrick's life was rife with sweat and grass stains. Two-a-day practices tested his endurance and strength in the late August heat. He met the challenge, but it was draining. He was bruised and sore. Through the reps on the hot, dusty practice field, he grew familiar with the movements and power of his teammates as chemistry formed among them. Then, when school started, his focus shifted from the grueling physical preparation for his first game to his sophomore classes. His attention to classes often waned, however, as his daydreams carried him back to the football field. Regardless of sport or school, Patrick's recollections of his summer with Lynn North lingered always close.

The Bishop Noll Crusaders blasted into the season with four dominating wins. The team was a balance of veteran seniors and talented juniors, with Patrick, the only starting sophomore, lining up as running back.

Their fifth game, held in a torrential downpour, was a disappointment. A lesser team from Valpo stymied Noll's running attack with quick, stunting linebackers, holding Patrick to a season low of fifty-two yards on twelve carries, with no touchdowns. Patrick fumbled the slick pigskin on Noll's only serious scoring threat at Valpo's seven-yard line. The ball slipped from his grip, flipped end over end in a neat little arc, and settled right into the hands of Valpo's speedy cornerback. Patrick wrestled free from the linebacker who had popped him, scrambled to his feet, and gave chase. Water squirted and splashed underfoot with every step as he sprinted the length of the field. Patrick gained ground on the cornerback, diving at the five-yard line, only to feel his opponent slip through his grasp. He ate mud and splashed water high around him as he sloshed face-down toward the goal. Valpo won the game, six-zero.

Noll's head coach, Lee Roy Rayborn, was livid after the game. His mood persisted through the following week of preparation, with extra sprints after each practice. By game time the following week, the team was leg-weary. The coach's strategy failed; instead of being motivated, the team was dispirited.

Fortunately, their opponent, Portage, feared the powerhouse private team from the big-city school. By the time they realized how flat Noll was, it was too late. Portage rallied to score twice in the fourth quarter, but with no skilled kicker on the team, failed on the conversions. Noll had scored after a twenty-seven-yard drive in the waning minutes of the first half, after the Portage quarterback tossed a stupid interception. And Patrick secured Noll's victory when he ran the kickoff back eighty-seven yards after Portage's second touchdown near the end of the fourth quarter. The game ended with a score of fourteen to twelve, Noll.

They rolled over their next two opponents.

The final three games of the season posed the biggest challenge: an away game at Chesterton, followed by a game against Hinsdale, a big, powerful team from a huge Illinois high school, and then the season finale at Michigan City. Patrick felt the morale rebuild in his team as they gelled for the final run.

He looked forward to the Chesterton game. He liked playing in front of Jack, who resented that his cousin had left him behind, recruited to Noll's big–school program. Jack constantly reminded Patrick that he could be playing for their hometown team, but Patrick just shrugged. He didn't regret his choice. He didn't have deep roots of friendship with the Chesterton players, and they weren't generally of the caliber of Noll players. There was, nonetheless, a strong rivalry between the schools. Chesterton hadn't played up to expectations during the season, but Patrick felt the anticipation building up within his team throughout the week of practice before the game.

∞

On Thursday, the day before the game, Patrick drove into Chesterton with Aunt Mary to pick up some groceries. Although the evening featured the clear, lovely skies of a warm Indian summer, Patrick took the opportunity to flaunt his Noll letter jacket around town. Strutting a bit arrogantly and quite absently down the cereal aisle, Patrick was looking at Mickey Mantle on the front of the Wheaties box. He wondered whether the Yankees, with Mantle's and Roger Maris's combined batting power, were headed toward winning another series, when he plowed right into someone he'd not noticed. It was Lynn North.

She staggered back a step or two, bumping exaggeratedly against a wall of Cheerios boxes, pretending to have been knocked off-balance by her clumsy friend.

A broad grin claimed his face. He saw through her antics, shook his head, and blushed like a ripened apple. "You did that on purpose," he blurted. He knew she was pulling one over on him, and her beaming smile acknowledged that she was enjoying it.

"Hey, buddy. You gotta watch where you're goin'," she teased, laying on her full Minnesotan accent. "You're wearing the wrong colors to be walking around this town like you own it, ya know," she added, looking down her nose at his letter jacket.

Patrick stood gawking, abashed, dancing little two-steps back and forth. She was really grilling him. He smiled like a loon.

She let up on her ribbing. Digging through her handbag, she pulled out a thick envelope and offered it to him. "It's from Kenny," she said. "You'll enjoy his letter. He talks about how making his canoe was one of the best things he's ever done. He's sending copies of the log he kept while building it."

Patrick started to unfold the letter, but she put a hand over his, stopping him.

"It's too long to read right now. Take it home and read it later. I do want it back though, please," she said. "Okay?"

Patrick nodded. "You bet." He was at a loss for words. Shuffling around the perimeter of a single tile of linoleum in front of the cereal display, Patrick wanted somehow to keep the conversation going. He'd seen her only twice since the start of football. She and Barry had hosted a Labor Day weekend wall-commemorating cocktail party for their Dunes neighbors, and Patrick, Jack, Aunt Mary, and Uncle Paul had joined in the celebration of the vaunted construction project. And he had seen Lynn from a distance when she and Harriet had accompanied his aunt and uncle to the Valpo game.

"You gonna come to the game tomorrow?" he blurted. His grin widened and his swagger returned as he added, "We're gonna kill Chesterton."

Lynn laughed. "I would expect you are. Definitely. I just ran into your aunt over in produce. She asked whether I would like to go to the game with her and Paul, and told her I'd love to. Maybe I'll take some photos, if they let me go down on the field."

"That would be cool," Patrick said. He thought a moment, then asked, "How did those pictures of the wall turn out?"

"Great," Lynn replied, lifting her eyebrows. "I sent some to Kenny. He wrote about them in his letter." She pointed toward the envelope Patrick held. "He thought they were beautiful. When you come over, I'll show you."

Patrick thought he saw a hint of blush flush Lynn's tanned face. He smiled. "Cool."

Lynn backed away. "Play your heart out tomorrow. I'll be watching." Turning, she looked back over her shoulder, adding, "Your aunt asked me to remind you to pick up shredded wheat."

And she was gone.

Patrick stood looking at the space she had just vacated. Her familiar fragrance lingered. "Shredded wheat," he mumbled to himself, turning back to the cereals stacked in the display.

∞

The kickoff arced end over end, the ball illuminated against the crystal clear, periwinkle-blue twilight sky. Facing the south goal, Patrick eyed the ball as it sailed up alongside the full October moon, then tumbled down into his limber fingers. The Chesterton kicker was good. Patrick had backpedaled to the eight-yard line before pulling in the kickoff.

Cheers from both sidelines formed a sound tunnel through which white-jerseyed Chesterton players darted and dodged as they ran toward him across the crisp green gridiron. He saw his team mates forming a wedge at the twenty-five. Patrick loped smoothly across the twenty, veering toward the right sideline, going wide of his blockers. Seeing his projected course, the Chesterton defenders sweeping in around the right flank of the wedge froze in momentary hesitation. Patrick planted and turned upfield, accelerating off his cut. He slashed to his left, needling through a sliver of a hole his teammates had sliced though the Chesterton defense. As he slithered through the tangle of movement, he heard the crunch of pads on pads and helmets on flesh, and the pounding of cleats on turf punctuating the grunts and gasps of players colliding in violent contact. He cleared the line of Chesterton defenders at the thirty-four, with only the kicker left to evade. Patrick adjusted his route, hitting max speed, heading straight for the last Chesterton defender.

The crowd gasped and roared as the kicker hesitated, shocked to see Patrick burst through the scrimmage, free, running directly at him. The defender adjusted his stance, bending at his waist and knees, balancing on the balls of his feet, preparing for the tackle.

The stands exploded on both sides of the field.

Patrick feigned right, a subtle dodge; the tackler committed to the outside, losing his balance. Patrick planted his right foot in stride, cutting to the left across the kicker's face, and felt gravity shift like a pendulum low in his belly, across his body and above his hips. He saw the Chesterton player trip, his knees buckling as his momentum carried him past Patrick on the right. Head down, the tackler swatted desperately at Patrick's right leg as he sprinted by.

The wall of sound flooding the field wobbled drastically. Quiet gripped the Chesterton bleachers as though the spectators had suddenly gasped as one. A few, singular voices called out. "Get him! Get him!"

From the Noll stands, the crowd exploded.

Patrick felt the surge of energy from the crowd's cheer sweep over him, spiriting him toward the goal line. The explosive cheering picked him up like cresting Lake Michigan waves as he rode the pounding surf into shore. He bounded across the goal line, pumped with adrenalin, sucking wind after the sprint. The air tasted sweet. Chambers and Mathews, fellow Nollies, followed him into the end zone, slapping him on the shoulder pads and back. He flipped the ball courteously to the ref, turned, and jogged to the sidelines. Coaches and teammates welcomed him back to the bench with handshakes and helmet-slaps. He sat back on the flimsy wooden bench, his arms draped along the top of the backrest, catching his breath. The cool, dry air felt good in his lungs. The lighting in the stadium was brilliant, the colors crisp, and motion wonderfully fluid. *This is how it should be,* Patrick thought. *This is perfect.*

Coach Rayborn found him on the bench, congratulated him again, extending his hand. "Nice job, Joyce. That was a beautiful run."

"The wedge, Coach," Pat panted. "Those guys rocked 'em." As Patrick shook hands with his coach, the geometry of a tripod behind the far end of the bench caught his eye. Lynn was busily winding the film advance on her Hasselblad, her face studiously focused on the viewfinder. She caught his glance and looked up from the camera, smiling. A slender smile momentarily eroded his stony game face. She clicked the shutter.

In spite of the Nollies' easy kickoff touchdown, Chesterton fought a tough battle. Neither team scored again before halftime. The Nollies tightened up and were playing anxiously, particularly after three consecutive calls from the referee that blatantly favored Chesterton. The Noll stands grew restless, with loud, brazen hoots chiding the officials.

"Homer! Homer!" the fans yelled. Fan behavior concerned Patrick's coach enough that he turned to the stands, raised his arms, and attempted to quell the crowd's anger.

"We'll beat them on our own terms," he told the team at halftime. "Just play our game and don't let the refs get into your heads."

It was not to be.

A flagrant call on the second-half kickoff gave Chesterton an extra fifteen yards for piling on. Starting their drive at Noll's forty-five, they ran off tackle, and then looped a long, graceful pass just over the hands of Cliff Chambers at cornerback. He'd been sucked in, anticipating another ground play. The Chesterton receiver strode untouched into the end zone.

Patrick's runback after the extra point put the ball near midfield, but the Nollies had trouble advancing against Chesterton's big defensive line. Hefty, oversized linemen, the sons of steel mill workers, the aggressive Chesterton defensive line closed down any hole the Noll offense attempted to punch through their line. Patrick caught a flair pass on third and eight to keep the drive going, with a gain of thirteen. The line clamped down on their offense, however, and the Nollies were forced to punt from Chesterton's forty-six. The punt spiraled from Charlie Hinton's foot in a line drive, not long. The Chesterton punt returner nabbed the ball on a dead run, several blockers in good position to cover him.

Patrick cut a sharp angle towards the runner. Just as Patrick aimed to make the tackle, a Chesterton defender shoved him hard from behind, accelerating him involuntarily. Patrick grabbed at the swift little scat-back, his forearm bashing across the runner's face. He latched on to his shoulder pad and wrestled him down at the forty.

Flags flew from several refs, landing at the heap of players. Patrick untangled himself, springing to his feet. He'd clearly been hacked from behind, and he expected to hear a clipping call in Noll's favor. The blocker was still pushing and shoving, caught in his feet as they untangled from the pile.

The head linesman listened briefly to the refs who'd thrown the flags, turned to the sideline and pulled down on an imaginary bar across his face.

"Personal foul, face mask," the ref started to say. "Fifteen yar... ugh!"

Patrick heard the call and instinctively lunged for the ref, reaching out to grab his arm, wanting to explain and protest. Adrenalin, excitement, and anger combined, and his momentum carried him too far, his hand missing the ref's arm and socking him squarely in the stomach. The ref fell backwards, landing plunk on the seat of his pants, the breath knocked out of him.

The crowd screamed and hollered from both sides of the field.

Instantly, more flags were flying at Patrick's feet. The umpire and line judge ran to him, taking both his arms and turning him toward his bench.

"I didn't mean it," Patrick stammered.

"You are out of this game, son!" an angry ref told him. They walked him toward his coach. One of them yelled, "Your player is disqualified!"

Patrick's coach stood, astonished, his arms spread at full width. "What the fuck do you think you're doing? You can't so much as touch an official!"

"Watch your language, coach, or we'll tag another unsportsmanlike on you," the official spat, daring the coach to respond. "Get him off the field."

"Time out," Coach called. As the team assembled, the coach said to Jerry Dillon, his assistant, "Get him out of here. Take him to the bus."

The backs coach put a guiding hand on Patrick's left triceps and steered him toward the end of the field, to where the team bus was parked. The hoots from the Chesterton bench were loud and taunting. The Nollie side was mixed, with some fans' anger directed at the refs, while others shouted meager words of encouragement to Patrick.

Coach Dillon forced open the folding doors on the big yellow bus. "Get in," he said simply.

Patrick climbed into the bus. He tossed his helmet on a seat and pulled at his jersey to rip it off over his shoulder pads. Having shed the jersey, he unstrapped the pads. He grabbed a towel from the stack in the front seat and wiped his face.

"I didn't mean it," Patrick said. "And I didn't facemask him." His voice rose in anger.

"I know," Coach Dillon said. "The facemask wasn't there. But the ref, Patrick. Man, that was not a good thing."

Patrick nodded, his anger quelled by the realization of his impetuous act. He was in trouble.

Dillon looked out the bus window toward the game. Patrick saw that his coach wanted to get back to the sidelines. He felt like being alone, as well.

"I'll be okay."

Coach Dillon didn't know whether to stay or to leave. He watched him a moment, then nodded. "Yeah."

"Go on. Honestly."

The coach left him, jogging back to the sidelines.

Patrick stepped down the stairs of the bus. He sat on the bottom step. Cheers and the noise of the dueling pep bands filtered out from the stadium into the darkness of the parking lot. He draped the towel over his head and buried his face in his hands. Anger once again welled up within him, then subsided. He felt absolutely alone. A sob wracked his breathing. Then another. Inhaling deeply, Patrick hung his head and wept.

∞

The conference sports administrator came down hard and fast on Patrick with a two-game suspension. He could have no contact with the business of the team. Essentially, he was barred from playing ball any more that season.

"It's a shame," Coach Rayborn told him. "For a sophomore, you were having a hell of a season. You definitely would have made all-Conference, at least on the second team. You may have even gotten a little attention from the All-State team. Honorable mention. I don't know." He looked away, disgusted. Patrick's action had not lost them the game against Chesterland. The Nollies found strength to battle back after Patrick's ejection. They held Chesterton on the drive following the thirty yards of personal foul penalties. The teams traded a couple of punts. In the fourth quarter, the Nollies put together one unstoppable drive, scoring on Martin Matthew's scamper around end to win the game.

The greater loss was Patrick. With their two toughest games of the season looming big, his suspension was a major factor. His coach let him know that he had let down his team.

"Clean out your locker," he said curtly. "You're done."

∞

In school, his fellow students were supportive. Some claimed he'd been screwed. Others said they thought he did the right thing, decking the damn ref. Everyone, he felt, looked at him like he was a marked man.

∞

At home, Uncle Paul's reaction to Patrick's humiliation was rational and comforting. "Patrick, just remember that it's only a game. You play by the rules. If you break the rules, you get penalized. If you get penalized, you learn," Uncle Paul rhapsodized over coffee one morning shortly after his suspension. "Games are an imitation of life, Patrick. They're a good way of learning how to control yourself and conduct yourself in the real world. Remember that. A few years from now, you won't be playing football anymore. You'll be getting on with your life. And you have to be aware of what you are learning along the way, how you are interacting with your teammates and your competition. You have to know what you're learning in order to meld your knowledge and experience into wisdom. In the end, games don't really count."

Aunt Mary was not as philosophical. The event embarrassed her, and she didn't know how to explain Patrick's actions to her friends, much less to her sister. She didn't speak directly to Patrick until football season had ended.

Jack, on the other hand, hounded Patrick mercilessly. While openly admitting that he regretted Pat's suspension, he nonetheless railed and ranted about the call, claiming that the facemask was flagrant and carrying on about Patrick "punching out" the ref. At one point, he even stopped grabbing for the breakfast cereal in the morning, expressing his "terror" that Patrick would knock him out if he was left without his regular whole-wheat biscuit and fried eggs.

In a wonderful sort of irony, Jack's insanity restored an element of humor to Patrick's perspective. Jack, quite simply, was nuts. If anyone was out of control, it was Jack. But when he was just kidding, when he wasn't in a mean streak, he was a hell of a lot of fun. Only Jack would talk so absurdly to him. It was reassuring.

Chapter Twenty-Seven

Jannie

October, 1962

DAVID AND PADDY stood in the suddenly-spacious barnyard, watching the big cattle truck pull away with most of their herd. After a long, silent moment, David left his uncle to the solitude and solace of the barn. He finished his evening chores quickly, then hustled to the house to grab a bite to eat and clean up. He hardly noticed as Rosie slipped out of the kitchen and quietly walked across the farmyard to the barn.

Jannie was waiting for him in town. If he was speedy, they could catch the Friday night eight o'clock movie, *That Touch of Mink.*

David showered and dressed in a hurry, and let his foot ride heavy on the Packard's gas pedal on his way into Baraboo. His hustle paid off. They were in plenty of time to get good seats for the film.

Afterward, they picked up a couple of root beers at the A&W on Highway 12. Sipping their sodas, they drove out past David's old schoolhouse, cutting over on Klemm Road to Hoot Owl Hollow. The hollow was their favorite place to park. David pulled the Packard along the side of the road and shut off the engine. Rolling down the window, he drew in a breath of clear, earthy autumn air, rich with the scent of fallen leaves. They hopped out and climbed up on the hood, leaning back against the windshield. Jannie tucked her sweater behind her on the glass to keep warm, although the hood itself was toasty from the engine. She snuggled up close under his arm, and they looked up into the night.

The bluffs enclosing the hollow rose dark and tall against the clear, star-speckled sky. Pines and old white oaks stood like sentries atop the rocky walls. The harvest moon cast its rays from beyond the easternmost bluff, sending shimmering beams through the boughs of the pines. The hollow's shadows swallowed so much light that the navy blue sky appeared remarkably bright in contrast with the black of the gorge leading down to the Baraboo River. A late peeper or two sang in the stillness. David felt safe and happy, his arm warm around Jannie's shoulders as she leaned her head upon him.

"Can you believe that Doris Day?" Jannie started.

"What do you mean? She was funny. Didn't you like her?"

Jannie nodded enthusiastically. "Oh, yeah. The movie was cute enough. I laughed a lot. But I mean, I can't imagine her character. It was like, she wanted Cary Grant. She thought she even loved him. I mean, he really moved her. But she didn't want to do it. She didn't want to make love to him. That's what I can't imagine. Breaking out in hives at the thought of it! Forget it. Too much."

She looked into David's eyes. "That is not the way a woman feels about the one she loves."

They sat quietly, gazing into the night. When the hollow's breeze took on a sharper chill, David slid off the fender. Jannie climbed down after him. They slid into the Packard, lying intertwined on the deep, cushioned backseat. It was their favorite lair. In no time, they were breathing heavily, making out, their hands roving all over each other's bodies.

David kissed her as he undid the buttons of her blouse. She leaned forward, helping him with her bra and lifting her hips so he could slip her skirt and underpants off in one movement. He kissed her breasts, his hand wandering across her smooth belly and into the warmth between her legs. He leaned back, removing his pullover shirt, kicking off his loafers, stripping down his pants and socks in a single move. He fished into the pocket of his trousers, pulling out one of Father Jack's condoms.

Jannie touched her hand onto his wrist, stilling him. Her eyes invited him to take her. She smiled slightly.

"No. Just you."

David trembled with desire. "Are you certain? I mean…."

"It will be okay. It matters to me, really. I just want all that is you." Jannie's voice was soft, but firm and certain. She leaned to him, kissed him, and drew him to her.

∞

Their passion spent, David held her, stroked her face and the soft, smooth skin on her neck and shoulders. The scent of their bodies filled the autumn air with a humid muskiness that pleased him.

"How come you love me so much?" he whispered.

"It is who I am. I am love for you. I know nothing else."

"And I love you," he replied, kissing her lips, then setting his face softly upon her breast. With all his gentleness, he caressed her eyes, her face, her neck. His fingers ran up her neck into her scalp. Her hair was as long as his fingers now, and was silky and fine. He rubbed little circles on her scalp, moving from the crown of her head down along her ears. He knew how she loved when he caressed her scalp and neck. His hand stroked the smooth, cool skin of her face, moving down her cheek, then up along her neck. His fingers split, three along the front of her ear, with his little finger slipping under the lobe. It was his pinky that felt it first. The lump was almost small enough to go undetected. But it was there, and he noticed it, recognized it, his fingers stopping, probing, exploring the pea-sized mass.

She lay below him, calm, her eyes intense, reaching to him, into him. She let him probe, watched as recognition came into his face. She nodded once, slowly, definitively. She reached up, taking his hand, leading his fingers to a spot deep within her armpit. David felt another gland there, harder, a bit larger. She moved his fingers again, to a third mass down between her legs, on the inside of her thigh.

David felt a wave of fear race through him. He sat bolt upright, alarmed. She gathered him back to her breast, holding him in her arms, calming him. They lay, entwined, for a long time.

An owl hooted from up the draw. David heard animals, large hoofed animals, moving through the dried grass and leaves near the base of the bluffs. He heard and felt Jannie's heart, beating evenly, vigorously under his cheek. He felt the wetness of his tears between his skin and hers. And he heard her say, softly, again and again, "I will always love you."

∞

On Tuesday, after milking, David drove into town to watch the end of Game Seven between the Yankees and the Giants with Jannie.

Jannie hated the Yankees. She jeered Mantle each time he got to the plate, though David sensed her tension as she watched each pitch tempt the mighty Yank. He'd had a sluggish Series, but he was still the Mantle. With a one-run game going into the seventh, she cheered the Giants' every pitch, every batter. David smiled, amused by her enthusiasm. He enjoyed playing baseball, and missed the hours he'd spent catching for Patrick in years past. But his interest in the major leagues was fueled primarily by his girl's fanaticism. He chuckled at the realization that she knew most of the players' names. All of them on the Braves. Many from other teams, too. A funny slate of knowledge to pick up at Bethesda, but she had.

During the seventh inning stretch, Mrs. Whitman and Wendy went to the kitchen to make popcorn and cut up the batch of brownies cooling on the baker's rack. As soon as they were alone, David turned to Jannie.

"Did you tell them yet?"

She looked quickly over her shoulder to the kitchen. "No. But I will, soon. Look, I have another one of these," she said, flipping her lip down, exposing a large, spreading canker sore deep in the tissue at the base of her gum.

David winced. "You'd better," he said, "before...."

She looked, tipping her head and peering out from under a raised brow. "Davey, I'm not going back to Bethesda. Or Madison."

"You sure?"

She simply nodded. The aroma of the popcorn wafted from the kitchen. "I hope they don't put too much salt on it," she said, rubbing her lip with the tip of her finger.

"What do you think is going to happen?" Davey asked.

She shrugged, lifting both downy new eyebrows high on her forehead. "I don't know. I guess I'll be like the other kids back at Bethesda. I wrote M.C. about it. I haven't heard from her since the fair. I don't know, though. I just know that these damn Yankees are going to win if McCovey doesn't belt one. "

She pretended to turn her attention to the game, but David could see her flash surreptitious glances toward him. At first, he thought she was holding back a grin. But as she got more into the game, she began to grimace at the duel. The Yankees were closer to taking the Series. The Giants did little in the bottom of the seventh.

Jannie's mom set the popcorn on the table alongside a plate of moist, luscious brownies. David took a handful of the hot, buttery popcorn and stuffed it into his mouth. Jannie looked apprehensively toward him, and he shook his head slightly. She reached instead for a brownie.

"Want some milk? Or soda, David?" Helen Whitman asked.

"Milk, please," was the muffled answer from both full mouths.

"Too salty?" Jannie asked when her mom went for the milk.

David nodded, stuffing his mouth again. "Good, though."

"Rub it in," she teased.

By game's end, the Giants had done nothing. McCovey's best attempt was to swat a bullet out of the infield, only to be snared by a lunging shortstop. Inning, game, Series over.

"Oh, well," Jannie sighed. "Next year."

The game ended fairly early. David asked if Jannie needed help checking on the horses before he left. She leapt at the excuse to be alone with him again, and they pulled on sweatshirts before heading to the barn.

The horses were in good stead. David sat with Jannie on a horse blanket draped over a stack of hay bales.

"So, you have to tell them," he said.

"I will. I just don't want to drop the bomb on them," she admitted. "I guess I'm just kind of afraid. I mean, more for them than for me."

"How's that?"

"Well, Dad will go nuts. He'll want to try everything medicine can do. That is what he knows best. That is how he'll... cope... with his feelings. With what he knows," she said, lifting her eyebrows with apprehension. "I've seen too much about what all that medicine can do." She shook her head. Not again, he understood.

"What about your mother?"

"It will break her heart," Jannie said simply. She looked down into her hands. "But I'm pretty certain she suspects, anyway. Just the way she looks at me. She sees me. She knows. I'm just glad she has Wendy, yet."

They sat quietly for a time. David leaned back, his arms up, his fingers interlocked behind his head.

"How about you?" Jannie asked.

He looked into her eyes, taking a deep breath.

"I don't know. I'm gonna die a thousand deaths, I think. I feel like I'm dying now."

"A part of you is, I suppose. Or will. Don't let it die before me, please. I need all of you," she said.

"How can you be so… calm about this?" David asked, leaning forward, the heels of his hands digging into the edge of the hay bale. "I mean, you're almost blasé about this, and you could die."

She looked keenly into his eyes.

"I'm going to die, David. Face it," her voice was suddenly brittle, shaking, a bit fearful, but filled with caring. "I understand how you feel, how you can't believe…

"But I have seen it too much, at Bethesda. I saw how easy—well, not easy—but how inevitable it was for kids to die. It just got them. It beat them, this cancer." She shook her head slightly, then smiled in resignation.

"And it is going to beat me, too."

"But you can fight it!" David protested. He was sorry he said it. They had had this conversation before, but usually in more confident moments. She often rallied with his support.

Not this time.

"David, you have always said you have to choose your battles," she said softly, taking his hand in hers. "This is not my battle anymore."

Again, they sat wrapped in stillness. Ashen shuffled in her stall, her shod hooves thumping in the dust. David watched a mouse scurry from the grain room into the stack of hay bales.

"So, have you quit fighting?" he asked.

"No," she reflected. "I don't feel that way. It's more like I've just… accepted. What else can I do? M.C. and I talked a lot about this. She wrote about it, too, in her last letter. I wonder if she, too, hasn't had recurrence, sometimes. I mean, she just talks so bravely about living to the fullest with what we have, and not regretting what we don't. That's M.C. all the way. Her way of saying, live it now. You won't have it tomorrow."

She fell quiet, pondering. Silence comforted them.

He asked, "What do you suppose it will be like?"

She laughed lightly. "You know, I've thought about it a lot. I'm alright with death, itself, really. I mean, when you think about it, we are all going to be there, right? Sooner or later."

She paused, contemplating.

"You know, at Bethesda, I couldn't help but see how all those kids who died, well, they just died. Some had family with them. Some were all alone. But they just went ahead and died. And you know, once they actually were gone, it was like, peace. It was like they were... okay, anyway. It is really not death that scares me. Once you're there, well, you're there. It's the dying that frightens me. What I know I have to go through just to die. That's what always made me feel so bad for the kids who were so sick. They suffered. In a way, I'm kind of lucky that I got to see all that. I mean, I'm a lot older than most of the kids that were dying at Bethesda. A lot of them were real young. Five, or eight. Or just toddlers. How could they understand what was happening to them at all? I felt so... privileged to know them, to see them die. They helped me understand."

David wondered. He didn't understand at all. Why did she have to die? He asked her.

"No, no. I don't mean I understand why it is me, why out of all the kids everywhere, I got cancer. No. I don't understand that at all."

She looked at him, first with uncertainty. Then, with clarity.

"I just know that it doesn't matter how we die. We will. All of us. I just know how I'm going to die. I don't really know when. Soon, I suppose. Sooner than I want. But that's not for me to say, I guess. That I can accept.

"So. There it is," she said, simply, smiling kindly, taking his hands.

"Do you believe everything your Church tells you about life after death and all?" she asked him.

He chuckled softly.

"Well, I don't really know what I believe about what the Church has taught me," he said, smiling broadly. "Father Jack has been warping my head, testing everything the Church has ever said."

They laughed at the thought of David's wild-looking friend.

"Well," Jannie resumed, "I think once you've been, you can never not be. I have been. I am. I don't know all that much about what happens... next. But if there is an ounce of truth in what your Church teaches you, I'll still be, right?"

David nodded.

"Well, I will always love you."

He nodded again, squeezing her hands.

She kissed him lightly.

"I'm going to miss you," she said simply.

∞

The following Monday, the world learned that Russia had installed nuclear missiles in Cuba. The world was in crisis, and fear fell upon the American people.

David wondered, as he milked the last of his cows the next morning, whether that would be how he would die, in a nuclear war. Then he and Jannie would both die. Unbelievable, he thought.

He knew deep down that this crisis was unreal, beyond the potential of reality—just games being played by the heady leaders of the world. He could not bring himself to believe that the threat of nuclear war was as real as the threat that cancer posed to someone he loved more than he loved himself.

∞

The nuclear threat seemed trivial to Jannie, as well. She rolled her eyes when the teacher instructed her class to crawl under their desks for protection from the blast of radiation. At first, she thought it humorous. Then, preposterous. She remained in her seat, defying her teacher's instructions to get under the desk.

"Jan, you have to, like all the other students," Mrs. Straubler commanded. "It is for your own protection and safety."

David couldn't help but snicker from under his desk. He found it most amusing to be hidden from the wrath of nuclear explosion by the sturdy, four-legged desk. Being small, he fit nicely underneath the metal desk. He could actually sit cross-legged fairly comfortably. He chuckled at Warren Beasley under the desk next to him, kneeling on all fours, his torso, rump and legs protruding out where his chair normally stood. Warren was a tackle on the football team. At six-foot-five, two hundred forty-six pounds, Warren was vulnerable to nuclear blasts, regardless of emergency school desk protection—but then no more than David himself, he mused.

Beyond Warren, Jannie sat smartly in her chair, glaring at Mrs. Straubler, the social studies instructor. Not only was Mrs. Straubler an ineffective teacher, but she had a sour personality. Jannie had little time for her, or for the exercise the teacher now demanded.

"I have no time for this nonsense," Jannie said firmly. "This is just an exercise in fear and stupidity. I prefer to use my God-given time in a more productive way." She took out her history book, opened to a chapter in the last half of the book, and buried her nose deep within the text.

Mrs. Straubler struggled with her anger. David watched as the plump, middle-aged teacher flushed deep red, perceptibly trembling. She reminded him of Margaret Hatcher.

"Young lady, if you have no time to do the things that common sense dictates in times of emergency, then you had better spend your time in the principal's office. Right now. Go!" she commanded.

Jannie neatly stacked her books, picked them up, and, glancing over at David with a flicker of a smile on her lips, turned to leave the classroom. From beneath the desks, cheers accompanied her on her way.

∞

After classes, David looked for Wendy coming out of school to offer her a ride home. Racing up to Whitmans' to hear what happened to Jannie after she'd gone to Mr. Ackerman's office, David recounted his version of Jannie's stance during social studies to Wendy, who'd heard bits and pieces about her sister's misadventure. Jannie hadn't returned for math by seventh period, so David knew she'd probably gone home.

Indeed, her mother had been called into school after the principal found Jannie to be every bit as unreasonable as Mrs. Straubler had. Helen Whitman was at first dumbfounded by her daughter's stubbornness toward the safety exercise. After taking Jannie home, she learned her daughter's good reason for her rebellion. Jannie took her mother's hand, leading her away from the house toward the sharp white wooden fence lining the green grass of the pasture, littered with brazenly colored maple leaves. Leaning with her arms folded atop the corral fence, she explained to her mother about her recurrence.

When David and Wendy arrived, he found Jannie and her mother inside the house on the sofa, sitting together, both a bit red eyed—Mrs. Whitman more so—but chatting, sipping tea and sharing some of the brownies left over from the night of the last Series game.

"So what's up?" Wendy demanded of her sister, oblivious of the tear stains on her mother's cheeks. Helen wiped quickly under her eyes. Wendy threw her books on the kitchen counter and headed straight for the pan of brownies. "Everybody was talking about how you got sent up to Ackerman's office. How was it?"

David stood in the entry to the family room. He watched as Wendy moved across the kitchen with her strong, athletic stride, biting into the brownie, reading, slowly, the expressions on first her mother's face, then her sister's. She glided to a stop, sitting slowly down on the single step leading from the kitchen to the family room.

"No," she said firmly. "No. No." She repeated herself again and again, each time more quietly. Dropping the half-eaten brownie absently on the floor beside her, she cradled her face in her hands, and just looked at her sister and mother sitting together on the sofa.

David moved to her side. He put his hand gently on her back, between her shoulder blades.

"Wendy, it's okay," he said.

"No," she said, breaking into a sob. "It's not."

∞

When he returned from his rounds at the hospital that evening, Jannie's father was the last to learn about her recurrence.

Initially, he responded with determined professionalism. He examined the lumps behind her ears and elsewhere, palpating the masses. He looked concerned when she showed him the spreading sores in her mouth. He looked at the insides of her eyelids, and pinched her fingertips. He even took her pulse.

David watched with curiosity. Dr. Whitman was the most proper, dignified person he knew. He carried himself with quiet confidence. David often noted that whether he was working the horses, cleaning the stables, or mowing the Whitmans' expansive lawn, Jannie's father never looked ruffled.

Now, however, as he knelt before his daughter, his hands gently palpating the swollen glands behind her ears, David watched a shadow passed over Dr. Whitman's expression. Slowly, the Doctor became cognizant of the reality at the tips of his fingers. David wondered what thoughts, what diminishing hopes whirled through Dr. Whitman's mind. He prayed, silently, that her father would honor Jannie's will. He hoped that he would not resort to his faith in his profession, but love Jannie first and foremost as his daughter. He wondered whether acceptance would be easy, or even possible. And yet, although in his heart he knew better, David harbored slim hopes himself that perhaps Dr. Whitman would find one more medical technology, one last miracle that would turn the tide for Jannie. The look that had crossed her father's face only bolstered David's suspicion that her father knew they'd exhausted their medical options. He looked at her lovingly, seeing her as only a father can peer into the eyes of his daughter.

∞

By morning, after a sleepless night, Dr. Whitman had resorted to his professional knowledge to address Jannie's condition. She would return with him for evaluation by the cancer specialists at University Hospital in Madison. He took a blood sample to check her cell count, but otherwise, patiently compromised with his daughter, letting Jannie's situation ride time.

But, he stipulated with a raised eyebrow and half smile, she would comply with the school's civil defense programs, if for no other reason than to promote a sense of calm and normality among the other students.

Jannie didn't argue with her father about the classroom activities. She conceded, David found out later, in order to focus her arguments against further treatments at Madison—or more critically, a return to Bethesda.

∞

Sitting close together in front of the TV that night, while the President displayed aerial images of missiles stacked on transports bound for Cuba, Jannie shared her strategy with David. Talking in almost a whisper, which annoyed her eavesdropping sister, Jannie assured David that she would remain at home.

"Mom will stand behind me," she said. "And I really don't think Daddy wants me to have to stay away from home. If I have to take medicine, well, I can take it right here. Mom is here. And Dad is a doctor, after all. I just won't take that chemotherapy again. Or the radiation."

David keyed on one word in Jannie's explanation.

"If you have to take medications?" he asked.

Jannie half shrugged, inflecting a glimmer of hope. Then, hooking her lip with her left index finger, she revealed the smooth, pink tissue inside her cheek. Cankers spread evenly across the inside surface of Jannie's mouth.

Raising her eyebrows again, she finished her shrug.

"We'll see."

∞

Jannie stalled her trip to Madison. While Dr. Whitman pressed for her to go, he compromised just enough to let much of the week slide by. On Thursday morning, he said, "Enough."

"We've been camped around the television set every evening for almost a week now. If we don't get your tests done, Jannie, we may never find out how serious this is before the whole world blows up," he argued.

"Exactly the point," Jannie countered. "If Russia and America launch their nukes and we all blow up, then none of those tests mean a thing, really. And besides, I'd rather be blown away by nuclear bombs than go through any more radiation treatments."

"Jan," Dr. Whitman said emphatically, not a shred of patience left in his voice, "We are going to Madison tomorrow. That is all there is to it."

Jannie looked at David, a bit of a devilish smile in her eyes. She sighed, and shrugged resignedly.

"What we don't know won't hurt us," she said quietly to David.

By Friday evening, they learned all they didn't want to know.

David got a call from Jannie just before he headed to the barn for milking. She spoke slowly, soberly.

"Are you coming over?"

"You know I am. I was just going to feed the heifers before milking."

She paused, the silence coming over the phone heavy with anticipation.

"You okay?" he asked.

"Yeah. I'm me. You know. I just…. Can Paddy milk for you?"

David didn't hesitate.

"Yeah. I know he will. I'll be right there."

∞

David was surprised by the atmosphere in the Whitman house when he arrived.

Wendy had left to spend the night at Annie Sprecher's house. Dr. Whitman had already returned from driving his younger daughter to her best friend's. Jannie explained that her father had gone out to the barn to tend the horses and had not yet returned. Mrs. Whitman greeted David warmly, but made little effort to chat. After just a few moments puttering in the kitchen, Helen Whitman put on a jacket and went to the barn to join her husband.

Jannie took David by the hand and led him to the family room. He melted under the warmth of her smile.

"So, how are you?"

She sighed.

"Well, okay, but not that well, I suppose, if you know what I mean. Are we surprised?"

David didn't respond. He waited until she was ready to relate the findings from Madison. They watched absently as Edd Byrnes repeatedly swiped a comb through his hair on Sunset Strip.

The mystery unfolded with dramatic suspense on the television program, but Efrem Zimbalist, Jr., could not hold David's attention. He wondered about Jannie and what she would soon be telling him. But he felt he knew, more or less, the impact of the medical results. He considered the crisis that continued to unfold in Cuba. It did not escape him that no one in the Whitman home seemed concerned about the nuclear missile crisis. Indeed, they seemed oblivious.

"Too bad you missed *The Flintstones*," Jannie told him during a commercial break. "Pretty funny tonight."

David responded with a muted grunt.

She looked into his eyes, and he felt the familiar energy surging through him. She seemed to know how to reach his soul with just a glance.

"There is nothing new," she said matter-of-factly. "My blood count is very high—a lot higher than when Daddy took it. It is all we thought it would be."

She took her place on his shoulder again, and they watched the last few minutes of *77 Sunset Strip*. Kookie made his trademark whimsical remark to conclude the show. Neither of them laughed.

Dr. and Helen Whitman returned to the house just as program started.

"You kids want some ice cream?" Dr. Whitman called from the kitchen, where he was scooping chocolate from a big carton.

"Yes, please," Jannie called over her shoulder, hopping up to join her folks in the kitchen.

"You bet," David answered, following behind.

And together they moved on, living as if nothing of the moment was to change, as if life were as mysterious but predictable as on Sunset Strip, while the world teetered on nuclear disaster, and Jannie's bone marrow spewed out errant cells in a quest for immortality that would consume her.

From the family room, Rod Serling's familiar voice trailed behind them.

"...for you have entered *The Twilight Zone*."

October, 1962

PATRICK QUICKLY FOUND that although his suspension from the football field stung his pride and left him lonesome for the competitive camaraderie of his teammates, it also gave him a new degree of freedom. After cleaning out his locker, he took a few days off, kicked back, relaxed, and healed. He finished *To Kill a Mockingbird* and caught up on some class work. But toward the end of the first week, he was practically twitching with replenished stores of energy that he needed to burn off. He strapped on his running shoes and covered miles of dunes and shore.

On Friday, he went to the game and watched his team struggle to a tie with Illinois Hinsdale. Sitting in the bleachers was odd. He enjoyed watching the game amidst the fans' breathless, boisterous excitement. It was an atmosphere he'd never experienced before. But he felt out of place. He was a player, not a spectator. He made up his mind not to follow the team to their last game in Michigan City.

Instead, he ran the beach. He headed east, jogging lightly on the hard, water-soaked sand. Indian summer persisted, and the air was deliciously pleasant. He avoided the water. Lake Michigan lapped timidly at its shore. Its surface was almost still. What waves there were spanned just a few feet between ebb and lazy rush. He followed the shoreline all the way to the state park, haunting in its emptiness after the bustle of summer recreation. Patrick turned back at the old hotel at the far edge of the park and headed west, retracing his steps, the only footprints in the sand. The beach was still and peaceful.

Drifting down through the dunes from a house above the beach, the smooth, doleful notes of a clarinet hung melancholy in the air. Patrick recognized the tune. Acker Bilk. "Stranger on the Shore." It had been tremendously popular all summer. A perfect Dunes song.

The sky faded to lavender, then indigo, as he jogged further still. There was no moon, and the darkness grew richer and denser. Patrick's eyes searched the sand along the lake for darkened objects, piles, driftwood, hazards that could trip him up. Occasionally, he'd hurdle rather than dodge a dark mass washed up on the beach.

To his left, along the front row of dunes, motion caught Patrick's eye. Something in the dunegrass, perched atop the little mound of sand. A deer, perhaps. On his morning runs, he often found tracks from the herd that flourished in the woods and wetlands south of the beach. He eased his pace in preparation for the last mile before turning back toward home.

Again, along the edge of the beach away from the shoreline, he detected movement. He veered off the packed wet sand and worked his way through ankle-deep dry sand to the base of the dune.

"Hi, stranger." The voice was unmistakable. Lynn North.

"Hi, partner," Patrick puffed. "Whatcha doing?"

"Oh, watching the lake disappear into night. Watching Chicago turn on its lights. Waiting for the moon to rise. Figure if the Russians launch their missiles, it might be the last time we see the moon rise." She forced a laugh. "Where is that moon, anyway?"

"It's a new moon. It will take a couple days. Then it comes up at dawn this month, anyway."

"Really?" Lynn's tone was incredulous. "How do you know that?"

"Gabriel. David, I suppose. They were always watching the sky. You can't help but pick some of it up. I just find myself kind of keeping track of where it should be, when it's coming up. You know."

"Well, no. I guess I don't," Lynn admitted. "It's not something I ever paid much attention to. Join me?" She hitched over a few inches in the bare spot in the long, course grass atop the dune.

Patrick sat next to her. Sweat had soaked through his t-shirt to dampen his old sweatshirt with cut off sleeves. He tried not to muck the sweat running down his arms onto his friend. Lynn leaned casually against him anyway.

"Good to see you."

He nodded. "Yeah." He paused, then added, "Kind of makes me want to build a wall all over again."

They sat in silence, sharing their warmth.

Patrick slid his arm around her back. She rested her head against his chest. After a long moment, she lifted her face, slowly, tentatively. Patrick held her close. She kissed him gently, with a passion that electrified him.

She rested her head against his chest again, and they sat for moments in silence.

Finally, she said quietly, "Patrick, I have no right kissing you like that."

He squirmed, but held tightly to her.

"No," he admitted. "Neither do I. I mean, you're married, and all."

Again, silence.

She looked out over the lake. When she spoke, her voice was soft and clear. "Yes." Once again, she rested her head on his chest. "I'm going away for a while," she said.

"What?" Patrick blurted. The news set him off balance. "What do you mean, 'away'? And 'a while'?"

"Just that. Not too soon. But soon enough. Before Christmas, I think. My sister wrote. It's her idea. But it's a good one. The timing is good, anyway, for me."

Patrick gulped. "How can it be good timing to leave now?" His voice conveyed his hurt.

She looked up at his starlit face. As his eyes adjusted to her closeness, he could see her loving smile. But he could see, too, the tracks of spent tears glistening down her face. He wanted to kiss her again, and tightened his grip around her waist. She lowered her face and leaned once more against his chest. He waited for her to speak.

"Our timing isn't exactly great," she said. "I wonder if it ever could be?" she added, almost absently. "Things are happening in my life right now. Things that I was hoping to ignore. I have to deal with them."

Her head hung lower on his shoulder. He felt her stifle a cry. He felt the heat of her head on the skin of his cheek, and savored the fragrance of her hair as he hovered just above her.

"What?" he asked softly. "What is it?"

Slowly, she turned her head partially toward him, resting her hair against his lips. "Oh. My husband. My marriage. Or, maybe, my not-marriage." She chuckled slightly at her own joke. "It was never really meant to be."

"So why do you have to go away?" he asked. He couldn't see the sense in it.

"I need time, I suppose. I need to have something totally constructive that I can build on while I dissemble this other part of my life that never worked anyway. I need the enthusiasm and craziness of my sister," she laughed. Looking up into his face, she admitted, "And I need to get away from you, too. Before I do you more harm. You and me both."

Patrick began to protest. She felt his body stiffen as he mustered a rebuttal. She put her fingers to his lips, stilling him.

"It's not your fault. There's nothing you can do about this. It's just impossible. It's my fault. For falling in love with you. I do still love you, you know." Her voice both teased and pacified him. "Can you still love me, even if I do this to us?"

Patrick nodded, but he could not talk. A pain gripped him, ripping him apart inside. He inhaled deeply several times before he attempted to respond.

"How can you do this?" he asked. His voice shook with emotion.

"To survive," she said simply. "So that we both can survive."

They sat a long time in silence. She felt his breathing even out, and knew he'd regained control.

"You know, it is funny," he said, shaking his head and laughing slightly. "I don't even know why I feel this way. I mean, I think about you all the time. All the time. I have ever since the summer. I didn't mean to. I didn't even try to. I couldn't believe it when we kissed. You wouldn't believe how I've wondered about that. Why would you kiss me like that? How could I ever possibly do that with you?" His thoughts and feelings flowed from his heart.

She nodded. "I know. I couldn't believe it either. I felt so, well, like I was taking advantage of you. I knew my situation. I had no right to act that way. I did take advantage of you, Patrick. I'm so sorry. I know I hurt you. Forgive me?"

Patrick contemplated all she had said.

"But you love me," he said, his voice soft and sweet.

"Yes."

"Then you didn't take advantage of me, Lynn. You have nothing to be forgiven for. I would have been worse off never knowing. Never having kissed you. Always just wondering if it was just me. Me in my little adolescent mind," he joked.

They laughed quietly together.

He looked down on her face. Her eyes sparkled, deep and dark, returning his gaze. He slid his hand across her stomach, resting tenderly over her breast. She breathed deeply, leaning into him. He could see a smile cross her face, her eyes open to his. They sat for moments, still, content, accepting.

"So does this mean you're not going to show me how to build a canoe?"

He felt the rush of laughter burst from her lungs as she gently patted his face.

"That's the worst of it all, isn't it?" she laughed. "Well, I do have the copy of Kenny's log and directions. We could start soon. But we probably can't finish before I leave."

The last words cut into him again, but he didn't let it spoil the moment.

"That's okay," he whispered, kissing her forehead. "I finished the wall when you couldn't go on. I'll finish the canoe after you leave, too."

Lynn scrambled abruptly to her feet and extended a hand to help Patrick up.

"Come on," she said. "I want to show you some things."

They ran along the beach, pretending to race, pretending to shove each other into the water, laughing. When they got to the blowout leading to her house, they turned and climbed the path up the dunes, hand in hand.

At the house, Patrick went to the fridge and grabbed a couple Cokes. He glanced up at the kitchen clock. Just ten to eight. His team was probably starting halftime, he thought as he joined her in the study. She had pulled out several portfolios and a box of loose photos and set them on the coffee table. Curiosity coursed through him, tinged with anxiety, as he waited for Lynn to adjust the dial to the Valpo country station. When she had a clear signal, she hitched herself up on a stool by the wet bar. Swiveling back and forth, her legs swinging freely, she nodded at her art.

"Go ahead," she directed Patrick.

The pictures were primarily of him. In one portfolio, she displayed the photos she'd taken during the summer while he built the wall. The black and whites were on matted paper, some blown up as large as eleven by fourteen. Others were no larger than a post card. Each page contained either a single image, or a grouping of photos, sometimes as many as five in a series.

Interspersed with the candids of Patrick were settings from the yard. Shadows of dune grass slicing across the facade of sand, perfectly smooth, sculpted into curves and ridges by the wind. Footprints and tail tracks of a lizard climbing up an impeccably smooth wall of dune and disappearing over the sharp crease at the summit of a tiny blow. A jay peering at the camera from just a few feet away, jauntily perched atop a tie in the half-constructed wall. A wide-angle panorama of the horizon to the west in a timed exposure, capturing the haunting, steely light of the waxing summer moon dipping down over the wall of ties, highlighting the step-down architecture; above the wall, a pale strip of beach curved away in the distance toward a beadlike chain of lights from the turnpike far off on the horizon above the lakefront. Long continuous strands of headlights streaked the routes of cars speeding along the distant highway below the pendulous moon. Mostly, however, the images were of Patrick, sometimes capturing his youthful smile and eyes turned towards the lens, other times oblivious, intent on his own efforts.

A wave of humility filled Patrick's chest. The pictures were beautiful. And they were focused on him. In one image, intense July sunlight glistened off the sweat beaded on his tanned arms and back as she'd captured him, shovel in hand, sand flowing in a soft blurred plume as he'd cast it up onto the dune above the shoulder-high wall. In some shots, Patrick's labor was only a small part of a much bigger scene. In one early picture, with the wall only two tiers high, she'd caught him swinging the maul in a full arc, about to set an inch-and-a-quarter thick, foot-and-a-half long pin into the foundation ties. The muscles in his shoulders and back stretched and rippled at the strain of hefting the twenty-five pound hammer. In another, she'd snapped him wielding the chainsaw, woodchips flying from the blurred chain blade in a rooster tail of debris. An image from later in the summer showed him perched on the nearly completed wall, leaning back on his elbows, a can of soda in one hand.

Some of the photos were humorous, particularly those featuring both Patrick and Harriet. Lynn had caught the rapport between the two in a shot where he sat side-by-side with Harriet, a dictionary spread across his lap, his finger pointing mid-page, as they both studied a folded section of the Times, in which she marked the same word with her plump baker's finger. Another picture drew a loud guffaw from Patrick. Harriet had her back to him as he sat on a tie in the third tier. She was pointing toward the wall. Even in profile, she made her opinion clear, frowning slightly, her lips pursed. Behind her, the basket of sandwiches and treats stood open. Patrick held half a sandwich, with a crescent-shaped bite cleaved from the diagonal cut across the bread. He held his mouth as though something foul sat upon his tongue. His chin sagged and his lips pursed loosely, barely able to contain the repugnant mouthful. He looked away from Harriet, his eyes unevenly half closed. His shoulders slumped forward, with the tight, rippled belts of muscles across his belly meeting in an indentation dropping from his sternum to the band on his shorts. He crossed his feet, much like a little kid dangling his legs from an oversized rocking chair.

Patrick laughed again. "Eggshells," he said, studying the image. He turned the page.

The last series of images, the photos that Lynn had taken on their last day of work, were placed one per page. The first was of Patrick alone. His face was boyish as he looked sheepishly away from the lens.

Lynn had moved into the frame for the second picture. She sat in the planter, her knees tucked up under her chin, her arms wrapped gracefully around her legs. Her hair was wet and slicked close to her head. Patrick peered out over her shoulder, looking squarely at the camera, his face handsomely neutral. He looked older, more mature with Lynn at his side.

In the third image, they were similarly positioned. Instead of looking at the camera, however, Lynn looked up into Patrick's face. The light reflecting off her face illuminated the highlights of his lean cheekbone and straight nose. He held a wrinkle of tension in his eyebrows as he returned her gaze. His lips were open just a crack, as if he'd been startled. Lynn had cropped the image closer than the previous portrait. The couple was framed by the ties of the planter. The chemistry between them was palpable, and Lynn had captured it with her framing.

Patrick studied the photo closely, recalling the moment before the shutter had snapped. Lynn had been so gracious, filled with such immense gratitude. Patrick sighed, then turned to the last page.

In the final portrait, Patrick looked boldly at the camera, his jaw line square and even, his eyes confident and determined. He looked older, manly. His arm draped gently over Lynn's shoulder, his fingers entwined with hers, close to her breast, over her heart. She looked defiantly, happily at the camera. With her hair damp against her scalp, pulled back above her neckline, she was stunning. Resting against Patrick, her fine frame was dwarfed by the width of his shoulders and body. His forearm covered a quarter of her torso. His hand and fingers swallowing up her long, thin digits, poised gently over her breast. It was impossible to tell whether he cupped her in his palm. It looked as though she had drawn his large hand gently upon her.

Patrick studied the picture, reexamining his expression, then hers, and their posture. The portrait was charged. He felt the stirrings of arousal. He flushed, burying himself in a final inspection of the photograph.

He looked up at Lynn. She was sitting on the barstool, watching him, studying him. She'd drawn one leg up underneath her, the other bent at the knee and tucked up under her chin. Her arms were wrapped tightly around the uplifted knee. Her face radiated joy while tears streamed down her face. She met his glance, and they locked eyes.

"I'm going to miss you," she said simply.

Patrick could say nothing. He set the book aside. He wanted to go to her. Her eyes told him no, not then. She gestured toward the other book and the box.

"There aren't as many shots of football, but they are fun, even if some are pretty blurry."

Many of the football pics were fun, just as Lynn had said. Several were spectacular. The Chesterton game series was laden with emotion. She'd caught him stepping high, the hand and arm of a would-be tackler falling from his powerful thigh, as he broke away on the opening run. A jubilant team surrounded him, his coach shaking his hand, as he returned to the bench. His winsome smile as he glanced at her from the bench. Patrick clubbing the helmet of the Chesterton ball carrier with his forearm as a blocker clipped him from behind. Patrick, fully extended, almost horizontal, airborne, his hand reaching out, about to make contact with the zebra stripes of the unwary official.

Patrick startled when he turned to the last image of him, steam lifting from his dampened tee shirt, towel draped over his hanging head, alone and dejected on the steps of the bus. The photo was in high contrast, with Patrick sitting in the darkness away from the brightly lit stadium in the background. He was almost completely in silhouette, the side of the bus reflecting the lights from the field. His hands held the towel across his face. Patrick had not known Lynn had been close by.

He looked up at her. She wore an expression of caution, uncertainty.

"I hope you don't mind..." she began.

He shook his head, looking back at the photo. He couldn't find his voice, and the image blurred as his eyes teared up.

"I wish I had known you were there," he whispered. "I didn't know you were so close." He looked up at her. "I would have wanted to know you were there."

She nodded, then changed her gesture to the negative. "I thought you needed to be alone. I was respecting that."

He sighed softly as he examined the image. "You're probably right. Back then, I probably did want to be alone. It was the loneliest moment of my life." He shook his head again, and wiped his eye with the back of his hand. "Now, though, I wish I had known you were so close. I'm glad I know you were."

He sat, turning back through the images.

The radio purred a country ballad.

They sat quietly for a while. Then Lynn slid down from the stool and joined him on the couch. Carefully, slowly, they once again paged through the images, sharing their impressions, laughing, savoring the summer they'd had.

∞

In the weeks after the Cuban missile crisis passed, Patrick and Lynn set the keels for each of their canoes and began installing the ribs. She insisted that they do two.

"Perhaps we won't get either of them done before next summer, but I'd rather have two so that we can each have one after we're done with this project," she rationalized.

It didn't matter much to Patrick. Doing two would take longer, and that meant more time with Lynn. If that's what she wanted, that's what they'd do. What could be better?

Lynn bought all the necessary materials and the tools, a battery of clamps, saw-horses, and other necessities to do the job right. They set up shop in her garage the week after President Kennedy informed the world that Russian nuclear missiles were a mere hundred miles from the U.S. mainland. And while Uncle Paul, Aunt Mary, and every other adult he knew was totally absorbed in the missile crisis, Patrick didn't fret about it. Instead, he and Lynn focused on the project that kept them busy every evening and weekend until she would leave to join her sister for their winter trip. He only wanted whatever time he could have with Lynn before she left.

The Saturday they started, Lynn filled a large mug of coffee for Patrick and topped it off several times as she made him sit through a three-hour session during which they poured over Kenny's instructions for building the boats.

As they poured over the instructions, Patrick figured with the time he and Lynn had to put into the canoes, they'd complete a third of the project by Thanksgiving, four weeks away—and he hoped Lynn wouldn't leave before then. He was working on the hope that she might stall her departure until nearly Christmas, if they were making good progress. After a final review over the last of the coffee and some of Harriet's warm, crumbly cinnamon coffee cake, Patrick set the saw horses in place and together they laid the keels for two seventeen-foot cedar sided canoes.

"Got a letter from Davey," Patrick said as he fixed a rib onto the keel a couple of afternoons later.

"Oh?" Lynn replied, bent over the raw skeleton of the vessel, her eyes focused intently on the angle at which Patrick set the rib into the keel.

"Yeah," he said. "Jannie's not doing so well."

"Really," Lynn said, looking from her work. "Not her cancer again, I hope."

Patrick nodded, grimacing. He pulled his brother's folded letter from his shirt pocket and handed it to Lynn.

Lynn hitched herself up on the countertop alongside the vise and electric tools. She swung the bench lamp over to illuminate the letter. She recognized David's neat and uniform handwriting.

October 27, 1962

Dear Patrick,

Well, Jannie's sick again. Or still, I suppose. Only she's getting worse. She was down in Madison this week, and they did all the old tests again. Her white blood cell count is real high. She says she isn't feeling bad, except for the sores in her mouth, like big canker sores. She had them before, last time she went East. I guess I can see she's kind of getting tired easy again. And she's kind of puffy and swollen, especially her face. Not bad, but it just makes her look a bit different.

It is unbelievable. Especially the way Jannie just kind of takes it in stride. I mean, it is like she just accepts it as if it was just the way it is supposed to be. I suppose if it were me, I would see it like that too, maybe, if I had been through all she went through out East. She says she knows it was happening, that she just knew it was still there. That her body was losing quietly to this cancer. How could she have known?

It is kind of funny to be with her. She says she is so grateful for me to be with her and support her and make her feel strong about facing it, this cancer, again. Oh, I try to be strong for her sake, but sometimes I feel like just screaming and screaming. Why? Why Jannie? Why this? I just don't know who to scream to.

You know, she told me—well, really, I kind of figured it out after I found some swollen glands behind her ear—and we didn't even tell her folks for like forever it seemed. She told me the day of the auction, that night after we went to a movie. And she didn't tell her folks for more than a week! I couldn't believe it. She said it wasn't important when they knew, cause they'll know sooner or later. She said it was better for them to have the time that they didn't know.

I guess that I can understand that. I mean, if I didn't know yet, I think I wouldn't be feeling like I'm going crazy half the time.

I just don't know.

Paddy's taking it kind of hard, too. And now that we don't have all the cows for him to be busy with, he's going half nuts, I think. You know how he always is busy. Man, he's always working on something. Well, now with just a few head left in the milk line, he's got too much time on his hands. He is just cruising around looking for things to do. He's even tagged along with Father Jack on some of his cross country hikes around the county. He's been working on the house a lot, 'cause he says we got to get it in tip-top shape for when Mom comes home. Well, I'm sorry, but who knows when that will be? Soon, maybe? He's also been making firewood like there is going to be a hundred-year winter. I don't know. I think he's going crazy, too. He is just nuts about Jannie.

Father Jack was by this morning—early! Man, he walked into the barn just as we were starting to milk. It was still pitch black out. He looked like he'd been out for a leisurely stroll—like for about all night! He said he'd taken the route from North Freedom south to the Natural Bridge, down halfway to Sauk! Then he turned around and came up the highway past the powder plant. I asked him why he didn't just come straight over the rail trestle. He said if he had, he would have arrived about two in the morning and nobody would have been up. What sense did that make, he asked. Man, I think everybody here is going nuts!

Maybe not Miss Rose, though. She is something else. I just can't believe her, sometimes. I mean, when I told her about Jannie, it was as though she knew already. She surely wasn't surprised. Just like Jannie's mom. I told her, Rose, well, Jannie's sick. She may be going to die. Miss Rose just smiled in this kind little way of hers, and she just said, yes. She said everybody was going to die, just that Jannie knew she was going to die sooner. Jeez, I thought she had been talking to Jannie already. That's just how Jannie talks. Anyway, then Miss Rose said this really weird thing. She gets this look sometimes, like she is seeing about a hundred miles away. And she says, "Jannie's here to show us how to die." Then she looks right at me, like right into my head, and says, "Jannie is here to show you the way." Oh, man, Patrick. Sometimes Miss Rose is a real case. I mean, she says something at this level, and really means something at a totally different level, and you don't know if she meant it to be at the first, obvious level, or at something altogether different. She can be really spooky at times. Father Jack says it is no wonder she likes reading John's gospel the most. And right now, when I'm about half going out of my mind, sometimes I can hardly look at her for fear that she'll say something that will bend my head into a pretzel. You should be here when she and

Father Jack get going. Whew! Even Jannie gets going with Miss Rose sometimes, and you wonder what the heck they are talking about. Jannie really likes Miss Rose.

Well, maybe Mom should come home now. All the rest of us are about half crazy. She'll probably feel real comfortable. She'll probably be able to make some sense of this for all for the rest of us. I sure hope so.

Well, I'm going in to town to see Jannie, so I'll mail this on the way.

Hey, write, why don't you. Or give me a call or something. I miss you. I mean, you're never around anymore.

Love,

David

"Wow," Lynn said softly as she scanned the letter again. "Davey's really hurting, isn't he?"

"Yeah. Can you believe it? I mean, like, wow, I can't believe Jannie's sick again. I just about can't remember Davey without Jannie being around."

Lynn looked down to avoid his eyes, then returned his look when she caught her composure.

"I'm not surprised," she said bluntly, her eyes glistening. "I didn't practice nursing for very long, but I did enough to see kids who were sick with leukemia. I was really surprised that she was doing well at all during the summer. They were lucky to have the summer, she and David."

Patrick thought about it. He had shared all of David's letters with Lynn, enjoying Lynn's responses as she got to know his twin from his writings. But she did seem reserved, or reticent, sometimes, when she read David's optimistic and happy accounts of Jannie's return home and the fun they were having as she regained health. Now it dawned on Patrick what he had seen in Lynn's expression. He wondered why she hadn't shared her suspicions with him earlier. But he understood, he thought. It was her way of kindness.

Chapter Twenty-Nine
Homecoming

DAWN HAD YET TO TAKE COMMAND of the eastern sky, Elle noticed. Or maybe it was overcast. She bobbed her head, ducking under the valance that hung across her bedroom window. No, there were stars above. Not bright, and certainly not the entire Milky Way. But there were stars glowing softly through a thin, hazy cloud cover. In the southwest, a sliver of moon arched downward, hovering above the hills of Dane County. If the clock at her bedside was at enough of an angle that she could read the face, she could lean back, if she wished, and she would know what time it was. It didn't matter. *It is today,* she thought, *and that is all that matters.* Today. She knew today that she was going to go home. Sunday. The Holy Day. She was ready to go home. She had decided. Now, if somebody would just come by her room, she could tell them so.

∞

Nobody was more nervous about his mother coming home than Miss Rose, David thought. His teacher and mentor had been living on the Joyce homestead for more than four years—a quarter his entire life. He knew her as well as anyone could know her, he supposed. In company, she was often so quiet that she went unnoticed. She listened carefully to everything everybody had to say, and seemed to understand the true character of each individual she observed. When she did add something to an exchange, she often stopped the conversation in its tracks. Nothing more could be added. The truth had been spoken. She could sum up the entire discussion and deliver resolution with a quiet, sparse sentence or two.

She often gave town folk the willies, David noticed. More often than he cared to remember, he'd heard his schoolmates joke that Miss Rose was a fine replacement for his mother. Just as crazy, in a different way. Spooky, they'd say. He knew they were repeating things they heard older folks saying at home. He wished they could know her better.

If there was one thing of which he was certain, it was that Miss Rose was not crazy. She was different, yes. Removed, sometimes. Subtle, and very deep. He'd spent many nights in conversation with her, sharing intense, rapid-fire exchanges of ideas. At the end of these dialogues, he often found that he better understood his own outlook on life—without having hers imposed upon him. She'd taught him how to think, he reflected. Or rather, how to discipline his thinking. He had never seen her discomfited, neither in class when he first got to know her, nor since she had moved into the big old Joyce farmhouse.

Now, he chuckled, she was flustered. He could tell, because she had busied herself doing something that didn't come naturally to her. She was housecleaning. Normally, she cleared up after herself, and lent a hand with the shared household chores. She was innately neat. But now, she was deep cleansing. She was scouring.

Admittedly, the house had been looking more like Paddy's bachelor pad than it did when his mother was home, working desperately to keep everything tidy and in place. That's one of the things that drove her nuts, he thought. Trying to keep up with Patrick, the walking human tornado. Entropy in action. Patrick left a wake of destruction like a herd of cattle rampaging through harvest-high oats.

Miss Rose was just about the opposite. Nothing in the house ever really looked lived in since she'd arrived. She never left a trail. If she studied a book, or journaled in one of her spiraled notebooks, it was never left out. In the kitchen, she never left a trace of anything she ate. She'd pull the same cup or plate from the drying rack, use it, clean it, and return it to dry. She was frugal with misspent energy, and lived with a graceful ease of effort. Honestly, David thought, a deer in the bluffs was easier to track than Miss Rose's movement around the Joyce house.

Now, with Elle's impending return, David watched Miss Rose labor with chores she wasn't used to undertaking. She dusted and moved every lamp, book, knickknack, and piece of furniture. David chipped in with the vacuum cleaner, and helped wash the insides of the windows. He enjoyed it as much for the fun of watching Miss Rose vibrate with anxiety as to channel his own anticipation and excitement at having his mother due home the next day. But when Miss Rose started in on the chandelier hanging in the vestibule at the foot of the stairway, David laughed openly.

"You have to be kidding," he teased her. Sitting on the stairs, he watched Miss Rose, high up on a folding ladder, spraying and wiping each of the ornate glass prisms. "I mean, I never even saw Mom do that."

"No matter," Miss Rose said. "She'll be glad to see it done. Better yet, if it goes unnoticed, then she'll be most comfortable. But if she sees it dusty and in need, she'll think we've been neglecting."

"I guarantee you, my mother will never notice whether or not there is dust on those things. Heck, you could put manure on them, and she probably wouldn't pay any attention to them."

"What makes you say so?" Miss Rose asked as she buffed a glass orb.

"She didn't focus."

Miss Rose stopped polishing. "Don't think for a minute that she missed anything, David. Just the way things were when I got here tells me your mother knew exactly the condition of every square inch of this house."

David wrinkled up his face in disagreement. "I'm telling you, you didn't know my mom."

"And I am telling you, there was much to your mother that you don't know, either." She spoke quietly as she continued her task. "Your mother had every linen napkin folded perfectly, each set in precisely the same manner in the buffet. Every book on the shelves was in alphabetical order by author. Good Lord, the canned goods were even stacked next to each other by content and height. Have you ever looked in her bathroom medicine cabinet, David?"

"Yes," he conceded. He had seen the ordered arrangement of medicines, ointments, bandages, powders, and razors on the shelves of the cabinet. All labels faced out, and the containers were arranged first by category, then by size. He contemplated Miss Rose's argument. "You have a point. You should have seen how she organized her garden."

"Hand me those clean towels, please," Miss Rose asked.

David fetched a handful of old towels. Standing at the base of the ladder, he passed them up to Miss Rose. "So why are you doing all this?" he asked. "She's going to know we've been living here. You can't hide that. It will look unnatural if everything is exactly like it was when she left. Better, even. And it doesn't look bad."

Rose paused again and looked acutely at her young ward. "David, when your mother gets home, I want her to have her home be exactly as she wants it. Exactly as she expects it," she said. She looked down into her hands, folding the towel around her fingers. "Except that I am here. I am what will be different. I'm here, Patrick's gone. Somehow, she has to find that acceptable." The expression on her face indicated how severe the consequences might be if Elle wasn't comfortable when she resumed living in the Joyce homestead.

David looked around the vestibule and into the living room. "Is there anything else you can see that I should do?" he asked. Grabbing one of the towels, he swiped the rungs of the wooden staircase.

∞

What is the most frightening aspect of this next step? I can't seem to focus on it. Events just spin around in my mind as if they are being sucked down into a whirlpool, sweeping everything into a great homogenous slurry. What is so strange is that it doesn't upset me. I feel the fear, but almost with amusement. Intrigue, perhaps. I'm resigned to the fear, so the fear is idle. Toothless. It doesn't bite. I know it is there, but it doesn't rip me apart. It can't. How can it? Perhaps the surges of current with which they plied my brain left nothing contiguous to rip asunder any more. It doesn't matter. I know what is best. I think I always have, even though I chose the other. How narcissistic of me! So splendidly selfish. Hiding in the folds of my fear, simply to avoid facing the pain of sorrow and grief. How foolish. To think, opting for the pain of fear over the pain of sorrow! And accepting the pain of loneliness. Grief heals sorrow. I should have grieved purely. Love heals fear. I am going home to practice love. And to reap some as well.

∞

Elle inhaled the aroma of rich coffee wafting from the kitchen. It feels good to be alive, she thought. She listened to the subtle sounds of Rose's early stirrings. Her little friend was as quiet as a shadow. She had a good heart, Elle thought. Pure. Focused. One's perception of others is enhanced, sensitized, through removal in time and space, Elle reflected. She saw her home, her family, in a different light now that she'd returned. Things had changed. David was not a boy anymore, regardless of his size. He carried himself as an adult. He made decisions like an adult. Probably better than most adults. He communicated so easily. Her younger son was as intense as ever, and his energy was compounded by the grief that welled within him, contained behind levees of courage. Elle was glad to be home.

She neatly folded the afghan in which she had curled, wrapped and cozy in the big rocking chair, watching dawn bud through the family room window. She'd watched David cross the yard to the barn in the hazy moonlight. He arrived at the milk house just as Paddy walked across the road. Paddy. Dear dependable Paddy. He had raised her boys like a father. He had seen them through their days as youngsters, energetic, wild, and innocent. She held dear the close bond between Paddy and David. They shared so many interests. Perhaps David was attracted to the things he loved, the animals, the farming, because he was so drawn to the things that made up Paddy's world. She saw as they met in the light flooding the milk house door, saw the brief smile of a morning's greeting cross David's lips as he looked into his uncle's kind face. Paddy gently clapped his nephew on the shoulder, saying something unheard but doubtlessly encouraging, kind, nurturing. The men entered the milk house, and a moment later the windows of the barn spewed diagonal shafts of silver light, slashing through the fog that rose from the moist autumn soil.

Elle placed the wrap under the table alongside her favorite sitting chair. *Oh, how I missed you during my long exile from the farm,* she thought as she patted the chair's puffed pillow.

"Good morning, Rose." Elle greeted her friend as she entered the kitchen. She spoke softly, so as not to disturb Rose's concentration on her work. "You look so lovely this morning. And fresh. Are you planning a big day?"

Rose glanced up from the dough she was kneading, catching Elle's eye, a hint of blush in her cheek as she smiled shyly. "Nothing special," she replied. "David wants to go to the Whitmans' later this morning. I thought I'd go to the library. They have some books I requested from Madison. How about you? Would you like to come into town with us?"

Elle considered for a few seconds. "Yes. That is what I'll do." She poured a cup of coffee and brought the pot over to refill Rose's mug. "What is it you ordered?"

Rose glanced up from her work. "I've been reading the works of a priest that Father Jack knew from his early years after the seminary. A fellow named de Chardin."

Wiping her hands on a towel, she left her work and walked lightly into the back hall toward her room. She returned in a matter of seconds, holding a thin, worn book.

"This is Father Jack's," she said, handing the book to Elle and returning to the dough, which she spread into a metal pan and set above the oven to rise. Then, after quickly cleaning up her mess, she pulled up a chair and quietly watched Elle inspect the book.

Clad in a smooth, faded cloth cover, Father Jack's book looked more like a hefty journal than a printed book. Elle opened the cover. In fine, delicate script, a gentle hand had inscribed the words *Le Phénomène Humain* on the title page. Beneath the inscription, the author's name was centered above a date, 1952. On the opposing page, a note, written by a different hand, ran at a jaunty slant across the open space. It read, *Jacques, read this. Learn it. Translate it for others to read in English. Travel always with the speed of God, and dwell always at the Godhead.— Teilhard.* The pages were vellum, filled with handwritten script. The book was hand bound.

"It is in French," Elle said, slightly disconcerted, mesmerized by the smooth surfaces of the pages under her fingers.

Rose smiled kindly. "That's alright. I can read it to you," she reassured her. "Or we can pick up a translation at the library."

Elle wrinkled her nose. "What is this all about?"

"The book? Or de Chardin?" Rose asked.

Elle frowned as she carefully turned pages, then inspected the carefully crafted binding. "Well, both, I suppose. I've never seen a book like this. It's handmade."

"Father Jack made it himself. He knew de Chardin. Met him in New York. They were both Jesuits," she explained. "He traveled out west with him, to California and up into Montana. He was enamored with de Chardin's thinking, his philosophy and theology. He said that Chardin told him he could have a copy of this book, but that Father Jack would have to hand transcribe it himself. So Jack copied every word of it."

Elle paged through some of the inner chapters. The script was meticulously neat. Each letter of every word was perfect. She shook her head in wonder.

"He must have been possessed to have copied all this! Why didn't he just buy a copy?"

"At the time, there were none. It wasn't published until 1955. Chardin was controversial. The Church had a hard time with his ideas. Still does."

Elle lifted her eyebrows, rolling her eyes from the manuscript that she extended to arm's length.

"Oh," she said, knowingly. "Dangerous stuff, eh?"

Rose chuckled. "Not so dangerous. Liberating, perhaps. Challenging. Exciting," she said, her eyes gleaming.

"Well," Elle considered. "What does this Chardin have to say that is so provocative?"

Rose looked deep into Elle's eyes. Her expression was grave and sincere. She considered her words before sharing with Elle.

"He said that right now, this very moment, you and I are in God's mind. We are in the forefront of God's thoughts. We are part of his act of creation. And his creation is one continuous, evolving act. That all of creation has been as it is just so that we can be at this moment in life. And by being aware of this moment, by participating in this moment, we contribute to the way God creates. We contribute through our will, the free will God has given us. We have evolved into our role as participants in creation. Our intellect, our spirituality, everything we have been given evolves with the surging wave of God's creation. Our choice, our free will, is to fashion how that creation looks to us, right here, right now.

"That is what I take from it," she added, after a pause.

Rose shrugged, dispelling the moment of tension and excitement. She gently reached for the book, taking it carefully from Elle's unmoving fingers.

"Let me read a passage or two."

∞

Rather than keep the car and have to leave earlier than he might otherwise want, David asked that Miss Rose and his mother drop him off at Whitmans' on the way to the library. He'd walk home, he said, if he had to, before milking that evening. He wanted to be able to stay with Jannie as long as he could.

Miss Rose assured him that she'd drive back into town and pick him up in time for chores. Perhaps, she noted, she and his mother might be busy in town until then anyway.

David found Jannie feeling punk. She looked drawn and pale. For the first time in months, Jannie had a low grade fever. They played a couple games of cribbage. There was nothing on television. They read. David stayed close to her all afternoon. At times, he just held her.

When Miss Rose and his mother drove in to pick him up, Jannie was napping. He kissed her gently on the forehead. She stirred.

"Are you leaving?" she asked.

"It's time," he said.

Through her veil of pain, Jannie smiled warmly.

"Soon," she said.

He nodded.

"I'll be back. Soon as I can," he said. "Tomorrow."

She nodded, watching him until he was gone.

∞

November 2, 1962

Dear Patrick,

Well, things have sure changed around here. Mom's home. More than half the cows are gone. Jannie's getting sicker. Some things good. Some things not so good.

She is really different than I remember. She laughs more. She doesn't seem quite so nervous. Quite. I don't know if she is all that happy or not. I really can't tell. She just seems more involved. More engaged. She dresses kind of funny. Like some of the Jehovah Witnesses that come around the farm, apostlizing. Real old fashioned. I think she's wearing Gramma Joyce's clothes that have been hanging in the closet forever. Figure that one out.

She and Miss Rose hit it off like old friends. It's neat. Miss Rose is teaching French to Mom now. Thursdays are French-only days here in the Joyce house. Even Paddy is trying to learn a bit of the language. But Mom and Miss Rose really are going at it. They head to the library most every other evening. They're having a lot of fun, and it seems real good for Mom. It's been neat having Mom home again.

You know how I wrote you about being worried about Paddy? Shipping the cows and all. And Jannie, too. Paddy was really taking it hard. Well, not so much anymore. He's been doing all right—even when he's trying to speak French! Seems like he just one day decided to start getting on with life again. Keeps saying he's just happy hanging out with all of us good guys. He's even been going out hunting with Gabriel and me after I get home from school. We've taken a few grouse—our shorthair Basil really has a nose for finding those birds! Mostly we've been watching the deer herd. There is a tremendous buck that we've seen back in the hollow several times now. Gabriel says he's been watching it all season, since spring, really when it was in velvet. Paddy is just fascinated with that old buck. He is eager to go out with me every chance I get.

And I've been getting more chances than ever lately. Jannie is real sick again. I've been over there as often as I can. Most times, lately, I see her just a little while. We get to talk some. She hasn't gone out in like a couple of weeks.

The other night, she was telling me about what she thought it would be like in, you know, heaven. Well, she doesn't actually talk about heaven. We talk about the afterlife. The 'herenow,' she calls it. I asked her if she thought it would be like knowing everything, and knowing people like Dad, and that kind of stuff. She just kind of laughed. She said that she didn't know if that would really be important anymore. She said it is probably possible, but maybe just not what would matter. She talked about the compelling, all-encompassing presence of God. Sometimes, she talks at a level that I don't even know where she's at. Sometimes, I think she is in a different world already. Then other times, it is like she's buzzed up on the drugs that she's taking. The painkillers and such. I don't know. When I tell Father Jack about what Jannie's saying, he gets all wound up. He thinks she's a saint or something. He goes nuts about what she's thinking. Sends him out walking the hills and valleys all across the county.

She told me a few nights ago that she was absolutely sure that she'd be with me always, though. I don't know how I feel about that. Sometimes this pain I feel 'cause she's dying is so raw, so sharp, that to think of how she wants to be with me or thinks she'll be with me always is even more painful. I feel so bad for her. And, really, sometimes I feel so bad for me. I can't believe this is happening to us.

I don't know. I guess I write these things to you because, well, other than Jannie, I am closer to you than anybody else in life. Mom's been talking to me about Jannie, and she's trying to be real helpful. But, you know, it is kind of different having Mom back here. She's different than I remember. It is like getting to know her all over again.

I feel close to Paddy, of course. But we kind of have this way of agreeing not to talk a lot about Jannie. He'll ask just about every morning at milking, "How's Jannie doing?" But he really only wants to hear that nothing's changed much, or that she's sick. We don't ever seem to talk about what it really means to us, personally. I think it hurts us both too much.

Well, I gotta go. Mom was talking about calling you soon. That will be cool. It'll be good to hear your voice. But I'm glad I can write to you about these things. I really need it.

Your brother,

David

∞

On the Monday after he'd sent his letter to Patrick, David got a call from Mrs. Whitman.

"David, Jannie's asking for you," Mrs. Whitman's voice was both tentative and urgent.

"Is she okay, Mrs. Whitman?"

"Well, yes. I don't think it's critical, but she seems very restless. She's been asking for you all evening."

"I'll be right there."

He'd just showered after chores, so he quickly threw on some clothes and grabbed the sandwich that his mother had been making for him. He was always famished after evening milking and chores, but his hunger would have to wait.

∞

She didn't focus on him at first. He could tell, even though she looked toward him, that her mind was not immediately there. Or it was shielded behind the layers of pain that she fought. He had a moment to see her as she lay struggling with her disease. She was pale and excruciatingly thin. Gaunt in some ways, puffy and swollen in others. Her eyes were dull, focused far away. She breathed in shallow, even breaths spaced hauntingly by gaps of deafening stillness. A heavy, sweet odor of disease filled the air of her room.

In a moment, she surfaced. Her eyes flashed, almost twinkling. Her smile reclaimed her face, and sweetness illuminated her expression.

David smiled in return, going to her bedside, taking her warm, dry hand in his. They looked into each other's eyes, then he bent down and kissed her. She raised her face ever so slightly to meet his lips.

When she spoke, it was as if they were continuing a long, ongoing conversation.

"I have been thinking how I will be with you even after I am gone," she said.

David startled. He heard Mrs. Whitman leave the room and walk away down the hall.

"And how will that be?" he asked. He blinked his watering eyes.

"It's okay," she reassured him, reaching up and wiping a tear track from his cheek. She sounded absolutely confident, but her voice wavered in a quiet, high pitch, higher than her normal tones. "Davey, I... saw... him." She wrinkled a brow, her face warped in confusion. "Or her. I don't know. You know. The... source. The light. You saw him! You told me. I mean, I was there!"

She looked at him, her face radiant with hope that he understood what she knew. He looked at her, his eyes bound under a furled brow, afraid. He knew what she saw, and he understood what it meant. She saw through his fear. Shaking her head, she smiled again, taking his hands and pulling him closer. He sat on the edge of her bed, and she drew his hand upon her breast.

"Davey, you are my heart. I love you. I only wish I could tell you what it means to be there." She leaned forward, and whispered urgently. "I was there. I mean, I am there. And so are you."

She leaned back upon her pillows, nodding for emphasis. "We will always be there. We have always been there. There is here. It is here right now.

You don't have to be afraid, Davey. There is no room for fear there. Just joy." Again, she nodded.

David looked into her eyes, searching to find his Jannie. She returned his look intensely. What he saw was timelessness. Freedom. Peace. She loved him immensely. Eternally. He knew her love without doubt. A peace settled upon his heart. She held his soul in her arms.

Once again, she nodded.

He smiled, and she relaxed against her pillows.

"So, have you figured out why?" he asked.

She looked at him, weighing his question.

"Why us?" she asked in return. "Because. We were meant to be in this together. Why me, leaving you? Because. That was my role. My duty. I am here so that you know where you are in life.

"Why you, for me?" she continued. "Because I couldn't have made my way alone. You are my reward for being. We have been in this together from the beginning. It will only seem like we will be apart after I leave. For you anyway."

She smiled.

"I bet you that you won't live a day of your life without me in your heart, if not in your mind. You may try to forget me, but your heart won't let you. I'll be your elusive butterfly of love. You'll always be trying to catch me, and I won't be there in your hands. But remember, I'll be there, always. There will be signs, always, when you need them, along your way. Just look in your heart."

After a moment, she cautioned, "Let my memory help you live, and love. Not keep you from it."

She watched his tears run down his face and splash off her hand clasping his. She smiled again, and closed her eyes.

"You are so sweet," she told him, falling into a light slumber.

∞

Two days later, Jannie slid peacefully into a coma.

Her parents stayed by her bedside, sometimes together, sometimes in shifts, almost an entire week, until she died.

Wendy went to school when she could muster the energy to control her emotions. If she attended her classes, David drove her home after school. He would stop in to see Jannie, sleeping deeply, living only for her next breath. He would wonder, *where is she now?* Could she tell he was here with her? She said she'd always be with him, but as he stood by her bed, looking at the vessel that had carried her spirited soul, he knew, he felt, that she was as much in his heart as she was in the disease-ravaged shell of her body. More so.

He'd stay for just a moment or two. Then he'd take to the woods until dark, and sometimes past dark, right up until milking. He hunted, but never took anything. Mostly, he stepped noiselessly through the dried autumn leaves, watching for life, remembering everything he could about Jannie.

When, on Monday morning before milking, Mrs. Whitman called the farm to say that Jannie had passed just a short time before, David was prepared. After taking the call, he walked out into the clear, crisp darkness of the November morning, inhaled the clean cold air, and looked deep into the star-speckled sky. Exhaling long and slow, he stepped off the porch on his way to the barn, where the girls waited for him.

∞

Harriet was perched upon the top rung of a short step ladder, reading commentary from the *The New York Times* when Mary knocked on the window of Lynn North's garage door.

Patrick and Lynn glanced up from their canoe.

Harriet hopped down off the ladder to greet Patrick's aunt.

"Well, well," she said, holding open the door. "Such a pleasure. Come in, Mary! Come in! Would you like some tea, or coffee?"

Mary stepped through the doorway, a cool blast of air rushing in along with her.

"Hello, Harriet," she said, accepting a hug from her neighbor. "Coffee? I'd like that, please."

"Hi, Aunt Mary. What's up? I didn't expect to see you," Patrick said as he finished tacking in a strip of cedar along the smooth, curved hull of the canoe.

Lynn stepped around the canoe to greet Mary as well.

"Come in. Good time to take a break. Let's have some coffee. Harriet brought some brownies over. Would you like some?" she asked, leading Mary from the garage into the den. Patrick followed behind, eager for Harriet's treats.

"I sure would," Patrick answered.

Mary followed Lynn into the kitchen. She was anxious about delivering the news from her sister in Wisconsin. Elle had said that both she and David had tried reaching Patrick when they thought he'd be back from school, but no one had been home. Mary had just returned from Michigan City when the phone rang. The word of her nephew's friend's death was not unexpected. David had written Patrick regularly, and they had talked the week before. Nonetheless, she regretted bearing her message.

Lynn sensed Mary's apprehension. As she handed her a mug of coffee, she asked, "Is everything alright, Mary?"

Mary looked to her nephew. "No, I'm afraid not," she said. "David's friend died this morning, Patrick."

Patrick reeled as he absorbed word of Jannie's death. He set his coffee on the counter and looked around, bewildered.

"Man," he said softly. He looked down into his hands, shaking his head slowly.

Harriet, too, looked bewildered, but for lack of understanding of the situation.

"Is this somebody you knew?" she asked, looking inquisitively first at Patrick, and then at Lynn.

Lynn stepped close to Patrick, putting her hand gently on his shoulder, then sliding down his arm to take his hands in her own.

"You okay?" Lynn inquired. Patrick nodded, looking absently around the room.

Mary intervened.

"Pat, I told your mother that as soon as you got home, I'd be sure you called."

He looked at Lynn, pleading with his fraught gaze for understanding, clinging to her hands.

"I knew she was sick," he said, his voice raspy and breaking. "I knew she was dying. I just didn't see it coming…."

Mary stepped in and put her arm around her nephew and held him close to her side.

"Oh, Patrick. I know this hurts. No matter how prepared you think you are, it is always a shock when someone you know dies. Especially if it is someone close," she said.

"Let's go. I'll take you home. Your brother and mother are waiting to hear from you."

∞

That evening, Lynn dialed the Howards' phone. Jack answered, and she asked for Mary.

"Hello?" her voice came on the line.

"Mary, this is Lynn North. I was just calling to see how Patrick and his brother are doing."

"Oh, Lynn, I think he'll be alright with it. They talked. I think David did most of the talking. Patrick was fairly quiet. He'll be okay. He's sleeping now. I think it all just fatigued him so." She didn't add that he had wept when he heard his brother's voice. She had left him alone in the library, but could hear the mumblings of his conversation through the louvered doors. Patrick had not said much.

"That's good," Lynn said. She was uncertain how to proceed. She decided to go head on. "Mary, is Patrick thinking of going to be with David for Jannie's funeral?"

Mary paused a moment, gathering her thoughts. She had considered that briefly, but she had not discussed it with either Patrick or her sister.

"I don't know, Lynn. It crossed my mind. My sister didn't know when the funeral was going to be, yet," she said. "We'll be talking, I'm sure."

Lynn took a deep breath. She wondered for an instant whether, if she said anything, she would be committing herself to a path she might otherwise not take. *Oh, be damned*, she thought.

"Mary, if I can help… I am leaving, you know, to travel with my sister. I think it is a good time to head to Minneapolis… before winter really sets in and all. If it would be a help, I'd be glad to drive Patrick home. It is right on the way, I think."

Mary listened to Lynn's offer. She had briefly considered making the drive herself, and wondered whether she would need to pull Jack out of school to take him along. He was such a problem. So temperamental. He would hate to have to drive all that distance for the funeral, just to drive back. But she couldn't leave him home. Paul was deep into teaching his fall semester courses and had a grant due. He couldn't possibly join them. She didn't really want to make the trip herself without Paul. She'd have to cancel bridge club, which she was scheduled to host on Thursday, inevitably a travel day if not the day of the funeral. She'd thought of sending Patrick on the train, but what Lynn North was suggesting might be the easiest on her nephew.

"Lynn, that might be a help," Mary said after a pause. "I'll discuss with Patrick whether he wishes to be with David. I'm sure he will. He hasn't seen his mother, either, for a long time. This might be a real good opportunity, if you're sure you wouldn't mind?"

"Not at all, Mary," Lynn said, a sigh in her voice. "I'd best head north before the snow starts falling. And I'd be glad to help Patrick out. Let me know."

"I will. Thanks, Lynn."

"Good-bye, Mary."

∞

Patrick was a bundle of mixed emotions.

A road trip with Lynn North had to be a fun event, even if the road led to a funeral.

And to saying good-bye.

Lynn drove her Thunderbird with a heavy foot, speeding along the interstate at more than 70 miles per hour. Patrick commanded the radio dial, switching back and forth from WLS to some of the smaller local stations from towns along the way. He crooned along with Elvis—*I can't help falling in love with you*—and did a front seat twist to Chubby Checker, feeling the beat and rhythm of the music piped into the car several decibels louder than would allow normal conversation. Lynn laughed and sang along, occasionally begging him to change stations, sometimes demanding a different song, and other times imploring him to go back to a station that was in the middle of a good tune.

"How's Wisconsin look to you?" she asked as they passed the exit for Oconomowoc.

Patrick squinted as he looked out onto the autumn countryside. The pure, clean sunshine cast long shadows across fields turned by plow blades. A few tenacious maple leaves clung to mostly bare trees, flagging blaze red in the breeze. The oaks were clad in dried, brown, curled leaves.

"Kinda wide open, isn't it?" Patrick said. "A little flat around here. Pretty, though. Not like in the bluffs by Baraboo, though."

"Oh?" Lynn mused. "Must be nice there."

Patrick raised an eyebrow. "You'll see."

They rode in shared silence for a while, and then chatted again, exchanging their thoughts about his schooling, her family, what he wanted to be "when he grew up," her excitement about the trip with her sister, until they reached the Madison turnoff. Lynn swung the car north, following the signs for Portage, Wisconsin Dells, and Minneapolis. They were getting close. The pace of their conversation kept up with the speed of Lynn's car.

By four o'clock, they were off the interstate, heading west on Highway 33 into Baraboo. Patrick was chagrined that he could offer no help in directing Lynn to the farm. He knew it was further west of town, but until he saw familiar landmarks, she had to rely on the directions Paul Howard had carefully written down. Within a few minutes after passing through town, she turned the Thunderbird south onto Joyce Road, crossing the bridge over the Baraboo River. They had but a mile to go until she delivered Patrick home.

They passed the first two farmyards along the road, the Klemms' and the Kohlmeyers'. Patrick sat forward in his seat, looking off to the south.

"There it is," he said softly. Lynn saw excitement and joy in his expression. The farm stood off to the left of the road, toward the edge of the long, flat bottomlands rising from the river to the north up to the foot of the

Baraboo bluffs to the south, east, and west. The valley cut deep into the bluffs, carved by the snaking course of the river that ran to the southeast from the bridge over which Lynn drove. Between the farms, many of the fields stood open where plow blades had turned under the coarse fiber from the summer's bean or corn stands. In other plots, sun-bleached stalks of corn stood tired and haggard in the field, shabby and littered with broken leaves and bared, dried tassels. A flock of Canadian geese waddled and foraged along the edge of a corn stand. Rich yellow kernels peeked out from splitting husks on heavily laden ears. As they approached the last large field lying green with shriveled and frost-nipped late-growth alfalfa, Patrick perked up, pointing toward the dark, heavily wooded hillside beyond, to the east of the house and barn.

"There's Davey," he said. He fumbled with the switch for the electric window. A cool, dry blast of air gushed in around Lynn's shoulders and neck. It was refreshing, filled with sweet and acrid aromas of fall in the country.

Patrick could squeeze little more than his shoulder and arm out of the T-Bird's small window. He waved furiously, blasting Lynn's ears as he bugled his brother's name again and again.

Lynn saw three figures illuminated in the last rays of the late afternoon sun, one toting a gun, standing on the far side of the alfalfa field along the base of the hillside to the east. They were a good ways from the farmyard as she pulled into the drive between the house and the barn.

"Park there," Patrick indicated a spot near the walk. He threw the door open, leaped out, and sprinted across the farmyard.

"Come on," he called, spinning to face her, taking a step or two backward, waving for her to join him, running ahead to meet his twin. Patrick beamed.

Lynn watched Patrick easily vault the fence between the farmyard and alfalfa and sprint full tilt toward his brother. She could see David's features now, dark hair and light skin, much lighter than Patrick. He was slight, nearly a foot shorter than his brother, and of much lighter build. He, too, beamed a wide smile as they ran at top speed toward one another.

Lynn caught her breath when, just steps from his brother, David dropped low, spread his arms wide as if to hug Patrick, but rather clutched his brother just above the knees, wrapping Patrick's legs in a clean double leg tackle. Patrick's momentum carried him over the top of his little brother, and David turned and twisted as he swung Patrick onto his back. The smaller of the twins ended up on top, hooting and hollering, buffeting his twin with a flurry of playful punches to the shoulders and chest. Their laughter spiked the country air like the cackling of crows. Lynn had never seen a cleaner tackle take down her young friend in any of Patrick's football games.

Lynn watched the boys frolic while at the same time eyeing the two people approaching from across the field. She could see their smiles as they neared the brothers, rolling like puppies in play. She started, however, to discover a thin, dark-haired, pale woman standing next to her, watching the boys tumble in the alfalfa.

"Just like a couple of young wolves," Elle Joyce spoke. Her words flowed like a brook, little inflections rippling across snags and boulders beneath the surface of the water. Her tone was not lacking feeling, but emotion was not the current that electrified her statement. There was kindness, and there was affection. But there was something else, and it stirred melancholy deep within Lynn.

She turned to meet Patrick's mother.

"You must be Elle," she said. "Patrick's mother?" Her voice trailed up at the end. "I'm Patrick's friend Lynn. Lynn North."

She felt Elle sizing her, up and down, inside and out. Her eyes didn't wander, Lynn noticed, but stayed close upon her face, looking almost squarely into her own eyes, but up just a fraction, and center, as if peering at a point on her forehead. Lynn had wondered during the trip how she would feel meeting Patrick's family, particularly his mother. In the few seconds that passed in silence between them, she felt warmth and trust from Elle Joyce.

Elle extended her hand, and when Lynn accepted it, Elle closed her other hand over Lynn's, pressing gently, meeting her gaze.

"You are very kind, Mrs. North, to bring my son home," she said, shifting her eyes to the group of four who were now close to the farmyard. "David needs Patrick to be home now. We all are glad that he has returned."

With Elle's attention shifting back to the activity in the alfalfa field, Lynn looked closely at Patrick's mother. She appeared younger, much younger, than at first impression. Perhaps it was the one cluster of grayed hairs streaking from her right temple, standing in stark contrast to her deep brown, almost black hair, that gave the impression of age. Her attire certainly hid her youth. With a loose-knit, cabled Afghan snugly wrapped around her shoulders over a prim, high-collared blouse, Elle Joyce was engulfed in a fashion that seemed decades out of sync. Patrick had said his mother was not yet forty—slightly older than her own brothers, Lynn thought. Elle's clear, smooth skin vouched for her son's description. Just a hint of crows' feet around her eyes creased an otherwise youthful complexion. Much of her appearance suggested a young woman, but a woman of the 1930s or '40s, or even before. She could have been Mary Howard's mother forty years ago, Lynn mused.

Elle returned her eyes to meet Lynn's, still warmly clasping her hands. "May I call you Lynn? Certainly you'll join us for supper, won't you, Lynn?" she said. "And you'll stay the night before heading on to, where did Mary tell me, Minnesota someplace?"

"Minnetonka," Lynn said. "Near Minneapolis. I really thought I'd...."

Her protests were interrupted by Patrick's raucous clamor as he hurdled the fence into the farmyard, whooping it up, exuberant to be home with his family.

"Hey, Mom," he called from mid-air over the fence. "Wow! It sure is good to see you."

He wrapped his arms around his mother in a big bear hug, engulfing her in a squeeze that brought a huge grin to her face. He leaned back, lifting her feet right off the ground, where they hung useless until he set her back down.

"My Lord, Patrick," she said, her voice rising with excitement. Lynn noticed, however, the steady, even gaze of her eyes as she examined her oldest boy.

"You're a giant! What has my sister been feeding you?"

"Enough, Mom. Aunt Mary's a good cook. Ummm!" He turned to Lynn, stepping closer to her while keeping his mother wrapped up with a strong right arm. He reached behind Lynn, ushering her near with a gentle touch of his hand between her shoulders.

"You've met Lynn?" he asked rhetorically. "I've been telling her all about you. And David. And the farm."

Swinging them both around, he extended the introductions to the three hunters arriving from the field.

"Lynn, this is Davey. You know all about him. And Uncle Paddy. And Miss Rose, I believe," Patrick beamed. "Man, it is good to be back home!"

Rose nodded to the twin.

Lynn took in a warm welcome from each of the new faces. She felt as though she knew each of them from Patrick's description and stories. She thought from their expressions that they knew nothing about the closeness between her and their Patrick. She felt compelled to accept their demands that she stay for at least a meal. She was drawn to the chemistry of this family. She warned—commanded—herself to follow reason and leave immediately upon dropping Patrick off.

Instead, she listened to her inner voice. She felt the gentle warmth of Patrick's huge hand on her shoulder blade. She looked deep into the kind eyes of the round-faced, graying farmer carrying a small-bore shotgun and two ruffed grouse. And she felt the inquisitive, hypnotic glances of both of the small-framed, dark-haired people standing before her. Rose Truewater stood calmly, a bland expression on her dark face, her deep black eyes carefully, politely, but thoroughly examining her. And the twin, shorter than she, fair skinned, with keen, sharp eyes bearing a hint of sadness, but eager and excited.

It was David who turned her will completely, captivating her with energy and charm.

"The wall builder!" David laughed. "Come on in! You have to come in!" he said, taking her side opposite his brother. Placing a gentle hand on her elbow, he drew her toward the house ahead of the rest of the party. His tone dropped to conspiratorial. "You know, you just have to tell us how on earth you got my brother to do that kind of serious labor."

From behind, she heard a loud guffaw from Patrick's uncle, and she glanced toward Patrick to see him curl his lips into an embarrassed smile, his cheeks flushing red in the cool air.

And she let her mind surrender to her heart. She wanted to see Patrick with his family. She wasn't ready to leave him just yet. She wanted to know more about that which she was leaving behind.

∞

After dinner, Lynn helped Rose clean up while Elle put on a pot of coffee. Paddy oversaw the measurements of the boys as they added to their growth marks on the doorframe of the pantry.

"Wow," David said softly, inspecting the tape at Patrick's new mark. "Six one and three-quarters. Man." He looked down sharply at Patrick's feet. "What do you got on, some extra thick socks, or what?"

Patrick grinned boldly. Obviously, he'd grown a good bit since he left home, and the half-foot gap between his last two marks confirmed it.

"Nope. No thick socks," he said, holding up his foot to show the threadbare white cotton. "Let's see how you've done, Twinny."

David backed up against the door jam, stretching his spine for all it was worth. Paddy held the pencil level on his head and dashed the wall. David quickly spread the tape to see his new height.

Five feet, three inches exactly.

"Hmmmph," David grunted, satisfied. He, too, had grown, almost four inches since the last time they had marked the door almost two years before.

"What? Were you standing on your toes?" Patrick quipped, pressing down on David's shoulders and earnestly examining the mark as Paddy added the date. David swung his elbow back, whomping Patrick squarely in the solar plexus. Patrick coughed, then laughed as he chased his brother into the living room and administered revenge for the punch. The noise followed the boys away, leaving the kitchen with a moment's peace.

"You and Patrick," Rose addressed Lynn in quiet tones. "You've become close friends?"

Lynn considered the question, and decided to answer candidly.

"Yes. We worked quite hard together all summer. We've grown to know each other."

Rose nodded.

Lynn wondered where she meant to go with this.

"How is life for Patrick in Indiana? Is he... accepted? Does he have friends?"

Lynn again measured Rose's questions before answering them. She didn't want to embark on the strength of her friendship with Patrick. But, she realized that he probably spent more time with her than all of his other friends combined.

"I think so," she said. "He enjoys his teammates, his sports. He seems to be thriving."

"Would he do better coming home?"

Lynn pondered that question thoroughly. She sensed Elle was listening to every word as she busied herself with coffee cups, saucers, and dessert plates for the cake. She answered in Elle's direction.

"Better? I don't really know. We talked a little about just that notion on the way up here today," Lynn said. "He enjoys his aunt and uncle very much. And he has great dreams and aspirations for his football team next year. I think in his mind he is prepared to remain in the Dunes. On the other hand...."

Lynn didn't continue. She couldn't really think of anything Patrick had said suggesting he would prefer to come home.

"I think you answered it best," Elle suddenly entered the conversation. "He is thriving with my sister. Well, she nursed him at her breast. She seems to be doing a good job raising him as a teen. Maybe better than with her own son, from what she writes me."

Lynn gave Elle a smile. She was a peculiar woman, no question about it. Her voice did not seem to come from the same person who looked through vacant eyes. But Lynn was certain; Elle didn't miss anything that was going on around her. She seemed to be holding back the expression from around her eyes to shade them from... what, Lynn wondered? Fear?

"He is particularly close to his uncle," Lynn shared. "I think Patrick would be happy to come home," she told his mother. "Honestly, I think Patrick has learned how to find his place wherever he is. He has learned to fit into the Howards' home beautifully. And he would do the same here, if he was to come home. I just think you may want to ask him what he prefers. My guess will be that he wants to go back to the Dunes, if not for anything other than football next year," she said. She held back the thought that he probably looked forward to her return next spring. Perhaps. Maybe he would be over her by then. He was young, and things change quickly for teens. She realized, however, that in her heart, she hoped not. And in her mind, she didn't believe he would.

Elle was looking up at her forehead again, Lynn noticed.

Lynn wondered whether Rose, too, was looking into her thoughts when she said, "His friends are important to him. He will stay where his friends are."

"Yes," Lynn agreed, spellbound by Rose's dark eyes. "He'll want to be where he can find his friends."

"And you?" Elle interjected. "You will be gone now?

"Yes. I'll be traveling with my sister. South. Into Mexico."

Rose and Elle exchanged a glance. The idea of the two sisters traveling abroad struck a chord of interest. Elle tilted her head quizzically, and Rose lifted her eyebrows, pursing her lips.

"It sounds kind of daring to me. Maybe even a bit zany," Elle said, rolling her eyes. "I do look forward to hearing how your travels go. You'll have to be sure to tell Patrick about it when you get back. He does write me nice letters on occasion. Indeed, he's introduced you to me in his writings, and told me all about your wall. Another zany idea."

She widened her eyes, arching her eyebrows. It was Elle's most animated use of her eyes that Lynn had seen all evening.

"I'm sure he'll tell you all about it, when I get back," Lynn responded, surprised to hear that Patrick had written about her to his mother, and curious as to what he'd said. She knew David had remarked often enough in his letters to Patrick that his brother owed him a reply. She'd have to ask him about it. "I'll be back in the spring," she assured Elle.

Elle nodded once, her eyes closing, then opening with the bob of her head, the slightest of frowns impressed upon her expression.

Rose, too, nodded, almost imperceptibly, and Lynn wondered whether it was in agreement with Elle, or from a deeper comprehension and understanding about Patrick.

∞

That night, before falling asleep under a thick down quilt, Lynn North considered the events of the evening. She examined every word of the conversations she had had with Elle and Rose. Two remarkably perceptive women, she concluded. They both seemed to function on completely different wavelengths from each other, but their respective thought processes complemented in undulating harmony. She felt warmth from both women, and a special, determined strength from Rose. The diminutive Native American was protective of Elle. They were close, trusting friends. Lynn was surprised to find they had known each other well for less than a month.

As she reviewed the evening discussion and family dynamics, she exonerated herself from feeling guilt for staying the night with the Joyces in spite of her intentions to continue north. She cherished her memory of having the evening with Patrick's family. The talk had focused on Jannie. They discussed the funeral plans for the next morning. They spoke of the Whitman family. And they shared their memories of Jannie, laughing, speaking with awe and respect, nodding quietly, taking moments in silent recollection of David's kindred spirit. David brought her a photo of Jannie and him taken with Dante at the fair auction. He talked openly of his feelings for her, and how they had spent every possible moment together. He spoke of how their interests kindled one another's curiosity to learn and master music, science, their cattle and horses. She inspired him, he admitted. Lynn saw in the photo the pretty, bright face of Davey's friend, her eyes twinkling. David himself was an image of pride and hope, standing tall in the face of despair.

She had caught Patrick glancing at her as David spoke openly of his feelings for Jannie. Once their eyes met, Patrick struggled to break his glance. He finally turned his eyes away, frowning, his expression tense and near tears. They returned their attention to his brother.

"It is kind of hard to think of her being gone from my life," David said candidly. "It's unbelievable." His voice conveyed no bitterness or anger. There was no resentment. Merely a note of bewilderment, Lynn thought, as sleep tugged at her weary will. She slid into deep, dreamless slumber, cozy under the comforter, her last thoughts in awe of Patrick's brother and the courage he would need for the morning. And the morning after that. And every morning to follow.

Chapter Thirty

Farewell

LYNN SLEPT IN until the sweet aroma of fresh-baked coffee cake mixed with the pungent, rich fragrance of hot coffee wafted into her bedroom and beckoned her to meet the day. When she joined the family, Patrick and his mother were sipping coffee and chatting at the kitchen table. Rose was swallowed up in the big stuffed chair just inside the family room, reading an unusual looking manuscript. She did not miss Lynn's entry into the kitchen, however, glancing up and smiling as she turned the page in her book and continued her study.

"Mornin'" Patrick beamed. "Sleepyhead."

"Good morning," she countered, unabashed. "I did sleep like a baby. I feel wonderful. And you?" She directed her question toward both Elle and her son.

"Very fine, indeed." Elle words trailed downward on the scale from very high to very low. A whimsical smile crossed her lips as she spoke. Then, looking directly into Lynn's eyes, she asked, "Will you be attending the funeral with us this morning?" Her words were inviting and welcoming, not heavy with expectation.

"Oh, no. No, thank you," Lynn protested. "It was wonderful joining you and your family last evening. I believe that was enough of an imposition. I think I'd be obtrusive at the funeral."

"Obtrusive?" Elle picked up on Lynn's choice of words, redirecting them to her eldest son. "What does Lynn mean by 'obtrusive,' do you know, Patrick?" Her brows drifted up her forehead, forming inquisitive, parabolic arches.

Patrick rolled his eyes. "Not a clue. Have to wait until David gets in from milking. He'll know." He grinned, baiting his mother.

The arches met suddenly in a frown. Elle chided her son. "That is the exact attitude that got you in trouble in grade school, you'll recall. You know you can't depend on your brother to do your learning."

Patrick grinned. *Man, Mom's a different person. Still weird, but different,* he thought.

"Well, I could make a guess, then, I suppose. Obtrusive. Hmmm," he sat rubbing his freshly shaved chin, feigning intense concentration. "Sounds to me that Lynn thinks she'd be a big pain in the neck, sticking out like a sore thumb, prominently in the way and out of place at the same time."

Elle's brows reshaped into arches. She said nothing, but her expression reflected her pleasant surprise.

"But she'd be wrong," he added stubbornly, looking to Lynn.

Lynn was inclined to protest, but sighed, deciding to say nothing. There was no argument. She could see from his look that he was resigned to her leaving.

Elle intervened, her words dancing playfully across her tongue. "Obtrusive, is it? Now, who in their good grace taught you the meaning of so glorious a word? Are they schooling you well in the humble state of Indiana?"

Patrick chuckled. "Well, it came up in a reading one day last summer. Our friend, Harriet, often sat and read to us from *The New York Times,* or *The New Yorker,* or whatever, as we wrestled with that tie wall. Honestly, we would have finished it two weeks earlier, if Lynn and Harriet wouldn't have stopped after every big word and made me look it up. It was nuts! Harriet even kept a dictionary outside with her whenever she read. Obtrusive: big, noticeable, and in the way. Thank you, Noah Webster."

Lynn laughed, pouring steaming coffee into the mug that had been set on the counter for her. Almost magically, Rose was at her side. "This is good, what you have done with Patrick," she said quietly, setting her cup alongside Lynn's and allowing her to top it off. "All that you have done for him. I am grateful."

Lynn caught her nod, affirmative but almost imperceptible, and returned it.

∞

Lynn had finished her coffee and was about ready to leave when David and Paddy returned to the house from milking.

"What's your hurry, young lady?" Paddy asked, his voice kind, his nature gentle. He sat on a chair by the doorway unlacing his boots.

"This has been a wonderful stop," Lynn explained, "but I'm afraid it looks like it's just halfway between the Dunes and my folks' home in Minnesota. I have hours before I get home. It's time to go, and you have to be getting ready for the funeral."

Paddy nodded, gracefully accepting her explanation.

Patrick, however, had other ideas. "Well, I'm all cleaned up and ready," he said, drawing everyone's attention, although it was clear that he addressed only Lynn. "Just have to put my church clothes on. It's early. Wanna see a bit of the farm before you leave? It'd be good to stretch your legs before you go."

Lynn liked the idea. It wasn't easy to leave. She could easily put it off for another half hour and still be home by midafternoon. "Show me," she agreed.

David reversed his motions and started lacing his boots back on. "If you wait a second, I'll be right with you," he said. "You gotta see the new Holsteins!"

Paddy raised an eyebrow toward his younger nephew, and then toward the older one. Patrick had frozen in the act of opening the door to show Lynn out.

"David," Paddy rumbled a soft, deep tone. "You've plenty to do this morning, getting ready to head to town. Why don't you just let Patrick show the farm to Lynn?"

It was not a question, but David missed the point. "Won't take but a few minutes. And we don't have to be in town until eleven. We've got almost two hours." David eagerly tugged at his boot. He looked up toward his uncle, only to be met with the sternest of expressions. He started, looking first from Paddy, then to his mother, who sat expressionless at the kitchen table, and finally to Miss Rose, who stood, arms crossed casually, her eyes riveting him to his chair. A light went on. "Oh," he said, dumbly. "You're right."

He bent down, loosened the ties, and once again pulled off his boots. "You go on, Twinny. I have to shower up. Be sure to look at the Angus calves. They're starting to put on some flesh." He sat up to see Patrick and Lynn leave the farmhouse.

No one said anything after the kitchen door closed tight. David sat for a moment, tilting his head one way, then the other, weighing the variables in his confusion. Paddy, having tossed his boots in the mud room, poured himself a cup of coffee. David noticed Miss Rose watching him. "What?"

"Patrick's friend is leaving to travel. We should let them say goodbye."

David scrunched up his nose. "I'm confused," he muttered. He wondered what he was missing. Shaking it off, he skipped breakfast, deciding instead to shower and get dressed.

Jannie's funeral was this morning.

∞

They toured the barnyard. Patrick pointed out the machine shed, the granary, the corn crib, the silo. He was struck with the notion of being raised a farm boy, a simpleton, as he explained each building. Only Lynn's questions kept him from babbling like a moron. They paused near the barn, leaning against the broad boards of the swing gate as they inspected the calves and marveled at the size of the cows in David's Angus herd.

"Do you think you missed the farm more than you realized, now that you're back?" Lynn asked.

Patrick thought a moment. "It seems good to be back, sure," he agreed. "Yeah, I miss not being here. But really, I guess I miss my brother more than anything. Twin and all, you know."

She smiled, appreciating how different the brothers appeared. Yet they did share certain expressions. It was something about their eyes. When they laughed, she had noticed the night before, they resembled each other more than at any other moment. They had a remarkable sense for what the other was about to say, or was thinking, or even what they might want or need.

"What?" he asked, seeing the amusement on her face.

"Just you. You, and your twin. At times, it's hard to believe you're even brothers. Then, at other times, it's clear you are closer than mere brothers."

"You know, sometimes when I'm back down in the Dunes, I still feel like there are moments when I know exactly how Davey feels, or what he's thinking. I can just about predict when one of his letters will be in the mailbox. Like radar or something, I can see it coming. Sometimes, I just know he's gonna call, and wouldn't you know, the phone rings and it's him." Patrick grinned. "He'll say the same thing when I call. He'll say, 'I knew it'd be you.'"

It was precious, Lynn thought. They could remain so close. "Does it make you miss him all the more, feeling that way?"

"Sometimes," Patrick said, his eyes narrowing.

She let him weigh his thoughts before probing further. "Do you think you'd like moving back? Your mother was wondering, I think. Rose even asked about it."

Patrick shook his head definitely. "No. I don't think I'd feel good about that."

"Why not?"

His look teemed with anguish, edged with anger. "Just look at her, Lynn. She'd drive me nuts. She just keeps kind of staring at me. Did you hear how many times she pointed out how much I look like my father? I mean, it was spooky." He stuck his hands in the pockets of his letter jacket, a shiver quivering across his shoulders. He shook his head tightly back and forth.

She felt bad to have pushed him. She wanted to say something comforting. "I think she must be so proud of you, all grown up, big, and handsome. A man."

Patrick grinned, blushing. "Yeah. Yeah."

"Really," Lynn insisted. "She's proud of you. She told me about how much your letters meant to her. I didn't know you were writing to her so regularly."

Patrick shrugged. "Yep. Every other Sunday morning." The slight roll of his eyes revealed that he was not fully responsible for his own diligence. "Aunt Mary made me. Wouldn't let me do anything until she saw a letter to Mom. It was a pain, especially at first. But then it got to be all right. I could whip out a couple pages pretty fast by the beginning of last summer. 'Specially when we had so much going on, building the wall and all."

A look of apprehension flitted across Lynn's face. "You didn't write too much about me, did you?"

Patrick smirked. "Well, I suppose. I mean, I must have mentioned just about all the progress we were making, and all the things we were doing. I mean, what else was I doing, but being with you? Everything we did, all summer, was what I had to write about. You. And Harriet, too, I suppose. Why? She say something?"

Lynn nodded. "Not much. Enough to make me wonder. "

She thought about his mother's comments, and how insightful and understanding she seemed to be. She wondered what Elle's sixth sense—her maternal sense—told her about their friendship.

They looked out over the cow yard, across the pasture, out into the deep woods leading up into the hillside that framed the edge of the valley.

"I'd miss all this, if it were my home," Lynn said softly.

"I do," Patrick said. "It seems so vivid, so new now that I'm back. It's different than I remember. It never really will be the same as it was. But it is more like home than ever." He looked into her eyes, searching for hints that she understood him. "I mean, maybe it's me that's changed. I'm just glad you could see this place. My home. Where I'm from."

Lynn nodded. "I wish you could see mine." She reminded herself that she should be on her way.

Patrick sensed the spell breaking. He stood, nodding, letting his eyes focus on the ground in front of his feet. "Yeah," he said quietly.

They walked back to the house in silence. On the porch, Lynn graciously thanked Elle, Rose, and Paddy for their hospitality. Saying goodbye to David, she surprised everyone, especially herself, when she wrapped her arms around him, her eyes tearing, saying how by knowing Patrick she felt like she knew David, too, and how very sorry she was that his Jannie had left him.

As a family, they walked her to the Thunderbird to bid her farewell. At the car, abashed and flustered, Lynn again sputtered her goodbyes to David,

Elle, Rose and Paddy. Taking Patrick's fingers in her hand, she squeezed firmly, then let her fingers slide gently away. "Take care."

Patrick stood mute, nodding once. His eyes were fixed upon her, following her every move into the car. He felt hollow, emptied, abandoned.

The T-Bird roared as she turned the key. Jerking into reverse, Lynn hurried to back up the car, then jammed the gears into forward so she could drive away, quickly, as fast as she could. She felt his eyes follow her as she turned the wheel toward the road. Pressing the accelerator, she lurched the car forward, the wheels spinning on the gravel. She glanced one last time at Patrick's family gathered along the driveway, blurred by the welling of tears in her eyes. Elle raised her hand, her palm faced out as if in benediction. Paddy waved his big farmer's hand in a single, short arc. Rose calmly looked on.

David, too, followed Lynn with his eyes as she drove out of the farmyard. He wore a tired, pale, lonely expression, but he stood with his hand upon his brother's shoulder, supporting him, offering comfort. The last she saw of them, the two brothers were leaning against one another, watching her drive away. David looked up at his brother. Patrick's face was set with intense determination.

She turned the car north, toward Minnesota, toward Minnetonka, toward home. She drove blindly for the first mile, seeing Patrick's face in her mind. Blaming herself. Hoping that with time, with distance, they would find healing. And forgiveness.

∞

Patrick watched with solemn awe as his brother stood with the Whitmans, graciously accepting condolences and sharing in the grief of friends and family. It seemed like the entire town was at Jannie's funeral. Everybody Patrick ever knew in Baraboo and North Freedom had stopped by Edgar's Funeral Home at some point between eleven and noon. A long line filed through the visitation room to pay their respects to Jannie, with mourners congregating outside to make space for the horde of Jannie's fellow students, their families, and her many friends still waiting their turn.

Although he had never been to a funeral, Patrick had heard tales from a friend or two whose grandparents had died. From movies and television, he'd expected to see Jannie lying peacefully in an open, flower-bedecked casket, looking as pretty as he remembered her. He was a little shocked, then, to see only a small cherry urn set inconspicuously on a pedestal behind where David stood with the Whitmans. A photo of Jannie, her eyes joyful, stood alongside the urn.

Patrick watched with curiosity as a young black woman entered the visitation room and approached Davey and the Whitmans. She was with an older woman, who Patrick assumed was her mother. He was intrigued to see this girl in Baraboo; he'd noticed, in passing comparison to his high school in Gary, how overwhelmingly pale-skinned David and Jannie's classmates were. With poise and grace, the unfamiliar girl greeted the Whitmans, whose faces lit with joy and surprise as they embraced her. The mothers hugged, and tears slipped down their smiling faces. Mrs. Whitman turned to David and introduced the girl and her mother. David's smile burst across his face and he impulsively hugged the young lady, though she was fully five inches taller than he. She handed Mrs. Whitman a thin parcel, wrapped simply in tissue paper. Mrs. Whitman carefully unfolded the wrapping, and they all leaned in to examine the drawing. A shout of laughter rose from the group, leading to joyful tears. Helen Whitman took the drawing and placed it next to the urn, opposite the photo of Jannie. From where he stood, Patrick could see that the drawing was of a carton of eggs, each egg with a face, smiling, laughing, crying, glum. One of the front eggs was a brown one, bearing a striking resemblance—for a cartoon egg—to the young woman. The other egg in front was unmistakable. It was Jannie. Smiling, eyes twinkling, Jannie's caricature was exact. Patrick thought the drawing was quite clever, but wondered why the Whitmans were so taken with it as to display it with Jannie's urn and photo. Before he could inquire, the gathering mobilized for the drive to the cemetery. The community formed a mile-long caravan on North Street for the burial of Jannie's ashes.

By one o'clock, the urn was placed in a hole in the grassy hillside. Patrick listened vacantly to a eulogy delivered by a church elder who spoke kindly of Jannie, but really didn't know her at all. He spoke more to her parents about the love and life they had given their daughter than about her as a vibrant, lovely person, Patrick thought. Without even looking at David, he could feel his twin stifling a powerful urge. He glanced over at his brother, standing mute, eyes burning under welling tears. He could sense David's soul yearning to cry out the joys and virtues of his lost friend, rather than stand and listen to the banal, desensitized message of the droning stranger before them.

Afterwards, Mrs. Whitman handed Jannie's violin to David. She'd asked him to play, and Patrick watched his brother muster more fortitude than he could imagine, shoulder the violin, and touch the bow to the strings to play the first long, doleful notes of Bach's Air on the G String. The violin sang. No one listening was left dry-eyed. Many wept and sobbed as David continued through all the measures, tears streaming freely down his face. At the last note, a full, clear silence filled the cemetery. The chirping of a few titmice graced and complemented the stillness, along with a few muffled sniffles. David walked to Jannie's grave and set her violin and bow down beside the urn. He stepped back, standing like a sentry. The black girl walked up and hugged him, and took her place beside him with her arm around his shoulders, comforting him, whispering something for only him to hear. Mrs. Whitman, her husband, and their surviving daughter approached, scooping handfuls of dirt from the fresh mound next to the grave. They sprinkled the soil upon the urn. Mrs. Whitman turned and hugged David. Dr. Whitman put his arm around David's shoulder, gently leading him away from Jannie's grave. Together, they left the site where their loved one remained.

Patrick and his family climbed into the Packard and drove to the tennis club, where the Whitmans hosted a luncheon. Patrick felt numb. The club was bright and cheery, and from his perspective, the Whitman family seemed joyous and graceful, chatting, even laughing, in a hazy, warm aura. He watched his mother and David standing with a group of people he didn't recognize, nodding and talking. He saw the soft, golden November sunlight filtering through the large bay windows that overlooked the courts and pool. He felt a strange thickness in his head, behind his eyes, and heard a soft buzzing in his ears. He felt a tug on his sleeve.

"You need air." Miss Rose turned him toward a doorway leading to the courts, her hand on his elbow. "Come. You're pale." Patrick obediently followed her lead. Outside, the air was fresh and cool. She directed him to a white bench alongside the near court. "Breathe in. Breathe out. Loosen your tie and collar," he heard her say, as from a distance.

"Whew," he said, feeling her hand gently press his head down between his knees. He felt his skin tingle across his neck and scalp, and sweat break across his brow.

"Breathe," she reminded him.

After a few moments, he sat up. She was sitting next to him but looking off, far away. He leaned back, relaxing as the weakness subsided. Each breath of fresh air sent strength through his body. He felt a shakiness replacing the numbness, and then vigor seeped in to supplant the wobbliness that had sapped his strongly muscled frame.

He did not interrupt Miss Rose; she was distant, trance-like. After a moment, she stirred, turning ever so slightly, and said, "You are better now."

He wondered at her words. She meant no question, demanded no response. A statement of fact. Still, he replied. "Yes. I felt kind of dizzy."

"You forgot to breathe," she said, flashing a whimsical smile. "I looked over to see you tottering. It has been a day of overwhelming loss for us. For David. For the Whitmans." He felt her deep, dark eyes look into him. "And for you."

Patrick felt vulnerable and exposed. But not judged. He wondered whether this dark little woman could see right through him. She knew and accepted him precisely as he was.

He gathered his thoughts. He searched for words, but he could only stammer. "So much loss," he choked a raspy whisper. "I can't see... I mean, I just can't believe how David can... I dunno... I mean, how can he take it?" He hung his head, and shook it back and forth, slowly.

After a moment, he heard her soft, gentle voice. He wondered at first if she was talking at all. "... accepts his loss. His family is large, now, and heartfelt in their concern to help him through his grief. And Jannie left him whole, fulfilled, free to live, even without her."

She turned toward the bay windows next to the terrace doorway. Through the windows, David was visible, engaged in lively discussion, smiling, sometimes laughing with Jannie's sister and father and several others. They laughed heartily at David's expressive body language as he twisted and contorted, his arms flaying wildly, acting out the memory he shared.

She returned her gaze to Patrick's eyes. "It is not David alone who is left to deal with his loss. You, too, have a hole in your heart. David has many to help him—and Jannie prepared him to heal long before she left." She looked at him intently. "It is you who are surprised by your loss. You are suffering the loss of that which you did not know you had found. You are isolated in your loss. You are alone. It is you who should consider returning to your family."

Miss Rose said no more, but kept her eyes locked on Patrick with an intensity that sent a shiver across the muscles of his broad shoulders. Her eyes flowed with kindness.

He stirred, the cool November shadows creeping across the terrace and chilling his toes and fingertips. He pulled up his collar and bundled his arms across his chest. "I dunno," he said. "Aunt Mary's family. And Uncle Paul. Jack, of course." He paused. "And I play with a team. We've gotten really close. We're going to be really good." He paused, rationalizing his thoughts. "I have some things to finish in the Dunes," he said. "And I really do love living with Aunt Mary and Uncle Paul." He looked into the dark, warm face that studied him as he spoke. "And my friends down there...." He left off without finishing.

"Yes. Your friend. Just consider it," Miss Rose added. "You can see a way home, if you let it be. At the right time."

Patrick dipped his head again, and nodded. "Maybe," he agreed.

She looked into his heart, and he was riveted by her gaze. "Patrick, you must not let yourself behave as if you have no family."

He nodded again, wondering, *what has she just told me?*

∞

After the lunch, the Joyces headed back to the farm. No one said much, even after they'd returned home.

Only Elle commented. "Well, that was nice. Heartwarming. For a funeral, that is. It was like a parade. But sad."

The twins went to change. Still sharing his childhood bedroom with his twin, Patrick said little while he and his brother donned jeans and sweatshirts and prepared to head out to the hills east of the farm, maybe to hunt. Or just to wander. Patrick followed David to the mudroom, where they pulled on heavy boots and zipped up warm jackets. With little more than an hour of light left, the brothers stepped out to face the rest of the day.

∞

Patrick climbed into the dome car on the Hiawatha line from Wisconsin Dells, running through Milwaukee to Chicago. He rode along in solitude as his eyes scanned the dormant Wisconsin countryside.

His mind whirred with fleeting thoughts that spun in rhythm with the clacking and clatter of iron wheels rolling along rail. It seemed unreal that Jannie was gone. She should be there, at home, in Baraboo. She should be hanging around with Davey. Riding her horses. Playing her violin. In his mind, it was easier to see her that way. Not dead. Not having died. How could that be? *That just doesn't happen to young people,* Patrick thought.

He could barely remember David without Jannie. He remembered that very first time Mrs. Whitman had brought the girls out to the farm and they'd romped in the hay mow, climbing bales until he'd succumbed to a major allergy attack, and then David and Gabriel and Jannie's mother had played their fiddles. That was the beginning of David and Jannie. The start of their amazing friendship. If he thought of David, he was also thinking of Jannie as well. Kind of like David and Paddy, but even more so. It had just about always been that way, was meant to be that way.

But now it was different. It almost seemed easier to picture Davey separated from him, his twin brother, than removed from Jannie. How would David be, he wondered. *Alone,* he answered himself. *Very alone.* And he began to understand the chasm that being alone creates in one's heart.

He thought of Lynn leaving for Minnesota. Just driving away. To places he couldn't conjure in the images of his mind. Driving away. So easily. Leaving just memories. The thought of her absence was softened, he supposed, by the hope that she would be back. Soon, maybe, in the spring. One day. Maybe sooner. She was gone, but she was still there. Still possible. Just away.

He thought of what David had told him about Jannie, how she'd assured him that she would always be with him, always kept alive in his heart and mind. David spoke of Jannie as if she was with him. In the present. Still there. He thought of David, his brother, with his love for Jannie, who had died. He thought of David. Alone. He thought of Lynn.

From the dome, Patrick watched the shabby gray houses along the tracks cutting through the northern suburbs as the Hiawatha slowed for its approach into Union Station. His thoughts swirled and returned again to Lynn.

Her sparkling eyes. The dimple at the corner of her smile. Her glow. It had been so right, he thought, how she had become such a stabilizing, grounding force in his life. She was gone now. He felt the rift cleave deep into his soul. He'd left his home again. He knew he had a choice, and had chosen to return to Indiana. He thought of the canoes in Lynn's garage, unfinished, one hulled out, the other showing bare ribs, with cedar strips laid tightly in a half-dozen rows from the keel. Calling him. He thought of Jannie, gone. David, alone. He considered the notion of remaining in North Freedom with his family. What was there for him at home? In the Dunes, he knew, he had unfinished business. He wanted to finish the canoes before Lynn came home. He didn't know when she would be back, but he believed she would return. And when she did come home, he wanted to be there.

And, he had football.

The train rattled slowly into the Union Station yard. Patrick watched the lead cars pull into the dark mouth of the terminal tunnel. As he saw the gaping darkness swallow the cars ahead, a vision resolved in his mind. He clung to his thought. He would finish the two little vessels in Lynn's garage. He would complete the canoes.

∞

Patrick spotted his uncle waiting on the platform. Uncle Paul greeted him with a broad smile and wave. "Well, how'd it go?" he asked, extending his hand as Patrick stepped down the steep metal stairs from the train.

Patrick shrugged, screwing his mouth up in half a grimace. He shook his uncle's hand, reflecting that he had never done that before. "Okay, I guess." He was surprised by the tenor of his own voice, weary, subdued, worn with emotion. He sucked in a deep breath and straightened the slump from his shoulders.

"It's good to see you," he blurted candidly, smiling shyly. It was good to see his uncle. Paul treated him as a person. A human. A somebody. He always did.

Paul returned the smile, clapping him on the shoulder. "Hungry? Come on," he said. "I've got a place I'd like to take you for lunch." Flagging a taxi, Paul instructed the driver to take them to the Berghoff. "You'll love this place," he assured his nephew. "They have a wonderful bouillabaisse."

Patrick wrinkled his brow. "What is *booya bays*?"

Paul grinned. "Soup. You'll see."

At the Berghoff, Paul let the seafood soup nurture his nephew, and waited patiently for Patrick to open up and relate the events of the previous week. Gradually, in snippets, Patrick reflected on the trip. He described his twin's remarkable outlook. He told of David's playing the Air over Jannie's ashes. He readily admitted that he could not bring himself to even imagine so brave a response to so great a loss. He spoke of his mother, and the awkward feelings he had for her.

Paul listened, savoring the candid insight into his nephew's life. He heard every word that Patrick said, and saw beyond to the fiber of his nephew's soul. To extend the moment, he ordered them each a slice of Berghoff's cheesecake and a cup of steaming coffee.

The spell snapped, however, when Patrick glanced up to recognize an unexpected face. Paul watched curiously as Patrick's eyes focused toward the front of the restaurant. His nephew's eyes widened, and he blanched, then flushed with a deep, crimson blush that rushed up his neck and darkened his face. Paul studied Patrick's expression, resisting the inclination to turn and see what spurred so visible a response.

"Jesus," Patrick muttered. Shifting his gaze back to his uncle, he gestured toward a booth near the windows. "That's Dr. North."

Paul was intrigued by his nephew's reaction. He turned slowly, peering carefully over his shoulder. His occasional neighbor from the Dunes was engrossed in an earnest conversation with his companion. Both men sat, heads tipped together, along a far bench facing the back of the restaurant, where he and Patrick sat. Paul turned back to his table. Patrick sat with his forehead set heavily on his hand, his elbow planted firmly on the table. He looked up, however, from under his eyelids, watching the lively debate at the table near the front.

Paul picked up the tab, opened his wallet, and left a reasonable tip on top of the bill. "Well, let's head home, what do you say?"

Patrick nodded, shifting warily from his chair.

"Shall we say hello?" Paul taunted. He couldn't resist.

Patrick quickly shook his head. His answer was firm and fast. "Naw. Not unless he sees us first."

Hiding his smile, Paul led the way past Barry North's booth on his way toward the door. As he stepped alongside the table, Dr. North glanced up, his expression freezing with instant recognition as he made eye contact first with Paul, then Patrick. Paul adjusted both his pace and his expression, slowing his stride and assuming an appearance of pleasant surprise.

"Well, hello, Paul," Barry greeted him. Sitting at the back of the booth, Barry North had no opportunity to stand. His companion, sitting nearer the aisle, craned his small round head on his long, thin neck to see the interloper. Barry shifted his gaze back toward Patrick. "Ah! I see you have your young, industrious nephew along."

"Hello, Barry," Paul took command. "Yes, Pat's back home." He glanced at his nephew. "Just in from Wisconsin. I thought I'd welcome him home with a bowl of Berghoff's bouillabaisse. It was wonderful!"

"Indeed, yes," Barry agreed, somewhat absently. He nodded once toward Patrick. "I trust you enjoyed it." Then, shifting his attention, he addressed his companion. "Dr. Reims, I'd like you to meet neighbors of mine from the Dunes. Or, more accurately, former neighbors. Paul Howard and his nephew, Patrick Joyce."

The young physician slid from the bench to his feet and offered his hand to first Paul, then Patrick.

"Former neighbor?" Paul picked up on Barry's comment. "I hadn't heard—are you selling?"

"Not at all." Dr. North made no attempt to conceal his acrimony. "The house was always my wife's folly, really. She bought it, for the most part. Family money. She's quite the little princess, you know. The world is her toy." His voice was hard and bitter. "She's filed for divorce," he said abruptly, studying Patrick's response to his news.

Paul showed more surprise than his nephew. "No!" he said earnestly. "I am sorry to hear that." He glanced at Patrick, whose stony expression was directed toward the ornate gaslight suspended from the wall above the table. "Did you know?" He regretted asking as soon as the words left his lips.

Patrick leveled his eyes toward his uncle, nodding. "Yeah. Lynn... Mrs. North told me on the trip up to Wisconsin," he said, turning to meet Dr. North's stare. "Sorry to hear about it."

Barry North pursed his lips, his head bobbing once in an almost imperceptible nod. "I suppose it was inevitable. Perhaps I have been wed more to my career than to my wife all along." He leveled an appraising eye at Patrick, then stopped short of voicing a thought that appeared to cross his mind. Instead, he smiled wanly, saying, "I can't really blame Lynn now, can I?"

No one responded.

Before the pause settled into full-fledged awkwardness, Paul saw an opening and used it. "Well, Barry, I'm truly sorry to hear about this. But do please stop in when you're in the Dunes. Or call." He extended his hand in a quick farewell shake.

Outside the Berghoff, Paul glanced at Patrick from the side of his eye. "Well, that was interesting."

Patrick sniffed and grunted. He met his uncle's glance. "Let's go home."

Book Two

Butterfly

Oh very young
What will you leave us this time
There'll never be a better chance
To change your mind
And if you want this world
To see a better day
Will you carry
The words of love with you
Will you ride
The great white bird into heaven
And though you want to last Forever
You know you never will
(You know you never will)
And the goodbye
Makes the journey harder still.

– Cat Stevens

But those that will not break it kills.
It kills the very good, and the very gentle,
and the very brave impartially.

– Ernest Hemingway, A Farewell to Arms

November, 1962

ON THE TUESDAY before Thanksgiving, the door at the end of the alley slid open during the evening milking. Leaning out behind M21's hindquarters, I dodged her swatting tail to see a pair of figures slipping through the narrow opening. Down the aisle, Paddy stood up and looked across the backline of his cow toward the door.

"'Ello, cousin," Roger Joyce said. "Hi, Uncle Paddy."

Roger possessed the same charming smile as his father, but carried a touch more kindness about his eyes, with soft, boyish features that even the Marine Corps had not hardened during his first three-year tour. Now twenty-four, he'd enlisted in the Marines the summer after his graduation from UW Whitewater, where he majored in history and enrolled in Naval ROTC. He had been home only a handful of days since.

"Hello, Junior," Paddy called. "I'd heard you were in town. Here for the hunt, is it? I wondered if we'd see you."

"Yep, Pad. We've been after the elusive Wisconsin whitetail," Roger acknowledged, although his tone indicated that he'd been less than successful. With a nod, he indicated his companion. "Uncle Pad, my friend here is Steven Whitney. Major Whitney, in the Corps." He turned back to the major. "This is Uncle Patrick—or Paddy, as we Joyces all know him. And this is my cousin, David Joyce."

The major walked up the alley and shook first Paddy's hand, then mine. His grip was confident, without swagger or pomp. When he looked me in the eye, it was like he was drilling for the truth. No excuses, just the truth. He made me feel good just shaking hands.

"Nice meeting you. Pardon me." I bent to take the milking claw off young M21 and move it on down the milk line to another promising first-calf heifer, M28. Both these girls had come in on our first load of new Holsteins.

"You'll have to excuse us, Major," Paddy explained. "Our girls don't like waiting, and we don't want these suction devices to irritate 'em."

"Understandable." Major Whitney's voice was soft, with a mellow tenor note. Looking at his square jaw and muscled neck and shoulders, I'd half expected to hear a booming baritone. "My family are farmers—ranchers, really," he continued. "North Dakota. I know how finicky animals can be. Perhaps we best come back, or wait outside?"

Paddy waved off the notion with a flip of his hand. "We're not far from done. Then we're headed for some supper. Have you been up to the house, Rog?" His nephew shook his head. "Well, go on up and tell Elle and Miss Rose that I've invited you to eat with us."

"I got the heifers fed," Paddy announced twenty minutes later, as I finished the last of the chores in the milk house. "Let's go see what Roger and his friend are up to." His eyes glistened with excitement.

Over supper, we learned that Roger and Major Whitney were up to some serious hunting, with some pretty poor results. "We were south of the lake opening morning," Roger began his report. Paddy winced a bit and shook his head slightly. I couldn't help but make just a flash of eye contact with my uncle, stifling the urge to raise my eyebrows. The park south of Devil's Lake was a rough hunt in the bow season, just for the terrain. Opening day of the rifle hunt, it was worse. The animals hunkered down amongst the rocks and underbrush while scores of unwary hunters clambered over them. "We'd seen some real active sign of heavy rut when we cruised the area Friday morning. A couple of well-used scrape lines," Roger continued. "But Saturday, when things opened up, there was a hunter behind every third tree."

Major Whitney elaborated. "We saw a dozen or so does. I caught a glimpse of one small, forked buck. Nothing really that gave me a shot. What we did see was generally on a flat-out run." He shifted his glance to Roger, a sly smile spreading across his face. "Bonehead here," he continued in a tone that made all of us smile along with him, "he missed a six pointer. Plain out missed! Just about ran right over him. Disgrace to the Corps," Major Whitney chided. He turned to Roger. "How did you ever qualify, anyway?"

"Come on," Roger protested. "That was a darn hard shot at a running deer a good two hundred yards off. Okay, I missed, but give me a break!" His tone was apologetic, as if he was ready to absorb more of his fellow Marine's razzing. He knew it was coming.

"Well, how come you let him get that far off before you took the shot?" Major Whitney pressed. "Going for drama? Or were you sleeping when he sailed over your stand?"

Roger steamed. "It wasn't all that close to me."

"No closer than maybe ten feet straight overhead when he jumped you." Major Whitney pointed up at the ceiling. Even Mom laughed aloud at that.

"Anyways." Roger clearly wanted to move on. "We haven't seen much since. This morning we found a chewed-up carcass of a nice eight pointer over north of Brewster's land. Looks like the dogs and coyotes got to it. That's been the extent of our action."

"An eight pointer, by Brewster's?" I repeated. "Did it have heavy brow tines, with a broken fork in the right one?"

Major Whitney glanced over. I felt him kind of assessing me. He nodded. "Yeah. A nice rack. Pretty good girth at the base of the horns. Those brow tines would make real nice knife handles. The right one was split with about an inch and a half off the point, and one fork was chipped off some. Must have been sparring."

I nodded. "Gabe and I watched that guy challenging the Pony a couple weeks ago. Nice buck, but it was no contest."

Roger perked up. "Whaddya mean, he challenged the pony? He was jousting with a horse?"

A slow grin split Paddy's face. "Nope. A big, big buck that lives out back here. He looks like he's about the size of a Shetland pony. We've been watching him for a couple years now. We see him fairly often. By the end of this last summer, he looked like he'd even got a gut on him, like ponies do."

"He's got to be the alpha buck in these parts," I added. "He gives us a good look whenever he so chooses." I turned toward Miss Rose. "Remember him strutting around, showing off his velvet when we were baling the third crop, right before the fair?"

Miss Rose nodded, a smile confirming my report.

"He is massive," I went on. "And he just about always shows himself in the most dramatic ways. He'll appear out of nowhere and walk right next to us down the rows as we're picking strawberries or weeding the garden. When we were haying, it was late in the day, just about sunset. Miss Rose, Jannie, and I were sitting on the hay wagon waiting for Paddy to come back with the tractor and haul in the last load. The sun was setting right over where the road comes up from the river. We were watching the sunset, feeling a nice breeze. It couldn't have been more peaceful. Then all of a sudden, here comes the Pony, walking right in front of this big, red disc of setting sun."

Miss Rose joined in. "He stopped right there in front of the sun, holding his head high, his antlers thick in velvet. He looked this way and that, as if he were surveying his kingdom."

Roger's eyes widened, and he held his lips in a pursed O. Major Whitney watched me with an intensity that made me feel kind of proud, and special. He listened to every word.

I continued. "Yeah, and then after he'd made this grand entry, he leaped over the ditch and cleared the fence, no problem, then just sauntered across the fresh-cut alfalfa right toward us. We froze, watching him. He had to know we were there. He's a big show-off."

Roger's eyes sparkled. "Have you seen him lately?"

272 | The Good Guy List

I returned his look evenly. "Oh, yeah. All the time. I hunted him hard in the bow season." I looked to Major Whitney, explaining, "I do most of my deer hunting with a bow. The Pony's too wily to give me a shot, though. Last week when Patrick was here, we watched him rocking a tree while he rubbed his antlers. That's how we spotted him. We saw this tree just shaking back and forth. It was like a twenty-foot tree, maybe six or eight inches thick. I thought he was gonna knock it over."

"Damn," Roger muttered.

"He's a good twelve pointer. His brow tines are like the handle of a baseball bat, maybe nine, ten inches long."

Paddy added simply, "Biggest darn deer I've ever seen in my whole life. 'Bout the only time you don't see him, though, is during the gun season."

"Ain't that true," I agreed, nodding.

"Don't use that word," Mom said, fetching the coffee pot to top off our mugs.

We all kind of sat in our own thoughts for a moment or two. Then Roger came to the point. "Well, Davey, my dad was saying how you'd been in the woods a bit this fall. I—well, we, Major Steve and I—were wondering if you'd be willing to guide us around a bit."

"Well, you know, I got my license, but I didn't even go out opening morning," I replied slowly. I couldn't help but be amused at the thought of guiding Rog and the Major around the woods. And flattered, too. I wondered, though, if I could get my heart into it. "After last week ... I guess I really hadn't thought of going."

Roger looked at me anxiously. He was worried that I'd turn down his request. But I could also see that he was sympathetic, that he knew about Jannie's funeral.

Major Whitney had a different sort of look about him. He, too, seemed sympathetic. But his glance was more calculating. He was assessing me again. It was as if he was wagering within himself as to whether or not he thought I measured up ... or something. After a moment, his eye narrowed, and he nodded once, knowingly, almost imperceptibly, as if he meant for me alone to see it. He spoke sincerely. "We heard about last week. I'm sorry." He left it hanging, and I appreciated his candor. After a respectful moment, he moved on. He asked softly but firmly, "So, are you up for it? Can we count on you?"

I glanced up at Paddy.

"Nothing in the barn holding you up," he said. "Least ways, not that I can't handle."

"Milking's no worry," I said. "We'll be done long before light." I turned to Mom. "How about missing school?"

Mom rolled her eyes, pursing her lips while she considered. "I don't really know that it matters," she decided. "You are the valedictorian, after all, or are going to be." I saw Major Whitney raise his eyebrows a bit as he gave me another penetrating look. Mom continued, "You can make your own decision on this. Rosey was just saying how futile teaching was going to be tomorrow, anyway, with all the hunters' flu that the faculty expects called in. Just don't expect me to lie for you. If you want to go hunting, well, go hunting and call it what it is. None of their fake excuse business from me!" she stammered.

Paddy cut in, laughing. "I'll let them know you won't be in. They won't even ask why. Don't worry."

"Okay," I said, grinning more than I expected. "I'll find you some bucks. Maybe even the Pony.

"Wouldn't that be something," I added, half to myself.

∞

Thursday morning, I finished chores in the barn early. I thought I'd have a jump on Major Whitney, but as I came out of the milk house, he was unloading his gear from his car.

"Morning, David."

"Morning, Major Whitney."

"David, if it's all the same, call me Steve. We're hunting partners. Unless you enlisted since I saw you last."

I felt a sheepish grin cross my face, and shrugged. "Okay by me— Steve." It sounded pretty good, least ways for the first try. "You must be kind of eager, being up and out so early."

"I guess so," he admitted, looking to the sky. "Probably close to an hour and a half until there's enough light for shooting, I suppose."

"Where's Rog?"

The Major chortled. "I'm afraid he's a non-hacker this morning. Seems he decided his warm sack is a better venue than a rock in the woods. He mumbled something about his 'venison is hanging in the garage,' and pulled the pillow over his head."

"Hmmm. Well, come on in and get a cup of coffee while I get my stuff. It won't hurt to head out early to the bluff above the marsh." I looked up at the starless, opaque sky. "It'll take a while in the dark."

The Major followed me into the house. Miss Rose greeted us with steaming coffee and the sweet, inviting aroma of warm coffee cake blended with the delicious fragrance of her great scrambled eggs with cheese and mushrooms and onions. She wasn't going to let us go hungry in the woods this morning.

∞

In spite of the dark, we made good time across the alfalfa stubble, over the barbed wire fence along the east woodlot, and up onto the ridge heading south from the point where the Baraboo winds along the north forty of Klemms' farm. We crossed over the furrow in the leaves where we'd helped Roger pull his nice little forked buck from the hollow the previous afternoon. I looked back at Major Steve where he'd stopped to inspect the drag tracks. He glanced up, a humorous little smile matching the twinkle in his eyes. He didn't say anything, nor did I, but I couldn't help smile back, knowing what he was thinking about our hunting partner.

∞

Rog had tagged the yearling buck a half hour before sundown the day before. He'd been set up fifty yards west of us, at the south end of the bluff looking out over the hollow. From where I was set up on the hillside to the east next to Major Steve, I could see Roger's shot unfold—as well as what he didn't see coming at him. In fact, I think I saw that little buck picking its way up the creek bed a full ten minutes before Roger caught sight of it. The path it followed led right up to him. Once he spotted it, meandering towards him, browsing on buds and stem ends, I had to admire his patience. He must have seen it a hundred yards out, but it was pretty thick along the bottom. I don't suppose he was too eager to force a high-risk shot and come up with another miss for Major Steve to hound him about. He waited, and slowly, quietly got into position, raising his rifle toward the likely window in which the buck would pass. It took nearly twenty minutes for that buck to move the last seventy yards into his shot line.

I'd looked slowly over my shoulder at Major Steve to see if he'd spotted Roger's action. His eyes were locked on the buck moving up the creek bed. He glanced over toward me, barely bobbing his head in a subtle nod. I slowly started to turn my head back toward Roger, wondering if he'd take the little buck. It was prime time for deer to be moving off their beds to feeding grounds, and if this young buck was leading out in front of a herd, we might see some better racks come up the creek well before dark.

The ear twitched ever so slightly, but the motion caught my eye before I turned my head back all the way toward Roger. I froze, trying to make sense out of what I was seeing. Nothing was discernible in the shadows along the base of the dark, lichen-mottled bluff, a good hundred yards north of Roger. A tuft of sumac sprang up behind some tall marsh grass on the other side of the creek. There was absolutely no breeze, but something had fluttered just this side of the sumac, or in that vicinity. It could have been a bird, or squirrel. But an ear flip or twitch on the head of a deer is subtler than the flight of a jay dipping from limb to limb in search of dried grapes or seeds. And squirrels, well, they are anything but subtle. They can be sneaky and stealthy, but they are also acrobatic clowns. This motion was nothing more than the tease of a hint. My eyes burned, looking through the natural camouflage that hid the big buck. Minutes passed, and in the back of my mind, I prayed that Rog would let the little buck go by, or not take the shot until I resolved this optical puzzle before my eyes. I slowly readied the .35, carefully, quietly turning the muzzle toward the sumac.

The Major noticed my movement and followed my eyes toward the unseen distraction across the valley. In the periphery of my vision, I could see that he remained absolutely still, not even moving his rifle toward the target zone. Then, he stealthily moved his foot until he jabbed my leg with the tip of his boot. I shifted my eyes toward him, squinting to hide the movement of my pupils and irises. His gaze was locked near where I'd seen the flash of movement. He raised his nose a fraction of an inch, pointing, confirming that he spotted something.

Just as I turned my eyes back toward the sumac, Roger let go with a booming blast from his .308. The report echoed off the bluffs, filling the still air along the creek bottom with energy that I was certain I could feel as much as I could hear. The Pony flicked his ears toward the sound as the rifle boomed, and my eyes honed in on the shape of his head and rut-thickened neck. His instinct took command, and with the discipline of a veteran buck that had lived through gun seasons before, he didn't move from his bed on the far side of the sumac. He scanned the creek bottom, looking for signs of predators. Roger's rifle had stilled the birdcalls and squirrel chatter that made up the background noise of the forest, and in the sudden silence, the cracks and crunches of his steps filled the little dale as he climbed down the side of the bluff. I saw a single flash of polished antler as the big deer swiveled on his hind feet and silently, fluidly, disappeared into the dried autumn colors of the valley's flora.

I looked back at the Major, who was still following the path of the buck's disappearance with squinted eyes. When he turned, his eyes met mine, wide and excited. He smiled and mouthed a single silent word: *Wow.*

We climbed down the embankment to where Rog was standing over his kill. He hadn't started field dressing it yet, but was grappling with the buck's hind legs. To my surprise, the Major didn't mention the Pony making its escape up the creek bed. Instead, he was real gracious to Roger about tagging the young buck. When I heard Major Steve congratulate him on his first deer, the picture cleared up for me. I'd wondered what he was all about with the way he was flailing around with those hind legs. I clapped him on the shoulder and told him what a nice shot he'd made, waiting so patiently and all. Then I kind of offered to show him how to gut the animal, which he was more than willing to let me do. All the while I worked on that little buck, Major Steve never said a word about the Pony. Nor did he say anything as we dragged the seventy-pound carcass back across valley and the pastures, toward home.

∞

In the dark of Thanksgiving morning, as the Major inspected the trail where Rog had dragged his deer, I wondered about the evening before. Had he not wanted to take anything away from Rog's hunt? Seemed like it; he was so congratulatory. But to say nothing at all? I'd seen his eyes after he watched the Pony disappear into the sumac. I had an idea of what he might be considering.

We climbed the long ascent to the top of the ridge and followed the bluff as it wound along the river valley. There lay our stand, a spindly skeleton of a massive old pine, limbs splayed in all directions, its trunk stretched out parallel to the face of the bluff, just five or six feet from the edge.

"Get yourself comfortable," I whispered. "We'll be looking down over the whole marsh come daylight." Steve nodded, inhaled deeply, and peered out into the darkness filling the valley.

The only thing darker than the ocean of predawn sky above us was the sea of densely black terrain below, sucking in the faint light of a few hazy stars. We'd arrived by quarter after six. There wouldn't be enough light to betray our movements for a good forty minutes. The river ran straight out from the foot of the bluff underneath us, weaving through the tall, thick marsh grass and cattails that extended north for a good three-quarters of a mile. It looked like a long ribbon of quicksilver running over a swatch of rich black velvet.

Major Steve took out his knife and trimmed back a few straggly branches next to his stand. The pungent scent of pine spiced the cool morning air as he sliced through the thin limbs in virtual silence. Next, he scraped the leaves from under his stand so that his movements wouldn't rustle them later. The cool, earthy aroma of stirred moss wafted up, mixing with the fragrance of pine. With the best of my night vision, I watched in admiration as the Major considered all the variables of his stand. He set up near the bared, upturned root cluster of the downed pine. He quietly wiggled himself comfortable, and turned his head to survey his complete field of vision. Then, becoming completely still, he blended into the tree like he was part of it. He was about the only person I'd ever been in the woods with who was as quiet—quieter—than Gabriel. On the way up the ridge, I'd looked back several times, thinking I'd lost him. But there he'd be, three strides behind. He'd nod, encouraging me to keep up the pace.

Major Steve had been eager to get to this stand. When I'd laid out the options for this morning's hunt, he'd been keen to stake out the marsh. When I told him about this bluff, a fifty-foot ledge over the marsh just a hundred yards off the ridgeback, he was even more enthusiastic. He figured that if the big buck he'd seen with his own eyes was bedded down for the night in the marsh, like so many bucks he'd known and hunted back in the Dakotas, we might just catch it coming out from the lowlands toward the acorn-rich feeding grounds on the ridge early in the morning. I reminded him that the most certain thing I knew about deer was that they just about never did what you expected. But the marsh overlook seemed like a good bet, I'd agreed. And now, we'd made a pretty decent entry into the nighttime woods.

Settling into my stand, I peered into the sky as it began to brighten to a dark, pearly gray. Nothing to do now but wait, but that's okay. I've always been partial to the light before dawn. There's a peace about it, and promise as well. From the utmost darkness, shades of light brighten the land in increments, revealing the secrets of the night in graduated measures. Whether it was going to the barn in the biting cold dark winter mornings, or sitting on a hillside watching nature unfold, or opening the shutters and flooding the darkness with the subtle light of dawn, sunrise reaches into my heart. I love it even more than the sunset, hands down. There's no doubt about the romance of a fine evening sunset. Jannie and I shared many glowing moments, watching the scarlet sun fire up layers of violet clouds in the western sky. But the sunrise is personal. It is fresh. It brings strength and challenge and ambition. It grips my soul. All the promise, the potential for everything is awakened by the undeniable prying and creeping of the first rays of light. It is the hunter's finest hour, where all is equal and waiting, quiet and pure.

A rifle barked in the distance. It was still too dark to see fifty yards. Perhaps someone had an unwary buck walk right up to him. More likely, an accidental discharge. Major Steve tipped his head slightly toward the source of the report. His motion was barely noticeable. Then he slowly rolled his head to fix his ear on the hillside to the east, where the leaves had rustled just slightly a moment before. From the way I'd positioned myself on the bole of the old pine, I was facing southeast, directly toward the rustling. Through the veil of predawn darkness, I watched for movement. At the very horizon of my vision, I spotted a flicker of white against the curtain of lingering night. My eyes froze on the spot, but I could see nothing but dark woods. The early rays intensified a notch, and the image of a young deer, little more than a fawn, precipitated on my retinas. It stood, oblivious, twenty yards east of the Major, who was watching it intently. The nub buck turned and looked back over its shoulder along the trail. He waggled his tail, then bounded a stride or two westward along the worn deer trail that emerged from the woods.

The fawn walked right up to the upturned clump of pine root, not five feet from Major Steve. He stopped, turned his muzzle back over his shoulder and nipped at a spot on his rump. With his hind hoof, he scratched his side like a dog with a flea. Major Steve was as still as the pine trunk against which he leaned. The little buck spun around twice, chasing his tail, then once again, just like a dog who'd found the right spot for a nap, then dropped in his tracks onto a makeshift bed, sticking his muzzle snug along his underbelly.

Only then did Major Steve move. A grin spread evenly across his face. He glanced back up trail to the east, looking for any deer following along behind. I about snorted with laughter, but sucked it in. After Major Steve made certain that nothing was in sight, he stepped slightly forward, just touching the tip of his boot to the unwary fawn's spine. The youngster jumped from a tight curl to all four hooves in one seamless motion. Startled and bewildered, he looked right at Major Steve, incredulous. He stood stock still, little more than two strides in front of the Major.

Major Steve jerked his head just an inch, tipping it westward. He hissed in a whisper, "Get on. Get on now." He had to repeat himself before the fawn reacted, leaping almost effortlessly along the path in the direction Major Steve had urged. He stopped once, maybe twenty yards down trail, looked back toward us as if trying to unravel the mystery we presented, then sauntered away along the trail. He left us with a silly shake of his tail.

The Major shrugged and grinned, then melted back into invisible stillness. Within minutes, a small herd of does and young deer came following along the same trail as the young nub buck. The light was quite strong by now, and I spotted these animals a good hundred or more yards up the hillside. Major Steve had turned back to watch out over the marsh. I chirped once, like a chipmunk, and he slowly turned his gaze toward me, his eyes asking for info. I nodded once up the path. He raised his eyebrows. I unfolded four fingers from the stock of my rifle, then raised three fingers a second time. He mouthed, buck? I shook my head once, just a fraction of an inch, and he resumed his watch over the marsh.

The herd was led by a fawn no bigger than the one Major Steve had just chased off. The herd began to fan out as they entered the bright, open space around our fallen pine. The morning was bright enough now that I could see a number of beds flattened into the leafy carpet of the forest floor. We'd set up right on a favorite bedding ground. I wondered whether we'd have the herd at our feet as we hunted. If they did bed down, it would make our every movement precious. If we needed to get into shooting position, we'd have to be extremely careful not to spring the entire herd, or we'd have seven deer running helter-skelter, alerting everything in the woods that something had frightened them dearly. That was precisely why the Major had booted the nub buck, I figured.

The lead fawn seemed as anxious to bed as the little one that Major Steve had shooed away. But before it could find a likely nest in the leaves, a mature doe, a fine animal four heads back in the line of the herd, stiffened as she entered the clearing. She snorted a single warning whistle, then deliberately stamped a forehoof, thumping the packed ground of the trail. Major Steve and I both froze as she looked in our general direction, recognizing danger, but not seeing us. It was unlikely she'd scented us, with the wind at her tail coming toward us. Indeed, I could smell the sour fragrance of doe in estrus wafting from the herd.

Suddenly, she made up her mind. With another loud snort, she bounded up the slope to the ridge. The older does followed behind her, four animals flying between the oaks and maples on the hillside. Two of the young fawns skittered away along the path that the earlier fawn had taken. A single, nervous yearling doe stood confused, looking up the hill after her older harem mates. She glanced warily back across her shoulder, looking eastward up the trail on which the herd had been traveling. Then, uncertain as to where the danger lay, she plunged full speed down the steep face of the bluff, her hooves clattering on the rocks and rubble of the cliff. In three strides, she was down to the marsh. She fleeted through the light marsh grass and the darker, deeper tufts of cattail reeds. Only the diamond-shaped flash of her brazenly flagging snow-white tail broke her natural camouflage in the marsh.

It's hard to explain the intensity and vividness of the woods at a moment like that—there's so much build up, it feels like something big just has to happen. My body was tight with adrenaline, but I knew I had to have the patience just to wait and let it unfold. I exhaled, almost sighing, and I could see Major Steve's chest drop as well. The deer had been all around us. We could hear them, smell them. Yet I don't believe they ever saw us, or knew where we'd set up our stand. They were skittish, and they looked tired and ready to bed down. I wondered if they'd been chased during the night. Harassed, perhaps, by an alpha looking to breed. Perhaps. I'd watched deer many times without them being aware that I was close by, and this herd was definitely on edge. Maybe it was from the week's hunt, but there hadn't been much pressure since the weekend, and these deer looked pushed. I was thinking they were maybe just a little nervous about the big old Pony coming around, looking to be certain he'd made his mark on the gene pool as strong as possible. When a doe is at the height of estrus, she'll stand for a buck like a docile cow. A little past, or worse, a bit early, and they're jumpy and anxious. These deer looked just that. I took a deep breath and scanned the hillside above and to the east, watching for the slightest movement. Major Steve kept watch out over the marsh, sometimes scanning the bluff to the west. Occasionally, with the smoothest of movements, he'd slip his set of binoculars from a pouch on his red plaid field jacket, scanning the marsh thoroughly. I cleared my mind and focused, waiting for events to unfold.

All that caught my eye was a ray of sunlight peeking through a dip in the ridge top, catching the polished ivory tines of the Pony's massive rack. I couldn't see his body; he stood hidden behind an oak, his head craned out to see along the trail, his ears scooped forward to catch any sound that carried along the bluff. He was looking for the does he'd been following, and he sensed something amiss. He moved back out of sight behind the trees. Two deep grunts burbled through the forest. I glanced at Major Steve in time to see his eyes go wide. Slowly, he pivoted his gaze in my direction. I nodded, and felt my eyes close slowly in emphasis. The deer Major Steve hunted was here. As I righted my head and opened my eyes, I tilted my forehead towards where I'd last spotted the buck, a good hundred-fifty yards up the trail.

The Major slowly swiveled around a hundred and eighty degrees, using his body to shelter his arm movements from the deer's keen vision as he positioned his gun. By the time he'd got his feet in place, his rifle was aimed up trail to the east. He had made no sound.

We could hear the buck, however, working himself into the frenzy of rut someplace along the hillside. Occasionally, I caught a glimpse of movement between trees in the distance. To our east, the Pony was pacing back and forth along an arc the length of a football field. For half an hour, until almost eight o'clock, the big buck snorted and grunted and worked up scrapes along the hillside trail. I could hear him kicking leaves and dirt aside and venting his aggression on small trees. I'd seen bucks scrape often enough, and I recognized the earnest, dire scuffing sounds as dried leaves scattered and twigs snapped.

I caught one more flash of motion between the trees, and then there was nothing. Stillness. The whisper of the breeze through the bare limbs of the hardwoods on the ridgeback. A few squirrels rustling through leaves, recounting their hidden stashes of nuts.

Neither Major Steve nor I moved a muscle for more than half an hour. The wily old deer had sensed our presence, or simply known that something was out of place in the woods. Perhaps the scent of the does' fear had alarmed him. It seemed possible, but with the wind drifting lazily toward us from where the buck had worked the woods, I doubted it. I turned slowly, looking over my left shoulder, out across the marsh. The watery grey of dawn had matured into a hazy blue. Autumn had been easy on the northlands this year, and though the mornings were crisp and the leaves on the ground dry and brittle, the day promised to be unseasonably warm. I watched the marsh grass undulate gently in the morning breeze. Much of the marsh was still in the shadows of the southern ridge, and would remain so throughout most of the day. The sun would not rise high enough to bleach out the last traces of chlorophyll lingering in the reeds and marsh grass hidden in the shadows.

In the periphery of my vision, a slight motion rippled against the current of the sweeping breeze. As slowly as I could will my muscles to move, I craned around, peering past where the Major had leaned back, relaxed, against the pine. Again, it was the polish of the Pony's rack that exposed him. The buck had moved silently off the hillside and nestled himself behind a dark scrub brush amidst the reedy marsh grass. The light shifted and his tines became branches again, but now that I'd seen him, I could still pick out his mass, a different sort of solidness than the grassy hassocks and tufts of foliage around him. Buried in the shadows, he sat alert, warily surveying his domain.

Once again, I chirped. I thought the Major would burst out laughing when he read my expression. I smiled in return, realizing that my eyes were about as wide open as they could be. I checked the terrain, and catching no sign of approaching deer, I gingerly crossed the three paces to his side.

"It's him," I whispered, gesturing toward the lowlands with a hitch of my head. All the while, I kept an eye trained on the buck. So often, a deer could be standing in plain sight, and with the passing of a cloud or the shifting of the foliage in a gust of wind, it would simply disappear. Vanish.

The Major turned to see for himself. "Where?" he whispered.

"Fifty, sixty feet north of the bluff. Out a ways. Look between the bend in the river and that dark swatch of sumac right along the base of the bluff."

The Major squinted, looking hard. The buck lay motionless, surveying the marsh as intently as we were. Steve took out his binoculars and searched for endless moments, but resignedly shook his head. "Nope," he said softly. "I can't pick him up." Then, an ear flicked amongst the dried leaves of the sumac. The Major's eyes snapped into focus, he nudged the dial on his binocs, and he whistled, low, like the rustle of the wind through pine needles. He shifted his eyes to me and grinned in awe. "The Pony."

Major Steve looked me over thoroughly, inspecting me again. "You want to take the shot?" I didn't know if he was asking or telling. Or daring. His expression was open, inviting. He held out his rifle. "You earned it."

I shrugged, shaking my head. "Naw. This guy is yours. I don't know the gun, anyway."

He sized me up once more. From a simple glance, I saw that he understood. Not only did I realize that my .35 Remington was not the round to try and lob accurately at three hundred and fifty yards, but I also knew that shooting someone else's rifle for the first time should be for practice, so that when a shot presented itself like it did with the Pony meandering through the marsh, there would be no mistakes. Although this was exactly the kind of shot that his Browning was designed to make, I wasn't the man to take it. He smiled slowly, looking almost proud. I returned his grin. "You just better not miss."

His eyes widened with his grin. He shook his head, incredulous, and went to work.

The Major eased opened the clip on his Browning and removed the .300 Winchester Mag shells. The muffled metallic clinking seemed loud and out of place in the hush of the woods, but not even the squirrels scuffling around nearby seemed alarmed by the Major's discrete movements. Next, he cranked the bolt and removed the round from his chamber, and set the bolt back home. With an empty chamber, he wrapped the rifle's sling tight around his left arm, placing the stock of the barrel on his hand, resting on the downed pine. He leveled the optics of his rifle's scope toward the buck, adjusting the focus ring slowly. "How far?"

"Three-fifty. Maybe more."

He looked at the calibration ring on his scope, and straight-eyed the line to the bedded deer. "At least. Maybe closer to four."

He took off his glove and held his hand out above the pine trunk. Blowing softly against the back of his hand, he held it up to the wind again. Then he looked down off the bluff to the lowlands.

"Not even a click of wind up here," he whispered. "But the grass down below is moving a bit. I'd bet we have a breeze down over the marsh of six to eight miles per hour. That's a click," he said, turning to the adjustments on his optics. He shifted the horizontal hold on his scope one notch to the right.

"Three hundred sixty yards, maybe," he muttered, dialing the vertical screws for elevation. He looked up at me. "This round will drop about sixteen inches at four hundred yards."

With the optics adjusted, Major Steve set his rifle gently across the pine and resighted on the buck resting obliviously below. I heard the safety snap, and watched the Major time his breathing. After a long exhale and a three count, he gently pressured the trigger. With the sear polished, the firing mechanism sprung at less than a pound and a half of pressure. He continued looking through the scope, assessing his skill. Smoothly, he recocked the bolt, again with an empty chamber. He lined up his aim and took a second dry shot. He repeated the process once more, and was satisfied. The sound of the hammer seemed explosive in the quiet on the hillside, but it didn't carry down to the buck huddled out in the marsh. He never so much as pivoted his ears toward the clicking from the Major's Browning.

Major Steve fished a shiny brass cartridge from his jacket pocket. He inspected the round, looking for mars and nicks in the projectile. He fed the round into the chamber, checked to see that the safety was set, and then released the magazine catch. He fed two more rounds into the magazine, clipped it in place, and set the rifle comfortably across his lap. He sat cross-legged, facing away from the marsh. He relaxed his shoulders and slowly rotated his head first to the right, then to the left. He inhaled three times, exhaling fully, pausing between each breath. My eyes flicked back and forth between the Major's preparations and his prey. His method was fascinating, but I didn't want the Pony to pull a vanishing act while the Major was practicing deep breathing. Turning back toward his target, the Major positioned himself alongside the pine stump. He re-strapped the rifle's sling around his left arm and carefully lined up the optics on the deer in the distance.

The Major's rifle barked, and through the lenses I saw the Pony react almost instantly. In a flash, the deer was up off his bed. He bucked his hind hooves once into the air, then dashed westward, toward us. I heard the Major chamber a fresh shell as I set the binoculars down and raised my .35.

The buck had closed to within two hundred yards and was still on a dead run. I pulled back on the hammer and found the sprinting deer in my open sights. He was coming straight at us as fast as he could run. He'd closed to within a hundred-fifty yards when I squeezed down on the trigger, aiming a quarter-body length ahead of him. Just as I felt the recoil and heard the distinctive pop of my .35, Major Steve's .300 barked again.

The Pony dropped in a heap, twitching in death throes.

I turned to Major Steve, grinning. He looked sober and solemn at first, but a warm smile quickly softened his expression. We picked our way down the steep face of the bluff and through the thick fringe of the marsh to where the deer lay, a massive pool of blood running between the clumps of grass roots. Major Steve pulled his knife to slit the Pony's jugular and bleed him out. He stopped short, poking a finger into a bullet hole just where he'd aimed his knife. "Looks like he already bled out." He turned the buck's head by its lofty rack and examined a three-inch exit wound. "Yep. I think that might have been my second shot."

He moved to the deer's torso and found another fine hole just an inch or two behind and above the heart. His first shot. Liver, maybe lungs. A third bullet hole, larger caliber, entered at the base of the buck's thick neck, just above the shoulder. The Major poked his finger down into the bullet wound. The trajectory of the projectile drilled a hole straight into the neck, where it had struck the back bones. The slower, heavier .35 slug had smashed the spine, killing the buck instantly.

All three of the shots were fatal. The faster .300 had inflicted mortal wounds, and the Pony had run instinctively, not conceding his mortality to the puncture wounds of the high-speed projectiles. My .35 had simply brought him down at the end.

Major Steve knelt quietly over his kill. He hung his head briefly, his eyes trained on the big deer's glazing eyes. The moment hung solemn in the crispness of the autumn marsh. I felt like we were in church. After another moment, he nodded his head, his bottom lip protruding pensively. Then he gazed up at me, and it was like we'd entered a kindredship. We were brothers now, on a new and profound level. He nodded once, an unspoken acknowledgement. Then, finally, his face cracked into a wide smile, his eyes flooding with gratitude.

"That, my friend," he said, "was nicely done."

∞

November 22, 1962.

Dear Pat,

Man, am I tired! How often have you heard me say that? Not too often, I bet. Well, tonight, I'm tired to my bones, I tell you. What a day!

After milking this morning, I went out deer hunting with Young Roger's friend, Major Steve Whitney. This guy is a real good hunter, let me tell you. I've never seen anyone get around the woods like he does. Better than Gabe. And what a shot! He bagged the Pony, that big deer we saw rocking that tree when we went out after Jannie's funeral. He made a shot that was incredible. Almost four hundred yards. I was amazed. But then again, he's a Marine.

But then we found out how much work we'd made for ourselves! Man, the Major and I started down where the river bends near the point of the bluffs, just east of Klemms' farm, and pulled that buck all the way to Paddy's north alfalfa stand. It must have been about three-quarters of a mile. We pulled from about 9:30, after we had the Pony field dressed and all, until just after 1:00! More than once I wished you were here lugging that old buck with us. Man, we were soaking wet from sweat—and marsh water—by the time we got to Paddy's north forty. I left the Major sitting against a fence post, the buck lying alongside, and went and got the pickup so that we didn't have to drag that old deer the last six hundred yards. You should have seen Paddy's eyes go wide when we hung the carcass in the hay mow. We used the block and tackle, and it seemed like we were never going to get that buck's hind legs off the ground. Paddy said he'd never seen a buck as big. He figured it weighed well over two-fifty, just the way it hung. Gabriel thought closer to three hundred. I don't know. I just know that between Major Steve and me, it took us everything we had to pull that venison through all those clumps of marsh grass and up those hills and all. This was one grizzly old buck. Gabe said that even its gravy is gonna be tough!

Anyway, just about the time we got the buck all hung up, it was time to clean up for Thanksgiving dinner. Oh my Lord, did we eat! Everything was wonderful. I was so hungry. So was Major Steve. Everybody was teasing us about us never getting full. But we did, eventually. Mom's pumpkin pie put me over the top. I could hardly move! I could have napped big time after dinner. But you know how that goes. Gabe strung up his bow and was pealing tunes off his fiddle about as fast as you can imagine. He called me out to join him, which I did, even though I felt a little funny. I hadn't played at all, I guess, since I last played with Jannie—or at her funeral, actually. It seems so long ago, but it's really only a little more than a month since she and I last played together. Can you believe it? I can't. It is beyond me. I can't believe that just two weeks ago, she was still alive. And then she died. And we buried her. Just a week ago. It seems so unreal. Jannie was here, then she was gone. I mean, it's like, on one hand, nothing is real. Everything is turning upside down. Mom comes home. Jannie dies. You come home. You leave again. It's all so crazy! And on the other hand, life goes on. I get up in the morning and milk the cows. I go out deer hunting. Turkey day happens, just like usual. And no one misses a beat. Man. You know, Jannie used to talk about that, from her stay in Bethesda. People died and everybody else just kept on living. I guess you just have to do that. Just keep going on. So I rosined up my bow, and fiddled up a storm with Old Camp. And you know, it felt good. It felt real good. Only once, for whatever reason, I got a huge lump in my throat, and I could hardly keep on playing. But I couldn't just stop in the middle of the song—we were doing the Cannonball Express. I kind of felt Jannie there with me, then, and I was getting all choked up. But then it was as if she was whispering in my ear, telling me to just keep playing, keep making the music, just as she'd play it herself. And it was okay.

And then I had to go out and milk the girls. By the time I'd finished chores tonight, I'd pretty much run the course. Miss Rose took one look at me after I'd come in from the barn and said, "Davey, warriors must rest, even during the times of their most heightened awareness." I feel it now. Right now, I think I'm going to rest like a warrior. A real tired warrior.

I wish you had stayed home last week. I know you have your own life down in Indiana, but just now, it would be good to have you home.

I've said enough. I can hardly keep my eyes open to write. I'm going to bed.

Love,

Your brother David.

∞

December 7, 1962

Hi, Davey,

Got your letter. Sounds like a great hunt! I'd have liked to see that big old buck again, up close. Did you take any pictures?

I've been taking a few pictures lately myself. I'm not finished with the first roll yet, but I've been fooling around a little with a camera that Lynn left me, an old one of hers. I was real surprised to find it. She had it waiting for me on the canoes that we are building. She wrote a note saying that she wanted me to take pictures of the canoes as I worked on them. She left me about a half-dozen rolls of film, too. She's that way. She likes taking pictures. You should see some of the photographs she's taken.

I've been working on the canoes more. Progress is a lot slower now that Lynn is gone.

I decided not to go out for basketball. My coach went nuts when I told him. He said he had me figured for the sixth man on varsity. Coaches always say stuff like that, though. While you're on the team, they are always saying they don't know if they can play you. They are always doubting you. Then you find something more interesting to do and you quit, and they tell you the team can't get by without you. Coaches. They forget that the reason you want to play is just that, to play. They make it painful and hard, and they are always trying to make you feel guilty, or worse, to make you mad. They figure they can make you play better if you are mad. Get angry, play better. I didn't want that right now. I really am enjoying seeing the canoes come together. I get more out of it.

But quitting basketball has kind of turned out to be a major thing for the adults. Or for Aunt Mary, at least. She's all concerned. Uncle Paul is okay with it. He says my time would be better spent reading a good book. But they are both a bit on edge, mostly from trying to keep up with Jack. Jack has been so crazy lately that they are all concerned about him. They figure he's up to no good, and a lot of the time they're right. Man, Jack is wacko! He just keeps doing things that are more and more outrageous. Anyway, now that I quit basketball, Aunt Mary figures I'm gonna cause trouble just like Jack. She doesn't have to worry. But I guess she doesn't know that. Oh, well.

One thing Jack is up to that I think is a big problem for him is drinking. It's not like he drinks all the time. Just weekends, for the most part. I think. But when he does, he gets really blasted. He has a fake ID now and there is a liquor store in Valpo that will sell to just about anybody. He drinks a lot of beer, usually. But sometimes he drinks whisky. Man, sometimes he comes home just staggering. I don't know how he does it. I know I try to avoid being around when Jack is being Jack. He kind of lives in his own world. Jackland. I think the rules are different in Jackland.

Anyway, I gotta go. I'm headed over to Lynn's to work on the canoes. I have all day. I'm gonna run the roads to get there. The lake is just wild with the winds that blew in from the northwest the last couple of days. I'd be soaking if I ran the beach, and I'd freeze before I got there.

What do you want for Christmas?

Love,

Twin

∞

April 13, 1963

Hi, Davey,

Sorry I haven't written for a while. I've been real busy. But it's been fun busy.

We're still celebrating Loyola's national championship down here. You'd think Uncle Paul was full time at Loyola and adjunct at University of Chicago the way he's been carrying on these past few weeks. He says that he's got alumni privilege. What a game, though! Did you watch? Maybe it was that we were biased for the home team, but you may just have been able to hear us yelling all the way to North Freedom!

Man, did we get a snow last night. Kind of unexpected. I was running on the beach yesterday afternoon—yeah, yeah, I know, I should have been in church on Good Friday—and it was really kind of nice. Almost balmy. Then the wind shifted from the north, and snowflakes about the size of grapefruit come drifting gently down. Uncle Paul said it was lake effect snow, and that Valpo didn't get any at all, just ten miles inland. Well, whatever, it came down in bushels along the lake. We have about nineteen inches! And this morning, the sky was crystal blue, and it was the most quiet, peaceful morning I've ever seen. The lake looks incredibly deep blue, with the beach all white as snow. It is spectacular.

In a little while, I'm going over to Lynn's to finish the second canoe. It is really the better of the two canoes. I made a few mistakes on the first one, but that helped me learn things about finishing the second one. I want to put one more coat of marine varnish on both of them, and then I think they will be water worthy. Not that I would want to put them in the lake and try them out now. Too cold. I'll wait until Lynn gets back and we can launch them then. I don't really know when she will be back. I—well, we—have only heard from her twice. We got a Christmas card from when she was down in Oaxaca, Mexico. And then about three weeks ago, she sent a postcard from Japan. Jeez, can you imagine doing all that travel all over the world? Anyway, she mentioned coming home in the spring. Well, spring started almost a month ago, but no sign of her. I imagine that she'll wait until the weather is nicer. Wouldn't you? Just in case, I'll clear her driveway today, so she can get in if she's decided to come back soon.

Have your heifers started dropping their calves? Seems like you told me that some of those bred heifers you bought last fall should be calving by now.

Say hello to Paddy and everybody for me. I wrote Mom last night, and will send it out today along with your letter.

Your older brother,

T-1

∞

Patrick's uncle sipped his steaming latte as he curiously watched his nephew lace up his boots. "Where you headed?" Paul asked. "Are you really thinking of plodding through all this snow to work on your boats?"

Patrick shared a good-natured grin with his uncle. "You betcha. I should wrap up the last of it today. When this final coat of varnish dries, they'll be done."

"Wow," Uncle Paul mused, sipping again at the hot brew. "That's been quite a project." He rubbed his chin, looking vacantly out the kitchen window over the snow-covered yard. "Seems like you started these boats way back last summer, when the weather was still warm."

"October, really," Pat nodded. "But we had such a late fall. I'm really pretty happy that I have them done already." He glanced up from his boot straps. "You want to help finish?"

Uncle Paul looked pleasantly startled. He chuckled softly, and admitted, "Well, I'd normally be quite glad to take you up on your invitation, especially since you're at the finish line with this project. But," he added, raising his eyebrows, "I'm a little more intimidated by all that white stuff out there than you seem to be. You don't really expect to hike through thigh-deep snow all the way to Norths', now, do you? You'd need snowshoes, or skis!"

Patrick grinned again, and shrugged. "Well, I guess if that is what it takes to get me there, yeah, I'll plow through the snow. I was planning on jogging to Norths'. It might take a bit of high stepping. It would be a pretty good workout."

"Pretty good, indeed," Paul coughed. "Well, I'd offer you a ride, but...," he tipped the brim of his mug toward the snow. "...I concede to Nature with all her strength and beauty today."

Patrick pulled his knit cap down over his ears, pulled on his gloves, and stepped out into the snow. Uncle Paul stood in the opened kitchen door, laughing good-naturedly at his nephew. "You know, you could let those canoes wait a few days. They aren't going anywhere."

Patrick beamed over his shoulder. "I suppose I could. But it seems like a little snow shouldn't stop me now. It's time to wrap this project up."

The jog took perhaps three times as long as it would have on dry roads. Patrick was huffing when he reached the bottom of Lynn's driveway.

He was puzzled by a lump of snow mounded indiscreetly in front of the garage. As he approached, his heart leapt with hope that Lynn was finally home. The buried car was about the size of her Thunderbird. But with a swipe of his gloved hand across the snowy windshield, Patrick's hopes were dashed. The interior was dark and sporty, and the clutter on the bucket seats had nothing to do with anything of Lynn's. It was obviously not her car.

Whose was it? Patrick wondered. He kicked snow away from the license plate. Illinois plates, not Lynn's. But whose? It wasn't Dr. North's big Caddy.

Patrick let himself into the garage, where the two canoes stretched out over the sawhorses. He flicked on the garage light and stripped off his jacket and heavy, wet sweatshirt. He donned a dry, if not totally clean, t-shirt that hung in the garage. Then, he stripped off his running boots and snow-packed sweatpants and stepped into his work pants. He looked down, amused. The overalls had fit when he started the canoes in the fall, and he knew the denim hadn't shrunk over the winter, since they hadn't been washed. But the cuffs were an inch above the knob on his ankle. He'd grown over the winter. Things change, he mused. Nothing stays the same. Particularly his body.

Patrick moved to the door leading into the Norths' study. He listened closely, but heard nothing from within the house. He knocked softly, then a minute later, more firmly. After several moments with no response, he knocked again, then opened the door and called into the house. "Hello. Anybody home?" He couldn't keep a tremor from his voice. He wondered if he'd hear her call in return.

After a moment, he heard muffled sounds from up the hallway toward the bedrooms. He remained in the garage, his head and shoulders protruding into the hall. He called one more time. "Hello? Lynn?"

A silhouetted frame of a man entered the hallway above. "Who's there?" The voice was edgy, nervous.

Patrick strained to adjust his eyes against the bright backlighting to see who was approaching him. "It's me, Patrick Joyce," he said, his eyes resolving the shadowed figure. His heart sank, and a great lump formed in his throat. "It's just me, Dr. North, checking on the house. Lynn—Mrs. North—well, she wrote and asked me to make sure the furnace was working, and that nothing froze or anything." Patrick suddenly felt pressed to explain himself and his unannounced entry. "And to do things like keep the driveway shoveled. In case she comes home, I suppose." He felt suddenly very small, and he scrunched his shoulders and hung his head. Nonetheless, he towered over the thin man before him.

"Well, Patrick," Dr. North stammered. "It's good you're here to clear the driveway. Yes, definitely. This will help. I'll need to return to Chicago soon, and if you could just shovel the drive... well. Yes. Great."

Patrick looked up from where he'd fixed his gaze on the floor, gauging the tension in Dr. North's voice, far removed from the brusque, authoritarian tone he'd taken when he'd hired Patrick to do his yard work. The man seemed embarrassed, almost panicked. Patrick felt a surge of relief. Something was not quite right, but his presence wasn't the problem. The charged atmosphere in the hallway reminded him of being at the Howards' house when Jack was up to his shenanigans. He felt awkward and uncomfortable, but the guilty pang that had hit him when he saw Dr. North had passed, and now the doctor was practically fidgeting in the hallway. He wondered, *what exactly is the problem?* Was Dr. North even supposed to be here? Had the divorce gone through? If so, the house would be Lynn's property now, but he'd heard his aunt say that nothing could be finalized until after Lynn returned from wherever she was traveling. Patrick searched the doctor's face, surprised to see small beads of sweat forming on his brow.

"So, as soon as you have the drive open, we'll...uh, I'll be on my way," Dr. North continued in a rush. "How long do you think it will take?"

"Well," Patrick ventured warily, "I can probably get you to the end of the driveway by noon, easily." A wave of relief swept across Dr. North's anxious expression.

"But I don't know how much that will help in getting back to Chicago," Patrick went on. "I mean, it took me a good part of an hour just to get here from my house. The snow's this deep." He held a flat hand just above his knee. "I don't think you'll be going anywhere soon, unless the county comes in and helps plow. And I imagine they've had the plows off their trucks for weeks now."

"Damn it!" Dr. North burst, his usual abruptness returning. "I can't just be stuck here. I have to get back to the hospital. Goddamn it, this was not a good idea at all to come out here." He glanced back into the house.

Patrick started to back out towards the garage, when a voice filtered down the hallway from the bedroom.

"Barry, is everything all right?"

Barry North's head whipped around. A silhouette stood at the top of the hall. Squinting into the bright morning light flooding in through the bedroom windows, Patrick thought he recognized the man's round head and long, thin neck. The light was too bright to make out his face.

"Yes, everything's fine," Dr. North called back over his shoulder, his voice high and almost shaky.

He looked back at Patrick, and his bravado fell away to resignation. "Look," he began, falteringly. "Lynn..., well, she had to go... figure things out, she said. But I don't... I can't..., I have the hospital, and my patients, you understand. She has the leisure of removing herself from what she's... afraid of. I... don't. I don't think she'd mind me using the house, just to get out of the city. To get away."

He reached into his pocket and drew out his wallet. He fished through the currency and pulled out a single bill, folding it precisely with his surgeon's fingers, and handed it to Patrick.

"Here," Dr. North said, his voice hoarse and throaty. "Take this. For clearing the driveway."

Patrick looked at the bill. It was a fifty. He didn't want Dr. North's money. He took another step back, and shook his head. "Lynn's already contracted with me to keep the drive clean and check on the house. You don't need to pay me any more."

Barry North glanced back into the house once more, and then he met Patrick's eyes, pocketing the bill. "Fair enough. I'm sure you've worked out a suitable arrangement. But Patrick, when you see her... she doesn't really need to know that I was here." He looked into Patrick's face urgently, beseechingly. "She doesn't." He turned to walk back towards the bedroom.

"Wait!" Patrick blurted. "When I see her? Won't you..., do you know? Is she coming back?"

Dr. North turned back towards him, shaking his head. He smiled sadly. "I've instructed my attorney to contact me when she reappears. You'll probably know before I do. Give a shout when you're done with the drive, if you don't mind."

He walked back up the hallway, leaving Patrick to let himself out.

Spring, 1963

YOU DON'T REALLY KNOW there is a part of you that is beyond you, that grows and grows and becomes almost more important than the rest of you. You don't realize it's even there until you lose it. It's taken from you. And you're left with this gaping, gnawing hole that tears you almost in two. And there's nothing you can do. And you wonder if you'll ever find anything to fill it. You don't know that. At least, when you're young. And innocent.

I didn't see Mrs. Whitman much after Jannie died. When I did, I could see that her heart reached out to me. I knew she loved me like a son. I knew that just seeing me rent the wound in her heart anew. And I could hardly take it myself. So I guess I did things that kept me from seeing her. I stopped going to the library when I knew she might be there. Then I heard she'd stopped working there, too. At least temporarily. She'd taken a leave. I spotted her from afar a few times in town, and maybe she spotted me, too, but we respected each other's space, our mutual need to carry our own burdens.

It wasn't until spring that we talked. It was due. I think running into each other so unexpectedly at the co-op caught us both off guard. She was getting grain and salt licks for Cherub and Joker. I was hauling some fencing wire up to the counter, and didn't even see her until I literally bumped into her, startling us both. Just seeing her, smelling her lovely lavender scent mixed with the co-op's rich fragrances of grain and machine oil, well, it soothed me with peace and frightened me with a wave of pain revisited, both at the same time. She seemed smaller, thinner, but her face was radiant. I caught a flash of the same fear in her face that I fought in my own heart. But it was good to see her.

"David."

"Mrs. Whitman."

"You've grown," she said. We were almost at eye level to one another. I stepped to her, and we fell into one another's hugs. I thought for a moment that I'd cry, but after a deep breath or two, I knew I was okay. I think if I'd cried, she probably would have too. But we both held strong. If we had cried, though, I don't think it would have been for sadness. I think we were just so glad to see each other.

"I've missed you." I didn't even think what I was saying. I just heard my words flow right out of my mouth.

"It's been hard," she agreed. She stepped back and examined me with a careful eye, keeping my hands in hers. "I understand you'll be at Madison in the fall."

"Yes'm. Unless I go early, for summer classes. I'm going to study genetics."

"Genetics. You'll do well in genetics," she said. Her voice held a needed dose of kindness. My eyes welled up, and I almost lost it again. "David, are you so anxious to get to the University? Why would you go for the summer session? It's so beautiful here in the summer. And you have your animals."

"I know. It's kind of hard. I just thought I could get started."

She looked keenly into my eyes. I felt as though she was looking right into my heart. Sometimes, I could see so much of Jannie in her. "You'll have to be the judge of that," she advised. We stood, still hand in hand, and I felt as good as I had in months. I honestly thought I could make it. I felt a tickle of laughter trying to emerge from deep within.

"What?" she inquired, seeing that seed of humor in my eye.

" I don't know," I admitted. "It is good seeing you. I don't know why, but I think I've been hiding from… us."

"Yes. I have, too. I think we each needed to find our equilibrium. After Jannie… left." It was still tough, talking about it. We both got misty-eyed, but just for a second. Then our smiles took over.

"I've missed you, too, David. Why don't you come by, now? We'd all love to see you. And I sure could use your help with Cherub. I think he's missing Jannie as much as the rest of us!"

We agreed on it. I'd quit hiding out and avoiding the Whitmans. No sense missing out on being with my good guys. I'd come over and give that devilish Cherub a good workout at least once a week—and maybe have a few brownies afterward, while we visited.

And in my heart, I knew I wouldn't be going to Madison until the fall. There was still too much beauty here at home for me to rush away. I needed to savor it now, as it was. I didn't need to leave to start living again. I felt so glad, so relieved. When he picked me up at the co-op after his haircut, Paddy looked across the pickup's wide bench seat six times, at least, as he drove us back home. He must have been wondering why I was whistling.

∞

May 11, 1963

Dear Patrick,

Well, I'm just as disappointed as you that you can't make it home for my graduation. I always just took it for granted that you'd be here. I never even gave it a thought that your school year would run longer, or that you'd be taking finals when I was graduating. Oh, well.

Mr. Ackerman said he could tape my valedictorian speech so we could send it to you. Do Uncle Paul and Aunt Mary have a reel-to-reel tape player? I don't know. Perhaps you won't even want to hear it.

I've been thinking about what I should say. Every time I do, though, it kind of sounds stuffy and proper. Not like me, really. Maybe I should just play a tune on my fiddle and call it good. That would be most like me. Gabe won't let me do that, though. He said that would be taking the easy way out. He said my gift wasn't just fiddling, and this time I was being called upon to share the gift of my brain with my classmates. He said if I hadn't wanted to give the valedictorian speech, I should've planned ahead and flunked a couple of courses, but since I went for it and got it, I have to give the speech. Not fiddle. I told him he'd turned on me, and he just poked me in the ribs with his bow. No compassion there!

I suppose I should work on it. I have to have it ready to rehearse with Mrs. Everett by Wednesday. She said no later. I suppose she'll want to make any changes before graduation Thursday evening.

I asked Miss Rose what I should say, and she gave me one of her looks. She said, just talk from my heart. I dunno about that.

Mom says I should talk about the challenges that we have before us. Like with President Kennedy's goal of going to the moon by the end of the decade. I don't know. I'd rather talk about my cows hitting twenty thousand pounds of milk by the end of the decade. Least ways that will feed somebody.

I'm not going to summer school. I thought I might, but I finally figured out that I'd rather have this summer at home. You know, college is going to be real different, going away and all.

Father Jack is leaving. He's going to go abroad again. First he has to go back out to New York for some schooling and training. Then he'll be reassigned to someplace overseas. I'll miss him, but I guess I'd have missed him anyway after I left for school. But Madison isn't that far. I could always get back and see him now and again. He won't be leaving until the end of summer, anyway, I think.

Well, again, I'm sorry you won't be here Thursday. I'll be missing you.

Do well on your exams. You can't play football forever, you know.

Have you launched the canoes yet?

Love,

Your Little Brother

P.S. You know, don't you, that you're right on top of my Good Guy List.

∞

Patrick sat lazily on the porch swing, reading the letter for the fourth time. He always read and reread David's letters, three, four, even a half-dozen times. He could hear his brother's voice in each word of neat, boxed script. He wondered what he'd meant, his "Good Guy List"?

He picked up the square manila package that had come with the letter in an oversized envelope. He opened the flap and let the reel of opaque brown tape fall into his hand. David's graduation speech. Patrick was curious as to what his brother had said. David had written the letter prior to delivering his speech, and had not added anything further about what he actually decided to say. He turned the reel over and over, inspecting it, unrolling a two-foot lead, examining the tape, wishing he could read the words right off the shiny brown surface of the flimsy plastic film.

The only tape recorder that Patrick knew about was in Lynn North's study. Maybe later he'd jog on up to Norths'.

∞

He'd run twelve miles on the beach and was spent. Home alone, he showered. He'd skipped dinner. He tried to focus on a book, but slipped into drowsiness.

The waning light of the late May evening filtered into his room. Patrick dissolved into the oncoming darkness. He forgot his hunger. His mellow, post-run high buffered the fatigue in his legs. He smelled the sweet fragrance of soap lingering on his freshly cleaned skin, and the smooth coolness of his cotton sheets. As he tumbled into slumber, he focused on the image of Lynn North standing before him, leaning into him, looking into his eyes. He remembered her fragrance, her presence of being, her touch.... Slowly, calmly, he succumbed to sleep, a fuzzy, nonsensical dream escorting him away from reality.

He heard the phone, but it made no sense. It rang on, so distant and remote. The ringing pulled at him, drawing him from his slumber. Night had settled in. Darkness filled the room, and then the ringing. Again. And again. Patrick struggled to clear his head, sitting in a stupor at the side of his bed. The phone stopped ringing, then, a moment later, started again. This time, he was awake enough to respond. He staggered to the desk under the window. Plopped his naked body down in the desk chair, he flipped the earpiece off the receiver.

"Hello?"

He listened to a pause of silence.

"PJ." Her voice was little more than a whisper.

Patrick jolted awake. "Lynn?"

"Of course. It's me."

"Lynn! Oh, God, Lynn."

She laughed softly. He thought he'd remembered that soft, lilting laugh so vividly, but now, hearing it, it seemed like forever ago.

"How are you?" she asked.

He nodded several times. "Good. Good. Fine," he grinned. He couldn't have been better. "And you? How are you? Where are you?"

"I'm fine," Lynn said, a tremor in her voice. "I'm here. In the Dunes. I saw you sailing today."

"That was you!" He'd been sailing with his cousin at the helm, and had done a double take at a woman walking alone on the sand. Jack, in one of his dangerous moods, had held Patrick captive on board, refusing to sail in toward the beach to confirm the walker's identity.

"So you did see me!" she teased. "And you wouldn't even sail in to say hello!"

"Damn Jack," Patrick muttered. "I'd have swum in, if I'd have been sure it was you—and if the water wasn't an ice cube."

She laughed again.

"When did you get home?"

"Two days ago. I have to leave again on Monday," she said. "I just had to come for some papers and things. I have some business to finish in Chicago. Then I'm going to fly to Minneapolis next weekend for my niece's christening. But I'll be back soon."

"When can I see you?"

"Tomorrow?" she offered. "I saw your aunt and uncle at the Chambers' cocktail party. They said you'd be around. Would you like to come over tomorrow afternoon? I have something for you. I brought it back from Japan."

Patrick's mind whirled. He could see Lynn tomorrow. No. It was too much.

"Tonight," he insisted.

Again, she left him in silence for a lingering second. "Yes. Tonight."

Patrick's mind raced. He'd have to get dressed and run the road. It wasn't even fully dark yet. Just twilight. He could be there in twenty minutes, tops, he assured her.

"No, Pat," she said. "I'll come to you. I can drive. I'll be there soon. Are Paul and Mary back from Chambers' yet? They were partying pretty hard."

"Yeah, they always do. I don't think they're home. I haven't heard them. I was kind of nodding off."

"You sounded like it," Lynn teased. "I'll come up the stairs in the front. To the porch. Meet me on the porch, okay?"

"Yeah. Sure," Patrick said, dreamily. Anything. Anyplace. He'd meet her anywhere.

"See you soon."

∞

Patrick waited in the darkness of the Howards' screen porch. He looked through the porch window into his bedroom at his bedside clock. Eleven minutes had passed since he'd hung up the phone. He sat pensively on the end of a lounge chair, his elbows on his knees, his fingers kneading the dips between his knuckles. His head turned to the sound of a car driving along East Road, coming over the crest of the dune to the south. The car cruised down to the beach, pulled into the East Beach parking area, and stopped, its headlights shining down onto the beach. After a minute, the lights died and the engine shut off. The doors opened on both sides and the voices of a couple young men carried, muffled and deep, on the still evening air up to where Patrick sat waiting. He glanced back at the clock. Thirteen minutes. *Was she coming?*

Tires crunched on loose gravel as the car slowly crested the dune to the south. Patrick stood and went to the screened wall of the porch as the headlights turned into his driveway. They went off, and the engine stilled. He heard the door open, then close. He switched on the lights to illuminate the stairs.

Lynn's movement flashed through the pine trunks, dune grass, and tiger lilies that grew thick along the face of the dune next to the long flight of stone stairs. He could hear the soft grating of sand beneath her feet on the fieldstone. She stopped at the landing halfway up, and he could hear her inhale deeply and then sigh. She continued up.

Patrick tried to find his voice to call a greeting. He could say nothing. He watched her climb the steep ascent, her steps strong and even. She carried a wrapped box, her left arm cradling its mass, her right hand balancing the package. Even with her load, she moved smoothly up the steps. When she got to the three wooden steps to the porch, she stopped. The top light on the stone stairway was behind her now, and she stood in silhouette, her hair glistening in the bright white candescent light. She looked curiously into the unlit porch.

"Patrick?" she asked softly.

He moved toward the door. His voice was trapped in the dryness of his throat.

"What are you doing in the dark?" Lynn asked, her cadence bouncing with gentle humor.

Patrick opened the door and held it for her. Her fragrance filled his nostrils as she stepped in.

She turned to him, the package prominently between them.

"I brought you something," she said, her voice as soft as the gentle lapping of waves along the beach.

Patrick tried again to speak, but could only whisper her name. "Lynn."

He took the box from her, set it on the lounge, and faced her.

The edges of his vision dissolved into the darkness. Voices drifting up from the beach, lights from the skyline rimming the lakeshore, and the crickets chirping in the dune grass outside the porch… all was gone. Lynn stood before him, gazing into his eyes.

He watched as her hands moved from her sides, taking his fingers, holding them briefly, then sliding between his arms and his body. She closed the last step between them. He felt her hands pull him gently to her, and she reached up to kiss him warmly on his lips. She held him, and he wrapped his arms around her and kept her close. He exhaled a long, slow breath and rested a kiss upon her hair.

"Lynn," he said again, his voice more fluid.

She looked into his eyes again, keeping her arms snug around his sides. "Yes. I'm me. Did you expect otherwise?" A twinkle lit her eyes, evident even in the shadows of the porch.

Patrick shook his head quickly. "I just…well, I've wondered how it would be…." His words floated in the stillness. "I mean, I just wondered if you, if we…."

She brought her hand from behind him and placed a single finger gently on his lips. She looked deep into his eyes, and he thought he saw her shake her head slightly. A shock of electricity jolted through him. She moved her head more definitively, again shaking her head. Her eyes held kindness and warmth. She placed her hand behind his neck, pulling him gently to her lips. Patrick melted into her lingering kiss. He felt himself grow aroused, as did she, and she pressed her body closer to him. Slowly, she pulled back, looking up into his face.

"Don't wonder, Patrick. I'm here now. This very moment is how we are. That's what you need to know. We don't need to worry about what we will be, or how things could be. Right here, right now, we're being true to ourselves. That's all we need to go on."

She brought her hands around and placed her open palms high up on his chest, leaning back into his strong arms as she looked at him. "You've grown since I last saw you, haven't you?" Her eyes shone with delight. "You must be another inch taller."

She ran her hands up onto his shoulders and down the sides of his arms. "You haven't gotten any smaller, that's certain."

Patrick chuckled self-consciously. "Yep, I guess I did grow a bit more. I was wondering if you hadn't shrunk, or something." His voice remained tight in his throat.

"No. Not me," Lynn laughed. "In other ways, perhaps."

She turned her head and laid it on his chest, and he snuggled her in his arms. They stood quietly, swaying with the rhythm of the tiny waves lapping upon the beach.

Patrick lost all sense of time. He felt as if he and Lynn could hold each other forever. Finally, though, he sighed, and his voice felt relaxed and under control. He spoke with his lips pressed against her hair. "I thought of you every day. Almost every moment of every day."

He felt her head nod against his chest.

"I wondered where you were. What you were doing."

She looked back up into his eyes.

"I did so much. I have so much to tell you about," she assured him with a smile. "My crazy sister dragged me halfway around the world! It was incredible. And Patrick, I thought of you, too. Every day. You were with me all the time. I...." She left her words hang unfinished. Instead, a broad smile swept across her face.

"They're beautiful, Pat." Her eyes glowed.

It took him a split second to understand. He grinned. "Yeah. I love 'em. I did them for you."

Once again, she shook her head with a tiny movement. "For us, Patrick. For us. There are two canoes. They are both beautiful."

He welled with pride and satisfaction. He drew her tightly to him again, and felt her move her body in response. Then she stepped away gently from his arms. She took his hand and led him over to the lounge chair on which he had placed her package.

"I want you to have this. I brought it from the other side of the world for you," she said, adding, "I was thinking of you."

Patrick stepped over to the door and switched the porch light on. They both squinted and shaded their eyes.

"Whoa!" Patrick cried. "Sorry. It seems brighter than I thought it would be."

"Don't worry," Lynn laughed, trying to keep her eyes open while they readjusted to the light. She sat on one of the upright wicker chairs and pointed toward the box. "Come on," she urged. "I can't wait. I brought it for your birthday, but I just couldn't wait."

Patrick brought the box to the matching wicker chair next to Lynn. He sat on the edge of the seat, sat the box on the decking at his feet, and started to fumble with the ribbons. The bow had been tied inexorably tight. Lynn dug into her white denim shorts and extracted a small, single-bladed pocketknife.

"I figured you'd need something to cut it."

Patrick smiled. It was so like Lynn to plan every detail. He unfolded the blade and slit the ribbon with two easy motions.

"Nice blade," he commented, testing it with the tip of his finger before folding it and returning it to Lynn.

"Got it in Sydney," she said, adding, "Australia."

Patrick looked up from the wrappings he was tearing apart. "Australia! Wow. You must have gone about everywhere."

Lynn shook her head in resignation. "No. But we would have, I'm sure, if Ingie had her way. The place I liked best was New Zealand. Maybe. Mexico was incredible too, but so different. Come on," she urged, watching him pause as he listened to her report. "Open it! I'm dying for you to open it."

Patrick tore the paper off and opened the box. The box held a leather case. He pulled the case out by its strap, letting the box fall to the floor. He rubbed his hands across the smooth leather surface and glanced up at Lynn, who was bubbling with anticipation.

"It's so soft."

She nodded, scrunching her shoulders up. "It's kangaroo. Isn't it lush? But go on. Look what's inside."

Patrick detached the pair of snaps that held down the top flap of the case. Underneath was a zipper, which he pulled open, noting how smoothly the brass zipper moved along the rows of metal teeth.

Inside, tucked into the center compartment, was a single lens reflex camera. Patrick removed it carefully, tipping and turning it to examine the fine instrument. A chrome plate above the lens read *Nikon*. He held the camera to his face and looked through the view finder at Lynn. He turned the focus band on the lens, and her image became crisp and clean. She smiled broadly at him, her hands clasped palm to palm, fingers spread electrically, the index fingers touching her lower lip. He found the shutter and snapped it.

Lynn burst with joyous laughter.

Patrick looked at her over the top of the camera. "Wow. This is incredible," he said. "You brought me this? You're amazing. Thank you."

"There's more. In the bag." She reached out for the camera, which he handed to her. Before he unfastened the long, heavy lens from its secure compartment, he heard his camera click. Lynn was peering through the lens, focusing, and snapping the shutter.

Patrick examined the heavy lens he extracted from the satchel. On the retainer ring, *300 mm* was stamped in white.

"Man, this is a whale!" he exclaimed.

Lynn chuckled. "There're two more. And some filters."

Patrick fished the other optics from the bag. There was a mid-sized portrait lens. The last lens was a wide angle. Short and compact, its glass bulged slightly from within the metal tubing.

"That may be the hardest lens to learn to use," Lynn said. "But it can be really fun."

They handled and exchanged the photo equipment. Patrick listened as Lynn explained about the camera and lenses. She'd bought it for him in Japan, along with a similar set-up for herself. She'd lugged the heavy optics through three countries for more than nine weeks.

From the upper landing behind the house, he heard car doors slam. His uncle and aunt were coming up the short staircase to the back side of the house. He could hear his aunt laughing and talking loudly, and recognized her tone. *They'd really enjoyed the cocktail party,* he thought fleetingly.

The side porch door swung open and Patrick's relatives let themselves in. He and Lynn sat facing each other in the chairs, the pile of photo equipment and wrappings stacked on the floor between them. Lynn had been too engrossed in the photo equipment to hear their approach, but she turned at once, and smiled in greeting.

"Well, good evening once again, Mrs. North," Uncle Paul said, his enunciation thick and melodic. His voice remained kind and friendly, but Patrick noted his curious expression.

Aunt Mary was less discrete. Her brow furrowed as her mind decoded the signals from her eyes. Her lips had frozen as if in mid-word, but no sound came from her mouth. She looked confused, and the sheen across her eyes indicated the fog of her thought process. After an awkward moment, she coughed, "Oh!"

Patrick held up his camera. "Can you believe what Lynn brought me?" He turned to Lynn. "This is awesome."

Uncle Paul teetered across the decking and reached for Patrick's camera. "This is quite a camera," he said, inspecting the F2. Concern accented his words. He turned his head at a funny angle to face Lynn. "You *gave* this to Patrick?"

"And these, too." Patrick held up the lenses.

Paul's eyes widened further.

Aunt Mary was less stable on her feet, and she groped for Paul's arm as she stepped closer to her nephew.

"Whadja want to give all that to Patty for?" she slurred. "What kind of a gift is that, anyway?"

Lynn gestured to the camera, still in Paul's hands. "It's a single lens reflex," she explained, undaunted. "I thought it would be good for Patrick to learn photography with an SLR."

Patrick wondered at the defensiveness in Lynn's voice. Alarm crept up his spine like a centipede.

"This is quite a generous gift," Paul offered, diplomatically.

"Gift?" Mary said. "How can you even think to give something so valuable to this young boy?"

Patrick recognized the anger rising in his aunt. He'd seen her get angry often before, but almost exclusively at her own son. The flashpoint of her fury was dry tinder when she was drunk.

Lynn trained her calming nurse's gaze at Patrick's agitated aunt. "This is really more than simply a gift to Patrick," she said calmly. "It's for his help looking after the house during the winter. And for his work on the tie-wall, and... ."

"I thought you already paid him for that wall," Mary snapped.

"I did. I paid him fair wages. But building our wall was far more valuable than any wages could be. I brought him this because it was special, just as his help was more than expected. And also, I gave it to him for building the canoes for... me." She glanced at Patrick.

"The canoes?" Mary asked, diverted. "I haven't seen those canoes since they were hardly more than ribbing." Her tone softened, her expression looking concerned but confused.

Patrick grinned. "They're done, now, Aunt Mary. And they're beautiful."

Paul intervened, his voice resonant and his words no longer thick. "Yes, Patrick did an exceptional job on the canoes. I've been over to see his progress a number of times—even helped with the sanding more than once or twice," Paul said evenly. He extended his hand to return the camera to Lynn.

"Well, young man, you have much to be thankful for," he continued, reaching up and placing a hand reassuringly on Patrick's shoulder. "This is not a trivial gift. It is an opportunity to learn. I just hope you'll be generous in allowing your uncle to learn on this fine equipment, as well." His eyes focused intensely on his nephew, and he wore a grin meant to bring finality to the discussion. He turned to Lynn. "This is a most generous gift, Lynn. Thank you, on Patrick's behalf." He returned his glance to his nephew.

Patrick saw clarity and understanding in his uncle's eye. Paul's jovial, somewhat intoxicated wit had sobered and sharpened as he stood examining the camera. Patrick had watched him weigh judgment, and was relieved by his words.

"You bet, Uncle Paul," Patrick said softly. "It's the least I can do for all the help you've given me. And not just on the canoes."

Paul patted Patrick's shoulder and stepped toward the door. "Well, Darling," he said, "shall we retire?"

Aunt Mary moved with him in resignation. "Well, it should be 'good evening,' after all," she said stupidly, following her husband. They both hesitated at the doorway.

Lynn also turned to leave. "Thank you again for the canoes," she murmured to Patrick.

"Aw, really...," he began, then collected himself. "I'm the one who's thankful. This is an awesome gift." He nodded sincerely. "Hey, I meant to tell you. I was going to head over to your house tonight anyway, before you called to say you were home. I got a tape from Davey of his valedictorian speech. I was going to use your tape deck to play it."

Lynn smiled eagerly. "Oh, that would be wonderful! I'd love to hear it, too." She turned to Mary and Paul. "Why don't you all come over tomorrow afternoon? We could all hear David together."

The last of Mary's bitterness dissipated. She, too, wanted to hear the tape. "Well, if it isn't too much of an imposition...."

"Not at all. I really would like to hear him, too. But if tomorrow isn't convenient, you can use the tape deck any time next week. I'll be leaving on Monday for Minneapolis for my niece's christening, but Patrick knows how to use it."

"I think tomorrow would be perfect," Paul replied. Thank you, Lynn, for asking us. But I'm wondering, will you be christening your canoes tomorrow as well?"

Patrick's eyes widened along with his grin. "Oh, yeah! Let's! Whaddya say, Lynn?"

"Let's!"

May 29, 1963

DEAR BRUDDER,

Well, the last of the calves dropped this morning, least ways from our home-born stock.

Sounds like a nice camera setup that Lynn got you. Are you lucky, or what? It sure took some nice shots of your canoes. From the pictures, they look beautiful.

I'm glad you liked the tape from graduation. Did it really make Lynn cry? I tell you, it was real scary having to stand up in front of a big crowd like that and talk.

Well, you gotta let me know what you'd like for our birthday. Now that the cows are milking pretty good, we have a little more cash to do things with. If you don't tell me what you want, I'll choose something myself. Then you might end up with a new lead halter, or a set of nice leather work gloves. I suppose if you build any more walls or something this summer, that wouldn't be a half-bad idea.

We should talk. Give me a call sometime.

Love,

T-2

∞

June 15, 1963

Dear Davey,

I hope you're getting the same kind of weather we've had this past week. If you are, you're probably making hay to beat the band. It has been perfect. About 85 every day, sunny. Maybe a cloud or two in the afternoon, just to make the sky look bluer than it already is. The lake has been incredible. We haven't had a wave more than three inches high for almost a week. In the mornings, it's like glass. I've had one or the other canoe out every day. This morning, the canoe just glided across the surface. I headed straight out, just kept paddling without ever looking back for I don't know how long. Maybe an hour? Maybe more. When I finally turned around, the beach was out of sight. I couldn't believe it! It was so amazing! When I was way out there, just floating around, not even paddling, this big old seagull flew down and landed on the other end of the canoe. Like it needed a place to rest its wings. It just sat there, giving me the eyeball, squawking now and again, and peeking over the side of the canoe into the water like it was looking for fish. Too cool. Then, I watched a huge iron ore freighter come sailing in from way out in the lake. It was tiny at first, breaking across the edge of the horizon to the north. But as it got closer, it just kept on growing bigger and bigger. It really didn't take too long before it came within about a few hundred yards from me. The guys on the boat must have seen me a ways off, 'cause four or five of them were standing along the rail, watching me. Looked like they were wondering what the heck I was doing so far out on the water. The captain of the boat, or at least the guy at the wheel, he blew this incredibly loud horn when they were just about as close to me as they would get. It was LOUD Three times, he sounded the horn. It was incredible, though, to watch that big ship cruise through the water. It must have been a couple of football fields long. Just about the time that the tail end of the boat passed by, its wake hit me. What a roller coaster! From sitting pretty on a surface as flat as a table, all of a sudden I was going up and down these nice six-foot swells. The guys on the deck of the ship all laughed and yelled something to me, but I couldn't hear what they were saying. I think it was in another language, anyway.

For a while, I tooled around and caught on to a bit of that big old boat's wake and paddled like a bandit and rode the crest of the wake's swell for a good ways. Maybe a hundred-fifty yards or so before I slid off the back end of the wave. It was cool. Well, I had to paddle for at least an hour before I got back in to shore. By then, though, I could see people on shore, and I could see that a few people had gathered right out in front of East Beach. One of them was waving frantically, and sometimes even doing jumping jacks and yelling. The closer I got, the more I recognized the movements of that person. It was Aunt Mary, and she was madder than hell at me! By the time I got almost to the second sandbar, well, I knew my goose was cooked! Did she rip into me. She said she spotted me heading out and ran upstairs and got the binoculars. Then, she watched me paddle out until she couldn't really see me with the glasses. Oh, was she mad. So, she came running down to the beach and started yelling at me and calling for me to come back in... lot of good that did! I know voices carry over the water pretty well, especially when it's so calm. But I never heard her once. By the time I got back to the beach, I couldn't recognize her voice anyway, it was so hoarse and raspy. That didn't stop her from giving me an earful, though. I don't know why she was so mad. I guess I was gone for a pretty long time. It was nearly one o'clock when I got back in. But all I was doing was paddling the canoe. And I even had a life jacket with me. I wish I'd worn it more. I got really sunburned out on the water like that for more than five hours. I'm like a lobster. Aunt Mary chewed me out about that, too.

So, I'm grounded. I don't know for how long, really. She said a week, but we'll see. This is the first time I've been grounded. It's nothing for Jack to get grounded. I think he's grounded until he's about thirty-five. But he never really takes being grounded very seriously. If he gets grounded for a week, well, he's gone after a day. It used to be that Aunt Mary, particularly, would go bananas when he'd come back home after he'd breezed out while he was grounded. But then Jack just wouldn't come home at all. He'd come back a day or two or three later. So it got to be that Jack would get grounded, but he'd just leave. Then, when he'd come back, nobody would say anything at all. Kind of like nothing had happened and that Jack wasn't grounded at all in the first place. Like he had just gone into town for a soda or something and come back an hour later, rather than two days of who knows where? Anyway, so after Aunt Mary grounded me for a week—until our birthday, much less—Jack just kind of waited until she wasn't around, and he told me to just lay low 'til tomorrow and then ignore that anything had happened. I don't know. With this sunburn, it won't hurt staying inside for a day or two anyway. I'll see. Maybe I'll go as stir crazy as Jack does. I doubt it, though.

I'll just probably catch up on some reading. Uncle Paul has been after me to read this Rachel Carson book, Silent Spring. *He said it would make me appreciate the lake and the Dunes even more. I think I'll give it a try. I had to laugh. He wasn't even bothered by my paddling trip. He never even came down to the beach while Aunt Mary was doing her histrionics. He was working on some writing that he wanted to catch up on. When Aunt Mary confronted him and wanted to know his thoughts on my "absolutely irresponsible, thoughtless shenanigans," Uncle Paul just said, "Wow, you went so far you couldn't see the beach?" It was like he was disappointed because I hadn't asked him to go along. That really burned Aunt Mary up. As did the sun. Man, I may be sunburned, but I already had a fairly good base tan to work from. You know how fair-skinned Aunt Mary is. Probably more than Mom. Well, she's a whole different color red than I am. She's pure red. She's been in bed since late afternoon. She looks like she's got sunstroke. I took her up some ice water, and she looked so bad I felt pretty horrible. Oh, well. She really didn't have anything to worry about.*

You were wondering what's going on between her and Lynn? Well, not much, lately. Lynn's been gone for a couple weeks now. Ever since the day after we launched the canoes. Those were the pictures I sent you. I don't know when she'll be back. I don't know why she got Aunt Mary so mad, either. Not really mad, I guess. Nasty. Kind of rude, and real cold, too. It's kind of embarrassing for me, though. I can't imagine anybody wanting to treat Lynn so mean. It started Memorial Day weekend, when Lynn came over to give me the camera. Man, I have to tell you, I was so glad to see her. I couldn't believe it. I gotta tell you, Davey. I did kiss Lynn. I mean, it was like, hello, I'm so glad to see you again type of kiss. Well, maybe more. But it was perfect. And it was so natural. But that's all. A kiss. Or two. Well, Aunt Mary and Uncle Paul weren't even home, they were off drinking and partying at the neighbors. But they got home while Lynn was still here. I mean, we were on the porch, just sitting there. And we were behaving ourselves and everything. Just happy to be with each other again. And looking at the camera gear she brought me. But when Aunt Mary got home, she got real snide and sarcastic. It was so embarrassing. Uncle Paul was cool enough, although he was looking at me with his one eyebrow perched up about halfway to the top of his head. You know what I mean. Well, anyway, nothing much became of it. And the next day, we listened to your tape. Then we went canoeing. Uncle Paul and Aunt Mary took my canoe, and Lynn and I took hers. We paddled the lake for an hour. But Aunt Mary was kind of cold that day, too. And by Monday when she called Mom, she was just nasty about Lynn. Said she had no business fooling around with a "child" like me. I didn't hear all she had to say to Mom, but from what Mom asked, she didn't sound too concerned. And she doesn't have to be. I mean, Lynn is about as cool a person as there is. And that's what I told Mom. Anyway, it has all kind of cooled off since Lynn left, although I think Aunt Mary might have thought that Lynn had snuck a kiss to me when we were all leaving her house that day after canoeing. I mean, Lynn did give me a little kiss, kind of a peck, really, but I don't think Aunt Mary saw. She just suspected. And that's what lit her fuse. She's been like a time bomb lately. And I guess I'm easier to catch than Jack. He never did come home until Tuesday that week. He called once or twice. He often does, and he says when he'll be home. But he never gets here when he says he's going to. I don't know. I can't figure out why they are so tough on me for when I haven't done anything wrong, and they just gloss over how Jack's behaving. Maybe it's that I stick around too much.

I suppose Aunt Mary's being extra protective of me since she doesn't want to let Mom down and let me get in trouble or anything. But I don't know. I really can't see how being with Lynn is any sort of trouble. We do so many good things together. The wall was a work of art. And the canoes, too. Yeah, I know, she's older and all that. Almost seven years older. But she's so different. I mean, I can really talk with her. We can talk for hours and not run out of things to say. Or, we can just sit there, and be still, working side by side, and be comfortable with being quiet around each other. And she's so interesting. She has done some cool things, and she has all these great ideas. I mean, imagination, or what? I guess you'd know, Davey. She's like Jannie, kind of. I remember you telling me how, instead of hanging out with me and the guys from the baseball team, you'd rather be with Jannie. Well, I never used to know what you meant, even though I thought Jannie was cool and all. I couldn't see it. I do now, though. I hate it when Lynn is away. I can't believe she's gone again. But just the little time that she was home over Memorial Day was so wonderful. I felt so wonderful. And when she goes away again, it is the worst. I think of you so much, with Jannie gone, how you must feel. It makes me sad. But somehow, I always feel that you are okay, and strong and willing to go on. I don't know. When Lynn leaves, I feel empty. Hollow. And I never really know when, or if, she's coming back. And if she does, I never know just how I'll ever even be able to see her. Especially now that Aunt Mary has her sights set on us.

Well, you can tell I'm grounded and have a lot of time on my hands. My first day of being grounded. It's just getting dark. That wonderful twilight above the lake. Normally, I suppose, I'd be cruising the beach. Maybe going for a run. Tonight, I'm sitting here, my skin still hot to the touch, taking it easy, writing you. I feel good.

Wish you were here,

Your big brother

∞

There's nothing like sitting high atop a wagon mounded with fresh baled hay. After we'd been haying all day, dusk was creeping across the June sky, the air dry and the sky clear and clean. The warm, herbal aroma of alfalfa scented the air like incense above the groomed pasture. I watched the blaze-orange sun dip beyond the bluffs to the northwest. With plenty of waning light on one of the longest days of the year, just a few days before my birthday, I felt like lingering in the field long after Paddy and Rose hauled the penultimate load back to the barn, leaving it to unload and stack in the morning. It had been an excellent week for haying, and I couldn't remember ever putting up more bales from one cutting.

I pulled Patrick's letter from the rear pocket of my jeans. Mom had brought it out with the lemonade and snack mid-afternoon. I'd scanned it briefly earlier, between loads, but now I had the time to sit back and savor a good read.

A pair of sandhill cranes trumpeted and chattered down in the marsh. I looked up from the letter, gazing toward the source of the cranes' cacophony, but my thoughts drew me away.

It didn't surprise me that Patrick had such intense feelings for Lynn North. I mean, the whole family noticed there was something there when she'd dropped him off for Jannie's funeral. Even Mom seemed to key into it. I think she thought it was innocent enough. Probably harmless. Friends. Or maybe it was real. I don't know. I know Mom observed them, though. I mean, it was pretty much right out there in the open, but where was it going to go? We could just kind of see that Lynn and Pat related. So natural. Kind of like the way Jannie and I were. I didn't really see it for what it was, at first. It just seemed to me that they were comfortable with each other. They fit together. She didn't really look all that much older than Pat, but then again, Patrick is a beast. She looked pretty young to me, but she was a woman, not a girl, no doubt about that. Older than Jannie. Patrick looks older, too, though. Probably why so many people can't believe he and I are twins. He's about twice as big, and he looks about ten years older. He looks at least as old as Lynn in the pictures Uncle Paul took of them in their canoe. Especially since it doesn't look like he'd shaved in a day or two. I don't even shave twice a year! I don't know, maybe seven years isn't all that much. But on the other hand Miss Rose is only in her late twenties, almost six years older than Lynn. But Miss Rose seems so ageless. She's so wise. Miss Rose is unique. Mom would say they broke the mold when they put her together. But isn't that what Patrick was saying about Lynn, that she was unique? But in a different way.

I know Jannie was unique. There will never be anybody like Jannie.

I just hope Patrick knows what he's doing. With love, there is no time to waste.

As twilight sapped the last of the day's brilliant rays from the sky, I neatly folded the letter, placed it back in the envelope, and carefully tucked it in the pocket of my jeans. I wouldn't want to misplace it, and have Mom or somebody find it and read it. It wouldn't be good for Patrick. My brother had trusted me with his thoughts, and I would not be careless with them. The letter would go with the others that Patrick had sent me, into the old metal lockbox that Paddy gave me years ago, the box that kept my letters from Patrick, and from Jannie—her letters from Bethesda, and from home after she returned. She never stopped writing me, even when we saw each other almost daily.

I jumped down off the mound of bales and landed with a thump on the hard, dry field of alfalfa stubble. We baled good hay today. Good feed. I gave it an approving glance, then turned west toward the last of the azure sky. The walk home was but a quarter mile. I strolled, alone, toward the farmhouse, its windows aglow with the golden hue of lamplights in the kitchen, blurry through the tears welling in my eyes.

∞

The week of being grounded did little to infringe upon Patrick's lifestyle. Uncle Paul intervened on the first full day of the punishment to make an exception: Patrick could continue his running program as usual. As for his weight lifting program at the high school, Uncle Paul drove Patrick into town and either ran errands or waited for him to complete the prescribed workout.

With Uncle Paul on vacation, Patrick actually found the grounding to be somewhat of a treat. His time with his uncle was consumed with lattes, chess, reading, and discussion. The week swept by gently, as only lazy summer days can do. About the only thing he missed was the social time on the beach. Over the weekend, as a few of his friends noticed his absence along the lake front and Jack relayed word of Patrick's punishment, several of his buddies made the long climb from the beach, up all sixty-four stairs from the road, tapping at the screen door of the sun porch, asking if Patrick was available. The redness from her sunburned having faded to an amber blush, Aunt Mary flushed a deeper shade of scarlet when she heard the clamor of young voices buzzing on the front porch. Her flash of anger, however, quickly receded when she discovered the first visitors to be the O'Connor twins. She was particularly fond of the girls, and thought that Patrick would be best served by spending time with kids his own age, rather than having all his time consumed by that older married—no, divorced—woman from the west end. As more kids streamed up from the beach during the course of the week to visit Pat, as well as for the sodas and treats that Uncle Paul made available, Aunt Mary second-guessed opening the floodgates by allowing the darling O'Connor twins to visit her nephew during his sentence. By Wednesday, however, she had mellowed considerably, and seeing Patrick's good-natured compliance with the punishment, she began enjoying the bustle of youthful life accenting the otherwise quiet summer days.

∞

Patrick finished *Silent Spring* late Wednesday night and found Uncle Paul waiting for him the next morning as they sipped coffee and shuttled the chess pieces around the board.

"This is as profound a piece of literature as has been written since the War," Uncle Paul proclaimed, flipping Carson's book over and glancing at the rear cover. "It flies in the face of the massive economy that was spawned by the industrial revolution and has been nurtured by two world wars." His voice was passionate, typical of when he challenged Patrick with academic debate. He subtly slid his queen's bishop along a diagonal that threatened to pin Patrick's knight and prevent it from abandoning his black queen.

"Well, I like *Exodus* more," Patrick said, advancing a pawn one space closer toward his uncle's rook.

"Trite passion plotted on the framework of historic reckoning," Paul said, hastily shifting his white queen to the mid-board square adjacent to his exposed king. He looked up to see a placid, calm expression on his nephew's face. The hint of a smile indicated that the end-game was upon them. It bothered the professor that he didn't see the sequence.

Patrick advanced his remaining knight, attacking the white queen and exposing a rook along his vacated queen's column. Paul was in a bind. His queen was pinned by Patrick's rook. He now had to defend the queen without moving her—she protected his king. Paul suddenly recognized that perhaps Patrick's lackluster opinions on Carson's oracle had been a direct result of his attention to the chessboard. He looked over to see his nephew studying him with a smug expression.

"Your move, Unc!" he taunted.

Paul flinched. It infuriated him that he couldn't see Patrick's end game. He took the knight, freeing his queen from attack.

Patrick paused, feigning uncertainty. Then he slid the pawn, snatching the vulnerable rook and setting it ceremoniously with the other captured pieces along the edge of the board.

Paul studied the board. His best move, he thought, was to shore up the mid-board defense of his king, perhaps working to free up his queen. He slid his bishop over next to his queen, one square diagonal to his king.

Without hesitation, Patrick moved his queen across the board to the black square immediately adjacent to his uncle's queen. He sat back in his chair, crossed his ankle over his knee, and folded his arms smugly. "Check."

Paul saw it now. Had Patrick challenged his king directly, there was a single escape route. By sacrificing his queen, Patrick set up a cross fire of attacks from his rooks and the rogue knight that had earlier probed and picked apart his pawns' first line of defense. It was hopeless.

"Mate in two," Patrick snickered.

"Verfluchen!" Paul muttered, tipping his king to the board. He looked into his nephew's confident face. "Nicely done."

Patrick smiled graciously. "Well, now I know how to beat you," he said, sipping a last, cooled swig of latte from his mug. "Wait until you've read a good book, then let you get all worked up about it while your board game goes all to hell."

"You are developing into entirely too political a young man," Paul assessed. "You're willing to sacrifice your debate on the most important book of the century, all for the sake of winning a contest on the chessboard."

"Hawrhh!" Patrick guffawed. "You simply have to choose your battles, Uncle Paul," he chided, parroting his uncle's oft-voiced advice. "After all, this is about the tenth book you've told me was the 'most important work of the century' in the last week! You just need to curb your enthusiasm and focus on what's really important...."

Paul burst into laughter upon hearing his own favorite lessons turned back on himself. Patrick sat grinning at his uncle.

"Well, it's good to know my wisdom is not wasted on deaf ears," Paul conceded. He cast a sharp, definitive eye upon his ward.

Patrick's eyes widened. He knew that he was about to be offered yet another dose of his uncle's wisdom.

Paul let the moment hang, ripening. When his nephew met his eye, he candidly broached the subject that he'd been awaiting the right moment to discuss.

"Patrick, about Lynn North," he began, again letting the words set in during a long, pregnant pause. He observed his nephew, and saw that the young man remained open. Patrick's eyes focused, and his expression sobered, but did not harden. He remained engaged. Paul felt confident to proceed.

"Patrick, are you playing with fire with Lynn? Are you in over your head?" Paul asked. He paused, looking into his empty coffee mug, wishing it was filled again with warm, frothy beverage. He set the mug aside. It would have to wait. He glanced again at his nephew and saw the depth of his introspection.

Patrick gazed out across the expanse of Lake Michigan extending north toward the city. The lake was up this morning, rolling waves cresting over the sandbar, washing the shoreline with lines of white froth. Patrick pursed his lips, thinking. He looked down at his victory on the chessboard. His black queen stood brazenly exposed, but untaken by the resigned opposition. He mindlessly lifted the piece from the board, turning it gently in his large fingers.

Paul wondered if he'd lost the moment of openness. He resisted the urge to speak, or to disrupt the moment by going to refill the coffee mugs. He sat, listening to the silence of his nephew's concentration, buffered by the wash of the surf.

After several moments, Patrick looked straight into his uncle's eyes. Paul pressed his lips tightly together, holding his tongue with all his will. The discipline paid off.

"Yeah." Patrick said. "I am. Totally, hopelessly over my head," A warm, confident smile spread across his face. He leaned forward, placing his elbows on his knees, perched on the edge of the chair. "Lynn makes my head swirl. I can't stop thinking about her when she's away. And when she's here, there's nothing better than just being with her. We do so much." He heard what he'd said, and shook his head vehemently. "I mean, we don't do things we shouldn't be doing. We just do things that are fun, and meaningful. Like building the wall, or taking photos, or canoeing. We work together, and we talk all the time we're working. Being with her is like being with you, kinda," he blurted, amazed at the comparison he proffered. "I mean, we talk about interesting things. Important things. I couldn't help but think about her while we were talking about *Silent Spring*. She would have loved to be here and discuss it with us. I mean, she gave me the copy of *Exodus* I read. And it's not trite passion. It's real passion. It's about more than just life and death and love. It is about real, living passion."

Paul smiled deeply. "Real living passion in fiction," he interjected.

"Well, yes," Patrick said, his hands flying wildly. "That's why it's so great. I mean, those people in *Exodus* are like real, even if they're not. They're are alive, if only in my mind. That is what makes it so good to read."

Paul sat back and let his nephew speak his mind and vent his emotions. Patrick spoke evenly and passionately. When, after several moments, he came to the silence that follows deep thought, Paul set the hook for a longer discussion.

"I'm going to get a dividend on my latte," he said, getting up from his chair and grabbing both mugs. "How about you?" The question, he knew, was rhetorical. It would keep Patrick riveted in the conversation, but let him alone with his thoughts on the questions that he'd not fully worked out.

Paul could whip up a couple of lattes in just a few minutes, but this morning, he didn't rush. While the water came to a steaming boil, he looked out the back window to where Mary weeded the flowers in the long strip of garden rimming the yard. He carefully brewed the espresso and steamed the creamy milk, consciously letting Patrick steep in his thoughts on the enigmatic Mrs. North.

When Paul finally returned to the porch, Patrick remained deep in thought, his gaze distant, but sharply focused, looking far across the waters of the lake. Paul set his nephew's mug smack in the center of the chessboard, disrupting the pieces as they stood in mocking deference to the shameful loss he'd just suffered. He sat back in his chair, kicked his feet up on the top plank of the bookshelf under the windows, and waited patiently for Patrick to share his thoughts.

Patrick picked up the coffee and sipped. He looked frankly at his uncle. "So, there it is. What I have with Lynn is real," Patrick said softly but firmly. He looked evenly at his uncle. "Do you think it's wrong?"

Paul considered the question. He shook his head.

"No, I don't think it's wrong. What is, is. A measure of a man is how he accepts that which is, rather than dream futilely of that which is not." He shook his head in understanding. "It does concern me. I sometimes think that you are growing up way too fast, but in this case, I don't know if I could see it any other way. I think it's a burden for you, and a challenge. I do think you're right. For whatever reason, what you and Lynn North have together is real. I can see that. I can feel that, the chemistry between you, when you two are together with us. I don't know if it's right. I don't know if it is truly good for you. But I think it is real.

"Your aunt, well, she doesn't understand that. She is principled. Dogmatic. It is easier for her that way, to see black or white. There is no gray zone. But that's where you are, in a great, wide gray zone, where convenient and conventional definitions of what is right or wrong don't exist."

He shifted his glance out over the expanse of the lake. "Your feelings for Lynn, and her obvious feelings for you, well, I don't know how to advise you to proceed. I don't know if you should go on. Can it lead to anything good? Anything lasting? I don't know. I believe, however, that it is real. How can you just stop that which is real?"

He turned to look his nephew in the eye. "My concern is that it will not be easy for you. Your differences, your youth, well, it will be difficult. And I hope it doesn't make you unhappy. Or take something from you before you know you have it."

Patrick listened to his uncle, and then sat with him in silence. It was a comfortable moment. He felt reassured that his uncle would discuss Lynn with him so candidly and with such understanding. He nodded several times.

"Well, since she seems to be gone more than she's here, I guess it's pretty hard to see her at all, much less play with fire," he grinned.

Uncle Paul looked up from under his bushy eyebrows. The hint of a mischievous smile flickered across his face.

It didn't escape Patrick's notice. "What?" he demanded. "What's going on?

Uncle Paul nodded. "I ran into Lynn in town yesterday. At Smedman's." Uncle Paul's grin spread evenly across his face. He had done the grocery shopping the day prior, while Patrick was lifting at the high school gym. "We had a nice chat, standing there in the produce isle. She is quite a lovely woman, Patrick. She asked about you. Asked me to tell you hello. She said that she had arrived home on Sunday evening."

Patrick sat up, tensed and excited. "Wow," he muttered.

"Patrick," Uncle Paul said, caution in his tone. "Be careful, son. Be careful."

Patrick nodded, stood, and walked over to the screen walls of the porch. He studied the waves pounding the beach. He wondered, *how will I get together with Lynn again?*

"I'm still grounded?"

"'Til tomorrow," Paul said lightly. "'Til tomorrow."

∞

Since Monday, when his skin had cooled down enough to move comfortably, he'd been running early in the morning to avoid the mid-day heat. On Thursday, after his chess game with his uncle, however, he elected to run at the height of the afternoon. He'd put up with the heat and the intense rays from the sun, gambling that he might find Lynn on the beach. But the sand was nearly deserted. The canoes were in place high up against the small dunes below her house. No footprints or signs of activity were evident in the sand alongside the sleek little vessels. Patrick scanned the water. Only one Cat skimmed the lake's choppy surface, dipping between the rolling swells on the far side of the sandbar. Lynn was nowhere to be seen.

That evening, he jotted a note to his mother, another to Davey, and then made a lame and futile attempt to get into Michener's *Tales of the South Pacific*. Mostly, though, he just pined.

Early on the morning of his birthday, he went back to running in the cool air and soft light of late dawn. The sand at the state park bore the dimpled imprints of the previous days' sunbathers, but no one was on the beach. Patrick reversed course, picking up the pace for a short mile to Porter Beach, where he cut over to the road behind the beach houses. He ran through the blow-out dune and out East Road toward the highway. At the shelter alongside the South Shore rail, he slowed to a walk, then hit the ground to pump five dozen quick pushups. He walked on his hands across the station's parking area, then vaulted upright to his feet. He hit the ground at a jogger's pace, heading north toward the guardhouse. He kept stride as he turned west along the trail leading back through the woods to the deserted golf course.

The air in the woods hung heavy with fog that the morning sun had yet to burn off. Patrick felt the waves of misty vapor settle on his sweat-coated skin. By the time he breached the crest of the dune, his lungs burned as he sucked in the cool, clean morning air. He broke stride at the raspberry patch, coming to an halt, leaning, his hands braced upon his knees. When his breathing settled to an even, quiet exchange of air, he gazed out across Lynn's pool toward the lake.

On the far side of the deck, looking out toward the beach, Lynn North sat cross-legged, her elbows perched upon her knees, holding a large pair of binoculars to her eyes as she scanned the beach and waterfront. A coffee cup steamed beside her. She hadn't heard Patrick sprint up the south slope behind the raspberries. She sat facing north, toward the lake. A pair of sunglasses perched high upon her head, she wore a blue cotton shirt with short cut-off jeans. She was barefoot, and her hair was pulled back in a ponytail.

Patrick stepped evenly across the pool deck toward where Lynn sat scoping the lake. He watched her peer through the glasses. He stood quietly, taking in the scene. The sun had risen ten degrees above the eastern horizon, and the intensity of its rays forecast the afternoon heat. Sunlight glistened from the smooth, neat strands arcing in a sassy cascade from the back of Lynn's head. Her ponytail bobbed and danced as she scanned the beach with her glasses. As he watched her, she grew still, dropping the glasses a few inches from her eyes. She had sensed him. She sat motionless for several passing seconds. Her shoulders tensed, then relaxed. She slowly turned her head. Patrick could see her profile appear, radiant in the long rays of the early morning sun, as she peeked over her shoulder. When she caught his shape at the edge of her vision, a smile tweaked the corner of her lips. She swung around toward him.

"Ah, the birthday boy!" she said tenderly. As lightly as a flame on a candle, she stood and turned to face him. "You startled me."

"Didn't mean to." Beads of sweat trailed in glistening streams down his arms and shoulders, dripping from his nose. A sheepish smile crawled across his face, and he instinctively took a step toward her.

She smiled, stepping next to him, placing her hand above his elbow, steering him across the deck. "I was hoping to see you today." She gestured with a tip of her head back toward the lake. "I thought I might see you running the beach. You tricked me." She led him toward the house, alongside the pool.

Patrick shrugged, searching for words among the swirl of thoughts whirling around in his mind. "Didn't mean to trick you," he mumbled. "I guess that's why I ran the old golf course this morning." He stopped walking and turned to face her. "I just was hoping to see you, too. Uncle Paul told me you were back."

She studied his eyes, then looked up and down his tall frame, smiling mischievously. His heart raced as he watched her take the single step that closed the gap between them. Gently, she placed her hands on his chest, stepped up on her toes, and kissed his lips ever so lightly.

"Happy birthday," she whispered, her eyes shining into his as she shoved mightily against his chest and pushed him backward.

Already spinning from her kiss, Patrick teetered for a long moment on the edge of the pool, wildly helicoptering his arms, before toppling helplessly into the water. His eyes wide in surprise, he watched her throw her head back with laughter just before he broke the surface of the cool, refreshing water. Lynn appeared distorted in the wake of his splash, but he could see her leaning over the edge of the deck, delighting in her prank. He pushed off the bottom, building momentum with strong strokes as he surged back up through the water. He breached the surface like an orca onto an ice floe, snatching an unwary seal from the safety of its berg. Erupting out of the water, he closed his fingers around Lynn's ankle.

Lynn's laughter screeched into a squeal of alarm. "Oh, no you don't!" she protested, reaching down to pry open his grip.

As she bent down towards her trapped foot, Patrick swept his other arm in a long arc, reaching over the top of Lynn's back to grip the waistband of her cutoffs. He tossed her over his head as easily as if she was a large pillow and laid her gently upon the surface of the pool. She hit the water squawking in protest, her tirade fading to bubbling babble as she sank into the pool.

For a second, he heard only his own winded guffaw. Then, she surfaced with a flurry of splashing, squealing laughter. Gasping for air, she launched a counterattack, clambering onto his shoulders and neck like a cat climbing a pole. She shoved with all her might, trying to dunk her partner, all while Patrick gasped for wind between rounds of belly-gripping laughter.

He let her submerge him with her play, holding her gently but firmly, his hands on her back and shoulders. She followed him helplessly under the water, unable to escape, the muted muffle of her voice carrying through the water as she continued to clamor and shout while he pulled her fully below the surface.

He felt her respond, however, to the tenderness of his hold upon her, and as they surfaced, she no longer struggled. They both gasped, still coughing choked-off laughter.

"What kind of a birthday present was that?" Patrick laughed, pretending to threaten her with another dip under the surface. She held him tight, her head rocking back as she laughed loudly.

They jostled and played, pushing gently and posturing back and forth as they feigned threats to dunk one another again. Soon, though, they simply held each other, their chests heaving as they caught their breaths, little chuckles and whimpers escaping between exhalations and gasps.

Lynn lay her head against Patrick's neck. He felt her hand slip behind his back and lift his buoyant body, and she floated him toward the shallows where the steps led from the deck into the pool. He glided weightlessly, letting her take him. She pulled his t-shirt up to his shoulders and stripped it over his head, bundled it, and laid it underneath him on the steps. They had caught their wind and were breathing easily. He could hear the sound of his breath moving through his nose, mixed with the singing of birds in the raspberry bushes.

"That was not what I have for you on your birthday," she murmured. She nestled next to him, and they lay entwined in the shallows.

Patrick considered. He held her close in his arms. Could he ask any more from her than all she had already given him?

"You gave me my camera," he spoke into the wet, warm hair atop her head. He kissed the spot where he left his words.

They floated quietly. Lynn set a hand upon his belly, pushing softly to prop herself up, looking into his face. The intensity of her gaze moved him. He was looking into the kindest, most loving expression he had ever seen.

"I have so much more to give you," she said, her voice breathless and subtle, barely more than a whisper. "Your camera is a token of my love for you." She sighed. "I have so much more...."

Patrick felt his breathing deepen as he looked into her eyes. Her expression was apprehensive, hinting of fear. Her eyes glistened. Her look was as intense as any kiss he had shared with her, and he knew his only response was to meet her lips with his. The tenderness of her kiss sent waves of passion coursing through him. She leaned back, returning her gaze to his face. He felt the pounding of his heart and glanced down, certain the pulsing would show. It did.

"Wow," he said, smiling at the little ripples forming as the water bounded from the skin above his ribs. She laid her hand on his chest where his pulse pounded through his rib cage, then kissed him again, her tongue darting lightly, flickering against his lips, exploring, probing, searching. She closed her lips smoothly upon his, and leaned once again back to where she could look into his eyes. Her gaze was bold and confident.

Slowly, she slid her hand down across his navel, her eyes locked on his. Her fingers moved with certainty across the belt of his baggy running shorts as she reached into the opening of the loose pant leg. He felt her fingers touch the skin inside his thigh, linger for but a second, then slowly inch upward, tenderly cupping him, her fingers snug upon him. She tickled the tightness of his skin, and moved her hand up, finding his full, firm penis. She held him gently yet firmly, stroking up, then back down, slowly, almost imperceptibly, no more than half an inch along the length of his flesh.

Her eyes held him. He dared not break the gaze they shared, yet in the periphery he could see her lips curve into a smile. She nodded once, and then again. Again, she brought her lips to his, more passionately than before, gauging his urge through her touch. Again, he felt her tongue softly probe his lips, just barely touching the tip of his own tongue. Patrick arched back, his eyes closed, and he felt her grip tighten, her movement quicken. He heard himself gasp. Then she loosened her hand, pulling it from his shorts.

Patrick opened his eyes wide, startled, wondering.

Lynn said nothing. Her expression remained determined and confident.

She stood in the shallow water, her eyes still taking in his every expression. Gripping the elastic band of his running shorts, she lifted his buoyed body. With a muffled, nasal, "Hummph," she indicated for him to float while she tugged the wet shorts down around his buttocks and over his erection. She rolled the pants down around his legs, then cleanly pulled them over his feet. He lay nude in the water before her.

Patrick watched as she stepped away, just beyond the reach of his arms. Slowly, she fussed with the buttons of her wet denim blouse. She pulled the fabric over her shoulders and slid the sleeves off behind her back, letting the shirt drop into the pool. She next removed her bra, again letting it fall into the water.

Desire racked his body as the sunlight swathed Lynn's creamy skin. Her breasts stood firm and high, her nipples wet and erect in the morning air. She kept her eyes trained on Patrick's face, but her gaze did not demand that he lock his eyes with hers. She needed him to view her, to run his eyes over her skin, to see her naked body.

She loosened the button of her cutoffs and slid her thumbs under the waistband of both the shorts and her underwear. Smoothly and evenly, she stepped out from the last of her garments, leaving them adrift below the water's surface.

She stood a moment before him, breathing evenly and deeply. Then she laid her body atop his, wrapping one arm under his back, and the other around his neck.

He held her close, then drew his hand evenly across the skin of her back, her buttocks, and back up along her side to where he caressed her breast. She turned slightly so he could feel her easily, then kissed him again on the lips and face, his neck and chest.

She reached down between his legs and found him hard and erect. She worked him more deliberately than before until his breathing was deep and fast. Then again, she stopped, and he felt her slide her hand up his body to his shoulder. His eyes sought hers. She reached across his hardened body, gripping his shoulder, pulling herself up over him in the water. He watched her swallow, her eyes again begging that he lock his gaze upon her. She straddled him, and let go of his shoulder, never taking her eyes from his. She reached down and found him, arranging him with one hand, and herself with the other. Slowly, she slid down upon him.

He felt her take him in. She took him, and the soft warmth of her body surrounded him. Their eyes remained locked as she slowly rocked her bottom upon him, and he moved with her. He watched her eyes lose focus, and her lips draw together, then slightly part. She rocked and pressed, slowly bending forward, her eyes rolling back beneath her lids. With the slightest of moans, she touched her lips along his face from his neck to his lips and flickered her tongue on his lips as she thrust more rapidly. She took him as she gave herself to him.

They lingered in each other's arms, coupled, half submerged in the pool, until the water chilled their bodies enough that they felt compelled to move.

"So is that my birthday present?" Patrick quipped as they helped each other up.

Lynn grinned.

"Just the beginning," she laughed. "Just the beginning."

At the top of the steps from the pool, she reached her arm around his neck and pulled him to her again. He felt himself against her, still firm and responsive. She looked into his eyes and repeated, "Just the beginning. You have all of me."

Patrick felt suddenly abashed.

"You know, I'd never…"

She moved her fingers to his lips.

"Yes," she said kindly. "I know. Of course." Her eyes sparkled as the sunlight reflected off her tanned face. "Not so anymore." She smiled lovingly. She pushed her hips firmly against him. "We have so much to learn about each other," she said.

They stood, and all that was around them didn't matter for a moment. Patrick could not imagine being more happy. Until she mentioned breakfast.

"You hungry?" she asked, taking his hand and pulling him toward the house. He was easily led.

"Oh, yeah!" he said. "I hadn't really noticed, but I'm starved."

Lynn laughed aloud.

"How about some scrambled?"

"Yum!"

They walked naked to the kitchen and started to make breakfast. Patrick measured the coffee grinds and plugged in the percolator. Lynn cracked half a dozen eggs into a bowl, sautéing scallions and mushrooms slowly as she grated the cheese. As Patrick turned away from his coffee making, Lynn noticed that he remained large. Moved, she set aside the cheddar. Taking him in her arms, she kissed him, pulling him close to her as she leaned back on the counter. He took her there, quickly, before the onions burned.

No breakfast ever tasted better. They ate, then sat in the living room, still nude, sipping coffee, saying whatever came to their minds. They made love on the couch, then moved into her bed, where they again came together. By half past ten on the morning of his birthday, Patrick had made love for the first four times in his life. Then, he and his lover fell deeply asleep in each others' arms. When they awoke from their nap, they made love again.

"Hi, sleepyhead," Lynn had said, watching him rise from the depth of his slumber. She'd been awake just a few minutes herself.

Patrick forced his eyes open wide, then shut them tightly several times in succession, He felt disoriented.

"Wow. What time is it? Is it still today?"

She snickered.

"Of course it is." She kissed his forehead lightly. "It's 12:30."

"Wow," he sat up suddenly. "I betcha Uncle Paul and Aunt Mary are wondering where I am."

Lynn reached for the phone on the table beside her bed. "Oh, I'll call them and let them know you're just fine…"

Patrick lunged for her hand on the phone.

"You gotta be kidding," he exclaimed. He knew she'd had him when he heard her laugh fill the room like music. He grabbed the phone from her hand and jammed it down on the receiver. He had her firmly under his arm, wedged in by the weight of his chest on her side.

The touch of her skin was electrifying.

They both laughed, and kissed, and came together again.

Afterward, she lay relaxed in his arms.

"Lynn," he said. "I love you."

She looked up into his eyes.

"Say it again."

"I love you," he said, a smile spreading on his face.

"Again," she said, first returning his smile, then a more sober expression.

Again, he shared his feelings.

She repeated, "Again."

Patrick looked into her eyes. She meant it. Abandoning his lighthearted grin, he said earnestly, "I love you."

She said, "I love you." Still, her eyes remained locked on his.

"I love you," he offered once again.

"I love you," she said.

"I love you," he said, holding her in both his arms.

Lynn nodded. Her eyes welled with tears.

"I know, Patrick. I know."

"I love you," he whispered.

He felt her nod against his chest. He turned her onto her back and once again, for the last time that day, he took her, vigorously and powerfully, kissing her face as her tears freely flowed.

When he was done, he held her close as she stifled choking sobs. Her tears confused him, and he rocked her slowly in his arms. When, after she drew in several long, staccato sighs, he asked, "What is it, Lynn? Why do you cry?"

She took her time in choosing the words of her reply.

"On the one hand, Patrick," she started, "well, you've told me you love me more than anyone else has ever told me in my whole life. And meant it, too. I know you, and I trust you. I believe you."

She paused, and Patrick waited.

She looked at him, a weak smile forcing the tears running down her cheeks to alter their course.

"Patrick, remember always what we just said, and what we've just done. Always. Remember," she pleaded. "Because I love you so much, sometimes I will act as though I don't. As if you mean no more to me than... your uncle, or your cousin." She rolled her eyes. "No. I mean, well...."

Patrick smiled kindly, and resorted to one of Lynn's gestures. He softly put the tip of his index finger upon her lips.

"I love you."

"I love you."

"I believe you."

"Now, go."

∞

Patrick could not remember ever having strolled the length of the Dune Acres beachfront. He'd always run it, or at least jogged. But that afternoon, he did little more than amble along the water's edge. He didn't feel like running. It was enough that he occasionally had to sidestep a wave that swept farther up the beach than most of the small waves that roiled the surface of the lake on the solstice.

He stopped and chatted with Brad Sanderson, who was rigging his Cat for a sail, and initially declined the offer to crew. At first, he didn't feel as though he wanted to muster the energy to sail all afternoon. But he knew his aunt would be wondering of his whereabouts, and sailing would be a convenient alibi. He dug his heels in the sand, tugged on the coarse nylon ropes, and helped drag Brad's sailboat across the hot sand, rolling the boat on huge, inflated cylinders.

"I can only sail an hour or so," he told Brad as they aligned the Cat, pointing its twin bows toward the depths of the lake.

"That's cool," Brad assured him. He told Patrick that he thought he'd surely be able to find somebody interested in sailing as they cruised the beach. Conditions were near perfect, even with the little surf generating breakers cresting along the sandbar. Once they pushed out past the shallows, the waves were merely soft, rolling swells, but the nice breeze from almost due west caught the sail and zipped the Cat swiftly along the shoreline. The sail ballooned as it caught the wind, and there was little to do but sit back and enjoy the ride. *This,* Patrick reflected, *was even better than walking.*

As they approached East Beach, Patrick spotted his aunt and uncle sitting on their beach chairs in the shade under the large parasol planted in the sand behind them. *So they'd come down to the beach,* he thought. Amazing. He waved happily at them as Brad piloted the Cat swiftly along. Patrick smiled, relieved that they spotted him. He would need no explanation of his time. They had seen for themselves. Aunt Mary adjusted her sunglasses, then looked back down into the magazine she had spread across her lap. Uncle Paul waved casually, and watched the Cat fly by in the wind, carrying his nephew and friend rapidly toward the building throng a mile down the beach at the state park.

Chapter Thirty-Four
Disclosures and Liberations

IN THE DAYS and weeks following his birthday, Patrick and Lynn found innumerable excuses to be together. For the first time, Patrick found himself concealing his whereabouts from his aunt and uncle, giving vague explanations about afternoons on the water or evening bonfires with the Sandersons and the O'Connors. He'd worried that Jack might blow his cover, until one morning when his cousin, unbidden, told Mary a long, involved tale about a neighborhood party they'd attended together the night before—that had never occurred. Pat had stared at his cousin for a moment, baffled, before realizing that while Jack might not know where Patrick had been, he also didn't really care, as long as he could rely on Pat's complicity and appropriate his alibis.

Feeling a little guilty, and wanting to make up for his unexplained absences, Patrick tried to be as candid with the Howards as he felt he possibly could. When he and Lynn drove into the library in Valpo or took the canoes out on the lake, he'd make sure that Mary and Paul knew exactly where he'd be—and he'd often invite his uncle and aunt to come paddling with them. On two occasions, they took him up on the offer, and in spite of the protective eagle eye that Mary kept trained on her nephew, the foursome enjoyed their hours on the water.

On the second of their trips, after they'd tied up the canoes at the base of the dunes, Lynn surprised the Howards and their nephew with an invitation up to her home, where she'd presciently stocked the fridge with steaks and vegetable skewers ready to grill. Famished and thirsty after paddling the lake, the Howards graciously accepted the invitation and thoroughly enjoyed the margaritas and rib eyes that Lynn served as they lounged on the deck. Patrick smiled contentedly as he watched his aunt recline in a lounge chair next to the pool steps, her reservations about Lynn North melting into the ice of her third cocktail. He tuned out Mary's friendly chatter and Lynn's polite responses, amusing himself with recollections of his birthday. Lynn caught his eye from across the deck and glanced down at the water, reading his thoughts, or maybe his face. She grinned wickedly and turned back to Paul and Mary. As the sun slid down beyond Chicago, the weary Howards gladly accepted Lynn's offer of a ride home. Patrick could only fit in the front passenger seat of the T-Bird, so Paul and Mary wedged into the rear, and Lynn taxied them across the community. The Howards sent her off with heartfelt gratitude. She glanced at Patrick as she slipped her Thunderbird into reverse, and he nodded, a smile affirming their understanding.

At home, Aunt Mary immediately crashed, spent from both the physical exhaustion of canoeing in the summer heat and the half a pitcher of margaritas she'd ingested as a cool-down. Paul, who not only held his liquor better but had also governed his intake to just a couple drinks, was good to accept Patrick's challenge on the chessboard. Patrick's playing was distracted and perfunctory, however, and Paul executed what he thought was a clever and relatively quick mate. He deferred the rematch until the morning, excusing himself and bidding his nephew goodnight.

Patrick shrugged, smiled happily at his uncle, mentioning that, well, he thought he might just go for a run. Paul returned the shrug, gave his nephew one curious glance, and headed to bed. The first winking stars pierced the azure and navy sky above Chicago's skyline as Patrick pounded the sand heading west along the beach.

He found her on the mogul-like dunes near where they had beached the canoes. They made love on the sand, still warm from the afternoon sun, and again while they skinny-dipped in the lake. Then they rolled up in her fluffy beach blanket, clinging to each other's warmth, and talked until the Big Dipper had moved a third of the way across the sky and threatened to descend upon the twinkling city to the northwest.

When he returned home, all was quiet. He knew his aunt and uncle slept soundly. He wondered whether Jack had even come home.

He fell asleep thinking of his moments with Lynn, swept away in the passion that flowed between them like a river, unchecked.

∞

Just when he would begin to fret that he'd run out of plausible excuses to visit Lynn, she would call Aunt Mary and ask if she could hire him for yard work, or offer to include him on a trip in to Chicago to go to the Art Institute, or maybe a Cubs game. While Mary raised a skeptical eyebrow at the suggestion of the baseball game, she enthusiastically supported any activity that was culturally enlightening for her ward. In exchange for permission to watch the Cubs take on the Mets, Patrick promised earnestly that their next outing would be more staidly educational and enriching. And on their third trip, they did spend nearly two hours touring the Shedd Aquarium, after which Lynn hired a taxi to deliver her and Patrick to the Lakefront Hilton, where she claimed her reserved room and they made love madly and tenderly until late in the afternoon.

Patrick had never experienced a hotel before, and his concept of service and amenities was forever tempered by the baseline set that day. In the waning hours of the afternoon, they'd toyed with the idea of ordering room service and eating dinner in bed, but had eventually showered together, dressed, and left the hotel. They walked hand in hand up Michigan to Adams, fighting the current of harried pedestrian traffic on the crowded sidewalks, sauntering along, stopping to view window displays, watching the bustling of humanity scurrying home after a day's work.

Up the block, Patrick spotted the landmark sign above the restaurant his uncle had taken him to the previous fall. The Berghoff. "Hey, I know that place," he said. "They have great food."

"I'm famished. Let's eat," Lynn smiled, and together they picked up their pace, Patrick using the breadth of his shoulders to open passage routes through the streams of pedestrians, holding tightly to her hand as she followed in his wake.

After they ordered, they chatted excitedly. The maître d' had shown them to a table near the window, through which they watched the bustling commuters outside.

"Kind of like the Shedd, huh? All those schools of peoplefish?" Lynn puckered in her cheeks and flapped her hands like fins, starting them both chuckling and giggling until the inquisitive glances of other diners reined them in.

"So your uncle brought you here," Lynn said, steering their banter toward less raucous topics.

Patrick nodded, his face deep red with mirth. The thought of his last visit to the restaurant, however, quickly grounded him.

"Yeah," he said, looking down at his hands. He thought a moment, deciding what he would share with her. "On the way back from home, last Thanksgiving. After Jannie's funeral. Uncle Paul picked me up at Union Station, and we came here."

He paused, took a deep breath, and sighed. "I saw your..." he checked himself. "Dr. North was here. We ran into him. He was sitting right over there." He looked across the dining room to the booth Barry North had shared with his companion.

Lynn grunted, casting her eyes down, examining her own hands. She looked up again, however, when Patrick continued.

"He wasn't alone," he said. He held his gaze on her, gauging how much she might want to hear.

"Patrick," she said, "I have no feelings at all for Barry. He was an egocentric, self-absorbed, self-made surgeon who had to control everything. But he never really treated me badly. He just never really treated me any way. There was nothing there. It was just a mistake that we ever married in the first place. He was... different, I guess. And I was just too young, and I thought he was something that he wasn't, and I wanted something that wasn't real, either." Her eyes focused keenly upon him. "I was too young. Like you." She stopped, letting the impact of her words settle upon them.

Patrick considered what she'd said. Too young. He didn't feel too young. He didn't know what too young meant. He glossed over contemplating her meaning, choosing to push on with the conversation at hand.

"Dr. North was here with another doctor," he said. "A man."

He let that thought situate itself in her mind, and then added, "I saw them both again another time. Last Easter. At your house. They were there."

Lynn's brow furrowed in wonder. She registered his message, and a curious smile spread across her lips.

"Barry?" she asked. "Another *man?*"

Patrick nodded shortly.

Lynn tipped her head back at the ceiling as she processed Patrick's information. Then she met his eyes levelly, with determination. "Okay. Tell me everything."

When he'd finished, he watched carefully as she considered everything he'd told her. He felt a smile spread across his face as he watched her eyes light up mischievously, twinkling, incredulous.

"I guess I should be shocked, but..." she mused, reaching across the table to clasp Patrick's hands. "Oh, my! Why did I not see that? Bless him. Oh, Ingie will have a field day with this! She'll say she told me so from the very start. Ha! Well, she did say he was rather odd and... different. I'll grant her that. But she never... I never... Ha! Oh, wait until she hears. She's coming out for the Fourth, you know. I don't know that I can hold this from her 'til then, though. I cannot believe it!" She paused, and her focus drifted away.

Patrick wrapped his thick, long fingers around her fine hands, squeezing just enough to encourage her.

"Pat, you don't know how relieved this makes me feel," she said. He cocked his head in concern, and she hurried to explain. "You know, from the very beginning, I always wondered what was wrong with me. I figured it was me all the time. I couldn't meet his expectations, or his needs, or his... desires! Poor soul! Ha! I certainly couldn't. This explains it, though! It wasn't really me. Not at all. I thought sometimes that he married me because I was a prize, a trophy wife, you know? That's exactly how I felt when he'd take me to functions at the hospital, or even out with his friends. I always felt he was showing me off. Putting me on display as some kind of catch, some kind of validation for himself. Oh, my God, I am so relieved. I am so relieved. I couldn't explain it, or understand it. After we got married, he quickly got... well... disinterested in me. Bored with me. I couldn't understand it. It was such a failure—I was such a failure, I thought. Now I understand! Oh, thank you! It's such a relief!"

Their waiter bustled about the edge of their table, ready to serve their meals. Patrick returned a quick squeeze to her fingers, they unclasped their hands, and the waiter set their bowls of bouillabaisse before them.

"I've never been hungrier," Lynn said as she dug in to her meal. Patrick watched her closely; she was more brilliant than ever. He had worried about telling her what he knew, but had he known the impact of his information, he might well have shared it sooner. After their meals, they charged out along the streets of the Loop, heading for the South Shore subway station.

They double-timed the steps down into the station and hurried to the platform where the South Shore was already loading its passengers. Most of the cars were only half filled, and Lynn climbed aboard and found a window seat. Patrick sat down across from her, as had become their usual arrangement on their train rides back to the Dunes.

"Anxious for your sister to arrive?" he asked as they watched South Chicago roll by.

"Kind of," she nodded. "There's always a moment of nervous anticipation before Ingie shows up. Well, you never really know if she will show up. Once, my whole family expected her home for Christmas break. When she didn't arrive on the day we'd planned, my Dad was beside himself. The next morning, she called from Amsterdam. A friend invited her, and Ingie said, Why not? That's Ingie."

"Seems like you two had a pretty well-planned trip last winter," Pat pointed out. "She must be pretty well organized."

"Oh, my God," Lynn said. "You would not have believed! My sister is a maniac. If I wasn't along to administer daily doses of common sense, I don't know if she'd ever come home from her adventures alive. I mean it. She's nuts. No discretion whatsoever. She'll just walk into anything without a thought about it."

She looked sharply at him. He wondered for an instant if she would hold back. They looked squarely at one another, and he saw her arrive at a decision.

"Like in Mexico," she said. "Oaxaca. I don't know how she gets drawn to places like that, but she just had to go to this little mountain village, Huautla de Jimenez. Honestly, it was like a different world. I think she'd heard about it from some of her friends at Madison. Anyway, just about all she did there was to use these herbs, these drugs that grow down there. And sometimes mushrooms. The native Indian people have used them for years. For centuries. Ingie was just nuts about them. They made her hallucinate. I mean, she was seeing all sorts of things, and seeing everything around her in new and really weird ways."

Patrick frowned. He wasn't certain what Lynn meant by "hallucinate." He asked her.

"Well, when Ingie would drink this tea, she would be bizarre. She'd talk a hundred miles an hour, about things I couldn't see, or about the way she was thinking or feeling. I mean, sometimes it was beyond imagining. I'd stay with her, and listen to her and talk with her. Sometimes she'd have the most amazing, astute observations, or she'd speak with incredible lucidity. She'd have ideas that were brilliant, and she'd explain them perfectly. Her vision was awesome. She'd explain the whole universe! But a lot of the time, it was just way too much. I got tired of watching her get a vacant look in her eyes, or she'd fall into a stupor. It got pretty boring. Or scary. I just got tired of it."

Patrick wondered, "Did you ever do it? The stuff that Ingie was doing?"

Lynn considered carefully. "Yes. The herbs, three times," she answered honestly. "And mushrooms. I smoked weed a few times, too."

"What was it like?"

"Well, Patrick," she said guardedly. "It was remarkable. Maria, this Mexican lady we met, she was a shaman, kind of like a medicine woman. She was like a guide, kind of, who showed me things, and helped me. I don't know how to explain it, really. I mean, I don't even know enough Spanish that I could talk with her. Spanish really didn't help, anyway. She spoke Mazatec, the native language. Yet somehow, she was able to communicate with me. I knew the meaning of her thoughts, sometimes, without even understanding her words. And sometimes I realized that I knew the meaning of my own thoughts in ways that I'd never understood. There was clarity, an unbridled, unbounded clarity of thought. Thoughts were free from words. It was amazing."

He sensed her reservations. "Were you scared?"

"Well, yes, the first time, definitely. But Maria was kind and powerfully caring, so I trusted her. She was my guide. And she never encouraged me to take the drugs. But she always seemed to know when I was ready to try them. The first time was like, well, just something new. But the other times, it was different. Meaningful, in a strange, weird way. It was profound."

She looked at him, trying to convey understanding through her eyes.

"You know, the native people in Mexico use those drugs as part of their religion. Some of them do, anyway. Like Maria. I felt she was a very deeply religious person. Like a priestess."

"Is that why you took the drugs?" he asked.

"I suppose," she agreed. "I think it was kind of like a... meaningful adventure, and I feel like it was right at the time. It made me think about my life, and what I've been doing and should be doing, all from a different perspective. About what's important. And what is real. It helped me face what I feel about you. I guess if I'd have gone wild like Ingie and some of the other foreigners we met down there, it would have been bad. It was so powerful. I wanted to use the drugs, but only carefully, and Maria sensed that, and was with me as I took them.

"Not Ingie, though. She was doing it all the time. Maria would only let Ingie take them as a tea, she never let her eat the leaves like I did. Maria could see right through Ingie, and I think she could tell that she's too goofy, too compulsive. It became her daily routine. She just tossed herself to the wind, with no reservations, like she always does. Mostly, I felt I was there just to watch out over her. Make sure nothing bad happened to her."

"What could have happened to her?"

"Oh, Patrick, we were in a strange place. A foreign place. I mean, there were enough Americans around, but honestly, you had to be as careful about them as anybody. Maybe more so. I just didn't want anybody to be taking advantage of Ingie. Or me, either," she added.

Patrick listened, wary. He wondered how threatening it could have been.

"Well, anyway, finally I just told her we were leaving. We'd been there more than a month, and she couldn't really argue. I hired a driver and he took us down out of the mountains to Oaxaca City, and we flew from there to Mexico City, and then to Los Angeles. From there, we took off right away for Hawaii, and then Australia. I mean, Ingie was just as crazy in Australia as in Mexico. Ingie is a party waiting to happen. But in Australia, it wasn't drugs, it was beer. You would not have believed how we—she—partied in Australia. So, I'd find other things to drag her to. I mean, I had to beg her to leave the resorts and bars so we could go to the Barrier Reef to go diving. Oh, my, Patrick, how you would love to dive on the Reef and see the fish and sea life. I loved it so much! And Ingie did, too, once I got her to go. But it was always kind of like I balanced the equation for her, and if I hadn't been there, she would have been consumed by her own craziness. I felt like I was there to save her and keep her healthy and safe."

"Didn't you get kind of tired of it, I mean, watching out for her and all? Sounds like you were babysitting."

Lynn considered it. "Well, yes, it was really tedious at times. I mean, bars get boring! And sometimes we'd fight, like only sisters can. I almost left her in Sydney, actually. And then she'd go to bed and sleep things off and wake up and be bright and cheery and do whatever I'd planned. And we'd have a wonderful time. Until she'd find something else to get into, some other kind of trouble. She just can't seem to stay away from it."

"Sounds kind of like Jack," he said.

"I've thought about that comparison myself," she agreed. "But Ingie's a sweeter person, really. Not as angry as Jack. I mean, you'll just love Ingie. She's kind-hearted and lovely and full of fun. And bright. She's real smart. No sense, though. None. She just knows no lines, no limits."

Patrick leaned his head back on the seat rest. He thought about how his own brother, his twin, had looked out for his well-being. But that was a lot different. David had worked with Patrick to keep his grades up in school. Or to keep out of trouble at home when Mom was falling apart. But nothing like what Lynn described. It was as if she were trying to keep Ingie alive. Patrick reflected that he could probably try harder to help keep Jack out of harm's way, too, but Jack really would have none of it. They got along fine, and even did things together from time to time. But Ingie sounded much more pliant than Jack, and the sisters were clearly much closer than Pat was to his cousin. When Jack wanted to separate himself from his family and delve into the dark side, there was no opening for Patrick to pursue.

The steel wheels of the South Shore squealed and screeched, gripping the rails as it rolled to a halt at the covered shelter alongside Mineral Springs Road. Patrick hopped off the steps of the coach ahead of Lynn, then offered her his hand as she took the last step down to the platform.

The bright light of late-summer afternoon dappled the leafy canopy over the driveway when she dropped him off at the lower landing of the Howards' house. By unstated agreement, they always parted with no more than the most casual goodbye. He thanked her politely for the day's trip into town, turning back for a single final word before bounding up the stairs.

"Later?"

Lynn smiled, bobbing a nod. "I hope so."

∞

By the first of July, Patrick had shared Lynn's love and bed every day since his birthday. He learned quickly to be gentle with his partner, and to listen to the murmured hints and suggestions that revealed her mystique. She, in turn, studied him intently, and asked him many questions about his masculinity. Each day, they deepened their understandings of each other's bodies, desires, and satisfaction. Whenever he assured himself that he finally understood her, she amazed him with new revelations. She whispered to him how he could please her, or tease her, in ways that took her to new levels of bliss. She carefully, tenderly, placed his hand, or his finger, or his lips and face, so that he learned and mastered the art of lavishing pleasure upon her. And she generously returned the joys to him. Together, they devoured all that they could learn about one another.

Chapter Thirty-Five
Ingie

Tuesday, July 2, 1963

"WHEN WILL YOUR SISTER BE HERE?" Patrick asked lazily. He looked down at her head cradled in his arms, her body snuggled alongside his, a fine layer of moisture beaded upon her skin from their lovemaking in the humid July afternoon.

She tilted her face toward him, her eyes opening a sliver. She closed them again, nuzzling her head against his chest. "Tonight. In the morning," she mumbled. "I dunno."

Patrick watched her eyes flicker back and forth beneath her lids. He wanted to kiss her face again, as he'd already done many times that day. But he let her slumber. He looked out the bedroom window across the dune, watching the surface of the lake in the distance. The lake was raging that day, roiling, jagged blue-black waves churning relentlessly onto the sand. From nearly half a mile below where he lay, the roar of the surf funneled up the dune, loud and thunderous—almost loud enough to drown out the sound of Lynn's breathing, softly, in and out, as she fell deeper into sleep.

He studied her face. She was a picture of peace. Her eyes were as beautiful softly closed as when they looked deep into his own. The bright afternoon light reflected off the white sand of the dunes north of the house, falling upon the skin of her cheeks, and shoulders, and breasts…. Patrick let his eyes follow the smooth curve of her hip to where the light fell into shadow on her stomach. He looked at her skin, smooth across her flat belly, punctuated by her navel, and bracketed by the slight protrusion of hip bone, down to where her abdomen converged into a wedge between her legs. Her fine hair twisted and curled, still moist from their union. He reached over, softly laying his hand upon the divide hidden within her curls. She stirred, murmuring, and fell still. He held his fingers quiet, gentle upon her. He had heard her words.

"I love you."

As he held her, listening to the rumbling of the lake and watching the shadows of the dune grass stretch long toward the east, a creeping sense of loss cast anxiety upon him. He could not explain it. Perhaps it was his increasing awareness of the guilt that he carried. He brazenly ignored the tension crackling between himself and his aunt when she'd complain about how little he was at home anymore. He noticed the slight cant of his uncle's arched eyebrow. He wondered how long he could maintain the secrecy of his relationship with Lynn. This morning, as he'd left for his run, Uncle Paul had quipped, pointedly, that he'd been wondering whether Patrick was running the same routes as Jack, since the Howards now saw their nephew about as much as they saw their son. Patrick sensed that discretion was essential, but he couldn't figure out how to be more careful about Lynn and still be with her as much as he wanted.

∞

Ingie arrived on Wednesday, mid-morning. She walked into Lynn's house as though she'd just made a short run into town and come home with milk and bread. She caught her sister unaware, wrapped in Patrick's embrace. He'd arrived just three-quarters of an hour earlier, having run up the long way through the old golf course. After a swim, he and Lynn returned to her bed with nary a thought of her sister's arrival.

"Hi, Sis," Ingie called sprightly as she followed Lynn's voice to the bedroom door. Stepping in from the hall, she caught Patrick scrambling to cover himself with the bedding that had been kicked down off the end of the bed. Patrick was mortified, and his embarrassment was magnified when he heard both sisters giggling.

Lynn sat up in bed, cross-legged, tucking the sheet around her waist. "Ingie! How can I possibly wait for you forever, and still have you surprise me?"

Ingie sidled cheerfully into the bedroom, finding a seat on the overstuffed armchair at the bedside next to Lynn. She kicked off her sandals and lifted her feet up on the edge of the mattress. Making no effort to be discrete, she peeked over Lynn's bare shoulder to get an eyeful of Patrick. "So this must be your little Patty." Her tone was equally balanced curiosity and teasing humor.

"He is," Lynn said brightly. "Patrick, this is Ingie." She looked around to find him cowering below the bedding. She grabbed at the sheet to turn it down and expose more of him than the upper half of his face, but he still had a good tight grip on the linens. She turned to her amused sister, and together they belted a hearty laugh that embarrassed Patrick even more and made him realize how silly he must look. He relaxed a bit, lifting himself on his elbows into a sitting position against the pillows and headboard, the sheet slipping down across his belly.

"Oh, my," Ingie said, rolling her eyes and pursing her lips. "There's more here than meets the eye!" Again, her sister joined her in peals of laughter, which flowed easily into a rapid dialogue of questions and explanations as to where Ingie had been and why she was delayed, and Lynn's plans for canoeing on the lake. The sisters bantered joyfully, but neither let Patrick think that he was forgotten. Lynn subtly but persistently drew him in, explaining nuances of their sisterly in-jokes and asking him his thoughts on their plans for the Fourth. Ingie, meanwhile, made no effort to conceal her curiosity about the man in her sister's bed. Her appraising gaze, leveled on him even as she laughed and gossiped with her sister, made it difficult for him to steal looks at her.

Ingie was more striking than she appeared in any of the photos Lynn had taken of her. She had the looks and lines of a model. Lynn had caught that in many of her photos. Nonetheless, Patrick was awed at her stunning beauty, and even more so by the presence with which she filled the room. Lynn had told him that her sister was much more beautiful than she, a suggestion that Patrick had rejected out of hand. Seeing her in person, however, he had to reconsider. The two sisters closely resembled one another. Whereas Lynn's beauty manifested itself not only in her appealing prettiness but in her grace and charisma, Ingie had perfect symmetry of features. She was breathtakingly beautiful. But she held an air of coolness and hardness. Lynn had said she didn't have a mean bone in her body, but Patrick wondered whether she was as kind and caring a person as her sister. She seemed jaded, her words laden with hints of cynicism.

"So, Patrick, how is it that I find you here in my sister's bed?" Her directness flustered him. "Did she seduce you, or you, her?"

Lynn shrieked with laughter, but put her arm around him and drew him closer. Patrick was amazed that Lynn made no attempt to cover her upper body. He had seen her nude so often as she walked about her house or even outside on the deck by the pool, but he was taken aback to be sitting beside her, with nothing but the bed sheet, in the company of another person. He felt self-conscious about his nudity—thank God for the sheet—in front of anyone else, much less Lynn's sister. He didn't know Ingie, just about her, and she sat inspecting him, her eyes clearly indicating that she'd love to assess his entire body. Lynn noticed it as well.

"You look as if you've never seen a man before," she teased.

"Not this one," Ingie replied coyly. "Your descriptions were lacking, from what I see." She tugged at the sheet, leaning to peek underneath. "You didn't sell him short, did you?"

Again, Lynn laughed. "You're embarrassing him."

"I suppose I may be, but he's the one in your bed. And neither of you admitted yet as to who the seducer was."

Lynn was about to chide her sister, but Patrick intervened. "'Twas mutual," he said.

The sisters exchanged a glance, and tittered yet again. Patrick grinned sheepishly.

"Well, tell me then, did my sister do well by you?" Ingie eyed him deliberately, an eyebrow arched in mock severity.

Her matter-of-fact forwardness had Patrick reeling. He inhaled deeply, recognizing that he could well be the butt of Ingie's humor indefinitely, if he didn't make a stand of some sort. He decided that a hint of self-depreciating ridicule might satisfy her, so he answered, "Well, Lynn was a lot more than I expected. I mean, I kind of thought it would be more like, you know, what you see on the farm. If you know what I mean." He shifted his position, rolling over onto all fours, being certain to keep the sheet pulled up over his back. He thrust his pelvis forward, like David's bulls servicing the heifers.

The girls sat momentarily gape-jawed, then unleashed screaming gales of laughter.

Between gasps, Ingie struggled to ask her sister, "I hope you accommodated him?"

Lynn held her sides, tears running down her face, shaking her head in disbelief at the conversation they were having. She was laughing too hard to respond. Only Ingie would maneuver the discourse so glibly.

"Stop!" she gasped.

Patrick, however, did not let the ball drop.

"Most certainly," he boasted, puffing out his chest in an exaggerated show of pride.

Again, Lynn screeched, and Ingie fell back into the chair, writhing.

From the back of the house, the sound of a door slamming rang through the hallway, followed shortly by a lilting voice. "Hel-lo-o! Lynnie, it's me, Harriet. Are you home?"

Ingie quieted, looking inquisitively at her sister, who sat upright, like a cat startled by a sudden movement. Her face blanched, and she spun around to Patrick. "Quick, down there!" She indicated the floor next to the bed.

Patrick hurtled over the side of the bed, not failing to notice Ingie's eyes following his movement until he was out of sight between the bed and wall. In a single motion, Lynn pulled the comforter up over him, letting it fall as if it had simply slipped off the side of her bed, too hot to use in the summer warmth. The last thing he saw before ducking his head beneath the mattress and under the comforter was Lynn tucked snugly under the sheet, much like he had been when Ingie entered the room. Just her head was exposed above the bedding. Her eyes remained wide as saucers, startled by her neighbor's unexpected visit.

"I'm in here," Lynn called.

Harriet's reply came from the hallway immediately outside the door, and then became even louder as she, too, joined them in the bedroom. "What have we here? Aren't you feeling well?" Harriet's voice was full of concern. "You're still in bed? That's not at all like you."

"Oh, I'm just fine," Lynn was quick to answer. "I was just feeling lazy. I read too late last night, waiting for my sister Ingie to arrive. And here she is, just having shown up. Ingie, this is my dear friend, Harriet Hamilton. Harriet, meet my wild and reckless sibling, Ingrid Knote."

"Oh, Ingie! I've been so looking forward to meeting Lynn's little sister! I've brought you both some fresh cinnamon cream cheese bars."

"Thank you so much, Mrs. Hamilton. You are so thoughtful. How could you have known I'd just arrived?" Patrick heard a new tone to Ingie's voice. Softer and gentler than the sharp, incisively sarcastic tones she had directed toward him and Lynn, Ingie sounded truly grateful.

"Call her Harriet," Lynn interrupted. "Or she might cut us off from her bakery. Harriet always knows when I have visitors. Her kitchen looks right down over the driveway. She's my friend, and my security."

Patrick envisioned his wizened friend bobbing and bowing, turning back and forth between the sisters. He could also smell the wafting cinnamon aroma from the cream cheese bars, one of his favorite of Harriet's treats. He was suddenly aware of the sharp hunger pains he felt, and listened in horror as his stomach rumbled and groaned.

Lynn might have heard it as well, for she quickly suggested, "Harriet, will you stay for coffee with us? I don't have any brewed yet—I'm just getting up. Would you please show Ingie where the coffee grinder is, and if she'll listen, how to use it? I'll get right up and be dressed in a moment."

The idea was well received, and Patrick breathed a huge sigh of relief as he heard Harriet and Ingie's conversation fade away as they made their way up to the kitchen.

After a minute, Lynn yanked the comforter off of him. If she was frightened by Harriet's near discovery, she didn't show it. Instead, she grinned widely. "Can you believe it?" she whispered. "She was almost in here before you were covered!"

Patrick shook his head warily. "Wow," was all he could say.

"Quick," she said, rummaging through the bedding on the floor at the foot of her bed, trying to find his running shorts. She handed them to him, then pointed to his shoes, set obtrusively next to the chair where Ingie had been perched. Had Harriet noticed? They exchanged a wide-eyed glance, and he picked up the large, worn canvas shoes and bundled them with his shorts.

"Get into the bathroom," she directed. He was already headed there. "I'll come get you when it's safe, okay?"

He nodded as she found her own clothing and quickly dressed. She ran a brush through her hair, shrugged, and disappeared into the hallway.

Patrick sat in Lynn's bathtub, re-reading her copy of *Snoopy Come Home*. He finished it twice before he heard the muffled slam of the garage door, and then the chatter of Lynn and her sister coming up the hall.

"Coast is clear," Lynn said, opening the bathroom door.

Patrick emerged, clad in his running shorts, his shoes laced, looking as if he were ready to run the beach as soon as he could break away. Ingie faced him, and he realized how much taller she was than her older sister. She came just to his eyes, whereas Lynn measured just to his chin, or perhaps his mouth, if she wore her sandals.

Ingie smirked. "Close one, wouldn't you say?"

Patrick grinned, nodding his head in agreement. "Closest yet."

She glanced at Lynn, startled. "Have you had other close calls?"

"Just one," Lynn said, lifting her eyebrows. "Harriet again. She knocks, but then she lets herself right in. The last time, though, it was easy. Patrick was already dressed, and he just slipped out by the pool and down to the beach."

Ingie cast a scrutinizing eye upon him. "So, just exactly how old are you?"

"Seventeen," he replied. "And thirteen days."

Ingie shook her head in disbelief. "Jesus. You certainly don't look that young." Then, turning to her sister, she grinned. "Isn't there a law against this?"

Lynn winced. Patrick blinked hard, twice. "Naw! Really? What kind of law?" he asked.

"Well, maybe some sort of cradle-robbing law, I suppose. I don't know if statutory rape laws cover males, too. But remember how much trouble Karl Bjornstead almost got into when he was doing me? I was fifteen, but he was nineteen. He almost got in a world of trouble."

Lynn cringed. "Yeah. Whatever happened to Karl?"

"He enlisted. I think that was the best option he had. Say, you get caught, maybe you can enlist, too," Ingie quipped, but the joke fell flat, and they quickly moved on to making plans for the holiday.

They decided that Patrick would run home and spend the afternoon around the house, maybe playing chess with his uncle. Then later, Lynn would call and ask whether he and Jack could meet her and Ingie to take the canoes out on the lake. Patrick figured the plan would go over well, especially if Uncle Paul answered the phone when she called. He was keen on canoeing, and might even offer to fill in for Jack if his son was not available.

Patrick left the house by the deck doors, ran down the path through the dunes to the beach, and headed east. Several hundred yards along, as he high-stepped through the waves lapping up onto the clean flat sands, he realized that he didn't get a cream cheese bar. Or a cup of coffee.

∞

While Patrick had marveled at how quickly Jack and Ingie hit it off, Lynn was not at all surprised. "It's a natural fit," she said through a benign sneer. "They were made from the same mold, cast from the same smelted ore. I'd have been more surprised if they didn't get along."

They could hear the pair laughing and flirting in their canoe, thirty yards astern. The late-morning swells were rolling and gentle, waves breaking gently against the shore. They beached at the very edge of Dune Acres, along the boundary of the Bethlehem Steel property, far from the crowds that gathered at East Beach on the other end of the Dunes' lakefront. Since the Fourth was on a Thursday, many of the Dunes families were arriving from the city for the long weekend, but the crowd was not yet much denser than on a normal July weekday. At the West End, there was no one.

Patrick had lugged along a jug of iced water, which they chugged. Hungrily, he tore open the layers of aluminum foil from the brownies Lynn had baked for their excursion. Her brownies were even better than Harriet's, he thought, but Lynn had made him promise never to share his opinion with her neighbor. He popped a rich chocolate square into his mouth and handed pieces to Lynn and Jack. But when he offered a treat to Ingie, she waved him off. Instead, she dug through a small satchel she toted over her shoulder. Fishing through the contents, she voiced a deep sigh as she found the object of her search.

"Ahhh," she breathed softly, carefully extracting a long, roughly rolled cylinder about the girth and length of her fine-boned pinky finger. "I'll save my brownie for later," she smirked. "How about this kind of treat?"

"Oh, I should have figured," Lynn rolled her eyes.

"What's that?" Patrick asked.

"Wow!" Jack was entranced. He reached out for the blimp-shaped joint, which Ingie released to him. She turned back to her bag and rummaged through it again until she found a pack of matches.

"Glad these stayed dry," she observed happily.

Jack was running the joint under his nose, sniffing deeply. "Wow," he repeated. "This smells rich. Good stuff?"

"Excellent," Ingie said, turning to Lynn. "Wouldn't you say?" she asked, putting her sister on the spot.

"Is that from Mexico?" Lynn asked. "How'd you get it?"

"Sure is. Same that we smoked in the Sierra. Luther sent it, the darling. It was waiting for me, shipped in a package with several knickknacks and souvenirs, all wrapped up as cleverly as could be," she said. "He'd positively stuffed one of those precious black Oaxacan pottery animals with the richest, most laden buds you could imagine. It was like my own little piñata."

"What is it?" Patrick repeated.

"Dope, dopey," Jack chided.

Patrick's expression revealed his confusion. He didn't have a clue.

"It's marijuana," Lynn explained. "Weed. One of the drugs I told you about, remember?"

Patrick's baffled expression softened slightly. He had heard very little about grass, and what he knew was mostly overheard in locker room conversations, or in the lunch hall, or from Lynn. Other than the anecdotes that Lynn had told him about her and Ingie's use of the drug in Mexico, he'd never known anyone to use it. He looked curiously at Jack. "You know what this is all about?"

Jack raised his eyebrows sagely. "You bet!" he bragged.

Ingie took the joint back from Jack and struck a match, drawing in deeply as the flame kindled the tightly wrapped paper. She exhaled a plume of smoke, and Patrick smelled the sweet, novel fragrance.

Ingie tipped the cigarette toward Lynn, who simply shook her head once, blinking slowly. Jack took the joint, inhaling with enthusiasm and experience, and returned the cigarette to Ingie. Glancing at Patrick, Ingie offered him the smoke, taunting him with a smug look.

"Uh," Patrick grunted. "Naw. I, uh, you know. I don't smoke. Training and all...."

Lynn chuckled softly, and Patrick turned to see a look of pride on her face. Ingie dragged again on the joint before bursting into a fit of laughter as Jack exploded in a spasm of coughing from his long, smoke-filled inhalation.

"Wow!" Jack coughed, reaching for the joint again. "Wow," he repeated. "Dynamite."

Ingie dissolved into laughter.

Lynn took Patrick's hand and led him aimlessly along the beach, away from his cousin and her sister. The sound of the smokers' chortles and gasping coughs drifted in bursts down the quiet beach.

"So that's what you were telling me about, when you were in Mexico?" Patrick inquired.

"Yep. Some of it."

They continued strolling. She was deep in thought, and he let her be. A quarter mile down the beach, she turned to him, looking keenly into his eyes. "So why didn't you try it?"

Patrick hemmed and hawed, collecting his thoughts. "Well," he said, finally, "you didn't. So I wasn't going to. And really, I don't know much about that at all. I guess I'm ignorant. But it seems kind of dumb for me to do all the training I do for football, and then smoke. Anything. It just doesn't seem right."

She looked into his face, admiring his honesty and innocence. She rewarded him with a smile. "You'll have plenty of time and opportunity to explore and adventure."

He wondered what she meant, and asked, "Did you think I should have tried it?"

She shook her head, but added, "It isn't for me to decide that, I guess. I tried it, and some other things, enough to know what I think about it. That was enough. I don't need it. I hope you never need it, either, if you do try it." She looked down the beach at her sister and Jack, both of whom were lying flat on their backs, looking straight up into the bright afternoon sky.

"Like Ingie needs it?" he asked.

She gave him another deep look, and nodded. "Jack, too, I bet."

They turned and headed back to the canoes and their excursion partners, who were as giddy as children for the rest of the canoe trip back down toward East Beach.

∞

Later, after the canoes had been stowed, they climbed the path up the dune to Lynn's. Patrick was relieved when Jack talked of heading into town. But Jack sagged into inertia as they cooled off in Lynn's pool. And then Ingie lit a second joint. Patrick watched as they smoked, joking and laughing goofily. They were indeed funny, and he was caught up in some of the belly laughs, egging them on with his crisp, sober wit. After a while, though, Ingie yawned and abruptly announced that she was heading into the house for a nap. She pulled herself from the pool, wrapped a towel around her waist, and gave Jack an ambivalent glance. With a shrug and the flicker of a smile, she left the deck.

Patrick noted the stupefied expression on his cousin's face. With a clearer mind, Jack would probably have followed Ingie into the house. Patrick glanced at Lynn, who was watching with apprehension. She, too, had seen her sister's lingering glance at Jack. The moment hung in the balance, and Lynn held her expression tight as she awaited Jack's move.

Jack, however, was too stoned to act. He blinked repeatedly, then frowned. After a moment, he looked across the pool to where Patrick floated lazily on a kickboard. Lynn, he could see, was watching him from the lounge on the deck above where Patrick hovered in the water. Jack chuckled, then muttered, "Wow. That is some really good stuff." He glanced briefly into the darkness beyond the sliding door where Ingie had disappeared. Then, as abruptly as Ingie had departed, he sunk like a rock into the water to the bottom of the pool. He surfaced with a splash, riding his momentum, staggering up the steps of the pool to the deck. "I'm gone," he announced.

"Where you headed?" Patrick asked blandly.

"Town. I'm gonna go into Chesterton. Maybe get some six-packs for the fireworks tonight. I dunno."

"See you," Lynn said. "Later."

As Jack trudged off the deck down toward the beach, Patrick found Lynn looking at him with a quizzical expression.

"What?"

"I didn't know if I should offer him a ride home."

"Naw. Looks like he'll do better by walking. He's sure loaded. And now he's gonna go get some beer? Wow. He'll be just fine when it's time for fireworks," he said, giving her a measured look. "I was kind of wondering if he wasn't gonna get in too deep with Ingie there. Whew!"

Lynn acknowledged his concern with a nod and a smile. "Yeah, me too. But then, would that have been half bad?"

"Well, I dunno, but it made me kind of uneasy. Like it would complicate things even more. You're right. Those two are two of a kind. And I think with Jack so blasted, it was a powder keg. He didn't know what he was doing. Thank God."

"Yeah. Well, I hope Ingie's straight by the time she wakes up," Lynn said, frowning. "I told the Drapers that I was bringing her to their cocktail party. Your aunt and uncle going to be there?"

"I imagine," Patrick said. The thought struck a chord, and he floated his way to the edge of the stairs. Climbing out, he walked over to Lynn and shook the pool water off his arms onto the smooth browned skin of her back.

"Ah," she gasped. "That's a shock, but it feels so good. I was just thinking of taking a dip," she said, rolling over on the lounge.

Patrick bent over and wrapped his arms under her knees and back. "Well, here," he teased. "Let me help you."

She grabbed his neck reflexively, arching her back and struggling as she felt the shock of his cool, wet skin against her body. "Don't you dare!"

"Oh. That was not a good thing to do," he shook his head gravely. "Daring isn't to your advantage." He held her close, walking back toward the stairs into the pool.

Lynn relaxed in his arms, sensing that at least he was not about to simply dump her into the cool water. She loved the strength of his body. She felt like a whisper of wind in his arms. She snuggled close to his chest and let him make his teasing threats as he slowly entered the water, dipping her ever closer.

As he descended into the water, she slipped gently from his arms, turning her body to meet his. She pushed him back into the water and reclined upon him, laying her cheek upon his shoulder and her forehead up under his jaw. She felt him stir. He kissed her golden hair before pulling smoothly at the tie string that let her bikini bra float loose in the water. Slipping his hand under the fabric, he gently teased her breast, plucking softly at her nipple.

She smiled. "You're gonna drive me nuts."

"Can't help it," he shrugged, lifting her buoyant body and setting her down, straddled, across his lap.

She slipped off the dangling bra. The dripping skin of her shoulders and breasts sparkled in the sun.

Patrick leaned back against the stairs and let his eyes course across Lynn's body, resting finally on her eyes.

She smiled. "Want to make love?"

"Always," he replied, making no move to advance toward her. "Tonight."

Her eyes opened wide in surprise, her eyebrows arching. "Tonight? Not now?"

"Yes, now," he said, laughing. "Of course, now. Always. But maybe I should head home for a while. Especially if Jack is going home. Aunt Mary will be wondering, if I don't show up with him. You know."

Lynn did know. She pursed her lips, considering. "I bet it takes Jack a while to stagger on down the beach," she offered.

Patrick grinned, nodding knowingly. "Yep. And I can run it in seven minutes."

"So what's your hurry?" Lynn asked, sliding down his legs and teasing her fingers into the elastic beltline of his shorts.

∞

The sun stubbornly hovered over the Chicago skyline. Patrick figured that there were still at least two hours before sunset, and the fireworks wouldn't start for an hour after that. He strolled aimlessly down the beach, absorbing the buzzing energy of the crowd. Members of the Dunes Fourth of July committee scurried about like industrious ants on the sand, setting up launching tubes and arranging canisters of fireworks. The lake was speckled with cabin cruisers and ski boats, many cutting wedges of white foam behind them as they jockeyed for position along the shoreline. A small fleet had already set anchor off East Beach, where the fireworks were traditionally launched.

On the shore, families claimed their turf as well, creating a multihued checkerboard of blankets and beach towels at the feet of the dunes. The younger children chattered and played, kicking sand onto the blankets and running up and down the dunes. Parents helped their little ones roast hot dogs and s'mores over small fires in pits dug into the sand. The aroma of the sweet browned marshmallows mingled with the scent of the roasted hot dogs, reminding Patrick that he was hungry again.

A girl's voice cut through the festive hum, discordant in its anger. Glancing toward the source, Patrick was less than surprised to see his cousin. His girlfriend, Debbie, stood angrily over him as he sprawled on the sand near the Sandersons' catamaran.

"Yeah, well, you're not one to talk," she raged. "You stink like you've been drinking all day. What a slob."

"Fuck you," Jack snapped, looking away from his girlfriend. "What a pain in the ass," he said to no one in particular.

Debbie's eyes burned with contempt. She glared at Jack. "Prick." She stormed away as Patrick approached.

"Having another little spat with Debbie, are you?"

"We're done. I can't take any more of her bitching." Jack's lips were drawn taught and tense, his glassy, bloodshot eyes narrowed. Then, distracted, he looked up at Patrick hopefully. "So, you expecting Lynn and Ingie for the fireworks?"

"Maybe. I dunno," Patrick hedged. He could see where Jack was heading, and hoped to derail that train of thought, if he could.

Jack wouldn't be put off, though. "You know damn well they'll be down here later. You see them, let me know. I'm gonna hang right here." He lowered his voice. "I bet she has more of those doobies with her."

Patrick shook his head in disgust. "You can't smoke that stuff here with all these people around."

Jack snorted a laugh. "Didn't say we would. We'll move off a ways, where nobody'll bother us." He jerked his head toward the west.

Patrick bit his lip. Toward Lynn's, that meant. "Yeah. Well...."

"Just let me know if you see her," Jack repeated. He looked past his cousin, staring fuzzily at the mesmerizing motion and color of the water under the twilight sky.

"Yeah," Pat agreed half-heartedly. "Sure."

He had no intention of hooking Jack back up with Lynn's sister. Forget it, he thought, drifting off to fetch a soda from the cooler tanks.

∞

Paul Howard snatched a beer from one of the ice troughs as he plodded through the sand. As he moved across the beach, nodding and calling out greetings to his neighbors, a brilliant gold firecracker burst in the sky, illuminating the sea of upturned faces below. From near the water, Patrick waved and called to his uncle, and Paul headed over to stand next to his nephew.

"Oooh!" the crowd sang in chorus as the next volley of fireworks exploded in the clear July sky. The night was spectacular, the Milky Way twinkling softly behind the blazing fireworks.

"Pretty decent," Uncle Paul said, looking up at the shimmering, flying embers.

Patrick nodded, smiling broadly. He loved fireworks.

Suddenly, a deep, resonant *huWUMPHF* belched from a canister not more than forty yards down the beach. A trail of sparks marked the rocket's path as it soared into the sky, slowing, slowing, and finally tipping northward out over the lake at the apex of its flight.

"Uh-oh," Patrick muttered as the canister arced downward, regaining momentum as it fell.

"The boats!" Paul gasped. The live firework was headed directly down onto the armada anchored just beyond the sand bar.

A blend of screams and astonished laughter rose from the beach, crescendoing in both volume and pitch, until a fiery spider burst over the water just yards above a pair of yachts. In the strobe-like flash of the explosion, two revelers hung silhouetted in midair, leaping from the decks of the boats, martini glasses in hand. Beneath them, the reflection of the blast spread gloriously across the placid surface of the lake. The report thundered, so close that Patrick could feel the compression of air against his cheeks.

The boom from the explosion was echoed by a great roar from the spectators on the beach. The pyrotechnic team—volunteers from the Dunes community, all heavily plied with beer from the ice troughs—responded by sending another volley of canisters skyward. Their efforts were met with further cheers, and the show went on.

"Wow," Patrick whistled, his shoulders shivering involuntarily. By the light of the next burst, he watched the sodden passengers climb back aboard their respective ships, which now showed the etching and scarring of char marks. On the larger yacht, a sailor sprayed a fire extinguisher onto the smoldering deck. Several other boats from the flotilla already had hoisted anchor and were backing away from the hot zone immediately in front of the beach.

"Man," he said to his uncle. "Who would have expected?"

Paul glanced over with a grin, then sipped from his can of beer. "No port is safe," he quipped. "You never know when lightening will strike."

He tipped the can up for the last sip, then tossed it toward a trash can fifteen feet away. He missed by a yard and shrugged.

Patrick drained his soda, and with a fluid motion, chucked the can in a high arc toward the barrel. It clanged loudly inside the receptacle. He glanced at his uncle, his eyebrows raised.

"Lucky," Paul muttered, but he knew that it wasn't. Patrick made it look entirely too easy. "Have you seen your cousin?" he asked, turning to look down the beach at the spectators lined up along the perimeter of the launching zone.

Patrick nodded. "Over there, where the Sandersons have their Cat pulled up on shore." Another explosion lit the shoreline, and Pat gestured toward where the twin-hulled sailboat with its naked mast stood silhouetted along the waterfront. Several people sat on the edge of one pontoon, and others lingered about on the shore.

Paul trudged through the soft, deep sand toward the shore, Patrick close behind him. Halfway to the boat, he recognized his son's voice, ringing out louder than usual from the midst of the group. A round of laughter floated up from the boat. Jack's unmistakable cackle mixed with a woman's softer but nonetheless hearty laughter. Patrick recognized Ingie's voice, and then he heard her calling them.

"Hey, Patty, we're over here. We were looking for you, but we found Jack first. We thought you'd lost us." Her little joke seemed remarkably funny to Jack, who snorted and guffawed.

Paul shifted course toward his son's voice just as another firework popped, illuminating the beach with pale green light. "Hello, Paul," Lynn North called as he approached. "You met my sister Ingie at the Drapers', I believe?" She looked back toward her sister. "Ingie, you'll recall Jack's father, Paul Howard."

Ingie giggled. Sitting cross-legged on the sand next to Jack, she struck Paul as charmingly different than she'd appeared at the cocktail party. She looked much younger than she had a few hours before. As another canister of fireworks lit the sky above them, attracting her attention and lighting her face with a cool, blue glow, Paul saw that she was strikingly beautiful, more so than he'd noticed that afternoon, when her expressions were more measured. Here, he observed, she was having fun, laughing and applauding the light show, leaning against his son, joking and relaxed. In fact, his son had his arm around Ingie's back, and she was leaning comfortably against him. It wasn't as if they were snuggling. Just comfortable. Amazingly so, considering they'd just met that morning. Where was Debbie, he wondered.

"Hey, Jack, where's Debbie?" Paul blurted.

Jack's eyes widened, and he ducked his head low. Ingie giggled quietly, then murmured, "Uh-oh."

Patrick sidled closer to his uncle. "I think they're taking a break," he whispered.

Paul cringed. He seldom said the right thing to his son, anyway, but now he'd embarrassed him in front of his friends. He wished he'd not said anything at all. Instead, he added, "I see. Well. Hmm." Finding himself stammering, he excused himself quickly, retreating back to the house.

As he walked back toward the road, stepping carefully among the spectators carpeting the beach, he reflected that now both his wards seemed entangled with the lovely Lynn North and her glamorous sister. That Patrick had remained behind had not escaped him. He'd last seen him taking his place at Lynn's side, their faces illuminated by a burst from the first volley of the grand finale. Their eyes were trained upon each other, however, rather than the spectacle exploding above them.

∞

Harriet found them deep asleep in each other's arms.

"Oh, darlings," she whispered, covering them with the sheet that was flung in disarray from the bed. She'd have to waken them, but she wanted to spare them as much embarrassment as she could.

She felt like an interloper. She'd entered Lynn's house stealthily, without her normal chatter and noise. She had known how she might find them, and had listened first for sounds of intimacy before proceeding through the house without so much as turning on a light. She'd heard nothing, until she arrived at Lynn's bedroom door. There, she could hear the sweet, gentle sounds of their breaths, mingled in slumber. They'd fallen asleep. They'd been lovemaking, it was clear. She paused to savor a moment of their peace and beauty as they slept. They were graceful and so full of love, and she was to break that grace, spoil their peace. Possibly forever. Probably.

She looked at them intently, embracing every detail. Their clothes lay discarded across the floor and the arm of the chair. The bedding was cast aside, draped upon the floor. They lay motionless, their lovely, young bodies cast in the silver and blue light of a half-moon streaming through the windows above the bed. She watched them silently, hearing their breathing, smelling the soft, warm fragrance of their bodies. She hated to disrupt them. She loathed bringing the word to them, the ill-boding, the bad message.

She laid the sheet gently over them. She watched Lynn stir and held her breath, hoping her young friend would not waken just yet. She retraced her steps, leaving the bedroom and moving back toward the study. She took a deep breath, and then embraced her mission.

She switched on the lights in the den, and those that lit the hallway leading toward Lynn's bedroom. She waited a moment, hoping to hear her young friends awaken to the unexpected light.

Nothing.

She walked again down the hallway toward the bedroom. "Hello, Lynnie," she sang out with the melody they'd come to know as her signature greeting. "Lynnie, it's me. Harriet."

Still, nothing. Like children, they were anesthetized by exhaustion. They had been busy all day, paddling the lake, swimming, making love, watching the fireworks, partying, making love again....

Harriet decided that it would be rude to waken them by turning on the bedroom light. Instead, she stepped close to Lynn's bed, and kindly laid her hands upon each of their shoulders, shaking them gently.

"Darlings," she murmured. "Children, wake up."

Lynn stirred first, then startled like a fawn. The shock that reverberated through her body woke Patrick. They both instinctively pulled the sheets up to their shoulders, their eyes widening as they recognized and read the sad, kindly face of their closest friend.

After her initial moment of alarm, Lynn smiled up into Harriet's eyes, like a child smiles as she rises out of sleep and peers into the loving gaze of her mother. As her thoughts untangled from her dreams, Lynn's expression twisted from a smile to quizzical concern. *What was Harriet doing here?* She looked so loving, yet so sorrowful. Was she upset that she'd caught her here, sleeping with Patrick?

Patrick awoke befuddled. Indeed, he wondered whether he was dreaming when he saw Harriet standing alongside them in Lynn's bedroom. His throat tightened with panic, but Harriet's benign expression steadied him. She was not angry about finding him with Lynn this way. She seemed to have expected to find them together, to have long since given her blessing to their union. What drew Patrick rapidly into alertness was not the fright of having been caught, but rather the deep sadness that Harriet so visibly bore.

When she saw that they were sentient, she spoke softly, carefully. "Darlings, you must get up now. People will be looking for you. They will be needing you."

Patrick heard the urgency cloaked in Harriet's gentle tone. "What is it?" he asked. "What's wrong?"

Harriet sat on the bed alongside Lynn. She took Lynn's hand in both of hers. "There's been an accident." She waited, watching the meaning of her words take shape.

Lynn understood first. "Ingie? Is Ingie all right?"

Her question focused Patrick's thoughts. "An accident?" he asked. "What do you mean?"

Harriet nodded.

"Jack?"

She nodded again.

"There's been a car accident." Harriet inhaled deeply, and when she spoke again, her voice wavered, then cracked. "It is not good, darlings," she said. "I'm afraid it is not good at all."

Looking into Patrick's eyes though the seeding of her tears, she explained what she knew. Jack had been seen by several residents driving his VW at speeds far too excessive for the arrow Dunes roads. Slightly more than an hour and a half before, just below the clubhouse where East and West Roads branched, he'd apparently simply lost control. His Beetle had flipped at least once. He'd been thrown from his car, and crushed beneath it as it rolled.

Harriet moved her eyes to Lynn's. "There was a young woman in Jack's car. She is badly hurt. Very badly hurt. And they don't know who this young woman is, but I believe she is your sister, Lynn. We need to get going. I don't know if it is too late."

Lynn sat in horror, pale and incredulous.

Patrick shook his head repeatedly. "Jack?" he asked. "What about Jack? Is he... okay?"

Harriet's eyes closed. She shook her head once. "Jack is dead." She looked back at Lynn. "And we must hurry," she demanded. "They took her to Valparaiso. We must hurry, Lynn. She may die, too. She may already be dead."

∞

At Jannie's funeral, there was warmth. And light. And, yes, joy. The entire community came together like one big family. We were all sad, sure. Devastated, really. But everybody there seemed to take their own loss and grow from it. And we all kind of put our losses together and came out of it together, maybe even stronger in some ways. She had given us so much. She was a Giver.

I remember how helpful it was when people came to support Dr. and Mrs. Whitman, and me, too. It was remarkable, really. I hadn't expected it. I don't know how, but it was like they could transfer their energy and power to me to keep me going. I noticed the same thing happening with the Whitmans. How many times during that day did I see each of us, even Wendy, laughing and smiling with those who came to share our loss? We really celebrated Jannie. She gave us something uplifting in her life, in her courage, in the way she faced things. We were better because Jannie lived and died among us. The whole community. We came together because of Jannie. At her funeral, we mourned for ourselves, I think, because we had to say goodbye to a friend. A bright soul who would be in our hearts forever.

Not so for Jack.

With Jack, people mourned a lost soul. There were friends and neighbors who came to support Aunt Mary and Uncle Paul, but the sadness of the people at Jack's funeral was dreary. Like they had failed Jack. They'd lost him. Jack was a Taker. He'd voraciously taken everything from life that he could, and it was never enough, and he didn't give back. People who knew him had nothing to celebrate, it seemed to me. I wondered if it was simply because I didn't know anyone. I wanted to ask Patrick about it, and reminded myself to bring it up later. That wasn't the time, although Patrick looked like he could use somebody to talk to. He pretty much stood in the background, nodding to those friends who sought him out. He looked almost physically crushed, like he carried a heavy burden. I wondered if it was guilt. It was very dark. I just stuck around Mom, though. I knew we'd have lots of time to hash things out when we got home.

I think it all kind of spun Patrick's head around. He even said, later, that he felt like he took a dunk in the lake when it was high with waves and sucked down water and came up gasping, wondering which end was up.

I think he wound up on his feet. Even if he didn't exactly know which direction he was going.

Chapter Thirty-Six
Home Again

August, 1963

PATRICK WONDERED if he'd ever see Lynn again. He'd heard nothing from her, although he'd written several letters and called many times. The phone just rang, endless and empty.

Harriet's note arrived at the end of his second week of two-a-days with his new football team. He'd forgotten nothing, but the hard work on the gridiron in the hot August sun had numbed him, until he walked into the house between practices to find the envelope lying conspicuously on the kitchen table. The sight of Harriet's slanted script on the envelope jolted him back to the tragedy still unfolding in the Dunes. He snatched a half-full pitcher of lemonade from the refrigerator, called a quick greeting to his mother and Miss Rose, who'd tactfully busied themselves in the family room, and fled to the shade of the porch, steeling himself for Harriet's news.

> *Friday, August 16*
>
> *Dear Patrick,*
>
> *The summer seems so vacant with so few of my favorite people in the Dunes.*
>
> *As you must know, your uncle and aunt left last week for his sabbatical. There was a nice farewell gathering for them at the Smiths'. Your uncle looked good, full of hope and courage. Mary still seems quite wounded, as any mother of a lost child would. I suspect she will need more time to find some peace.*
>
> *Lynn writes to me regularly. She remains in the Twin Cities with her family. Ingie has not regained consciousness yet, but they are hopeful. Some of the injuries to her legs, ribs, and face have healed, but the brain and spinal problems have yet to be resolved. Lynn says that she expects to stay with her sister indefinitely. She has no plans to return to the Dunes, except to pick up the things she might need for the coming months. I told her I'd be glad to send her anything she desired, and she may take me up on my offer, although I'd much love to see her. She indicated that she'd like to do a road trip, take care of some loose ends and business, as soon as—if—Ingie becomes stabile enough for Lynn to leave. It all depends.*
>
> *Please feel free to write and update me on your well-being. I miss you children so much. Life is certainly lacking some of its vitality without you here in the Dunes.*
>
> *I hope this finds you well,*
>
> *Sincerely,*
>
> *Harriet Hamilton*

∞

Saturday, August 24

Dear Harriet,

Thanks so much for your letter. I was real happy to hear from you.

Life in Wisconsin is a lot like it would be if I were still in the Dunes, at least since football started. Hot and sweaty. My new coach is pretty good. He isn't quite as mean as Coach Rayborn was. He seems pretty happy to have me on the team. He even kind of cuts me some slack when I goof up. He looks at me like he thinks my mind's about a mile away. Which it often is, which is why I miss plays and stuff. He's pretty good about looking me in the eye and getting me to focus. He'll kind of tap me on the side of the head, like he's reminding me where I live. Like he knows my mind is likely to wander these days. I can't get it out of my mind, really. The Fourth is just kind of always there. Is it with you?

So it's kind of the same, playing football all the time, but it's not. It's different being back here, playing with some of the guys I knew before I went to the Dunes. Some of the guys aren't too happy that I'm here, though, 'cause they're friends with the guy who I beat out for the starting halfback job. A kid named Ronnie Schumann. He's a senior.

I can't believe that I'm here, sometimes. Everything happened so fast. I can't believe Jack is gone. I think about Ingie all the time—well, and Lynn, too. I hadn't heard anything until your letter. I sent Lynn letters at her house in the Dunes. Maybe you're taking care of her mail, if she's gone. Did you forward them?

Life on the farm is pretty good. My twin left for school in Madison about the time I started football practice. He won't be home again until next week, for our first game. My mom is still a little goofy, but in a fun sort of way. She has her friend, Miss Rose, and the two of them are inseparable. I think they're good for each other. She seems happy to have me home again, which is nice.

I still can't help in the barn much. The animals really make me allergic. But I did do a lot better than I used to helping make hay, especially out in the field. I got pretty sneezy in the hay mow, but not as bad as around the cattle. I kind of like putting up hay. It's a good workout. My uncle Paddy and I made a lot of firewood in July. Six full cords.

Well, I really miss the Dunes. I miss you, and Lynn, of course. I'm really grateful for how considerate you were, you know, when Jack died and you had to come get me and Lynn. Thanks. Those were bad enough times.

I don't know if you'll be seeing Lynn, but if you do, tell her I'd really like to talk with her, or see her. If that's possible.

Thanks,

Patrick

∞

God, I love watching Patrick play football. I'm so glad he's home. And he's so much better than he was when he left—he was just a farm-league kid then, and now… he's a machine. He's been playing against lots bigger teams, and it shows.

I could tell the difference right away in the opener against the Dells. Patrick ran the very first kickoff back for a touchdown. In the first half, he caught two passes for touchdowns. The first one, on our first possession after the kickoff, was for eighty-three yards! The score was 21-zip after the first quarter, and everybody in the stands was going just nuts. We clobbered the Dells, and that was nothing compared to what we did to Mauston the next week. I wish I could have seen that game, but I stayed in Madison to keep up with my class work.

Aunt Kate and I drove up to see the Sauk game, though, and brought my buddy Trong along. Wow, he'd never seen a football game before, so he didn't know what the heck was going on. Just like Trong, though, he asked about a million questions in the first half and by the second half he was Patrick's biggest fan, except maybe for me. Aunt Kate was laughing at the two of us. She said the two smallest guys in the stadium were making the most noise. Well, it was kind of hard to contain ourselves, with Patrick running wild like that. He scored five touchdowns, three running and another two pass receptions. He really likes the passing game. He said his team in Indiana didn't let him catch much, but from what I can see his coach here is trying to get him the ball every way possible. Patrick is happy. He said the only drawback is that he hasn't played much in the fourth quarter. Ha! No kidding. Baraboo is creaming their opponents. Well, our homecoming game against Reedsburg will be tougher. They're our biggest rivals, and they're still undefeated, just like last year. I think they won the conference championship every year I was at Baraboo. I hope we kill 'em. It's homecoming. It'll be wild.

∞

October is perfect football weather, Patrick thought as he lay on his back on the soft turf in the end zone. He stretched his hamstrings and quads, savoring the scent of dry leaves in the cool, crisp air, listening to the buzz of the fans filing into the bleachers and the warm-up tunes from the Baraboo marching band. For a little high school in the middle of the boonies, he thought, the band made some pretty good music. It wasn't as polished and loud as the band at Bishop Noll, but to be fair, it was only about a quarter the size. And the band's enthusiasm really worked on him. He loved it when they played "On Wisconsin," which they did about three or four times a night. They didn't have a big repertoire, but what they did, they did well.

"Get 'em, Patrick! Run 'em over!"

Patrick recognized his brother's voice. He rolled his helmet to the left, catching sight of his family threading through the crowd lined up at the stairs to the bleachers. David's Vietnamese friend was along as well. Funny guy, that one.

"Keep focused, son." Coach's calm, encouraging voice came from directly above him.

Patrick looked up at the hulking figure silhouetted against the field lights.

"C'mere," Coach gestured. He turned and walked out of the end zone. Patrick sprung up and followed. He waited as Coach looked off into the darkness above the river flowing into town. "I'm making Ronnie co-captain tonight," Coach told him.

Patrick nodded several times, his hands perched on the web belt running above his hip pads. "Sounds right."

"He's a senior, and he's worked hard in this program all four years."

Patrick nodded again, waiting to see if Coach had anything more. Then he spoke his feelings. "Why don't you start him?"

Coach looked deep into Patrick's eyes, narrowing his own in a measured gaze. A slow, sincere grin spread across his face. "I was hoping you'd see it that way."

"Aw, hell, Coach. Why not? You've been playing him fourth quarter every week anyway. What difference does it make? Let him play the first quarter, and keep me in for the fourth. We may need it by then, anyway. Do it. I'll knock 'em dead once you put me in there."

Coach's expression hardened and he gripped the back of Patrick's shoulder pads. "I'm hoping it won't make a difference. But you listen here, son. This Reedsburg team is a cut above everybody else we've played so far this year. And they will be up for this game. They're coming in here undefeated, and they intend to remain so. They have a couple of real tough linebackers, and they'll be keying on you every play. This may not be the cakewalk you've become accustomed to the last few weeks, so you keep your focus." Coach tapped him alongside his helmet. "Okay? Especially if you're watching the first series or two. Don't let it distract you. You got it?"

Patrick heard his coach's intensity. He bobbed his head, jogging in place.

"Go on, now. Get loose. We have a game to play."

∞

Standing on the sidelines gave Patrick a new perspective on the game. He seldom watched his team play, except while settling into the mellow glow of endorphins in the waning moments of comfortable victories. Tonight was different. His muscles were stretched, warmed, and ready. His adrenalin titer soared, and he twitched, craving contact. He glanced back at the packed stands, bustling with motion and excitement. The fans had responded enthusiastically when Ronnie was announced with the starting lineup. The buzz of homecoming stirred Patrick's love for the game.

Across the field, the Reedsburg stands were loud and full. People lined the entire circumference of the wooden snow fence that arced around the ends of the field.

Watching his teammates break huddle and spread out for kickoff, Patrick suddenly realized how small they looked. Many were no more than one hundred forty-five pounds, and most were several inches shorter than he. Playing alongside them, he'd never noticed, but from the side of the field they looked like, well, a bunch of kids.

The sounds of the game took on an entirely different tone from off field, too. At the kickoff, when his ears would normally be full of his own heartbeat, and the breathing and jostling of the players around him, he heard the thump of the kicker's foot against leather and the rising cheers from the bleachers behind him. The fans screamed in crescendo as the ball arced toward the receiving team. Another tiny player, wearing the deep navy jersey of the opponents, centered himself under the descending ball, trapping it against his body with his arms instead of catching it with limber fingertips. Reedsburg's deep man, Donnie Craker, slipped through two of Baraboo's better tacklers and was off, untouched for the remainder of his ninety-one-yard touchdown return.

It happened quickly. The sounds from the stands changed with the swinging mood of the fans.

Patrick watched in frustration as his opponents lined up to kick their extra point. Pacing, he turned away from the field for three long steps, then pivoted back towards the action. He stopped.

At the far end of the field, seventy yards off and centered directly in the frame of the goalposts, a figure stood behind the snow fence. She had on a tawny-colored Norwegian fisherman's sweater. A matching wool cap was on her head, but even at that distance, Patrick could see loops of golden hair sweeping gracefully across her shoulders. Patrick wiped his eyes with the back of his hand and blinked hard. He took several steps down the sideline, trying to get a better look at the woman along the fence.

"Hey," Coach's voice boomed. "Where you going? You can't go beyond the thirty-five without a penalty. Stay focused."

Patrick returned to his teammates, but he couldn't help glancing back toward the figure alongside the perimeter fence. This was nobody from around Baraboo, he was sure. Maybe she was a Reedsburg fan. Perhaps his eyes were playing tricks on him, but Patrick felt almost certain that the figure along the fence line was Lynn. For months, he'd longed to see her. But not once during that time had he actually thought that he was. He'd never mistakenly glimpsed her in a crowd, or been caught up by a blond shimmer in the corner of his eye. *There was no mistaking Lynn,* he thought.

Ronnie Schumann took the kickoff out to the twenty-four-yard line, where Baraboo's offense took over without their premier running back in the lineup. Patrick tried to focus on the game, to let go of the distraction of the mysterious woman. But it was hard. He missed the first play, a loss of a yard, as he scanned the perimeter looking for her. At the next snap, he quit his search just in time to see Ronnie hit the hole, running high, straight up and down. Reedsburg's middle linebacker ripped into Ronnie, his helmet spearing into his ribs. The ball spurted from Ronnie's arms like a greased melon. It caromed off the helmet of Baraboo's right tackle, bouncing high above the pile of players who'd converged on the running back. Reedsburg's outside linebacker lunged at the free ball, nabbing it with his fingertips before it hit the grass. Without breaking stride, the hulking athlete lumbered gracefully into his own end zone.

With the extra point, Reedsburg was up fourteen to zero, a minute and twelve seconds into the first quarter.

"Jesus Christ!" Coach hollered. "What the hell is happening?" He turned toward Patrick, yelling, "Take the kickoff—and stay in there."

Patrick yanked on his helmet and snapped the chinstrap tight as his team regrouped. They huddled, and the special teams' captain, Ricky Green, called a return up the left side. Breaking from the huddle, Patrick jogged back toward the far goal line, near where he'd spotted the mystery woman. He glanced up, but she was gone. He shook his head, slapping his hand against the side of his helmet, forcing himself to focus. At the ten-yard line, he turned to face upfield. Patrick held his hand high, and the ref whistled the play into action.

His pulse ramped up and he sucked in a deep breath as the kicker trotted toward the ball. But instead of launching a booming, high-arching, end-over-end kick, the kicker stutter-stepped, pooching the kick, and the ball dribbled sloppily off the tee. The entire center of Reedsburg's kickoff team converged on the haphazardly bouncing football.

Jeez, Patrick thought. *Onside kick.* Reedsburg recovered. The groan from the Baraboo stands ached in the cool fall air.

Reedsburg controlled the ball and the clock masterfully during the drive for their third touchdown. Only thirty-four seconds remained in the first quarter after they kicked the point to take a twenty-one point lead over Baraboo.

Reedsburg's coach continued to stay one step ahead of Baraboo, directing his kicker to squib a low, bouncing kickoff away from Patrick. Billy Green, Ricky's lanky sophomore brother, covered the ball at the twenty-eight, where Baraboo started their second offensive drive of the game. By then, the

Reedsburg defense was screaming with determination, eager to drive Baraboo back on every down. Coach was right. The linebackers were keying every move Patrick made. He felt as if he'd come head-on with a pile driver on a dive over center for two yards on first down. He ran into a wall at the line of scrimmage as he cut off Hintz's block on second down, but gained five tough yards on pure second effort. Back in the huddle, he questioned the call for a screen pass to him on third and three when Roger ran the play in from coach. They hadn't run enough offense to set up a cleverly timed screen pass.

"Zip it in there," he told Stevie Pritchard, his quarterback, as they went to the line. Steve nodded, but Patrick saw only a distant, unfocused look in his teammate's eyes. Stevie was shaken. *Don't lay up a duck,* Patrick thought as he locked into the set position.

The right defensive end was coming strong, and Patrick pancaked him to his back before sprinting to the right flank behind the linemen setting up the screen. Reedsburg's outside linebacker, Stan Kent, read the play beautifully, and attacked at the point where Baraboo's blockers were forming the wall. But it was Nick Olsen, Reedsburg's middle linebacker, who made the miraculous play. Fleet as a receiver, the athletic linebacker sprinted toward where Patrick headed to receive the pass. Olsen anticipated delivering a crushing blow to Patrick to stifle the drive. Had Stevie zinged his pass to Patrick, Olsen could have dropped him for a loss, unless Patrick broke his tackle.

Instead, Stevie lofted a soft rainbow pass that forced Patrick to break stride and reverse field and come back toward his quarterback. Olsen was a step closer, and, with the ball hanging up in defiance of gravity, the agile linebacker nabbed the pass at the tip of his fingers as he ran full stride toward the goal line.

Patrick braked as his momentum carried him away from the play, and watched the interception unfolded before his eyes. He reversed field and pursued with a sense of doomed panic. He caught up with Olsen at the fifteen, his momentum knocking his opponent awkwardly off balance. As he drove his facemask into the middle of the big 61 on Olsen's jersey, Patrick wrapped his arms around the linebacker's chest and pumping arms. Patrick felt the hard, grainy pigskin in his hand and yanked with all his might. As they tumbled, the football popped up, spinning end over end in an awkward trajectory over the ten yard line, where it bounced erratically more or less parallel to the goal line.

Patrick scrambled to untangle from Olsen. The linebacker grasped and grabbed, fighting to hold Patrick from the fumble. The ball, bouncing as only footballs can, reversed its course and in one bobbing hop, delivered itself into Patrick's outstretched hands. He wrapped it firmly in his arms and folded it to his chest.

The referees conferred for several minutes before determining that in spite of the momentary possession by Reedsburg, the ball remained in Baraboo's possession. Fourth down, thirty-one yards to go, at the seven.

Patrick sauntered back toward the goal line to await his teammates as they straggling down the field for the huddle. His chest heaved as he sucked the cool October air. He circled slowly in place as the refs conferred.

Beyond the goal, twenty-five yards away, across the end zone and on the other side of the snow fence that kept the spectators from the field, he spotted her again. He was sure she was there. He thought she'd even smiled slightly when his gaze fell upon her. She stood behind several rows of cheering fans, and though she appeared for just a moment, he knew it was her. And then, she was gone.

"Huddle! Huddle!" Patrick's teammates called to him as they gathered just inside the goal line. Bobby Brecker was in the huddle to call the punt, and he relayed the instructions he'd gotten from Coach. He was going to try to angle a high floater toward the right. Coach was certain the Reedsburg team would make every effort to block the kick, so Bobby pleaded with his teammates to make solid blocks before releasing downfield to cover the kick. The last thing they wanted, Bobby said, was a safety.

Patrick was bewildered as he lined up to block for his punter. He was certain he'd seen her. But what would she be doing here? He heard Bobby calling the snap, and suddenly the pigskin spiraled sharply past him. Reedsburg was indeed coming strong, and he felt an instantaneous flash of anger surge from deep within him. He drove hard into big number 61, shoving him into another dark jersey that charged across the line of scrimmage. Patrick released and sprinted downfield, veering toward the right, where Bobby said he'd place the ball.

Reedsburg came at the punt with ten of their players, leaving only a single safety back to field the ball. Bobby rushed his punt, but kicked it cleanly and solidly. The ball sailed very high, almost above the rays from the field lights perched high atop the poles around the stadium. Reedsburg's Craker was back to receive, and he drifted in from his position at midfield toward the forty yard line, eyeing the ball, moving continually to his right as the spiral curved infield.

Patrick could hear the Reedsburg coaches screaming "Fair catch! Fair catch!" But Craker, focused on catching the booming punt, neglected to hold his hand aloft to signal for the free catch. Patrick accelerated with all the energy he could muster. All of his power converged as he drew a bead on the receiver awaiting the lofty punt. His motions seemed effortless, as if he were floating. He understood the geometry of the descending ball, his opponent, and his rapidly changing position on the field. He was flying toward his target. He could tell from Craker's concentration that the ball was coming down quickly. The receiver readied his arms to bring the ball into his body, just as he'd caught the opening kickoff. He was going to trap the ball against his chest. Timing would be everything, Patrick sensed, as he lowered his head and shoulders and he took another stride—then launched himself horizontally toward Craker. He saw the ball meet the bright yellow numbers on the dark jersey… and instantly delivered the crushing impact that jarred the ball from Craker's arms and sent the smaller receiver flying head over heels. The hit was impeccably timed and explicitly legal. Patrick tumbled and rolled, watching the ball bounce rapidly downfield. He saw only his teammates' gold jerseys converge on the ball, with few of the Reedsburg players in pursuit after their failed attempt to block the punt. Indeed, in their determination to get to the punter, several had knocked into Bobby, and the refs had tossed penalty flags all across the end zone.

But now, with Ronnie and Billy Green and several of his teammates smothering the ball at Reedsburg's thirty-three, the penalty would be assessed at the end of the play. The Baraboo fans were wild in the stands, and a pall of quiet settled upon the Reedsburg bleachers.

A shift in momentum in a football game is often tangible, and Patrick felt his team restoring its confidence. He knew they would make a fight of this game. He picked himself up, and offered Reedsburg's number 24, Donnie Craker, a hand getting up. Craker accepted the gesture, and Patrick pulled him up easily. He said nothing, but the look in his eye delivered a message that Craker could not mistake. He saw the panic in Craker's expression, a tension around his eyes, as the Reedsburg player tried to break his gaze away from Patrick's. If there was a second in which the game was decided, it was in that glance. Patrick's calm confidence spread quickly to his teammates, and was noticed by each of Reedsburg's players as they returned downfield to muster another defense. Olsen, Kent, and others each glanced furtively at Patrick, then quickly shifted their eyes away. They, too, had sensed something subliminal in Patrick's expression.

Patrick would not quit. He would not concede this game. And his teammates were with him. They had been rocked by the best assault that Reedsburg could throw at them, and they had not quit. It was not yet midway through the second quarter. Though behind by three touchdowns, Baraboo was undaunted. The game was on.

Patrick jogged over toward his sideline as the chains were brought downfield and the ref set the down markers. Coach watched him as he slowed to an amble.

"Run the screen again," he suggested.

Coach reflected no more than a second, then, with a sliver of a grin, nodded.

"Tell him to deliver the ball."

Patrick nodded, and headed back to the huddle. He met Stevie a few yards away from where his team huddled.

"38 screen right. Dammit, Stevie, zing that ball to me. Call it." He looked deep into Stevie's eyes until he was certain his quarterback was focused and unflustered. They exchanged a little grin, and Stevie took control of the huddle.

Reedsburg was still reeling, sitting back on their heels when Stevie brought his team to the line and called the snap. Little Peter Vulkovich, Baraboo's fleet but miniscule wide receiver, cut back in from the right flank to throw a cross-body block on Reedsburg's outside linebacker. Olsen read the play as clearly as he had the first time Baraboo ran it, and was almost in position to repeat his interception. This time, however, Stevie whipped the ball on a line like a frozen rope to Patrick, who caught the pass in stride behind his two pulling guards and the right tackle, Joe Hintz, Baraboo's lumbering, lanky lineman. Joe keyed on Reedsburg's outside linebacker, Kent, who tumbled toward the play after having his legs cut by Peter's block. Joe ran through the linebacker, dashing him to the turf with powerful thrusts of his thighs. Olsen's momentum took him out of the play, but he reached back with a desperate attempt to grab at Patrick's leg. Patrick accelerated past Olsen's lunge and wedged in behind his tackle as Hintz bowled over Kent. Joe pancaked the linebacker, but kept his feet churning and escorted Patrick downfield. Patrick patiently slowed his stride to allow Joe to set up a devastating block on Reedsburg's cornerback, who was backpedaling in vain hopes of containing the screen until his safety or linebackers arrived. Hintz drew a bead on the corner, never breaking stride as he trampled the diminutive defensive back. Patrick sidestepped the corner's desperate grasp, and opened up to top speed as he picked his way between Hintz and the Reedsburg sideline. There was no one between him and the goal, and he loped smoothly into the end zone as the roar from the Baraboo bleachers swept the field.

After the extra point, the score was Baraboo, seven, Reedsburg, twenty-one, with four minutes to the half.

Reedsburg managed a consuming drive that gobbled up most of the remaining time in the first half, but Baraboo finally held on forth and two at their own thirty-four yard line. With forty-six seconds left, they fashioned a drive of their own that consumed twelve yards, then seven, then another seven, with time outs after each down that didn't end with Patrick going out of bounds. With a first and ten at Reedsburg's forty-two and twelve seconds left in the half, Coach sent in a play that put a smile on each of Patrick's teammate's faces as they broke from the huddle.

Stevie brought his team to the line of scrimmage and barked out the signals. At the snap, Reedsburg came full out with a blitz. Baraboo's guards pulled right, just as if they were setting up a screen. Patrick, too, started right, making solid contact with the rushing defensive end, then releasing to the flats. He caught a glimpse of Peter sprinting past him in the backfield, heading the opposite direction. Reedsburg's defense was screaming "Screen! Screen!" as were the coaches and players on their sidelines. The entire defense sagged to the right to stop Baraboo's star running back.

Stevie pumped convincingly toward Patrick, then gracefully handed the ball to Peter as he rounded the backfield behind the quarterback. Patrick feigned as though he were about to catch the ball, then watched as Peter sprinted to the other side of the field. Joe had pulled from his right tackle spot to set up blocks downfield on the safety and corner who would be the last defenders to prevent Peter from scoring. Joe ran them over one after the other, and Peter dashed into the end zone to the roar of Baraboo's fans.

The extra point was converted with no time on the clock, and Patrick's team went into the locker room at halftime down by just seven points. Baraboo had completely reversed the tide of momentum, and the energy in their locker room rocked.

∞

I milled through the crowd lined up to get hot dogs, popcorn, and sodas. I wasn't in line, but I was looking around among the people gathered at the south end of the field. Some of the townsfolk I knew greeted me and wanted to talk about my twin's performance, but I disengaged from conversations as quickly as I could. I was looking for someone I had spotted from the stands.

It was my brother's interest in the spectators standing along the snow fence that drew my attention to her. I watched her study Patrick as he lined up near the end zone for the kickoff. Patrick had been distracted, I could see. He'd been absorbed with the figure. He had stood, facing the wrong way on the kickoff, looking out the back end of the end zone, like he was lined up backwards. Clearly Patrick had confused the official, who stood, whistle in mouth, awaiting the signal to resume play. I'd wondered whether the ref was going to call a delay of game penalty, but then Patrick kind of woke up, slapped himself up on the side of the head, turned and raised his hand above his helmet, and the ref blew the ball in play.

I wondered whether Rose had homed in on Patrick's distracted focus. Or Paddy. It was so obvious to me. But now, they were standing with Trong and Aunt Kate, waiting in line for hot chocolate. I didn't say I'd be gone for a bit. I just left.

She was nowhere to be found. Perhaps I was imagining. Maybe Patrick had not noticed her. Something convinced me to think otherwise. I strode toward the south end zone in search of Lynn North. I was certain I had spotted her watching the game.

A buzz rippled through the spectators as the halftime performances of the schools bands' filled the stadium with brazen fight songs. Fans walked about, exclaiming the turn of momentum in the first half. Everywhere, debate sparked the chatter between Baraboo fans and their Reedsburg kin and acquaintances. I listened distractedly as I searched the crowd.

In the rows of vehicles parked along the tennis courts east of the field, I caught sight of movement, a light-clad figure between cars. I strained to see, searching the lot, then broke into a jog toward the parking lot. I stepped quickly between the cars parked one after the other, looking up and down the rows for movement. I'd gone to the far end, where my pickup was parked, when I spotted the low sports car moving slowly between the last rows of cars. She didn't see me standing between the cars as she drove by. Instead, she was looking at the vehicles in the far row. The brake lights of her Thunderbird lit brightly, and she rolled to a stop behind my pickup. I watched her get out and open the trunk of her car. She pulled a medium-sized box from the trunk, balanced it first on the fender of her car, then carried the parcel to my truck. She set it behind the driver's seat in the bed of the pickup. She returned to her car and retrieved a second parcel.

I quietly walked the distance between the rows of parked cars. I made no attempt to hide, but I didn't think she saw me. I was surprised, then, when she looked up from the boxes she left in my pickup and smiled kindly.

"Hello, David," Lynn North said.

A smile claimed my face.

"I thought you might follow me here. I spotted you looking through the crowd as if you had seen me."

"I did," I nodded. "I thought it was you. Only by the way Patrick looked at you from the field."

Her smile melted, replaced by the hint of a wince narrowing her eyes.

"You think he saw me?" Her question was laced both with hope as well as concern.

I nodded. "Yep, Ma'am. I kind of think he figured you out about as soon as he saw you. He almost left the sidelines when he first spotted you. Strange way to start a game, that's for sure."

Lynn stepped close, extending her hand. I reached to her, and she took my hand in both of hers. Riveting me with her gaze, she explained her mission.

She had arrived at the game early and watched as people came to the stadium. She had seen Patrick and his team arrive by bus before their warmup. She stayed back, out of sight, not wanting to distract him. Later, she had seen me and Trong arrive in the pickup, followed by Mom, Aunt Kate, Paddy, and the old fellow, Gabriel, in the Packard. She noted where we parked because she was here, after all, to deliver some things to Patrick that belonged to him.

"Why don't you just give them to him yourself?" I interrupted. Her touch calmed me.

She looked at me keenly. I wondered what thoughts she weighed sharing with me. She appeared lovelier than I recalled from meeting her last fall, when she'd delivered Patrick to the farm for Jannie's funeral. She'd been slighter when we'd first met, a year before. Sadder-looking back then, too. Not sullen, but certainly bearing sorrow. Maybe it was her divorce, and all the things she was going through. Or perhaps I had remembered her through my own grieving and loss. A hint of sorrow remained in her eye, but it was fresher. The events of the summer. More profound, perhaps.

She knew her purpose. She stood facing the flow of energy pouring from the stadium. She glowed, illuminated by the stadium lights. Her hair sparkled golden, and the light fell warmly on her skin. Her eyes were kind and grace filled, and hopeful.

"I kind of hoped Patrick might see me," Lynn admitted. "I thought it was a long shot, in a crowd like this," she said, gesturing toward the stadium.

"He was like radar," I said. "He picked right up on you. He knows you are here. But he doesn't know why. Why are you here, if not to see him?"

A shadow crossed her face. She gestured at the boxes in his pickup, but kept her eyes on me.

"I wanted to see you, David," she said. "I knew I couldn't... see him. Not now. Not... now." She withdrew her hands and wrapped her arms across her body, holding herself. I looked into her eyes and listened as she explained.

"I don't think it is fair" she paused, taking a deep breath, "for him... that I see him now," Lynn continued. Her voice was kind, but strong. "I don't know that I have been fair to him all along, so I can't see making him go through it all again."

She watched as I slowly shook my head, but I remained quiet. She gathered her thoughts and continued.

"I have these things, and they are his," she said, gripping her arms snugly. "But now may not be the best time for him to have them. I don't know when that time will be, but it is not now. I want to ask you to take them. They are photos and things. And maybe when it is right, you'll know, and you can give them to him. Maybe that way he will understand...."

I watched her rock slightly, to and fro, rotating back and forth, holding herself. I wanted to take back her hand.

From the stadium, the roar of the crowd in the bleachers announced the return of the teams to the field. We looked toward the commotion under the lights.

"Will you do that for me... and for Patrick, please?" she asked.

I nodded. Of course.

"When will the time be right?" I asked.

She shook her head and shrugged. Tears welled. "I don't know. Maybe Patrick will let you know." She implored with a smile, "Just don't wait forever." Her voice broke off in a whisper.

The band struck up the alma mater, and all of the Baraboo fans stood and sang along.

"Thank you," she said.

"Aren't you going to watch the second half?" I asked.

"Of course," she said with the certainty of a judge.

"Then join us," I urged her to stay.

She shook her head decisively. She had gambled enough and was fortunate to have gotten me aside without alerting the others.

"It is not the right time," she said simply. "Not fair to Patrick. Not fair to your family. Not fair to me.

"I will watch Patrick play the rest of the game. I want that, at least... for myself. But that is all. I'll be on my way home, to Minneapolis, by the time the teams have cleared the field."

I inspected her expression carefully. She knew precisely what she had come to do, and she would live by her plan. As she looked toward the activity in the stadium, I knew she could not change her mind. I knew that Patrick would want to see her. He would anguish to know that I'd talked with her—much less had accepted things from her that belonged to him. I recognized the burden she was putting upon me. And I instinctively knew that the best thing for my brother was to agree to what she asked.

"So why did you come tonight? Why not later? Why now?"

Again, she hugged herself, slowly closing her eyes, then opening them and focusing deep into mine.

"This just seemed the best chance...," she said. "The best chance to watch him, and leave him, and be on with our lives. We have no choice but to be on with our lives."

She nodded, then gestured toward the bleachers.

"Go on now. You'll miss the game. You don't want to miss your twin being the star."

We smiled, and she hugged me, and I nodded goodbye.

Jogging back toward the bleachers, I was grinning like a cat. I wondered how much of the truth I could keep from my brother. And how long must I hold the secret? I hoped I'd know the moment when I should share the secret Lynn entrusted to me. I would do what she asked.

The roar raging from the crowd in the bleachers on Baraboo's side of the field announced the kickoff. I raced toward the snow fence in time to see Patrick sprinting headlong toward the end zone with three blue-shirted players in ragged pursuit. I grabbed the wooden slats of the fence and jumped up and down, screaming wildly for my brother. Patrick finished his run a mere ten yards away in the end zone. He held the ball out, pointed end aimed right at me, his head nodding confidently inside the hard shell of his helmet.

As my twin was pummeled by his teammates, I glanced back toward the parked cars. A lone figure in a light-colored sweater and cap leaned against the hood of a car not sixty yards into the dim lights of the parking area. I raised my fist, screaming and cheering. The figure by the cars spread her arms wide and lifted her face to the sky. I listened, but could not hear her cry above the din from the crowd behind me.

∞

By the time Trong had revisited every play of the game at least four times with the Joyces, Patrick had savored the homecoming victory and was ready for bed. The game was particularly hard fought, and as the target of two all-Conference linebackers—Olsen would likely be all-State—Patrick felt his muscles and joints ache with fatigue and bruises. Excusing himself and bidding good night, he left for his bedroom.

I followed right after him.

Patrick looked up with an expression of weary joy as I sat facing him from the side of his own bed.

"Well?" he asked expectantly.

I startled. "Well, what?"

"Did you talk with her?" He raised an eyebrow as he tugged off his shoe. I collected my thoughts, but Patrick pressed me to filter nothing out.

"You saw her, I'm sure," he said assertively. "Didn't you?"

I grinned, sheepishly.

"Yeah."

Patrick's expression transformed, the joy melting to pained loss. He looked across to me, hoping for more. I offered little.

"Why was she here?"

I considered how to answer. "To see you. To watch you play."

"Why didn't she stay after the game? Didn't she want to talk to me?"

"I think so. Probably too much. She said she didn't think it would be fair. She thought it would be easier if you hadn't seen her at all."

Patrick said nothing as he yanked off his other shoe, then his socks. He stood, popped the snap on his Levi's, pulled down the zipper, and let the jeans drop to the floor. He plopped back down on the mattress, fell backward, his head sinking deep into the pillow. He pulled it up over his face.

"But I did see her," he muttered from under the pillow.

I didn't reply.

Patrick pulled the pillow away and faced me.

"What did she say to you?" he inquired.

I hemmed and hawed.

"Well, nothing much. She was on her way back home from Indiana. She said Harriet sends her love." I paused. In a lower tone, I continued, "I kind of surprised her. I noticed her from the way you were watching her down on the field. Wow! I thought you had forgotten you were in the game!"

Patrick smirked.

"Almost had. I couldn't believe it when I spotted her. Like, normally, you don't see anybody off the field during a game. Nobody. Hell, I couldn't see anybody else tonight, either, but her. There she was. I couldn't believe it. Why did she go? Without even saying hello. I can't figure it out."

I thought about it. Then I improvised on what she had said.

"She wanted to see you play, Patrick. She wanted to stay and talk, too, she said. But she didn't think it would be right. She said she thought it would be too hard for you... and for her, too. She said she couldn't do that."

Patrick wrapped a heavily muscled arm across his face, his elbow propped in a peak above his nose.

He said nothing for several minutes. I stood to return to the others chatting away in the kitchen.

"David," Patrick called behind me. "Did Mom see her? Or anybody else? Miss Rose?"

"Don't know. I don't think so."

"Good." Patrick said after a pause.

I turned out the light as I left the room. I was hoping Gabriel had not left. I felt like fiddling.

Chapter Thirty-Seven
Transitions

I'M SURPRISED by how strongly Lynn's boxes attract me. I admit, I used to bear a hefty guilt about going into Patrick's things. At first, I wouldn't let myself crack open the albums, or even shuffle through the loose photos. Not at all. I felt too much responsibility, too much honor in the task Lynn gave me. But I was just drawn in. My curiosity got stronger and stronger, and once I gave in to it, it seems that now I'm going back to look at them a couple times a week. And I don't feel a shred of guilt anymore. Those things exude happiness and love, and I can't stay away from them.

I brought Lynn's boxes back to my room at Aunt Kate's and stashed them at the back of my closet. I figured that if I left them at home, somebody might snoop. It would be okay, I suppose, if it was Patrick who discovered them. I even thought about taking them home just for that reason. Maybe that would be the best way for him to get them. But then, Lynn asked me specifically to wait for the best time to give them back, and I don't think she meant for him to just stumble across them by accident. I wonder, though. I mean, what did she mean by the best time? What is the right time? How am I supposed to know?

At first, looking through the photos, I couldn't see why he shouldn't have them right away. I mean, it's mostly just photos that they took of each other. Mostly of Pat. She did a beautiful job of picking out the best ones, cropping them, and arranging them in the albums. The pictures tell so much about their lives. I know all the adults were concerned about how much older Lynn is than Patrick, but you sure couldn't tell that by the photos. She doesn't look older than him at all, maybe because he's such a giant. But more than that, they look like equals. Equally happy, the same joyous excitement shining in both of their faces. And in some of them, the more private ones, the intensity I see in Patrick's gaze is just as mature as the way she responds to him. The photos make them look perfect for each other, though. I mean, they look so natural and happy together.

The photos are works of art, and I can page through them anytime without feeling the tugs of conscience. They're mostly just shots of Patrick working or playing football. And there are some portraits of him around the Dunes and in Lynn's house, and in Chicago. Those are the most intimate ones, the ones that maybe would have made the older folks feel vindicated in their worrying, if they were to take a look. Man, they get pretty steamy! Just Patrick's body language reveals a lot. And what he was or wasn't wearing. There is the one, though, that is really special. Totally them. They must have used the shutter timer, but they weren't looking at the camera. Patrick was looking down at Lynn, who pointed at something on his chest. Or maybe she was just playing with a twist of his chest hair. It's hard to tell. It was clearly an intimate moment. And with his arms folded around her, you can't really see if she has a bikini top on. I mean, you can't see any straps at all on her shoulders or around her neck. Or around her back. It is really mysterious. And since they're standing in the pool and the reflections block out just about everything underneath the surface, you can't tell whether *either* of them has on anything at all! Honestly, it is as erotic a picture as I've ever seen. Or it would be erotic, I guess, if it was meant to be seen by just anybody. But this isn't. No. This is meant to be private. And if it weren't so, well, beautiful and appealing, I'd feel more guilty about looking at it again. I just can't help it, though. It's my twin, after all. And his woman. Man!

But it's one thing to look through the pictures. It's another thing to read her thoughts. Some of her writings are in there, too, and those are what hold me back from giving Patrick his boxes. Her writings carry a tone more clear than even the most explicit pictures. The daily log from building the wall, and the one from the canoes—that one was filled out in Patrick's coarse script—detail the building of their trust and their friendship as clearly as they noted the progress of their work. But Lynn's other, personal writings, while not as erotic as a few of their pictures together, make it obvious that their relationship evolved well beyond platonic. If Patrick were to read these things, it would reach right down and grip his heart. And I don't think it's time for Pat to deal with that just now.

Aside from Lynn's writings, though, there are two sealed letters. They both simply say Patrick on the envelope, with the date. One is dated July 10, 1963, the day after Jack's funeral, when we came back from Indiana with Patrick. The other is dated simply October 5. That would be the day I saw Lynn. I haven't opened them. She didn't seal them very tightly, just the tip of the point on the back flap of each envelope. I've tried peeking under the flap, but I really can't make anything out. It's enough seal to say, *Stay out.* Unless your name is Patrick, I suppose. He is my twin, though. It is driving me nuts.

∞

For opening morning of deer season, I had planned on taking a stand out on the bluff where Major Steve and I took the Pony last year. He wasn't able to come back to Baraboo for the hunt like he'd hoped. He's gone over to southeast Asia, to the country of Vietnam, Trong's homeland. I got a note from him a few weeks ago, saying he was in the jungle and doing some hunting of his own. Whew! I know what that means. I'd rather go deer hunting, I think.

Anyway, the day before the season opener, I got out of my last class by eleven and hightailed it to Aunt Kate's for a sandwich before we headed home.

We were all packed and ready to go, so we got an early start. We were just past the turn to Lodi at about noon when we heard on the radio about the President. I couldn't believe it. We kept on driving, the wipers slapping out a pace that made the trip seem endless. We drove on and on, not saying a word, hoping the radio would stay tuned in as we wound up and down the hills on Highway 12 leading to Sauk and then north to Baraboo. Sometimes we'd lose the signal, and I'd turn the dial to find a stronger station. Most of them were just playing music, like nothing out of the norm had happened. It was so unreal. Looking out the car window, everything looked the same, like nothing earthshaking had happened. A herd of Holsteins lay chewing their cud on the flats just before the bridge leading into Sauk. The Wisconsin looked as bored and placid as usual, just filling space, passing time, moving downstream toward the big river, and then on to the big pond. In town, though, hardly anybody was on the streets. And when you did pass somebody, they'd look up, kind of puzzled and surprised, wondering if maybe we hadn't heard, wondering if they could believe what they'd heard themselves.

When we got home, Mom and Miss Rose were huddled together at the kitchen table, working on Mom's French. They hadn't heard. Neither had Uncle Paddy, who was out in the barn keeping things tidy, working with some of the young stock, getting them used to grooming and the lead halter. It was amazing just seeing their faces when we told them Kennedy had been shot. I could see my own emotions mirrored in their faces: confusion, disbelief, and then shock. No room for grief, yet, even. We turned on the TV right away. He'd already been declared dead at the hospital. We watched all afternoon. Patrick got home just after three, and he said the school had interrupted classes and piped in the radio broadcast over the loudspeaker. He said kids were crying and real quiet, except for some who acted like asses, saying that it was about time they got him. Patrick said he almost got into a fight with Donny Warton over it. He would have crushed him, he said, except for Wendy Whitman, Jannie's little sister. Patrick said she just kind of appeared out of nowhere in study hall, when Donny was carrying on and Patrick had told him to just shut his face. Warton was within an inch of getting thrashed by my twin when Wendy got between them, facing Patrick, and simply shook her head and whispered, "Don't. He's not worth it. Let it be. Don't give him the satisfaction of a whooping. It's not the honorable thing." Then she just walked away. Patrick stood down then, even after Donny kept taunting him. He said it was the first thing Wendy had said to him since he got back. He still seemed stricken by the whole event. But then, everybody seemed stunned by what happened that Friday.

I didn't go out hunting Saturday morning, although I made it out for a while in the afternoon. I saw a couple does, and one nice buck. I just didn't feel like shooting him. Mostly, we just watched the television and things going on in Dallas and Washington.

Sunday afternoon, the Packer game was on. It was weird to be hearing the game in the middle of everything with the assassination. Like, well, should we just pretend to go on as if nothing really happened? Or, maybe football was more important? Or was it just that we didn't know how to act with something so big as the President getting shot, so we just tried to stuff some of the normal things of life back into place? I don't know.

Paddy and I were planning to work over some of the breeding plans. We'll probably put Flash and Lightning—the two half-brothers sired by Orbit with some of the new line we brought in last year—in with our young heifers again early next spring. I dunno. Maybe we're being too aggressive with too much of our herd. Paddy doesn't think so. He says we've got the most front-line genetics available. He's excited to see if the offspring from these young bulls are going to be as special as we hope. It's kind of funny. Things just go on. The President isn't even laid out in his grave yet, and here we are planning for things that we'll set in action next spring, which will result in calves dropping almost a year hence, and then we'll have to wait out another two years just to see if these young bulls can produce daughters that will really milk. It'll be 1966 before we know it. Heck, at the rate I'm planning, I'll be out of college before then. I'll be back home on the farm in time to see just how fancy those heifers turn out to be. I can't wait!

I wonder where my brother will be by then. He ought to be going into his second year of college, I suppose. I wonder where he wants to go? He'll probably be able to go anywhere he chooses, at least anywhere that has a good football team. After this past season, undefeated and all, with him making all-Conference and getting honorable mention for all-State, he's getting a lot of attention from recruiters. I suppose it depends on him having another good year next year. I can't wait to see him play again.

Chapter Thirty-Eight

Leaving North Freedom

Fall, 1964

TRONG HAD ME.

"Check," he said softly. His voice was humble, but a sparkle in his eye told me that he savored his win. He didn't often take his end game to mate against me, but it was coming. Two moves and I'd be done. At most. He'd earned it this time. My only option was to insert my queen between his bishop and my king, which only prolonged my agony. It would be mate after that.

I tipped my king over, and smiled warmly at my Vietnamese friend. "You want to go again?"

Trong bowed his head deferentially. "Thank you, David," he replied. "But, no. Not at the moment. I think I prefer to enjoy this win for a few moments before you unleash your revenge on me." He laughed, his shoulders jerking up and down. He pushed his chair from the table and rose. "Instead, I think I will go visit your 'girls,' and perhaps enjoy a walk under the harvest moon. Care to join me?"

The outing sounded appealing, but I begged off. "Sorry, Trong. Not this time. My twin is looking like he could use a little deep muscle therapy before he crashes."

Patrick grinned wanly. His eyelids had been drooping as he followed the action on the chessboard.

"Thank you for the excellent game, and even more excellent victory," Trong teased as he wrapped himself in a bulky sweater, moving toward the porch.

"Well, you want a backrub? You wanna stretch out and get comfortable before I work on you?" I asked.

Patrick looked resigned to his fatigue. "Why don't you just rub my neck for me while I sit here?" he asked. "I'm too tired to move into the bedroom."

I chuckled. Patrick's post-game adrenalin high had peaked and ebbed in the hours since the game. I was a bit surprised that he was still up. Mom and Miss Rose had long since retired, and they were usually the night owls. I think we all felt a little letdown after Patrick finished the last game of his senior season. While he did it in grand style—one hundred ninety-three yards rushing, one-thirty-seven receiving, a couple good returns—the excitement of his last home game, and his last high school game, with several college scouts in the crowd, well, it had us all pretty wound up. But when the whistle blew for the last time, we all felt it. Especially Pat. He'd been quiet all evening.

I stepped behind my brother as he stripped the t-shirt over his head. He slouched back in the sturdy wooden chair, letting his long, heavy arms drape across the armrests.

"Sure you don't want to lie down?"

"Yeah. I'm fine here. I don't really want to go to bed yet."

I laughed. "By the looks of your yawns, you could've hit the sack a while ago."

Again, he smiled gamely. "Probably," he admitted. "I guess I'm just hanging on. It's hard to believe it's all over."

He winced as I dug into the cords of heavy muscle along his neck and shoulders. "Damn, that's sore."

"They sure keyed on you tonight," I said. He'd had two linebackers on him every snap, making him earn every yard. I had to give his coach credit. He kept Patrick in the game until the end. He knew that the Baraboo fans probably won't see another player like Pat for a while, and they wanted to see him play it out. His teammates fed him the ball thirty-four times, the most in his entire career. Plus, they threw to him for seven receptions. The more he carried the ball, the harder he fought, running like a raging bull. I imagine Reedsburg is glad they won't have to face Patrick Joyce again. They played him tough, though, the entire game.

"So whaddya think about Reedsburg, now that it's over?" I asked as I worked the hot, thick bundles of his left shoulder.

"I think those assholes were trying to kill me," he snorted. "Man, do I hurt."

"That had to be one of your best games ever."

Patrick considered it. "I don't know. I'll always remember that first time against them, last year. That was such a comeback." Then he was silent.

I wondered whether he was remembering Lynn's surreptitious visit. I wasn't going to ask him. I focused on the muscles running parallel to his spine, prying between each vertebra with my thumbs. I wondered if I should tell him about the stuff I had in my closet down in Madison. I didn't think so. I surprised myself with that. I don't know why. I trusted Lynn, and I didn't see certain things in Pat that made me think it was time. I figured it would probably throw him for a loop if he saw it. That didn't seem like what she'd want.

"How's that?" I asked, driving my fingers up the muscles that ran alongside his neck to the base of his skull.

"Oh, man. That's it. Man, that's sore."

I changed the subject and told him about the progress the herd was making and about the prospects of our young bulls.

"The A.I. co-op is testing a couple of 'em," I told him. "We have one particular fellow out of one of our Morningstar heifers bred back with Flash. Flash was out of Orbit, remember? Uno's grandson. Well, this young bull is our first bull out of Flash. He looks real good. On paper, anyway."

"Oh, yeah. What do you call this one?" he asked. I was surprised that he'd ask. He usually had little interest in the cattle.

"Elevataur," I said. "Like, the bull that elevates your cows' milk production. Spelled with an 'a-u-r' at the end, like in Taurus, the species name. Nice, eh?"

He snorted a laugh. "Where do you come up with these names?"

"That's half the fun," I grinned. "The hard part is figuring out the breedings. After that, once the girls are settled, I have about ten months to think about it. And it eventually pops up. Elevataur. Man, I like that one. I think that young bull has a future for us."

"Whaddya mean?"

"Well, it has to do with the A.I. co-op. If we breed a good bull that the co-op tests out and accepts, and if that bull becomes popular with other breeders, well, it can mean a lot of money."

"What's a lot of money?"

I thought about it. I'd figured it, dreamt about it. "I don't know. Depends. If he's real popular, lots. More than milking brings. Lots more."

I felt him shrug. "Milking doesn't seem to bring all that much."

"More than you'd think," I countered. Patrick didn't know anything about the cash flow of our dairy business. He'd never been interested. "It's steady. And it keeps on coming, and as we breed higher-producing cows and heifers, it keeps getting bigger."

"Well, how much more would the bull bring than all those cows?"

"Over time, lots," I said. "Thousands. Tens of thousands. Maybe even hundreds of thousands."

He turned and looked at me. "You're kidding?"

"Nope."

"Really?"

"Yep."

"Man!"

I could see him turning it over in his mind, so I juiced it up a bit for him. "Yeah, and if the young bull shows a lot of promise, the co-op might buy him outright for a hefty price—like, maybe, a million."

He sat upright. "No! You are shitting me now."

"Nope. No bull," I laughed. I shook my head with certainty, though I really was talking through my dreams. It was a pretty tough task, getting the co-op to go after a young bull. But our genetics were good, so I had hope.

"When will you know if they like this Elevataur, eh?"

I considered it for a moment, then explained. "He's eighteen months now. We turned him out on two of our fanciest heifers, but he's a bit young still. He'll go into testing next spring, I suppose. Then it will take a couple years for them to see the return results. I don't know. Maybe in three or four years. Probably '67, maybe '68. We'll see."

Patrick let his heavy muscles relax again. "Oh. That's a long way off.""Who knows where we'll even be by then?"

I knew were I'd be, but I wondered about my brother. "I'll still be in Madison. In graduate school. How about you? You gonna come down and play for the Badgers?"

I could see him reflecting. "Depends who offers what, I suppose. There were a couple new scouts there tonight. They introduced themselves up at school before the game. One was from Ohio State. I'd never play for them. I hate Ohio State."

"Why? They're big winners."

"I dunno. I just don't like the idea. Ohio, you know. I don't know anything about them. Plus, they have that Woody Hayes guy. I hear he's crazy."

"He's a winner."

"Winning isn't everything."

"That's not what Vince Lombardi says."

"What does Vince Lombardi say?" Patrick asked. His tired voice rose a little in challenge.

"Vince says that winning is everything. The only thing."

"Nope," he corrected me. "Vince said that *the will to win* is everything. Big difference. See?"

I nodded, giving up on any more massage. The strength of my milking hands had waned during my time at Madison.

"Had enough?" I asked. "Because I sure have."

"Yeah. Thanks. It felt great."

"So where are you going go to school, then?"

Patrick tightened his lips, thinking. "I dunno. I'd like to see if Notre Dame is going to recruit me. They had a couple scouts up here at the homecoming game. Southern Cal is interested, too. There've been a few schools. Some of them smaller. Ripon. St. Norbert's. That's where the Packers train in preseason."

I nodded that I knew. "Maybe you should just go be a Packer."

Patrick's eyes lit up. "Wouldn't that be excellent!" He grinned, then shook his head. "That doesn't happen, though." He took on an earnest look and bobbed his head as he said, "You remember me telling you about that coach of mine down in Indiana? Coach Dillon? He called me last week. Said he had a friend who would be scouting me at tonight's game. He asked me not to commit to anyone before he talked to me." He leveled his eyes at me seriously. "I'd play for him again. He was great. Totally up."

"Is he still in Indiana?"

"Nope. He said he was moving out west, and he'll let me know more later. I guess I'll wait to hear from him."

We heard stomping on the porch, and then the door jangled open. Trong stepped in and slipped off his shoes as he quietly closed the door. He grinned in the direction of the chessboard. "You ready to go at it again?"

I looked up at the clock. Eleven-thirty. *"You walk into the den of the tiger,"* I quipped in his native tongue. He'd been teaching me, as had Lee from China and others from Aunt Kate's long string of boarders from east and southeast Asia. Lee and Trong, her current students, seemed to be in a competition to see which one could get me to learn their language first and best.

"I will cut off the tiger's balls and feed them to the vultures," he replied, his grin never wavering.

"You guys start talking like that, I'm outta here," Patrick said, lumbering to his feet and arching his back in a long, slow stretch. "I'm done. Goodnight."

"Goodnight, Patrick," Trong said.

"'Night," I said, placing the chessmen on their squares.

∞

Spring, 1965

Patrick is going to go to Colorado to play ball! Wow! That's a long way from home. I mean, for me, it would be crazy to go all that way to college, especially just to play football. I did try to get him interested in being a Badger. Two years ago, when Ron Vander Kelen led Wisconsin against Southern Cal, I think Patrick would have done about anything to play ball at Madison. The Badgers haven't been as good, though, since. And what really did it was being recruited by his old coach, a guy named Dillon, from down in Indiana. Gyro Dillon, Patrick calls him. Seems like Coach Dillon got a job as a backs coach in Boulder, and he came calling on Patrick. They even flew him out there to tour the campus. Man, that Patrick is something else. He is totally unintimidated by the thought of getting on an airplane and flying halfway across the country. I guess I'm just more of the homebody. And to think that everyone thought I was so daring to go down to school in Madison. I was always so impressed with Trong and Lee, being able to up and move around the world so they could study at the University. I'm glad Madison is so close. I mean, I can get about the best education there is, and still be home to see the girls and help Paddy with the milking and breeding on weekends.

∞

June 21, 1966

So, we're twenty today.

Kind of hard to believe. Twenty. I remember going from single digits to double digits. Nine to ten. Seemed like such a big deal at the time. One day, nine. The next, ten. Double digits. That was important stuff back then.

Now, still double digits, but the twenties. Twenty years old. Kind of neat. Old Camp told me he just turned ninety-five. I don't know how he knows that. In all these years, I've never once heard anyone say they knew when Gabriel's birthday was. I didn't think he knew himself. I kind of remember asking him about it when I was little. I think it was when he gave me my first fiddle. He gave me a vague response, something like, well, it's all just one big day anyway, so every day is his birthday. I wouldn't take that for an answer, I recall. How could it all be one big day? I distinctly remember him telling me to consider myself as a seagull flying high above the North Pole.

"When would the sun set?" he asked. "When would the new morning dawn?

I thought about it for probably a whole week.

"It never sets," I told him the next time he came down to the house.

He picked up the thread of our conversation right away. "Yep. One big day is all. Just one, big, glorious day."

Well, by my count, I figure I've had seven thousand, three hundred and five sub-days to divide up this one big glorious day that I've lived so far. Man, that's not even about a quarter of the days Old Camp has lived.

So why do I feel in such a rush to get at things in my life?

I haven't been home more than four weeks since graduation, and it's been one of the most beautiful late springs I can remember in my whole life. Seventy-six degrees today, a breeze barely kissing my cheek. Life is good. The cattle are milking great. The new calves are looking tremendous, and we got a bundle of heifers—sixty-four percent of the calf crop. That bends the stats all to hell. I suppose we'll get our due next year. So why am I feeling so uneasy?

I wish Patrick had made it home for our birthday, but I guess I have no space to complain. This is the first summer I've been home since leaving for college. And I'll be back down in MadTown sooner or later anyway, for graduate school. I'm going to enjoy taking a break and farming and being home now that I've graduated. I guess I'll just enjoy the summer and being with Paddy, Mom, and Miss Rose. If I'd have planned better, I could have prepped a show calf to enter in the fair. I haven't done that since Dante and Bruno, since before Jannie died. I guess I've left that part of my life behind.

I wonder what else life will bring me? It is so peaceful and beautiful this summer here on the farm. I can't imagine ever having to endure anything like losing Jannie again. I hope I don't. I'm really kind of feeling, well, healed, finally. Kinda.

∞

June 22, 1966

Hey, Patrick. How you been?

Well, I have strange news, and good news. And I have bad news. But mostly things are pretty good here on the farm.

The strange news is that Old Camp has gone. We hadn't seen him since a couple days before our birthday. Miss Rose hiked over there yesterday to invite him down for birthday cake, but when she got to the cabin, he was gone. All she found was a note he'd scribbled in that ancient script of his. He'd written, "Gone camping in the mountains." I guess you'd have a better handle on how close the mountains are to here, but just looking at the map, I can't imagine he meant the Rocky Mountains. Paddy thinks so, though. He says Old Camp is gone, headed for Montana. He says that as long as he's known Gabriel, he's always talked about getting ready for that final Big Hike in the mountains. His one last camping trip. I asked Paddy how long he's known Gabriel, and he said as long as he can remember. He's been living out in that cabin for at least fifty years, Paddy thinks. You know, Paddy turns fifty-five this year. He says he remembers growing up thinking Gabriel was old back then. He says that Gabriel was always an ancient one. Always old. But spry and young at the same time.

I'd noticed him getting that cloudy look in his eyes this spring, like he was looking beyond you, out into the distance. Mom said it was probably cataracts. Maybe. I think Gabriel used more than his eyes when he was seeing, anyway.

The co-op wrote me about our bulls. They are done using Flash and Lightning. He says they have more current genetics than those old boys can bring them. You know, between them, those old boys have sired more than eighteen thousand daughters. Not bad! Flash's daughters ended up with a plus-one-twenty-five-pound predicted difference in their milk production. They still have another couple hundred straws on nitrogen from him. Lightning wasn't quite as good, but he gives his daughters more style, more sleek dairy look about them. Dairy character, it's called.

The big news, the good news, is that the co-op is going to contract Elevator. (They changed the spelling to "-or." They said their marketing people thought it looked better.) They haven't spelled out the details. But when I told Paddy, he about popped his eyes out. That's something, isn't it?

Well, the bad news is the pits. I got a notice to report for a draft physical. Can you believe it? I really didn't think that would be a problem. I thought that by coming home and working the farm, I'd be exempt, like Paddy was during WWII. We called the draft board and inquired. But they said, well, had I been working the farm the whole time I'd been a student at Madison? I said, what kind of sense did that make? But they said that the farm obviously got along without me all this time, and it can get along without me for another couple years.

I really don't know what to think about it. It just doesn't seem real.

Give us a call, would you?

Your twin,

David

∞

Miss Rose called through the porch screen, "David, your brother's on the phone."

I hurried in, stripping my barn boots and jeans off as quickly as I could. Didn't matter much. Mom was chatting with Patrick, so I ducked into my room and pulled on a pair of cut-offs so that I didn't have to stand around in my shorts in front of the women. Mom was about done when I returned to the kitchen. She held the phone out to me.

"Hey, Davey," Pat said. "Mom tells me you did all right on your physical."

"Well, if passing a draft physical is all right, that's what I did."

"Damn."

"Right. Guess I didn't expect much else. I'm pretty darn healthy all the time. Can't hardly remember ever missing school, or work in the barn, for being sick, I guess."

"Yeah, but...."

"Yeah."

We listened to the silence across the wire.

"Have you considered Canada?"

I shrugged, knowing he couldn't see me. Yeah, for about a minute. "Wouldn't work for me, Patrick. I mean, what have I got up there? I talked to Miss Rose about it. You know she's from Canada, don't you?"

"Yeah."

"That's where she gets her French. Up near Montreal. But she says she doesn't know anybody up there anymore, either. We agree. Our home is here."

Again, we got caught up in the silence between us.

"Davey?" my brother asked.

"Yeah."

"Have you considered if you could, you know… fight? Kill a man?"

I couldn't answer right away. Sure, I'd considered it. I just hadn't come up with an answer. I didn't know if it was really a question. "I've thought about it."

Again, a pause.

"Could you?"

"I dunno. I haven't figured out yet."

I could hear and feel my brother thinking on the other end of the line.

"Davey. I could."

"What do you mean? How do you know?"

"I just could. Think about it. If it was somebody and me, and that somebody was trying to kill me, I could sure kill him first."

"Hmmph." I couldn't see Patrick fighting. No matter how intensely and violently he played football, he was simply *playing*. I couldn't see him hurting a soul, on purpose.

"I mean it. I could," he insisted. "I just don't ever want to be in that situation, is all. I don't want to go looking for it. I want to stay away from anything to do with it."

I thought about it. "Yeah. I see. I wish it was that easy."

"Think about it, though."

"Yeah."

"Let me know."

"You betcha."

"See you."

"Yeah."

∞

I wish Father Jack was here. I need somebody to talk some moral sanity into my head. Damn. Most everybody I know is wishing me well. Telling me how proud they are of me. I wonder if Father Jack would be saying the same.

∞

I said goodbye to Mom and Miss Rose at the house. Paddy took me into Baraboo to meet the bus for Madison. I didn't want them to drive me down. It would have been way too long a drive for all of us.

On the way to town, I asked Paddy why he didn't go into the service when Dad did.

"Different times, I reckon," he said. "I guess the government thought they needed somebody at home to raise food. I was a bit on the old side, too."

"Did you ever miss going?"

He glanced sideways toward me. "Never once."

We rode the rest of the way in silence.

At the bus stop, he got out and pulled my satchel from the back seat. He set it down on the sidewalk between us. He was frowning big time, like he was intent on saying something that he was rehearsing over and over in his mind. I waited and let him work it out.

When he was ready, he kind of bobbed his head, and took a deep breath. "David, I want you to remember this. In the service, you don't want to stand out. Just do what you have to do, and don't make a show of it. This will be one time in your life where you're going to want to excel at not excelling, if you catch my meaning. And for God's sake, don't ever raise your hand or voice to volunteer." He nodded again for emphasis. "Your dad told me that. He said it was key to surviving in the service." I could see his eyes mist up.

"I'll be okay, Paddy."

"You goddamned better be," he barked. He stepped close and engulfed me in his arms. "You are a son to me, David. I'll be praying every day for you."

"I'll be okay," I repeated. "And I'll be home after boot camp, by Labor Day, I suppose."

"Good," he said, stepping back. He looked me over good once more, then offered me his hand.

I took his hand firmly and we shook. He picked up my satchel and handed it to me, and nodded one last time.

I turned and walked toward the station office. I couldn't even say, "Take care of the girls," for the lump in my throat.

∞

July 19, 1966

Dear Patrick,

Well, by the time you get this, I suppose you'll have heard about where I am anyway. But this is how it happened.

Paddy dropped me off at the bus station so that I could report for duty, and I rode down to Madison thinking the goodbyes are all done with and I'm on my way. But when the bus pulls up to the place where we were supposed to report in, there was a big demonstration going on. The bus was full of guys from Tomah and Mauston and the Dells and Sauk, all the stops along the way, and all these guys ready to report for the draft. There were about thirty of us. So, the bus is going to drop us all off. That was the deal. But the bus can't get anywhere close. There must have been about a thousand people all packed up tight to the doors of the place where I'm heading, and they are all yelling and shouting, "Hell no, please don't go," over and over again.

All of us guys reporting had to practically fight our way into the induction center. Just before we got to the doors, there was this flight of stairs, maybe ten steps. There were maybe half a dozen soldiers lined up on each side of a clearing where we could climb up those stairs and go into the induction center. It took us nearly ten minutes to get from the bus up to the steps. I was one of the last ones to reach the stairs, and the crowd was jostling and shouting and raising all sorts of hell. Man, a lot of them were students, and a lot of hippie types. There were all these young women crying and yelling, and some of them were mad, too. Screaming at us as if we were criminals to even report for the draft. A lot of the guys were mad, too. Just as I started climbing the steps, the soldiers who were cordoning off the stairs kind of lost their hold and the crowd collapsed in on us. I suppose they picked me 'cause I was smaller and lighter. They could have picked up the big fat guy behind me, but he would have been a load. Anyway, they grabbed me and lifted me up over their heads and started passing me back away from the induction center. The soldiers, they grabbed on to me, too, and started tugging. I was like the rope in a tug of war! I mean, at first, it was a little bit funny, and even some of the people who hoisted me above their head were laughing and joking. But once the soldiers got into it, it was for real. Man, I think they stretched me to at least five foot five! You know who was going to win that war, anyway, so eventually I ended up inside the induction center. But the crowd never did give up. We could hear them shouting and wailing the whole time they processed us.

And did they ever process us. Then, when it looked like we were all about ready to get on another bus and head to an Army base somewhere, they made us all stand in alphabetical order with our toes on this long yellow line. One of the officers said, 'Gentlemen, count off by fours, starting from this end." I heard the other guys tick off the count and I could see I was going to be a four, and sure enough, I was the second four. When everybody got done counting, this officer says, "All fours, take one step backward." We did, and then he told all the others to pick up their gear, face right, and he marched them all out of the room.

Once they left, those of us who were fours stood there a minute, thinking we were all alone in that room. I could tell we were all thinking the same thing: Maybe they didn't need us and were going to let us go home. Then, from behind us, we hear the heels of someone marching pretty smartly. We all started to turn to see who was coming, but a voice like a cannon boomed out, "Eyes to the front, ladies." I gulped. That voice wasn't here to tell me to go home. So, this huge guy with shoulders like yours steps in front of us. He's wearing a crisp brown shirt and blue pants with a whole mass of stripes on his shoulders. He's got on this white hat, and both the visor and his shoes were absolutely polished. He looked us up and down, and when he came to me, his eyes burned right though mine. He took a deep breath, and very quietly but clearly said, "Welcome to the Marine Corps, ladies."

I about died.

They took us out to the airport in Madison and put us on a plane and here I am in San Diego. I was amazed, it happened so fast. But you know, the one thing that really blew me away was as we were getting on the plane in Madison, the sergeant who greeted us there waited until he had me alone for the briefest of moments before I boarded the plane. As I walked by, he caught my eye and said, real quietly so that none of the others could hear, "Colonel Whitney sends his regards." I couldn't believe my ears. I stopped to ask him what he meant, how Colonel Steve knew about all this, but he just ordered me on to the plane.

So here I am in sunny San Diego. I'm living with about forty other guys in this metal barn about a hundred yards from where the planes land at the airport. It's amazing that I can sleep through the noise of them landing, but I don't hear a thing. They keep us plenty tired.

So, I guess I'll be here into September, and then go to Camp Pendleton, which is up the coast of California. Then, I'll get a leave, and then I'll go to my assignment, wherever that may be. I won't know until I leave boot camp.

We haven't done much yet except process. We got uniforms. And rifles. And boots. And haircuts. That was like, first thing. I have no hair. Well, maybe more than Jannie did when she was bald. I have a bit of stubble that I can feel with my hand, but that's about it. Man, I'll tell you one thing. People sure look funny when they have no hair. No matter how ugly or good-looking all these guys are, they all kind of look alike without hair and dressed all exactly the same. It's weird.

Gotta go. My time is not my own anymore.

Semper fi,

Your twin

Chapter Thirty-Nine
Boulder

October, 1966

PATRICK WONDERED if he would ever forget Lynn North.

He tried. Or, he told himself, he lived like he was trying to put her in the past. But so often, she was there. He could see her now, as he remembered her, in her bedroom, in the Dunes, on a lazy summer afternoon, the sunlight dancing off her skin.

Patrick looked at the clear Colorado morning sunlight moving across the tanned skin on the girl's thigh and butt. She was sleeping now. He wondered for a second how many times they had fucked during the night. Jesus, it must have been eight. She was hot. She kept on coming on. He'd fucked her every which way, until she finally slumped into a heap in his arms, her face against his chest, one leg atop his own, her knee tucked in between his thighs.

Just the sight of her smooth skin in the sun stirred him. He wondered whether he should turn her and do her again. Instead, he let her rest. Maybe he'd had enough raw, powerful sex with her during the night. Let her rest.

His mind kept tripping over images of Lynn. Could he ever forget her? Could he somehow purge her from his memory? Did he really want to? It had been three years since he'd last seen her. And he hadn't even had the chance to talk with her then. She'd avoided him. She hadn't thought he'd seen her. But he had.

Patrick shifted his leg out from under the girl's and gently set her head upon his pillow, gingerly pulling his shoulder and arm from beneath her. She stirred, her eyes opening slightly, rolling beneath her lids as she dreamed. Her deep, peaceful breathing told him that she'd fallen further into sleep. He looked at her lovely body once again, then pulled the sheet up over her shoulder and let her sleep.

One of the cheerleaders, he thought. This one is a cheerleader. He must be moving up in the world. Only the stars get the cheerleaders, he mused. He tried, but couldn't remember her name. Shelly? Sherry? Cherry? Ha, he chuckled. That would be about right. Cherry. Whoo! Cherry.

Patrick slipped on a pair of gym shorts. He rummaged through the ashtray on his dresser, spotting a good-sized roach. Man, they'd left a lot of this one go, he thought, inspecting the brown-stained, tightly rolled joint pinched between his thumb and finger. He lit it up, took a deep drag, held it, and exhaled, the bluish smoke puffing against his image in the mirror above the dresser. He repeated the action, and then took the smoldering roach along with him to the kitchen, stepping around several of the bodies that were oblivious of him, sleeping where they lay across the living room floor. He took a third drag, his head swimming in the rush from the dope. He flicked the sour, nasty-smelling roach onto the edge of the sink, where it sizzled in the dampness. He jostled the kettle, then added water and returned it to the stove. He lit the burner and fetched the coffee from his freezer. Uncle Paul had always cautioned him to keep his coffee frozen, it didn't matter if it was whole bean or ground. Patrick poured a small mound of grinds into a fresh filter in the Melita and waited for the water to boil. He spotted the baggie left on the table and held it up to gauge the dent they had put in the lid the night before. About half, he figured. It was good stuff, really good stuff; fine, mostly bud and flower, no seeds at all. He reached for the papers, took a few pinches from the bag, and smoothly rolled a thick doobie. He stuck it behind his ear. The water was bubbling by the time he finished, so he filtered the coffee into the carafe. He poured a cup, topped off the carafe, and, taking a nearly empty pack of matches, went out onto the deck of his rented house.

It was a beautiful Sunday morning in Boulder. The first of October. Already, the temperature was climbing into the lower seventies. He pulled the lounge chair around to face into the sun and climbed carefully onto the thick, padded cushion that was forever sliding off the webbing. He was pretty stiff this morning. He'd taken a few good hits yesterday. He rubbed his left shoulder and rotated his arm in slow, wide arcs. Man, he should have taken something when he got up. The girl's head on his shoulder had awakened him. He knew it was sore, knew it would be sore almost as soon as he took the hit from Brushman, Oklahoma's all-American safety. The guy was a hitter, and he'd clocked Patrick head on, full speed, lodging his helmet up under Patrick's shoulder pad. It had burned last night, he remembered, but he'd been feeling no pain. He was glad he'd chosen not to drink, he thought. His mind was fuzzy enough from the numbers he'd rolled and shared with the cheerleader and her friends. He hated being hung over from alcohol, though.

The coffee was good—the beans a gift sent by David from California. He couldn't believe his brother had thought to send them. David. Always thinking. Always doing decent things. He had picked these beans up on his two-day leave, he'd written, when he got through with basic and before his infantry training. He'd found a coffee store in San Diego. These were great beans. From Hawaii. Kona beans. Some of the mildest he'd ever enjoyed, Patrick thought. Uncle Paul would certainly approve. Hell, he'd probably be jealous, if he knew. He sipped another slug, closed his eyes, and felt the rush of dope surge with the caffeine. The sun was warm on his face.

He heard the clink of a cup in the kitchen, then the refrigerator door opening and closing. A minute later, one of the girl's friends looked out the sliding glass door to the deck, spotted Patrick by the pool, and came out uninvited to join him. One of Cherry's friends, he recalled, the thin one. Tiny, really. No taller than five feet, maybe five one at the most. Pretty, though, Patrick thought as she sauntered toward him, sipping on a mug of coffee she'd helped herself to. She smiled shyly at him, and twitched a shrug.

"Hi," she said, her voice more solid than a squeak, but barely. "I'm Cindy."

Patrick smiled in return. He didn't know exactly what to say, other than the obvious.

"I'm Pat."

"I know." She actually did squeak this time. "We met last night."

He nodded. "Yeah. A friend of Cherry's?"

She frowned, then her brow arched with comprehension.

"Cheryl?" she smiled.

Pat grunted.

She sat alongside him in one of the captain's chairs.

"Good coffee," she said, holding the cup up to her chin and sipping frequently.

"Yeah. Thanks. My brother sent it to me. It's from Hawaii."

She nodded, and sipped, watching him curiously.

She was really more than pretty, Patrick noticed. Fine boned, and hardly tan at all. Her hair was loop upon loop of large curls, and it captured the rays of morning sunlight, shimmering as she moved her head to sip, or bob and nod at what he said. She smiled and shrugged timidly between comments.

"Everybody's pretty well out," she said, nodding to the house.

"Yeah, well, I don't think anybody got too much sleep," he chortled.

She paused, sipped, then smiled gamely.

"I did."

He looked at her quizzically.

"I was tired. I just kind of fell asleep early," she laughed at herself.

He smiled in return, and wondered. *Wow. How could anybody have slept through that party?*

He sipped his coffee and noticed her watching him with her vivid blue eyes, clear and sharp. From the captain's chair next to him, she looked down her straight, sharp nose. The sunlight glistened on her cheeks, and she smiled easily.

She was wearing a lightweight, sleeveless sundress, cut fairly low in the front and back, with two straps about an inch wide over her shoulders. Almost gauze, he noticed. Fine muslin. It captured her slight, delicate frame. Her breasts were not large, but her nipples held up the fabric smartly. She sat with her legs crossed comfortably, the dress draped gracefully across her thighs. For so small a person, her legs seemed long coming from under the sundress.

She seemed absolutely nonplussed as he looked at her. Indeed, he caught her looking at his chest and stomach. She sipped her coffee again, then nodded at the number perched above his ear.

"Are you going to do that?" she asked.

He nodded.

"Thinking about it."

"I love being a morning person," she shrugged.

She reached over, brushing his ear as she picked up the joint, and lit it with the matches. She took a long, smooth drag, held the joint, took another, then offered it to Patrick.

He smoked it, but before returning it to her, he asked through the smoke as he exhaled, "Ever do a turbo?"

She shrugged again, her expression indicating that she didn't know what a turbo was.

"Here," he said, pulling the last of the matches out from the matchbox and rolling the cardboard cover into a tube around the joint.

"Just inhale when I nod," he explained. "I'll turbo it for you. Just breathe in from the tube here when I tell you."

He got off the lounge, pulled the padded cushion from the webbing, and knelt on it before her. Her eyes widened as she watched him insert the lit end of the joint in his mouth, embracing the paper tube of matchbox cover in his lips.

He inhaled, filling his lungs with sweet scented-smoke, and then nodded at her. She carefully put her lips around the end of the paper tube and started to draw just as Patrick blew steadily through the joint. He watched her eyes widen and water, just inches from his own. He pulled back a few inches and carefully took the joint from his mouth, inhaling the fresh air deeply.

She held her breath just a few seconds, then coughed out the smoke from her lungs in a thick, white plume.

They both laughed, and he said, "Here, again," as he tucked the joint back in his mouth.

Her eyes watered heavily as she gripped her lips on the tube, close to his. As he started to blow evenly through the tube, he touched his fingertips gently on her upper arm on one side, and just above her hip on her left side. At the sensation of his touch, she softened and moved just a little closer to him before pulling back sharply to cough out the smoke in an explosion of laughter.

"Wow," she stammered between coughs, catching her breath.

Patrick joined with her laughing, then took a long, smooth drag from the half-burned joint. He adjusted the tubing, and said, "Again?"

She nodded, wiping the tears forming in her eyes.

"I guess so," she laughed, rolling her eyes merrily.

Patrick set the joint in place and offered her the other end of the tube. As she put her mouth around the paper, she touched her lips lightly against his and laid her hand up along his neck. He touched her gently again, this time down along her butt with his right hand, and under the arm that she reached to his face, setting his open hand on the soft, warm indentation under her arm, the heel of his hand feeling the rise of her breast.

By the time he'd finished blowing though the tube, her lips were flush against his. She broke away to exhale and cough again, but didn't remove her hand from his neck. Instead, she pulled him closer to her, arching her back and tipping her head to the side so as not to cough in his face.

Patrick, too, turned his head to the side and spat out the joint onto the pool deck. He followed the pull of her hand upon his neck until his lips kissed the skin on her neck and shoulders and above her breast between the straps of the sundress. He felt her coughing, but catching her breath. As she settled her breathing, he carefully put one arm under her legs and the other behind her back and picked her easily from the captain's chair and set her down upon the long cushion from the lounge.

She laughed and giggled with the rush from the marijuana, and held tightly where her hand was still on his neck. She pulled him toward her.

Patrick slid his hand inside the sundress. He ran it up across her buns, over her underpants, to the skin on her back. His hand moved smoothly without ceasing. He stroked her back, and side, and, leaning back, her stomach, and her breast. Her breast was not big, but nicely shaped, and her nipple stood firm under his palm. He rolled it slightly as he kissed her neck, her face, her lips.

She met his kiss with lips slightly open, and he tasted smoke on the wetness of her tongue.

He moved his hand slowly down from her breast, back across her smooth, tight belly. His fingers slid beneath the band of her panties. She lurched suddenly and slightly, and he slipped his fingers into the folds within her hair. Her tongue quivered against his, and he, feeling her writhe and respond, chose to play with her body in the ways he knew so well. He would take her, he knew, but first, he would let her know that he was grateful.

It was something Lynn had taught him.

∞

The stadium throbbed with excitement. The Cornhuskers brought in a team that was physical and well-disciplined and nationally ranked, but in the fourth quarter, CU held on to a two-point lead, fourteen to twelve. The Buffaloes weren't expected to win, but with the stand that the defense was making, there was more than a chance.

Patrick didn't touch the ball for most of the first half. But late in the second quarter, inside the two-minute warning, Patrick fielded a Huskers' kickoff at the eight. He caught it with three steps of momentum and accelerated toward the wedge forming at the left hash marks. The crowd saw the wall building, and the roar raged. He popped through the wedge at the thirty-seven with all the Huskers but two behind him. Patrick scanned the field to his right. He stretched his stride to full sprint and raced the final sixty-three yards to the end zone untouched in a hail of resounding cheers.

Patrick's score late in the half pumped the defense going into the locker room. They had the lead, and they held it tenaciously again after halftime throughout the entire third quarter. Patrick watched from the sidelines, though, as the Huskers pounded away at his teammates. As the whistle blew to end the quarter, the size and brute strength of the Huskers were beginning to take a toll on the defense. The momentum was changing. Patrick could see it in his teammates between plays on the field. And he could hear and actually feel it from the crowd. Their cheers were muted, almost as though their voices were lost in their throats. He could feel their confidence erode.

The big red machine was moving down the field, eating chunks of turf with each run now. Within the first four plays of the fourth quarter, Nebraska had crossed midfield and penetrated all the way down to the eighteen. Then they took it all in one fine play, a sweep that everybody in the stadium—the defense, the offense on the sidelines, the fans, everybody—could see developing. Nebraska's back was never touched.

Miraculously, their kicker missed the extra point—after nailing four long field goals earlier. But Nebraska was four points ahead. A field goal would not tie it, and it was unlikely Colorado would have the chance to kick two. The Buffaloes had to score a touchdown.

After the kickoff, Coach changed his game plan, turning to the pass. He sent Patrick over the middle twice, with Boyd lofting quick, short passes that Patrick latched onto and turned up field for gains of six and seven.

The linebackers adeptly adjusted, but so did Coach, telling Boyd to look for Willard, the tight end, releasing on a delay. Boyd hit him two or three yards off the line of scrimmage after Patrick had crossed through the middle and the wide receivers had run fly patterns. Willard ambled for seventeen yards before crunching their safety like a steamroller. On the next play, Boyd hit Charlie White coming out of the backfield as a safety valve, and Charlie turned it upfield for a nice gain of fifteen thanks to a neat block downfield that Patrick laid on the corner.

The crowd was perking up again. With more than six minutes left in the game, CU had charged down to the Nebraska thirty and was moving almost unchecked when Nebraska's coach called for a time out. He wanted to break CU's momentum and reorganize his team.

Patrick waited in the huddle, taking a slurp of water from the trainers, while Boyd went over to the sideline and listened to Coach. Nobody said much, just caught their breath and rolled their eyes back and forth, wondering. The linemen were spent, having battled the Nebraska defense that outweighed them by an average of thirty pounds per man. Some of them nodded to each other, muttering, "Come on. Come on, now. We can do this. Come on."

Patrick stood with his hands tucked into the top of the flaps protruding from his hip pads. He rested his arms and sucked in the thin Boulder air. He loved this stadium. Of all the places he'd played, he loved this place the most. It was beautiful, with the bright, clear sunlight filtering in over the Flatirons to the southwest. It was an intimate stadium for so large a building. He wanted more than anything to do what he could to make the people in this stadium rise to their feet, filled with all the excitement they could muster. Now was the time for it. He could feel it. They could beat the Cornhuskers. He had told Boyd to tell Coach to give him the ball down the middle, deeper this time, behind the backers. He knew he could get by their safety. *Tell him to deliver the ball, Boyd,* Patrick's inner voice repeated. His mantra. *Give me the ball.*

Boyd jogged back to his teammates and tightened up the huddle. At six foot six, he towered over them, so he had to lean well over into the huddle, his head ending up in the middle of the oval between all the players.

"Listen up," he said. "Joyce, run it short across their faces. I'll drop it in right between the outside linebacker and Spruskins in the middle. Hold on to it, and keep it short across this play. We're setting them, and we'll go for it all when we come back. Got it? Set right, eighteen sprint right slot in, on two. Go."

They broke the huddle, and Patrick jogged to his spot inside the wide receiver's position and three yards out from the tight end. Boyd called the snap, and he took two stabbing, choppy steps angling out toward the sideline, then shot across the middle four yards deep in front of the linebacker. The ball was right where Boyd said it would be, and Patrick snared it with both hands, covering the ball, expecting a blast from the Husker middle backer. Nothing. He turned instinctively up field and accelerated past the twenty. He made it to the fifteen when both the safety and a corner drilled him. He lowered his shoulder, knocking them both back toward their own goal line as he lunged to the eleven.

The crowd erupted. Patrick could hardly hear his own breathing as he sucked in the cool afternoon air. How'd the backer miss him? He didn't care. He snickered inside his helmet as he regrouped in the huddle, his hands on his knees, his ribs heaving as he caught his breath.

"Well, that changes Coach's best plans," Boyd quipped as he waited for a runner to come in with a new play. He set his hand on Patrick's back, patting him several times. "He was going to send you deep to the post after you sucked them up into the middle again. Guess we didn't expect a nineteen-yard gain out of that."

The runner came in, consulted with Boyd behind the huddle, and stood in at left guard.

"Patrick, you up for another?" Boyd said. "Sweeney, run a big loop out back along the far end line. Hug the line. Charlie, release left to the flat. Ozzie, run the out to the left flag. Patrick, you're going to sell them on your route across the middle, but cut it up to the goalpost just as soon as you clear the outside linebacker. God, you mules, hold 'em this time. We need an extra second to let this set up. Set right, nineteen sprint left, Z-whirl-flash, on set. Break."

Patrick once again jogged to his slot on the right. He feigned fatigue, jogging as if disinterested, as if he'd had his play, and he was done. He was tired. He was off duty.

The linebacker bit on his bluff, stepped back and in toward the middle.

Boyd took the snap and Patrick continued with his charade, taking just one slow, deliberate step downfield, then turning it on with a slashing dash across the center. He caught the linebacker flatfooted, and turned up field toward the goal line at a full sprint. He crossed the five before he looked for the ball, and what he saw sent a flash of panic surging through him. Boyd was being smothered. A lineman already had one of his legs pinned, and another massive body was hurling at him, about to clock him. The blitz was about to swarm him when he let the ball sail, aiming by instinct to the point where he thought Patrick would clear the middle linebacker.

The ball wobbled in a high, slow arc, beyond Patrick's route toward the end zone. He shifted his route, accelerating with all his might, his body angled almost parallel to the playing surface as he raced to the ball. He heard the pounding of his feet hitting the turf. The roar of the crowd sounded muffled, distant, drowned out by a warp in time, which slowed, stalled, stretched out between every beat of his pulse. He dove, reaching fully extended and watched as the ball dropped onto his fingertips. He could see and feel every nubby bump on the pigskin, and his fingers caught up on the rough white laces. He reeled in the catch, bringing it to his chest, protecting the ball. He saw it all unfolding.

His body was suspended, his hands gripping the ball, directly above the goal line.

He heard the thump.

And then all was white.

Chapter Forty

Marines

"JESUS! DID YOU SEE THAT HIT!"

How could I have missed it? I thought, stunned at the blow my brother had just taken. A knot of panic welled up in my belly, however, when Patrick didn't get up from the pile on the goal line.

"Goddamn, I hope they show that on replay." The officers had gotten louder throughout the game, gripped by the intensity of the play and juiced up by round after round of beers and cocktails.

I stood, numbed, holding a tray of freshly filled steins, oblivious of the calls from some of the officers. After a moment, during which CBS replayed the pass several times, Captain Hollings was at my side. He carefully took the tray from my hands, passing it to a table of rowdy leuies.

"You okay?" he asked quietly. Captain Hollings had arranged that I do KP and wait on tables in the officers' club so that I could take in snippets of Patrick's football game. I'd been real grateful that he'd figured out a way for me to watch the game, although with the orders for beers, burgers, and fries, I'd only seen smidgeons of it. I did see Patrick's earlier touchdown. And I'd just picked up the tray of beers for the demanding assholes—who, wouldn't you know, were Nebraska fans—and who'd kept me busier, it seemed, once they learned Patrick was my brother.

I felt the captain's hand gently grip my shoulder. He kind of shook me, just the littlest bit. I looked over to him. He nodded.

"Okay?"

I returned the nod, and looked back at the screen. Patrick was still not getting up. The announcers rehashed the action on yet another replay. Patrick made a tremendous move on the linebacker, then cut clean up the middle. The safeties had cleared, covering CU's swift wide receiver deep in the end zone. But the red jerseys of the huge Nebraska linemen swarmed in over Colorado's line, hurrying the quarterback, who bought every second he could before launching a pass as the defense toppled him backward like a flagpole. The football floated idly like a butterfly, wide of Patrick's route. Patrick darted left, then dove fully extended, making a fingertip catch just a split second before getting blasted by the Nebraska safety. Both Nebraska linebackers piled on instantly before either the safety or Patrick had hit the ground. The camera caught the angle from the sidelines that clearly showed Patrick's head snapping back, his neck bent at a right angle to the plane of his body as the safety rammed his shoulder into Patrick's helmet. The linebackers, however, came from behind, and their momentum added to Patrick's, and the heap of players landed a body's length inside the goal line. Patrick lay motionless, still gripping the ball. A ref stood by, arms raised, awarding the touchdown. Another rushed quickly to the pile, having witnessed the blast Patrick had endured. The replay ended abruptly as the linebackers and safety untangled themselves, and Patrick lay still, motionless, facedown in the grass of the end zone.

"Jesus," I whispered.

By then, even the officers who were Nebraska backers had quieted, realizing the impact the television had on me, not knowing what was happening to my brother. The television had gone to commercials, but when the cameras returned to the field, Patrick was still down.

The raucous celebration in the officers' club grew as quiet as a wake. We sat and listened to the meaningless prattle of the announcers, who were at a loss for things to say. They attempted to summarize the game, commenting on the intensity of the play leading up to this last hit. There was just over two minutes left in the game, but play was delayed almost fifteen minutes, until they'd removed Patrick from the field on a stretcher. I never saw him move the entire time.

Captain Hollings pulled me over to a table and sat me on a chair. He motioned to the PFC behind the bar, and said something I didn't register. The bartender brought over a couple of glasses and a bottle of Canadian Club. The captain poured a decent splash in one glass, and three times that amount in the second. He pushed the smaller portion in front of me.

"Drink it," he said. I took his words as an order. The whisky was strong and burned my mouth and throat all the way to my stomach.

"Bring us some water," the captain called to the PFC, who kind of glared at me when he brought a pitcher of iced water and two more glasses. The captain sipped from his glass, and after a few moments, poured another small dose in my glass.

"If you want it," he said.

I left the glass sit. The fire in my belly still smoldered, but I did notice that the knot that gripped my stomach had subsided.

After the cameramen followed the ambulance out of the stadium and play resumed, I took the second drink of whisky in my life all in a gulp.

Captain Hollings studied me, then the TV, then me again.

"We're going to find out what's happened to your brother. Let's go."

He shoved back from the table and set out from the officers' club in long, swift strides. I pretty much had to run to keep up with him all the way to his office back at the company. He didn't break stride until he'd slid into his chair, and the receiver of his phone was already planted in his ear as he scanned pages of a worn Marine Corps directory of some sort. He pointed at the straight-backed chair in front of his desk. I sat down. It looked like we might take a while to figure out how to get in touch with somebody, anybody, who could tell us anything about Patrick. After rummaging through the wrinkled pages, he planted a finger underneath a line of print and cranked the dial with the index finger of his other hand.

"I'm calling Denver," he explained. "Gotta find out who did the color guard at the beginning of the game."

Hmmm, I thought. My worries centered more on what I didn't know about my brother than about the color guard. The gentle buzz from the whiskey kindly smoothed the edges of my worries, and I let myself drift in my own thoughts as the Captain posed rapid-fire questions to whoever he got to answer the phone in Denver. I kind of wondered whether Mom even knew what was going on in Colorado. Or Paddy. The Captain made about a half-dozen calls over the next half hour before he looked up from his quest to update me.

"Those were Marine ROTC on that color guard," he said after one call, as he dialed a number he'd just scribbled in the margin of the directory. He got an answer at the ROTC armory on campus, where the color guard had returned following the game.

"Who is your commanding officer or non-com?" he requested. Again, he jotted information down. "Is the captain available?"

No, but there was another number to call. Then another, and another. Captain Hollings called a half-dozen numbers in Boulder before finally getting the home number of the officer in charge of ROTC at the University of Colorado. He tried that number, and I could hear a strong, loud voice drift from the receiver that Captain Hollings held loosely to his ear. The Captain inquired whether the person answering the phone was Captain Ernest Willis.

He was, and he got an earful from Captain Hollings once he identified himself. After briefing the Marine on the other end of the phone as to who he was, who I was, and my relation to Patrick, the Captain wanted to know first off whether the ROTC officer could report the condition of the CU player who went down late in the game.

"I have his brother here, Captain, and I'd appreciate any information you can get me regarding Patrick Joyce's condition." He listened, a ray of optimism highlighting his expression.

"I'd be much obliged, Captain. You can reach me here. I'll await your call." He read off the number, and bid the Marine on the other end of the line a gracious farewell. Captain Hollings rocked back in his chair, smiling in relief.

"Well, we got something here. A little recon, if I say so myself. Damn, that is what I love about the Marines. We're all just one big family, looking out for one another come hell or high water." He stretched back in the wooden desk chair until it clanked against the file cabinet behind him. "Captain Willis is going to drive on up to the Boulder hospital and find out everything he can about your brother. Now, isn't that something?"

We jabbered about nothing in particular for a while, just passing the time. We talked about the football game, and I thanked the Captain again for arranging my duty in the officers' club.

"So, Private Joyce," he said. I got myself ready to field his question. Anything to pass the time and get my mind off of Patrick. But it was my brother that the captain asked about.

"Is this your younger brother playing for Colorado?" he asked.

I couldn't help a grin from spreading across my face. I knew where this could go, and I wondered how much he'd believe.

"Well, Sir, no. Patrick is older," I replied, wondering if he'd let it rest.

He looked thoughtful. A slight frown furled his eyebrows. I could see him calculating.

"You've a degree, Joyce, don't you?"

"Yes, Sir. Wisconsin. Graduated last May."

"That's what I thought. I remember your record. You're the only college grad in the platoon. The whole damn company, for that matter." He studied the thought a moment longer.

"Your brother didn't go right to college, then? They said he was a sophomore on TV. Is he a veteran, or something?

"Nope. No, Sir," I corrected myself hastily. The whisky, coupled with the spent adrenalin and the wait for information, kind of dulled me and distracted me. I tried to remember that this was still the Corps. "It's kind of hard to believe, Sir, but Patrick is only about a couple minutes older than I. At the most."

I kind of winced, wondering if the captain would think I was bullshitting him. His eyes narrowed as he considered my statement, then widened in amazement.

"Are you telling me you are a twin?" he demanded.

"Sir, yes, Sir!" I straightened my back in the chair, and darn near shouted the answer, just like during drills. "The private is my brother's twin, Sir."

Captain Hollings laughed outright.

"Relax, Joyce. We're both off duty, for the moment." He grinned, then shook his head. "But how could that be? You, twins? I mean, didn't they say he was over six feet, and two hundred pounds?"

"Yes, Sir," I said, slumping back down in the chair a bit, but trying to keep a little edge on. "Six two, two sixteen to be exact, Sir. My brother is a monster, Sir."

He looked at me incredulously, and his expression invited any explanation I could muster. So, I gave it to him. From the beginning. We had the time, I reckoned, until the Marine in Boulder called back. I figured I may as well entertain the captain a bit, for all he was doing for me today. I told him about being the runt since the day I was born, and how Patrick was almost always twice as big as me, our whole lives long. I explained how I'd skipped a few grades, and then finished up college as quick as I could, and that Patrick had been held back, and, well, that put him still in college and me out.

"Hmmm," the Captain mused as he considered our story. He tilted his head, peering at me from a measured eye. "So, you more like your mother, or your father, Joyce?"

I smiled. "I guess I look a lot more like my mother, Sir. Dark-haired. Small-boned. Skinny, I guess. But they tell me I'm a lot more like my father in a lot of ways, like the way I think and the way I go about things."

"What do you mean?" he asked. "Who tells you? Don't you know your father?"

"No, sir, I don't. My father died before I was born. My uncles tell me that, and my aunt. Mom, too, for that matter. Dad died the week before I was born. He drowned trying to save my cousin. That would be Roger Joyce. He's in the Corps, too. I guess most all the Joyce men go into the Corps, if they go into the service at all. Dad was a Marine. South Pacific. Guadalcanal. Iwo Jima. He made it all the way through that, and then died less than a year later, at a picnic."

"Ain't it the way. A Marine, was he?" the Captain said, studying me. "That's what I mean. One big family. How come you didn't go for officers' school, Joyce, with your degree and all?"

The phone rang, and we both snapped to attention.

"Hollings here," the captain said. He listened, his eyes tensing to a narrow slit. "You mean to say, you have some fucking resident there who won't say anything at all about his condition? Jesus H. Christ! Well, give me the slime ball, if you think it would do any good. Okay. Thanks, Captain Willis."

He paused a moment, taking on a steely look that I'd seen several times during training, especially when he was giving orders on how he expected things to be done right.

"Yes, Dr. who? Dr. Dirschkie, good. Well, Dr. Dirschkie, this is Captain Armand Hollings, United States Marine Corps, and I have with me Private David Joyce, the brother of a patient you are treating," the Captain said on rapid fire. He didn't let up, but for a second when the doctor tried to butt in and explain his position.

"Well, I perfectly well understand that you can't release information to just anyone but family, and I'm not asking you to release any information to me or anyone else, but I'm going to put Private Joyce on the phone here in just a moment and you are going to give him a complete update on the condition of his brother—his twin brother, the closest person to him in the whole world. Do you understand me? Private Joyce has a right to know about the condition of his brother. What's that? No, I said 'brother.' I know Private Joyce is not his brother's mother. It doesn't take a damn professor to figure that out. Since these boys are twins, you'd kind of figure that they both would have the same mother, am I not correct? And Private Joyce here would... What do you mean, you can't give out information to just any family member? You just told me a moment ago that it had to be a family member, and now you are denying Private Joyce the right to find out the condition of his brother, who he saw get hurt in that football game on television, saw it ten times at least, with the instant replay, and now you just want to let him sit here and wonder how bad off his brother, his twin brother is, just because you have it up your ass to hold back information from a family member? I don't give a rat's ass if Private Joyce is not his brother's mother. He's a goddamn Marine, for Christ sake, and a good one. He's in training to go overseas and fight to protect your goddamn candy ass, and you're playing God with the information on how his brother is doing..."

The captain was in full stride, and the doctor didn't even know what he was about to hear. I sat back, kind of amused, but definitely annoyed at the prick, and worried about Patrick. All I wanted to hear was that he was going to be all right.

"What's that? Okay, yes, put him back on, you miserable son of a bitch," Captain Hollings spit the words at the doctor. He didn't look at me, and I figured we'd about run out of luck.

"Willis, that you? Good. Captain, I would ask you, as an officer and a fellow Marine, to please put your boot as far up the good doctor's ass as you can possibly bury it."

I could hear Captain Willis laugh on the other end of the line, and his response broke the tension that Captain Hollings wore in his frown. He listened closely for a moment, then broke into a wide smile.

"Willis, I owe you. Wonderful. Okay. You keep the doc busy then, and we'll be right here."

He set the receiver back in its cradle with a touch that exuded triumph. He looked over at me, smiling, and gave me a nod.

"Son, this is exactly why I love the Corps. Seems that a nurse at that hospital is ex-Navy. Well, let me tell you something, Joyce. I hope you never have to share in this perspective, but if you do, you'll know what I mean. There is nothing as heavenly as looking up into the face of a professional Navy nurse in a moment of need. Dressed all in white, kind and considerate, going about her business, she'll look like an angel of mercy. And we have just such an angel working for us now. Seems that she overheard Willis and me giving the good doctor a measure of common sense, and when she had a moment, she got Willis aside to find out the details. She's going to give us a call in just a minute or two. You're in for a good surprise, I think."

He sat back, gloating, muttering, "Damn, I love this Corps."

The phone rang an instant later, and the Captain lunged for the receiver.

"Hollings here. Yes, Commander Franklin. I do appreciate that more than I can ever tell you, Ma'am. Certainly. Yes. Yes. I will tell him so. Yes. And Ma'am, you can let Patrick know that his brother will be finished training here next week, and will be on a plane to Denver to visit him as soon as we can get him to the airport. Yes, Ma'am. That is certainly good news, Ma'am. And thank you again, Ma'am. You are indeed an angel. I will, Ma'am. Bless you too."

He leaned over the desk and handed the phone to me.

"It's for you," he smiled. "You'll want to keep it short. I'll update you later."

I wondered what the nurse would be able to tell me.

"Hello," I said. My voice sounded small and distant. I was uncertain, talking to another military authority figure who I couldn't see, and to whom the Captain spoke with such deference.

I was startled to hear Patrick's voice in response.

"Hey, Twinnie," he said, simply. His voice was quiet, strained, and a bit slurred, for having muttered only two words.

"Patrick!" I cried, tears filling my eyes. Man, I was so relieved to hear his voice. It broke the tension that had been building up in me since I saw him go down. "You're all right?" I intended my question to be rhetorical, but as Patrick struggled to respond, I sensed his agony.

"Yeah," he murmured. "Davey, I couldn't move, man. I was so scared. I couldn't move...."

He let it go.

"Are you all right now?" I asked again.

"Okay. I'm pretty snowed. I can feel again. I couldn't feel my arms. Or my legs. I mean, it was like there was nothing there. Just my face, kind of. I mean, except for being scared, I couldn't feel a thing. No pain. The worst part of it all was the grass that was sticking up through my bird cage. Man, it was poking me right in my eye, and right up my nose. And I couldn't move it. I couldn't move my head, even, to get it out of my face. Oh, Davey. Man."

He trailed off again. I could hear the nurse's voice, telling him to finish up.

"Davey," he asked.

"Yeah, Pat."

"Call Mom, okay. Let Mom know. I'm okay. Okay?"

"You betcha, Pat. I'll call her. And I'll be seeing you, soon, okay?"

"Yeah. Can't wait."

"See you."

"Yeah."

I listened to the stillness on the end of the line. And then a woman's voice.

"Hello?"

"Hello, Ma'am. This is David Joyce."

"David, this is Nurse Franklin. Your brother will be just fine. Can you call him again in a day or so? He'll probably be feeling much better, and he won't be so groggy." She gave me the number, and instructed me to pass it on to my mother

"I'll do that, Ma'am. Thank you. Please take care of Patrick."

"I will. And you take care of yourself, son. Good-bye, now."

I heard the line click, and set the receiver back on the cradle of the dusty black phone.

I sat for a moment, savoring the relief, before I looked back over at the Captain. I wondered, what now? Back to duty in the officers' club, I suppose?

The Captain had other thoughts, though. He waited until I met his eye, and then some. Then, he started in.

"Joyce, you were about to tell me about why you haven't considered Officers' Candidate School yet. I've got you here for another six days before you ship out. I think I'm going to need to hear a real good reason you haven't put in for OCS. Other than that you're a draftee, for which there is a remedy," the Captain said, leaning back in his chair and linking his fingers in a web behind his head. His eyes looked right through me as he waited on an answer.

I knew I was back on duty.

Chapter Forty-One

Boulder and Beyond

GETTING FROM STAPLETON AIRPORT to Boulder took longer than the entire plane ride from L.A. Isn't that the way? Seems like the closer I get to my destination, the tougher each step becomes. It's like climbing a mountain. And with the view of the looming mountains out the bus windows, I felt like I had a bigger climb still ahead of me.

Patrick said to get off the bus at the Hill, before it went down into the town. The driver remembered to tell me when we were there, and bid me farewell and good luck as I grappled my duffle bag down the steps of the coach. I think he was partial to my uniform. Not many of the people on the street looked at me with the same approval.

Patrick had left the hospital after just three nights. When I called the hospital before leaving Pendleton, they told me he'd been discharged, to call him at home. He'd been there since Tuesday, two days ago. I'd gotten my leave as of this morning, and HQ had helped me set up flights first to Denver, and then on to Madison on Sunday. I was real anxious to see my brother, if just for a couple days. I needed to reconnect with his world.

Patrick had instructed me to get off the bus and walk straight toward the mountains. He called them the Flatirons, and I could see why. Four rugged peaks, flat and triangular, jutted up in a row like the jagged cutting teeth of a hound. Leaning against the mountains behind them, they looked like they were just a ten-minute walk away. I was supposed to walk toward them 'til I hit Ninth Street, then go south for three blocks. His house was the third on the right from the corner of Ninth and Spruce.

I stood at the bus stop for a moment, feeling the pulse of the university community. Students streamed out of the three-story glass building across the street—the bookstore that Patrick had given me as the first landmark to look for. Kids, students, milled about, all lugging backpacks, co-eds looking tan and fresh, jocks, nerds, all the types I'd known in my days at Madison. Standing there in my uniform, lugging a duffle that was just about as heavy as me and certainly bigger around, I felt peculiarly out of place. The students flowing down the sidewalk cut a wide swath around me, like I was an Untouchable, banished to an island. Their curious, disdainful glances, like I wasn't their peer in age or interests, well, they made me feel horrible. And to hear one angry-looking girl no older than I mutter "baby killer" as she hustled by, the glint of hatred in her glance... I just felt beyond awkward. Desolate. I hefted my duffle strap over my shoulder and headed west past the bookstore. I could feel the anonymous eyes that followed me as I made my way toward Patrick's in this strange new world called Boulder.

∞

On Tuesday, after breakfast, I helped Paddy with a few barn chores. But as I'd figured, the barn was immaculate. The girls were looking real decent. Clean. Sleek. He had them so docile, they were like pets. I don't know any finer handler than Paddy. By ten thirty, we were done. He invited me to go into town with him, but I declined. I thought maybe I'd wander up into the woods.

I didn't take a gun. Didn't feel like even trying to hunt. I just wanted to sit out there and let nature walk by. It always does, sometimes dramatically, sometimes less so. That day was a quiet one. I set up alongside the downed tree where Colonel Steve and I had bagged that old buck a couple years ago. Hell, it was more like four years ago already. Man. How can I be so young and have so much time slip right through my fingertips?

I guess I'd seen a lot, though, when I thought about it. School. Jannie. Now boot camp, and language school next. In Monterey, California. I thought about Gabriel's one big day—sometimes now it felt like someone had swatted the Earth like it was nothing more than a classroom globe, and sent time spinning so fast it blurred beneath me. I just wanted to get my bearings. And my balance.

I was still mind-fucked from my visit to Patrick's. Man, between all the dope he and Cindy had to burn, and just the way he's living out there, I was reeling. Cindy was enough to make me spin, all by herself. I still can't believe she blew me. I mean, she's Patrick's girl and all, I guess. I sure didn't see that coming. Patrick zz-ing peacefully after taking his painkillers and smoking a joint, and she comes out and shows me how to do a "turbo." Something Patrick showed her, she said. Next thing I know, she's got her lips all over me, and her hand jacking me, and when she brings me to blowing, she sends my wad straight up over my head, hitting me right in the forehead. Man, I couldn't believe it. She smiled happily and cheered, "Wow, field goal! Three points," and rolled another one and started smoking it as fast as she could get it lit. Man, I don't think we were straight for more than an hour the whole time I was there. I mean, Patrick and I didn't even really talk a whole lot, him being so heavily medicated, and me being, well, drugged up too. I never would've thought. What a lifestyle! Missed opportunity. I do think he's got a good plan, trying to get into a study abroad program. Cindy's idea, really, but he's going for it. She's going to France next fall. She's cerebral, Patrick says. Doesn't even know what football is, except for her goofy notions about field goals.

Patrick seems pretty resigned to not playing ball again. I was surprised. The doc told him to forget it, and that's all it really took. He'll miss it, oh yeah.

He will. But he's still living with the fear of that moment in the grass. Man, what a scare.

I told him not to worry about paying for school if they yank his football scholarship, which he's certain they will. Ungrateful bastards. He just says, that's the way it is. Well, he doesn't need to worry. I set up a checking account for him at the Baraboo bank. He'll be able to draw from that, and I can be sure it always has enough in it. Paddy will help out there, too, keeping the balance in the black. Paddy and Mr. McDermott, my new estate lawyer. He helped me set up trusts and even draw up a will so that all the earnings from the bulls and the farm go where they should, if they need to. We set it all up yesterday. Patrick has no reason to sweat, even if he does go to Europe for the school year. Nobody should be in a bind. Not Mom. Not Patrick. Not Miss Rose. Not even Father Jack. Weird. Who'd have ever thought? I feel like a kid playing banker or lawyer or something. I'm too young to need to do this kind of thing. But I got it done, anyway. Now I guess I can just go back to the Corps. The Corps. They own me. Do my schooling. Learn some more language. Then on to Nam. What the hell.

∞

I strolled down the hillside, back toward the pasture and the house. The sun was drawing deep, long fencepost shadows across the stubble in the cornfield. Half an hour, and the sun would be set. It got dark so early this time of year, I reflected as I crossed the last fence line separating the sprawling fields from the feral hillsides leading down to the marsh. I stopped and turned, looking back at my path. Autumn's golden rays lit the hillside, catching the rust and amber and tawny shades that quilted the slope. I stood for a long moment, absorbing it, making it a part of me. Then I headed home.

Chapter Forty-Two
Context

CONTEXT is such a mind-fucker.

I find great solace in pulling out the worn and rumpled letters from everyone back home. I'm so delighted each time I get a letter from Mrs. Whitman. I think she's written every week since I've been here. And then her care package, complete with brownies and my old violin! Her letters are a lot like Mom's. A bit of Baraboo news. Tidbits about the family. A paragraph or two skimming the surface of her current philosophical focal point. She is such a heart, Mrs. Whitman is. I'm so glad we've been able to sustain this long, intercontinental conversation about all we learned from Jannie. I wonder if either of us will ever get over her. I suppose not. I can't say I ever want to forget Jannie. To get beyond her. But at times, the idea of her not being is overwhelming. Is she really not being? She's still in my mind. In my heart. But does that make her being? Being alive, no. But being? Where the fuck is Father Jack when I need an answer to the absurd?

Sometimes missing her is too much. That's when I feel most vulnerable. Those are the most hopeless, lonely times, and I fear them. They threaten to take me completely, to let me make a mistake. My greatest fear is walking into a mistake. Leaving myself vulnerable. I can never read Mrs. Whitman's letters in the bush. Not like Patrick's. I'll read and re-read Mrs. Whitman's letters when I'm back in my billet. That's okay, then. I can focus on them, savor them, in the long moments of downtime. I can inhale the last freshness of her scent off the stale paper. Then I can handle it. The memories. Not out here. Not when so much is at stake.

I can always read Patrick's letters, though. I don't know why. Maybe because it's like hearing from my other half. The half that's still back in the real world. The half that can laugh and play and think that getting laid is about the greatest challenge to accomplish in any given day. Christ, I don't know where Patrick gets his libido. Maybe I sacrificed mine, or squelched it, or repressed it. I just didn't have such a sexually free college career as he did in Boulder. I guess having met Cindy, I can understand why he finds it so easy to get laid. But then he was a jock, too. That's a different world altogether. No wonder I can read his letters over and over out here. It's like reading a wetdream fantasy. Not like here. Not like living a fantasy that is a nightmare. How the fuck did I ever find myself in the Nam?

I try to write Patrick to explain to him what it's all about. The trudging up and down the mountains here in the highlands. The heat. The rain. The stink. The fucking insects. Leeches. Goddamn leeches. Hiding out. Watching, always watching. I'm kind of glad Colonel Steve roped me into recon. We spend most of our time out humpin' hills, hiding out, watching out, not being seen. Invisible. In-fucking-visible. And man, we are really good at that. All six of us. We can go out for a walk in the jungle and disappear right into the hillsides. Trekking along on our little keyhole expeditions. A scattered, invisible, cohesive unit. I think sometimes that if one man has to fart, we all feel it, and if it's a threat, if there are gooks around, we all pucker our bungholes to help the one guy keep it in. We don't want anyone catching wind of us. Not if it means lobbing grenades and projectiles our way. I hate the unexpected stingray lash, when we have to duck and scramble and disappear. Or fight through it. I try to tell Pat that, and I wonder if he gets it at all. I suppose it's so unreal to him, like a TV show. He always writes back that he's so interested in what I'm doing. He should only know... It's like a perverted game of musical chairs. And someone always loses. In the four months I've been here, my six-man unit has gotten a whole rotation of newbies to replace another six who bit it. Well, really four of us have been here the entire time. But we keep losing the other two spots, time and again. Six of them, come and go. Of those six, four were from booby traps, run of the mill. The fifth was nabbed clean by the gooks, doing to us what we do unto them. That was Clement. From Missouri. A good man. Quiet as a whisper. Calm. Never made mistakes. Just once, I suppose. That's all it took. Once, and they got him. He was there, and then he wasn't. We found him, later. Strung up with bicycle chains. Eviscerated. His cock and balls looking out at us from his gaping mouth. They think they're so fucking funny.

The sixth guy, he got bit by a snake. Two weeks in country. A snake. Killed him deader than dead. I can't even remember his name. He was from Minnesota, though. That's what we all called him. Minnesota. Minnesota Dead.

The guys call me Squirrel, mostly. 'Cause of my size. I'm by far the smallest guy in my recon unit. So, of course, I get all the tunnel duty. I can't say I mind it. Scares the living bejesus out of me, I admit. But what a rush! Slipping through those tunnels like a snake in a rabbit warren, never knowing if I'm going to come face to face with a gook, knowing full well that that's exactly why I'm down in there in the first place. Sometimes, I wonder, what the fuck do they figure I'm gonna accomplish down there, anyway? But then I run into an office chamber and find a horde of info that we pilfer and send on down the line to intelligence, so that those motherfuckers can distort it all to hell for whatever use they're conjuring this week.

A couple times, I've run into sick bays filled with wounded VC. They look like their eyes are gonna go round, seeing me down in there. Like they're looking at the Angel of Death. I never waste them, though. Naw. Hardly ever. Why? I just saunter on up to where they're laid out on stretchers, dying, bleeding, hurting. Just kind of float over to them. And I ask them, why they are there, and where are their loved ones? I always ask them that. And they always tell me. Unless they aren't too hurt, in which case they sometimes try to fight. I don't put up with that, at all. Nope. I've had to do a couple of them, bastards. If they would only not fight. Why do we have to fight? I dunno. But if they wanna fight me, I toast 'em. Before they toast me.

Not too far back, I found a sick bay with a doc in it, tending his wounded. He looked up and saw me there, like I'd appeared out of nowhere. Like I was a ghost. He never stopped working, even after looking down the big dark hole of my .45 barrel. The doc took one look, then kept on tending this poor sonofabitch bleeder. Couldn't stop him from leaking out. I went over and inspected his handiwork, tucked away my piece, and then asked him, "Need a hand?"

He didn't even blink, just told me what to do. Didn't seem curious that I could speak to him and understand him. We chatted while I plugged up the guy's chest wound, trying to keep the blood from flooding out, while the doc made some real crude sutures, but damn if he didn't stanch the bleeding. The doc gave me a little grin. I wished him well and beat it. The odd thing was, he'd had a game of chess going on his little work desk. I glanced at the board and saw a quick and easy move, sending the black rook down the end row to put the white king into checkmate. I made the move and looked up at the doc. He snapped impatiently, "It was white's move. Not fair. Take it back." I just laughed and got the hell out of there.

So now, here I sit. Hunkered down, middle of the day, not moving at all for fear of twitching a leaf against the current of the breeze, taking a break while Brinkman, Huey, Mandoloza, and Sarge watch out over the trail. *The* trail. The fucking Ho Chi Minh trail. It's supposed to be a fucking highway. Looks like a little burned-out stepping path in the woods, from this vantage point. Comes east into the country from Cambodia, just a few miles from here. Supposed to be even bigger across the border. Not so big here, but pretty well used, for sure. Yesterday, we watched a whole fucking regiment of NVA regulars go by. Not more than thirty yards from our noses. Kelly kept count, he said. Four hundred fifty-five gooks. Sarge called in the info once they passed on by, and we heard the A1s torch them with napalm no more than three-quarters of a mile south. That always gives me the willies, when we break silence to call something in. I mean, I can't believe it out here, sometimes, with my buds. We can be out in the sticks for two or three days without uttering more than a whisper. We talk with our hands, our eyes, and our bodies more than anything. Except when we have to turn the fucking radio on, and we gotta talk loud enough that the motherfuckers back in Khe Sahn or Dang Ho can hear us. Then, after being so goddamn quiet for so long, it sounds like we're fucking yelling. I can't wait for Sarge to shut the fuck back up, and listen again to the wonderful silence that hangs so expectantly before the rounds hit. We can count on maybe a full minute. We all sit there, kind of wide-eyed, sharing glances back and forth, like, wow, man, these gooks don't know what the airmail is bringing in for them. It's just so wonderfully quiet, like the woods in summer. Bugs. Birds. Maybe the trickling of water, or the rush of rapids if we're near some. But then it happens. All hell breaks loose, and the gooks must wonder just how in the fuck we found them. How could we know where to lob a couple tons of incendiaries to land right on their noggins? Yesterday when it hit, I could hear the land burning. The land and the troops. I was glad the breeze was headed downwind, away from us. I hate the stink of charbroiled.

Context. Everything has such an amazing fucking context.

I write this to Patrick, and he must think it's nuts. Unreal. Can't be.

And so, for the twelfth dozenth time, I unfold Patrick's pages and live his life for a moment, and it is like a breath of fresh air. Real air. The kind that keeps me alive. The fucker is in Germany! Un-fucking-real!

∞

September 1, 1967

Hey, Twinnie,

Well, Germany is a blast, man!

I've got this room on an "étage," my German friends call it. I think that means floor, but maybe in French, or something. I think they think it's cool to use the French. You probably know if that's what it means. Most of my Kraut friends already speak English pretty well, so they're more interested helping me with my German than practicing English, which is okay with me. Man, that was the pits, getting here after, what, two years of high school German, and another two years of college German, and shit, I couldn't understand a word anybody said. It just sounded, well, not like the German I thought was German! Regensburg is in Bavaria, which is kind of the southeast quarter of Germany. Everybody says they have their own dialect. Kind of like how the people in Mississippi or Louisiana talk English, but nobody can understand them but themselves. They speak Hoch Deutsch at the Universität, but still, man, after a few minutes, I feel like I'm in the third quarter of the Nebraska game and their linebackers have been pounding on my fucking head. Everything is tunnel vision. I wonder if it will ever get better. Thank God the Krauts speak such good English. Oxford English, they remind me. They sound like they have goddamn British accents. They speak better English than I do, really. And you know the real killer? I have some Brit and Scot friends studying here, and they won't let me speak English. They say I'm desecrating the Queen's English. They take away my "speaking privileges!" Can you imagine? They only let me speak German. They really do want me to shut up.

You're not gonna believe what I did this afternoon. Here you are, in Vietnam, a fucking Marine. My brother. My twin for Christsake. And I went with my Kraut friends and marched in protest of the war! Ha! Unreal, eh, man? I haven't told any of my friends that I've got a twin brother fighting in the war that we're protesting. Couldn't do it. Nope. I think they are all kind of stoked up that I join in with them. Their token Amerikaner protester.

Only one of my friends really is in on you being in Vietnam. A friend from the Étage. I don't know why, but she's always interested. I let her read your letters. She saw me reading one—the one you wrote about what it's like to get lifted out by the choppers—when I was at the café down the street one morning. I guess I was so intent on you getting "sucked out of the jungle" that I didn't even notice when she stepped up to my table and said hi. I told her what I was reading and why I was so absorbed in it, and she asked if she could see. I let her read that letter, and every one since. Seems like she's there waiting for them, just like I am, when I check the mailbox. I actually let her read the ones I'd saved from earlier. She never says a thing about what you write, and hasn't told anyone else about you being there. But she takes them and reads them. Does that matter much to you? I hope not. Don't go censoring what you say now, anyway. I want to hear it all. Unreal, man! Do ya really spring a boner when the chopper sucks you up out of the jungle?

The rest of my Kraut friends, they haven't a clue. I'm sure that I'll tell them soon enough. But right now, it's kind of a blast. A game. A joke. Weird, man. The Krauts, they take politics real serious. I mean, we meet together at the Uni before classes in the morning, at maybe 8:30 or 9:00, and we have a beer and a hard-boiled egg and they talk about Johnson bombing North Vietnam and whether the Russians should be in cahoots with the NVA and all sorts of stuff. They live and breathe it. Then we go to classes—after having downed a pint of helles bier, kind of a light, spritzy beer, and chasing it with coffee that would knock your socks off—until we get done, maybe mid-afternoon. Then we meet for another beer—usually a pilsner, another fairly light brew—and get into more discussions about Europe, or the U.S., or the war, whatever. The Marshall Plan. Economics, you name it. Man, these people take things seriously. They all have these serious pipes, kind of like Sherlock Holmes, and they stoke them up and we sit in thick blue clouds of smoke and soak up the beers and philosophize and solve all the problems in the world, or at least figure out how to.

By evening, we head to Kneidinger's, the local brewery. Man, this is beer *that they make. A lot of the Krauts, the ones with hair on their chests, they'll drink the boch, or dopple boch. I like their lager. And we talk and gab and do more of the same. It's not unusual that we go to someone's apartment and light up some hash. Man, that'll knock your socks off! I kind of miss good old American weed. I mean, I'd like to roll up a nice doobie now and again. But whew! Hash is something else! Wish you were here. We'd blow your lid off—and not the way Cindy did! Ha. She told me about launching your fucking field goal. Nuts, isn't she? She was here last weekend.*

Well, I am always wondering about what you're up to, all the time I'm romping around Germany. You ought to come here sometime. It's a blast. We could protest together! Ha. Imagine that.

Take care of yourself. Nab a gook for me, would you?

Brudder

∞

21:50, September 16, 1967, six clicks north of Lang Vei

Jesus, we are in deep shit.

This little walk in the woods has been nothing but dust and flutter. We've been pushed since the moment we dropped in. Like they were waiting for us. It didn't help that we came in on top of their tunnels, just as they were getting in, or maybe out. Jesus. They have chased us.

Brinkman took it first. Then Sarge. Man. The radio, and the voice. Who the fuck is going to get us out of here? Kelly is healthy, still, and leading. Wouldn't you know. The worst fucking leader amongst us, and he's the one who stays whole. Huey is hurt. He took one in the belly, but it kind of went through and through, at an angle across the front. He's coping, but I can see it hurts. No shit and guts, though. Just a blaze of red meat and white insides in contrast to his ebony belly. Lucky, I guess. Brettan, the guy who filled in for Mandoloza after he went back to the real world, well, Brettan is gonna have one good arm, at the rate we're going. We aren't due to be pulled out of here until 16:00 the day after tomorrow, and we have no radio to call for an early extraction. He's got a through and through of his bicep. I can see the bone, white as china. We wrapped it up, but he's had to go through three streams on this chase, and if that wound doesn't rot, well, God bless him. The worst part is, he was lugging the second radio. The bullet that went through him lodged in the radio. We're voiceless. Totally.

Mine is just a nick. Burned like hell, but it's very shallow. Hardly more than skin. Damn. I can feel my thigh tightening up. But it really wasn't much more than getting poked with a sharp stick. Right on the inside of my left thigh. Man, two inches higher, and bingo. It's not bad, though. Hardly slowing me down. Lugging Huey is what's slowing me down.

If we can just keep our heads down and melt right into this morass, maybe, just maybe....

Chapter Forty-Three
Sunflowers

FUCK, WHAT A NIGHT.

I thought we pretty much slipped them yesterday. Or at least, it seemed like they lost interest in chasing us. We hardly saw them at all. Until last night, anyway. And that was probably a fluke. I think they just ran into us. Caught us with our pants down, kind of. Or more like, they caught us, and they pulled their pants down! Jesus. What a night.

They never did see us, thank God. Too much into twilight, I think. Maybe they were just unloading from their manholes over the tunnels. I don't know. They just all of a sudden were there, and we were hobbling along like a bunch of hikers in the woods. I don't know how they didn't see us. They couldn't have been more than a hundred yards away. Maybe they just weren't looking. We spotted them first, on the other side of this little river. Man, there was only one way for us to be, and that was submersible. We slid into the water like snakes. Hugged the bank on their side of the stream, where the grass stood tall and hung out over the water. Not a bad shelter. I thought they had us, though, when they stopped no more than five feet from us. Must've been a dozen of them. Standing around, smoking. Like a little garden party. I could hear them discussing shit. Complaining, just like we do, about their chow. Not like a home-cooked meal, one of them bitched. Just once before he died, he said, he wanted a good home-cooked meal. I almost laughed, hearing them talk like that. Made me relax, knowing their minds were far from thinking about us, looking for us. But, Jesus, when they whipped their little peckers out and started peeing right on top of the grass we were under, well, shit. Man. Just disgusting. The look on Huey's face, man. Pissed. Getting pissed on, and getting pissed. First they shoot him, then they piss on him. He was mad. Made me want to laugh, that's all. Totally fucking absurd.

It had to be well past midnight before we dared get up out of that river. Some trophy leeches, I tell ya. Big as pickles. Bastards, drinking up all our blood. Man, we poured out some blood on this little walk.

I knew we were still a click plus from our extraction point. And the whole area had been hopping for three days now. We pushed. I wondered if we'd get up here in time, but we did. Now we got nothing to do but wait and listen. Man, once we hear those blades scrambling sky, we'll start moving down into the zone. It's just maybe a hundred yards. Huey is hanging. I'm worried about Brettan. He's feverish. I think this is his first vertical extraction on a SPIE rig. Leastways in realtime. He's gonna pop his cherry on this one. He's gotta depend on Kelly to get him up-rigged. That's all there is to it.

I'm impressed with Kelly. Maybe 'cause he actually had to do some thinking, he's really stepped forward. Maybe all this time he's just been leaning on the rest of us to make the decisions. He's never been a bad recon Marine. Just kind of invisible. Kind of like how Paddy advised me to be. Kelly is good at it. But he's come through these past couple of days.

∞

15:48, September 18, 1967, Twelve clicks northwest of Lang Vei

The bird is coming in. We gotta move. Gotta put an end to this little keyhole exercise.

Jesus, Huey is heavy. He's hurting big time, now. Work with me, buddy. I got you. Work with me.

Kelly's got the smoke going. They're coming in. Jesus, what a sight to see!

Come on, Huey. Come on, man. Just another twenty yards. Kelly's already strapping Brettan in.

Jesus! All hell. Jesus. They're everywhere. Christ!

∞

No sooner had I snapped Huey in than he took one right in the fucking ear. His head just fucking blew up. Damn it!

I couldn't hear. It was too loud to hear anything. You can't hear thunder when you get struck by lightning. I yelled, and I could not hear the sound coming from my throat.

I snapped into the line and instantaneously felt the surging lift of the chopper pull me out of that fucking hellhole. The goddamn gooks were storming out from under every bush and rock. We were like a turkey-fucking-shoot. God, I hoped they didn't down the chopper. Those fucking gooks, man! They just stood out there and raised their .47s and took pot shots at us lifting off. Even with our Cobras hovering around to give us cover, cutting them into ribbons, those bastards stood there and plugged away at us, like they were invisible, or like they didn't count or something. They sure as hell weren't invisible to our Gatling gunners. They diced them, but they still stood in, shooting, shooting, shooting, 'til they got minced in a fury of dust from a zillion bullets raining on down around them. It was all so surreal.

I saw the one who plugged me in the butt. Standing there, taking good steady aim. I saw the flair from his weapon's muzzle just about the same instant as I felt the burn in my ass. Man, right through my cheek. Jesus, that ripped clear through me. No bone, thank God. But another one just a couple inches off my jewels! And then I felt a searing sting burn through my shoulder and up my neck. It felt like someone ripped a meat hook though my shoulder. The jolt bounced me back and upward in my sling. My head flopped to the side, yet I watched as the shooter was pulverized by the gunners. Bastard. He got me.

With my head flopped over like that, I could kind of see up the line. I knew Huey was wasted. Shit, I was still wearing half his head. He was hanging there, chest-to-chest with me, the whole fucking top of his skull gone. I felt his body take the impact of a couple more rounds. Better him than me, at this juncture. He just hung there, shielding me. His eyeballs hanging sideways off the front of his face. Like he was staring at me. Up above, I didn't like the way Brettan was splayed out backward, his head lolling like he, too, had taken one in the neck or head. Kelly was slumped, and his belly was all turned inside out. I could see loops of his guts hanging out, dragging in the draft from the chopper above.

Man, we'd had it.

I kind of screwed my eyes down toward the green canopy below. The sun was sinking over the hills to the west, and the clouds that were gathered in the east were puffy and billowy. The gorges were steep and wood-covered, deep in greens. Occasionally, along a river cutting through the valleys, the land flattened out, and lush green grasslands shone like emeralds on a glistening chain of crystal blue. A head or two of buffalo stood along the river banks. Funny-looking cattle, compared to my Holsteins. Rugged and boxy. Those horns arched back over their neck in perfect crescents. Low and squat and odd. But they fit right into this country. The land was old and the mountains were rugged and untamed. Venerable. It was truly a beautiful sight.

They flew us right down into Da Nang. I could tell, just seeing the size of the dust hole we'd created to camp in there, and the airstrip, all tucked in with the ocean right out there to the east. And the troops were all out along the side of the airfield, over at the amphitheater area. Looked like some civvy show going on stage. A thousand grunts sitting there, with some women dancing and a band playing on stage. I wondered if it was Bob Hope. As we neared the airstrip, the guys in the audience heard the chopper thumping wind. I could see them turn their faces up toward us, first a few, then some more, and then with a synchronicity like they were all controlled by the same electronic impulse, the entire crowd turned away from the stage and looked up at me and my buddies dangling from that rope, being dragged across the sky beneath the chopper. Looked like a field of fucking sunflowers. I wanted to wave to them, signal them, let them know I was still okay. Salute them. Let them know. One of us, at least, had made it.

PATRICK SAT STARING at the letter he'd read four times. He looked to the top of the page and started reading again.

> *September 27, 1967*
>
> *U.S. Naval Hospital*
>
> *Yokosuka, Japan*
>
> *Dear Pat,*
>
> *I keep popping up in places I'd never have imagined. I'm in Japan. Can you fathom that?*
>
> *Kind of an unplanned excursion, though. Unwanted all the way around. Although I'm lucky to be here at all. None of my buddies made the trip. I guess I can count my blessings.*
>
> *The Corps notified Mom right away. I already got a letter from her. I wonder, though, if you even know yet. Maybe you'll have heard from Mom. Anyway, I got hit. Nothing real serious. Some flesh wounds, really. To tell the truth, I got shot in the ass, man. Right in my left cheek. I'm still mostly laying on my stomach, but I've been able to sit pretty gingerly the last day or two. The worst is taking a dump. I also got hit in my left shoulder, right by the muscles running down from my neck. Another one clear through. Chipped a little notch in my collarbone, but didn't even break it. Makes it hard to lift myself up with my arms. So I'm too sore to hold my ass up off the pot when I have to shit, but when I sit, the pain is so much that I can't dump anyway. Life is such a buttfucker sometimes.*
>
> *They tell me I'm lucky. I'm gonna heal right up. Imagine that. Lucky. Heal up. Rotate back into the Nam as soon as I can function. They're telling me that will take a few weeks. I've got some R&R due, so maybe I can drag out the inevitable a week or so longer. Regardless, unless I get a stroke of divine intervention, I'll be back humping mountains by Thanksgiving. Maybe they'll send me back away from the boonies. Work with the spooks in interrogation in Da Nang. I don't know if that would be better or worse. Fucking spooks. They give me the willies. I don't know.*
>
> *Anyway, I know I'm blessed, in a way, when I look at all these guys in here who took it a lot worse than I did. And not just 'cause I've only got flesh wounds. They look at me and see that I've got all four of my limbs. And my whole face. My balls and pecker. I'm intact, pretty much. Scratched, is all. They know I'm going back in country. And a lot of them know they aren't. They're just processing back to the States, where they'll go to Bethesda, or some veterans' hospital, and they'll never see the Nam again. And they eyeball me and they get this zany look on their faces, like they got something over on me. Fucking crazy, is what it is. They don't have a clue yet just how fucked up wasted they are.*

I think that's the hardest part for me, really. The emotions. Man, it is hard to stay up. I mean, I watch my body healing. I just started working with the PT people to get my shoulder working good again. And I'm happy and all that I'm okay, pretty much. But it makes me sad that I gotta go back in again. Or I flash big-time on my ride back from the highlands, and I see my buddy Huey looking at me out of his dead eyes. Or I see the faces of a thousand fucking Marines, looking up at us as we came in. And even from a thousand feet up, I could feel the wave of exasperation and grief that those faces sent up toward us. I felt it, and it slammed me down, harder than the fucking round that hit my shoulder. Man, it is hard to pick it up after that image does a slow napalm burn on my cerebral cortex. It just kind of takes over.

And then some fucker here in the hospital will do something just incredibly kooky, and we'll all end up laughing, or crying, and bam, it's like the whole wing is a kettle boiling over. And then there is a moment of relief. And we cycle all over again.

It's hard to explain. It is harder to go through.

Do you understand? I wonder.

Anyway, I hope you're doing okay. I'm okay. Really. I am doing alright.

I'll be seeing you,

Twin

Patrick folded the letter and held it carefully. He glanced at the dateline of the newspaper he'd picked up outside the Universität. October 7. Two weeks since David had written. More than three since he'd been wounded. Patrick sighed. Man, he thought. His brother had been lying in a hospital for three whole weeks, and he'd had no idea. No clue at all. They were on two opposite sides of the world. Neither one was at home. And they had no idea what was going on with each other.

It was a foreign feeling. He'd always considered his twin to be somehow present, even if they were in different places. North Freedom or the Dunes. Madison or Boulder. Their lives had always had a symmetry of sorts. And it had been comfortable, and safe. They had always kept each other informed of what they were experiencing and learning. Throughout their lives, they'd each held one end of a long, invisible thread of knowing, and quietly marveled at its strength. It was always there, just part of being a twin. There had always been an echo of understanding and consciousness of his brother that whispered tidings in his soul. A link, unseen, not really felt, but there. Something he could rely on. Until now. This.

He looked down at the letter again. It was unreal, and he was blindsided. His brother had been hurt, and he had been oblivious of it. When David suffered so after Jannie died, Patrick had felt that he was there with him. He'd felt what David felt. And likewise, David had been the only one who could lift the burden of Patrick's own grief over Lynn. David was the only one who knew.

And now David was healing from bullet holes. And Patrick knew nothing of it. Didn't feel it at all. The notion bewildered him.

Tucking the letter safely inside his coat pocket, he downed the last of his pilsner and walked toward the art building for his nine o'clock lecture.

Chapter Forty-Five
Rehab and Reconciliation

I STILL DON'T KNOW exactly how he found me.

There I was, walking along with a couple other leathernecks, dumb Americans among a throng of Japanese, slinking around and gawking, just like we had been for the past week. Running out our R&R, keeping ourselves bored so the minutes before we went back into the bush would drag just a little longer. I looked up from the camera I'd been ogling in a storefront, and there's this lion-haired guy in a flowing ivory tunic, standing head and shoulders above the sea of dark heads bustling past him, just staring at me across six lanes of Tokyo rush hour traffic. And all the din of the street vendors and blaring horns and different songs pouring out of each of the stores that line the streets of this vibrant city just fell away, and there is Father Jack.

I stopped walking, and my buddies all looked back. And then I started laughing. Father Jack smiled his stupid little grin. He raised his arm and extended his finger, and crooked it twice, beckoning me. And across all that foreign cacophony, I heard his booming voice.

"I've been looking for you."

Well, getting across that street to join him was more of a challenge than I ever would have thought, but after about a half hour, we managed to reunite. My buddies were pretty amused at this wild-looking bohemian, who engulfed me in his long arms and hugged me like a son.

I was glad when my buds decided to go on into town. We were all the docile type of GIs in Tokyo, not the kind out whoring and carousing and brawling, but just trying to be as invisible as we could be, what with our uniforms and our weird, nervous energy and our thousand-yard stares and all. But even though they were pretty low-key guys, hanging out with a Catholic priest was a little less exciting than what they were hoping for. I don't know what they were seeking. I don't think they knew either. And they sure wouldn't know what they were missing.

That was the whole trouble with R&R. We all went around searching for something, we didn't know what, that would give us some peace, or at least a little satisfaction, all the time with Mick Jagger screaming about how he can't get none from the speakers playing to the ears of the money-laden American tourists and GIs streaming though the neon-bright commercial district. Circling, circling. I saw my buds later, and sure enough, they had just milled around, their unarticulated hopes dashed. Maybe God doesn't step in for amusement purposes only.

But He sure as hell intervened by sending Father Jack my way.

And I got a lot more peace in the days I spent touring with him than in the whole rest of the break. He showed me more about the culture of Japan than I would ever have seen walking around with a squad of other ignorant gyrenes. I'd meet him early in the morning at the Jesuit mission downtown. We'd have wonderful breakfasts in the Jesuits' dining room. Those guys really know the meaning of poverty, for sure. "Plush" might be a bit strong, but "elegant" works. "Comfortable" is an understatement. Nice settings.

Then we'd head out on foot, or sometimes by taxi, on excursions. Libraries. Parks. In our last few days together, we settled in the Buddhist gardens. The place exuded peace and sanctity. And of course, Father Jack knew the monks who lived there. They greeted each other with bows and words I wished I understood. I made sure Father Jack taught me a few phrases to convey my gratitude and respect to these gentle, accepting hosts. They let us remain in the gardens as long as we wished, talking, sitting quietly, just being. Just when I'd feel a rumble of hunger to remind me of my humanity, a monk would deliver a tray of lunch—fruit, dried garbanzo beans coated with pungent mustard, slices of fish on bars of sticky rice. And a couple times a day they'd bring cups of refreshing, cool spring water, or sometimes a light green tea with the fragrance of jasmine. They always arrived just when I'd notice my thirst or hunger, deliver their offerings, and recede. They were as stealthy as me and the guys in the bush. But they were waging peace.

Father Jack asked me about waging war. He listened with total focus and attention to every word I said about how I live in the Nam. Every word. He took it in. And I just poured it out. I felt like toxins were being drawn from my liver, from my blood and bones. Eventually, I felt something lift from my mind, like a shroud. I looked up at Father Jack, as attentive as he had been the morning we started this whole conversation—or really, this monologue. When he had interjected, it was with a precise question, as if he knew the key to unlock my next thought. At no point during those three days in the gardens did I feel that Father Jack was angry with me. He never seemed to judge or condemn my actions. I was so relieved. I'd been hesitant at first, afraid I'd lose his respect and friendship when he heard what my life was about. It was so radically different than how he'd known me in North Freedom.

∞

There's no free lunch with Father Jack, that's for sure.

After listening to my confession, he rallied to lob his thoughts and reflections back at me. His first salvo was straightforward.

"David," he asked softly. "Are you cognizant of how coarse your vernacular has become?"

Not the response I expected. I actually did a double take, glancing up at him to be certain he wasn't pulling my leg. His demeanor was sober.

"It's the Crotch, man," I blurted, immediately wanting to bite my tongue. "The Corps, you know. I mean, that's just the way we think. And talk."

It sounded lame even to me.

He looked deep into his palms as he considered my response. "What else has the Crotch taken from you?" Though his expression didn't soften, his use of my term assured me that he was still with me.

I hadn't really considered what the Corps drew from me. It was a weird give and take. It took my will. My innocence, maybe. But it gave me other things. Identity. Confidence. The Corps had torn me down and rebuilt me as a warrior, I explained.

He nodded again. "A warrior. Yes. I see." His words lingered a moment in the silence of the gardens. "David, I dare say, you have always been a natural warrior. A champion, of sorts. You have led your life and faced your challenges and battles as a warrior would."

He looked out over the manicured hedges and graceful trees, spreading his arms to encompass all we could see and much that we couldn't. "In this land, David, there once lived men who strove to become impeccable warriors. The samurai. They imposed the most stringent of disciplines upon themselves to achieve a state of near perfection in their ability to battle, and to conduct their lives. Bushido. Their discipline was pure."

We rode his thought for a moment. I knew about the samurais, and wondered where he was leading us. So often when we talked, I wondered if he even knew where he was taking us. Finally, I asked. "So, what became of the samurai?"

He studied the question for just a moment. "Well, there are a few vestiges of them. The yabusame and their horses. Others here and there. But mostly, they died out, of course." He leveled his eyes upon me. "They waged war, and they died. Some died at venerable old ages. Others died earlier, often at the hands of other samurai. Did it matter, really, when and how they died? The samurai died at their appointed time. As we all die. Like Jannie died."

Well, now, that was a thought from left field. I wondered again where we were headed.

He looked over at me with his eyebrows arched. "Waging war is really the most absurd act of the most perverse of romantics, you know. Explain to me, please, how mankind can honestly expect to gain that which we most desire, if we murder one another in the process? Is it wealth for which we kill and die? Or love? Or power? Perhaps love of power. Those in love with their power are so eager to send their subordinates to their deaths in order to feed their hunger."

I reflected on that line of thought for a minute, after which I told him that really, I kind of thought he was giving me a line of fucking horseshit.

"See what I mean about coarseness?" he reminded me. But he knew I was right. At this juncture, I had little patience for caroming around the mental labyrinths of his philosophical intellect.

"Really, Jack," I snapped, "Just what the fuck do the deaths of a bunch of last century's star soldiers have to do with me going back into the Nam and hoping to God that I come out without getting my ass blown off? Again?"

It was the first time I'd ever addressed him solely by his first name. He smiled warmly as he squared off, facing me directly, welcoming me. His next salvos were targeted at the essence, and he fired until he exhausted his munitions. "It is not that the samurai died, David," he said. "It is not even how they died. It was how they lived that mattered. Impeccably, in every facet of their lives. Not only were they impeccable warriors. They contributed to their communities as well. The impeccable ones did. Oh, I'm certain some fell short. They could have been mean spirited. Or bullies. Or tyrants. But those were not the ones that reached excellence. And the samurai strove to reach excellence. They did so by exercising their will. They made choices."

"That is my concern for you, David. Are you exercising your will? Do you still have your will? Have you really relinquished your will to the Corps? The Crotch, as you say?"

I felt my eyebrows furrow, and my eyes squint down.

"It is not like you, David, to be so coarse of tongue," Father Jack stated. "Not like you at all. It tells me that you've allowed yourself to… sink. To allow yourself the luxury of abdicating your own will. Subjecting yourself to the will of the Crotch will reduce you to little more than an animal, a pit bull trained to fight and kill, without regard for humanity."

I felt myself withering within as I considered my state of being. "Well, what can I do, anyway? I gotta go back to the Nam. You think I should desert or something?" I was taken aback by the whining tone of my own voice.

"That would be the easy way out, a desperate, desolate, aimless solution. No. That is not what I said."

I breathed in long and slow, closing my eyes as I exhaled. "How can I reconcile the demands of my circumstances to the range of will that the Crotch imposes upon me?" My voice had lost its whininess. Instead, it was low, calm, and resigned.

I sat with my eyes closed. Father Jack said nothing. My mind was still, and after a moment, or longer, I don't really know how long, I realized that I was feeling peace. I opened my eyes.

Father Jack's expression was ebullient. "David," he started, pausing for me to gather focus. "Why do you think that we didn't probe the morality of your situation? Why didn't we spend this time together considering whether the murder and mayhem that you embraced is right or wrong?"

It hadn't escaped me that he had not dwelt upon the guilt of my transgressions. At no point during our talks had my old friend leveled the title of "murderer" at me, and I was grateful for it. Rather, our discussions had penetrated to a more gravid level of morality.

The act of warring, in and of itself, was not the crime of my soul. That was a deed of necessity on the battlefield. I had not killed wantonly. I had not enjoyed the battles I'd endured. I made war well, I knew. As well as I possibly could. I did what I had to in the faith and hope that by warring well, I would live. I knew that at any moment I could be wasted as quickly and easily as Huey or Kelly or Brettan or any of the guys we sent home in the bags. But now I saw beyond survival to what Father Jack was claiming. It was my soul that was at stake. I had relinquished my will.

I had thought that was expected of me.

"So are you saying I should tell the Corps to shove it?"

Father Jack merely grinned.

"Okay. I see, I think. So what does this all have to do with me being foul mouthed?"

"For you, David, it means everything. You have the two gifts: Time and Will. That is what creation gives us. If you use your will effectively, you will not roughen your mind, your heart, and your soul with coarse living. You have control over that. The words you choose dictate the state of your mind. And further, the state of your soul. I have no idea how you can extricate yourself from this situation except by fulfilling your obligation and getting out of the service, thank you, amen. Desertion, of course, is an alternative, but it is an unlikely and unfitting one, unbecoming to you. I don't see it happening that way.

"So you must exercise your will. Fully. Conform your will unto the will of the Lord within the challenges set before you. And be dogged about sticking with it."

Again, the contradiction between his advice and the arena I was about to reenter sent me reeling. And I said so.

"It is not that hard, David," he said, his voice as kind as I'd ever heard. "Yes, you must go back and wage your war. Yes, it seems to be in your cards to do so. But remember the Rule, the only Rule that counts. Love one another."

I looked at him with impeccable astonishment.

He laughed.

"David, when the shit gets thick, you are going to be frightened and angry, and you'll be enthralled and ecstatic. For a warrior, that's natural. You can expect it. You can depend on it. You can—you must—use it. You will embrace it and you will live it with enthusiasm. You will fight back. You will wage war. You have been trained to do so, and you must be as good at it as you can be and hope to God you come through alive. The only provision is the single important message in the New Testament. Really, you can cut and cull all the extraneous noise out of the entire New Testament until you reduce it to just three simple words. All the rest shakes out, and you are left with the perfect Rule. Love one another."

He let me ponder that thought for just a breath. Then he added, "You can consider that Rule. And you can apply it to every situation you get yourself into, be it war or not. It is the responsibility of your will to reconcile that one simple Rule with every action you take as you add to this creation. That is all there is."

After a long spell, I asked him, "So just how am I going to wage war as I go about loving one another?"

"I have no idea. That is beyond my range of experience or comprehension. I am not a warrior like you. I do not wage war. That is not my calling. I champion peace."

A twinkle lit his eye.

"But I have every confidence that you are up to the challenge of your calling. It is your way. It would be unlike you to do anything less."

∞

On Thursday, Father Jack was scheduled to fly back to Afghanistan to resume his work with the Sufis. After one last lunch in the gardens, we shared a taxi back into town. At the hotel, he enveloped me in a farewell hug. Neither of us hurried to part, but finally, regretfully, we did.

"Be prepared to accept anything and everything that comes before you. Be impeccable." He smiled as he got back into the taxi. "The best part, David, has been thinking all these things through with you. I am grateful for that. Always."

He didn't look back as the taxi pulled away.

Chapter Forty-Six
Temporary Duty Yonder

THE NOTE was waiting for me at the hotel desk when I returned from the gardens: *Sergeant Joyce, call Colonel Whitney at the Tokyo Hilton, ASAP.*

Sergeant?

Call the Colonel?

Colonel Steve didn't answer right off, and I had a couple hours to collect myself and become impeccably ready for whatever he was about to throw at me this time. I prayed it would be something a lot more pleasant than a hot deal in the Nam.

None of my meticulous preparation helped, though, when I picked up my room phone and heard his voice. "Pack up your gear, Sergeant. We're going to Europe. Now."

He laughed as I blustered my way toward understanding.

First off, Sergeant? What was that all about?

Second, Europe? Sounded a whole lot better than the Nam. But why?

Third, now? Did he mean, like, now tomorrow morning, or now later on? Or could he possibly mean, like, right now?

"Yes, I mean right now," he replied, relief clear in his voice as he took my questions by priority. "If you hadn't gotten back to me this evening, I'd have had to leave without you. But you must've pulled your head out of your butt and picked up my radar.

"And yes, Europe. I've got some TDY in Paris. We might be there for three, maybe four weeks. Still has to do with the Nam. But since you're sitting around on that rosy patch of new ass skin you acquired, I thought you might be up for a little change of pace. When Olsen, my sergeant assistant, rotated back to the real world two weeks ago, I thought of you right away. Since you weren't rank quite yet, I fixed that. Congratulations, Sergeant. You packed yet? I'll have my driver swing by and pick you up at 17:30, sharp. Air transport lifts off at 19:00. We gotta move, son. I'll bring you up to date on the way."

He clicked off, leaving me wearing a stupid little grin. *Jesus,* I thought, my inner voice sounding a lot like it belonged to the Crotch again. *What the fuck now?*

∞

One good thing about hanging around officers is that if they aren't working on day-to-day field operations, or watching a football game, or venting about their wives back home, well, they clean their language up pretty good. In

Paris, Colonel Steve was dealing with a lot of intense, professional soldiers, who were officers *and* gentlemen. Their demeanors were all business, and any profanity was targeted and effective. Their example brought me back to Father Jack's admonishment. I was working hard to speak no evil.

Actually, for the first four days in Paris, I didn't have much of anything to say to anybody. I accompanied Colonel Steve to his meetings and then sat around until he was done. They'd start up by 7:30 and shoot straight though until 19:00, breaking for a quick half hour to have lunch brought in. Which left me doing a lot of reading—Solzhenitsyn's *Cancer Ward,* a hilarious western called *Little Big Man* that one of the other non-com aides had brought in from the states, and a couple other cheap paperbacks.

From what the colonel told me, we were expecting a build-up of troops coming in from the North. Well, no shit, gizmo. There'd been regular parade coming through the jungle for weeks, even before I left the boonies. I couldn't imagine much more traffic. But they thought there would be. Some of the guys in civvies that were meeting with the colonel were retired French military, veterans of their own war with the Vietnamese. I couldn't help but wonder: If the French were in country ten years ago, and they lost their asses, just what kind of advice were they capable of giving? Were we getting what we really needed here? But then, hell. Colonel Steve clearly valued whatever he was learning. And I can't say I minded the sit-around time.

Thursday morning, however, things got a whole lot more interesting. At a break, Colonel Steve took me aside. "Well, Joyce, you have an option here," he said. "I've been asked to accompany our hosts to the Mediterranean over the weekend. We may well continue our meetings along the Riviera for a while. So, here's your choice. You can come along, but it sounds like I'd be finding you billeting away from our 'meeting' site." A glint of humor lit his eye, and I got the impression that his meetings were entering a new dimension. They'd be just as intense, I was sure. But in a different setting. And maybe in shirtsleeves. I waited to hear the other option.

"Or," he lifted his eyebrows, "you can stay here in Paris until we get back. If you do that, what you see is what you get. Either way, you'll be on your own a lot of the time. The embassy might put you to some sort of duty there, if you like. Clerking or something. What do you think?"

I couldn't see reporting to the embassy, really. And billeting with the Marine guards? Not much draw there. Too much spit shine and ballyhoo. I thought a moment and went out on a limb, figuring the worst the colonel could do was say no.

"Well," I ventured, "It's clear I'd be extra baggage on the Riviera, Colonel."

He smiled, acknowledging that he wasn't keen on having a non-com tag along.

"So, what would you think of cutting me loose to go visit my brother near Munich?"

That caught him off guard. With all the time I'd had just sitting around, I'd already found out that I could get on a train in Paris in the evening and arrive in Regensburg the next morning, with only one changeover in Basel. Or I could fly to Munich, and be back in a flash on a return plane if I had to. I explained the possibilities to the colonel.

He mulled it over a moment. "You just chewed up your R&R in Japan, didn't you?"

I nodded.

"Let me figure this one a bit," he said. "I'll see if I can come up with some creative temporary duty for you." He nodded to himself. I could see his wheels turning. "Joyce, we may be tied up here for a couple weeks, and I might be running down to the Mediterranean with these fellows a couple times. Hell, we may even hop over to Morocco. Business can be pleasure," he winked. "And you can see exactly how much work I have for you here. So maybe we can work something out. Let's talk again in the morning."

FRIDAY AFTERNOON, I sat strapped in my seat, looking out the portal at the Alps passing beneath me. In an hour, I'd be in Munich. Colonel Steve had worked his magic again.

"When you get to Regensburg, call this number," he'd said, handing me a slip of paper. "Simply tell them you're reporting in and awaiting further orders from me. Nothing more. They'll ask you for contact information. Then all you have to do is call in every third day. I'll either leave you orders, or we'll get in touch with you. Got it? Now git," he said, clasping my shoulder in a fond dismissal. My fresh scar tissue twinged, but I didn't flinch. Hell, I'm a Marine. I'm tough. And he'd just cut me some slack. I sure wasn't going to whimper.

From Munich, I took the train to Regensburg, and then caught a cab to the address I'd been writing on envelopes for months: 17 Adolf Schmetzler Strasse. The taxi was a beautiful new Mercedes. Nice. My first ride in a Mercedes.

The doorbell was positioned curiously high alongside the door, as if it was designed to be out of the reach of children. A little higher and I'd have had to jump. Reaching up for it, I paused. A low rumble was building on the other side of the heavy door, as if a herd of cattle were clomping down a wooden ramp. The door flew inwards and Patrick and three friends came charging out.

My twin's eyes about popped out of their sockets when he saw me. The rest was autopilot. On his next step, Patrick swooped me up in his massive wingspan, hopping and hollering.

"Ja-heesus H. Motherfucking Christ! Davey!" he bellowed. He turned to his friends, pointing at me with one hand while holding me aloft with the other. "Mein Bruder! Mein Bruder ist gekommen!"

He set me down so I could meet his friends, Uli, Jorgen, and Franz. They greeted me in warm yet proper English while Patrick stammered away in German. Lugging my duffle and suit bag in tow, they reversed their path, herding me up three flights of stairs to Patrick's room in the Étage.

"Man, I can't believe you're here," Patrick repeated. "How come you didn't let me know? I might've missed you. We were just headed out—there's a recital tonight. A couple of our friends are playing in the Universitäte's chamber orchestra. You'll love it. You gotta come with us. I can't believe you're here! Let's stash this stuff and get outta here."

Pat's friends chucked my bags onto the floor of his apartment. They were visibly impatient to leave, but did give me enough time to yank a set of civvies out of my duffle. I wanted to escape the military look fast. And I don't think Patrick and his cohorts much cared for me to keep my uniform on, either. I was still fastening my belt as they hustled me back down the heavy wooden staircase and out into the dark of the Regensberg evening.

As we walked the cobblestone streets, Patrick demanded an explanation of my presence, and I gave him a quick and dirty summary of the past six weeks' craziness.

"I noticed you're limping a bit," he said, his eyebrows raised.

"Shoot a new hole in your ass and see if you don't limp too," I laughed.

"Man, Davey," he said in a low tone. "I couldn't believe it when I got your letter about getting shot up. I just couldn't believe it."

He said he wanted to hear all about it, but I filtered a lot out, for that initial telling anyways. He didn't need to hear about Huey and the others. Not like this, walking down the street. Maybe later. I just told him what it was like to be a target, to get hit. Hell, even now, it sounded unreal to me. How could I expect him to understand?

"We gotta fly," Patrick interjected. "Concert starts in twenty minutes. Maria will castrate us all if we make Uli late. It's a big honor for the orchestra to perform in the Regensburg Theater. The girls were pretty hyped—they live on the Étage too, so we've been hearing about it for weeks." He tilted his head toward one of his friends. "Uli's sweetheart plays the clarinet. Maria. She's played on the chamber orchestra for, what, Uli, three years?"

"Doch," Uli replied, his pride evident. "She's chamber lead this year."

"We've heard them rehearse pretty much the entire concert, but it'll be fun to hear the whole ensemble, especially in the Theater," Patrick said. "You'll dig it. They'll start with Vivaldi and a couple Bach pieces. Then I think there's a Mozart wind concerto, and finally Moonlight Sonata. He looked at me closely. "They'll be playing the Air."

I was touched that he remembered how much it meant to me. I smiled, reassuring him that it would be fine. It would be good to hear the Air. I hadn't thought about it for months. Not at all. Now, here in J.S. Bachland, would be the right time to revisit it.

∞

While we waited for the performance to begin, Patrick grinned at me, shaking his head.

"I cannot believe I am looking at you, man," he said. "You just showing up like this blows my mind."

I laughed. "Yeah, me too. Last week, Japan. This week, Paris. Today, Germany. Here with you. Some days, I wake up not knowing where the—" I caught myself "—just where I am."

"Yeah. No shit," Patrick replied. "So. Are you... okay then? I mean, you know, all healed up?"

I explained that I was doing well, and would probably be back in the Nam if it wasn't for Colonel Steve.

"How long you good for?" Patrick inquired.

"Dunno," I admitted. "I figure a week at least. But I'm just taking what the Colonel gives."

Patrick pursed his lips, considering.

"Why, what's up? Am I cramping your style, being here?" I asked.

"God, no!" he exclaimed. "I can't believe how good it is to see you!" He paused a moment, and continued, measuring his words. "I mean, I do kinda have plans... did have plans, anyway, to travel to Vienna in a few days. Leaving Friday, after Thanksgiving. Wanna come with?"

I steepled my fingers over my lips, considering. I was loath to ask Colonel Steve for permission to leave Germany; better I stay under the radar, out of sight and mind. What's more, I was travel-weary. And still healing. I couldn't generate much excitement for the thought of another journey.

"I don't think so, Pat," I answered. "Even if I could, I dunno...." Even without looking, I could feel his sigh of disappointment. "But don't worry about me," I reassured him. "Just go. If you don't mind me hanging out in your apartment, I'd be happy just to cool my jets for a while. Read. Sit back. Hide out, sort of."

Patrick looked relieved. "Oh, yeah. No sweat. That'd be cool."

"How long you figuring on being gone?"

"Well," he began, gathering in a breath. "I'm signed up for a river trip down the Donnau. The Danube. We're supposed to start here in town, and take a few days to sail to Vienna. Then we were gonna stay a few days and take a train back. A whole week. Minimum. But, man, with you here, I'll be glad to cancel out. I mean, I can do it later."

I waved my hand toward my twin. "Take your trip. I mean, this still gives us a few days to see each other. And who knows, I could get called back up any time. That would be a pisser to miss your trip and have me out of here a day later. Just do it, and don't worry."

"You sure?"

"Absolutely. I'd really like some time alone, to be honest. I mean, you wouldn't believe how little time alone there is in the Corps. You can't take a dump without somebody nearby. About the only time I have halfway to myself is when I'm out in the bush, being an eyeball. Even then, my buddies are close by. We all know exactly where everyone is…." I drifted off. My entire platoon was gone. When I got back to the bush, I'd be cycled into an existing group, a fresh body to replace for one departed. I hoped it would be someone who'd gone back to the real world. That would be so much better than filling in for someone in a bag. Or a wheelchair.

Applause filled the room as the chamber orchestra filed onto the stage. Patrick leaned closer, pointing out the two musicians from the Étage. Maria carried her clarinet to the first chair, while Eva held her violin and bow before her almost as if she was presenting arms. The lights dimmed as the company took their seats.

As the strings swelled, I let the rapture take me, remove me, elevate me. After each piece, I surfaced, opening my eyes, registering the soft murmur of the audience shifting in their seats, exhaling aloud after breathlessly embracing the music, then settling back to hushed attention as the musicians took up their instruments for the next arrangement.

At the opening measure of the Air, my eyes snapped open wide. The violin was eloquent, and it captured me. The lead violinist's long, lithe fingers danced across the neck of her instrument. Each note was seamless and laden with passion. My eyes captured the movement of her hands, her arms, her slight, fine shoulders. Eva, Patrick had said. Eva's eyelids were half-open, relaxed, her eyebrows arched ever so slightly as she rocked gently with the strokes of her bow. Her face was placid, a portrait of peace. Her eyes probed the space around me, toward me—as if she was seeing through me. Not the thousand-yard stare of my buddies. No. She was seeing into me.

Absolute stillness absorbed her last lingering note. Then the audience erupted, springing from their seats, saluting the orchestra with thundering appreciation. I remained seated as Patrick leapt to his feet, cheering and clapping. He glanced at me, and I realized that my face was wet with tears. I smiled at him and whispered, "I don't think I've ever heard it played more perfectly."

"Only when you played it last," Patrick answered, his eyes suddenly brimming. He dabbed at them with his sleeve and returned to his seat. "You okay?" he whispered. "Wanna go out and get a breath of fresh air?"

I shook my head definitively. "I wouldn't miss any of this."

The musicians played two final pieces, then an encore, and a second encore, before the crowd allowed them to retire. By the time the last note was but a memory, trod on by the rustling of people moving from their seats and the murmur of voices, I was physically and emotionally spent. I had never taken in a more moving concert.

"All right?" Patrick said, standing before his seat, his troop of friends lined up behind him.

I stood slowly. "Fine. Man, I could have listened to that all night."

Patrick laughed. "Well, we just about did. And enough is enough for me. I haven't heard that much music since you and Gabriel played all Christmas Day last year. Or the year before, was it?"

I stood back in the aisle and let my brother take the lead. *Three years ago,* I thought.

∞

He took me to Namenlos, a dark and trendy tavern. I found a seat on a wide bench wrapped around a fixed, low table, sipped the large stein of beer that Patrick handed me, and settled back into the shadows, a spectator. Before long, the musicians arrived. Maria entered with a flourish, Eva in her wake. Eva looked on, her arms folded, a smile on her face, while Maria fueled her friends' exuberance with deep, dramatic bows and curtsies. As Maria clowned, Eva drifted to the end of my bench. She was nearly close enough to attempt a greeting over the hubbub around us when Patrick's friends spotted her and drew her into their celebration. She was hugged and kissed, and everyone offered congratulations. She smiled self-consciously, nodding graciously, and eased her way back toward the wall.

At first, Eva focused her attention on the roiling cauldron of energy and cheer before us. But soon, I felt her glance probing into my shadowy perch. She nodded her head, little more than a bob of her straight, fine nose. I met her dark eyes and returned the gesture. Our eyes remained locked for just a breath before she turned back to the revelry of her friends. I, too, watched the party wind itself up as steins clinked, then emptied. But from the corner of my eye, I saw the slight violinist sit down at the end of the bench, just a yard from me.

Patrick noticed as well, and elbowed his way over. When he draped his muscular forearm around Eva's back, his hand wrapped completely around her shoulder and nearly down to her elbow. My brother was a monster, and he made her appear tiny.

"Eva, mein Gott! Du bist... eindrucksvoll schau! The Air! Oh my God! Ausgezeichnet!" he said, just loud enough for her—and me—to hear. I smiled at how sensitive and genuine my raucous brother was with this young woman. She beamed at her hulking friend, clearly grateful for Patrick's kindness.

He turned her gently and pointed toward me with his stein of beer. "Eva, this is my brother, David," he said, his English slow and deliberate. "David, this is Eva. She lives with us on the Étage. She's our sublime force on the floor. And she's read everything you've written to me."

Eva shook her head, laughing. "I am no force," she tried to explained, her English tentative.

"She keeps us honest," Patrick said. "Eva's a good Catholic girl."

She laughed again.

"The Air was heavenly tonight, Eva," Patrick repeated sincerely. "But you don't have to take my heathen word for it." He tilted his head in my direction. "David will support me. And he plays it every bit as beautifully as you." Patrick touched the end of her nose with his index finger, his arm still firm around her shoulder.

Eva peered at me, her eyebrows arched. "You are the violinist your brother says?"

I shrugged, hoping the darkness hid my flushed face. "More of a fiddler, really. I have played the Air. In the past. But never as you played it tonight."

"He's as good as you, and you were perfect tonight," Patrick asserted. "I've told you about David. Don't let him kid you."

He released her shoulder and reached for a stein floating by on a waiter's tray. Patrick grabbed first one stein, and then a second, and swung around to check on my beers. My second stein remained untouched on the table, and my first was still almost a third full. I grinned helplessly and shrugged my shoulders at him.

"This will go to you," he said to Eva, handing her the glass. "My twinnie isn't keeping pace."

"You're out of luck here," he said quietly to me. "Of all the people on the Étage, I'm afraid Eva's English is the shakiest. She can understand fairly well, and she can read, but…" he shrugged, and then his brow furrowed as an idea struck. "But she does speak French."

Turning to Eva, he explained, "Davey here is a polyglot. Speaks your language. Hell, he speaks a bunch of languages, except German."

"And Japanese," I added.

Pat shot me a curious glance, but his attention snapped back to his buddies' laughter, and he drifted away.

∞

I glanced back toward Eva. She was studying me.

"Multilingue?" she inquired in French. "I think what Patrick says is true. You have written so in your letters. What languages do you speak?"

"Well, Vietnamese and some Chinese," I replied. "I do know French— although I have no illusion that I speak it as beautifully as you."

She grinned. "You speak as a Canadian."

I couldn't help but laugh. "I learned from a Canadian."

"And your music? Your 'fiddling'?"

"My great-uncle, of sorts. Taught me as a youngster. Then a friend taught me more symphonic pieces. Less folksy works."

"We shall play. Yes?"

I considered the invitation. "We shall."

We sat quietly for several moments. Then Eva said, "I saw you sitting with your brother at the recital. I wondered who you were, though I knew. You resemble one another."

"Seriously? Do you really think so? Nobody's ever said that before."

"You both have kind eyes." She looked down into her beer and took another sip.

We said little, sitting quietly with one another, while the rowdier members of the group clanked their steins and downed their beer, sharing Patrick's orders of fried camembert and calamari.

"You are tired, no?" Eva asked.

I nodded. "I was just wondering whether I could find my way back to Patrick's room on my own. He looks like he'll be going for a while."

"Get his key. I, too, would like to go home. I'd be glad to walk with you."

"Oh, that would be wonderful. To get home," I explained. "I am exhausted."

Eva set down her half-filled stein and floated through her friends. She took Patrick's elbow, drawing his attention.

Patrick glanced over at me, understanding blooming across his face. He stepped toward the wall benches. "Jesus H, David, I wasn't thinking. You must be beat." His voice was loud, the beers ramping up his volume. "Goddamn, here I am keeping my brother out partying, not suspecting he was gonna be a wimp and wuss out early." He lowered his voice. "Sorry, man. I forgot. Your wounds... are you still healing?"

At my twin's mention of my injuries, I saw Eva recoil, just the tiniest bit. I didn't want to go there, didn't want to talk about it. My shoulder did ache, and so did my butt. I felt so weary. I didn't want to deal with being wounded. Healing. A warrior. I averted my eyes, though I could see her studying me.

I smiled at my brother. "I'm good. But I am tired. Can I get your key?"

"Wimp," he teased as he handed it over. "Well, Eva will get you home. I'll see you later. Then again," he laughed, looking over his shoulder at the young ladies still chatting with Jurgen and Franz, "maybe not until morning."

He laughed again and clapped down on my shoulder, and the two of them looked startled when I winced.

"'Night," I said, smiling sheepishly. I turned to Eva and saw concern in her eyes, and shrugged to indicate it was nothing. Together, we turned to leave.

∞

In the Étage, I fumbled with the key to Patrick's room. The lock was heavy and tumbled with a solid *ker-lunk*. I stepped in, stripping off my shoes and socks, my sweater, and my last somewhat clean civilian shirt, which I hung squarely on the back of a chair standing askew before Patrick's desk.

The room was big and comfortably furnished, and of course, being Patrick's abode, nearly covered with clutter. The end tables beside the bed and the sofa overflowed, spilling their burdens onto the floor. Magazines. Letters, some of which I recognized as my own. Wine bottles. A couple coffee mugs, one of which was half full, a fuzzy swatch of mold riding the surface of the dark liquid. A hash pipe.

I picked up the pipe and sniffed the bowl. It reeked, strong and bitter. I looked through the litter on the table and found a few pea-sized hunks of dark wax. I sniffed them, too. Resin. I set the pipe back down on the table.

I lugged my duffle onto the end of the sofa. From the neatly folded gear inside the green canvas tube, I pulled out my shaving gear, clean skivvies, an olive green t-shirt, and my flip-flops. I glanced around the room. Several crumpled and spent towels were stuffed into a rack on the side of the wardrobe. I dug deeper into the duffle, feeling for the roughness of the military-issue terry cloth towel. I pulled it out, gathered my essentials, and made for the water closet that Eva had pointed out on our way upstairs.

I stepped into the third shower stall of the communal "clo," as she'd called it, and pulled the curtain. I was used to quick showers, and within a moment I turned off the spray and toweled down. Wrapping the towel around my waist, I pushed aside the shower curtain and stepped out to the sinks. Lathering up my sparse whiskers, I took the razor from my toilet kit and scraped my cheeks. Why, I wondered, did I bother?

The door opened and Eva entered, wrapped in a heavy robe and carrying an armload of towels and plastic bottles.

I froze, the razor halfway down my jaw. Her eyes met mine in the mirror, and she halted, alarmed. Her eyes moved to the angry red scar high up on my back. She stepped to within arm's length and slowly reached out to touch the uneven tissue.

Blood rushed up my neck, heating my face. I stood frozen, the razor still suspended before me, watching her examine the tender new skin that ran along the back of my shoulder, over the top, and partially up my neck. She stepped to my side, running her finger to the top of my scar. From the side, she saw the single perforation punctuating my shoulder just above my collarbone. She set her finger directly on the healed entry wound.

I turned to face her. We were exactly the same height. She slowly removed her finger from my scar, but left her eyes locked on mine.

"War," she whispered. "You have no need to be there." Her French was deep and throaty. She turned away, walked to the shower stall, and stepped in.

I stood motionless, still holding the razor. I listened to the water run in the shower, but saw only the image of her eyes looking into my soul. I shook my head to clear my mind, turned to finish shaving, and as quickly as possible, gathered my things and retreated to my brother's room.

∞

When I awakened, I thought it was early. The dawn was dark and heavy with fog. I spotted Patrick's clock and was surprised to see that it read five minutes until eight. I was only slightly less surprised to see that my brother had not returned.

Jesus, I thought, stretching my arms and shoulders. I wondered how Regensburg's latitude compared to North Freedom's. The deer season was open in Wisconsin, and it would be light enough for shooting before seven. Man, it was dark here.

I felt so discombobulated. Eight o'clock in Germany and still dark. Was it earlier in Paris? Was all of Europe on the same time? Shit, no. They couldn't form a consensus on anything. Time would be too easy to disagree about.

It was probably well into the afternoon in the Nam. Christ, I thought, arching my back and stretching out my ribs and butt. I felt stiff and out of sync. How often had I been in the Nam, watching time march by, second by second, and wondered what time it was back in the World? I'd figure it out. I'd be watching spiders crawl on elephant grass on some damn jungle-covered hillside an hour before dawn, and I'd figure that Paddy was just finishing his evening milking. Or that Patrick would be getting high or getting head from his friend, Cindy. Although that could be any time of day, probably.

Now I'd come west of the East. I'd like to keep on going west, I thought. Right over that big fucking pond, back to the World. Seemed like it was shorter to there than back to the Nam. Yet the web of the Nam still had its silky threads stuck on my butt.

I worked my legs, tucking my knees to my chest and then pushing my heels out as far as I could. I rolled over on my belly and arched into a bowed, cobra-like pose.

The knock on the door was gentle. Four raps. Persistent enough not to be ignored, yet soft enough to show that the knocker respected my rest, had I still been sleeping.

"Just a moment," I called, feeling instantly like a fool. Did the person on the other side know English? Most of Patrick's friends spoke it, so I shouldn't worry, I reassured myself as I pulled on my wool dress trousers. I hadn't locked the door. I opened it, and Eva faced me on the other side.

"I thought you might want breakfast," she said. She offered me a steaming mug. "Or tea, at least. Perhaps you prefer coffee, no?"

"I love tea," I said, sniffing the aroma of pekoe. "That's so kind of you." My command of French was strong this morning, perhaps because she had greeted me in her first language.

"I have some breakfast cakes in my apartment, if you would like to join me."

"I'd like that," I said. "I was wondering what I'd do for breakfast. Can I take a moment? I just got up."

"Oh, certainly," she said. "My apartment is just down on the left." She gestured toward the hallway. "I'll leave my door ajar. Whenever you would like."

"I'll be just a moment," I assured her.

She lingered. "Bring your... fiddle, perhaps?"

"I'd love to. Will we wake anybody at this time of day?"

"We will breakfast first. But I think that we may play without disturbing anyone. Most everybody is at the Uni, and anybody still here is accustomed to us playing at all hours. Many of us on the Étage are musicians. We don't mind. Unless we play so poorly that we draw complaints." She smiled broadly and turned to go.

I watched her glide down the hallway to her room. She moved fluently, effortlessly, like the notes peeling off the strings of her violin. She was smaller than I. Not shorter, but very fine boned. I must have weighed thirty pounds more than she, and I still hadn't come close to one-thirty since leaving the hospital. I couldn't gain weight at all. I hadn't been hungry. But my stomach rumbled now. I changed into a pair of Levi's I'd bought in Japan, but all of my non-issue shirts were already soiled. I pulled on another clean green t-shirt, grabbed my fiddle and bow from their case and traced Eva's route down the hall to her open door.

I knocked, and she called me right in. I stepped into her apartment, a three-room suite much larger than Patrick's, looking down over the Danube River. On the table at the center of the room, a plate of kuchens steamed enticingly.

"Come in," Eva repeated, coming to the door and quietly closing it behind us as she ushered me to the table. The little breakfast cakes melted in my mouth, and I made an absolute pig of myself, eating at least eight of the dozen she had made. Maybe nine. I can't image she ate four. Yeah, I ate nine. They were wonderful, and I was hungry.

We chatted as we ate and sipped tea. I asked her where she was from, and how she came to speak French so well.

Eva paused, looking curiously at me for a few seconds. Then her features softened.

She was born in Munich, she told me. Her mother was a nun who, in the waning weeks of the war, survived the invasion of Russian soldiers from the east, and then the Americans from the west. She'd been raped by both. Eva had been the result. After Eva's birth, her mother appealed to her order to let her take her baby away from Germany, and in their mercy, they'd sent her to Paris to be with her sister, also a nun. The sisters in her new home in Paris helped her bring up the sweet, shy little girl. Thus, Eva had grown up speaking French with the many nuns who raised her, and German with her mother, who she never really understood to be her blood relative until a short time before the loving nun developed a fast-spreading cancer. She died at forty-three years of age, on Eva's fourteenth birthday.

When she'd finished, I set down the kuchen I'd been holding throughout her story and asked, "Do you always tell people you've just met how you came to be in this world?"

She smiled, then shook her head. "Never," she whispered. "No one knows. Not Maria. None of the people here. Your brother, certainly not!"

This was as stunning a revelation as her story itself. I looked directly into her eyes, rimmed with tears. She met my eyes and held my gaze. Then she shrugged, letting a timid little smile sneak across her face. A tear escaped her left eye, but she dabbed it dry almost as soon as it touched her cheek.

"Why did you tell me?"

"My heart told me I could. I did not know what I was going to say to you when I started talking, but suddenly my heart said, it is right. Tell David. I must trust you with this. I can trust you." She paused. "I know you, you know. Patrick has let me read your letters. I know your heart. And I knew you could be trusted when I saw, last night, how you felt my music."

"I know the Air," I said, my voice rasping from deep within my throat.

She nodded. "Patrick told me. When he first heard me practicing. He told me about hearing you play it… last."

Her eyes burrowed into my soul. Another tear escaped the pools welling on her lids. She let it drip down her cheek before wiping it away with a single finger.

I smiled. "He warned me that you would be playing it last night. He wondered if I would want to hear it. And you know, I thought it was perfect. I was really ready to hear it again."

I looked down into my hands, turning them over to peer first into my palms, and then back to inspect my knuckles. I looked back up to her. "I just didn't know I would be so moved."

She nodded, sitting impeccably straight, her delicate fingers steadying the cup and saucer resting in her lap. She set the china down on the table, and reached over to where I had set my violin. She carefully plucked the strings, fine-tuning the instrument.

"May I?"

I could not find my voice. I nodded once.

And, once again, she played for me the Air.

∞

Patrick didn't return that day, or the next. He wandered in on Tuesday, looking worn and weary. "I'm beat," he announced, slumping to a heap on his bed. He was asleep before he could tell me little more than that he'd taken an unexpected trip to Bonn with two of his friends to visit a woman he'd been seeing.

"You'll meet Courtney," he said, his eyes drooping. "She'll be down for Thanksgiving." With that, he laid his head back and fell asleep. While he slept, I perused the books that were strewn around his room. During his absence, I'd borrowed a number of good reads. Others remained inviting. *Beyond Good and Evil.* An English version of *The Tin Drum.* A book by Fowles, *The Magus.* Kosinski's *Painted Bird. War and Peace.* I found it amusing that my brother was reading philosophy and literature. Even more interesting was the number of books in German. He'd always liked to read, but I didn't know that his zone of comfort had expanded beyond James Thurber, O. Henry, and Michener. It was a long way from the X's and O's that he used to study ad nauseum during his football days.

Shortly after Patrick collapsed, I heard the familiar tap on the door, and Eva peeked in, just back from the Uni. Her eyes widened when she saw my brother.

"He's out," I said, making no effort to lower my voice. I knew Patrick well enough to recognize that he was in one of those fourteen-hour sleeps, like he used to fall into after a tough football game. He was good until late that night, or maybe even until morning.

I gathered my sweater and jacket and left with Eva. She had become a welcome, warm face, reappearing each day in my brother's absence. If she had later classes, we'd have breakfast. After class, she'd come fetch me and we'd visit the coffee and kuchen restaurants. We walked about the town, catching a bite to eat, and maybe joining her friends at a wine stube or one of the breweries. I'd been to Kneitinger's twice, and learned the full meaning of Patrick's descriptions of those exquisite beers in the letters he'd sent me in Nam. We talked and talked. Sometimes, we played our instruments together. Or played for one another.

We idled away our hours, often talking late into the night. I didn't know what time zone I was operating in, but I knew I was stretching Eva's day out. She didn't seem to mind. Indeed, she had apologized to me late one evening for keeping me up. I assured her that she hadn't by talking with her for another two hours.

Chapter Forty-Eight
Return of the Twin

PATRICK RESURRECTED early Wednesday morning, a man of renewed vitality. He was surprised, however, to see that his brother had gone. His clothes and bags were still there. The loose bedding on the sofa suggested that he'd camped there. But David was nowhere to be seen.

"Perhaps in the clo," Patrick mumbled to himself as he trudged off to shower. But the clo was vacant.

As he dressed, he scanned the clutter of his room for a note, or any clue to his twin's whereabouts. He couldn't hunt for long, though. The Americans' Thanksgiving celebration was the next day, and Patrick had promised to bring pumpkin pie. Of course, David had been the pie maker at home, even more so than their mother. He'd been banking on David's help with the pies, since he'd never made one himself, and at Namenlos, David had been agreeable enough to the idea. But where was he?

Patrick jogged down the stairs three steps at a time. He flung the door open and hastily walked the four blocks to the market along the Donnau. He'd searched fruitlessly for canned pumpkin in the grocery store on Schmetzler Strasse, and his German friends had openly doubted that he'd find it anywhere. They'd encouraged him to buy a fresh pumpkin at the early morning farmers market instead, but it closed at ten o'clock. It was already half past nine.

The crowd at the market was thinning as the vendors slowly packed up their products. He walked through the tables of produce, slain chickens still in feathers, pork jowls, shanks, and trotters, hanging strings of sausages, crafts and canned goods and many items he did not recognize and had never asked about. Towards the back, a truck farmer had set up her stand, and he headed in her direction, keeping an eye out for her long, traditional, blue-shaded skirt, dark jacket, and the black bonnet she always wore over her straight black hair. Patrick often bought his produce from her: Brussels sprouts, broccoli, beans, cabbage and lettuce, rutabaga and squash. In the months since discovering the market, he'd come to know her well.

He'd learned that she was a war widow, as were many of the vendors at the market. Her husband had defended Normandy. He had been seventeen years old, and she sixteen, when he left her behind on his family's farm outside Regensburg. His father and both brothers had been killed in the war as well. She had remained on the twelve-acre farm, taking care of her mother-in-law until her death seven years after the war. As the sole remaining member of the Bauer family, she'd inherited the farm. She'd been selling produce at the market since 1944. And, she assured Patrick, she held no grudge against the Americans who killed her husband. She was glad to take his Deutsche Marks every week, and often gave him ridiculously discounted prices on her produce.

Patrick hurried to Frau Bauer's display. If she didn't have a pumpkin, he would have to scurry around the market to see if any of the other vendors did.

Frau Bauer would have nothing of Patrick's haste, however. "Grüss Gott, Herr Joyce," she offered cheerily, ready to chat. "You come to the market in mid-week? This is not like you. Is it not so?"

Patrick hurriedly explained his mission, but Frau Bauer shook her head apologetically. She'd already heard about this American holiday of pies, she said. Indeed, she had sold her only pumpkin to another American just moments before Patrick arrived. It had been a rather small pumpkin, and the young man and his woman also took her last two squash, saying they might do even better than the pumpkin.

"And, I understand there are no other pumpkins," she informed him. "This young couple had searched the entire market." Frau Bauer lifted her eyebrows, indicating that Patrick was plain out of luck. She told him to take a stalk of Brussels sprouts as consolation—no charge, she knew they were his favorite—and not to be bothered by his shortcoming.

Well, he thought, if he couldn't find the pumpkin, he might as well go get his morning coffee. The café was just a block from the Étage. He could sip a latte and figure out what to bring to Thanksgiving, since he'd clearly be arriving pie-less.

He froze, however, as he entered the café and spotted David and Eva hands entwined, sipping lattes, absorbed in conversation. They didn't notice Patrick as he entered, walked up to their table, and stood before them with his stubbled stalk of Brussels sprouts for a dozen seconds, bemused. "Ahem," he announced himself, finally. The couple looked up, their expressions broadening in joy.

"Der Einschlafen Wonderchönkin," David surprised him with his makeshift German. Eva threw her head back in laughter. "She's been my teacher," David explained.

"I take no credit for his translations! Or blame, either!" Eva protested.

Holy Jesus, Patrick thought. *David and Eva! Christ, who'd have guessed?* The couple erupted with laughter at the big twin's astonished expression.

"Sit down before you fall over, you oaf," David said, kicking back a chair. "You need a cup of coffee? Man, you look like you're dreaming. Hey, I got good news. I found a pumpkin. Not much of one, but it'll do. And we got some nice squash, too."

Patrick lowered himself into the proffered chair, a slow smile spreading across his face. "Jesus Christ," he muttered. "I leave you alone with our young Eva for a few minutes, and what becomes of it? Amazing,"

Eva laughed harder than David, who shrugged. "Why fight it?" he said simply.

The waiter caught their eye, and David and Eva both called for him to bring Patrick a strong latte. Patrick was still mumbling in amazement when it arrived.

"Jesus Christ... holy shit... son of a bitch."

"So coarse," David chided him playfully.

Patrick just wagged his head back and forth. Finally, he took a swig of his steaming latte and swirled it in his mouth. The caffeine rushed into his system, and he gained a degree of equilibrium. Not entirely, but enough to open his mouth wide enough for both feet.

"So," he asked, "Are you two lovers?"

David and Eva turned to face one another, eyes wide, mouths forming matching circles of astonishment. Eva rocked back into peals of laughter, while David lurched forward over the table, grabbing his gut.

Jesus, Patrick thought. *These guys on something?*

"How can you even ask that?" David chortled. "Whaddya, nuts, or what?" He jolted forward again, bumping the table and splashing their lattes over the tops of their cups.

Patrick picked up his mug, nursing it while his brother and Eva regained control. Twice, their laughter calmed and crescendoed as they gasped for breath, then control. He watched them closely as they wiped their eyes, almost daring them to look at one another again. He knew that if David so much as glanced at Eva, he'd set her off again. He'd been there so many times himself, when they were kids. All David had to do sometimes was look at you, catch your eye for just a split second, and he'd send you over the top.

And it was clear that both Eva and David were over the top.

Patrick sipped his latte. He watched them begin to breathe easier, faces still rosy, their eyes moist. He waited until they'd regained their composure to ask, "Okay, children, can you explain what that was all about?"

He could see them resist the temptation to look at each other again. Eva spoke first, her English richly accented.

"Yes," she said softly. "We are lovers."

∞

He was like a puppy underfoot as I tried to get the pies made.

I mean, I walked to the pantry to fetch the flour, and he was right on my heels, yapping and carrying on. Then he'd be leaning over my shoulder, watching me cut the dough with a fork, his curiosity nibbling at his restraint.

"Jesus," he said again.

I reflected that Father Jack needed a word with my brother.

"I mean, holy fucking Jesus."

A strong word. Maybe a big stick, too. Beat some sense into this bugger, even if he was my brother.

"Like, everybody's been trying to do Eva, and you come along and knock her right over. Holy shit, man!"

"I wasn't trying to do her," I said. "I mean, neither of us was trying to do each other. It just happened."

"Yeah, sure. Like, turn around, count to five, and boom, you do her."

"Come on, Pat. It wasn't like that." I heard the edge mount in my voice. He'd been going on about this for fifteen minutes, ever since Eva had left for her afternoon class.

"Wow. Had me fooled. What is today? Mittwoch? What have you been here, five days? And you're already banging her? You're right on top of it."

I turned to my brother, rage sweeping through me. I struggled to keep my arms from coming up, from smashing his senseless grin. He did not know what I could do with my arms, my hands. My feet. "Patrick, I'm gonna tell you once. Leave it. You are way out of line. I haven't been just 'banging' her. I'm not just fucking her. It is not like that. Don't you ever say anything like that about her." I found my finger pointing into his face, steady and menacing. I breathed in, and out, controlling my anger.

He stood looking at me, his eyes round and astonished, and I saw recognition in him. For a moment, he found that he feared me. He had never had reason for that before. Even when I pushed him off his bike, when we were kids. That was a fluke. Now, however, he knew.

My breathing softened. My rage flattened. I felt abashed for having lost it, and forgiveness for his stupidity. He was just being a guy. A dumbass guy. I waved my hand off. "It's okay, Pat. I don't mean any harm. I just don't want this to be taken wrong." I looked sharply into his eyes. "By anyone."

He blinked, his eyebrows still high on his forehead.

"Especially you. You're my brother.'

His eyebrows relaxed. He nodded. But he still could not speak. I had the floor.

"Okay. Here it is. Eva and I have been together almost constantly since we left you at Namenlos after the concert. Not just at night, I mean. All day.

From the time we get up until the time we say goodnight, we're together. We're talking, or walking, or just being together. Playing our violins. Whatever. If she's not in class, we're together. We can hardly wait to wake in the morning, just to look at each other. To be with each other. I mean, it's like a wave that just bowls us both over. I don't know how, or even why. But I can tell you, neither of us saw it coming. It just happened."

Patrick still stood mute, a funny little smile squiggled across his face.

I watched him, and felt my smile mirror his. I shrugged. "I can't help it. Man, I love her."

Patrick nodded. "Yeah, man. I know," he said, finally. "That's what blew me away. I'm so excited for you. I'm sorry for being so damn coarse. I was just carried away. I can't think of anything better for you, Davey. Falling in love with Eva. Wouldn't you know. Man, everybody loves our Eva. But she's never had a love, like this, for anyone. And here you come. My twin. My brother. All I was really trying to say was, like, go, Bro. You deserve it. And so does she."

He leaned into me with a huge hug. Happiness coursed through me. After a minute, he set me down; when he hugs me he generally has to bend over to get a grip, then he always leans back and I'm airborne. The fucker had tears in his eyes.

He couldn't resist, though. Having set himself straight, he prodded once again. "So," he said, looking down at me out of the side of his eye. "You telling me that you haven't been knocking just a little bit of our Eva's sweet little ass off while I've been away? Wee ahr lowfers," he spoke with Eva's husky accent, bracing himself for another attack. When it didn't come, his eyes widened again, and his mouth formed a round of delight.

I found myself blushing, with my own stupid grin.

"Ohhh!" he cried. "True confessions."

I sprung, pummeling him with the softest, most loving punches and chops in my Tae Kwan Do repertoire. He took it all, laughing his ass off the entire time.

When we had spent our energy chortling and brawling, we stood, gasping, red faced and grinning.

"I'm happy for you, Davey," he said.

"Thanks." I took in a few more breaths. "So. You wanna learn how to make a pie?"

∞

Patrick's friend Courtney arrived from the University of Bonn by mid-morning. Patrick met her at the train station, brought her back to the Étage, introduced me and Eva, and then unceremoniously retreated to his room, where they fucked themselves silly for a couple hours before Thanksgiving dinner. Since it wasn't a holiday in Germany, most residents of the Étage were at class, and the floor was wonderfully quiet. Eva and I sat chatting, sipping tea, and occasionally rolling our eyes at the moans and muffled cries coming from beyond Patrick's closed door.

"Patrick has always been exuberant about life, but you know, I kind of remember him being shy around girls," I chuckled.

Eva raised her eyebrows. "And you?" she asked. "Are you any less passionate than your twin?"

She held my gaze, and shortly we, too, were embraced in a union that compelled cries and whispers of our own.

∞

Patrick hailed another sparkling Mercedes to take us to Thanksgiving dinner. The cabbie whipped through the maze of the city as though he was negotiating a race track, and in the back seat, we leaned into the curves, Patrick's big frame absorbing most of the load on right turns, me getting squashed as we rounded every left. We laughed and howled as if we were on a rollercoaster, cheering the driver as he made seemingly impossible maneuvers, which only served to make him more daring. At the end of the ride, Patrick handed the fellow a hefty Mark note and waved off the change.

A large, friendly group of American exchange students and their European guests had already begun to assemble at Patrick's friends' apartment, an airy, open dwelling located above a bakery, a butcher shop, and a café. Patrick introduced us to the hostesses, Becky, Bridgette, and Barbara, "the three B's from Boulder," and a few others among the crowd. He was particularly eager for me to meet his friend Jeremy Lang, who was about to embark on a pilgrimage through northern France and Belgium. Though no older than my twin and I, Lang was already a seasoned historian. For his Ardennes trip, he'd obtained diaries, military records, and local newspaper accounts of the Battle of the Bulge. His next six weeks would be spent hiking through the grounds of that critical World War II battle.

"My dad was at the Bulge," Lang said, in the slow, deliberate drawl of a Southerner. "He helped me plan out the route. I wanted him to join me, but he said he'd already taken that trip and didn't need to revisit it."

Patrick explained that Lang was a veteran of many hiking excursions with historical meaning. He'd done the Trail of Tears—from Georgia all the way into Oklahoma—between his junior and senior years of high school.

"I'm gonna do the Battle of Stalingrad after spring semester," Lang added.

"Holy mackerel," I said. "You gonna camp the entire winter?"

"Uh-uh," he said. "I'll be a fair weather warrior for that campaign. Besides, I gotta be back in 'Lanta before the fall semester."

"That where you're from?" Courtney asked.

"Nearby. Small town in the mountains. Right at the very tip of the Appalachian Trail."

"Ever do the Trail?" I asked.

"Oh yeah. One of my first walkabouts. Did it straight through with my Grandpa, when I was fifteen." Lang detailed some of the highlights of that hike, adamant that it was not only one of his favorites, but one that every American who had any desire to hike should try. "You can find your soul on the Trail," he finished.

Patrick laughed. "We ought to do that hike, Twinnie. Wouldn't that be a hoot!"

I shrugged. I'd humped a lot of hills the last half year. If humping hills constitutes soul searching, I thought, I'd found mine already.

Patrick was fascinated, though, by the details of the Trail, as he was already calling it. He and Lang huddled in conference, drifting towards a group at the far end of the apartment, where a cloud of blue hashish smoke filled the small alcove.

Courtney elected to stay with Eva and me. "I got no time for hiking," she murmured. "And it's too early in the day for hash." Sipping a goblet of a Rheinhessen Spätlese, she explained, "I don't do hash much. I know Patrick enjoys it, but it's a bit heavy for me. So coarse and sour. Not like a good hit of weed. Until I get back to the States, I'll stick with Pan's idea of a good time." She tipped her crystal glass in a toast.

Eva and I touched our wine glasses to hers. Her comment made me think of the dope I'd stashed in a tea tin somewhere toward the bottom of my duffle. Out of sight, out of mind. I hadn't thought about it since before I'd packed up to come from Japan, when a buddy laid it on me. I grinned, thinking how Patrick might react to seeing, much less smoking, some of Vietnam's finest weed. Later.

Topping off her glass with a nearby bottle, I queried Courtney about her studies at Bonn. She explained that she was immersed in the European perspective of the Marshall Plan, particularly the German experience. She'd been a history major at Boston College, and earned a Fulbright scholarship as a grad student at Emery based on a strong undergraduate thesis on the post-war recovery from the American perspective.

"The logical follow up was to look at how it shaped life during the recovery over here," she elaborated, her eyes sharpening with scholarly intensity. For half an hour, we chatted about her work. Both Eva and I were fascinated. I wondered aloud whether I might be interested in a Fulbright-type study after I got back to the real world, and how I might extend my genetics background in Europe.

"You could go to Belgium," Courtney suggested. "They do a lot of genetics there, both in animals and people. I know some students from the States who are working in Brussels. A lot of their work is in dairy cows, too."

"Perhaps there might be something you could study in Germany," Eva suggested, smiling. "Say, at Munich?"

I grinned broadly. "Yes," I agreed, as the Three B's started to assemble the buffet. I took Eva's hand. "I think we should figure out what we can make of life," I said, hesitating, "...after...."

I let the thought hang. It was the first time we'd acknowledged that not only would there be a later, but that it could be interrupted at any time by forces over which we had no control. Without stating it in so many words, we looked into each other's eyes with the sudden awareness that what we had would not last, not as it was. That I would be leaving. She squeezed my hand, and a shared sadness crystallized in the air between us. Courtney watched us closely, then turned to join Patrick as he came from the back room for dinner.

Patrick glanced at us, raised his eyebrows smugly, and commented to Courtney, "I think they're in love."

"You should only know," she said, her voice soft. He was oblivious, she was telling him.

I didn't think so. I knew my brother too well. He saw right through me. He knew where I was headed, and I think he was as concerned as I. Both for me, and for Eva.

∞

The Thanksgiving celebration was spectacular. A couple dozen Americans and as many Europeans gathered, bringing dishes enough to feed four times as many. Our two pies were sliced thin so that everyone could have a taste of the traditional American dessert. Most of us were so full that a sliver was all we could handle.

We ate too much. We drank too much wine. And we followed it with good Scandinavian-roasted coffee, contributed by friends from Denmark. We were stuffed, half-drunk, and wide awake as we taxied back to the Étage. Thankfully, the ride home was a gentler, sweeter experience than the road race of the morning.

The fog along the Danube was thick, as it had been every night. The damp air was bracingly cool. Stuffed to the gills, I didn't really want to go sit around the apartment quite yet.

I suggested to Eva that we take the river walk along the banks of the Donnau. Courtney and Patrick followed right along.

We ambled west along the river, Eva and I holding hands. We wandered aimlessly, using the river as our only guide. Perhaps three-quarters of a mile upstream, we arrived at an intersection where a half-dozen prostitutes stood along the street, waiting for johns to slow their Mercedes and BMWs, roll down their passenger windows, and arrive at an agreement. The girls hopped in the vehicles and rode off, while other cars stopped just long enough to deposit their passengers before speeding away. The returning girls fell back in line against the old stone walls.

We watched the commerce wordlessly from the opposite side of the intersection. Patrick leaned against the wrought iron fence separating us from a steep twelve-foot drop to an abandoned stone road below.

"Jesus," Patrick pointed at a plaque, barely visible in the shadows above the cobbled pass. "That road was made by Julius Caesar's slaves so that he could move his armies to battle." He looked down at the roadway. "Man. The Roman highway."

Eva nodded knowledgeably. "The armies of many nations crossed right here over history," she said quietly. She leaned back against the iron railing, looking down the street into the dense fog, punctuated by the hazy, diffuse globes of streetlights leading from the intersection across the bridge over the Donnau. "Frederick Barbarossa brought his army across that bridge in 1189, on his way to battle the Muslims during the Crusades."

We all turned and peered into the fog, imagining the tromping and rattling of men and equipment, marching hundreds of miles across Europe to this very spot, and beyond. I found myself straining to see the army emerge from the fog.

Eva turned around to face the building rising from the foundation above the Roman highway. She pointed to another plaque, just above eye level near the corner. It was in German, but I could make out the name "Napoleon Bonaparte" in the first line. She translated it for me. "At this site in the year 1809, Napoleon Bonaparte stayed in Regensburg after defeating the Austrians in the Battle of Regensburg. He spent the night in this building with a fräulein mistress from Regensburg."

"Wow. What a way to make history," Courtney commented dryly. She turned to Eva. "Any other famous Regensburg women?" Her sardonic smile indicated that she didn't expect a reply.

"Barbara Blomberg," Eva noted quietly, but didn't elaborate.

I looked down at the Roman highway, then back across to the old stone bridge, then again at the building where Napoleon had banged away at the dear fräulein .

"Can you imagine, all that energy and effort, just to wage war?" I wondered aloud.

Eva turned to face me. "I would expect that you could, David," she said sadly.

Patrick caught her soft words. He waited to hear my response.

I could think of nothing to say to Eva. How could I explain? How could I defend what I was doing, was trapped into doing? I looked into her probing eyes, thinking back to that other short warrior, the mad man who led thousands of young soldiers to their deaths. I was like one of Napoleon's foot soldiers, one of Barbarossa's crusaders, one of Caesar's legionnaires. Just a pawn in the fray.

Patrick pulled me from the mire of my thoughts. "Everybody trods their own road," he said, looking back down at the Roman stonework. He looked at Eva, then me. "Come on, let's head home," he said, taking Courtney's arm and guiding her along the street to the east.

Eva took my hand and stepped close alongside me. She whispered, "David, I know you must go. I know what you must do. You must know, though, that I love you not just as a warrior. I love you for much, much more."

Chapter Forty-Nine
Head Talk, Heart Talk

BACK AT THE ÉTAGE, Eva suggested a pot of coffee, and we drifted down the hall toward her door, hushed but in good spirits. I could tell that no member of our foursome was ready to break off yet, despite the long day we'd shared. I glanced at my watch and was pleasantly surprised to find that it was just after eight. Damn, I thought. It gets dark so early here in Germany. It had been dark for hours. I'd been afraid it was closer to midnight.

As we settled into the sofas in Eva's living room, Patrick stood back up. He'd remembered his hash pipe in his room. "Anybody care to share a bowl?" he said, moving toward the door. "Would you mind if we smoke in your apartment, Eva?"

She shrugged. "No."

I tried to read her expression, wondering if she really didn't care. Then a thought struck me. "Holy mackerel!" I laughed. I jumped to my feet, startling the women. Patrick turned, curious and amused. "Have I got something for you!" I pushed past him through the door. "Just wait here a minute."

"Well?" Patrick asked when I returned.

I handed him the canister. "For you."

He took the silver canister and examined the calligraphy on the cover. He spotted two small English words printed at the bottom edge of label. "Jasmine tea?"

"Open it," I advised. "Take a whiff."

Patrick worked the cap off carefully. At first glance, the contents looked pretty much like the label said. Tea. Jasmine, probably, at that. He stuck his nose down into the tin and sniffed. "Wow!" he laughed. "Holy shit."

Courtney was at his elbow. "What is it?"

He tilted the canister so she could inspect it. A broad grin flashed across her face. "No shit!" she said softly. "That smells real!"

"Happy Thanksgiving. Merry Christmas, too," I joked.

Eva came up on tiptoes to see into the tin in my brother's hand. "So this is… mar-i-ju-wa-na?" she asked.

"Yes indeed," Patrick answered. "Did you bring the pipe, Davey?"

"There are papers in there someplace," I assured him.

"Here, let me." Courtney slipped her long, thin fingers into the canister and fished out the pack of rolling papers. She flipped open the cover and used it to measure out a joint's worth, squeezing the sticky buds between her fingertips to pop out any seeds. There were none. "Sweet," she smiled, loading the cleanings onto the slip of paper and nimbly rolling it into a long, sturdy funnel.

"Der Joint," she announced, handing the number to Patrick and quickly rolling a second one. Good fingers, this woman had. She was even more dexterous than Cindy, I thought. Or perhaps more earnest about what she was doing. Not quite so silly a personality. If Cindy was cerebral, Courtney was the entire package.

Eva watched with rapt curiosity.

"Ever smoked?" I whispered to her as Patrick lit the first joint.

She shook her head. "You can show me."

I nodded, taking the joint from Patrick. He immediately sat back on the couch, still holding the draw deep in his lungs. I smiled, waiting for him to cough it back up. Sure enough, he'd barely handed me the joint when he erupted with a series of violent, spastic coughs, bluish-white smoke spewing from his throat. After half a minute, his coughs morphed into a gut-wrenching, rolling laughter.

"Whoa, baby, you aren't gonna need all those." He shook his head at the little pile of joints Courtney had neatly stacked like a cord of birch logs.

I'd tried a few pinches in Japan, so I knew the potency and richness of the smoke. I drew a careful toke, exhaled, and then took another quick one. I handed the joint to Eva, who took a quick hit, coughing almost immediately. She kept it, though, and tried a couple of times to draw the smoke without immediately coughing it up. She did alright.

Courtney, meanwhile, lit up a second number. That in itself set me giggling. Man, we hadn't even torched a third of the first one. Patrick was wrecked, and I felt it coming on real fast. Eva was grinning giddily as she passed the joint back to me. I smoked again, turned to hand it to Patrick, but saw that he was settling back as Courtney brought herself over him to blow into his mouth. Patrick's favorite trick, the turbo. We called them shotguns in the Nam, 'cause we often used a barrel of a 12-gauge for the blow pipe. Patrick's way was more intimate.

"This is something you could try," I said quietly to Eva. "Watch."

Courtney was straddling my brother now, blowing into his mouth, the joint encased in the cardboard cover from the papers. I looked on the coffee table for something suitable for Eva to use for the turbo. Before I could find anything, Courtney turned toward me and hitched her chin, joint still in her mouth. I lifted my eyebrows and widened my eyes as she inhaled. She came at me with the tube and started exhaling the smoke into my mouth as soon as I'd found the cardboard portal. Without missing a beat, she moved from me to

Eva, to whom she applied the turbo more carefully, so as not to overwhelm our rookie with too much at once.

After finishing with Eva, Courtney turned to give me another hit, but I was convulsed with coughs and laughter. "Where'd you find this wild woman?" I choked as I exhaled in preparation for another turn.

Patrick smirked happily, sipping tokes from the first lit number. "She found me. Oktoberfest in the Hacker Pschorr tent in Munich."

Courtney dumped the roach from the cardboard tube and collapsed, cuddling, alongside my brother. Her eyes swam with tears from the smoke, and she peered out from seemingly distant places. Grinning, she took up Patrick's story.

"Yep. I spotted this no-shit-he's-an-American guy standing around with an empty stein, gawking at the yodeling fräulein in lederhosen, and I just walked up to him and asked him if he wanted to fuck."

Patrick laughed, nodding. "That was it."

Eva stirred on the couch, where she lay with her head against my belly. "You Americans. So, how do you say, unpresumptuous?"

Her accent and tone put us over the top. We collapsed into fits of giggles.

∞

Courtney found it in her to lead us through another joint. It was like she was smoking herself into euphoria. Or oblivion. She and Patrick really carried the load. Eva took another puff, but I don't think the smoke went past her tongue. One more hit was it for me.

Patrick said, "Seems unreal, eh?"

I nodded. We were on track. He was thinking my thoughts again.

"What?" Courtney wondered.

"That they are here together," Eva whispered. "That we are all here together."

I glanced down at her face and swept a lock of hair back from her cheek. She looked into me, and smiled gently.

Patrick asked, "So do you still miss her as much?"

Courtney wrinkled her brow. "Who?" She rolled her head back onto Patrick's chest and closed her eyes.

"Naw," I answered him. "I've learned that she's with me when I need her. She's here. Here and now. If I'm missing her, it's 'cause I'm wallowing in some sort of self-pity. That's all. When it's over, she's still right there where she's been the whole time." My hand rose from Eva's face, and I touched my chest with my fingers. As I moved my hand back down to Eva's neck, she took my fingers in her hand and kissed them lightly.

"How 'bout you?" I asked. "Lynn?"

Patrick's eyes narrowed, measuring his thoughts. "Always," he said. "Always."

Courtney sighed deeply. I looked to see if she was sleeping.

Eva asked me in French, "Who is Patrick's Lynn? He has told me much of you and Jannie. But he has never mentioned Lynn."

I answered in her first tongue. "She is his soul mate. And he must be apart from her. She had to leave him. She was older. He was too young then. She had to let him go. It was not their time. Like us."

She nodded, understanding.

I turned to Patrick and asked, "What are you going to do about her?"

Again, he studied his answer. "I dunno. I dunno if there is anything to be done. Is there?"

"If there is, only you can do it."

He shook his head.

"Patrick," I began. "If I'm not home when you get back to the States…"

His eyes flared, and he cut me off. "Don't even say that, Davey. I mean it. Don't say it, and don't think it."

I was taken aback. His fear was much closer to the surface than I'd realized. I laughed, and he glared at me incredulously. "I mean it," he snapped.

"I wasn't even going there," I replied. "That's not at all what I meant, really. I mean, I could be anywhere. Jesus, I've been just about everywhere I never expected in the last year anyway. I was just saying that you might get home before I do, and if you do, you gotta look for a couple of boxes I got stored in my room at Aunt Kate's. In the closet, under the stairs. They've got your name on it. You'll see. It's things for you."

He looked confused. "What kind of things?"

"Just things I've been keeping for you. Hey, if I get home before you, I'll get them ready and take them back to the farm. Just don't forget, okay?"

His brow still furrowed, he shrugged and nodded. "Yeah. For sure. I'll remember." He looked really stoned.

Eva looked at me, curiosity stamped on her face.

"Remind him, please?" I asked in French. "Before he goes home? Okay?"

She nodded. "What do you have for him?"

"Things his soul mate left for him. Pictures of him, of them, together. Doing things together. Loving each other. Their life together. Some letters. He'll need to figure out what they are to each other. I just wonder if she has been patient about him."

She studied me a moment. "I will wait for you, Soul Mate. Always."

I nodded. "I love you," I whispered to her. "Soul Mate."

She nodded, a gentle smile returning to her face.

∞

The women dozed peacefully, their heads on our laps. But my twin and I were energized. The hard edge of the dope had dissipated, and we were still buzzed from the coffee Eva had made. We talked and talked and talked.

"You angry?"

"'Bout leaving home? Naw. Seemed like it was for the best." He looked over at me. "I'd have had to leave sooner or later anyway. It's yours. You're the farmer, anyway, eh?"

"You know it is always your home, too."

"Yeah. Yeah. I know what you mean." There was no bitterness in his tone. He really knew. "You know, I have freedom from the farm. From home. It's not just that I have to go, I can go. Nothing's holding me. Tying me to the old place. That seems like the best way for me. I got weaned right off the farm when Mom got sick and I had to go live in the Dunes." He bobbed his head a couple times. "I loved living there. Uncle Paul was the greatest. Kind of like you and Paddy, in a different sort of way. We really were close. Tight. You know."

"But there was never getting over missing you," he said abruptly, looking directly into my eyes. "Yeah, sure, there was Jack. I mean, he was okay. But he was nothing like you. He was on a death spiral. That was his trip. Not like you. Or me. Like we were on the same wavelength and all." He laughed, a smile lighting his face. "I mean, Davey, you were such a crazy little fucker, after all. All those times you had us laughing our asses off, never even saying a word. Just acting out something that would split our sides. Or worse, when you'd get us in trouble. Like the time with Ol' Mrs. Hatcher." He guffawed at the memory, tears of laughter rising to his eyes as he reminisced about the desks in the old schoolhouse.

"Yeah," I joined in. "Imagine if we'd been caught in the bell tower?" And there we were again, holding our sides, trying to top each other with stories of the goofy things we'd done as kids together.

Like blowing off Patrick's tennis balls by igniting lighter fluid in the bottom of his tennis ball can, like a mortar. One perfect time, I'd caught him looking down the clothes chute upstairs when I'd called to him from below. The ball hit him square in the face, just above his eyes. The seam left a red mark curling above his eyebrows. Mom couldn't figure that one out at all. She was always puzzled by the sooty smudges on the sheets when we tossed them down the chute to the laundry room.

Or waging war on the beavers, destroying the dams that plugged the creek and flooded Paddy's lower pastures. We attacked those sturdy dams, feeling the power of destruction as the twigs and branches and mud gave way and the backwater flowed freely, washing the broken dams away... and then having to do it all again a couple days later when the beavers had repaired our damage.

"Jesus," Patrick muttered, a shadow darkening his eyes as he thought back to the dam that had nearly claimed me, right before I got pneumonia. "That was a scary one."

I grinned. "Something else, man. Turned out okay, though. Wouldn't have, but for you."

He held his gaze steady. "Wouldn't have happened at all, 'cept for me."

I shook my head. "You don't still believe that, do you? The dam would have gone regardless." The look in his eyes indicated he still held himself responsible. I shook my head adamantly. "No way, man. I wouldn't have gotten out of there without you. Really."

We let it rest a moment. Then I turned back to the more whimsical shenanigans we pulled, and we easily found our way back to laughter. Remembering the harebrained schemes of our childhood: slipping salt into Aunt Kate's sugar jar when we visited her on April Fool's Day, and greasing her toilet seat. Putting plastic wrap over the privy hole in the schoolyard outhouse. Sliding our hands under the hens to squeeze the newly laid eggs while they were warm and wet, shaping them before they set.

"Jesus, Davey. You are a crazy fucker. Everything is always full-go with you. If you're gonna be a bear," Patrick laughed, "be a fucking grizzly." He sat reflecting, a peaceful, content expression on his face. Then he added softly, "I really was happy, Davey, going to the Dunes." He looked up, his eyes earnest. "Meeting Lynn. It was all worth it, just knowing her. And finding out what life was like away from the farm. From Mom. And even from you."

I nodded. He was right. His path had already ranged wider and farther than my own. I wondered where it would take him next.

"How about you?" he asked. "You pissed at Mom for being so crazy?"

We both laughed. How easy it was to say about our mother!

"Nah. Not any more. If I ever was. I mean, I don't recall ever being particularly angry with her. Sad. Real sad. It seemed like such a waste of her time. And ours. But, man, I always wondered why she was that way. For so long, it seemed that the way she was, was normal. Wasn't until I got to know

Jannie's mom that I kind of figured out that Mom wasn't running by the manual."

Again, we were taken by laughter. The dope still had us loopy. Patrick eyed the remaining numbers stacked on the table, and I wondered if he was tempted to light another. I hoped not. I was liking the trend of our conversation, the harmony of our thoughts. He must have sensed it, because he met my eyes, grinned, and nodded. No need.

"But you know," I added, "she really was a lot better after she came home. Goofy as shit, definitely. But not so sad. Gotta give Rosie credit there. If it wasn't for her, I think Mom would've been a basket case for quite a while."

Patrick considered that thought. "What do you think of her? Rosie, I mean."

I looked at him in surprise. I didn't think my fondness for my old teacher was hidden from anyone, and I told him so.

"Yeah. I see that in you," he agreed. "Kind of a spooky little thing, though. You gotta admit that."

I grinned. Yeah. He was right about that. Spooky, but good. Plenty good for Paddy, I figured. An image formed in my mind of the four of them, Mom, Rose, Paddy, and Father Jack, sitting peacefully on the porch, looking out over the pasture to the woodlot.

"You ever hear her and Father Jack get into it?"

"Never met him," he reminded me. "But feel like I know him from your letters. Now there's a loon if there ever was one!" Patrick guffawed.

I grinned and told him about seeing my friend in Japan.

"Cosmic," Patrick shook his head in awe. "He showed up in the middle of Tokyo? Un-fucking believable."

"No shit," I laughed. I considered sharing one of my secrets about Father Jack with my twin, and before I could open my mouth, he heard my thoughts.

"What?"

I laughed. "You know, he was supplying me with condoms that summer before Jannie died."

"No way! No fucking shit!"

I explained how it had come to be as Patrick rocked his head back, laughing that only I could get a Catholic priest to provide me with birth control.

"Didn't matter, though," I said, soberly.

He looked at me sharply.

"Jannie wanted me to stop using them."

His eyes widened. "Really?"

I nodded.

"Whoa," he said quietly, registering the nuances of that. "Neat."

"Yeah." I looked deeply into my twin's eyes. Eva sighed deeply, stirring under my arm. She reached for my hand and snuggled it upon her breast.

Patrick watched her move closer to me. He dropped his head, looking at the woman sleeping upon his lap. Then he returned his gaze to meet mine. He nudged his nose toward Eva.

I nodded in understanding. My brother considered me the luckiest fucker in the world, having found love again.

"You better not hurt this woman," he said.

Again, I nodded. Not to worry.

Chapter Fifty
Airmail

January 29, 1968

DEAR EVA,

If I figure right, this is the fortieth day since I left you. I wonder, is this the fortieth letter I've written? I guess not. A few lines scribbled while I'm out in the bush can hardly be considered an entire letter, and on those days, I'm always sorry that I can't send you more. I can tell you though, my darling, that I am constantly writing to you in my mind. Can you hear me, I wonder, as I write you lines in my thoughts? Maybe just the energy that I'm using to think those thoughts somehow makes it to you, so many miles away. I hope so. I hope you know I think of you always.

What can I tell you about life in the Nam these days? I've been out of the bush for nearly a week now. Word is we'll be heading in again in a couple days. Back up to the northwest. We've seen so much troop movement recently. Something big is up out there. Doesn't seem to have discouraged Uncle Sam too much. What did our brilliant man at the top say? We've crossed the point at which the enemy can no longer replenish his troops as fast as we're wasting them? Westmoreland. What a moron! Fuck him. He doesn't like us Marines anyway.

I think you are right, what you said in your last letter. The last letter I got from you, anyway. The one dated New Year's Day. I think that as soon as I'm out of here, I'm going to buy a ticket and fly right to Europe and look into those schools you wrote about. In Munich. Or Basel. Or Brussels. Somewhere near you. No, somewhere with you. That could be America, too. If you wanted to try America. But maybe we could do that later. I think I would like to live in Europe for a while when I get out.

Eva, darling, I still find my brain just spinning around in my head, thinking that I was in Germany. In Regensberg. That I went there to see my brother, and I met you. How come it was so easy to love you? How could you possibly love me so easily? It's like we have always been two parts of a greater One, and didn't know it until we came together. And now that I am away from you, I feel that I know what Oneness is. I cherish that feeling. And I look with all my heart to when we can be One again, together. Always.

Love,

David

∞

What the hell? Patrick thought, as he watched the postman drop a packet of airmail envelopes into Eva's box. Doesn't that guy ever write me anymore? He rifled through his own mail. A note from Courtney. Damn, she'd been a worry. He hadn't seen her for five weeks, and this was the first contact she'd made. He felt a shiver of guilt; he hadn't called or written, either. The letter was brief and, like Courtney, liberating.

Bonn, February 10.

P,

I'm sorry. But I had fun.

C

Jesus, Patrick thought. *What the hell did she mean by that?*

What else could she possibly mean?

Patrick was still looking at the note when he heard Eva behind him. "Is everything all right?" she asked. "Is that a letter from David?"

"No," he answered absently, trying to reel in his thoughts, and then added gently, "You're the only one getting letters from David." He folded the single page and looked down at Eva with a smile. Her appearance startled him. She looked drawn and tired. "You okay?" he asked.

She dug out the envelopes from her mail box, and her pallid face brightened. "Fine, fine," she said. "Queasy is all."

"Oh," Patrick said. "Flu's been going around." He craned his neck to catch a glimpse of his brother's handwriting on the pages she leafed through like treasures.

"Mmm." She was already engrossed in the first letter.

"I was wondering, maybe you want to let me take a look at some of Davey's notes? Just like I let you read his before you stole all his attention?

Eva laughed at his teasing, and held her own. "You may look." She waved the letters at him. "But you will blush."

Patrick stopped short. "Damn. David getting mushy?"

She nodded smugly. "Always."

∞

April 4, 1968

Dear Pat,

Got your letters. Thanks. This is a twist, isn't it? Me apologizing to you for not writing often enough! Ha! Well, it's not that I've haven't been thinking of you. I have. Lots, really. It keeps me close to sane out here, thinking about the world that is not Vietnam. Thinking about how much fun we had in Regensberg. What a riot. Man, I'm sure glad I had that opportunity. Led to Eva, after all. Of course, that's why I don't write you. I start thinking about Thanksgiving, and your life at the Étage, and all. And then I get to thinking about Eva, and write her instead! Tough beans, Bro! But, man, all that time in Regensburg with you... it was great. It was like we had more time there in one month than we had at home in the past eight years.

Life with the Third Recon goes on. Man, things have changed in the Nam. Charlie has cranked things up a notch these past couple months. I'm out in the bush most all the time now. My squad is pretty tight. Not like before, but pretty good. We have a lot more rotation than before, guys coming in green all the time. Right now, four of our guys have a total of two months in-the-bush experience between them. Two guys with just one recon apiece, and another just busting his cherry. We insert in the morning, and he's about white with fear. As he well should be. But with almost half our force damn near brand new, we have to be extra careful. Got to have our eyeballs out double time. Looking for Charlie, and watching over the Cherries. That's the way it is. I was green, too, once.

Odd thing is, we haven't had a lot of wounded or casualties in our squad in the past month or so, since Charlie focused his Tet craziness on the cities. One guy is short—twenty more days and a wake up. That's Georgia. Byron Baker. Gonna miss him. He's tops in the bush. All eyes. Like a shadow. He's nothing but grins these days. I was telling him about your buddy, Lang, and how he walked the Appalachian trial. Georgia liked that idea so much, he's planning to do it, soon as he gets out. Crazy fucker. I had to ask him, with all the bush time he's put in, why would he want to jump right back in at home? He said being in the bush was the best part of being in Nam, which I guess I can understand. But even more than that, he said he figured he'd air it out, exorcise all the demons. Beat the bush back in the States, where peace rules and he wouldn't have anybody climbing out of bunkers and tunnels trying to zap him. No ambushes. Nothing but freedom and beauty. He says he's gonna walk all the way to the tip of the trail, and then cut on over to the ocean and eat fresh Maine lobster till he pukes. Sounds good to me, too! At least the lobster.

So Georgia'll be gone soon, and we've had a couple other seasoned guys that had to leave for medical reasons. One guy, Dubois, came down with this skin rot, where the insides of his thighs and armpits and elbows kept getting progressively redder. Then the skin under the rash sloughed off and he was raw to the flesh. It hurt to look at. And it smelled. Man, we were out in the bush when it really deteriorated, and I could smell him rotting from six feet away. I knew if I could smell him, so could Charlie. He was a good Marine, good Recon. He left in early February, right after all hell broke loose in the Tet. Good timing. I hear they took him back to the States, to Bethesda. Trying to figure out what's making him rot like that. Man, it was like leprosy.

Another guy, Zonie, rotated back after his tour ended last month. Randall. A Navajo. That's the way it is. The experienced guys who you can trust with your back, well, they get short and then they wake up, step on a chopper, and head the hell out of here. Four months left for me. Not that short. Not short enough to flaunt to the newbies. Georgia's our short man. Then Buckeye, a guy from Ohio. He's got less than a month. Then me. Four fucking months. Not even. One-oh-three and a wake up. Fly the big bird, then muster on out. Get my life back. Home. Here I come.

So no more Courtney? What's the deal there? Man, she was a wild woman in some ways, much to your benefit. I liked her, though. So intense. Passionate. I imagine you liked that about her, too. But she's out of the picture now, eh? Well, too bad. She was all right. But was she for you? I dunno. Sorry about that, though.

And Cindy's found herself the One and Only, eh? A professor, much less. Makes sense, her finding someone cerebral enough to fascinate and entertain her. Wonder if he can make field goals, though? I imagine. Least ways with Cindy holding his balls for him! Ha.

Maybe it's time you stuck to your own treasure hunt. Remember the stuff I told you about, in my closet under Aunt Kate's stairs.

Well, I gotta go. Help the Cherries figure out how to tape things down and run silent in the bush. Last thing we wanna hear is lots of click and clack out there.

Take care, Twinnie. Keep an eye on my Eva for me. Tell her I love her. That's the hardest part, man. Just thinking, the Corps owns my ass. I'm on hold. I have no life of my own. And there is a lot of living I want to be doing. And I want to be doing it with Evie. Tell her that for me, will you? Shit, I know, I tell her that in all the letters I write her. But you're my brother, man. My twin. Make it real for her. Tell her for me.

Thanks,

David

∞

April 4, 1968

My dear David,

When I receive your letters, my heart leaps with joy and relief. We heard so much on the news about that Tet offense and how the North Vietnamese attacked so aggressively. Can they keep on? I am concerned every moment of the day, David. Only when I get one of your letters do I have a moment when I feel free from the oppression of fear. I hear your voice in each of your words. I feel your love. I need you so.

Your letters bear also your angst and frustration. Is it not unjust that you must do this duty, you ask? Is it not contrary to your nature, your character? Your creed? I know it is. And yet, you choose to conform. This is a strong decision. You ask yourself, are you placing a false god, your government, the Marine Corps, before the One God? I think this is so. You wonder if you would have been more true to your ideals and beliefs had you fled to Canada? I say that is a moot question, because what you have now, you have chosen. And by doing so, you met me. And that was meant to be. I believe you when you say that no accidents happen, that fate is not a whim. I believe in purpose in life. I believe, too, in purpose in love.

This love of ours has indeed become bigger than both of us, David. It has taken on its own purpose. My suspicions are true. Your child is with me. My doctor tested me. I am so grateful. And I feel strongly that the baby is a girl. If I am correct, David, I know in my heart that we will name our daughter Janet. I hope you find joy in this. We will call her Jannie.

I hope I am worthy of being your child's mother. I know how difficult it will be if you don't return to me, but I trust with all my heart that you will. I know that if you can, you will. Knowing that gives me peace. And joy. I know you will. You must!

In the darkest moments, I admit, I fear your never returning. I fear that you have left your child as my father left me, and as yours left you, with nothing more than a mystery, an echo ringing in the fog. Who is my father, this child may ask. And why did he make me if he could do no more than leave me? Like me, you know these questions well. I pray our child never does. But my faith is troubled, David. I have no vision of us ever having more than the vivid days we have already shared. I am worried, my love.

If I must, I will tell our child of our love, of your love for me, and mine for you. But will my words be empty to her, if she knows you only through your genes? And my memories? I cherish your letters, which remind me that you are real, and alive, and that you were here with me, not just in my imagination. I read and reread of the passion of our life together in the pages of my journal. And now I carry you both in my heart and in my womb. I shall never be able to separate myself from you. For that, I am grateful. I never felt more alive than when we were one together. My life is marked by our being one. If I have no more than the ringing echoes of your life and love, I am better for it, my love.

I believe that I am meant to be the mother of our children. I believe that, David. And I long for you to be with me, to be the father of my children. They will have such a good father in you. That, I am sure.

I am with you always. You are in my thoughts and heart always.

There is no other way.

Your loving Soul Mate,

Eva

PATRICK SAT ON A WOODEN BENCH in the nearly abandoned rail station in Bonn. He had never felt so alone. Not when he moved out to Boulder. Not when he came over to Germany. Not even when he'd left the farm for the Dunes. Now, he was absolutely on his own.

Courtney had turned on him. She'd gone berserk, hitting him and slapping at his face. Telling him how much she hated him. He couldn't figure. They'd had such a good time together, he thought. It'd be a nice surprise to come up to Bonn to be with her for Easter. Have some fun. Cheer her up. Not the way she saw it, evidently. She was so bitter and angry. Kept on telling him he was so selfish, self-absorbed, self-centered. Didn't want to do anything but get stoned and screw. Or drink. Patrick shook his head. That was what she was all about, too. He hadn't seen it coming.

He rummaged through his pack for David's last letter. He opened it up and skimmed it once, and then again. He didn't know how many times he'd already read it; he practically knew it by heart. He heard David's voice with every word. His brother was out there, fighting in a goddamn war, doing what he had to do, and just keeping on. And Patrick could hardly figure out how to keep himself going.

Four more months, David had. Four lousy months. *That's all I have here,* Patrick reflected. And even though things had turned to shit in Germany, it was still nothing like the time Davey would be putting in.

Patrick didn't know how his brother could put up with four more months in Nam. Just having him there was killing Patrick with anxiety. There wasn't much that worried Patrick, but David's presence there hung suspended in his consciousness, gnawing at him. He couldn't image handling it himself.

Hell, he could hardly handle the little things. His brother was dealing with tunnels and Tet, and he couldn't even deal with classes and girls. David was always saying, don't sweat the small stuff. Shit. Small stuff. Davey would explain, its only ten percent real, and ninety percent how you react to it. Damn. Sometimes it seemed more like a hundred-ninety percent real. Like this Courtney thing. Jesus.

He reread the letter dangling in his fingers. He and David were both having a problem of keeping friends. But Davey's friends all had to go, one way or another. They were desperately hoping to escape. Make it out of the Nam, or else leave in a bag. His friends, well, that was a different case. They were fleeing as well. Fleeing him. Trying to make it, to find some sort of peace. Some sort of stability. Some semblance of reality.

How will I? Patrick wondered.

An engine fired up at the very end of the terminal. A single, brilliant light shone from the nose of the train, filling the vast, empty rail house with a silvery sheen. The light was blinding, even from a distance. He closed his eyes and considered his options. Maybe it was time to start anew.

What was the thing about the stuff under the stairs? He'd have to write Davey and ask. He had a vague recollection, but couldn't quite recall what he'd said. He sat, wondering.

He recalled Lang's words about hiking in the States. Doing the Trail. Sniffing the fresh mountain air. Seeing the light at daybreak. Finding your soul.

After a few moments, he got up, shouldered his duffle, and headed back toward the ticket clerk. He bought another ticket, not to Regensburg, but to Luxembourg. From there, he could catch a Loftleiðir flight back to the States. To Bangor, Maine. From Bangor, he could catch a flight south. To Georgia. To the Trail.

He felt immediate relief. He was heading home.

Chapter Fifty-Two

Butterfly

AT DAWN ON THE FOURTH DAY, we heard the stirrings of troops on the move, a muffled shuffling in the jungle to our west. It was our first contact since the drop on Thursday morning. Holy fucking Thursday. That would make this Easter. And that wasn't a bunch of Easter bunnies coming down the mountainside.

The slow, determined pace of the enemy chilled me. They weren't traveling. They were hunting. Had they detected us? How? We'd been pretty much invisible since hunkering down late yesterday afternoon. Had they spotted movement when we'd taken our turns relieving ourselves? Had they caught scent? Often enough, I'd picked up Charlie's presence by no more than a change in the air, the hint of organic, humid, human scents, sweat, the sweet smell of urine, wafting carelessly in the breeze, betraying soldiers who were otherwise meticulously discriminate in their invisibility. A rice fart is pungent in the bush. So is a C-ration fart. Worse. Exponentially worse. Break wind after Beans and Motherfuckers and it had *USA* printed all over it.

Had they detected us?

From the hill on my left, the trail ran down toward the creek bottom on my right, with its closest point no more than fifteen yards from our observation point. The foliage in front of us was dense, but it cleared around the path a short ways downhill. In the dawn light filtering through the canopy, I studied the patterns of the breeze flickering the tall grasses and jungle plants. A crosswise movement caught my eye; as the sun breached an opening near the trail, it spotlighted a butterfly slowly flapping its wings, drying off the night's dew. It had best get clear of here, I thought. Something more ominous was moving in from the left. The sounds filtered down the hill, dispersing into the jungle. Charlie was tiptoeing along the hillside on our left flank.

Georgia was dug in on the left point. Damn, I wondered if he regretted coming along on this trip right about now. He was shorter than short. Extract in two days, debrief, two more wake-ups and outta here. He had a ticket waiting for him. He could have stayed back in. The Captain even made the offer. Georgia's nuts, though. He couldn't see sitting on his cot, knowing we were out here making do without him. I'd bet he wasn't even thinking about it now. He'd be nothing but ears and eyes, not thoughts, not regrets. Georgia was the real all-here-right-now. I knew I could count on him. We all did. That's why none of us were surprised when he just saddled up like nothing was different.

So now he held down the left flank with the Cherry, then Rueben a couple yards in, and then Doc, then me. Buckeye with the radio and Nesmith flanking me on the right. I was less than six good strides from Georgia, but I couldn't see him at all. Reuben turned his head slowly, his eyes wide. He tipped a finger to point uphill. I couldn't see them. Not a flicker in the brush, nothing. Just the soft rustling of organic matter brushing aside as they inched down on us.

The butterfly took to wing in the sun filtering through the branches to the east. It fluttered aimlessly, testing its wings, then suddenly steered our way, dipping and rising as if drunk on the pure morning light. I swear, I felt the breeze from its wing as it fluttered past my face.

To my left, a footstep scuffled on the jungle humus.

The grenade landed with a gentle thud, rolling clumsily through the brush to stop a couple yards in front of Reuben. The flash was brilliant white. Buckeye lit up the Claymores and everybody opened up, the bark of AK-47s and the snap of our 16s roaring in the morning stillness.

ᴙ

December 21, 1967

Dear Mom,

Well, if you're reading this, you know I've died. This is that letter that we all dread writing, and that I'm sure you've dreaded reading.

I'm on the plane right now, with Colonel Whitney. I left Germany on Monday by train, arrived in Paris yesterday morning, and now I'm somewhere over India, I suppose, heading back to the Nam. I can't say I feel good about it. From what the Colonel says, we can expect a whole basket full of woe from Charlie once we get back in the bush. We'll be trying to figure where he's going with all his troops. He's really stepped things up the last few weeks. What's he up to? I'm sure we'll find out....

I'll be back in the bush pretty much right away, Colonel Whitney says. I guess I figured as much. I'll finish this letter up, and give it to him, in the event... which I hope will never happen. If it does, well, he'll send it on to you, he's promised.

I'm pretty well healed and rested up now, and have gotten back in decent shape. I suppose I'll feel the strain when I get back to hiking those mountains. But I'm ready for it. Physically, anyway. Mentally? Emotionally? I don't know. I don't know if anybody can ever be ready for it, that way.

Mom, I have more reason than ever not to want to go back to the war. I met a friend of Patrick's in Regensburg. Her name is Eva. And she has filled my heart with a love I've never known before. She has filled the void in my heart that was left after Jannie died. I feel whole again, for the first time, really, since Jannie. I have always known that Jannie taught me how to love in such a special way, and before she died she often told me that I would find someone whom I could love the way she taught me to. I was never sure that I could do that—love someone more than I love Jannie. I still love her. And yet now I know that she was right. I have found Eva. I feel like Jannie knew I would, and is smiling because I did. I found someone to love again. And now I have to leave her. I can't believe that I found her, and I'm going back to war. I have no right to choose to stay with her. I have no will of my own right now. And I think that's a shame. And a sin. I gave my will away. My will, and my life.

And now I'm writing you this, confessing to you that I believe I did wrong. If I have any luck at all, any blessing, I know you'll never see this. But if you're reading this, then you know. No such luck. No such blessing.

It's a funny thing. I've always felt blessed. I mean, look at what I've had in life. You. Paddy. My Twinnie. Auntie Kate. Gabriel. Jannie. Our home, the farm, and all that I've been able to do there. I can't believe I built up one of the best dairy herds in the state. I'm grateful that I was lucky enough to breed Flash and Lightning, and then the Elevator. I know that between the girls in the herd and the co-op contract, you and Patrick will never have to go wanting. I'm grateful I could do that.

I think of how life was, growing up without Dad. I realize now how lonely that must have been for you. And I understand why it was so hard on you. I can only imagine how your heart hurt all those years. And I understand. I'm sorry that I may be leaving you, too. Like Dad left you. With just memories, with just the echoes of our being. I want you to know that all the memories I have of you, good times and tough times, are filled with love. I'm so grateful that you are my mom. I'm so grateful for the past couple years, since you got home. I'm so grateful for Rosie. For her being such a good friend to you. Seems like she showed you the way through the woods. I took care of Rosie, too, in my will. You'll see. I am so grateful for her and the education she gave me. And how she was there for us when Jannie died. And when you came home.

If I do die, if you are reading this, then you'll know that I will have regrets. Not for what I did—except for the big one, choosing to give away my choice. But for things I won't get to do. I will regret not being able to share old age with you, yours and mine. I'll regret not having the time to run into Mrs. Whitman in the Co-op, or to feed Cherub another apple. I'll regret not shooting the breeze with Father Jack again. Thank God for Father Jack. He is one of the greatest blessings in my life.

And Paddy. I'll regret not being with Paddy. I think of the hours and hours that Paddy and I were together. Often not saying much. Not needing to. Going through the entire milk line without more than a word or two. Just being with each other. And then, when he did share his mind, it was so heartfelt. So clear. Like the St. Mary's bell knoll tolling in across the pastures. Soft, clear, pure. Paddy was my Dad. He is how I know the meaning of that word. I hope you don't take that wrong, or that it wounds you further. Paddy is Father to me. And I'm grateful for him.

Mom, writing this is odd. It is like I'm breathing the Truth. Basking in the Truth. Facing the Truth. Why one has to wait until he writes "The Letter" to confront and admit what is good and meaningful in life, I don't know.

Mom, I also want to confess something else to you. I read your writings. While you were away, I read them all. You write so beautifully. You inspire me. I know that I transgressed into your mind and heart where I was not invited. I want to say, Mom, that at times—just sometimes—I wanted to shout at you, tell you that you were wrong. Absolutely wrong. The guilt you bore, the blame you cast upon yourself for being a "lousy, frail mother" was wrong. I have loved you every day of my life. Every day you were home with us. Every day you were away. I loved you then, and I love you now. And I forgive you for bearing that guilt. I know it was just one way you loved us. But it was needless guilt, Mom. I love you for all you have given me. For all that you are.

And I know my twin feels the same. We talked about it in Germany. Patrick still wonders about why he was sent away, but he is not angry. He gained so much by leaving, and he knows it. If anything, he feels too much guilt himself. He believes that he drove you crazy. That is something I know you'll be able to fix. Neither of you need to keep carrying the guilt that you feel about abandoning one another. We all did what we had to, and we are all better for it. We did the best with what we were given, and we were given a lot. Starting with one another. We were given the best.

Mom, I feel so ALIVE! It is hard to imagine that you will have to read this because I am not. It is hard to imagine what it would be like to be dead. I have so much to live for. Remember that night when you first came home, and you and Rosie and I sat around the kitchen table and talked and talked? And you told us how you felt alive again? I feel that way now. I can't imagine never sitting with you at the kitchen table again, or watching a sunset from the porch, or sipping lemonade atop a wagonful of hay bales.

I believe that if I am not blessed to do all that—physically, anyway—that my spirit, my soul will be with you. And Paddy. And Patrick. But particularly with you.

Listen for me.

I'll be there.

You will never be alone, Mom.

I will be there.

And I'll always be grateful. Thank you for life.

Your loving son,

David

☙

On Mother's Day morning, the warm fragrance of coffee permeated the crowded kitchen and living room of the Joyce farmhouse, mixed with aromas of sweet cinnamon and rich roast beef. A soft murmur of voices burbled through the house as friends and family convened in David's honor.

When it seemed that the old farmhouse could hold no more, Paddy stood and cleared his throat, and the group fell silent. He spoke more softly than ever, although strength rumbled from deep within his chest. "Father Jack sent this along. He found it in his readings, and said that it must have been written about David. He asked that I read it for him. I only wish he was here to read it himself." He cleared his throat again, then took a deep breath, and read Jack's letter.

"He died for Nothing.
For Nothing could stop him from dying.
It took the force of war for him to die,
So strong was the spark of life,
So bright the light of life,
So vital the vigor of life
Within him."

Paddy folded the page and tucked it safely in his shirt pocket as he looked around the room. Beneath their tears, a glow of love shone from the eyes of those around him. He nodded his recognition. "I think we're all here because we are grateful for having David in our lives," he said. Then, he sat quietly in the chair at the table.

Rosie poured a steaming cup of coffee and offered it to Paddy, and another to Elle. She made the rounds among the guests, refilling cups and encouraging everyone to enjoy the treats, many of which were David's favorites.

Soon, the gentle hum of polite condolences was spiked with bursts of laughter, as a friend or relative related a uniquely David moment. Disappearing school desks led to a steer wearing a babushka on its docked tail, and then fond recollections of a runty boxer in gloves bigger than he was, taking on opponents twice his size. When Paddy surprised them all with an amazingly accurate and vivid rendition of Davey miming his brother feeding his face, the entire group was reduced first to tears of joy and laughter, and then tears of love. They spent the day, celebrating, feasting, and feeding off the love focused within David's family.

After dessert—gallons of homemade ice cream and the famous Joyce chocolate sauce—the guests lingered in the house, while Paddy, Elle, Kate, Rose, and the Whitmans walked together across the alfalfa stand before the woodlot, following a swath that Paddy had mowed through the lush first crop, due for harvest in another week. Paddy carried the cherrywood urn as Rose led them through the fence line into the marsh, along the deer path leading back toward the hillside. They trooped up the slope, huffing and puffing, pacing themselves together, letting no one lag. When they arrived at the bluff overlooking the marsh, the sky was hinting at a delicate, rosy sunset.

Without a word, David's most beloved huddled around Paddy and the urn he embraced. They wrapped their arms around him, and each other. They stood in silence, strong in their love for their son, their friend, their loved one. Together, they began to sway, warm in their shared embrace. Sweet, thrumming notes arose from Helen Whitman's chest, growing as they reverberated outward. With her eyes closed, rocking with the others, Helen hummed the melody of their children's favorite, the Air. After a few bars, Steven Whitman joined in, taking the lower cello's part over which his wife's voice floated.

When the final measures had fallen away, Rosie opened the urn. She looked into Elle's eyes. David's mother reached into the urn and scooped a mound of her son's remains into her hands. She turned and walked to the edge of the bluff, and as if she were setting a bird to wing, she tossed the ashes into the breeze. David's ashes flowed upward in a wide arc, then drifted downward to the earth.

Rosie followed Elle's lead, as did the Whitmans, and then Kate. Rosie took the urn from Paddy, allowing him the chance to sow David to the earth. She tipped the last of the ashes into Paddy's big, calloused dairyman's hands. He cupped the remains as he would the most tender of babes. Tears streamed down his face as he held the ashes before his heart. He moved his eyes from Elle to Rose, then to each of the Whitmans, and finally to his sister.

"My life would have meant little, but for this boy," he whispered. He turned away from the bluff, taking several steps toward the hillside. He spread the ashes among the ferns, trillium, and May flowers along the deer path running past the downed bole of an ancient pine tree. He took back the urn from Rosie, turning it upside down to empty any last ash on the hillside. He turned back to his kin and friends.

"I am honored to have been a father to David."

Then, with Rosie on one arm and Kate the other, he led David's funeral procession home.

∞

While the guests rummaged on the leftovers of the feast, Elle gently laid her hand inside the arm of her friend, Helen Whitman. She led her toward her bedroom in the back of the house. "Helen," she began, "David sent me a letter. I thought you might take joy in it, as well as sorrow. David loved you, and he loved your daughter. I think he would want you to know what he shared with me before he died."

She offered the pages to Jannie's mother, and sat with her on the edge of the bed, slipping her arm around her friend's waist as she let her read the last message from her son. Helen struggled to get through the letter, pausing several times as her shoulders shook with sobs. When at last she finished, she folded the letter along its creases and set it in Elle's lap. Wrapping her arms around David's mother, Helen wept, memories of her daughter and Elle's son keen in her heart. Elle hugged her close, and they nurtured one another with the special love of mothers who bury their children.

When she could speak, Helen asked, "Elle, what do you know of Eva? What can Patrick tell us?"

Elle tilted her head and looked into the distance. "We don't know where Patrick is. He seems to have left Germany. We don't even know whether he is aware that David is dead." Helen caught her breath, both at Elle's words and her matter-of-fact demeanor.

Calmly, Elle reached to her bedside table for another envelope. "But this is more about Eva. It is a letter from her to David. It was in his belongings, which were delivered on Friday. Helen, it hadn't been opened." She carefully extracted the letter from its envelope and unfolded the pages. She held Eva's letter out for Helen to see.

Helen glanced at the letter, then back to Elle, puzzled. It was dated April 4, 1968, and it was written in French.

"I can read it for you," Elle said. She took a breath and focused her eyes on Eva's script.

"My dear David…,"

Book Three
The Good Guys

…If you are none of these
you can be sure it will kill you too,
but there will be no special hurry.

– Ernest Hemingway, A Farewell to Arms

June 21, 1968

HERE I AM, sitting in the dark side of dawn, waiting for the sun to peek up in the east, bringing on a whole new day of I don't know what. More Trail, I suppose. Or maybe I'll savor the solstice all day, right here, on top of the Pinnacle. Some days, I just don't feel like moving on, and that's okay. Moving on to what? I ask myself. Today feels like that kind of day. Just sit back and see what it brings.

It's our birthday today, mine and Twinnie's. I like our birthday being the longest day of every year. All the days leading up to it get a little longer, the sun gets a little higher in the sky. I've never noticed it as much as this year, though, being out on the Trail from dawn until dusk, every day, rain or shine. The longer the day, the more ground I put behind me.

It's worked to my advantage, too. The shorter days of April meant I had more time at night to rest and recoup after a day's hike. I mean, when I first hit the Trail, I couldn't even go the entire day. I did it all wrong, of course. Tried going ten miles a day right off the bat. Yeah. Ha. Day two, hot spots. Day three, blisters erupting like mushrooms. Day four, bloody socks. Days five through nine, sit on my ass in a soaking spring rain, watching the Georgia hillsides turn blue and green through the mist. Smoking like a chimney. I must have gone through half of what Davey left me in Germany in those four days. I thought I was soul searching. I think now, I was hiding from it. Smoking till I was numb. Smoking until I dreamed of Rosie, telling me I was acting like I had no family.

But I've aired out a bit since then. A bit. Still, I'm sitting here, looking out to the east over the patchwork quilt of the farmland below, lit up all silver by the last rays of the full moon dipping behind the ridge to the west. A soft blue tinge creeps up from the horizon in the east, absorbing the low-lying stars, letting me know that there will indeed be a dawn today. And I can't keep out the thought, wouldn't this be even better if I were high? Wouldn't it be so fucking far out that it would blow my mind? I look around and answer myself, how could it be? How could it be any better at all? It might be. Just light up. Just free up my mind. Fuck. No. Not today. Not my birthday. Not yesterday. Not tomorrow. I've had enough. For now, anyway. It's nice that I can go miles now without thinking about it. Letting it rest. Having it let me rest. Five weeks, I've made it. I don't think there were five days I haven't been rocked out for the past two years. Now I've gone five whole fucking weeks. And yet it still gnaws at me. Not as hard. Not as persistent. But it's there.

I'm anxious for the sun to come up this morning. I want to look at the map. From here, I can see the lights of Allentown, due east. I know the highway heads north from there, then meets the Trail, maybe forty miles from where I sit. I might get off there. It's been almost two months, and it isn't even my dream, after all. It's Lang's. Or Barney's. It's somebody else's. I'm tired of chasing somebody else's dreams.

That's one thing I've come to on this pilgrimage. I don't want to chase somebody else's dreams anymore. I want to make my own dreams happen. I'm pretty clear on that now. After five weeks of fresh air to my brain, I feel pretty confident that my own dreams are sweet. My own dreams are more real. How could I have ever lost sight of them to begin with? It wasn't just the dope. Nope. That didn't help, for sure. But I'd lost focus long before I started the wake-and-bake routine. That's pretty clear to me now. I left my dreams along the way, surrendered to whatever circumstances I encountered. I got used to accepting the limitations of my experiences, rather than exploring all my options.

What do I mean by that? I ask myself that all the time. I've always done it that way. But I want to do something else now.

It's like when I moved to the Dunes, to Aunt Mary's. I just constantly reacted. I figured out everyone else's expectations, and I met them, precisely. I stepped right up to the boundaries of those expectations, and never crossed over them. I responded to how everyone perceived me, a big, dumb jock, and I fulfilled their vision. I knew all the parents looked at me from under their brows, thinking, *this is the son of the crazy woman*. It mattered. I reacted to it. In Indiana, and even more back home, playing ball for Baraboo, being the star.

That's all I was then: the jock. The running back. I ran to the cheers of the fans. And the fans made me their hero. They didn't want to know about the head inside that helmet, or the heart under the pads, covered by that Baraboo jersey. They wanted to see themselves as number twenty-one. They wanted to project everything they could identify about winning from within themselves, and pin it on number twenty-one, and have me carry the ball for them. And I did, with all my heart. I wanted to do it more than anything, I realize. I wanted to be their hero. I wanted to be my hero, too. But I sold myself short.

It was even worse in Boulder. I mean, that was a full-time job, training and playing at CU. Davey asked how I could walk away from it so easily? Walking away from football was like sucking in the greatest breath of fresh air I'd ever taken. I felt liberated. Free. Yeah, it took some getting used to. I mean, I thought of myself as the jock, too. It made me wonder, who the hell am I, really, without football? How long had I put all my energy into playing sports? All of my focus? So long that anything really important to me evaporated right in front of my eyes, like the heat waves above the beach along Lake Michigan.

Clarity dissipates, and with it, the things of most importance. Like Lynn. I mean, she was like the best birthday present I ever got. Seeing her for the first time on my birthday. Having her for the first time on my birthday. I mean, Lynn—it was meant to be Lynn for me. With her, those expectations, those boundaries, they didn't exist. We just… were. How could I have ever let her out of my life? How could I ever have kept her in my life? I don't know. Were there answers to those questions once, long since evaporated? Will I ever know? I don't know.

From the valley below, the lowing of cattle rises to urgent crescendo as the dawn casts rosy hues in the east. The cows want in. They want to get milked. So they sing. As if in response, my hiking partner sighs and hums a note, seated on a rock alongside me. He was already up and keeping a vigil, facing east, when I awakened an hour ago. He doesn't sleep much.

We joined paths a few days back, on the other side of the ferry north of Skyland, in Virginia. Together, we've kept a swift pace. Yesterday, we started at dawn, a few miles west of the Susquehanna and covered more than thirty miles to get here in the late afternoon. Over the campfire, we shared a few stories and a little grub, watching night capture the Trail. The moon didn't rise until almost midnight. It didn't get high enough over the canopy to pour its silver light down into our campsite until the very early hours before dawn. Maybe that's what awakened me. Barney was already up, though, keeping watch.

I don't know whether I'll move on with him this morning, if he keeps hiking north. I may just stay here till mid-day, then head over toward the highway. I'll consider it a little more. But it feels like the right thing to me. I think it's time to go home.

∞

By the time the sun breached the sky, my new partner and I were ready to resume our daily routine. I fumbled through my pack, looking for a few breakfast provisions. I watched him stretch, pull on his socks and boots, and roll up his bed with an ease of movement that reflected his experience in the woods. He was traveling extremely light, a skill I'd grown to appreciate wholeheartedly. He had some sturdy hiking boots, military issue, but not like the kind you can get at the Army surplus store. His were jungle boots, the kind with the camouflage sidings, and they were worn. He toted only a small pack with a few essentials and a bedroll comprising a lightweight wool blanket and a wrap of parachute silk he'd "procured," he said, when he was on active duty. Traveling unencumbered, he claimed. A couple days earlier, he'd mentioned that he'd just gotten out of the service. He'd not said much more.

"Java?" I asked quietly. I'd started a small fire and was heating water to brew coffee.

"I'd be most appreciative," he smiled, drawing his words out like soft, stretched yarns of taffy. He hadn't said a whole lot along the Trail, but he'd loosened up some around the fire each night. I'd immediately been charmed by his southern drawl, the way his words slid right into low, rumbling chuckling and rolling rounds of laughter as he talked of life along the Trail, or his family back home in Georgia.

He offered his empty tin cup, and I poured the hot brew from my cup to fill his. He sipped his coffee, looking out over his steaming cup to survey the farmland below. He nodded, first at his coffee, then at the land below. "Makes for a mighty fine day."

"Yeah," I agreed. "And it's my birthday, to boot."

A pleasant grin spread slowly across Barney's face. He projected his emotions much like he spoke, long and deliberate, complete but with no wasted energy. He extended his hand. "Well, happy birthday, Pat."

I took his hand, which he held firm but not tight. Some men grasp fiercely, clamping down to assert their character. Others offer limp fingertips like boneless trout fillets, leaving me uneasy and alarmed. Barney's handshake was reserved, respectful, defined. It told me that he knew his position in this world, and was comfortable there. His grip was honest and open, inviting but not imposing. True. Last night, by the light of the embers and the silver illumination of the rising moon, he spoke of redefining himself on the Trail. I didn't know what he meant; he already seemed decent and genuine to me. The real thing.

"So how old are you?" he enquired.

"Twenty-two."

"Sweet Jesus," he chuckled. "You had me fooled. I'd have guessed a few years older, maybe 'cause you're so damn big. I'll be twenty myself, come July."

I laughed. "You should have seen me at the beginning of the Trail," I said. "I was a lot bigger. This dirt path has melted forty or fifty pounds of German beer and sausage right off me."

He let his eyes seek the far ridge. Barney often scanned the distance, probing the shadows under trees and alongside rocks and ledges. His eyes moved smoothly, taking in detail I knew I was oblivious of. When he rested his gaze on my face, I felt as if he measured every cell within me.

"I did spot you a couple times, early on," he admitted. "No doubt, you've burned off your baby fat. But it only makes you look older. More mature."

I asked him when he'd seen me, and he explained that he first caught sight of me within a hundred miles of Springer Mountain, sitting in the woods, smoking a joint. So probably in my first week, I figured, right after my blisters had calmed down. A couple weeks later, he'd felt the urge to sit a spell and found himself a place of power amidst a pine grove overlooking the Trail. He set up under an improvised lean-to, taking in the sky. He'd been camped there for three days when I trudged by again.

"You were stepping a whole lot more comfortably than the first time I spotted you tip-toeing off the Trail," he laughed. "But you looked like you were still stoned out of your mind. I'm surprised you got this far without getting lost."

I felt a blush warm my face. I had been that easy to read? Why did I ever think that nobody could tell when I was wrecked?

"Pretty lucky," I admitted. "I've aired it out since then. Haven't lit up in over a month."

Barney nodded. "Me neither." His gaze focused on me another moment. "It was getting in the way."

"Whaddya mean?"

He scanned the horizon again, then studied the ground in front of where he sat with his legs folded comfortably underneath him. He looked as though he could nestle in among the rocks and boulders along the ledge of the Pinnacle and disappear completely. "Means that I started this old Trail in pretty rough shape. I kind of figured I was, just getting outta the service and all. But it wasn't until I heard myself fucking up the peace along the Trail that I realized I was out of control."

"I never heard you," I reassured him. "I can't say I even noticed you. Wasn't like you were bothering anyone. I never knew you were there."

He grimaced, glancing at me quickly, then back at the far ridge. "Wasn't like... noise." He spit. "Maybe inner noise, more likely. I was screaming so loud on the inside, I couldn't suck in the peace all around me. Shit, it's not like I disturbed other hikers. Maybe the wildlife. The deer. Even the fucking birds were scarce, at first. But not the hikers. Hell, there haven't been more than a couple dozen hikers anyway. I don't know that more than a couple even picked up on me at all, anywhere."

I sure hadn't. I wondered why. He'd seen me several times, by his account. I asked why he stepped up and joined me just before crossing the Virginia state line.

"Looked like you were making the walk through to the end," he replied. "And if you are, I thought we might as well get to know one another. I'm figuring on being in Maine by mid-September. You?"

I paused, looking out to the east. The sun had risen, and the day was warming. "Funny you should ask just now. I dunno," I said. "I figured I was, when I first started out. Hadn't really given much thought to not finishing. I figured, if you start it, you finish it." I plucked a stem of mountain grass from a crack on the boulders against which we were leaning. The tender end was slightly bitter between my teeth. "But just this morning, before dawn, I kind of figured that I've done as much of the Trail as I needed to. Like it wasn't really my idea to do it in the first place. I just took someone else's dream, and used it to fill some time, get my thoughts straight. Now, I'm feeling the call of other things. Home. I guess."

He nodded, his gaze measuring me once again. He looked at me with a curiosity that could have made me paranoid, were he not so calm. "What?" I asked, amused. "You're looking at me like you recognize me."

"Naw," he grunted. "Not really. You seem kind of familiar. You talk like someone I knew. You from Wisconsin? You kind of sound like it."

I laughed. "You betcha! That's where I think I'm heading. Get off the Trail up near Lehigh. Hitch a ride to the interstate and turn west. Heading home. I haven't been home in over two years."

He nodded, plucking his own shaft of grass and inserting it between his teeth, twitching it up and down with his lips.

I told him about having been out of the country since the previous summer. He shrugged, saying, "Yeah, me too."

"Oh, yeah? Where?" Would he talk about his service, I wondered?

"The Nam." He looked again to the distance.

I'd suspected as much. But he didn't offer any more.

"My brother's there," I said. "My twin." I grinned. "It's his birthday today, too!"

"That so," he said without a smile. "Celebrating his birthday in the Nam. Happy birthday, bro. Where he's at?"

I shook my head. "Don't know, exactly. He's with the Marines. Someplace up north, I think. Third Recon, or something like that? He says he's in the highlands a lot."

Barney paled in the early morning's light. The blade of coarse grass sticking from his mouth suddenly stilled. He narrowed his eyes, examining me again. "Your brother. What's his name?"

"David," I answered. "David Joyce. You ever heard of him?"

Barney's eyes blazed, still narrowed, glistening in the light from the rising sun. He nodded. "Squirrel," he said. "We called him Squirrel." He leveled his eyes, looking directly into mine. "He was the real thing, man. Your brother, he was there all the way."

He lowered his head, and a tear trickled down his cheek. I felt my heart collapse inside my chest. A great, painful void lurched open within me as I read Barney's face.

"Of all the fucking people in the world to run into on this godforsaken Trail, I meet up with you," he said. "Squirrel's fucking brother. His goddamn twin. He told me about you. Lots of times. Played football, didn't you? He just saw you in Germany, what, at Thanksgiving?"

I nodded. I couldn't speak. The burning in my chest rose to my throat, lodging like a lump of dry, hard bread.

He grimaced again, then softened around his eyes. "He's dead, you know."

I shook my head. I didn't know.

"Yeah," he paused. "I was there." His eyes returned to narrow, angry slits. He rummaged through his pack until he found a baggie with a joint. "I was with him." He rolled the number carefully between his fingers and thumbs. "Yeah. I helped pull him out," he said softly. Then his eyes widened in astonishment. "Man, you better get off the Trail. You best go home. Jesus tits! How could you not even have known?"

Barney—Georgia, he told me, is what David called him—broke camp with me. He stuck his number up behind his ear and trekked along the Trail with it as though it were a reminder. Something he wanted to remember, but not yet touch.

We hiked together to Lehigh, sharing everything we knew about David as we hiked. We covered the forty miles in two days. At the crossing, we shook hands, and I thanked him. He nodded, turned, and walked on up the Trail, heading for Maine. I watched him go. The joint stuck out from under his shaggy hair, untouched.

Then I turned on the shoulder of the road, stuck out my thumb, and caught the first semi heading north to the intersection with the interstate.

I was heading home.

∞

As I rode semis across Pennsylvania, Ohio, and Indiana, or hunkered down in campgrounds and rest stations to wait out the rains that made it so hard to hitch rides, I pieced together a timeline. Davey must have died just about the time I left Germany. I wondered if Eva knew. And what about Mom, and Paddy, and all the folks back home? They had to know already. I tried calling from a couple of different truck stops along the way, but no one ever picked up the phone. I guess they weren't expecting me to call.

Chapter Fifty-Four

Home Again

NO ONE WAS HOME. Walking up the road, I thought for sure I'd see Mom in the garden, or on the porch, writing her endless letter to herself in her notebooks. Or Paddy cutting hay, bundling hay, putting up hay. But there was no one. The hay had been cut and the fields were gleaned. Paddy must have just finished baling the second crop. Where were they? I wondered.

Familiar earthy smells wafted from the double doors at the head of the alley as I stuck my head into the barn and gave a shout. The cattle were all out to pasture. A few sparrows flitted among the leftover grain in the mangers, and a couple of sleepy-eyed cats perched on the sills in the sun. But there was no sign of anyone.

The house was abandoned. The kitchen was immaculately clean, which I guess isn't all that surprising, what with Rosie and Mom after it all the time. But more than that, it didn't look lived in. The fridge had nothing in it. A box of Velveeta. A few jars of condiments—mustard, olives, mayo, some pickles. In the parlor, the bright June sunlight streamed through the windows. The fields outside bled verdant summer hues. The air was a bit stuffy, and I pulled open a few windows as I wandered back toward the bedrooms.

My own room remained almost exactly as I remembered. My books were there, and the buck Gabriel whittled for me, standing proud on my dresser. The ball from my last Reedsburg game, senior year. The MVP award. My jersey, hung on the wall with tacks. Seemed like it should be on my back, over my shoulders, bulging with pads. Not mounted on a wall, like a trophy buck.

The only thing out of place was a large cardboard box, sitting on the chest at the end of my bed. I lifted the flaps and peered inside. Two smaller, open boxes contained books... albums? I picked up the one on top. It looked familiar, but I couldn't place it.

I opened the cover and gasped. The image took the strength from my knees, and I had to sit down on my bed. I was looking at Lynn, sitting atop the tie wall, distracted, looking away. One of the first photos I'd ever taken. I'd not seen it printed before. I turned the page to a shot of me, taken when we first started building the wall. I was looking back over my shoulder, straight into the camera, grinning, as I placed a tie onto the footings of the wall. It was the first tie we had set. She'd focused right on my eye, but the depth of field was deep, maybe an f-11 aperture. Damn, I looked young. And innocent.

I flipped several pages of the album. I knew the photos. They were all here. I turned to the last pages. All of them. The best of them. Some I hadn't seen, and others just like I remembered. I closed the book, and glanced into the box. There were several more albums. The football album was there, and others that were unfamiliar. A stack of loose images was piled below.

Everything. She'd left me everything. Not exactly as I'd once seen it all, with her sitting at my side. She'd duplicated everything, and put the prints in new books. Some of the images were cropped differently than I remembered. And there were so many more.

I remembered Davey telling me about a box he had waiting for me. This box. Lynn's box.

I sat back on the bed, flipping through page after page. When I pulled another album from the box, the pages separated naturally in the middle. An envelope was wedged between an image of Harriet, holding a hose as she sprayed me with water, and a picture of a sand lizard perched on a tie.

The envelope was open, revealing folded pages inside. I recognized the writing immediately, from the cards Lynn had sent me while she traveled the world with Ingie.

October 5, 1963

My darling Patrick,

I'm going home, Patrick. I'm going back to Minnesota, to Minnetonka. I am going back to live with my family, to take care of Ingie, to be with those who love me. I'm so grateful that my father wants me to come back. I need my family now, more than I ever have, and they need me.

Patrick, I can't tell you how lost I feel without you. I know it was stupid of me to let us get so out of control. I know I had no business getting you so involved with me. I know it, yet I regret not a moment of the time we had together. I loved every moment of our time. I loved how we worked together. I loved how we could talk all night, all day, as long as we wanted. I loved how we could be together and not say a word for hours, just being there, gazing into each other's eyes, sometimes just touching fingertip to fingertip, and feeling One.

Was I so wrong, being this much older, to share my love with you? Was I being selfish? I can't think so. I believe what we have, what we had, was real. In the depth of night, I just wonder why we couldn't keep it.

I had to let you go, didn't I, Patrick? You have so much to discover, so much to learn. So much to find out about yourself and the world. I wonder what you have before you. I wonder if you will get beyond the jock thing and discover the greatness of your heart and the depth of your mind. I think so. My regret is that I will not be there to share your experiences and all that you will learn. My heart longs to share every moment with you. Every second. Every heartbeat I have, I wish to have with you.

So why am I leaving you and going my own way?

Because I see no choice.

Ingie needs me. If she makes it, she will need help all her life. She will never be the same. Even if I didn't feel some responsibility for her accident, even if it had happened on the other side of the world, she is still my sister. I love her so much. I will be here for her in whatever she needs. So now, I can use this education I earned. I can nurse Ingie, and I will. It will keep me busy and give me a noble, worthy purpose. And it will keep me away from you.

I need to be out of your way as you grow, as you conquer your challenges. I know how important football is to you. I so enjoy watching you play and photographing you playing. It is so thrilling to see you play. Patrick, your athleticism is not your greatest gift, but you truly are a gifted athlete. I hope to see you play again and again. I can't tell you how it makes me feel to see you run against a wall of opponents clamoring to bring you down, only to watch you tromp them or elude them! That is just one thing I will miss. There will be many.

I will miss your voice, deep, gentle, and sweet. I will miss the way you look at me, your eyes soft and caring. I will miss your touch, your smell. I will miss your presence.

This is how I feel about you now. I ask myself, how will I feel in the future? Years from now? I wonder how you will feel about me. I wonder if we will ever see one another again. I write this letter with hopes that we do.

Patrick, we must see each other again, at one time or another. I know full well that you will go on and have your life, and that your path may take you places where you will never be able to be with me again, ever, as we have been. I accept that. You must know, though, that I take with me part of you. I will always, God willing, have something of you that cannot be denied. Patrick, I carry our child. And I tell you from my heart, I will love and cherish this child. I am so grateful that I have this part of you to take with me.

Some tell me this is a mistake, keeping the baby. Some say the baby itself is a mistake. I admit that I made mistakes with you, that I should never have led you to where we went. I do not know how I could have done differently. I didn't plan, didn't expect things to be the way they were. I regret if I did you wrong. Somehow I think that I didn't. Ultimately, all I did was love you with all my heart and mind and soul. Patrick, if that is doing you wrong, then forgive me. I meant no harm.

I hope I gave you something, too.

I believe I did.

Yours always,

Lynn

∞

I don't know how many times I'd read Lynn's letter when I looked up to see Paddy leaning against the frame of my bedroom door. I'd not heard him approach. I was startled as much by my response as by his sudden appearance. I leapt from my bed and with two quick strides, engulfed my uncle in a bear hug. No sooner had I reached him than I surrendered to the sobs that had been building within me since Georgia told me about David.

Paddy was surprised by my response as well. He took a step back, regaining his balance. Then, wrapping his big, burly arms around me, he murmured comfort in my ear. I felt like a little kid on his shoulder, except I had to bend over to bury my face in his collar. He let me cry, like he'd let a horse have free rein to run itself out. I wept until I could weep no more.

∞

Once I'd calmed down, Paddy herded me out to the kitchen table, and parked me in a chair while he brewed a pot of coffee. He asked me what I knew of my brother, and was fascinated by my encounter with Georgia. He drank in every detail that Georgia had shared with me. What David had been like in the bush. Where they had dug in to observe the trail. How Davey had tried to get to the grenade, but was cut down by the cross fire. Georgia said that one of the first rounds had hit him square in the forehead. Paddy knew from the med reports that David had taken at least fourteen rounds, plus the damage from the grenade. He had been the only guy on the squad who died that morning. Paddy couldn't believe I'd met a guy who was with Davey when he died, who'd actually helped carry him out.

"I'd like to have met your trail partner," he said.

"Still can, I suppose. I got his address."

Paddy nodded purposefully, and I knew he'd look up Georgia someday. I hoped I'd be with him when he did.

After a few moments, Paddy gestured back toward my bedroom. "Seems like you have some business to consider."

"You know what she wrote?"

He met my eyes squarely, a slight frown creasing his brows. "Yep. I read that letter. And I make no apologies for it. I argued that we should've read it long ago, but the women said it was personal for you and we should keep out of it, even if it wasn't sealed. But once they left me here by myself, well, I guess I didn't feel compelled to abide by their ethics. I went ahead."

"Can't say I mind," I confided. "I'm overwhelmed, to be honest. I didn't know...."

"How could you have? She made it that way because she knew it was right. Now you need to reckon what you can do to make it right, as well."

I dropped my glance to the floor. I knew what was right. I just didn't know where to begin.

Paddy fetched the coffee pot and refilled our mugs. When he returned to his chair, I asked, "Whaddya mean, left you here alone? Where's Mom? And Rosie?"

He trained a keen eye on me again, measuring what he thought I might know. "When did you say you left Germany?"

"Easter. From what Georgia said, I probably left Bonn the same day Davey died."

"Just a moment." He rose and walked into the living room, where he shuffled through the papers on Mom's old rolltop desk, returning with a couple of envelopes. One was an airmail envelope, like Davey had used. The other was white, with fine script inked on the front. The stamps looked European.

Paddy took a deep breath and began telling me all he recalled about learning that Davey had been killed, and getting his belongings, and his body being returned home, and choosing to cremate him, and the funeral on Mother's Day with the kin and friends and the Whitmans. Then, with no further explanation, he simply handed me Davey's letter to Mom. I read, and then I wept again, as hard as I had when he first discovered me in my room. This time, Paddy wept as well.

After we'd calmed ourselves again, he hemmed and hawed and fidgeted for a moment. There was something more, and he didn't know how to bring it up. He fingered the white envelope, then handed it over to me. Inside was Eva's letter, in French, accompanied by a page in Mom's handwriting. Her translation. I read it through slowly, my head pivoting back and forth between the two versions.

"Oh, Eva," I cried. "Eva." I looked into Paddy's face and saw my pain mirrored in his face. "I forgot all about Eva and Davey," I admitted. "I didn't know she was pregnant. Oh, my God." I didn't think I had any tears left, but they flowed just the same.

I felt Paddy's big, soft dairyman's hand on my shoulder. "Well, Patrick, that's where your mother is," he said.

I looked up, confused.

"Elle and Rosie up and flew to Munich. They're with Eva right now. Kate is with them, too. They've been there since late May, and they'll stay to help her with the babies when they come. They wouldn't leave Davey's loved one to be alone."

It was too much to take in, all that I'd read and heard in the past hour. I shook my head. Then it hit me. "Babies? Did you say babies?"

Paddy grinned and nodded. "That's what Eva's doctor thinks. Seems Davey kept the Joyce twin streak going."

"Good ol' Davey. When will they be born?"

"September. Maybe early October," he said. "Davey wasn't in Germany all that long, was he? You can pretty much predict they'll be September babies."

"Wow." I couldn't believe what he was telling me. I was an uncle. Then the thought struck me. I was already a father.

Judging from the expression on his face, Paddy was reading my mind. "You have a lot of thinking to do, my boy. You have a lot of important things to consider. And some decisions to make."

I nodded in agreement.

"First thing you do," he continued, his thoughts right in stride with mine, "you call your mother. She's expecting you." He chuckled. "Damn if she doesn't know you. She said you'd be home by the Fourth of July. And here it is, not even the first. You're early."

He looked at the kitchen clock, calculating. "I think it's about eight p.m. in Munich right now. It'd be a good time to catch her."

It was only the first of several phone calls I was eager to make.

∞

She met me first with her eyes, dark with caution. Her anxiety was clear, and just. I saw it written on her face, the first thing I absorbed as they approached.

The twins were at her sides, each holding closely to their mother, gripping her hands and examining me shyly.

And the ring, the oval diamond, flanked by emerald green. On her finger, she wore the ring.

I looked from her hand back to her eyes. She read my expression, and all of her apprehension vanished.

Chapter Fifty-Five
The Good Guy List

"I HAVE SOMETHING FOR YOU," Lynn said. "From David."

The twins had finally gone to sleep. I think I won them over. They were first intensely skeptical, then curious, then playful, then demanding, and when their physical needs eventually overwhelmed them, they fell into deep, peaceful slumber. Now we had time for ourselves.

Lynn led me to the patio, stopping to pull an envelope from the desk next to the sliding door. The evening sun was still high in the Minnesota sky as we settled on the swing. "I was near you in Chesterton, when you endured loneliness by yourself," she said softly. "I will not leave you now. I am here. You don't have to go through this alone." She paused.

I met her gaze and shook my head, but couldn't find my voice. I looked down at the envelope. It was thick, and had been opened carefully. Inside, my brother's familiar script filled the pages of a letter. I glanced up at her. She nodded, and stayed by me.

December 24, 1967

Dear Lynn,

I want to let you know that I did tell Patrick about your albums and letters. Several times, I thought the moment had arrived, but it hadn't, and I waited, until recently. I told him last time I saw him, in Germany. I think it was right.

I'm writing this because I don't know if I will be going home. For that, I am frightened and sorry. Frightened that it may happen. And sorry for not having more time. I would like more time to talk with my brother, to tell him things that I haven't had the opportunity to say yet. Which is why, after harboring our secret for so long, I am going to ask you to return the favor. I know my brother, and I know he will find his way to you. He will find your address among your letters, as I did. I apologize for succumbing to the overwhelming temptation those boxes offered, but in this respect I'm glad I opened them. You left him your address, and I found it. And now I can send you this.

Another reason I'm glad I read your letters is that it gives me more insight into the love you have for Patrick. And for this I am very grateful. I would like to know you better. I may get the time to know you well. I may not. But I know what you did for my brother. And that gives me an understanding of you that brings me great peace. I know you'll always do well for Patrick.

Lynn, I regret laying this burden on you, to give Patrick this last letter. But I have no doubt that you will be by him. And he will need you.

Thank you, again, Lynn. For everything.

Love,

David

I set the page aside. Lynn put her arm around me and rested her head on my shoulder as we began David's letter.

Dear Pat,

Forgive me for not coming home.

I want to tell you what I know about getting through grief. I already know the loss you are feeling. I wish I didn't. I wish it was something we didn't need to know about, being so young. But the good do die young, sometimes. Jannie did. Now, if you're reading this, me.

I hope that as long as you live, you find the kind of joy that Jannie did. And that I have, too. Even with the emptiness of growing up without you, I feel joy. It's part of what Father Jack called being a warrior. I think he got it from Rose, although she prefers to say champion, especially when she's talking about you. I'm the warrior, to her. Either way, it's about how we live our lives, with purpose and intensity. With joy. We talked about that a lot on the farm. Lots of crazy thoughts. A lot of our goofy ideas came from Father Jack and Rose. Or through them.

The best thing I can tell you about making your way through grief is something that I learned from Father Jack. It's called the Good Guy List. I mentioned it to you a while back, when you asked me how I got on after Jannie, but I really didn't explain it all that well. I was still learning how to use it then. And I think you thought I was kind of flaky. Well, a lot of the things we talked about on the farm were kind of out there, but they were good. And the Good Guy List was definitely among the best.

The List is really pretty easy. I compose my lists intermittently, whenever I need to. Seems like a lot, lately. Almost as much as after Jannie died. Takes longer now, too, since it kind of tends to grow.

Anyways, there are no set rules for who goes on the List—part of the point is to make up your own criteria. Mine includes people who have had a positive influence in my life, or are just decent people. Nice people. I don't look for perfection, or anything close to it. None of us would qualify, if that was the standard. Warmth, kindness, good-heartedness—those folks are in, easy. People I admire, people I aspire to be with, or to be like. People I know firsthand, or sometimes people I don't know at all, who I've only read about or heard about from a friend.

So all I do is come up with these names, and then I jot the list down and reflect on it. I can't say I keep any of the lists after I write them out. Sometimes they get stuck in a book, or a pack, and carried around a bit. A lot of time, I just think the List, anyway—don't bother even putting it on paper. I mean, it pretty much lives in my mind. And heart. I just focus on being cognizant of it. That's why I don't need to keep the old lists. Writing out the lists is like taking in a breath of fresh air and then exhaling, leaving it behind after I've taken in its nourishment. Breathing in, breathing out, again and again.

Treat the List lightly, with as little judgmental discrimination as you can. Plenty of good people emerge, and there is something that strengthens my soul to go through and realize how many Good Guys comprise the List. It is a testimony to the goodness of people. And over time, it does tend to morph and evolve, but usually not because anyone turns nasty. That hasn't seemed to happen much. Even when it does, the List helps you find forgiveness, and you can see the good in those people, too. They usually stay on. More often, people fade from the List by moving on with their own lives, and just growing distant. Death is not an eliminator, although I do give anyone who's passed sort of an 'emeritus' status. Those people don't tend to evaporate away from the everyday working List. Like Jannie. Or Gabe.

One of the innate properties of the Good Guy List is that everyone on it loves you. They are aware of you, even if not specifically. It's an awareness that is timeless and all encompassing. Possessing it, in one way or another, is why those people made your List. On that very important level, which is more real what our eyes filter out into vision, the people on your Good Guy List share with you all the energy of eternity. Father Jack called it the communion of saints—the common melding of all spirit into and from the Source. Other people have other names for it. Peace. Grace. To me, the energy is love, the currency of the universe. When you look at your Good Guy List, you can't help pumping love into those who are on it. And at some level, some very important level, that love is a transfer. It comes right back to you. That which you give to them, they are constantly giving to you. It works both ways.

Jannie taught me that.

Father Jack taught me about the Good Guy List after Jannie died. He learned it from Rose, he told me. She got it from Paddy, can you imagine? Told me so herself. Paddy used it, too, after Jannie. He wrote that to me here in Nam. And you know where he learned about it? From Mom. Really. It's how she learned to calm her fears enough to leave the hospital. The Good Guy List. She's the one who figured it out, and named it.

We've all been doing it. And now you, too, will use it. I should have shared it with you a long time ago, but I guess I was just learning it myself. And saving it for you now, when you'll need it.

Patrick, I hope I'm always on your Good Guy List. I'll be there for you. My love will be, anyway. You can always tap into my love for you. It will be there.

Beyond that, be a champion. Always.

Love,

David

I let the letter dangle from my fingertips. I looked to Lynn; she was here. Her face reflected my hope, and gratitude.

Chapter Fifty-Six

Elle

I SEE HIM NOW and I understand. I should have named him Michael, after his father. He looks so much like him. I don't know if I could have told the difference. Or maybe it's just time that blurs my memory. Time, and all that has happened during its passage.

I see him now and I watch him move like his father moved. Gracefully, with strength and poise. The swagger of a champion. He has always been a champion, a fighter. Both the twins were fighters. This one came out on top, though. He came out alive. He chose his battles. He is a winner, of life.

I see him, and he looks at me and smiles, and he looks like his father. He sounds like his father. He gestures like his father, and his expressions unfold like Michael's did. He is more than his father, though. More than his father and his brother both. He came back to her. He came back to her and stayed. To her and her children. His children. His twins. He's a good man. He has a place on the List. They all do.

I see him now, walking hand-in-hand with his twinnies, his little ones. He between them, his huge hands swallowing up their little mitts. She, before them, looking though her lens. She has done such a fine job of mothering them. Much better than I did with my twins. I look into her eyes and I see strength and grace, and I am grateful. She answers my gaze with kindness and openness. I sense she is fond of me. And grateful. Goodness, she hardly knows me! But she is so candidly grateful. She has told me so. Grateful for her Patrick. And she directs her gratitude toward me. Heavens. Patrick is hardly my doing. She had as much to do with bringing him up as I did. More, perhaps. I abandoned him. Left him for the narcissism of my illness. Such a tragic waste of time. His and mine. But he has thrived, in spite of my cowardly mothering. Perhaps because of it.

I see them now, Patrick's family. How that little girl loves him so! And her brother adores him! How well she raised them, to never lose faith in their absentee father. She left him, too, didn't she? For so different a reason. How loving she was, to grant him the freedom to grow, and discover, and choose. How rewarding that he chose well. Chose correctly. Such a risk! Such a gamble! Yet there she is. There they are. I don't know how she lived with it. The fears would have smothered me. They did smother me. I let them bring me to my knees. I let myself succumb. Such a tragic waste of my time. And theirs.

Ah, well. I tried. Can worse be said?

I see them now, and I see my daughter, her head upon my shoulder, snoozing in the warm October sun. We bask in the Munich sun as we sit upon this park bench, watching my surviving son and his family playing on the grass. My little French-speaking German daughter. I am so grateful that she has opened herself to me. To us. To become part of our great family. How trusting she is. How helplessly, hopefully trusting. My, she is big. I see myself in her, and her in me, once upon a time. Once, so very long ago. But not that long, I suppose. Twenty years, and then some. Just half my life, so far. Half my life ago. She seems so big. Her twins must not wait much longer to be born. They must give her some relief. Will she ever know relief? I wonder. If I can be of any use to her, I hope to bring her relief. To free her of worry. Of fears. I hope that I can be of help to her.

Rosie writes that we need all come back to the farm. Me. Eva and her babies. Patrick and his family. All of Michael's family. Eva will come, I know. I sense it. She seeks to live among David's roots. Perhaps it will come to be. Let her give these children birth, and we shall see. In the meanwhile, Rosie and Paddy can build upon the time they have alone. It is meant to be. I can see it, have seen it for years. I am grateful. Imagine, two of the first of those who grace my List. And now they are together, as one. They who were the first with whom I shared the List. And they believed in it. Added to it. Yes. Life and love blend back into one another, if you let them linger long enough. I am grateful.

Oh, dear. My little Eva is stirring. And dripping. I believe it is her waters.

So it goes.

∞

Thanksgiving

I have a List of those for whom I am deeply grateful. Without the encouragement, suggestions and advice from those on this list, this story would remain untold.

I give thanks to Annie Vanderboom who, as my first reader and ultimate editor, suffered through all the typos, misspellings, lapses, and other shortcomings in my writing—and honed a polished gem from a crude stone.

My gratitude goes to Michael, my son, and to Catherine, my wife.

Zita Knific, Ohio's finest English teacher, Philly friends Kathy Case, Morgan Robinson, Brianna Gallagher, Karen Forte, Janet Thompson and Joel Levinson, I value your objectivity and precise critiques. Kim Sabelko, thanks for the beaver dam idea. Sam Fiegenbaum in San Francisco, Barb Brown in Eaton, Colorado, Helen Strader in Denver, and Bob Aronson in Jacksonville, Florida, your encouragement is cherished.

John Bunce, and our Memorial family, Mary Kay Holzman, Donna Rae Mordini, Candy Stapleton, Pat McCabe, Bob Bluhm, and Father Paul Esser, I am obliged. Pat Quinn, I treasure your sharp eye for editing and am grateful for your encouragement.

Chuck Weber, you're the king, and I love how you nailed the twins with the stroke of your paint brush.

Gustavo Estrada, thanks for your cover art.

I'm grateful to Harry Petrakis. I my youth, I was fascinated by how Harry gave life to the characters in his book. More recently, Harry taught me about overwriting and clarity. He taught the power of words.

In Rochester, Minnesota, Mike Kalmbach and my fellow writers in the Rochester Writers Group, thanks. Laurie Mona, thanks. Brad Zeller, I appreciate your help. Dwight Ruff, your keen eye is a blessing. Jan and Kathy Shepel, thanks. My Sauk County friends, I tip my hat to you.

Cousins Juliana Kottke, Chris Hanahan, and my sister Gretchen Geimer, thanks.

I'm grateful to whoever wrote the words to "He Died for Nothing" on a post-it and stuck them to the Wall in Washington where I found them when I first visited the memorial.

Every List grows and changes, and sometimes skips over those who truly belong. This List is no exception. I remain truly grateful.

Russ Vanderboom
Rochester, Minnesota
Thanksgiving Day
November 28, 2013

Acknowledgements

Book Plates quote and lyric permissions:

If people bring so much courage to this world...
Reprinted with the permission of Scribner Publishing Group from A FAREWELL TO
ARMS by Ernest Hemingway. Copyright © 1929 by Charles Scribner's Sons.
Copyright renewed © by Ernest Hemingway. All rights reserved.

Oh Very Young
Words and Music by Cat Stevens
Copyright © 1974 Cat Music Limited
Copyright Renewed
All Rights Administered by BMG Rights Management (US) LLC
All Rights Reserved. Used by Permission
Reprinted by Permission of Hal Leonard Corporation

Elusive Butterfly
Words and Music by Bob Lind
Copyright © 1965, 1966 (Renewed) EMI UNART CATALOG INC.
All Rights Controlled by EMI UNART CATALOG INC. (Publishing)
and ALFRED PUBLISHING CO., INC. (Print)
All Rights Reserved Used by Permission of ALFRED MUSIC

About the Author

Russ Vanderboom was born and raised in Wisconsin. He served as a Marine in 1970, where he was trained as a journalist, and later built a career in agricultural journalism in Wisconsin as a reporter and managing editor for a weekly newspaper. At a key moment in the course of his career, he realized that if he was to flourish in journalism, he would do well to become a subject matter expert in an area of agriculture about which he was passionate. At the time, dairy cows captured his imagination. At the University of Wisconsin in Madison, he studied dairy science—particularly genetics, reproductive endocrinology, and mammary physiology. Molecular aspects of endocrinology swept him away; his passion for estrogen-regulated mammary gland physiology in bovine mammals evolved into a keen interest in the pathology of breast cancer in humans. Medical science became the focus of his second career. After researching breast cancer during his post-doctoral fellowship at Mayo Clinic, he combined his interests in science and journalism as the medical science writer for research at the Cleveland Clinic, and then as the senior science writer at the American Association for Cancer Research in Philadelphia. He concluded his scientific career at Mayo Clinic, Rochester, Minnesota. He is married and has two grown children. *The Good Guy List* is his first novel.